The Intake of Br
Was Audible As Tana Stood
Poised in the Archway. . . .

Her entrance was stunning, and she knew she looked particularly well dressed in simple clinging black accented only by pearls. "Hello, everyone. I'm sorry we were detained."

She smiled and tossed her head in her accustomed way. "It's really good to be back." Her smile froze as she looked across the room into what seemed a mirror. The face looking up at hers was her twin. The entire dinner party watched, fascinated by the strange encounter.

Emmalina rose. She was a fraction taller than Tana and wore her hair differently, but their similarity was striking.

Every eye in the room was on them. Emmy smiled and extended her hand. "Since everyone seems so stunned at seeing us together, let me introduce myself. I'm Emmalina Griffon. I must say, my dear, no matter what anyone says, I don't do you justice. No one could. You are divinely beautiful. It's the rarest of compliments to have been compared to you. . . ."

THE WAYWARD WINDS

EVELYN KAHN

PUBLISHED BY POCKET BOOKS NEW YORK

Another *Original* publication of POCKET BOOKS

POCKET BOOKS, a Simon & Schuster division of
GULF & WESTERN CORPORATION
1230 Avenue of the Americas, New York, N.Y. 10020

ISBN: 0-671-83128-3

First Pocket Books printing May, 1981

10 9 8 7 6 5 4 3 2 1

POCKET and colophon are trademarks of Simon & Schuster.

Interior design by Sofia Grunfeld

Printed in the U.S.A.

*To my mother who knew I would
and to my husband who believed I could—
with grateful thanks to Harvey Klinger, Ann Patty
and Meg Blackstone whose combined efforts
helped to make it all come true.*

The environment fosters and selects
the seed must contain the potentiality
and direction of the life to be selected.

GEORGE SANTAYANA

PROLOGUE

"I DON'T WANT to die, Lord. I'm afraid—please don't let me die. Please, Lord—not yet—please!" Mary Ann was cramped and rigid with fear; only her lips moved as she mumbled fervently.

Daniel Beauford didn't like the feel of it. A situation like this could mean disaster. Mary Ann and the kids had been good so far, but he knew they were frightened. The winds had grown in intensity, drowning out the chug-chug of the old Model T motor. The few words he'd exchanged with his wife had had to be shouted over the roar of the gale. The sweat was pouring down his back. A powerful man, he needed all his strength to hold the car on the road. The world around them was a swirling nightmare of choking red silt. The old man in the roadside town who'd helped him with gas earlier that morning hadn't mentioned there was bad weather brewing.

Mary Ann huddled in her seat and the children began to whimper as the force of the winds increased. They were alone on the road, although he knew the town of Brightwater couldn't be far off. He poked Mary Ann. "Get the kids on the floor . . . throw the blanket over their heads. The way this dirt is piling up, they'll choke."

Quickly she turned to help the children as he had ordered.

He wondered if he should stop and wait out the storm or drive on to the town, but the problem resolved itself as a fierce gust tore the steering wheel from his grasp, skidding the car across the road into a rut. The girls were badly shaken. He tried to revive the motor, but it died with a gasp. This was a helluva predicament . . . they'd have to find shelter. If they remained here they'd surely die.

He was a resourceful man, but he'd never been caught in such a situation. He'd have to seek help on foot. The winds buffeting the car suddenly cleared the windshield and for a moment he thought he saw a light not too far off. There . . . he saw it once again! It meant there was a farmhouse nearby. They'd have to try for it, walking or crawling; it was their only chance. He leaned over to his wife. "Mary Ann, I think I see a house over there . . . can you make it out?"

The anxious woman strained to see through the window. "I think so, Danny. . . . Yes, I do! Thank the Lord!"

"We're not there yet." He grimaced. "Do you want to stay here till I check it out, or shall we go for it together?"

She stiffened. "Together, Danny—don't leave us here."

He nodded. "Okay, then. . . . I'll carry Polly. Mary Ann, you, Emmy and Amy, hold each other's hands. Don't let go! You hear me, girls?"

He heard a muffled "Yes, Daddy" and went on. "Use all your strength; don't let go of each other! Keep your heads down and your mouths shut. . . . Mary Ann, you hang on to me. Get ready. Hand the baby to me . . . put the blanket over her head."

Then they stepped into a world gone mad. The placid prairie country—gently waving grass, clumps of trees and grazing cattle—had disappeared; they were caught up in a churning maelstrom of hurtling sand and debris, orchestrated by a wailing din. Struggling with all their might to hold on to one another, they fought to reach the flickering light that beckoned through the terrifying red gloom. Raging gusts forced them to their knees. Crawling and gasping for breath, they found momentary respite next to the trunk of a huge tree that groaned in the wind above them. There, they saw the house looming in the distance; with hope now, despite being torn and pushed about at the gale's will, they fought on. When it seemed they had exhausted their last ounce of strength, one more desperate effort brought them to their goal, and within minutes the Beauford family found themselves inside the welcoming warmth of the Widow Fields' home.

Part I
CHILDHOOD

Chapter I

◦─◦◦◦─◦

THE BEGINNING

THE TEN PLAGUES were upon them! At the last town meeting the Fundamentalists had spelled it out: "Sinners—sinners all! Ye've sinned, and the Lord is wreaking his wrath upon ye!"

The few hardy souls who had ventured out to attend had left more shaken than when they'd come. God-fearing or not, they found it hard to dispel the notion in view of the catastrophes that were now becoming daily occurrences.

Brightwater, Oklahoma, had been a peaceful, sleepy farming community that early summer. Its people had welcomed the clear and sunny days as they went about their normal pursuits, tending crops and livestock. But as days passed and the skies remained cloudless, it became apparent that the excessive heat portended drought. When they woke one morning to see and give thanks for the black cloud in the distance, their gratitude quickly dissipated. It proved to be an onslaught of locusts that blanketed everything.

Brash invaders, voracious foragers, the locusts ate the land bare; wilting crops became stubble, cattle were starving. For miles and miles, as far as the eye could see, there had been no escape from their blight. Trees recently resplendent in spring array stood starkly skeletal against the blue, sun-drenched sky. Night and day, the crunching mandibles gorged; they would not finish their carnage until they had wreaked total devastation.

As if that had not been enough to bring the townspeople to their knees, the winds had come. They raged in their wild

3

dervish dance across the land, picking up the precious soil and hurling it about so that night could not be told from day. And the timeless land, so richly fruitful, blessed by sunshine and prairie green to the horizon, abundant without end, rose as if in wrathful retaliation to join its helpmate, the wind. The great cornucopia of undulating plains that had for so long sheltered those with a reverence for nature, a love of earth and sky, struck back against the farmers who had been wanton in their use. Strong-spirited men, they had wrested what they needed for survival, heedlessly tilling year after year, not understanding the soil's need for rest and replenishment.

The wild marriage of wind and earth grew in ferocity as clouds of red silt rampaged across the sky. There was no surcease; their song of rage was an incessant howling that brought man and beast to the edge of madness. Accusations and resentments flared; bickering and fistfights became commonplace. Each man sat in judgment of the other's sins, attributing the coming of damnation to his former friends and neighbors. The situation grew more acute with each passing day; reason and any semblance of sense had fled.

With each new gust, Father McGurdy's house shook, adding to his apprehension. As he peered through the thickly coated window, he could barely make out the small band of figures groping their way against the wind. He knew the Fundamentalists were going to nightly prayer meeting. He admired their zeal but worried about their denunciations against those of differing faiths. He had cause for concern. His was the only Catholic parish in the entire region, and long ago it had been forcibly brought home to him that he existed only on sufferance. If it hadn't been for the efforts of a few courageous friends, any attempts to remain would have come to naught. It had taken prodigious efforts to gain a tenuous foothold, since the prevalent feeling was that Catholics, Jews and Negroes were not welcome. He'd been burnt out twice and harassed in ways that would have sent a less resolute man off in flight.

He heard the faint voices through the gale. Why weren't their mouths choked with the sand? As they grew nearer, their importuning became more distinct: "Repent, ye sinners! Repent!" It was a frightening accompaniment to the wailing of the winds. He shuddered and murmured a prayer.

The priest was a brave man of temperate and reasonable

nature, but he was sorely troubled. As things were now, the town was a tinderbox; emotions were raw, and anything could happen. He turned from the window and watched as the sand floated around the dim light of his desk lamp. Red silt coated everything. His throat and mouth were dry and bitter from the feel and taste of it. Moving from the window, he was halted by the sound of horses' hooves. That could mean only one thing. He pressed his head against the glass to make out the familiar figure of Dr. Robinson coming into view. "Lord help him," the priest prayed as he watched the worn figure huddled on the carriage seat disappear down the road.

Father McGurdy sighed. He had tried to take hope since the past few days had seen the winds abate a little, but a brown cloud covered heaven and earth as far as the eye could see. Sand and grit were everywhere, in everything. He moved his fingers over the open pages of the Bible, and watched the deep ridges as he tried to clear the pages of dust. Lost in thought, he was startled to hear voices close at hand. Sean Corrigan burst through the study door. An oak of a man, he struggled to catch his breath. "Come, Father . . . come! Hurry, please! Doc says the child'll not last the night."

Father McGurdy felt the pain shoot to his heart as he saw the tears streak the grime on Sean's face. He gathered his strength. "Yes, Sean . . . I'll be but a moment." He made ready, praying fervently as he moved. "Father, spare them. . . . Spare the child. 'Tis their only one. They waited so long for your grace. She is all they can have. . . . Please, Father—"

As Father McGurdy entered the small, dark room and saw the piteous mother tending the limp form of the child, despair overtook him. The colorful patchwork quilt covering the babe had been stitched such a short time before; its gaiety mocked them. "Let us pray," he said.

Crowded around the bed, they clung together as if their combined strength could breathe life back into the child. Each time the doctor reached for the lifeless hand to check the pulse, the priest held his breath. He felt helpless: there was so little he could do to comfort them. They anguished together, but their long vigil was in vain. He watched as the baby's eyes opened, and then he saw the light dim in them. As he went to the keening mother's side, he muttered, " 'Tis true—now the firstborn are going too."

He and the weary doctor did what they could for the inconsolable parents. It was a tragic time and the suffering seemed to be bringing them to the breaking point.

After midnight, when Father McGurdy was readying himself for bed, Dr. Robinson knocked on the door. The priest was shocked at the doctor's pallor. "Come now, sit down. Let me get you a bit o brandy. You look all done in."

The doctor slumped in the chair, stretching his legs. "I'm afraid the worst is yet to come. The Grim Reaper's abroad."

The proffered whiskey glass slopped over as the shaken priest turned ashen, and the doctor continued glumly. "The diphtheria's spreading—we've got an epidemic on our hands. No telling how many more families are going to be decimated . . . it hits children the hardest. Darn disease is contagious and almost impossible to combat. It won't stop until it wears itself out."

Crossing himself, the priest murmured almost inaudibly, "All o this is affectin my mind. Doc, can you imagine what the Fundamentalists will make o this?"

A mocking smile crossed the tired doctor's face. "I've no doubt they'll tell us. But don't lose heart, Father; we'll weather it somehow. Keep putting in a good word for us nonbelievers. . . . Well it's very late, and we'd best be getting our rest. God knows, we're going to need it."

One morning not long afterward the rampaging winds disappeared as mysteriously as they had come. The air was clear, the sun shone and the sky was blue. What was left of the poor, bruised earth lay quiet, barren and waiting for new growth. The miracle of rebirth had begun.

Father McGurdy greeted his parishioners who were straggling in for early mass. He shared their joy and thankfulness. His poor, benighted flock were but a handful compared to the other denominations, but, God be praised, they made up for it in their goodness and devotion.

Slowly the sap and the vigor of the townspeople returned. Hesitantly at first, as if fearful of something new befalling them, they began to take stock of what the disaster had wrought. As best they could, they began the cleanup and rebuilding, amid talk that the government in Washington might give them help. There was hope; the worst was over. The sound of laughter began to be heard again. Beset and tormented, they had suffered together; and now they were eager to show each other kindness. Thus it was that, when the Reverend Jenson extended an invitation to Father McGurdy and Dr. Quenton to meet with him, the good father rejoiced. It was evidence of the new spirit abroad in Brightwater.

For the beleaguered Catholic priest, commonly vilified as "one of them Pope boys," to be included in a meeting with the two ministers of Brightwater's leading denominations was momentous. "The Lord be praised," he commented to his housekeeper. "We've been tested, and at long last we men of the cloth will join hands in leading the way to new understanding and brotherhood."

His step was jaunty as he proceeded to the appointment. Stocky little Reverend Jenson greeted him cordially as he ushered him into his well-appointed study, where Dr. Quenton was already seated. Father McGurdy could not help but reflect on the luxury around him. The impressive green horsehair-covered furniture and the imposing desk all bespoke the affluence of the Reverend's parishioners.

Indicating a seat to the priest, the Reverend settled himself, saying affably, "Make yourself comfortable. Tea will be along."

There was an air of expectancy as they chatted about mundane matters over the delicious, still warm pecan buns and cake. Having had his fill and brushing the crumbs from his hands, the Reverend Jenson addressed the father. "Have you heard what's been going on at the Widow Fields'?"

Father McGurdy looked at him questioningly. "Nothin's come to my ears. I hope all's well."

Exchanging a conspiratorial glance with Dr. Quenton, the Reverend exclaimed, "Good! The news hasn't spread. It has to do with the purpose of our meeting. Dr. Robinson suggested you be included in what we're hoping to undertake, and after what we've all so recently endured, Dr. Quenton and I believe the Lord would approve our sharing this with you. We're counting on the wisdom of your counsel in reaching a solution."

Gratified by the priest's look of astonishment, the Reverend launched into his story.

It had begun at the height of the windstorm. A family had been stranded and sought shelter from the Widow Fields when their car had broken down on her land. The young parents and their three children were in poor circumstances, and the widow had kept them in her home, doing what she could to assist them. When the winds had lessened, the father, a Mr. Beauford, had helped with the chores. However, he'd felt it unfair to burden the widow without more suitable recompense, so he'd headed for town in search of work. That had been the last anyone had seen of him . . . he'd vanished without a trace.

After days without word from her missing husband, the worried Mrs. Beauford had pleaded with Mrs. Fields to keep watch over her children and gone to town in search of him. After making inquiries in the few stores on the main street, she'd gone into the town's only hotel, a flimsy, two-story wooden building, and found the proprietor, Tom Hadrop, in the lobby–dining room that was used as a restaurant by traveling salesmen and other guests. He'd sympathized with her and offered her a job; his wife was still recovering from diphtheria, and he needed help. She would have room and board, some salary and a half day off. Once again the widow was prevailed upon to keep the children until a place closer in could be found to house them.

The woman had been at work not much more than a week when her oldest child came down with diphtheria. The poor widow had her hands full and asked Dr. Robinson to notify the mother to come at once. When Mrs. Beauford failed to appear, the widow again sent a message with her handyman, and to her amazement received the shocking news that the woman had also disappeared.

Here, the Reverend paused and said, "It was at Mrs. Fields' urgent request that I verified the story with Tom Hadrop. The man was furious; Mrs. Beauford had gone without a word to him. He figures she left with a traveling salesman who had spent the night."

Reverend Jenson, seeing the shock on the priest's face, said significantly, "It's plain the town has three abandoned children on its hands. It's been six weeks since the mother's disappearance, and, with no sign or word from the father, it doesn't seem likely either of them is going to return."

By the expression on the faces of the other two men, Father McGurdy knew they expected some comment from him. "'Tis a strange story you've told, Reverend. Certainly a sad turn of events. What has the sheriff to say about this?"

Impatiently, as if the priest were missing the point, the

Reverend replied, "It's his opinion the parents have flown the coop!"

For the first time, Dr. Quenton spoke. "We might as well get to the crux of the matter. As men of the cloth, we ought to be doing something to assist the Widow Fields. It's not Christian to expect her to be bearing the care of three abandoned children. I'm sure we all agree."

Startled at the turn the conversation was taking, Father McGurdy inquired, "Gentlemen, begging your pardon, has no one thought to contact the orphanage in Towana? Would that not be the likely place for the poor little tykes whilst they're waiting for their folks?"

Smugly, Reverend Jenson replied, "Indeed, yes. Dr. Quenton spoke with them, but, as matters stand now, it will be a long time before they can accept the children. The diphtheria's spread through the orphanage and it's been quarantined. We feel the matter can't wait, and that is precisely why, my brothers in Christ, we're meeting here today. Let me tell you about the children—all females. There's a babe, no more than fourteen, fifteen months old; another almost four and the oldest probably about six. Helpless little things, too young to know what's happened, and, more to the point, no idea of their faith, so—"

At this point, the Reverend looked probingly at each of the men and, placing his palms upward on his desk, spoke with deliberation. "It's apparent the solution lies in our hands. The way is clear, since, in each of our flocks, there are families recently bereft of a beloved child. Do you not think this is God's will?"

The priest stared at them in stunned silence.

Shifting in his chair, hands folded prayerfully, portly Dr. Quenton, in his most unctuous voice, said, "Can you imagine what this would mean to the Wilkersons? While they have a son, the loss of their little daughter has left them inconsolable. It's as if the hand of God were reaching out to them."

"Indeed, yes!" Father McGurdy suddenly exclaimed. "My poor Corrigans! Lost their one and only little lass, with no hope of more to come. 'Twould be God's blessin for them to have one o the despairin little lassies. They'd probably be happy to take all three—"

The instant hostility on the other faces made him offer quick amends. Chuckling, he added, "Now, I know you wouldn't be wantin to turn the lot o them over to my Catholic charge, but I'm grateful for the chance o one. I'm sure the Corrigans will bless you for the havin o one o them. A beautiful plan, Reverend Jenson. May the Lord preserve you for this day!"

Appeased, Reverend Jenson beamed as he told them, "The Widow Fields has intimated to me she would not be averse to keeping the eldest child, Emmalina. There already seems to be a fine affection between the two. The way she's nursing the child through the illness tells me she'd do a fine job of raising her. With each of you placing a child with a family established in town, the children could see each other and not feel as if they'd been separated. It's not likely the orphanage would find a family willing to adopt all three. What do you say, gentlemen: are we agreed? Shall we proceed with our little plan?"

"One thing," Father McGurdy interjected. "What happens if the parents return? 'Tis possible they've been prevented from makin contact and in good faith may be intendin to reclaim the children. What then?"

Dr. Quenton smiled cynically. "Let's be practical. There's little likelihood of that. However, in such a case, I believe they would have every right to them. I discussed the matter with Judge Maughan over in Towana, and he wisely suggested we inform each family they're not to consider the child theirs until a full year has passed. Then, if they so desire, they can apply for legal adoption. Stress the fact with your family that, painful though it may be, in such an event they would have to relinquish the child."

Seeing the concern on the Father's face, Reverend Jenson asked, "Do you think your Corrigans will agree? If not, we can find someone else."

Hastily Father McGurdy assured him, "No need o that . . . 'twill be fine. 'Tis the only right way to do it." Smiling broadly, he said, " 'Tis difficult to play at bein Solomon, isn't it? 'Twill be a hard thing for the Corrigans to have hangin over their heads, but the decision will be theirs to make." Pondering for a moment, he asked, "Do you suppose there might be any kin wantin them?"

Reverend Jenson shook his head in feigned dismay. "You're a cautious man, Father. Mrs. Beauford told the widow they had no kinfolk. They were on the road seeking a place where Mr. Beauford could find employment." Sighing, he looked at both men and waited. "Well, if there are no more questions, the sooner we get the children settled, the better off they'll be."

When no one spoke, he concluded, "Shall we get on with it? I'd appreciate your speaking with the prospective families and letting me know the results."

The men rose after they had decided to meet again the following evening.

Chapter II

DISPERSEMENT

THE SEQUENCE OF events had been arranged beforehand. The
baby, Polly Sue, went eagerly into the outstretched arms of
Deirdre Corrigan. Enjoying the warmth and sweet scent that
enveloped her, she squirmed a bit in the tight embrace and a
hand wiggled free to explore the tears that welled from
Deirdre's eyes. When finally she was passed to Sean, she
spoke, almost as if she were questioning. "Dada?" Sean
laughed and gently lifted her in the air above his head.

The onlookers felt a catch at their hearts. Father McGurdy
put an arm around Sean and silently blessed them all. If he'd
had any misgivings, the little scene in the crowded room made
it all worthwhile. The Corrigans expressed their humble
thanks to those assembled and left.

Amy Beth stood pressed against the wall, mute and
frightened. She did not understand what was happening. The
days that had passed without their parents had left her
bewildered. She'd been waiting, looking for her laughing
father and mommy. Who was this tall, thin lady looking down
at her, like the wicked witch in the picture book, who spoke in
a funny high voice? "You're to come with us, Amy Beth."

The child hung back, terrified. She didn't want to go
anyplace; she wanted to stay right where she was and wait.
She wanted to be near Emmy, from whom she'd been kept
apart because Emmy'd been sick. Mrs. Fields had explained it
to her.

Who was this strange, angry-looking man staring at her?

12

He was talking, and she tried to hear what he was saying. He kept repeating, "Pick up your head, Amy Beth . . . look at me!" She didn't want to look at him. Now he was saying, "You're to come with us, child. Our home is to be your home, and you're to be our daughter. We'll do everything we can to be good parents."

His words frightened her. What did he mean? She stood trembling, trying to control the water that poured from her, making a puddle where she stood.

Mrs. Fields took the child's shaking hand and said to the Wilkersons, "She's just a babe; she can't possibly understand what you're saying. Just comfort and love her. This must be very frightening for her."

The Wilkersons remained silent and grim, rooted where they stood. The widow bent down and put an arm around the tot. "Now, now child, don't take on so. You'll be fine. You'll like it at the Wilkersons'. Soon as you're settled in, you'll be able to visit Emmy. Very soon Emmy'll be fit and ready for visiting."

Elizabeth Fields hated herself at this moment. She should have kept the three of them together. It was a heartless, ugly thing they were doing. These little ones had only one another for family. She shouldn't have given in to Reverend Jenson's admonitions about the problems she would face in raising all three children and what it would mean to the bereaved families to have one of them. She'd been cowardly; she'd have managed somehow, she told herself, even though reason told her otherwise. She knew that once word got around they'd never have allowed her to keep the three of them.

She was certain the baby was in tender, loving hands, but the Wilkersons disturbed her. Unyielding and distant, they seemed to be carved out of granite. Good, yes . . . but loving? She could only hope so. Stiff as ramrods, they seemed indifferent to the child's suffering. Premonition assailed her, fear for the child; it was as if a baby chick were being wrenched from her keep. She was momentarily tempted not to give her up, but a look at the faces around her told her it was a lost cause. Reluctantly she said, "Be back in a minute."

She plucked the child up and took her into a bedroom. Murmuring softly all the while, trying to calm the shaken youngster, she changed her rapidly. "You'll see, Amy Beth, it's a fine place you're going to live in, and they'll have lovely toys for you. They've a big house and garden; maybe you'll even have a pussycat. Wouldn't you like that? You'll get used to them in no time. Just wait and see." She put the child on her feet and held her closely.

Amy felt the finality in Mrs. Field's words. If she'd had any spark of rebellion, any resistance, it flickered out. All hope gone, Amy Beth left to live with the Wilkersons. She never cast a backward glance.

Elizabeth Fields couldn't help weeping. Normally she was a woman who did not give way to open emotion, but she was overcome by pity for Amy Beth.

After they'd left, the silence seemed to shout. The Reverend Jenson tried to fill the breach. "A good day's work, Elizabeth. Give it time . . . don't suffer it so. The little girl will be fine. The Wilkersons are an excellent family. I daresay the child will have a better future with them than she might have had with her own parents. You can see that, can't you?"

She refrained from answering, and Dr. Quenton, who had been sitting quietly in the background, broke in. "Lord, yes, Mrs. Fields!" He paused prayerfully. "I think we've done a fine job caring for these little souls. The Lord will bless all of you."

"Amen to that," the Reverend added and asked, "Elizabeth, have you told Emmalina about her sisters?"

The woman dried her eyes and looked at the earnest faces of the men awaiting her response. They really don't mean to be so insensitive, she thought; they're intent on fulfilling their mission. She sat back, trying to get her emotions under control. "Not yet I haven't. The child's been too weak to be bothered by such things. As soon as she has more strength, we'll have our talk. It's a bridge I'm going to have to cross when I come to it."

Reverend Jenson nodded sympathetically. "Now, Elizabeth, you know I'm here to help if there's anything you want me to do . . . to talk with her, anything. You just call on me."

"Thank you, Reverend." Mrs. Fields smiled at him. "I do appreciate all you've done, but it's my feeling that if Emmy and I are going to make our lives together, it had better come straight from me."

The Reverend had known Mrs. Field a long time; he knew that when she said something, that was precisely how it was going to be. He rose. "I guess we'd best be off and let you tend the child. It's been a wearing day but a gratifying one. Take care now—and remember, don't hesitate if I can be of service. Again, our grateful thanks for all you've done.

You're truly one of the Lord's shepherds; may his sun continue to shine on you."

She ushered them out, glad for the respite of peace and quiet. She could do with a cup of hot peppermint tea, but first she'd have to check on her patient. She'd made certain Emmy had been napping before the guests arrived. She dreaded the time, soon to come, when she'd be obliged to tell Emmy that her sisters were no longer with them.

Emmy'd been uncomplaining throughout the illness. She had persisted in worrying about her younger sisters, their missing parents and, amazingly, about Elizabeth contracting the disease. As each day had brought no news of their mother and father, Emmy's disappointment had grown keener. Elizabeth's compassion had driven her to tell the child that her parents would probably send for them as soon as they had relocated.

Elizabeth felt it was false hope, but, under the circumstances, it was the only panacea she could offer. A pragmatic woman of strong and upright character, she had a no-nonsense exterior that covered a warm and loving heart. Ultimately the girl would have to face the tragedy that had befallen her, but she couldn't have been in stronger, more supportive hands than those of Elizabeth Fields.

As soon as she had finished her tea, Elizabeth bustled about, preparing a tray for Emmy. She tried to put out of her mind the disturbing events of the day. Though Amy Beth's face haunted her, the little one was now beyond her help, an added reason she would always secretly despise the Beaufords for their desertion. Foremost she had to concentrate on her goal to strengthen the child in her charge and bring her through the period of convalescence.

Elizabeth well knew how destructive a depressed state of mind could be. When her beloved husband, Thomas, had died, she had lost all interest in living and had become an old woman overnight. Bereft and grief-stricken, she had needed every ounce of will to withstand her loss; with his passing her world had blown away like dust in the prairie winds. The early years of back-breaking hardship had conditioned her to survive, but all incentive had gone; she'd become a recluse. She recalled how everyone had tried to help and she wouldn't budge; but now her experience would give her guidelines for dealing with Emmy.

Bustling about the sink, she caught a glimpse of herself in

the little mirror that hung over the kitchen counter and saw
the gray that streaked her once luxuriant black hair. She
heard herself humming—things were going to be different,
she had a reason for living. Childless, she had found a focus
for her deep-seated maternal frustrations. Elizabeth's heart
reached out to the youngster so sorely bruised in mind and
spirit. She would dedicate herself to providing the balm and
patience that would guide the child and help her outgrow the
shocking loss of her parents.

As Emmy slowly regained her strength and could remain
out of bed for longer periods, Elizabeth knew the time was
approaching when the matter of her sisters had to be
resolved. One afternoon, summoning her courage, she took
Emmy on her lap and, in the gentlest way possible, told her
what had happened. But it was impossible for Emmy to
grasp. Instantly overwrought, she implored, "Why didn't you
wait for my mommy and daddy to come and get us? You said
they'd be back soon. Why didn't you let Amy Beth and Polly
Sue wait here? Why did you send them away to live with
other people? When will I see them? Why were you so
mean?"

Elizabeth tried to reassure her, but the girl wouldn't listen.
Her frail little body became contorted with the unhappiness
she was unable to express. Young as she was, she seemed to
grasp that something cataclysmic had taken place; something
so awful that life would never be the same. The world she'd
known had disappeared. This story wasn't like the fairy tales
that Mrs. Fields read to her where everyone lived happily
ever after. A dark cloud, like those awful winds, had
descended, and everyone dear and familiar to her had gone
into some never-never land.

Elizabeth grew increasingly worried. The child had grown
cold, almost rigid, wringing her little hands in helpless
gestures. Elizabeth pleaded, "Lovey, please believe me—
your sisters are with people who'll love and watch over them,
just as I'm doing with you. I'd have tried to keep them, but it
would have been very hard, and what I can do for one, for
you, I couldn't have done for all three. Try to understand and
take heart. I promise you'll be seeing your sisters. They're
nearby, and in time you'll be meeting them at school and
other places.".

Lost in her own attempts to console the child, Elizabeth
couldn't realize that Emmy had crossed over the barrier of

trust; she was thrashing for her life in a fathomless sea, unable to believe anyone. The foundations of her young life had wafted away without rhyme or reason. It would take long years before Emmy would ever place trust in anyone again.

Collapsing, the youngster buried her head against Elizabeth and sobbed until her broken heart had no more tears left to cry.

Elizabeth held her close, kissing and rocking her in her arms. "Emmy, darling, I understand. A long time ago, when my mother and I were parted, I too had someone else to love me, and, in time, my bad feelings passed. You just be patient, child, and you'll see—as the days go by, the feelings you have won't be so painful. Dearest little Em, I love you very much and I promise you'll have no regrets being my little girl."

Hesitantly the child picked up her head and studied the woman's face. She remembered, through the sick and feverish haze, that when she'd called for her mother it had been Mrs. Fields' face that had hovered over hers. She'd been so gentle and kind, reading to her and caring for her. Tentatively a small smile crept across her tear-streaked face. "I like you very much, Mrs. Fields."

A sigh of relief escaped from Elizabeth. Thank God the worst was over. She pressed the girl close. "Emmy, take your time about what you want to call me, but you don't have to call me Mrs. Fields—all right?"

Weakly Emmy shook her head in acknowledgment. "Yes, ma'am." But there was a lump in her throat, one that would never quite go away until she was long grown. For many years it would occur each time she silently screamed for the handsome face of the man she'd known as Daddy—the one who'd lifted her up in the air until she'd squeal for him to stop—and the laughing, rosy-cheeked, dark-eyed lady who'd been Mommy. The lump was suffocating her. Where had they gone? All the days of her life the feeling would come back to haunt her, and she'd remember, wonder and mourn.

Deborah Wilkerson's face showed surprise as she peeked out through the screen door. Since the woman obviously seemed reluctant to let her in, Elizabeth motioned with her free hand to the pie in the other. "Brought you one of my lemon pies. May I visit for a moment? Can't stay but a short while since I left Emmy with Mr. Hovak . . . he's fixing a leak."

Hesitantly, the gaunt, hollow-cheeked woman opened the

door. "Come in, please. Here, let me relieve you o that. Mighty nice o you to bring us one o your pies. Mister will sure be pleasured."

Elizabeth had never visited the Wilkersons before. Though the old lilac bush resurging into leaf at the back door gave the weathered clapboard house an inviting look, that quality was dispelled by the drab appearance of the stained, slat-walled kitchen. She suppressed a cough at the overpowering smell of smoke and grease. This oppressive odor was unrelieved by the closed window over which washed-out red gingham curtains hung framing a view of the outhouse. In an adjoining dark hallway, she glimpsed, nailed to a wall, an unframed picture of the Savior.

Deborah said brusquely, "Have a seat." She motioned to one of the wooden chairs set around an oilcloth-covered table. The woman was awkward and constrained, and Elizabeth knew she was unwelcome. "I can see you're surprised at my being here, Deborah, but I was anxious to chat with you about our little ones. How's Amy Beth?"

The child was nowhere in sight. "It's her nap time. She's a puny little thing . . . needs lots o buildin up." Deborah was visibly disturbed.

Elizabeth chuckled. "Oh, I'm sure you're the one to see she gets just that. How are things going? Everything sort of settled down?"

Deborah looked at her coldly. "Course things are settled down. Everythin's just as it should be. Sorry I'm goin to sound rude, but I'm in the middle o gettin supper ready."

This was an outright lie. Elizabeth knew it was common practice for preparations to be long made for the evening meal, as was evident by the simmering pots on the black iron stove. "I'll be running along in a moment, but before I do, I was wondering if you'd be agreeable to the little ones getting together . . . They'd be comforted knowing they're near to each other."

Deborah snapped as if she'd been lashed, "Well, I never! Lan sakes, Elizabeth Fields, are you crazy? Why'd you want to do a silly thing like that? Mr. Wilkerson never'd agree to such goins-on. I can't speak for you, but Amy Beth's our daughter now and we're the only family she's got or goin to have! The sooner you and your Emmalina get over these kind o notions, the better off you'll be. Can't you see the faster these children forget the people that birthed them, the happier we'll all be?" She paused for breath, her face florid.

"Lord forgive me, but you must see plain as day how no-account they were, runnin off and leavin them children the way they did. It's best they forget all about them quick as they can. We intend to raise Amy Beth so she'll never act or think in any way that'd show what kind o folks they were. They was just no-good people, if you was to ask me. Besides, Amy Beth's got Theodore for a brother, and she won't be needin any sisters!"

Elizabeth looked at her in frozen shock. Shaking her head in disbelief, she said, "Do you mean, Deborah, you and Horace never want Amy Beth to see her sisters? The child knows Emmy's her sister as well as that darling baby, Polly Sue. Aren't you being heartless?"

For answer, Deborah marched over to the door and swung it open. "I'll bid you good day, Elizabeth. Thank you for the pie. I've said my piece!"

Incensed at the woman's rudeness, Elizabeth flared, "Just a moment, Deborah Wilkerson! I'll be leaving, but let me understand. What happens if we meet on the street? Do you intend to ignore us? Am I to take it you wish me to stop trading at your store? Will that contaminate you too?"

The compressed lips and beet-red face were answer enough, and Elizabeth sailed through the door. Her mind was spinning. In a whirl of dust and chickens, Elizabeth pressed her foot on the car's accelerator and headed for the Reverend Jenson's. He'd offered to help in need; maybe he could handle matters. In her heart, though, she knew it was hopeless. The Wilkersons were a strange breed and known for their cussedness; they'd never change their stand. This was the way things were going to be. She was grateful she hadn't told Emmy where she'd been headed.

As things turned out, she'd been right in her conjectures. The Reverend Jenson explained apologetically, "I'm afraid there isn't a thing we can do about this. After all, they have the right to decide what's best for their child, and they don't want her or themselves to be reminded of the past. However, I will speak with Dr. Quenton; maybe he can prevail upon Horace Wilkerson to change his mind. But, Elizabeth my dear, we both know we can't count on that."

Elizabeth snapped, "Do you call this Christian behavior, Reverend? What in tarnation happens if those parents come back and want their children?"

He looked at her in amazement. "Elizabeth Fields, I assumed you were a smart woman. Do you really, for one

moment, believe after all this time those people are ever
going to reappear? Do you believe in fairy tales too? They're
long gone and relieved of their burden."

Dismayed at the turn of events, Elizabeth went over in her
mind what the Reverend Jenson had said as she drove
homeward. She wondered what she would do if the Beaufords returned. Would she be able to pick up the pieces of her
life again? She couldn't abide the Wilkersons' behavior, but
deep in her own heart she began to understand what lay at the
root of their callousness. She was torn too, but fate alone
knew whether the parents would return. In the meantime, she
would live day by day, prepared to do the best she could to
make Emmy's world a warm and loving one.

Emmalina's face floated before her eyes; the child was
winsome and lovely, and Elizabeth was fast becoming her
slave. Well, no matter what the future held, she was grateful
for the moment and what it contained. If she had any regrets
it was simply that her husband, Thomas, wasn't by her side to
share Emmy.

It would have come as a surprise to everyone but Deborah
Wilkerson's immediate family if they had caught her un-
awares following her insolent dismissal of Elizabeth Fields.

Seated at her kitchen table, she sobbed as if her heart were
broken, and indeed it was. She had never stopped mourning
the loss of her own beautiful daughter, and there was room
for only one daughter in her heart. She didn't care what
Horace or Dr. Quenton said about it being the Christian thing
to do. No one understood the struggle she was going through
having to take the sulking child of those awful strangers into
her home.

Her own dear little Mary had been the joy of her existence;
loving her had thawed the bands of Deborah's frigid heart.
The child's sweet ways had transformed them into a family.
Horace had been easier to get along with, not so insistent on
everything being done exactly as he ordered it. He'd been
kinder and more lenient with their son. Poor Ted! Life wasn't
easy for him with a father who ordered his every move.

If this Amy Beth wasn't such a listless, puny little thing,
maybe they'd be managing better. As it was, she seemed to
hover around, never opening her mouth, spiritless. It was all
Deborah could do not to shake her. She was docile beyond
bearing, speaking only when spoken to and having to be
scolded repeatedly so that she would speak up.

Deborah tried desperately to cling to her faith without question, but it seemed strange that she had to settle for someone's castaway when the Lord saw fit to take her beloved child.

Horace had spelled things out the very night they'd brought Amy Beth home. He expected no deviation and was a watchful taskmaster. "Amy Beth's ours, our daughter now and forever. The Lord's seen fit to send her, and she's to be reared as we would have our Mary. There'll be no talk about her past and no contact with any o them other tykes. Comin as she does from them kind o folk, we'll have to do all in our power to see she follows the straight and right path. Now hear, Deborah, you're to tell me anytime you see a sign o anythin that don't smack just right. She's ourn and we're bound to do the Lord's work for her." He had paused. "She don't seem a contrary mite, but it's too soon to tell. Just keep a tight hold, walkin in the Lord's ways, and I'm sure we'll earn our just reward."

Deborah had nodded and bitten her lips, a habit that her husband detested. She knew that, for herself as well as for Amy Beth, there were no choices. If Amy Beth was the Lord's way of testing her, abhorrent as it was to her, she would do what she could.

The difference between the Wilkersons and the Corrigans was instantly apparent to Elizabeth. The sweet chatter and gurgling of the baby permeated the front room as Deirdre happily showed her inside. "How nice to see you, Elizabeth. Whatever brings you this way, 'tis the good Lord's work. Sean and I were but talkin o you this last evenin."

Elizabeth always delighted in hearing the young woman's brogue. When she and Sean had arrived in Brightwater, they'd come to Thomas for assistance in the purchase of their farmland. Not long departed from their native Ireland, they had seemed like a fresh breeze in the midst of the Oklahoma plains and its characteristic drawl. Their love for the land showed in the way they worked and prospered, and their joy knew no bounds when Deirdre gave birth to their baby daughter. Her labor and delivery had been complicated, and Dr. Robinson had told them Deirdre would be unable to have more children. When they lost the babe during the diphtheria epidemic their lives had been shattered. Immersed in grief, it had taken them time to realize the toll the winds had taken upon their land. Their back-breaking work had been swept away, and it would be years before the soil could be brought back to any appreciable fertility.

As Elizabeth greeted Deirdre, she was comforted by seeing little evidence of their travail. It was obvious Polly Sue had become the symbol of new hope. Deirdre's shining eyes and happy voice made that evident. Deirdre plucked the baby off the blanket and placed her in Elizabeth's arms. Happiness radiated from the sunny, chubby child who snuggled up to her in contentment.

Deirdre maintained a steady stream of chatter while setting the tea table. "Elizabeth, you'll not be off before a warmin cup o me brew and a piece o your own good pie. 'Tis good o you to think o us. Sean'll love you twice as much for it, you already bein one o his favorite ladies—o course after me and that angel you be holdin. Here I am clackin away and not after askin you about that darlin little gel—sick as she's been. Is she already as precious to you as this lass is to us?"

Elizabeth avowed that Emmy was her heart and then she related what had occurred at the Wilkersons'.

Deirdre grew angry and her eyes brimmed when she heard the story. "Poor little waif. To think o that sweet Amy Beth in the hands o sich people jist makes me blood boil. Elizabeth, if you think your darlin Emmy would be the happier for seein our Polly, bring her here. This little smilin jewel would make the angels laugh. We'd be pleased as could be . . . anytime. How about that, me darlin Polly Sue? Would you enjoy seein Emmy?" The baby smiled as if she understood.

Elizabeth felt better. "You know, Deirdre, I may do just that. Perhaps we'll come by one day next week. But remember, don't breathe a word to anyone about the situation with Amy Beth. I wouldn't want Emmalina any more upset than she is already."

Deirdre nodded. "O course not, but 'tis a shame. 'Tis not the woman, though, Elizabeth; 'tis more likely that man. An old beast o a man he is, a hand and a back o iron. He and his Bible-preachin all the time. I fergot to tell you: did you know that Father McGurdy's been talkin to a lawyer about the doption?"

This piece of news surprised Elizabeth. "Isn't it a little soon? It's to be a year before we can do anything."

Deirdre nodded in agreement, busily absorbed feeding Polly bits of cookie. "Yes, I know, but 'tis my Sean. I'm sure he's been at the good father, naggin away. Sean'll niver rest easy till Polly's ours—not that she isn't right now, bless her."

A tremor of fear ran through Elizabeth. They'd been cautioned about the possible return of the parents but had blocked it out of their minds. There was no question, they were certain Polly Sue was theirs. Elizabeth prayed it would be so.

As matters evolved, it was quite a time before the visit to the Corrigans took place. Dr. Robinson's final checkup of Emmy gave Elizabeth an opportunity to tell him what had happened. She couldn't believe her ears when she heard him say, "Why are you so anxious to have them meet? I'd postpone the visit for a while."

Crushed, Elizabeth asked, "Why, Doctor? That'd be cruel."

He shook his head at her sternly. "Now, now, woman, don't talk nonsense. I'm only suggesting you give the child a chance to settle down. It's apt to be more difficult for her if you open that whole kettle of fish again. Don't be in such a rush. It's too soon. She's bound to still be very upset."

That unsettled Elizabeth still more and he scolded her. "Don't get yourself in a tizzy over what I'm saying. It's only natural for her to still be anxious. For one thing, she's the oldest, and I'll wager she still feels a responsibility for the younger ones. Give her time to grow accustomed to you and her new situation."

Abashed, Elizabeth explained, "I didn't intend to upset the cart, Doctor. I just thought she'd be more at peace if she knew the others were safe and happy."

He looked at her sympathetically. "I understand your good heart, Elizabeth, but try to see it this way. You know better than I what the child's endured, and certainly each day that passes helps to ease the pain. As she gains strength and is able to run about and take part in life, her memories will recede. Remember, Elizabeth, hope dies hard, and it would be the worst kind of cruelty to do anything to encourage it."

Not understanding, Elizabeth asked, "You mean about their parents' returning? You figure seeing Polly Sue would start her being anxious again?"

This time the good doctor lost patience. "Lan sakes, woman, you can't think she's given up yet? You even told her—I heard you myself—they'd probably be coming after them as soon as they were located someplace. It'll take a lot longer time than this to get her over the hurdle. You know very well the heart heals slowly. Just let things be; take one day at a time." He paused for a moment. "Why don't you get her a puppy?"

Elizabeth laughed. "Doctor, of all things! What's a puppy got to do with this?"

His face broke into a smile. "I've a hunch it could do a sight more for her than you or I. She's fine physically and she seems a bright, sensitive youngster. A puppy'll do a lot of things for her. It'll be a soft and loving thing that needs her. It'll keep her mind busy giving it care and petting. It can't hurt none and may go a long way towards easing her heart."

The doctor was busy, and it was time for her to go. Elizabeth rose. "Thank you, Dr. Robinson, on behalf of Emmalina and myself." She laughed girlishly. "I guess, Doctor, it's one of the rare times you've prescribed a dog as medicine. Would you also know where I can pick one up today?"

In the late afternoon Elizabeth told Emmy they were going for a drive. It was to be a surprise, so Elizabeth didn't tell the girl where they were headed. Turning off the road, she drove through a lane dividing the pasture for the Swensons' large herd of dairy cows and stopped in front of an attractive blue-roofed house. Elizabeth hailed Mr. Swenson, who was high on a ladder applying a coat of whitewash to its exterior. Emmy exclaimed, "It's real pretty! It looks like the houses in my Hans Christian Andersen book."

Elizabeth concurred. "You're right, Emmy; the Swensons came from Denmark. Come along, now, I want to find Mrs. Swenson."

After a short chat with Mr. Swenson, they made their way toward a big blue barn, maneuvering through noisy ducks and hissing, lunging geese. Inside the capacious, well-kept barn, Mrs. Swenson, a warm and pleasant woman, led them to a stall in which romped a playful litter of pups, all soft fur and squeaks. Ecstatic, Emmy flopped down in their midst, squealing with delight when one pup clung to her. It was love at first sight; and when Emmy looked up appealingly and saw Elizabeth's nod of agreement, her joy could hardly be contained.

The ride home was filled with happy giggles. Elizabeth decided that the dog would not be kenneled in the barn as was usual, but instead would be Emmy's responsibility to housebreak and feed, close at hand. "He's all yours, Em, and it's up to you to see that he's fed and has water. He's depending on you."

Elizabeth bent down to kiss the earnest little face as Em promised, "I'll do it, ma'am. I'll take good care of him, you'll see. Can we call him Fuzzy?"

The child and the dog became inseparable companions, and as the summer days slipped by, they worked their magic. Emmy gained weight and with it a return of her vitality and spirit.

But, unbeknownst to Elizabeth, there was a day when Emmy slipped back. Romping through the fields with Fuzzy, she caught sight of a particular tree that struck a chord, reminding her of the terrible time when she and her family had found refuge beneath it. Stopping, she looked around, wondering where their old car had gone. She walked to the tree and pressed her head against its trunk as if to draw comfort from its rugged bark. Achingly she recalled how her parents had urged them on to safety. Through her tears she dimly heard Fuzzy whining. Stooping, she gathered him into her arms, and her sobs wet his coat. She was lost in misery when she heard Elizabeth's voice calling across the distance, and she knew it would be wiser to hide her feelings. Walking slowly back to the house, she wondered why it was that she and her sisters had been taken in by strangers when they had not even been wanted by their own mother and father. They must have been awfully bad children for their parents not to have wanted them. Filled with loneliness and longing, she turned to look back at the tree.

When she reached the house, Elizabeth stared at her curiously. "You've been gone so long, child, I became concerned." Laughingly she added, "I wouldn't want to lose you."

Emmy forced a smile and moved past her. "I'm sorry, ma'am. Fuzzy and I took a long walk."

Shortly after this incident, Elizabeth resolved to fulfill her unkept promise. One morning, girl and dog were bundled into the car for the visit to Polly Sue. Emmy's reaction totally surprised Elizabeth. After giving Polly Sue a joyous hug and kiss, she seemed perfectly content to wander outside with Fuzzy.

The truth was that being with Polly Sue had brought back a flood of memories and Emmy wanted to escape from them; the hurt was too painful. She tried to suppress her feelings as she and the dog explored the Corrigans' farm, which looked to be a poor place, with the land stretching flat and dreary, and nothing growing on it. She did discover a little vegetable garden in the back that was just beginning to sprout, and then she wandered over to a large shed where firewood and farming tools were stored and found a chicken coop. She was restored to laughter when Fuzzy began to chase the squawking rooster.

Elizabeth was thrilled: the visit seemed to have gone without a hitch. Soon Emmy was routinely addressing Elizabeth as "ma'am," and one day when "Mammy" inadvertently slipped out she saw the child's surprise. Elizabeth pretended not to have noticed; Emmy's reticence had to do with reasons embedded in her heart. *Mammy* was but one letter from *Mommy*. There was no doubt their relationship had improved; Emmy was outwardly content and more relaxed with her.

The Wilkerson encounter had produced another problem. For years Elizabeth had traded at the general store in Brightwater. Horace Wilkerson, its proprietor, prided himself on being the supplier of everything from farm tools and groceries to what he termed fancies. Usually the shopping expedition was something she enjoyed as she leisurely explored the store's cavernous interior. It was customary for her to pass before the shelves lined with goods and stacks of colorful fabrics, loitering before the sewing accessories and peeking into the kegs with their nuts, bolts and nails as well as looking into the barrels holding tea, coffee, sugar, salt and other basics. She would examine the racks with their array of ladies' bonnets and men's caps. When she had circled the store she would come to the long counter with its scales and place her order. But now she was in a quandary whether her patronage would be welcomed.

Her supply of staples was running low, and it was becoming imperative to shop for more. After thinking it over she decided to follow her usual procedure, so one morning, shopping list in hand, she set off. Quaking, her mind conjuring up all sorts of dire things, she resolutely walked into the store, prepared to face the fray. Momentarily blinded by coming in from the sun, she was soothed by the familiar aromatic scents as she peered through the darkness. She jumped when footsteps approached and turned to hear "Howdy! Good day, Mrs. Fields."

It was difficult to judge his countenance in the dim light.

"Good morning, Mr. Wilkerson. It's that time again, and I'll need to be stocking up for the fall canning."

She moved toward the light and saw what passed for a smile on his face. He seemed almost obsequious. "Yes, of course. Glad to be of service. Got a new line of jars just come in. Better'n we ever had before . . . a good buy too."

Together, as they always had heretofore, they moved from shelf to shelf, he jotting down what Elizabeth indicated she wanted. She had just about concluded when her eye was caught by colorful bolts of cloth stacked high on a shelf. "Oh! Those look new, Mr. Wilkerson. They're right pretty. I believe I'll take a yard and a half of each of them; they'll make up into darling school dresses for Emmy." She caught her breath. She'd sworn she'd make no mention of the girl's name, and now she'd done it. She was astounded to hear him say, "How's the little gel doin', ma'am?"

She responded hesitantly, "All things considered, she's doing very well, thank you."

He scowled as he said dolefully, "Wisht I could say the same for ours. The one we got—that Amy Beth—she's a mopey sort . . . downright spiritless, you might say."

Since he seemed disposed to talk, Elizabeth asked, "Been ailing, has she?"

His face grew sullen. "No . . . nothin like that. Just seems hangdog all the time. Is yours like that?"

It was as if he were talking about a chicken or a mule. She tried to summon an answer that might touch a tender spot, but it was difficult to disguise her dislike of the man. "No, Mr. Wilkerson, my Emmy's not like that. However, I believe these little girls need a sight more loving and understanding than might normally be called for. It may just be a question of more time for Amy to fit into your family. She's really such a little one . . . hardly out of babyhood. She must be confused after having just been through a really difficult time. Pitching them around the way we did didn't help—don't you agree?"

It was clear that he was contemptuous of what she'd said. Horace Wilkerson had not been raised to observe the niceties where womenfolk were concerned; however, a good, cash-paying customer such as Mrs. Fields had to be handled with some deference even if she stood up to him. "No, ma'am, can't say as how I agree. It's plain to see, womanlike you got one view 'n' I another. I don't abide with mollycoddlin. It's my feelin these gels should be grateful the Lord seen fit to put them in homes with food enough to eat and someone to instruct them in his ways . . . purtickly, you might say, seein as where they come from. I don't see that white trash needs all that special lovin and understandin!"

Color flooded her face; her resolve to keep calm dissolved in anger. "Mr. Wilkerson! You, a deacon of your church—how can you talk that way? Can't you realize these children are too young to understand what's happened to them? They're poor little innocents. Believe me, a little tender love such as you showed your own dear Mary would go a long way towards brightening Amy's spirits. Amy's not responsible for what her parents did; she's sorely tried, poor little babe, lonely for the life she knew."

He leered down at her. She'd said too much and it hadn't touched him even minutely. His look was worse than his speech. "Well, ma'am, meanin no disrespect, I come from a school that says, 'Spare the rod and spoil the child.' She'll come round or elst! Will there be anythin else you'll be needin?"

As the clerk helped to load the car, she caught a glimpse of Mr. Wilkerson watching her through the window. She was certain he was smirking at her. She shuddered. Judging from what she'd heard, she imagined that living at the Wilkersons' was a miserable hell for the child.

Chapter III

◦──◦◦◦──◦

AT THE WILKERSONS'

IT WAS TRUE. Amy Beth was miserable. Terrified and bewildered by the strange surroundings and the harsh, unloving people who made up this cold world, she tried in the best way she could to comply with their demands. She withdrew into herself, fear making her mute and clumsy. Sleep brought only a succession of nightmares. With no hope of rescue, without love and understanding, she was willing herself to die. The Wilkersons were totally incapable of comprehending it.

Despite Deborah's antagonism toward the little girl, she struggled to maintain an appearance of doing what would be considered right. Above all, Horace had to be appeased. Ever mindful of the way neighbors and church congregants viewed their charity, she resigned herself to proving what good, practicing Christians they were.

Born and raised on bordering backwoods farms, Horace and Deborah had in common childhood days of harsh and rugged circumstance. Insulated by region and bigoted by ignorance and fear, their sole enlightenment had come from itinerant preachers. Instilled with rigid values from which they rarely deviated, they aspired to put Amy through the same smelter to forge her into the same mold. Pity was a sentiment alien to them. The conviction that Amy had derived from a cesspool of sin only served to strengthen their contention that a lessening of their tyranny would be a sign of weakness. They had seen their duty; now they had simply to do it.

Although only in his thirties, Horace appeared older. He was a tall, thin man with glacial blue eyes. Early exposure to the elements had given him a desiccated, leathery countenance that was unaccustomed to smiling, and his gruff, stern manner made him a forbidding figure.

Thin and angular, Deborah—two years younger than her husband—had once been a pretty girl. A life of austerity had given her no incentive to enhance her appearance. She pulled her thick ash-brown hair back into a tight bun that accentuated the chronic discontent etched upon her features. She was too young for the lines that creased her face, evidence of the incessant nagging and complaints to which she was prone.

A deacon of the church and proprietor of his own business, Horace Wilkerson was adjudged an outstanding citizen of Brightwater. Those who knew of his irrational temper and occasional bouts of intemperate drinking thought none the worse of him. Both Wilkersons took pride in the knowledge that they were held in high esteem.

The church was the pivot of their lives. Its activities and their occasional visits to and from other congregants were their sole social outlet. The horsehair sofa and stiff-backed chairs set in their parlor were kept polished and gleaming in readiness for such visits.

The evening of Elizabeth Fields' visit to his store found Horace irritated. The woman's imprudent words had lingered all day. When he entered the kitchen of his home, the family was seated around the table finishing supper. His terse greeting sounded gruffer than usual, and Deborah, who knew the danger signals of his temper, hastened to serve him. Amy had found that aping Ted, the Wilkersons' son, sometimes saved her—the boy understood his father's ways. Since Ted kept his eyes glued to his plate, she followed suit. Tonight, this only served to enrage Horace more. He smashed his fist on the tabletop, scattering cutlery and dishes as he roared, "Pick your head up, gel! Don't you learn her better manners, Deborah?"

Tittering nervously, Deborah whined, "You knows I try, Horace, but, I declare, nothin stays in that child's head." She snapped at Amy, "Hear me, gel! Get your head up afore it gets slapped off! Look at your father when he's talkin!"

Amy swallowed and choked, gasping for breath. Quietly Ted slid a glass of milk toward her.

"Stop that!" Deborah shrilled. "She knows she's not to drink with the meal."

Horace ate steadily, staring balefully at them. Finally, shoving his plate away, he growled, "It's enough to spoil a man's food, this carryin-on at the table. Ifn you can't eat proper, you can eat with the hogs. Hear that, Deborah? If she don't learn, let 'er eat with the pigs."

At that moment, Amy Beth thought that sounded preferable to being at table with the family.

Routinely Deborah's conversation with Amy consisted of orders that were accompanied by slaps and threats. Saintly sadistic, she was seldom content until she brought the child to tears; she'd then launch into a favorite theme: "Snivelin ain't gonna help you none. You best learn what we tells you or off you go to the orphanage. You know what they do to kids in the orphanage? You works from mornin till night, and ifn you don't do it right, they use a hot iron on your back." Amy would listen in a state of absolute terror.

In desperation, wanting to find surcease from the beatings and bellowing that seemed to be her lot, Amy tried her utmost to placate them. She yearned, with every fiber of her being, for some sort of acceptance—a kind word, approbation, a pat instead of a shove—but it was not to be.

Any spark of tenderness Deborah had was expended on Ted. Amy's earliest lesson had been to learn she was excluded from the inner circle—the "family." Repeatedly Deborah pointed out, "You been lucky to be placed here. Who else'd want to put up with the likes o you?"

She was to find out that, no matter how she excelled, it would not alter their attitude. She would receive the only accolade they were capable of offering: "It be no more than what is right, Amy Beth. Keep it up!"

Several times a day it was Amy's task to pump pails of water from the well for household use. They were heavy and unwieldy, and she had to struggle not to have them slop over. If perchance Horace caught her at this, it amused him to belabor her back with a twig he kept handy. Already a mass of welts, the child's poor flesh would rarely have time to scab before another whipping would add to them.

She learned quickly that making a mistake earned incredibly cruel punishment. It was as if Horace and Deborah vied with each other in devising torments to humiliate and hurt her.

Necessity sharpened her wits and experience became an ally. Shortly after starting school, she'd made the mistake of coming home excitedly waving a spelling paper on which she'd made but one error. "Look, Mother, look! I got everything right cept one letter in 'good morning'—'n' that's cause I was in a hurry. Teacher said it was very good."

Amy had not realized Horace was home. His shadow loomed over her as he pulled the paper from her hand. Amy cringed; she could see he was in one of his fits. His voice boomed. "Why were you in a hurry? Careless—that's what you are! There'll be none o that! Spell the word for me now!"

Her voice was gone; her mouth was locked; her senses had fled; terror blocked her mind.

His voice was like thunder. "Stubborn, ornery critter— spell the word!" He was dangerous now; she knew it, but she was helpless. Beseechingly she looked toward Deborah. Horace's voice roared through Amy's head. "This is your last chance! Spell the word!" Amy tried, but no sound came. He reached over and picked up a piece of heavy stove kindling. She knew what was coming, but there was no escape.

He beat her in drunken frenzy, shaking her as if she were a rag doll. The pain tore through her, excruciating stabs of fire on the already badly lacerated back. "You'll never try this with us again, youngun. You'll do what you're bid right fast and proper!" He flung her to the floor. "I'm not through with you . . . you'll talk! A switch'll see to that!" She lay in a crumpled, sobbing heap as he tore out the door.

She didn't see Ted, who pulled up her hand and whispered, "I writ the word in your hand—don't let him see it. Look at it! Spell it afore he kills you."

She was too befuddled when she was yanked to her feet and dragged outside. Holding her as if in a vise, Horace raised the switch. It keened as it flew at her. She was bathed in blood when she lost her senses. The water Horace doused her with brought him some calm and helped to loosen her tongue. In a barely audible whisper, she repeated over and over, "g-o-o-d-m-o-r-n-i-n-g."

His fury sated, he listened until satisfied. He told her, "Remember this, gel! Never show that stubborn streak again! Never! Not so long as you live in my house. Now git up and out o my sight!"

Observing from the doorway, Deborah spoke her orders. Her face was expressionless, but her voice was filled with annoyance. "Take you shoes off—don wan you messen up my clean house. Mop yourself with this!" She threw her a damp rag.

With no other recourse, Amy slowly began to build an

inner strength, developing hidden resources that provided padding for enduring the brutality of her life. She wrapped herself in a cocoon of dreams. Little as she was, she knew that one day she would be grown and rid of these people. In the meantime, she suffered and survived, scrambling for a foothold.

In a household where children were seen and not heard, she had no problem being secretive. At school, her classmates sensed something intangibly different about her, and that, reinforced by her shyness and timidity, made them leave her alone. She didn't resent them; she understood they had "real families." It was enough to be allowed to go to school. Sooner than most, she learned to read, and books became an escape from reality.

Through the early years of her life, Amy assumed the word *dopted* was part of her name, since the Wilkersons commonly used it to refer to her. The word seemed to proclaim their goodness, as if it conferred saintliness.

There came a day when, by chance, Amy found what she considered a hideaway, a secret place. About a mile distant from the Wilkerson house, she came upon a dried stream bed surrounded by thickets of berries and flowers, the habitat of tiny animals, birds and insects. Chores and weather permitting, she would steal off to this tiny oasis of enchantment, filling her mind with sweet creatures of her imagining in the peaceful knell. Lulled by the humming of the insects and an occasional bird call, she would be overcome by lassitude. The unaccustomed quiet was a restorative from the hell and brimstone of her life. Deborah was habitually preoccupied with Satan, and it pleasured her to describe to the child what surely awaited her in the hereafter.

Doing the dishes one evening, Amy overheard Horace telling Deborah, "If you be wantin to, we can make the doption official."

Amy knew it had to do with her and was not surprised when, before sending her to bed, Deborah offhandedly announced, "For now, at any rate, we're not gonna be sending you to the orphanage. Since you be tryin to improve your ways and since them trashy folks o yours ain't comin back, we're agoin to keep you."

On her daily walk to school, lagging behind the other children, Amy would play with the farm dogs who, barking their greetings, would run along with them, adding to the small commotion. She would time her arrival at the small, one-room stone building to coincide with the ringing of the bell. She was captivated by Miss Ashwood, the teacher, who, pretty and neatly dressed, always greeted her class with a happy good morning. Young and conscientious, Miss Ashwood strove to make the classroom attractive and conducive to learning. A chilly place in winter, with only a small potbellied stove for heat, the room was nonetheless warm with cheer, bestrung with colorful cutouts, students' drawings and sheets of exemplary work, among which Amy's efforts often hung.

The young woman enjoyed teaching, and her attention had been drawn to the solemn, sad-eyed little girl. The child reminded her of a plant struggling to grow out of barren soil. It happened that, shortly after Deborah's news about keeping Amy, Miss Ashwood asked her to remain after school for the singular honor of cleaning the blackboard. The girl's total despair at what the Wilkersons' decision meant showed in the black rings that shadowed her haunted eyes. Watching as the child scrubbed diligently, Miss Ashwood remarked, "You're a lucky little girl to have such a loving mother."

Amy's astonishment wasn't lost on Miss Ashwood as she added, "Every day your dress and hairbow are so fresh and clean. Your mother must care about you a good deal."

Her face hot with color, Amy stood respectfully waiting for the teacher to dismiss her. Smiling warmly, Miss Ashwood reached into a desk drawer and extracted a candy, a rare treat. "Here, Amy; you deserve this. Thank you for a fine job. The board hasn't been this clean in a long time."

At this, a timid smile appeared on the child's face and she said shyly, "Thank you very much, ma'am." It was the first compliment Amy had ever received.

The teacher put an arm around Amy's shoulder as they walked to the door. "By the way, Amy, don't you have a sister in school?"

Amy's surprise was evident. "I don't know, ma'am. I never seen her here."

"Your sister's in the higher grades in the other building, and they have recess at a different time. Maybe one day you'll get to see each other. She lives quite far away, doesn't she?"

"I don't know, ma'am," Amy replied. "I never seen my sister when we got separated." She hesitated and lowered her head as she said, almost in a whisper, "My folks don't want me to see her."

Taken aback, Miss Ashwood said, "Well, I don't imagine it will matter if you run into her here. Now you'd best run along; I don't want your mother worrying about you. Tell her I said you're a good little girl. I'm sure she'll be happy to hear that."

Amy blushed. "Yes, ma'am. Thank you, ma'am. 'Bye."

The teacher remained watching as the girl walked down the road. There was no doubt the child was unhappy, and often she came to school with dark bruises plainly evident on her soft flesh. She wondered about the Wilkersons; everyone thought them excellent people. Amy seemed a good, pliant child; she certainly applied herself to her schoolwork. The Wilkersons should consider themselves fortunate to have been given such a youngster to rear. Well, it was an enigma.

Not long after the episode at school, Deborah became ill—so ill that Horace was forced to send for Dr. Robinson. After several visits, Amy heard the doctor telling Horace, "It's in the Lord's hands now, Horace. All's been done for her that can be tried. You'd best be doing a lot of praying."

Unobserved, Amy scuttled outside to hide in the tall field grasses and pray. She was filled with excitement and happiness as she implored, "Our Father in heaven, take my mother, Mrs. Wilkerson. Let her die and go to your heaven." It became a litany she repeated over and over until it suddenly dawned on her that if Deborah died she'd be left alone with Horace. Horrified, her heart sank at the thought of what she might be bringing on herself. Hurriedly she rose and tore into the house. To Horace's astonishment, she flew to Deborah's bedside sobbing, "Don't die, Mother . . . please don't die! Get well, Mother!"

Shocked by the sight of the lifeless, emaciated face, Amy was reassured as Deborah's eyes flickered open. Too weak to answer, she was obviously pleased by the girl's entreaties and Horace's visible amazement at what he was hearing. Deborah was only too glad to accommodate Amy and eventually made a good recovery. As a result of this odd occurrence, for quite a time after both Deborah and Horace were easier with Amy. The indisposition also offered Deborah an alternative way of living. She employed ill health as an expedient means of getting Horace to do things her way.

She was propped up in bed one night during her convalescence reading her Bible as Horace readied himself for sleep. Then he casually let drop a line that made her look up. He seldom shared gossip with her and could see how eager she was to hear what he had to impart. Unbuttoning his shirt, he asked, "Remember them folks . . . Corrigans I think they was called? Did you know they been gone from the area for quite a piece?"

For a moment she looked at him vacantly, not recalling who the Corrigans were, and then she remembered. "You mean them folks that took the little one—the baby?"

He nodded. "Them's the ones. Never shopped none at our place. Just as glad too . . . don't like those popery people. Only goes to prove what they're like—took off and never told a soul!"

Deborah's eyes were big with the news; now she was excited. "Who told you, Horace? Ain't the law gonna be after them?"

He shrugged. "It was Father McGurdy's housekeeper told me. Came in after some thread today and asked about you. She's a talkative biddy. Asked about Amy and one word led to 'nother. She told me they upped and left without so much as a good-bye. She thinks they done it cause they was worried about someone takin the babe from 'em."

Deborah looked at him questioningly. "Ain't it late for somethin like that?"

"Sure—more the fools they are." He grunted. "I don't think that's the reason. They was awful hard hit, probably couldn't make it work—their land was blown to Kingdom Come. The biddy told me the old priest took it right hard."

Deborah was pleased they were having a discussion; such an event was rare. "Don't he know where they've gone? Horace, don't they have that confessin thing? Ain't they supposed to tell things like that?"

He thought for a moment. "Don't know and don't much care. The way I figure it, it's one less for us to worry about."

She didn't understand what he meant. "Why should we worry about them, Horace?"

He shook his head at her stupidity. "The less o them sisters is hereabout the less apt Amy's gonna remember where she's from."

Deborah concurred hastily. "O course, Horace. That child owes you her life. What woulda become o her if you hadn't taken her in?" She nodded soberly. "You did a good thing, Horace, and I'm proud to tell you so!"

He was flustered and embarrassed. It was a rare occasion

when Deborah complimented him. "Thank you, Deborah. I only seen my duty and done it!"

They were pleased with each other. She watched as he stretched luxuriously; her lips compressed as he began to scratch himself.

He felt good all over as he got into bed. He picked up her Bible from the bed, put it on the table and blew out the light.

Chapter IV

THE CORRIGANS

Chapter IV

◦◦◦◦

THE CORRIGANS

THE DAY HAD been so hot the flies were still numb, and the simmering heat lingered on as twilight approached. The sinking sun was painting the prairie rosy red as the Corrigans sat companionably on the porch step seeking a breath of cooler air. Suddenly Sean broke the quiet with frightening news. He'd heard in town there was a plan afoot to look for the Beaufords. Some new lawyer in Towana had suggested it be done. The terror in Deirdre's eyes was all the impetus he needed to broach his plan. If she wanted to keep the baby, Polly Sue, they'd have to leave Brightwater. A small breeze stirred, filling the air with the fragrance of sage, and early stars glimmered as Deirdre, filled with guilty fear, quarreled with her husband.

It was their first big argument, and he won. The threat of losing Polly Sue finally glued her mouth tightly shut. Twice before they left she feigned illness so she wouldn't have to go to confession. Her usually sunny disposition was beset by nerves as she worried that Father McGurdy might make a sick call. For his part, Sean behaved as if there were fire at his back. He handled all the windup details, and, three weeks from the time he'd first told her of his intentions, they were ready to depart.

It was a heart-wrenching moment for both of them as they bade their home good-bye. It was on these now untillable fields they had struck their first roots and in this house seen their first precious child go to her eternal rest. Sean could see

38

what effort it was costing Deirdre, but he was unrelenting. He had decided there would be no good-byes to anyone. He offered one concession, promising Deirdre that, once they were resettled, she could write to Father McGurdy and Mrs. Fields. He banked on time and distance, knowing she probably never would do it.

Driving off in the middle of night as if they were criminals depressed Deirdre still further. She sat unspeaking, and despite Sean's attempts to cheer her up she remained remote. He whistled happily because he felt no guilt. He knew it was better this way. She turned to him, and at the unexpected bitterness in her voice his hackles rose. " 'Tis not like you, Sean, to do things this way. 'Tis underhanded and mean! 'Twill give us a bad name and make things ugly for the good father."

He stared at her angrily. "I've no likin for me wife to be thinkin these things o me. Did you niver think it's you I be thinkin of when I be plannin this? This babe be your lifeline. Do you no think I know what would be happenin to you if they take her from us? I could no take the risk."

Head bowed, she sat despondently, replying so softly he could hardly hear. " 'Tis true, Sean, 'twould break me heart, but—"

Curtly he cut her off. "Think, woman! The law won't be havin concern for your heart. This babe already be part and parcel o us."

Raising her head, she sighed deeply. "That be so, Sean, I canno deny it. I jist be wishin it had not to be done so."

His anger dissolved. " 'Tis done! It be behind us now, so be liftin your spirits and lookin forward to Mike and Montana. There's anither thin—it'll no be necessary for us to be tellin the lass she be not ours. Where we be goin there'll be no one knowin diffrunt."

She looked at him speculatively, slowly nodding. "I guess you be right."

He felt better. "See, Deirdre, kind fates be lookin after us. Who'd a thought we could rid ourselves o that land? Them oil people cum in the nick o time. Who else'd be wantin land with no respect for a man's sweat and toil, picking up and blowin off the way it did? 'Tis God's hand lookin after us. 'Tis a blessin me cousin Mike be needin me for his business. You'll see, 'twill all be well."

He grinned at her and she smiled back as he said caressingly, "You be the heart o me, me darlin . . . and you might as well be knowin, anyone takin that babe from you would be doin it over me dead body!"

Sean had no regrets, but he was not a man to disrespect a magnanimous God who'd sent them such a blessing. Late one night, while Deirdre and the baby were asleep, he wrote Father McGurdy a note.

The words made the priest weep when he read them. He found it difficult to disagree. He could almost hear Sean's voice as he deciphered the scrawling hand: "You see, Father, may the Lord forgive us, we canno be takin the chance that those people turn up and take our babe from us. 'Tis sure that Deirdre would sicken and die, and I'll not be sayin I'd handle it any too good meself. 'Tis better for all our sakes we take no chances. Bless us, Father, and the Lord be with you. We'll niver forgit you. Forgive us, Father. Sean Corrigan."

As the Corrigans wended their way north and began the corkscrew climb through the foothills of the mighty Rocky Mountains, their spirits lifted. Sean thrilled as Deirdre responded happily to the wonder and novelty of all they saw. Free time was a luxury they had never known before. Coming from the old country, Sean had worked his way across to defray the cost of passage; and when Deirdre had followed, locked in a crowded steerage during the worst of the rough Atlantic's tempestuous months, she had been so seasick she had prayed for deliverance. But now, as they grew accustomed to the release from work and chores, they sang their Irish ditties, and laughter came easily. Even their cranky old car, as if sensing the journey's importance, ran like a bird. Their joy was unbounded; even a flat tire was cause for hilarity. Driving through virgin forests of pine and spruce and meadows of wild flowers, they stopped at sun-dappled, blue lakes and were awestruck as they skirted a torrential river to see that it dropped in a great spray-filled falls. The weather was changeable, but when it held they camped by a sparkling stream and spent the night under a star-crammed sky, awakening at dawn in brisk and invigorating air. They climbed higher and higher through the ranging mountains, surrounded by the majestic silhouettes of towering peaks, until they were above the quivering aspen trees, walled in by granite and rock. Struggling and straining, the little car made its way around turns so narrow and precipitous Deirdre feared for their lives even while exclaiming at the verdant valleys spread so far beneath them. Crawling at snail's pace, ever upward, they finally reached the lofty summit. Standing on the pass in the crystalline, bitingly cold air, with only the sky as witness, they gave prayerful thanks for having reached it. They felt it an omen, as if their life were now cleansed of the past.

For a while their journey took them through towns and cities until they reached the northern plains. There a vast panorama of purple, cloud-shrouded mountains folding into one another loomed in the distance. The sky and the land seemed to stretch to infinity, and Sean's anticipation heightened as he realized that ranches ran for miles and miles and a man could dream of one day sharing in such wealth. Their disappointment was keen when they arrived at the small mining town of Ironore in western Montana that was their destination. It was here Michael O'Rourke welcomed them and showed them to the tiny, run-down house he had rented for them at the edge of the grubby little town.

But once they were settled they felt better. In Ironore no one knew or cared one whit about their origins. The baby thrived; Deirdre was busy making a new home and Sean worked long hours, but at least they were free of worry and they were happy.

Chapter V

ELIZABETH AND EMMY

THE DAYS SHORTENED and the sky was a palette awash with red and purple, portending fall. The last few mornings the fields had shown a rime of frost, and wood smoke rose high, perfuming the sparkling air. It was the time of year when energies were at their highest, and the women scoured the countryside gathering every bit of fruit and edible greenery to preserve and store for the lean winter ahead.

Mr. Wilkerson was obliged to extend more credit than ever before. The farm families were forced to depend on him for livestock feed and for the supplies their devastated lands could not yet provide. However, there was a glimmer of hope: government agricultural specialists had come to the area to advise them about crop rotation and soil conservation, so the future seemed promising. The Indian summer days brought a flurry of activity, despite the paucity and hard times.

In the Field household, Elizabeth busied herself readying Emmy for school. Betwixt the pinnings and fittings of new clothes Elizabeth was preparing, Emmy was excited and anxious. It would be a momentous step, leaving Elizabeth's side. The girl was drawn and nervous with anticipation as the first morning of school finally arrived.

Emmy was dressed in a favorite yellow-sprigged blue gingham dress with tiny pearl buttons from neck to gathered waist. Elizabeth declared she looked pretty as a picture, trying in every way she could to bolster her. Off in the distance peals of childish laughter could be heard. It was time to go.

Elizabeth and Fuzzy accompanied Emmy to the gate to wait for the group of neighboring children to appear. As they neared, Elizabeth hugged and kissed the girl so that all could see and urged Emmy into their midst. She watched as Emmy shyly sidled up to them and stood silently observing as the little band meandered along the dirt-rutted, tree-lined road, disappearing behind a bend.

Elizabeth worried; she knew how cruel children could be, particularly since knowledge of the strange children in their midst had been bandied about. This was a big hurdle for Emmy, and she prayed that the girl would be able to cope with it.

. Occupying herself with chores as the hours waned, Elizabeth was startled by Emmy's voice calling to her from afar. Hurriedly she ran to the door, to see the girl waving and running toward her. She sighed with relief: her fears had been groundless; Emmy was returning triumphant and happy. From that time forth, school and new friends absorbed the child. Elizabeth had coached Emmy in reading during the summer; she'd been an apt pupil, and it hadn't taken long before she read effortlessly. For Elizabeth, it was vicarious joy to see her curled up with a book, of which there was an ample supply.

As an early snow whitened the ground, there was peace and harmony in the Field household. Thus it came as a surprise when Emmy's difficulties surfaced again. She had been doing homework at the kitchen table while Elizabeth cleared the remains of dinner, when suddenly she spoke as if talking to herself out loud. "I must have a birthday too. The kids say everyone has a birthday."

Elizabeth stopped and turned. "What? Who are you talking to, Em?"

Startled, Emmy turned a reddened face to her. "They laughed at me. Helen told me I was silly not to know when my birthday is. Her birthday's next week and she invited me to her party."

Without hesitation Elizabeth blurted, "Of course you have a birthday, Em."

As if a weight had been removed from her shoulder, Emmy brightened. "I do? When is it?"

Elizabeth put everything aside and walked to the table, trying to think quickly. This could be a crucial situation for them, so she had to handle it with as much tact as she could muster. "Listen, child, of course you have a birthday—we all do. Mine's in April . . . lilac time. What do you remember about yours? Was there any way you marked it so you can recall?"

The girl stared, looking at her in desperate appeal. She sat quietly.

Elizabeth spoke encouragingly. "Think, Emmy. Was it cold? Were there leaves on the trees?" She watched as Emmy, her brow furrowed, tried to recall. Elizabeth sat down beside her, looking on helplessly as the child painfully probed her store of recently buried memories.

Only the dripping of the faucet intruded on their silence until Emmy's voice, sounding as if she were talking in her sleep, said, "It was cold. We were all inside around the table. I remember Daddy telling me what a big girl I was." Her voice droned on. "There was a cake and a candle and Amy Beth wanted to touch the flame. Mommy grabbed her hand away." She stopped, perplexed. "I think it was Mommy. Polly Sue was new . . . tiny like my dolly . . . she was in the little brown rocking cradle." Suddenly the child's voice rose. "The cake had chocolate frosting and it had white writing on it. Mommy said it spelled out my name . . . E-M-M-A-L-I-N-A. She said it was hard to squeeze the whole name on. Mr. Collins was there—we lived on his ranch—and he brought us a pumpkin . . . it had a scary face. He put it near the window and said it was for Amy and me. I remember Daddy told him we were having a party and he asked, 'Whose birthday is it?' He patted my head and gave me a penny."

Desperate to do something to alleviate the child's misery, Elizabeth put her hand on her shoulder. At the touch, Emmy jumped from her seat and threw herself at Elizabeth, pounding at her as if beseeching her to stop the pain. They rocked back and forth together as the words tumbled out of Emmy. "They're not coming, Mammy . . . they're never coming back, are they, Mammy? Why did they leave us?"

Elizabeth held the child tightly, letting her pour out the long-stored grief, appalled that Emmy had not given up hope despite all the time that had passed. She had to try to do what she could to salve the child's wounds.

As the girl's sobbing lessened, Elizabeth spoke. "Emmy, darling, it's hard to see you so unhappy. You've been such a brave little girl. I'm sad that you're so troubled. Maybe you'll feel better if we talk all this out. Promise me that if you don't

understand what I'm saying you'll stop me so I can explain."
Emmy nodded her head, buried against Elizabeth's chest.
"Maybe some of what I'm saying will cause you to hurt, but if
we get it out in the open you'll feel easier. First off, I want
you to know I love you very much." ·

The girl snuggled closer into her arms and Elizabeth went
on. "Now, I met your folks same time I met you and, as I
recall, they seemed good people who cared about you and
your sisters. . . . It was your daddy got you all here through
that terrible windstorm. It was a fearsome night. I'll never
forget how you all looked, covered with dirt and brambles,
cut and bruised. It was a miracle you made it to my door. The
little I know about you is what your folks told me. I
remember your mother telling me they had no kinfolk and
that she and your daddy were looking for a new place to settle
so's your daddy could find work and take care of you. The day
he left here, he was hoping to find work. I wish I could tell
you I know what happened, but the plain truth is I don't.
Maybe he had to go a long way off. Maybe he intended to
write but something happened that prevented him from doing
so . . ."

Emmy stirred. "What happened?"

"I don't know, Emmy. I can't even guess. When you're a
little older we can talk about a word I call responsibility.
Seems like some folks can't deal with it too well. They think
being free of it is an easier way to live. What they don't
understand is they give up a great deal and cause others lots
of unhappiness. It's sort of like when you throw pebbles in the
pond and make ripples . . . things that people do make
ripples that touch others without their realizing it. When your
mother didn't hear from your daddy, she naturally became
very upset. I think she needed your daddy to look after her
and you girls. I truly believe she was afraid she couldn't do it
alone."

Elizabeth felt Emmy's hand pinching her arm. "Now,
child, your mother wasn't being neglectful of you—no, not at
all! She had asked me to watch over you. She knew you were
in good hands, a roof over your heads and food in your
stomachs. You were safe for the time being, and she could
find your daddy easier without three little ones hanging on."

Emmy shook with renewed sobs and Elizabeth plowed on.
"Now, Emmy, it's a long while they've been gone—certainly
time enough to have had word from them. Because of that, I
decided to do something about the matter. I have a good

friend in Oklahoma City, a lawyer, like my late husband. He's a fine man; he used to be a judge, and everyone still calls him that. Knowing how much I've come to love and care about you, he agreed to help us. For the last two months he's been making what we call a search to see if we could turn up any information about your folks. . . ."

Emmy bolted upright. "What did he find out, Mammy?"

"Nothing." Elizabeth shook her head sadly. "I'm sorry to say there's not a trace of them. We know no more today than when they left. So, Emmy, I'm going to tell you right out what I honestly think: wherever they are, whatever they're doing, for now at least they're not coming back."

Emmy became rigid with anger. Elizabeth stroked her hair. "Now hold on, Emmy; hear me out. Come spring of the new year, I'm apt to get the finest birthday present of my life. That is, if you're agreeable. We can team up. You need a mother, I want a daughter; and if the law says it's all right for me to adopt you our problems are solved." She cupped Emmy's chin in her hand and raised her head so that the child could look at her. "You see, Emmy, more than anything in the world I've wanted a child. The Lord saw fit not to provide me and Thomas with one of our own. Instead, in his mysterious way, he sent you."

For a long moment Emmy sat motionless, staring at her, unable to comprehend. How could Elizabeth become her mother when she already had one? What did *adopt* mean? Her throat felt suffocated. She squirmed and pushed back from the embracing arms, only to see the question waiting for answer in Elizabeth's eyes. Suddenly Emmy realized that without her she'd be alone. She'd have to go along with being adopted; there was nothing else to do. She'd pretend to agree while she waited for her mother and father to return; she knew they would—they had to! She saw, without hearing, the words coursing from Elizabeth's lips. "I've come to love you, child, as if I'd borne you. You're as dear and precious to me as if you were flesh of my flesh. I understand you'll always remember your own folks, but I'll be the best substitute I can . . ."

Emmy's fingers were touching her neck. Elizabeth looked down at her and said, "From what you've remembered, Emmalina, I think we've discovered your birthday. It's got to be on or near Halloween. That's pumpkin time, and, since we have a choice, I suggest the thirty-first of October. That's Halloween and time for trick-or-treating. It's a fun time for a party. We could have apple dunking and all the stuff that goes with it. How do you feel about that?"

Emmy put her hand to Elizabeth's face, looking at her as if seeing her for the first time. She scrambled to her knees and put her arms around her neck. Elizabeth's heart leaped as she heard the muffled words. "I love you, Mommy. I'd like the party, and I'll be your daughter."

Torn between tears and laughter at the outcome, Elizabeth hugged the girl. "We have to make each other a promise since we're going to be mother and daughter. I suspect there'll be times when you'll be unhappy, and when that happens I'd appreciate it if you'd try to tell me about it. It'll help both of us to talk things over. Agreed?"

Solemnly Emmy nodded. "Yes, I promise, Mommy."

That night altered their relationship: they went from Mammy to Mommy.

With Emmy's eager acquiescence, Elizabeth made arrangements for old Mrs. Pierce to instruct the girl in the basics of piano. Though the old upright in the parlor was sadly out of tune, Emmy loved tinkering with it. She took to the lessons and astounded both women by how quickly she learned to play simple and then more complicated tunes.

The months blurred busily into one another until the day came when Elizabeth received a call from her lawyer, Max Esquith, with the information that the adoption proceedings would take place in two weeks. Arrangements were made for their meeting at the courthouse in Towana.

Elizabeth told Emmy, and, as the days passed uneventfully without comment, she assumed that whatever Emmy was feeling she was keeping under cover.

As Elizabeth laid out their clothes the night before they were to go to Towana, Emmy watched her soberly. Elizabeth smiled compassionately. "Honey, even though I'm trying, I can only imagine how you feel. Is there something you want to say?"

The girl choked up and Elizabeth turned her back, pretending to look for something in a drawer until she heard Emmy's voice. "It's all right, Mommy. They didn't want me anyhow and I know I'm lucky to be your little girl. I love you!"

The morning broke bright and clear and Elizabeth kept up a steady stream of chatter as they rode toward Towana. Entering the business section they met traffic—horse-drawn wagons and cars. Driving along the busy main street, Elizabeth was relieved to see Emmy diverted by the people on the street and the display of merchandise in the store windows, particularly fascinated by the big red Woolworth storefront. Parking the car in front of the granite building flanked by impressive columns, Elizabeth saw Emmy tense at the realization that this was the courthouse. Taut, the woman and the girl left the car, walking up the long row of steps to meet Max Esquith, who was awaiting their arrival.

Emmy liked the tall, smiling man at once as he joked and put an arm around each of them while escorting them into the courtroom. It helped to find that, aside from the clerk and judge, they were by themselves. After talking with Esquith, the clerk motioned to them to approach the judge and stand before him. For what seemed an interminable time, they stood quietly as he pored over papers in front of him.

Elizabeth was certain the beating of her heart was loud enough to be heard throughout the room. Finally the judge leaned over to study the solemn-faced child and the doughty little woman who held her hand so tightly. Clearing his throat, he spoke. "Mrs. Fields, it is unusual for a widowed person to petition the court in the matter of an adoption. However, I note in these papers your outstanding character estimates. I must say they weigh in your favor. I also see you are financially well able to provide for the child. All this speaks favorably. Therefore, the court asks: Are you certain that you have given this matter every consideration and do you fully understand the responsibilities you are undertaking?"

Elizabeth's voice quavered. "Yes. Indeed I do, Your Honor."

He peered at her a moment longer and then turned to Emmy. "Emmalina Beauford, do you understand what is happening here?" There was a trace of a smile as he observed the child shaking her head vigorously as she answered, "Yes, sir, Your Honor."

In a gentle tone he asked, "Do you understand that from this day forth you are to be the daughter of Elizabeth Fields? Is this satisfactory to you?"

Emmy didn't hesitate. "Yes, it is, sir."

Satisfied, the judge stamped a paper, wrote something on it and concluded by saying, "Henceforth you will be called Emmalina Fields. Adoption granted." He smiled broadly and said, "Good luck to you, honey, and to you too, ma'am." He turned to the clerk. "Call the next case, please."

As Judge Esquith shepherded them from the building, Elizabeth caught a glimpse of the Wilkersons and Amy Beth entering the courtroom. Emmy had not seen them. Elizabeth was dazed. It seemed incredible that such a simple procedure had altered her entire life, had consummated such an earth-shaking event.

Reaching the street, Judge Esquith announced, "A celebration's in order. I've arranged for luncheon at the hotel. Come along, you two."

Under his kindly ministrations, it didn't take long for their tensions to ease. When they had finished and Emmy had scraped her ice-cream bowl for the last time, Elizabeth said, "Maxwell Esquith, Emmy and I want to thank you from the bottom of our hearts for what you did for us today. We'll never forget it. Would you care to accompany us on a shopping expedition? Emmy's in need of shoes."

Max demurred. "Thank you kindly, Elizabeth, but I'd best be on my way. Let me know when you're coming to the city. By the way, may I be the first to tell you that, having officially been pronounced a mother, you're noticeably prettier. Don't you think so, Emmy?"

Emmy giggled as Elizabeth blushed and said softly, "Well, Max, that's what happens when a dream comes true."

The following Sunday, after church services, the Reverend Jenson congratulated Elizabeth. During their chat, as Emmy wandered away, he informed her, "All went well with the Wilkersons; Amy Beth's theirs now. I've been meaning to tell you that Father McGurdy's been in to see me. Poor man, he's been very upset. He's never had another word from the Corrigans, and he's received notice they could file for their final adoption papers. They're being held for them at the county courthouse. It's too bad there's no way of letting them know."

Chapter VI

<o—⟩o⟨—o>

THE CORRIGANS AND
POLLY SUE

DEIRDRE AND SEAN had long since put out of their minds any question of their right to Polly Sue. The little one grew, and they basked in the light of her beauty and brightness.

The raw and rugged little town in which they lived had sprung up as a result of the digging operations that scarred the bordering slopes. But beyond this was a vista of plains and rolling hills dotted by horse and cattle ranches. They worked hard, and Sean's partnership with his cousin Mike in a small bar and restaurant prospered. The neighboring mines ran full shift and they had as much business as they could handle. Deirdre had transformed the small house into an attractive abode and they lived comfortably.

In recent months, however, Sean had not seemed entirely content. One evening, when Deirdre pressured him, he admitted, "You be right, me sweet. 'Tis not that I'm ungrateful for the Lord's bounty to us, but I've a hankerin for a piece of the ould sod under me feet to tend. I miss the workin outside, havin the feelin o things growin. Wouldn't you like that too, Deirdre?"

She looked around the cozy lamplit room and repressed a little sigh. She rather enjoyed living in the small town and having neighbor women with whom she could chat, but if land was what Sean wanted, she would not stand in his way. She smiled at him. "Surely, Sean, 'twould be a joy to have me flower garden agin and the little one with place to run and play. Do you think we can do it, m'love?"

He laughed confidently. "We can and we will, me darlin. If we're a mite more careful we'll git the money together."

There was lots of land available, but Sean was very careful about what they would acquire. One day, when he was told about a ranch several miles out of town that had a good house and barns, his dream materialized. Once the purchase was made, they stayed on in town for a while to work and accumulate some money for their new life.

Eventually the day came when Sean felt financially secure enough to leave town and make the change to his beloved ranch. He and Mike parted amicably and, free at last, Sean was now able to devote full time to working the ranch. Deirdre had her sunny house and garden, and Polly Sue roamed happily wherever her little legs would take her. They were filled to the brim with contentment, back to a life they loved.

Under the tutelage of Sean and old Pete, the caretaker, Polly quickly learned to sit her own horse. Sean had acquired a small, gentle animal that she could control. She adored Pete, who doted on her, and she followed him everywhere, learning skills that would stand her in good stead. Deirdre worried, but Sean assured her, "'Tis best she learn how to take care of herself. She be learnin good things, care o the animals and respect for nature."

Even though Deirdre recognized the need for this, she scolded. "'Tis a shame! 'Twill be hard to know whether Polly be boy or girl despite all me efforts to make a lady out o the lass."

They indulged the child with single-minded devotion; she had only to open her mouth to have her every wish gratified. From her earliest conscious memory she had been conditioned to winding her mother and father around her little finger.

There was no Catholic parish within miles, so the Corrigans had done without, although Deirdre felt the lack. She lived with an occasional twinge of guilt, but with nothing to prod her she had pushed away the thought of writing to Father McGurdy.

Polly Sue was getting on to school age, and it came as a shock to Sean when Deirdre brought to his attention a matter that had been bothering her. "'Tis time, Sean, we give thought to the child's first communion. 'Tis not fair to be deprivin her o the faith. 'Twill do you no good to try and talk me out o it. I've made up me mind. You'd best inquire round and find the nearest church."

Upset, Sean fought the idea, but Deirdre was intent upon not compounding their sins and he soon saw the futility of further argument.

He noted with dismay how exuberantly Deirdre went about her chores in the days that followed. She was filled with plans for Polly Sue's first communion and took every opportunity to talk about it with the child. Deirdre's insistence and her awe of the occasion communicated itself to Polly, and reluctantly she allowed her mother to coach her in what Deirdre assumed would be required. But after a while the process palled and Polly would impatiently squirm to be off and riding.

A bright, mischievous youngster, whose greatest difficulty was sitting still, Polly possessed a quick mind, but diligence and application were not her strongest points. Since she was catered to and indulged, it was not within her scheme of things to exert effort if it could be avoided. There was every sign she was growing into a beauty. Everyone who encountered her fell victim to the flashing violet eyes fringed by dark lashes. She was blessed with even teeth and perfectly chiseled features, topped by curly black hair. It tickled Sean when folks insisted she resembled him.

At last the time came when Deirdre felt Polly had mastered enough of the catechism, and Sean arranged for them to travel to Butte. There, to Deirdre's joy, Polly had her communion. But it mattered to the child only momentarily; once done, she lost interest in the entire matter. At Deirdre's prodding, she would grudgingly say grace at meals, but the idea of religion bored her. She was a hedonist at heart, and if she had any sense of worship, it was for the land surrounding her and the breathtaking beauty she saw anew each day. The expanse of sky, the ever-changing patterns of the sun on the earth, the varied forms of the convoluted hills framed by the mysterious snow-topped mountains in the distance were her natural element.

She went to school, but except for what interested her she learned little. Bright and intelligent, she was no student. She hated to be confined. She mastered reading because long-suffering Deirdre plied her with colorful books about horses. The teacher moved her along, anxious to be rid of the disturbance and turbulence that Polly constantly created.

As far as Polly was concerned, life was to be lived and

learned anywhere but in the prison of a classroom. Deirdre never gave up trying and hoping, but it was useless. Deirdre would reproach her: "Someday, Polly m'darlin, you'll be sorry you didn't take advantage o the opportunities offered you. You'll be wantin to do things and won't know how."

For reply, Polly would hug her mother and laugh. "Don't you be worryin, Mother. 'Tis not me cup o tea. 'Tis a ranch I'll be runnin anyhow, now won't it?" Polly adored her mother and loved to tease her and imitate her brogue.

Deirdre's greatest pleasure was in making the girl's clothes. She was constantly sending for the latest pattern books. A dainty piece of fabric was a treasure to be bought and transformed for Polly Sue, who came to be known in school as "the fancy kid."

Polly Sue secretly gloated over the appellation. It helped her to lord it over her schoolmates, for whom it was common practice to dress in hand-me-downs. Polly was the envy of all the girls her age, with the added distinction of having neither sister nor brother. Occasionally when she became overbearing, they would gang up on her, but she quickly learned how to beguile them into doing what she wanted. Soon she had wrapped the world around her little finger just as she had her mother and father.

Deirdre made a habit of giving Polly's outgrown clothes to the mothers of neighboring ranches and, despite her admonitions to Polly about showing no recognition when she saw them on other children, the girl had her ways of letting it be known she was their benefactor. If they were embarrassed or angered, it behooved them not to show it, since she might use her influence and Mrs. Corrigan might give the lovely things elsewhere.

Polly was the queen of her dominion, picking and choosing her friends at will. Doted on at home, the center of subservient friends, she ruled her little world without mercy.

Chapter VII

◦─◦│◦─◦

AMY BETH AND EMMALINA MEET

EMMY FELT A moment of sheer joy when she realized at school that the little girl in a far-off corner, standing by herself, was her sister Amy. It was recess and both the upper and lower grades were on the playground. She ran closer to be sure and then breathlessly called out, "Amy Beth! Hi, Amy Beth!"

Startled, the little one turned around; she had been busily preoccupied bouncing a ball. Emmy felt as if her heart would burst. She wanted to hug Amy but was suddenly shy. "How you been? You growed a lot. I wasn't sure it was you."

Amy Beth stared, not believing her eyes. "Emmy, oh, Emmy, where you been? That lady, that Mrs. Fields, the one who took care o us, told me you was comin to see me . . . but you never did."

All the longing, loneliness and despair welled to the surface as Emmy cautiously looked to make sure they were alone. She spoke urgently. "Amy, I wanted to, so much. I knew we was supposed to see each other, but I think your folks didn't want to let us."

Shifting from one foot to another, Amy gaped, enthralled at the nearness of her lost sister. Apologetically Emmy gushed on. "Amy, it wasn't that I didn't want to see you. I miss you! Mom—my new mother—told me she was going to fix it so's we could visit. I got to see Polly Sue. Didn't you know we wasn't allowed to visit you? I know it for sure, cause when Reverend Jenson came to our house I heard Mom telling him 'n' he said it was a shame the Wilkersons didn't think it was a good idea."

Hearing this, Amy looked about furtively. Obviously frightened, she seemed about to back away. "Mebbe it ain't all right for us to talk."

Instantly protective, Emmy wanted to reach out, to clutch her. Didn't Amy understand they were family, they belonged together? She stoutly assured her, "Sure it is, Amy. We're sisters, aren't we? Nothin makes that different. We'll be sisters forever 'n' ever, so can't be any harm if we just talk—all right?"

Scared, Amy was still not certain, but another look around confirmed that no one was watching. "Okay, I spose so. I got a pig. I wisht you could see my pig."

Emmy desperately wanted to talk about what had happened to them, to ask Amy what she thought, but the words stuck in her throat and she was afraid she might cry. Next time they met she'd do it. She smiled. "I got a dog—Fuzzy. I love him to bits. My new mommy loves me a lot and I got dopted. My name's Fields now." She hesitated, hoping mention of this would prod Amy into saying something about their lost parents, but her little sister just gawked wide-eyed, so Emmy went on. "I take piano lessons and she says next year she's gonna take me to Towana for dancing lessons. They got a school just for dancin over there."

As Emmy drew breath, Amy, unguarded and safe for the moment, felt she ought to contribute. "I got dopted too and my name's Wilkerson. My pig's a sow and her name's Tippy cause her ears got black tips." After a moment she added, "I don't get to dance. Our church says we're not sposed to. Emmy, I got a secret . . . but I can tell you. I got a place—" She broke off as the school bell pierced the air. Recess was over.

The children in the yard broke off their play and ran toward the school doors. Emmy took Amy's hand in silent affection. "We can see each other now, Amy, long as we're in school together. You can tell me your secret next time. Cross my heart and hope to die, I won't tell anyone. You look real good—that's a pretty bow in your hair."

Amy regretfully watched Emmy run off. She was filled with the wonder of it, and she called out softly, " 'Bye, Emmy!"

For the first time in a long while, Amy had a happy feeling inside herself. She had a real honest-to-goodness sister who'd told her no one could change that—forever and ever. The thought was warm and comforting. She hoped no one had noticed them together, because she wasn't going to tell anyone, no one at all, about this magical meeting.

Chapter VIII

❦

ELIZABETH AND EMMY FORGE THEIR BOND

AT THE END of the school day, Emmy tore through the back door of her house calling, "Mommy, Mommy . . . guess what? I saw Amy Beth today. I spoke to her."

Entering the kitchen and seeing the child's excitement, Elizabeth immediately gave her undivided attention. "That's marvelous. Tell me all about it, darling. Was she pleased to see you?"

Emmy was aglow with happiness. "Mommy, she's growed a lot . . . and she's got the funniest skinny legs. She's got long blond hair with a big pink bow in the back and big eyes. She don't look atall like me."

Chuckling, Elizabeth asked, "In that case, how did you recognize her?"

Her little face sobered up immediately as she replied, "Oh, Mommy, I knowed her right off—she's my sister. She's sort of just like when I last saw her—only bigger She's 'dopted too, and she's got a pig named Tippy."

Elizabeth picked up some apples she was about to pare. "See, darling, you've been worried about her and she seems real fine."

There was a pause for a moment and then Emmy asked hesitantly, "Mommy, what kind of family are they? Are they like us?"

Elizabeth swallowed nervously and turned to look at Emmy, trying to determine how much she could say. "I don't know them well, child, but from what I understand, I'd have

57

to say they're not like us. For one thing, they're very religious, closer to their church than we are. I've heard they try to live strictly by the Scriptures. Do you know what I mean, Emmy?" She could see the girl was puzzled, so she hastened to assure her. "I don't think you have to worry about Amy Beth. She's in good hands."

She was astounded at Emmy's retort. "Well, if they're so good, how come they didn't let us see each other?"

"Look here, Em," Elizabeth said firmly, "folks don't all think alike. Each family makes its own decisions, believing them to be right. They probably figured it was better for Amy not to see her sisters right off, so she wouldn't be reminded what had happened. I'm sure they felt they were helping Amy. You said she seemed happy when you talked today."

Emmy looked at her pensively. "I don't know, Mommy. She seemed real glad to see me after she stopped being frightened. She was upset we'd never been to visit her. I told her we couldn't come cause her family didn't want us to visit."

Dismayed, Elizabeth shook her head. "I see, Miss Emmalina; little pitchers have big ears. It's the plain truth and she's probably better off for knowing it. It'll be more of a comfort than thinking you didn't want to see her."

Emmy shook her head emphatically. "She was afraid to speak to me, I could tell, but I told her we were sisters, forever 'n' ever, and no one could stop that. Even if we're not together we're still real family. She's got black and blue marks on her arms. I wish you had kept her. She could have shared my bed."

Elizabeth studiously sugared the apples. "I explained all that to you, Emmy. There was just no way."

Emmy sighed and seemed lost in thought as Elizabeth attempted to change the subject. "I've got a surprise to tell you."

"What?" Emmy asked, flopping into a chair, schoolbooks scattering over the table.

"Please, Em, tidy those books up before they land in the pie. Judge Esquith called. He's invited us to visit him in Oklahoma City."

Interested, Emmy's concern for her sister was diverted. "Oh, Mommy, can we go? What fun! Where will we stay? At the judge's house? Does he have a wife?"

"Hold on, girl! One question at a time," Elizabeth

laughed. "First off, we'll be staying at a hotel. The judge's been married, but he's a widower. His wife passed on about the same time as Tom. We've been good friends for many long years and he takes care of my business affairs. From what he tells me, Em, we're going to be rich . . . richer than we are now. Seems all the land my Tom bought up is soaked in oil. We're going to be free to do lots of things I never even dreamed about. But first off, you get your hands and face washed and get to your practicing. We can talk more over supper."

As she left to do Elizabeth's bidding, the image of Amy Beth's fear-ridden face once again distracted Emmy. Their encounter had ripped open her wound and the bitter reality of their circumstances surfaced again. Emmy had striven to put the past behind her. In truth, she'd had no other recourse; she'd resigned herself to the cruelty of the adult world around her. But today the realization of how powerless they were gnawed at her. Elizabeth would have been shocked to know that Emmy held her culpable. The child didn't doubt for a moment that Elizabeth could have held them all together. She had even once heard her say she should have done so. She had been selfish and mean, Emmy thought, and hadn't wanted them to remain a family. They might just as well not have struggled against the winds that fearsome night—they'd been blown apart anyhow. At this moment, the intensity of Emmy's feelings mounted and with her whole heart and soul she hated Elizabeth. It was one more thing to be borne and suffered in silence.

Seated at the piano, she absentmindedly picked out a tune that seemed vaguely familiar. She worked at it, trying to recall where she'd heard it, and suddenly the memory returned. Her father had sung it as she and Amy Beth had playfully marched behind him through the fields. In mournful remembrance she silently mouthed the words: "One for all—All for one—Together the world is won."

Elizabeth began to hum as she worked in the kitchen. In the past months she had begun to regain her old zeal for living. The miracle of having Emmy and living vicariously through her had wrought miraculous changes. She was constantly amazed at Emmy's precocity. There were times when the age barrier between them seemed not to exist and Elizabeth would be startled to find herself discussing affairs normally beyond the level of a child's comprehension. It tickled her when Emmy would proffer advice that often fit like a hand in a glove.

The kitchen had become oppressive, and she looked up. The sight that met her eyes through the kitchen window sent a shiver through her. The bright, clear day had gone, and in its place was a mustard-colored sky, with the sun a burning orb, barely able to filter through. She ran to look out the kitchen door. The air was still and menacing. Her worst fears were confirmed. Sure enough, there it was, still a distance away, but there was no mistaking the huge funnel-shaped cloud wildly barreling toward them. The door slammed shut. The wind was beginning to blow hard. Panic took over and she screamed for Emmy, who came running at the sound of her voice. Quickly she issued instructions. "Pick up Fuzzy and follow me."

Frightened by Elizabeth's tone of voice, the girl watched apprehensively as Elizabeth scurried about, closing windows. That done, she grabbed a kerosene lamp and a covered pitcher of milk which she thrust at the girl. "Hold on to it; no telling how long we'll be stuck down here. Follow me!" She grabbed the child's arm. "Come on, hurry!"

Stumbling and struggling to hold on to both the squirming dog and the pitcher, Emmy tailed Elizabeth out the back door to confront a horrifying spectacle. Racing toward them from a mottled gray and yellow sky was a huge black cloud wildly whirling from side to side, dipping to and from the earth, accompanying its mad dance with a high-pitched keening that blotted out any other sound. The sky was now turning ominously dark as the fringe of the tornado winds approached, and Emmy tried to reach Elizabeth, who was heaving and tugging at a heavy wooden cover that lay flat on the ground bordering the kitchen. It seemed an interminable time before Elizabeth succeeded in raising and propping it. Blinded by the hurtling dust and tumbleweeds, Emmy felt herself firmly grabbed as Elizabeth took the dog from her and screamed to make herself heard: "Get going down there! There's twenty steps—count 'em as you go. There's a rail to hang on to. Move, hurry!" Emmy had no time to lag even though the pitch-black hole beneath her was terrifying. She hadn't gone more than a few steps when Elizabeth loomed above her, working to release the overhead cover, which dropped with a thud. Panting, she called, "Keep going, Em . . . keep moving. We'll have light in a minute." There were no more steps and Elizabeth almost fell over her. "Move child . . . there's space . . . out of my way." Emmy staggered back in the blackness, not knowing what was happening, and Elizabeth thrust the dog into her arms. She remained rooted to the spot as Elizabeth groped about, and then, thankfully, there was a flicker of light. Elizabeth had found the matches carefully placed on a ledge and kept for such times.

Bewildered at the quick turn of events, Emmy looked around at the small gray stone room in which they stood. Gasping from her exertions, Elizabeth tried to smile reassuringly. Mopping her perspiring face, she regained her breath. "It's all right, child; we're safe here. It looks to be a big one, but we've nothing to worry about. We've weathered some bad ones tucked away down here. You can put Fuzzy down now."

The dog whined and clutched at Emmy's leg. Looking at the child's white face, Elizabeth kept up a line of reassuring chatter. "We've everything we need. Look about you."

Despite Elizabeth's forced cheerfulness, Emmy shivered as the thick cover securing them thumped and rattled and the sounds of the whistling winds high above could be heard. She remained standing as Elizabeth busied herself lighting other lanterns standing on shelves. As the light brightened, Emmy was flabbergasted to see they were in a little room complete with chairs, table and a pile of blankets. There were neatly stacked jars of fruits and vegetables, though not as many as in the big cellar where Elizabeth stored her produce and countless preserves. In one corner there was a big shovel and ax. As the lantern flames settled, they cast a cozy glow, and Emmy began to feel easier, even though the wind had picked up its tempo and they could hear its roaring voice growing louder. Emmy had not known this place existed.

Dusting her hands off, Elizabeth said, "Sit down, child. No need to worry now, although that was a close one. Like as not we'd have been safe in the house. That old gray pile of stones has withstood some mighty awful ones, but no sense risking it."

Seeing the confusion on Emmy's face, Elizabeth grinned as she said, "I'm sure getting absentminded; it was wrong of me not to have shown you this before."

Trying not to show how scared she was, Emmy asked, "What is it, Mommy? Why're we down here?"

"The tornado, honey. Didn't you see that big cloud racing towards us?"

Emmy shuddered. Everything had happened so fast; it had all been so frightening, particularly being shoved into what seemed to her to be a black hole. Her teeth chattered as she asked, "What's a tornado, Mommy? Is it like that other time?"

Elizabeth shook her head. "No, Em. Those winds were bad enough, but tornadoes are something else. Fortunately our house is not in the main path, but whenever they come, you've got to move fast. Whenever you see a cloud that looks like a funnel, you head for cover. They can pick up houses and cars. I remember one that made kindling wood out of one of the Swensons' barns. They're nothing to fool around with." Seeing she had thoroughly frightened the girl, Elizabeth said, "It's one of nature's ways of making us respect her . . . same as lightning. I've come through a lot of them. We're safe here."

Emmy moved her chair closer to Elizabeth's and asked, "What would I have done if I'd been in school or walking down the road?"

Elizabeth shook her head in disbelief. "Em, I can't believe I never told you before this. School's got tornado cellars and so does everyone else who lives here. You just run for the nearest house and down their cellar. All the children know what to do. If you're not near home, you go along with one of them."

The earth seemed to be heaving above them. Elizabeth picked up the panting dog and petted him. The air was suffused with a sulfuric smell that made them cough and gag. Elizabeth rose and took some glasses from a closed box and poured milk into them. "It helps to ease the smell. Drink up while I tell you how we came to build this cellar."

Emmy loved Elizabeth's stories; she had an endless supply of tales about her childhood, her parents and her brothers and their exploits when they had lived in a town in Massachusetts.

The child snuggled close as Elizabeth began to relate the story of how, as a newly married bride, she and Thomas Fields had traveled to the Oklahoma Territory and crossed into it before the prescribed time. She looked down at the little head leaning against her and said sheepishly, "We jumped the gun, so to speak. That's how we got to be called

Sooners. This very land we're on is where my Tom elected to settle. We've been here ever since. But that's only part of it. It was the second morning after we'd made camp; I was mixing the biscuit dough and Tom was off collecting firewood when I turned around and saw two Indian men looking at me. I hadn't heard them come—they just appeared as if out of the air. They were wearing tanned leather shirts and pants trimmed with fringe, and round their heads they had wide bands with feathers sticking out. They were something to see. Land, they scared me. Tom was just coming back with firewood, and when he saw them he put the wood down and walked up to them with his hand outstretched. They spoke a little English, and since they seemed in no hurry to leave, we invited them to eat with us. In no time at all we were sharing breakfast. It was one of the best things ever happened to us. They stayed around a few days and showed us how to make straw bricks. Would you believe, that's how we got our start here? Made our living for quite a while supplying bricks to the other settlers. That was one gift they gave us, and the other was this. They managed to get it across to us that we had to dig a deep hole. In their way, they tried to tell us about the big winds. They helped us line the hole with stones; some of these around us are from that time. That's how I first learned about tornadoes."

Elizabeth's voice faded away and Emmy stirred. "What happened to the Indians?"

Lost in her reverie, Elizabeth said softly, "One morning when we got up, they'd gone, just as mysteriously as they'd come. We never saw them again."

Emmy perked up. "The kids make fun of the Indians."

Elizabeth snapped, "I know. It's something I hope you'll never do. There's so much to be learned from others if we be but willing. Remember, Em, never turn away from a person if he's different-looking from you. The only important thing is how a person behaves."

They had been so involved in the story that they hadn't realized the wind had ceased. Emmy stood up. "Listen, Mommy, the tornado's gone. Can we go up now?"

Elizabeth remained seated. "Not yet, Em. It's not safe yet. It'll be a while; they twist and turn so much there's no saying if it's left the area."

Relieved and easier, Emmy sat down again. "Tell me another story."

Once started, Elizabeth described the early days when there were no roads or maps, and their difficulties in fording streams and herding cattle, and how they had braved their first norther without adequate shelter. As Emmy listened enthralled, she told about young Dr. Robinson traveling for miles to do emergency operations on kitchen tables, and how everyone worked together helping one another. When they had built their sturdy gray house with stones collected from the land, their neighbors had come to help them with raising the roof and putting in the window glass, which had come all the way from Kansas City. She explained that as more people had settled in the area there had been land quarrels and her husband Tom had hung out his law shingle. She smiled in pleasant recollection. "Things got easier, and in time we founded a town here. The old stream bed gave the place its name: Brightwater. Tom found out that's what the Indians called it."

Insatiable, Emmy asked, "Are all the people here the same ones that came when you did?"

Elizabeth chuckled. "Some, not all. The old town's seen a lot of changes and been through a lot of good and bad times. One time, I recall, we had a bunch of silly men here who used to dress up in white sheets. They gave themselves some fool name and tried to order other folks around, even tried to run them out of town. They looked like ghosts and terrified the people they went after. It was a nightmarish time, and it left a lot of bad feelings. Imagine, they wanted a law so no Negroes, Catholics or Jews could stay in Brightwater. If they came through, they were supposed to be out of town by six at night. There was a big hullabaloo over that, you can bet."

Puzzled, Emmy asked, "Why were they afraid of those people?"

Chuckling scornfully, Elizabeth said, "Exactly, Em—afraid's the word. It's hard to understand what winds other people's clocks, but as long as Tom and I had anything to say, those fool white sheets never got a foothold here. We had friends, the Levinsons; they'd also come to the territory from the East. Doc Levinson had the pharmacy—and what a blessing that was, not having to go all the way to Towana for medicines and such. Well, one night those white-sheeted lunatics rode into town looking like a wall of fire with their torches and they burned their store down. It was a miracle the whole town wasn't set ablaze. That was a bad time. I'll tell you, I never saw my Tom so roused." She looked sad as she continued. "The Levinsons were proud folks and I can still remember the day they came to us and told us they were leaving to go back east. They refused to stay where they weren't wanted. Believe me, the townspeople had good cause to regret that . . . more the fools."

There was silence now and Elizabeth cautioned, "Stay put, Em. I think the storm's over. See how relaxed Fuzzy is. But I want to make sure."

Emmy watched as Elizabeth climbed the stairs and pushed the heavy door open a crack. From where she was Emmy could see it was night and a star twinkled through. Pushing with all her might, Elizabeth raised the door and held it with the heavy stick set there. She returned to put the little room back to rights, blowing out the lanterns that would remain there. When everything was in order, she picked up the dog and the lantern and, with Emmy following close behind, they came out into a starlit night. They stood quietly for a minute or two, inhaling the freshness of the air. Elizabeth looked around. There had been no major damage as far as she could see. The tornado had coursed its way some miles from them; it would be the next day before they'd learn what it had done.

Just as they entered the house, they saw John Hovak driving up. "Everythin all right, Mrs. Fields?" he called out.

"Just fine, John. We just came up."

"Wal, I wanted to make sure. It sure was a devil. Swung off apiece just afore it touched Brightwater. Won't be till mornin we know if anyone got hit."

Elizabeth smiled. "It was good of you to come, John. Thank you. Would you like a cup of coffee?"

"No, ma'am, thanks. I'd best be off. See you tomorrow." Returning to his beat-up old jalopy, he drove away.

Elizabeth turned to Emmy. "He's such a good man. I've some mighty good friends here. Now, young lady, how about some bread and jelly, and then bed. It's late and you've got school tomorrow. Remember, we're going off to Oklahoma City in a few days. Dream about that tonight."

It was difficult for Emmy to fall asleep. The tornado had been unsettling, and she wondered about Amy Beth and if she had been protected. As for Polly Sue, she felt certain the

Corrigans would not let any harm befall her. Elizabeth had not yet told Emmy they'd left the area.

As luck would have it, arriving at the school grounds the following morning, she caught a glimpse of Amy Beth entering the schoolroom, her big bow neatly tied in her smooth hair. Amy Beth didn't turn around, but it made no difference as long as Emmy knew she was all right.

Chapter IX

❖❖❖

AMY BETH FINDS SUPPORT

"AMY BETH, AMY BETH! Where are you?" Dang that girl, she's never around when you want her. Deborah Wilkerson was peeved. This afternoon she'd planned to have Amy untangle some skeins of yarn for her.

"Ted!" she whined. "You seen Amy Beth on your way home from school? I declare, she gets later all the time. She be needin another good whuppin. Where you suppose she lags about?"

Ted walked into view of the kitchen door from where he'd been piling logs handy for the stove. "She don lag none, Momma. It's Miss Ashwood keeps her at school ahelpin—cleanin the boards and such. She tole me ony las week to tell you what a good student Amy Beth is—said you had reason to be right proud. 'Nother thin—she sayed you and Poppa should be right proud o the good job you done with her. She thinks Amy's the best-kept child in the whole primary grade and it's a wunnerful reflection on you."

Deborah was pleased, although she'd sooner have died than show it. It was a great feather in her cap that such complimentary notice had been given her. "Humph! 'Tain't been easy, son, I'll tell you that. It's good to know someun preciates my efforts even if Amy don. That child sure was a lot o nastiness to bring into line . . . but you know that, don't you, boy?"

Ted smiled; if she wanted an answer, she'd have to be

content with that. "Thar she comes, Momma . . . she's acomin now."

Ted turned back to his work. He knew where Amy Beth spent most of her free time, but he wasn't about to let his mother know. An introverted, taciturn boy, he understood a lot more than he let people know. He had no special fondness for his adopted sister but he had sympathy for her lot in life. She bore the brunt of his parents' ill temper and his father's drunken beatings. No need to give fuel to his mother's fire. Of late he'd begun to feel good about the way Amy looked up to him, tagging along behind him and, despite her shyness, finding opportunities to do little things for him. When they were alone together she'd hang on his every infrequent word. It made him feel manly to be protective of her.

He hoped the girl wouldn't be caught. As soon as he safely could, he'd have to tell her to be a mite more careful about stopping off at that old Injun woman's shack. What he'd told his mother had, in part, been true. He'd told the truth about what the teacher said about Amy Beth, and the teacher did keep Amy a lot, but not as frequently as he'd implied.

Ted had accidentally stumbled upon Amy's secret. He'd been in search of a special plant root and gone to the wooded area that was also a back way to their house. He'd been passing the old woman's shack and heard Amy's voice. She'd been laughing, and he'd been surprised—it had been the first time he'd ever heard her do that. Stopping behind some brush, he'd listened, and a few moments later she'd come out and run toward home. Purposely, several times after, he'd taken the unfrequented path to see if Amy was there. It didn't do any harm, but there sure would be hell to pay if his folks ever found out about it. They couldn't abide Injuns.

Later that afternoon, as Amy and Ted were at their tasks in the barn, he checked to see that they were alone and then signaled her to come closer. "Don't be afeared, Amy. I ain't snitchin on you, but if I seen you with the Injun, others folks might too."

Torn between horror that she'd been caught and gratitude to Ted, she mumbled, "Thanks . . . gee, thanks! I'll be more careful. Aunt Tina's a kind lady, Ted. She's lonely too. She tells me lotsa interesting stories."

He shrugged, feigning indifference; he'd done his duty. "It's okay, Amy. Whatever you do's okay so long as you don get caught. Watch it—you know what'll happen if they find out."

She knew! Yes, indeed, she knew! Aunt Tina was the church pariah. Faithfully attending services, she was relegated to a seat apart from the other parishioners far back in a corner. Amy'd heard her mother describe her: "That filthy trash . . . dirty old Injun . . . It's a mercy she's allowed in our hallowed house of worship. More's the wonder she comes to church."

In the town of Brightwater, Indians were seen and not heard, the prevalent attitude being that, since they had once been the cause of trouble, they were troublemakers. Their plight was of no concern and they were dealt with summarily if they caused any disturbance. Thus it was sheer chance that had brought about the meeting of the old Indian woman Tina Ondinka and Amy Beth.

Exploring a new way home, Amy had come upon a back lane that wound through a heavily wooded area. Pushing her way through the thick tangle of brambles and overhanging trees, she had gone a distance when she was met by the heady fragrance of flowers. Curious to find the source, she reached a small clearing and was astonished to see, set back in a copse, a house, barely discernible under an overgrown blanket of honeysuckle vines and wild roses, and apparently deserted. Thrilled with her discovery, for many days thereafter Amy would stop and linger, trying to summon the courage to go closer. Finally she had determined to walk down the grass-grown rocky path and peek inside. Bolstering herself, she pretended it was the woodcutter's cottage from "Hansel and Gretel." She was Gretel fleeing from the wicked witch, Deborah, and the little house would provide safety. The quiet was broken only by the incessant buzzing of bees reveling in their flower work as she stepped onto the path. She was startled out of her wits as a soft voice close by greeted her. "Hello, gel. Ain't you de Wilkersons' 'dopted gel?"

Amy turned to run as a smiling Indian woman appeared from behind a bush. "Don worry, gel. 'Tain't no one but yo 'n' me roun here." She beckoned invitingly. "Come in, don be fraid. Come see de new litter o pups out back. Satchu done it agin. Mebbe yo folks be lettin yo have one."

Shaken but tempted, Amy hesitated only a second. "No, ma'am, for sure they wouldn't, but"—she glanced around—"I'd like to see them."

Tina Ondinka extended a hand into which Amy trustingly put hers, and they walked to the back of the house. "Yo kin call me Aunt Tina, chile. What's yo name?"

"Amy Beth, but you can call me Amy."

They laughed and became instant friends. Amy recognized Aunt Tina from church and remembered Deborah's harsh words; but looking into the smiling, gentle face, Amy saw only kindness.

Wise and perceptive, Tina Ondinka was drawn to the pathetic child. She had been observing her for several days. She was lonely herself, and her warm heart went out to the sorely abused girl whose anguished screams she'd heard many times. "If yo got a minute, Amy, come into de house," she said after they had visited the pups and their mother. "Bring dat little pup dat's lickin yo han."

Quivering with anticipation, Amy followed Aunt Tina through the overhanging bower of flowers to find herself in a room lit by a flickering oil lamp that cast glimmering shadows on a strange and fascinating world. It was as though she had stepped into an enchanted land. In a corner there was a bed covered by a great buffalo hide, and above it hung a weaving of oddly shaped people and animals. Everywhere she looked her eye was caught by something intriguing. There were plaited strands of yarn and brightly colored beads with little dangling feather charms suspended from the ceiling, and on the floor around her were strange-looking baskets holding mysterious roots and leaves. Shelves bulged with jars and bottles filled with colorful liquids and uniquely carved wooden dolls. In front of the fireplace was an old, deeply indented easy chair covered by a leather hide, and next to it a small table holding a pottery jug from which a variety of well-smoked clay pipes protruded. An appetizing aroma permeated the air, and on an old wood-burning stove Amy saw something was frying. Seeing her sniff, Aunt Tina went to the pot and extracted a chunk of fried bread. "It's hot . . . try it, gel. It's real good. Here, sit down." With a motion of her broad hand she swept the clutter off a leather-topped stool and Amy perched on it, munching the delicious tidbit, feeding crumbs to the pup.

Studying the girl, Aunt Tina said, "Lemme put somet'in on dem bruises, gel." Selecting a jar, she rubbed a sweet-smelling ointment on the child's discolored arms and legs. As if it were the most natural thing in the world, Amy asked, "Could you put some on my back?"

Raising the girl's dress, the old woman gasped at the mass of angry red welts. She reached for another bottle. "Stan still, gel . . . it'll burn fo a minute but den it'll be better." She muttered to herself, "Dey calls us savages, but we don beat our chillrun."

Amy gritted her teeth as the unguents were applied. In a few minutes the sting was gone, and the salve was cool and comforting. "Thank you, ma'am . . . it feels better."

Smiling sympathetically, Aunt Tina said, "Yo kin come anytime and I be glad to take care o you. I makes dem medicines. When I was little like yo my mudder taught me. I be glad to show yo. Now I don like to be rushin yo but mebbe it be time for yo to go. Come agin tomorrow. I be here all de time."

Amy lingered, reluctant to go, but, finally rising, she impulsively kissed the old woman. For the emotionally starved child the invitation to return to this bewitching world was a gift from heaven. From that day forth every chance she got she would hurry to Aunt Tina's, and though each time together was brief, those moments were like magical balm.

One day Aunt Tina surprised Amy with a gift. "Yo'll have to leave it here, chile, but it's yos. My ole teef ain't what dey was, but I chew the pelt specially fo yo dolly."

It was the first gift she had ever received, and Amy was ecstatic as she clutched the little doll to her. It was dressed Indian style in beaded leather jerkin and pants, with a tiny silver chain around its neck. "Thank you, Aunt Tina. I'll love it forever. It's so beautiful. I know it'll bring me good luck."

Smiling at the girl's pleasure, Aunt Tina said, "Yo is right. Remember, Amy, if yo stan in good relation to de eart', to de gods, to all dat is beautiful, it stan in good relation to yo."

Free to ask questions, Amy never got her fill. "Where did you get the buffalo hide, Aunt Tina?" By now the girl knew that any question she asked would bring on a story.

"When I was young and live wit my tribe on de great plains, de buffalo were everywhere and we never wasted 'em like de white man. We had everytin we needed and made everytin ourselves. Life was good den."

"Did you have schools? How did you learn things?"

Aunt Tina chuckled. "We was taught many tins. I never learn to read or write, but we had many people who did. Dere was de great Sequoya . . . he invent de Cherokee writin— and, chile, in de Five Civilized Tribes dere was men could read Latin and Greek."

At the surprise on Amy's face, she asked, "Do you know

de great Choctaw leader, Allen Wright, give de state its name? My special tin is bein good wit leaves and herbs for helpin ailments."

Amy was impressed. "Are you a doctor?"

In the amber light reflected on her face, Aunt Tina resembled a wise old Buddha as, puffing on her pipe, she slowly shook her head, "No, chile. We had great people to look after us . . . de chief, de priests and de medicine men. Onct when my sister was sick wid bad spirits, a medicine man from anudder tribe come to our tipi. He make a big pitchur outa sand . . . all colors—and he sang prayers to drive out de bad spirits and my sister got better."

Amy's eyes were big with wonder. "What did you do with the picture?"

Seated in the shadows, her eyes closed, Aunt Tina seemed far away as she explained, "De wind blows de sand away 'n' takes de bad spirits wid it."

Many times Amy was convinced Aunt Tina was a good witch sent to watch over her. This was particularly true when she would watch the old woman pad around concocting her medicines and setting them to simmer, reminding Amy of witches' brew.

Parting from each other was hard, but the old woman knew how fraught with danger their association was and took every precaution to keep the girl's visits hidden. For the solitary Indian woman the visits were a blessing. "My chillrun be grown and gone, my people scattered, so, Amy, yo be my chile now."

Hearing this, Amy broke into a hopeful smile. "Can you dopt me, Aunt Tina? Can I be your child?"

"Dey wouldn't let me," Aunt Tina admitted sadly.

The day following Ted's revelation of their secret, Amy rushed frantically to tell Aunt Tina. Calming the anxious girl, she assured her, "He ain gonna tell, chile. In his way, he be yo fren. Don worry. But mebbe fo a day or so yo don come—till yo be sure. So as yo won be tempted to stop, take de udder road."

It was a great sacrifice, but Amy did as Aunt Tina requested. Miraculously, nothing came of Ted's discovery; it was as if Aunt Tina's good spirits kept them protected, and their meetings went on unknown and unheeded by anyone else.

This release from the rigid, puritanical tyranny under which she lived brought about a change in Amy. But if the

Wilkersons noticed it, their only reaction was, "The gel's settlin in."

The Wilkersons had other things on their minds; they were beset by new problems. The Depression was making an impact on their lives; times were very hard and every penny counted. Ted was to be sent to high school in Towana, and it required every sacrifice they could make to manage it. In order to pay for his board there, Deborah and Amy would secure work cutting cotton during the summer months. Amy's wages went directly into the can set aside for Ted's care.

The work was cruel and hard, and more often than not, returning home at night, Amy would tumble onto her cot too exhausted to eat. She would be roused by Deborah's rough shaking to begin another day's round. She rarely saw Aunt Tina during this period.

Matters reached a crisis when Horace was brought home one night stretched out in Dr. Robinson's buggy. He had collapsed at work. Dr. Robinson warned him, "You've had a mild heart attack. You'd best take care, Horace, and hew to my instructions. Another attack could be fatal. For at least a month you've got to stay home and take things easy. Deborah'll have to look after things at the store."

Amy continued to pick cotton, but this time without her mother nearby. She knew, sleepily crunched in the truck jolting along the rough road, that the long green rows were there, waiting—rows of the thick white stuff whose pods cut through her callused fingers. In the coolness of the dawn she would work quickly, her mind a blank, and the burlap bag slung from her thin shoulder would soon bulge. It was when the relentless sun beat down and the sweat poured from her, or after a rain when the moistened soil made the going hard, that she worried she couldn't maintain the pace. She knew how many lined up each morning looking for work, and she pushed her aching, cramped body along the endless lines, thinking of Aunt Tina, of songs she'd learned in school, of anything to distract from the exhaustion and monotony of the work.

Horace had no choice and was left alone to fare as best he could. It was during the period of his convalescence that he made a decision that would alter their lives.

One night, as Amy wearily assisted Deborah in the preparation of their evening meal, Horace announced: "Gonna sell out soon's I can find some fool to buy. We're movin! Goin west! Had a man in just afore I got sick said

Californy's the land o milk and honey. If the good Lord lets us, that's where we'll be aheadin . . . all o us—Ted too! You, gal, you been real steady bout workin, and since you've a mind to continue your studyin, you'll get better schoolin there."

They were stunned. When Deborah finally found her voice, she asked him, "When, Horace? How we gonna get the money to go?"

"Don be a fool woman! Ain't you listened? I'm agonna sell the store—lock, stock and barrel. Mind you, just as soon as I find a buyer, we're lightin out. Now hear, don' go spreadin this round the town . . . don none o you say a word. Awready writ Ted to quit his lookin round Towana for a better job and board. We'll be needin him here. You kin look for him to be acomin in soon. I ain't sellin the truck . . . that's how I'm plannin fer us to get there."

"But, Horace," Deborah persisted, "how you gonna sell the store—partikly if no one knows your plans?"

"Don you concern yourself with that; I awready got someone in mind. You just lissen and do as I says. Start stackin some o them empty boxes we got in the store. We'll be takin your preserves and such, long with our personals. I needs to see that Injun . . . Ondinka. We gonna be relieved o givin her that forty dollars a year for this place. Mebbe now she'll have to git off her fat ass and do some work."

Amy had had no idea their land belonged to Aunt Tina. She'd have to see her; she'd have to manage somehow to tell her about their leaving. With all her heart she wished they'd go and leave her behind in Brightwater, but she knew they wouldn't.

The realization that she would be leaving Brightwater, losing the last link with her big sister Emmy and Polly Sue somewhere nearby, as well as her beloved Aunt Tina, was almost more than she could bear. Moving west put the stamp of finality on it. She would never escape the Wilkersons; she would be forced to depend on them, tied to them forevermore. Her sisters would never be able to find her. Desolate and miserable, she lost her last shred of hope when, emptying the trash, she picked up a torn scrap of paper that had blown to the ground and saw Emmy's name on it. She had been unable to retrieve the other pieces without attracting attention.

It was her night to go to the library, but instead she rushed to Aunt Tina's, the tears flowing before she was through the door. "We're leaving, Aunt Tina! They're taking me to California. I'll never see you or my sisters again. Emmy wrote me a letter and they tore it up!"

The shocked woman tried to comfort the child, but Amy was verging on hysterics. Sobbing, she complained angrily, "Emmy knows what they're like . . . keeping us apart. She shoulda tried to see me herself."

Hiding her own dismay, Aunt Tina consoled her. "Mebbe she tried, Amy, but wit de Wilkersons she had no chanct. Keep hope, chile; one day yo'll fin each udder. Don carry on no mo, it don help. One day yo'll fin each udder."

Chapter X

◦━━◦◦━━◦

THE FIELDS DEPART

ELIZABETH FIELDS WAS in shock. She couldn't believe she'd actually decided to pull up roots and leave Brightwater. But their trip to Oklahoma City had brought about just such a momentous decision.

Max Esquith had been the propelling force. He'd been insistent. "Get out! You owe it to the child. Emmalina needs new ground to grow and develop. What can Brightwater offer her? Put your old ghosts to rest. The city'll offer you both new stimulation."

He'd been adamant, pounding away at her, and after much deliberation she'd finally agreed. Once decided, she could hardly wait; each day that passed made her anticipation keener. Although fearful, she looked forward to the challenge of a new future. Emmy had been the catalyst; without her as the incentive she'd never have done it. Good friend that Max Esquith was, when she'd faltered, he'd not given up; he'd bolstered and encouraged her, made her overcome her fear. "Elizabeth, you may be tiny, but you don't fool me. I know your strength."

She'd really been terrified at the prospect. "Max, at my age it's frightening to make such a move. How will I make a place for myself and the child? It might be bad for Emmy."

He'd scolded her. "Don't tell me you're scared! You're a Sooner, lady—you can accomplish anything you've a mind to do! As for the obstacle of your years, let me remind you that, at your age, you adopted a young child; anything else should

76

be easy." His eyes had twinkled and he'd grinned at her. "You're intelligent and adaptable. It's time you started to live. Besides, you're rich enough to do anything you want . . . even to be eccentric! The rich can get away with anything."

He had made her come back to the city on the pretext of some urgent business, and that had been the clincher. He'd driven her around, pointing out some of the lovely living areas, and then stopped near the entrance to an elegant private school. He'd said emphatically, "This is where Em should be going to school. They have an excellent curriculum and a fine music department." He knew her weakness. "Stop your hedging; don't keep stalling. Make up your mind and do it. You'll see how easy it can be done. I'll put you in the hands of a good realtor. Find yourself a house, enroll Emmy in school and give her the exposure and education that a wealthy young woman needs in the world today."

That had done it. She'd looked at him, smiling. "Max, you old devil, you've about got me convinced."

He'd laughed flirtatiously. "I'm glad. There's a lot of life left in you, my dear Elizabeth. . . . Tell the truth, isn't that why you wouldn't marry me? Max Esquith's too old a fuddy-duddy for you . . . isn't that so?"

"You know that's not the truth, Max." She was blushing. "You'd have made yourself a laughingstock with all your fancy friends if you'd had me for a wife. I'm a country bumpkin and you know it."

Angrily he cut her short. "Elizabeth, you never cease to amaze me. A woman of your sense and values talking such nonsense! I'd never have believed it of you."

"Max, you didn't let me finish. What could I do for you? What will I do here amongst these people? I don't want to be an embarrassment to you and Emmy."

He looked at her in derision. "Do you hear yourself? Do you really mean what you're saying? You're talking drivel. Every water seeks its own level. There are good, decent folks here, with your kind of values. Give them a chance—they'll be only too happy to take up with you. We've known each other so long, I'd have thought you'd have trusted my judgment."

She looked at him, surprised at the emotion he stirred in her. "Max, please, I do trust you . . . you're my best and dearest friend. What would I have done without your help and friendship? For goodness' sakes, don't make me feel worse than I already do. Look at me, Max—a dowdy little woman in home-sewn clothes."

He'd burst into laughter. "I see Elizabeth Fields! You're a very pretty woman who, with a little fixing up and some smart clothes, will turn herself from Cinderella into a fashionable-looking lady. Now just relax and take my word for it. And while we're on the subject, I'm ready with the glass slipper whenever you want to try it on. I'm warning you, I'm a lusty old codger and just having you close by will mean a lot to me. Let's stop wrangling—are you agreed?" He didn't wait for her reply.

He had all the answers before she raised the questions. "I wouldn't sell the old house. It's a landmark. Keep it and rent it to the Hovaks; they'll be only too glad to give it good care. Take only your most precious things and show me some of the old spirit!"

She sighed. "How can I fight you? Maxwell Esquith, this will be on your head. All right! I'll do it! You've convinced me." She reached over and kissed him on the cheek. "Max, Max . . . I have to tell you. Emmy asked why we don't marry."

Grinning sheepishly, he said, "The child's got more sense in one finger than you have in your whole head. What'd you tell her?"

Smiling coquettishly, she blushed. "I told her we might, but let's wait, Max, and see if I make the grade. All right?"

Putting the car in gear, he'd snapped, "Liz, you're a hammerhead—a stubborn, ornery critter. But we'll settle for this for now."

He'd put his hand out and she'd held it. "Thank you, Max. Thank you for everything."

The news was on everyone's lips; the town was agog. Elizabeth hadn't planned on people finding out so soon, but John Hovak's wife couldn't keep it a secret. It wasn't every day that the likes of poor folks such as them got to live in a house as grand as the Fields' graystone, and Mrs. Hovak spread the word that, once the Widow Fields departed, the Hovaks were going to be its new residents.

Now, driving toward town, her mind was awash with memories. She recalled the first time she'd driven the old dirt road, so fearful and proud. At Tom's insistence, she'd learned to handle the stubborn clutch in the then-new Model T. What a sense of pride and triumph she'd felt when she'd seen the faces agape at her driving. The men had snickered, and she'd heard the women talk, gabbling like a lot of foolish geese. Actually she'd never been too concerned with what her fellow townsfolk thought. Thomas Fields had been the town's first mayor, and after his death the main street had been renamed in his memory. They were considered the "first family" of Brightwater. Most folks stood in awe of Elizabeth and kept their distance; she was known to have a sharp tongue if circumstances warranted it. She had maintained a pleasant relationship with some of the old-timers, but with her husband's passing she had gone into seclusion. She knew she was a source of interest and that everything she did gave rise to gossip. Through the years her only close friend had been Pauline Levinson, and the two women had been inseparable. Both Tom and Elizabeth had adored the well-read and witty wife of the pharmacist. A fiery, dark-eyed beauty, Pauline had roused the enmity of most of the farmwives by her stylish dress and her indifference to them. Due to Brightwater's disproportionate share of bigots, the Fields had maintained a close watch over their friends, since Pauline was quick to fight back at the slightest slur. Elizabeth's last miscarriage had been difficult and dangerous, and Pauline had never left her side, nursing her through the harrowing hours, cooking and caring for both the Fields during Elizabeth's convalescence. Once the Levinsons had departed, Elizabeth never developed a closeness with anyone else.

She knew every stick and stone of the region; she had been here from the town's beginning, and it was an integral part of her. As the crowing of the roosters rebounded against the sky each morning, she could pinpoint where each farm began and where its boundaries ended. The most precious years of her life had been lived here, and every tree and rock was etched in her memory. It was only natural that she worried about adapting to a new locale. Brightwater had insulated her from the outside world, although she'd outgrown the town long ago.

As she drove slowly down the old main street, past the small weather-bleached hotel, past the little white building that housed the library she had helped found, past Father McGurdy's lace-curtained windows, past all the familiar landmarks, she was assailed by nostalgia. She had to get herself in hand; she was here to settle her accounts. She pulled up at her first stop, Horace Wilkerson's store. After she had paid her bill, she decided to tell him firsthand of their departure. "I guess you've heard the news, Mr. Wilkerson. Emmy and I are moving to Oklahoma City."

He shook his head affirmatively. "Sure was a surprise, Mrs. Fields. You're one of the pillars of the town; we'll be missin you."

"Thank you, Mr. Wilkerson. I'm sure we'll miss all of you too. We won't be that far away, and I'll be returning from time to time."

He seemed embarrassed. "Yes, ma'am, but it won't be the same."

She looked up at him as she made one last appeal. "Mr. Wilkerson, will it be all right if Emmy writes a note to Amy Beth with our new address? It would be very nice if you and the family would visit with us one day."

A little smile played on his lips. "Thank you, ma'am. Thank you kindly for the invitation, but it ain't likely we'll be gettin over that way soon. I cain't see any harm in Emmy writin a note if you think it all right. It'll be fine with us."

She couldn't make him out; his guard was down and he seemed ill at ease, not his usual gruff self. Elizabeth extended her hand. "I'll tell Emmy, Mr. Wilkerson. I'm sure she'll be happy to hear it. Will you be good enough to say our good-byes to your family? Good luck to you and stay well."

It was inexplicable, but Elizabeth felt near tears. Theirs had always been an adversary relationship, but, even so, saying good-bye was not easy. The man shook her outstretched hand and he too seemed moved by the emotion of the moment. Abruptly, Elizabeth turned and left the store.

Everywhere she stopped that day people expressed their sorrow at her departure. It became almost too much for her to handle.

Sparse gray hair pulled back in a knot, wiping her tears away, little Miss Harding—who filled in as the town librarian—whimpered. The tiny network of wrinkles at the corners of her eyes worked to curb her feelings. "Oh, Mrs. Fields, you leavin us . . . what's the world comin to? Who'd ever thought the town's leading citizen would move away? What will become of Brightwater?"

Elizabeth swallowed the lump that rose in her throat. Their ties went back a long way. Sooners too, the Harding family had followed close behind them when they'd jumped the line. "Come now, dear Miss Harding, it will go on exactly as before. I want you to have our address, and if you get to the

city, I'll expect you to visit. If there's a book you especially
want, you're to let me know, hear?"

That evening when she told Emmy of her conversation with
Mr. Wilkerson, she was surprised as the girl retorted bitterly
she doubted they would let Amy write.

In the few days remaining prior to their departure, Emmy
began to realize how much the old gray house meant to
Elizabeth.

Anxious and filled with sadness, Elizabeth talked constantly, as if by doing so she could avoid the imminence of change.
Each object seemed charged with significance and brought
forth a new flood of memories. "See there, Em, in that
wall—that odd-shaped stone. I remember when I found it.
It's hard to believe that I was a slip of a girl not dry behind the
ears yet, and that Thomas and I built this house stone by
stone. Those were hard years, but we had each other, and we
laughed a lot. We were so tickled when we added the porch;
Tom carved the gingerbread trim and rail by himself. Soon as
Thomas did well, we were the first to have an indoor
privy—you can tell it's been added by the way it juts out.
Folks came for miles around to have a look. I didn't mind all
the cooking that entailed; it was fun to have company. My
Thomas always worried I'd catch my death from pneumonia
due to my weakness from the babies I lost. He worried about
me a lot. Oh, how I yearned to hold a babe in my arms, I had
so much love to give. I tried hard not to let him know how
much I missed having a child."

Emmy nodded sympathetically, confused about what Elizabeth meant. She was tempted to ask but felt the subject might
be too sad. As if sensing this, Elizabeth explained, "Poor
man, he wanted children so much. It made me feel guilty
never being able to carry them full term."

At the look of tender concern on Emmy's face, Elizabeth
couldn't resist kissing her. "Here, now, my sweet, I didn't
intend to make you unhappy. My Thomas would have adored
you."

Emmy was happy to hear that; it made her feel she
belonged. Of late she had begun to feel a sense of importance, proud of her role as Elizabeth's daughter. Only
recently she had learned just how important the Fields really
were and noticed with what deference her mother was
treated. It had begun to reflect on her as well. Miss Harding,
the town librarian, had shown her the section in the history

book on Oklahoma covering their area—and, big as life, she had seen for herself the names of Elizabeth and Thomas Fields.

Miss Harding had beamed. "You're a mighty lucky little girl. The Fields are important folks in this area."

Elizabeth took special pains to see that Emmy didn't feel it was something she took as her due. Emmy had discussed the special treatment accorded her mother, and Elizabeth had explained, "It matters to me that people think highly of the Fields—but, mind you, Em, only because it means we've been of service to others. Had my Tom not died so young, he might have been governor of this state. He had a way with people and faith in what this region offered. It's due to his foresight we're rich and, according to Max, going to be richer still. If folks want to pay court to me, I can't stop them—but it's nothing for us to get bigheaded over."

Emmy understood, but it didn't rob her of increased self-esteem. She enjoyed being the crown princess.

When the last of the packing had been finished and the cherished bric-a-brac and keepsakes were carefully tucked into boxes, the letdown came. Tired but not sleepy that last night in the old house, Elizabeth shared her favorite memento with Emmy. It was an old, much-thumbed album filled with faded and yellowed photographs, and it seemed to Emmy better than any story because it showed those who had peopled Elizabeth's life.

Seesawing between laughter and tears, Elizabeth regaled Emmy with anecdotes about the pictures. For a long time they quietly studied the stiff and faded picture of Elizabeth's parents. A lot of sniffling ensued as both tried to contain their tears. Elizabeth said softly, "You know, Em, I never saw them again after we came to Oklahoma. It must have been very hard on them to have their only daughter go away. We wrote each other all the time. When my mother died, Tom asked my father to come to us, but he didn't want to leave the East."

Drying her eyes, she turned the picture quickly. "Look—those are my brothers. The swing they're sitting on was hung from the big old elm in our front yard. See the peony bush . . . my mother was famous for growing huge ones. The shorter boy is Herbert—he was killed in World War I—and the one with the smile is John. He was a missionary in Africa. Someday I'll show you his letters; they're so interesting." She sighed. "I heard only last year he'd succumbed to some tropical disease." She paused, sadly pensive.

Turning the page, she averted her head and Emmy felt bad as she watched Elizabeth stroke the few pictures she had of her husband. He looked to have been a tall, handsome man with a smiling countenance. Her voice was choked when she spoke. "We were such good friends. From the moment we met, we shared everything. I'd have followed him to the end of the world, and I guess I did. He never gave me cause to regret it. Through good times and bad our love for each other never changed."

She straightened up and snapped the book closed. Looking tenderly at Emmy, she said softly, "You see, darling, why you're so special to me. You and Max are all I have left."

Strongly moved, Emmy threw her arms around Elizabeth and for a few seconds they held each other closely. Then Elizabeth said resolutely, "This will never do! We've got to look forward to all the new things awaiting us."

As if in keeping with the difficult change, the morning of the move dawned overcast. All the good-byes had been said, the last walks taken, and Elizabeth fought to keep her feelings from overwhelming her. The Hovak youngsters hovered in the background, watching as their father loaded Elizabeth's car with the baggage. The moving van would arrive later to pick up the crates and boxes. The moment arrived, there was no further excuse for delay. With as much determination as she could muster, Elizabeth handed John Hovak the ring of keys to the house. "Take good care of the old place, John; it's part of me and I wouldn't want any harm to come to it."

"Don't fret, ma'am . . . we'll be doing our best to keep it in shape. Now you just take good care o yourself and that little one—we're agoin to miss you both."

She could hardly see the road through her tears. As she slipped the car into gear, she turned for one last look. There it sat, immutable, the weathered gray stone receptacle of all her past dreams, its two guardian pecan trees waving their branches in farewell. No looking back, you old fool, she told herself; the die is cast. Through a fog she heard Emmy. "Mommy dear, don't cry. It'll be fine. We'll be coming back. Everything will be all right, Mommy; you'll see."

She reached over and drew the girl close to her. "You're right, Em—absolutely right. I'm behaving badly."

Emmy's little face was sober as she said earnestly, "No,

you're not, Mommy. It isn't easy to leave something you love."

Elizabeth was instantly consumed with guilt. "My God, darling, you're right. You know, don't you?" The drive was long, and for most of it they sat in silence.

"There it is, Em. What do you think?" Elizabeth swung the car into a hedge-lined circular driveway and stopped at the front door of the grandest house Emmy had ever seen.

Set in the midst of spacious landscaped grounds, the imposing Tudor manor house exuded a gracious, welcoming air. Elizabeth had purchased it, complete with furnishings, from a family who had moved to Texas. As Emmy stood by her side, she put the key in the front lock and the door swung open. Even the dog seemed subdued at the elegance that met their eyes.

Emmy stood speechless until Elizabeth laughingly said, "Cat got your tongue? Don't you like it?"

Emmy gulped. "Mommy, it's so big. How are we going to find our way around?"

Chuckling, Elizabeth said, "We're going to have to, so let's make a get-acquainted tour. We'll do the downstairs first." Walking through the spacious paper-paneled hallways, they entered a walnut-lined den through whose stained leaded-glass windows the sun filtered, creating a filigree of colors that danced over the floor-to-ceiling bookshelves. There were wonderfully woven throw rugs and a large brown leather couch with several matching easy chairs. The cigar humidor in the corner gave the room a masculine scent. Beside the fireplace, which looked well used, there was a stack of wood in a handsome brass container. Surveying it appreciatively, Elizabeth said, "Max calls this the library. Imagine, Em, having a library in our own home." Taking Emmy by the arm, she led her toward a niche. "I have a surprise for you . . . look!" Before her stood a grand piano. "That's specially for you, Em." Face shining, Emmy ran her fingers over the keys. "It's beautiful, Mommy! I can hardly wait to play on it." Moving toward the door, Elizabeth said, "You will, child; it's all yours. Come along."

At the entrance to the next room, Elizabeth paused, momentarily intimidated by the grandeur spread before her. The salon's walls were covered in flocked gold paper, and the floor to ceiling windows were hung with shimmering gold and green damask draperies whose fabric was utilized in two handsome couches flanking a beige marble fireplace. On its mantel were gold candelabra and an ornate French clock. Placed throughout the room were delicate gold Louis XVI tapestried chairs and graceful tables holding exquisite bisque pieces. A huge rug designed to complement the appointments completed the decor. Elizabeth shook her head in mock dismay and, turning to Emmy, she remarked, "What could Max have been thinking of? When will we ever have use for this? I feel completely out of place. I hope the kitchen is more practical!"

Despite its huge size, they instantly felt more at home as they stood in the sunny kitchen. Elizabeth said happily, "I believe it's as big as our entire house in Brightwater."

Gasping excitedly, Emmy asked, "Mommy, are those for cooking?"

Hanging above a large white range was an array of shining copper pots. Elizabeth laughed. "I guess they are; we could feed an army."

Opening and closing cupboard doors, they kept exclaiming over their finds. Elizabeth's great delight was the big ice chest. "Em, it looks big enough to hold a side of beef."

From there they inspected the cheerful breakfast room and formal dining room. Its crystal chandelier and heavy silver epergne were in keeping with the grand living room. Finally they made their way upstairs and, pointing to a door, Elizabeth said, "I believe that leads to your bedroom." Emmy screamed with delight as they entered. "Mommy, it looks like a garden!"

The floral paper on the walls was topped by a trellis pattern on the ceiling, giving just such an illusion. The four-poster bed and rocker were covered in raspberry and rose chintz, matched by a cushioned seat fronting a large bay window. Flower-shaped pillows were scattered about, and completing the furnishings were an ivory-tinted bureau and vanity table. Squealing rapturously, Emmy discovered the private bathroom. "Mommy, is this really all for me? Oh, Mommy, I love it—I feel like a fairy princess."

Thrilled at the girl's delight, Elizabeth urged, "Come along, Princess, we're not through . . . you've got to see my quarters."

The master bedroom was a stately, comfortable suite, complete with mirrored dressing room. As she walked about inspecting the burnished walnut furniture, Elizabeth wondered if she would ever grow accustomed to the luxury of such surroundings. Opening closet doors, they heard the sound of a bell pealing through the house.

Hurriedly they made their way down the staircase to open the front door and confront a smiling Max Esquith. Always cavalier, he stood, gaily triumphant, a bouquet of flowers in his outstretched hand. "I've come to welcome you, ladies, to my land. Now that you're officially here, what are your plans for dinner?"

Elizabeth and Emmy looked at each other and giggled. Elizabeth said, "Come in, Max . . . welcome. Truth to tell, I hadn't given a thought to eating, but I'm sure we can put something together."

He laughed. "No, indeed . . . I've come to take my two favorite ladies out to dinner. Get yourselves ready."

The day, begun in sadness, was winding up with bright promise for the future.

The physical acts of settling in were accomplished with amazing rapidity. Elizabeth tried with every means at her disposal to keep busy and concentrated on readying Emmy for school. There came the morning that a freshly dressed and scrubbed Emmy awaited the private bus that would launch her on a new life.

As the bus disappeared, there was a hollow feeling in the pit of Elizabeth's stomach. She had to combat the encroaching loneliness; without Emmy at hand to keep her spirits buoyed she was miserable. She took herself off to the kitchen, the most familiar place in the cavernous house. As she reheated the morning coffee, she heard a timid knocking at the back door. Peering through the window, she saw a tall, smiling black woman. Opening the door, she was amazed to hear herself greeted by name. "Hiyuh, Miz Fields. Hiyuh all? De judge says I was to wait till yoh got yoh tootsies warm, and now heah I is. . . ."

Confounded, Elizabeth asked, "Who are you? The judge never said a word to me."

The woman put her bag down and walked over to the stove to turn the flame down. "I guess he done forgot. I comes with de house. I'se worked for the folks dat lived here till the day 'dey left foh Texas. Now youse is goin to be my folks. Where's yoh little gal at?"

Elizabeth didn't know whether to laugh or cry, but she found herself delighted with the presence of this friendly, matter-of-fact woman. She laughed. "Well, I never! I just don't know what to say . . . I wasn't planning . . ."

The woman was making herself at home, picking things up and putting them away as if she had long been accustomed to handling the objects surrounding her in the kitchen. She turned and beamed at Elizabeth. "Now, looka heah, Miz Fields, yoh cain't be expectin to tend 'dis place by yohself . . . doin laundry and all dat. Dat dere judge tole me I was to give yoh a day or so, and den I was to move in . . . and here I is. Fum the looks o it, yoh be's lonesome—but don yoh fret none, now yoh is gonna be Pearlie Mae's folks . . . and everyone'll tell yoh, Pearlie Mae's folks got demselves real good help."

For the moment she was exactly what Elizabeth needed: cheerful, wise and competent. It marked the beginning of a deep and loving relationship. With Pearlie Mae's coming they sank their first roots in the strange new soil. Her warm and happy presence helped to counteract the wrench that had been growing in Elizabeth. For the first time in her life, she needed a capacious bosom and warm shoulder to lean upon, and Pearlie Mae supplied both. She became a fixture in their lives, mothering them both. Emmy adored her on sight. If Elizabeth hadn't felt the same way, she might have become jealous. When Emmy confided to Pearlie Mae that she'd been adopted, Pearlie Mae laughed gleefully. "Sho nuff? Well, chile, now yoh done been dopted agin . . . only dis time yoh's got company. Yoh and Miz Lizbet bot my chillin . . . we's family . . . de tree o us!"

Elizabeth conceded that Pearlie Mae's culinary skills were unequaled. Her biscuits and rolls melted in the mouth; her okra soup, fried catfish and grits, Max declared, were nectar from heaven—to say nothing of her currant and raspberry jellies. She could make a molasses sweet potato pie that had them raving, and Max would go home laden with jars of her cucumber pickles. But beyond all of that was her sunny presence. The house was filled by the bright sound of her singing as her white-uniformed figure made its rounds.

Almost immediately Emmy's life took on broader dimensions. She was totally absorbed in the transition to her new world. Within a short time, a subtle refinement took place. She stood straighter and taller, moving with more grace. Her voice lowered, she drawled less, and her vocabulary broadened. She was receiving special tutoring in music, and it

wasn't long before Elizabeth and Pearlie Mae were aware of
the child's improved skill at the piano. She loved the
instrument and it responded to her touch. Elizabeth was
amazed at how thirstily Emmy drank up all that was set
before her, academically and socially. The new exposure
brought out facets Elizabeth had been unaware the girl
possessed.

As for herself, Elizabeth found it a struggle to adapt to the
new ways. Pearlie Mae became her counselor and guide,
tactfully advising her which hairdresser to consult and what
shops were in vogue. Slowly her appearance altered, and she
was pleasantly amazed as she studied her new image in the
mirrors of her bedroom.

It was a rainy, bleak morning and Elizabeth paced the
house. Max had been called out of town and time hung
heavy. Pearlie Mae would not tolerate her helping with the
housework. "Don yoh be interferin none wit me, hear, Miz
Lizbet? Yoh makes me feel I ain't doin my job right when yoh
comes peckin along behin me." Finally, in disgust, she
resorted to what she had always done when in need of solace:
she set about baking an apple pie. Its aroma brought Pearlie
Mae on the run. "Mah goodness, dat sho smells good. Do it
taste dat way too?"

Elizabeth took the coffee off the stove and filled two cups.
"Come and join me, Pearlie Mae, and try the pie. You know,
my pies have taken prizes all over this state."

Pearlie Mae needed no urging. "Yoh sho can bake." She
studied the woman across from her who seemed so unhappy,
and said, "I don mind a hand 'long dese lines, pies 'n' all, but
yoh got to get yohself goin . . . how long yoh gonna keep
hangin roun here? Dey's lotsa people hungerin to meet wit
yoh."

Surprised, Elizabeth asked, "How do you know that,
Pearlie Mae?"

A smile of impish humor lit her face as she chuckled. "I'se
got my ways. Dat gal works next doh done tole me her lady
kin hardly wait till it's decent to come callin, and the one fum
acrost the street done tole me the same thin. Now don take
on, I don mean anythin bad, but it's mightly impotan foh yoh
to git yohself agoin in dis heah sassiety."

Elizabeth's glumness began to dissipate as she eyed Pearlie
Mae warily. The woman had eyes in the back of her head
besides being a mind reader. "Why is it important, Pearlie
Mae?"

Pearlie Mae shook her head at Elizabeth's incredible stupidity. "Cose yoh's gotchu a child that needs yoh to open the right dohs. It's gettin t'be the time foh us to has a Sunday tea, and invite de right people. The judge kin hep yoh."

One evening as Emmy was readying herself for bed, she stopped what she was doing to study Elizabeth. As Elizabeth became aware of her gaze, Emmy became sheepish, as if caught doing something she oughtn't. "What is it, hon?" Elizabeth queried.

You look so different, Mommy. . . . Do I look different to you too?"

Elizabeth was instantly apprehensive. "What do you mean? How?"

"You look so pretty. I like your hair that way, so short and wavy. Your dresses are so nice and you smell so sweet all the time."

Elizabeth had taken to wearing a light flower cologne Max had given her. She had been pleasantly surprised to find that she enjoyed shopping for modish clothes. Although she wouldn't have admitted it to anyone, she was immodestly pleased that her figure was trim and slim enough to wear them to advantage. Her newly bobbed coiffed hair made her look much younger, enhancing her big brown eyes. She had taken to applying creams and light touches of makeup to her pert features, and it thrilled her to receive compliments on her altered appearance.

Studying herself in a mirror, Emmy remarked, "We don't look at all like we did when we lived in Brightwater." At the mention of this, she gasped. "Oh no, I never wrote to Amy Beth!"

"Shame on us! You're right Em. If you're not too tired now, write a note to Amy and I'll enclose a note to the Wilkersons. I'll invite them for a visit."

The letter was mailed the next morning. It was a long time before either of them realized there had been no acknowledgment.

It was after the new year when Elizabeth, accompanied by Max, made a return trip to Brightwater to check things over. She delighted in the Hovaks' undisguised surprise at her appearance. Her eyes sparkled, her skin glowed, and the fit of her suit emphasized her figure. Mr. Hovak clucked like an old hen. "Mrs. Fields, you don look like the same woman. I'da never knowed you. You look right pretty, like them magazine pitchurs."

The house and farm were in good shape, the barn had a new coat of red paint and the fields were readied for early spring planting. After going over the accounts, Mrs. Hovak brought Elizabeth up to date on the news of the town, which gave Elizabeth an excuse to ask if she ever saw the Wilkersons.

Grimacing, Mrs. Hovak said, "They be the same ornery lot they always been. Beggin your pardon, ma'am, but they sure is a mean, unfriendly bunch. There's a rumor they be leavin here too."

Startled, Elizabeth asked, "Do you know where they're going?"

Mrs. Hovak shrugged. "They're kinda closemouthed. I jist heard it recentlike at church meetin. They was sellin some o their stuff."

A few miles away from Brightwater on the drive back to Oklahoma City, Max turned to Elizabeth. "Well, Liz . . . any regrets?"

"About what?"

"About the conversion of Elizabeth Fields. What do you think of Brightwater now?"

"Max, you're a mean man! I'll always love it, it's a part of me. I'll admit I find it hard to believe I'm two such different people. Don't you?"

"No, ma'am! You've always had the potential! All you've done is take the basic material and bring it to fruition. Now I've another step I'd like you to take."

She looked at him archly, understanding his meaning. But she was too straightforward to play games with him. "Max, you can't mean it . . . at our age?"

A full-blooded young woman when widowed, Elizabeth had suppressed any feelings of sensuality. However, Max's proximity and constant show of affection brought on sensations she had thought long dead and gone. In the privacy of her mind she was ashamed and embarrassed; it was unbecoming to a person of her years. She decided that, if their long and deep-rooted friendship was to endure, the wisest course was to resist his attempts to involve them romantically. She had not reckoned on Max's determination and her own mounting needs. She had despised herself for the jealousy she felt when she discovered that an attractive spinster was in pursuit of him.

Now, sitting beside him, she saw his lips twitching and was uncertain whether this was a sign of concealed laughter or impatience. It occurred to her that she might lose him, and the thought made her uneasy. He was such a distinguished man, tall and lean and exceedingly fit for his years. She knew he was studying her and raised her head, unable to read the expression in his metallic blue eyes under their bushy eyebrows. They had such good times together, and she enjoyed his companionship and his outlook on life; she had learned he perceived the world with tolerant humor. He was widely revered and respected for his fairness and resourcefulness, and she basked in his attentions. As he shook his head at her mockingly, she had an impulse to run her fingers through his long, iron-gray hair. She saw the set of his jaw and her heart leaped. He was going to win. The train of her thoughts suffused her face with color, and he broke into a wide grin.

As if reading her mind, he picked up her hand and squeezed it. His voice was husky when he spoke. "I agree that, at our age, we have no more time to lose. I meant what I said . . . all your misgivings are nonsense!"

He drove directly to his home. "There's no one here. We have the place to ourselves."

He was romantic about simple things, and his gallantry made her feel relaxed and secure. He led and she was a willing follower, and under his tutelage she lost her constraint and was astounded at her ardor. She felt treasured and cared for, and there seemed to be a spirituality about their relationship. After long hours of lovemaking, tender and delighted, he teased her . . . "If you hadn't been so stubborn, we wouldn't have wasted all this time."

"Dearest Max, it just didn't seem right for people of our age. Oh, Max, bless you and darn you, I've become a bad woman!"

He laughed until the tears ran from his eyes. "Coming from you, that's a joke. You just wouldn't admit you had it in you—it's the most natural thing in the world, so to hell with all that! My dearest, you couldn't be a bad woman if you tried. I love you twice as much, if that's possible, for what you've done for me."

Wrapped in love and attention, Emmy slid into the changed patterns of her life effortlessly. She enjoyed the new school and her classmates. Ardmore Seminary for Girls catered to the elite and wealthy, preparing its young charges for an ultimate destiny of cotillions, debuts and high society. The faculty at all times stressed grace, decorum and discretion, special attributes necessary for the handling of wealth. The school prided itself in the knowledge that its alumnae were recognizable throughout the select circles of the world in which they lived and traveled.

Compliant and easily molded, Emmalina pleased her teachers by her studiousness and facility in academic work. She made friends easily, and it wasn't long before she was busily involved in the extracurricular activities of her age group—birthday parties and the small social events then current. Elizabeth saw to it that Emmy did her share of reciprocating. Pearlie Mae took special delight in fussing for the occasions, and the house often rang with the laughter of young girls.

It was about that time Elizabeth had special studio pictures taken of Emmy. As she studied the proofs, trying to decide which to choose, she felt a tug at her heart; there was something about the look on Emmy's face, despite its smile, that projected a haunting bewilderment. The fashionable Buster Brown haircut that framed Emmy's face and the big violet eyes that looked out from under the bangs were somehow wistful and sad. Showing the pictures to Max, she commented, "She's a little old lady, but I think she shows promise of being a beautiful woman. She has lovely features. You know, Max, I worry about her."

He looked at her as if she were out of her mind. "Worry? About what in the world?"

"She's a real goody-two-shoes . . . so sober and serious."

"Land sakes, what's wrong with that?"

"She's so young to be so burdened." Elizabeth grinned. "But, you know, despite everything that's happened, I think she's come to believe life is a fairy tale. You know, for a long time she wouldn't trust me—or anyone else, for that matter. I worked on her so long that now I think I've swung her the other way. I honestly think she takes every word I utter as gospel truth."

"Well, what's wrong with that? Do you lie to her?"

"Of course not! You know what I mean. I would hate to be the one to disillusion her. At this age she sees things sharply, either black or white, good or bad. Laughter doesn't come easily to her. You know, it's difficult to describe, but that's what I mean . . . that sort of thing."

Shrugging at her foolishness, Max grinned. "Elizabeth, what do you expect? She's a little girl. Give her a chance. In her own way and time, she'll learn."

"That's for sure, but she's extremely sensitive and I have to be very careful what I say."

"What does Ardmore's dean have to say about Em?"

At this, Elizabeth broke into chuckles. "I guess that's what's behind all this. I met with her for our monthly conference yesterday. I arrived at the school as the girls were on their way to lunch; there was such a gabble, it was hard to believe they ever behave with decorum. But, really, they look so adorable in their navy uniforms. I peeked into Em's classroom, but she'd already left. It's a delight, so sunny and bright, filled with plants and marvelous maps and globes. I'm happy to report there are inkstains from the wells all over the desks—but the school is beautiful. Anyhow, I'm digressing. . . . I have to confess, Max, I use every ounce of self-control when I'm in the presence of her eminence. She's so regal, I feel as if I'm in the presence of royalty. The ritual commences with tea being served . . ." And then Elizabeth's voice changed as she mimicked the dean. "Your daughter is an utter delight, Mrs. Fields. She's certainly to the manor born. We all take great pride in her."

The two broke into gales of laughter.

It was some time after Elizabeth's visit to Brightwater that Emmy reminded herself to ask her mother if she'd checked on why she hadn't heard from Amy Beth.

As delicately as she could, Elizabeth told Emmy what she'd heard about the Wilkersons' moving and that she'd taken steps to find out their destination. Elizabeth was appalled at the look of utter desolation on the girl's face. It was as if her lifeline had been taken away. She felt so helpless in the face of this that she resolved not to tell her about Polly Sue's disappearance.

Elizabeth could not be blamed for her ignorance about Emmy's obsession. Outwardly the girl seemed normal and interested in the life she lived. But despite Elizabeth's willingness to believe that Emmy had made peace with her past, it hung over the dark recesses of the girl's mind like an ugly cloud. With the news of Amy Beth's move, she felt her family slipping away, like sand through the fingers of her hand, and an overwhelming sense of emptiness possessed her. She had a feeling of unreality about herself, as if she dangled in space. The assurance she manifested, the routine functions that took up her time, did not diminish the specter of what had befallen her. The only catharsis available was her music, and she would give vent to an outpouring of emotion when she was alone playing her beloved piano. There were times when she was sorely tried. An odd word from a playmate, reference by one of her friends to a difficulty with a parent or a sibling—and the chains would start clanking in her mind.

The most traumatic experience had taken place at a pajama party in a friend's home when one of the giggling girls declared she was sure she'd been adopted because everyone in her family was so mean to her. Amid much hilarity she confessed she'd reached this conclusion because she'd originally been refused permission to attend the party. No one noticed how Emmy paled.

There was much romanticizing about the future among the girls. Peggy, who had become Emmy's special friend, announced she was going to marry a professional man. "A doctor or a lawyer, you know, Em, like your Uncle Max. By the way, what did your daddy do?"

Blanching, Emmy gulped as she said, "He was a lawyer too. . . ." She paused as the others looked at her and added defiantly, "He was the mayor of the town we lived in before we moved here." She saw the sympathy she evoked by being forced to discuss her dead father.

Suitably impressed, the girls went on comparing notes. Emmy wished she were someplace else; she was stricken by the bald lie she had told. She wanted to cry, and, what was worse, the old lump in her throat was suffocating her. What, she wondered, would have happened had she revealed the truth? Disaster . . . she could imagine the consternation she would have caused. Well, what she had said hadn't been altogether a lie—if Elizabeth was her mother, then by all rights Thomas Fields could be claimed as her father. Somewhat relieved by this rationalization, her mind wandered. What had her own father done? Had he been a common field hand, a rancher? Somewhere lurking in her mind she recalled him reading—hearing the tinkle of her mother's laugh as she'd said, "That's a pretty piece of poetry." She smiled to herself at the recollection and was startled to hear Peggy ask, "What's so funny, Em?"

She replied softly, "I was remembering my father."

At this, everyone quieted, obviously ashamed of having again trespassed on such sensitive ground. Hastily the subject was changed, and before long they were animatedly discussing prospects for another party.

The following night, home in her own bed, Emmy had a nightmare in which she vividly saw herself rocking Polly Sue's brown wooden cradle so roughly that the baby fell to the floor. It took a while before Elizabeth could calm the upset girl.

Part II
ADOLESCENT YEARS

Chapter XI

◦◦◦◦◦

POLLY SUE
DISCOVERS POWER

MIRACULOUSLY POLLY SUE reached the first year of high school and at long last, to the delight of her parents, showed some interest in her studies.

It was late spring when, at supper one evening, Sean gave them a piece of news. "What would you two ladies be sayin to our havin a young dude with us over the summer? If you're of a mind to it, Deirdre, we'll board him and he can sleep in the bunkhouse with Pete."

Instantly excited, Polly began to babble. "Who is he, Father? How old is he? Is he coming alone?"

Sean was pleased at his daughter's interest. "Hold on there, daughter o mine . . . git your bridle on till I'm through. Deirdre, the poor lad's had a bad time of it, been serious sick. His father, Mr. Griffon, be one o the owners o the Ace Mines, and when I was in havin a bit o the draft with Mike, he came in. 'Twas then Mike tells me he's been askin for just sich a place as ours. He's willin to pay handsomely for the lad's keep."

Deirdre was almost as excited as Polly. "Where'll he be comin from? What's been the matter with the poor lad?"

Leaning back, pleased with the effect his news had had on his family, Sean elaborated. "Seems the boy's had a pneumonia and is slow recoverin from it. His dad says he gave 'em a bad scare and the doctor thinks a bit o the outdoors will do wonders buildin him up. He's acomin from New York

City, although he's been up to college Boston way. I'd say the lad's about eighteen."

Polly was beside herself with anticipation—she'd be the envy of every girl in the school having a college boy at her beck and call. She was enthralled, and had to hear more.

"What's his name, Father?"

"Well, me girl, get this . . . 'tis William Griffon the Third. A mite fancy, aye? Well, Deirdre, what's your answer? If 'tis agreeable to you we can be expectin him about the fifteenth of June."

Unable to control herself, Polly blurted, "Oh, it'll be such fun having a boy here. I can show him around. Can he ride, Father?"

Deirdre interrupted sternly. "Hold on there, Polly Sue. Since I'll be tendin his needs indoors 'tis true you can lend a hand. Remember, there'll be none o your neck-breakin tricks taught to the poor lad. You dast not forget he's been sick and weakly, and if he comes he'll be needin buildin up. If I say yes, 'twill be on the condition you promise to do as we say."

Sean immediately concurred. "'Tis true, Polly. He's bad off, lass. He's been awful sick and poorly. We wouldn't want to do anythin to hurt him farther. You just take things slow and easy. If 'tis agreeable to you, Deirdre, I'll be needin to tell Mr. Griffon." He smiled. "It'll be a nice piece o change for us, Deirdre, help towards that new bull we been wantin."

Time seemed to move at a snail's pace for Polly. Deirdre couldn't understand what had gotten into her. "Stop wishin your life away, child! Settle down and do what's expected o you and everythin will fall into place. If you light a moment, I'll show you the letter his mother writ about how to tend her son, what medicines he's to take and when."

Deirdre was astonished at how eagerly Polly perused the letter. She understood it was cause for excitement in their routinely quiet life, but Polly Sue's interest in a stranger she hadn't even met puzzled her. She hoped the girl would calm down with his arrival.

When the day came and Sean arrived back at the ranch with the young man and his belongings, Deirdre couldn't help being impressed with her daughter's appearance and behavior. She had no idea Polly had been up at dawn to begin her primping.

From the moment it had been decided the boy was to come, Polly Sue had fantasized about him. She planned that he would become instantly enamored of her, finding opportunities to sweep her into his arms so that he could declare his undying love, saving her from peril at the risk of his own life. At the first glimpse of him she was certain he more than measured up to her dreams. The fact that he was painfully thin and wan made him seem even more romantic. She was sure that he reminded her of someone, though she did not know who.

Tall and gangly, young Bill Griffon showed the ravages of his illness. Against his fair complexion, the dark shadows beneath his sensitive brown eyes looked like smudges, and his sunken cheeks emphasized his aquiline nose and long face. When he smiled, his gentle, full mouth showed even teeth set off by a bony, elongated jaw. He looked like a dude in shirt and tie, and his rumpled blue wool suit was much too warm for the weather. Every inch the gentleman, he apologized for his loosened tie and collar, open at the throat. "I hope you'll pardon my appearance, but the heat's been a bit much for me."

Filled with compassion and motherly at once, Deirdre insisted, "Come right inside, lad. Polly, m'dear, git the pitcher o milk and cookies. I'm sure 'twill restore the lad after that tedious journey."

Polly, a picture of pretty docility, hastened to do as she was bid, and as she poured the milk she studied Bill. Her heart began to pump as it struck her that he resembled the picture of the poet Byron in her English book. She'd fallen in love with it, and now here in her own house was someone just like him. She became tremendously excited at the thought of how her girlfriends were going to react to him. Lost in her woolgathering, she was snapped back to reality at the sound of her mother's voice. "Sean, if Bill's up to it, it might be a good idea if you showed him to his quarters so he can rest a bit. Supper'll be at six, Bill, and we'll send Polly to show you the way back here. For now, you'd best lie down and nap."

" 'Tis a sweet lad, don't you think, Polly?" Deirdre asked as Sean led him away. "Real nice and not the least uppity, askin us to call him Bill right off like that. As I recall from me days in New York, he speaks in the same way . . . kind o up in his nose."

Dreamily, Polly said, "He is very nice, Mother. He doesn't look as sick as I expected."

Deirdre spoke sharply. "Now, Polly, mind you—remember

what we said. The lad's poorly . . . and if you had an eye in your head, 'tis plain to be seen. Just go easy with him, lass. Don't be tryin to show him everythin at onct."

Immediately contrite, Polly assured her, "I'll keep my promise, Mommy . . . don't go worryin about it. I mean to be helpful; you'll see."

Polly held to her promise despite Bill's eagerness to see and do everything. Sweetly maternal, the girl insisted he take things slowly.

Bill charmed them all. Courteous and friendly, he had a way about him that pleased everyone he met. Sean was nonplussed and hard put to contain his amazement at the way Bill would draw out Polly's chair at meals and rise to do the same for Deirdre when, after serving, she would join them.

On an overcast morning during the first week of Bill's stay, he drove into town with Sean to buy himself more appropriate clothes. Deirdre laughed to herself as the boy, resembling an ungainly stork, paraded before them in his new wardrobe. His cowboy boots, Levi's and work shirt of the yoke and snap-button variety, along with a Stetson hat, at least made him blend into the landscape. Self-conscious at the compliments being given him, he was glad for old Pete's practicality. " 'Taint how pretty yuh look . . . leastways now yuh won't be mindin the cow cakes and horse manure."

Since he was still on the weak side, Polly kept Bill close to the ranch, familiarizing him with his immediate surroundings, the bunkhouse, the barn with its horse stalls and hayloft, the corral, the great fields of alfalfa and the orchards. Watching Polly work a rope, Bill was amazed at her dexterity. He looked around him at the rambling ranch house, attractive despite its uneven carpentry partially disguised by Deirdre's wild rose vines and blooming flower garden, at the fields, at the grazing sheep and lowing cattle—all steeped in sun. He breathed deeply. "What a great way to live. It's so beautiful here, I could stay forever." Polly grinned with delight as he exclaimed, "Hey . . . would you look at that?"

Turning, she saw he was pointing to the huge horseshoe nailed to the upper portion of the ranch gate. "What size horse ever wore that?"

Laughing, Polly said gaily, "I dasn't tell you what the men say; 'tain't ladylike. Daddy had it made at the forge and hung it there for good luck when we moved in."

Young and with a good constitution, Bill found his strength returning and his appetite increasing with the excellence of

Deirdre's cooking. She had a deft hand with biscuits, Irish stew and fried chicken. Bill gorged himself on her pickled peaches and on watermelon rind and on the homemade vanilla ice cream that she would pile high for him on a generous slab of peach or apricot pie. He would smother his morning cereal with homemade blackberry and plum jelly. The sun and air, the bracing mornings, warm days and cool nights, brought color to his face, and tone back to his muscles and imbued him with an eagerness to be active again. He had learned to ride as a boy and, under Polly's tutelage, it wasn't long before he was able to spend time far out on the range. At Deirdre's insistence, Polly remained solicitous, refusing to tax his newfound strength too far.

As the days lengthened into deep summer, Bill became impatient to explore the surrounding countryside. It became a daily occurrence for Deirdre to prepare gargantuan picnic lunches for the two young people to take along on their trips.

When Sean questioned the advisability of their going so far afield, Deirdre scoffed. "If 'tis the distance you be worried about, you know better'n I how well Polly can take care of herself and the lad too. If it be anythin else on your mind, you've no cause for worry. The lad be fine and decent; you've no cause to fret on that account."

Sean smiled. "'Twas not that I had on me mind, me darlin . . . Polly be but a child. 'Tis just that they be spendin their time so much alone. 'Tis a surprise Polly hasn't been up to invitin any o the others she's been pal to."

Deirdre shook her head at him. "Always worryin. The lass for once be followin my instructions. 'Tis peaceful and quiet for the lad alone. Sean, there be somethin else. Have you not seen how the girl is changed? The boy sets a fine example, him so polite and respectful. Polly's a changed lass, that she is. 'Tis a wonderful thing we've done, havin the likes o the boy here."

For the first time Polly had a youthful companion who shared her enthusiasm for the natural beauty surrounding them. Their daily expeditions into the wild and rugged countryside heightened Bill's senses and his appreciation of the pretty and capable girl who was such a competent guide and so knowledgeable about all they saw. They would ride in quiet companionship toward the jagged mountains that hemmed the horizon, their dagger-bladed peaks piercing the vast blue cumulus-clouded sky. They would stop at one of the shimmering cerulean lakes whose quiet was broken only by the jumping of hungry trout and the winds that splashed the wavelets on the brooding pine shore. They would spread a blanket near the water's edge and invariably the loons would shatter the air with peals of eerie laughter, never failing to send chills down Bill's back. Filled by Deirdre's ample food supply and relaxed, he would lean back and watch the hawks vaulting through the sky. They would talk of many things, his life at college, hers at school, and he never tired of drawing from Polly's inexhaustible supply of nature lore. She would watch as he would doze, the pungent aroma of the pine foliage and the steady music of the lake riplets curling and breaking on the shore, filling them with peaceful contentment. Polly would rouse him for the leisurely ride back and he would never fail to say, "This is one place we must come back to . . ."

There came the day when Bill and the Corrigans agreed that his recovery seemed complete and Polly was allowed to change their routine. She could now take him to the Grange socials, and from then on they made a point of seeing each new movie that came to town. Movies were a recent innovation in the area and were shown every Saturday afternoon, when the townspeople and young folks would jam into the old barn, equipped with benches, to participate in the fantasy world unreeled before them. Bill found it a fascinating experience to watch as the audience would hiss, stomp and cheer the action along. Urban and sophisticated, it amused Bill to see the simple reactions of the people around him, although he was careful not to say so to Polly. In this instance he became the guide and expert, explaining to Polly how movies were made as well as satisfying her insatiable curiosity about the film stars appearing in them. Listening to him one day, she suddenly exclaimed, "Maybe that's what I'll do—become a movie actress. It doesn't seem hard to do."

"It's not that simple, Polly," he interjected kindly. "You have to know how to act. Of course, if you really decide one day that's what you want to do, there are drama schools that can prepare you. You're pretty enough." He blushed at his forwardness and she dimpled with pleasure at the compliment. It touched him to realize how each romanticized the other's world. It seemed odd to Bill that his preference was for western films, while Polly and the others in this backwoods region preferred stories that dealt with life in the cities.

The two had become inseparable, and Polly was the envy of

all her girlfriends. The tall, handsome Easterner made all their hearts flutter. Polly gloated; she was in her glory.

Sean took note of the things that Deirdre had pointed out. It was true: all at once Polly had become ladylike, polite and delightfully coquettish. Her tomboyishness was reserved for the back of a horse. He thought, appreciatively, She's suddenly blossomed into the promise of her beauty—it's as if she's all aglow. He felt a twinge of sadness as he realized Polly, his darling babe, was on the verge of womanhood.

In his turn, Bill was experiencing a reaction to this unusual girl who seemed to him the most fascinating creature he'd ever known. She was captivatingly both child and woman and the best companion he'd ever had. The first time he had seen her astride a horse, streaking across the horizon, fearless and exultant, he'd felt as if the breath had been knocked out of him.

What no one had foreseen was the physical impact he had upon Polly. Her feelings for him puzzled her; her nights were disturbed with sensual sensations. His proximity was a delicious torment. She had started her menstrual cycle early and a reticent Deirdre had tried desperately to explain the facts of life to this blossoming young girl.

Exceedingly embarrassed and discomforted, Deirdre had tried to answer Polly's questions, but the girl could not make head or tail out of her responses. "Mother, how do you make a baby? How did you and Daddy make me?"

In desperation her mother resorted to the only answer she felt Polly would comprehend. "Polly, 'tis plain to be seen with the eyes in your head. You've watched the animals here on the ranch."

It made no sense to Polly but, seeing her mother's reluctance to discuss it further, she dropped the matter. Subsequently, she was made even more confused by what she gleaned from her girlfriends. Sexual sensations had no understandable meaning to her until she encountered Bill Griffon. Her body's turmoil made her curious and excitedly she planned to find out what it was all about with him.

One afternoon on one of their explorations, Polly and Bill had ridden a distance when great sulky black clouds gathered on the horizon. Thunderheads were piling up and a lurid and ominous light lay over the sky. The air was sultry and the sky rumbled as great flashes of lightning sundered the midnight blue ahead of them. The wind began to blow and claps of booming thunder echoed across the valley. Rapidly the storm moved over the distant cattle and fields, and before long they were caught in a vicious squall. Hastily Polly scanned the area for shelter and signaled Bill to ride quickly after her toward a nearby hill formation. Tethering the animals close by, she found a small cave and urged Bill in beside her. She fussed over him, rubbing his hair and shoulders as dry as she could with her jacket. "The folks'll kill me if you come down with a cold. Stay close so you can be warm. Here, put my jacket around you so's your shirt will dry. Are you very chilled, Bill?"

His face was flushed and he seemed to be breathing with difficulty. Polly was instantly alarmed, but when he suddenly pulled her into his arms, her senses fled and nothing else seemed to matter.

He kissed her long and hard. She felt her temples pounding as she responded with all her heart. It was a moment of ecstasy she wished could go on forever. Suddenly he released her and stretched out on his stomach beside her. She followed his example, waiting breathlessly. Her body felt as if it were on fire; she wanted him to go on holding and fondling her . . . kissing her . . . but it seemed he had no such intention. Instinctively she knew it was wiser not to make any move on her own. This was just the beginning; there would be other times.

What she did not know was that Bill Griffon was faced with a difficult problem.

He had been reared as a gentleman and could not be forward in his behavior with a "good girl." Certain standards had to be maintained; above all, a "good girl" had to be shown respect. His care and regard for the Corrigans and their daughter certainly fell within that realm. He could do nothing that would violate the Corrigans' trust in him.

In the days that followed, Bill made that his prime consideration, taking pains to avoid situations that might jeopardize this decision. He hadn't figured on Polly Sue. She was determined they would have a repetition and sought excuses to fine one area after another where they would be safe from intrusion. She couldn't understand why Bill was suddenly so against going off on long trips, feigning excuses to stay close to the ranch. He managed to convince her he wanted to watch old Pete bulldogging and bronc riding, cheering Polly on as she worked with him. He insisted she

teach him some of her rope tricks, at which he eventually
became clumsily proficient. Over the years, Pete, who had
been an expert rodeo rider, had taught Polly everything he
knew and she'd become outstanding at stunt riding and the
use of a lariat.

For a while she basked in Bill's praise and admiration of her
skill. But after several days, she persuaded him they could no
longer put off their trip to the canyon and river country which
she had been saving to show him when he could make a full
day's journey. He couldn't find a reason to avoid the trip, so
early one morning they rode off.

They headed in a different direction than on their prior
excursions, and his excitement grew at the colorful buttes and
promontories along the route. Slowing, Polly hailed him to
draw close. "We're going into the canyon now. Keep a good
grip and give your horse his head . . . you can trust his
footing." The next hour, Bill decided, was the most unbelievable of his life. It was breathtaking working their way down
from precipitous cliffs with the swirling river winding beneath
them and the sun beating on their backs. The wind- and
water-eroded buttes around them were dazzling in their
varied hues. When they finally reached a plateau, Polly asked,
"Are you too tired to go to the river? It's only another half
hour's ride." He was filled with enthusiasm. "Let's go! God,
I'm glad you insisted; I wouldn't have wanted to miss this for
anything."

At the bottom, the turbulent river, foaming and tumbling
over boulders, roared madly, its sound echoing against the
cliff's hemming them in. Bill closed his eyes, wanting to etch
the unforgettable scene on his mind forever. It took a
moment for Polly's voice to reach him. "Get down. We'll
tether the horses over here."

They had hardly finished spreading the blanket when she
plopped down, pulling him alongside her. The scent she
exuded made his pulses race. He saw the tiny beads of
perspiration on her brow. Her eyes were shut but the flutter
of thick lashes told him she was awake. Her tongue flicked out
to moisten her lips. . . . Taut with her proximity, he leaned
over to kiss her. She turned to press herself against him; her
tiny breasts were like flower buds, and the pain of how much
he wanted her was excruciating. He fought for control as she
continued to rouse him. He sat up, holding her in his arms,
his pulse beating wildly. She clung to him and he knew if he

didn't resist now, he would take her. He kissed her hard and forcibly pushed her away. She opened her eyes in surprise. "What is it, Bill? Am I doing something wrong? Tell me."

Gasping for breath he tried to explain. "Honey, you're wonderful. It's not that. We can't go on . . . we have to stop."

A cry rose to her lips. "Why? Don't you like me?"

He held both her hands. "I adore you . . . but, Polly Sue, we have to stop. I can't do this to you. I'm not prepared and I'm in no position to marry you. Supposing you become pregnant?"

Startled, she looked at him as if he were crazy. "What are you talking about? I want you to go on."

Placatingly he explained, "Polly, I don't want to get you into trouble. You wouldn't want to have a baby until we're married. I have to finish college. Besides, I have to leave here at the end of the month. It wouldn't be fair to you or your family."

Helplessly he watched as her eyes grew red and weepy. He sat down next to her. "Polly, listen, please. I want you more than anything in the world. It hurts to want you the way I do. Please help me; don't make it so hard for me. I'll be back. Maybe you'll be able to come East for Christmas. I'll ask Mother to write your folks and invite you."

In her mercurial fashion, she turned sullen and angry, her face convulsed with rage. She rose and brushed herself off, looking down at him scornfully. "You don't want me . . . you had your chance. Let's get back."

Seething, she strode off, mounted her horse without a backward glance and, once out of the canyon, galloped for home.

In the days remaining before his departure, no one could figure out why Polly took such pains to avoid young Bill Griffon. It was exceedingly embarrassing for the boy, who had no idea why Polly was so stubbornly angry. He hung around the paddock chatting with old Pete, who commented wryly, "See you've fallen from favor. Whatcha do to our miss? She's a one for temper, that one is."

The Corrigans were embarrassed at Polly's blatant display of ignoring Bill, pretending he wasn't at table when they sat down to eat. They tried to cover it up, but it was plain Polly wouldn't relent.

Deirdre was distressed. "What d'you spose's gotten into her, Sean? One day she be sunny and fair, and now like this. Don't seem fair to the poor boy, him tryin his best to be friendly and all."

Sean, eating a wedge of pie, grunted. "Trust your lass, Deirdre m'dear. 'Tis probable he done somethin he oughtn't. Lads is like that, you know. Polly, bein young as she is, took it as insult, more than likely. Not unlike her old mom, who slapped this here boy's face onct pon a time."

Blushing at the remembrance, Deirdre shook her head, puzzled. "Still and all, 'tis no cause to be so rude—unkind is what 'tis—with the lad goin so soon. I've a mind to speak with her."

"Try it, lass . . . see where it'll get you. The gal's a set mind when she gets goin."

As Sean had predicted, Deirdre's entreaties were to no avail. Polly would neither reveal what had happened nor alter her behavior toward Bill.

The morning of Bill's departure, he once again tried to make his peace with Polly Sue. He found her saddling her horse, preparing to ride off. "Polly Sue, I'm ready to go, but I can't leave this way. Please let me talk to you a minute."

She turned to face him, anger dancing in her eyes. "There's nothing you can say that I want to hear. Good-bye."

Crimson with embarrassment, the picture of contrition, he tried. "Polly, you'll never know how grateful I am to you for all you've done—and no matter what you think, I do care about you."

She tossed her head mockingly. "You had your chance to show your appreciation." Her fury hovered just beneath the surface.

"I couldn't do it to you—it wouldn't have been fair. Don't you understand?"

She gave a contemptuous snort as she mounted her horse and without a backward glance cantered off, leaving him standing alone like a fool.

Observing this, Deirdre was filled with shame. As Bill walked toward her, Deirdre said, "I be sorry, Bill, our daughter be so badly behaved. I've no idea what divil's gotten into her." She hugged him and bid him a good trip, waving to him as the buckboard drove off. She turned to call Polly back and give her a good speaking-to, but the girl had disappeared in the distance.

That night at dinner, as Sean recounted the trip to the train station, Polly cut in. "Well, he's gone. Good riddance to him is all I can say. Out of sight, out of mind."

Deirdre looked at her sorrowfully. "Well, lass, with the way you've been behavin', 'tis likely we'll never set eyes on the lad again. There be no use fumin and frettin over it. Let the matter be."

Nubile and inquisitive, Polly's appetite to learn more of the pleasures of sex had been whetted. She had new worlds to conquer. Titillated by the movies she saw, she had discovered an exciting new pastime. Male conquests intrigued her, and the boys at school were willing to oblige, not concerned with her welfare as Bill had been.

For a while it was fun being tussled in the hay, and she enjoyed their clumsy fumblings and callow lovemaking. But always, in the back of her mind, she imagined what it would have been like with Bill Griffon. She had really cared about him. Compared to the lovemaking she saw in the movies, she knew her present companions were clods. One day, she vowed, she'd have a more suitable choice.

Polly had come to a decision; she knew better prospects awaited her and she had decided on the process to attain them. Everyone said she was beautiful, and the mirror told her it was true. She would become a movie star—and the quicker she could get away from all the hicks around her, the better for her future. She tried out for the school plays and applied herself so diligently she actually became quite proficient in the parts for which she was chosen. The Corrigans were impressed with their daughter's newly discovered ability, and Polly began to take the first step up the ladder toward her goal.

Every penny of her allowance went toward the purchase of screen magazines, which she read avidly, accepting as fact all that was spewed forth on their pages. She wrote endless letters, asking her favorite stars for advice on how to pursue her career. In return she received stereotyped thank-you letters and glossy photos. Her frustration had reached its peak when, to her astonishment, an actual reply arrived bearing a handwritten signature. One of Hollywood's current and prominent lady stars, Miss Illona Lassen, had sent Polly an answer to her request for information.

Thrilled, Polly read and reread the letter. If she was really serious about pursuing an acting career, it said, she should enroll in a professional acting school, most specifically the one described in the attached brochure. (Needless to say, Polly had no idea that the eminent star was plugging her brother's business.) The letter urged Polly to fill out the enrollment form at once to ensure her place in the new semester. Enticingly the folder described all that would be offered and included a list of hotels offering economical accommodations. Polly was impressed by the italicized lines recommending that the prospective student be prepared financially to stay with the school until the completion of the curriculum, thus ensuring the aspirant the best chance for work.

Through the wintry nights preceding Polly's high-school graduation, the Corrigans pored over stacks of brochures sent to them. It was difficult to determine which offered the most, since each claimed the success of someone high in the movie firmament. The choice was narrowed when Deirdre announced determinedly, "You'll not be choosin the most expensive, me girl. You'll be needin a tidy bit o money for livin and all."

Sean agreed with the wisdom of this and the result was a selection of the most sensible-sounding school, in the Corrigans' judgment. Polly watched breathlessly as Sean made out a check for the deposit the school requested.

In due time an acknowledgment was received informing Polly she had been enrolled for the summer session. Thereupon, the Corrigans sent another letter, this one to the Hollywood Women's Hotel reserving a room for their daughter. Polly was now set to pursue her dream. She talked about it incessantly, which began to upset Sean. " 'Tis eager you are to leave us, daughter."

Contrite at once, Polly hugged him. "Oh, Father, that's not true. I thought this was what you wanted me to do."

As they prepared for bed later that evening, Deirdre studied Sean with concern. "Is our Polly not a beautiful young thing, Sean? Them violet eyes and curly black hair . . . Lord, is she not somethin special?"

Sean nodded glumly. "That she is, Deirdre—sometimes I think too much so. She's a rare beauty. Men's eyes follow wherever she goes. 'Tis a good thing she's not aware 'tis a great power she holds in those eyes."

It never occurred to them that their daughter would willingly give vent to her sexual desires whenever the mood moved her. No one could have convinced them she would indulge herself in such a way. Innocents themselves, they perceived Polly Sue in the same light—unblemished, virginal and pure, the receptacle of all that was fine and upstanding.

Sean paused for a moment, looking at his wife. " 'Twont be easy lettin her go, will it, my love?"

Poor man, Deirdre thought. It's even more difficult for him than 'tis for me. "Sean, m'love, we can get to seein her whenever we can't bear it. 'Tis not far—and she'll be havin holidays and vacation time. Set your sights on that. I'll be takin her there, Sean. I want to see the place and get her settled in."

He grinned. "That's a fine idea—it'll be a bit o change for you too, Deirdre."

She gently kissed him on the cheek. "I love you, Sean, and I thank the Lord. You've been the best husband a woman could have and a mighty fine father to boot. Now, 'tis gettin late; we'd best get to bed."

He stood staring off into space, his expression sad and drawn. She was instantly concerned. "What is it, me darlin? What's botherin you?"

He kept his head bowed as he said, " 'Tis been botherin me o late, Deirdre . . . those other ones. With our lass comin along the way she has, how old would you say the othern be?"

It took her a moment to grasp what he was referring to, and with an intake of breath she replied softly, "Of all thins, Sean, why would you be plaguin yourself with that now?"

He looked at her and smiled embarrassedly. "I don know, darlin, but I be wonderin at times if the lass ought no to know she has other family in the world."

For a long moment Deirdre did not answer, thinking over what he had said. When she spoke, her voice was a whisper. " 'Tis so much water under the bridge, Sean. I'm no sure how the lass would handle it. 'Tis best to let the sleepin beastie at peace . . . do you not think?"

He smiled at her. "Deirdre, fancy if they was to meet someday and never know they be sisters, real and true?"

The conversation was making her unhappy. "If that be eatin at you, Sean Corrigan, then you sit your daughter down and tell her best you can."

Reluctantly he shook his head as if to clear it. "I dunno why 'tis botherin me now. No. Deirdre, for now, as you say, we'll let the beastie sleep a bit longer. One day, though, when she be full grown, it might be a better thing we tell her fair and square."

Perplexed, Deirdre said, "Sure and we will one day. 'Tis

me hunch Polly won't be much for havin sisters, and I canno see how it would be helpin to fill her mind with sich as that when she's got so much to do ahead o her."

"All right, me darlin, as you say. Anither day, anither time. I wonder if they all be back there in Brightwater."

" 'Tis enough, Sean! Come t'bed." She kissed him lightly, as if to stop the distressing flow of words.

Chapter XII

❦⊷∞⊶❦

BRIGHTWATER BECOMES A MEMORY FOR THE WILKERSONS

IT HAPPENED AS he had predicted. Horace had found a buyer for the store. A man in Towana wanted it. Smirking, Horace told them: "Never haggled a bit . . . more's the fool. As they says, there's a sucker born every minute. Deborah, now's the time to spread the news. Tell your frens they can buy our furnishins for a song. Here's a list o what I want for 'em . . . cash only."

At her wit's end, Amy sought desperately for a way to contact Aunt Tina. Time was closing in on her; there were only two days remaining to pick cotton and then she'd be chained to the house helping Deborah. She looked forward to the release from the backbreaking work and the humiliation of the foreman's jibes at her. For quite a time she had not been able to maintain her former pace. She'd been feeling poorly, with cramps throughout her body and a great weight of misery in her heart. She attributed it to her distress about leaving Brightwater and her last link with her sisters and Aunt Tina.

The cotton picking was done at a distance from Brightwater, and a truck provided by the owner picked them up each dawn. The following morning when the truck rumbled up, Amy lagged behind the sleepy group, and as they made their way to the tailgate she dodged behind a bush. She knew she wouldn't be missed, since everyone dozed until their destination. The moment the truck moved, under the cover of darkness she ran for Aunt Tina's house.

Reaching the now familiar old house, she scratched on the door. Awakened from her sleep, Aunt Tina embraced her. Alone, they would have an entire precious day to lavish on each other. Aunt Tina had not heard they were getting ready to leave; obviously Horace was waiting until the last moment to tell her. Tears trickled down her cheeks as she prepared breakfast. She looked at the girl sorrowfully. "Amy, I wisht there was sometin I could do to keep you wit me, but you knows dats impossible . . . sides, it would be selfish. I got a feelin dis is gonna be a good tin for yo. Yo gonna be in a new place wit a lot o new chances to make sometin o yo'self. Anudder tin . . . dey ain't gonna be able to beat you like dey been doin . . . not in Californy. My daughter says dey got laws, and she be smart. I gonna gives yo her address. Now yo hear me: yo gotta learn yoself one tin . . . yo gotta use yo guts!"

"What's guts, Aunt Tina?"

"What yo did dis mornin . . . dat's guts. Yo gotta stand up fo yoself. If dat old man gits riled ginst yo and tries beatin yo wit kindlin or anytin, you tells him yo agoin to the police. Out dere in Californy dey gots police. Now if tings get real bad yo gits to my daughter and tells her yo my child too . . . hear? Now, I caint read—yo knows dat—but onct yo agoin from here, dat teacher yo got be my fren, and she gonna read me yo letters. Yo be sure yo writes me evertin goes on . . . hear?"

Amy wanted to show her friend she had guts, but despite her efforts the tears kept coming.

Aunt Tina tried to comfort her. "Don yo give up, Amy. I don ever wanta hear yo gives up. Let me tell yo, chile, yo gonna be fine. Yo's a wise chile. Yo got more streng' dan yo know. Yo ain't never gonna fail." Suddenly Tina paused. "What's dat blood comin down yo leg?"

Amy looked at herself in shock. "I don't know."

"I spected it . . . yo look poorly."

Amy knew she would remember this wonderful, exceptional day forever. She had never heard about menstruation, but here, in the gentle care of her guardian angel, she listened intently as Aunt Tina informed her about the ways of a woman. The old woman busied herself preparing a special herb tea, insisting that Amy rest. Propped up on the bed, covered and warm, sipping the hot drink, with Aunt Tina close by, Amy found her discomfort eased and felt everything else was a bad dream. But the moments flew by, bittersweet, and she saw the sun was beginning to sink. It would soon be time for her to leave. As if reading her mind, Aunt Tina reached into the chest drawer and withdrew Amy's doll. "Kin yo hide it, chile? I like fo yo to have it wit yo."

As she took the doll from the woman's hand, Amy's face crumpled in misery. "I'll try . . . it'll be a comfort to have it near me." Rising from the bed, she looked at the old woman imploringly. "I love you with all my heart, Aunt Tina. I'll be back one day . . . you can be sure of that!" Aunt Tina smothered the child's head against her breast. "Be brave chile . . . it's gittin time."

Struggling not to break down, Amy said, "Aunt Tina, if you ever hear that my sister Emmalina be lookin for me, please tell her what's happened and give her my address." The old woman promised.

Amy lingered until the last possible moment before she was due back at the truck stop. It was a heart-wrenching parting, but Aunt Tina finally pushed the tearful girl out. Tears coursing down her face, Amy ran, thinking, "I'll remember Aunt Tina as long as I live. If God will let me, I'll come back to see her."

She reached the road just as the truck was pulling up. She'd made it in the nick of time. There was no mention by anyone that she'd been missed. When she returned to the house Deborah said, "It'd be a bad time for you to be comin down with somethin—you look awful peaked. Guess it be the excitement o gettin away from here."

Amy made no reply. One day she would come across some lines written by Elizabeth Barrett Browning and that particular day, with all its intensity, would come back to her and she'd think how aptly it expressed her feelings: "The child's heart curseth deeper in the silence than the strong man in his wrath."

The last tearful sight Amy had of Brightwater was the church steeple showing on the rise as their old truck, piled high with the family and their possessions, trundled down the road.

The Wilkersons had lived in isolation for so many years that they had no comprehension of what was happening in the outside world. They were unaware of the terrible economic problems that now prevailed in most urban and rural areas, and they were puzzled when they reached the main highway to find themselves part of a procession: old jalopies, trucks and makeshift vehicles, piled high with household goods, people and pets, all heading in the same direction. In its way it was a new American exploration—whites and blacks, skilled and illiterate, young and old—with the spirit of hope not yet gone. The Wilkersons unwittingly became part of those who walked, hitched rides, rode in boxcars, weathered the elements and struggled to reach a new place, to build a more secure life. Under the regime of President Herbert Hoover, whose philosophy was individualism and who believed that governmental assistance would undermine this essential ingredient of American character, unemployment and despair had taken over and dispossessed these sorely pressed people who were now vagrants on the roads.

The Wilkersons' astonishment grew with each stop for gasoline and supplies. The word *Hoover* permeated the bitterness they heard everywhere; the paper shacks they saw were called *Hoovervilles*, even the newspapers utilized for covering were called *Hoover blankets*. But despite this, as their old truck moved on across the great sweep of land unrolling before them, Horace seemed almost cheerful. This was the closest he'd ever come to a vacation and, relieved of his irksome daily tedium, he made attempts to be genial. Uncertain at the turn in him, his family remained wary.

The weather remained clear and mild, and they were fascinated by the cloud-locked mountain peaks, the flowing rivers, the plateaus and the valleys, the familiar small-town streets and the endless miles of desert, the cacti the only relief from the flat expanse of land. Camping near the roadside, they would watch as the others rolled by waving greetings to them. Deborah commented wryly, "It sure beats all how many be goin our way. Yo spose they all thinks it's the Promised Land?"

Horace shook his head soberly. "It can't be worse 'n' what they left. From what I hear, things is bad, real bad. That man in Washington talkin o chickens in every pot . . . we need new people in the government, that's for sure!"

Despite the separation from Brightwater, Amy's spirits lifted as she found herself enjoying the novelty of the trip. Each nightfall Horace and Ted would select a campsite. While Amy and Deborah spread the blankets and readied the food, the men prepared a small fire. Their simple fare tasted better than anything Amy remembered eating.

One day, seated near the fire, Amy mused about the difference in the family's behavior. They seemed almost lighthearted as they bantered and occasionally laughed. It amazed her to see the alteration in Deborah and Horace, who were like two children joking and teasing each other.

The old truck whined and grumbled as they climbed, and from where she sat in the back Amy caught the tang of pine. Peeking through a crack in the slats, she saw they were traveling through a forest. Shortly after, they ground to a halt, and when Ted came to let down the back, he told her excitedly, "We're at the Grand Canyon—it's probably the eighth wonder of the world!"

As they approached the rim they were struck dumb at the sight before them. The view so overcame Deborah that she sank to her knees to pray.

The majestic panorama was almost too mammoth for Amy's senses to absorb; she was exultant. This Grand Canyon had given them no warning. Sitting in its isolated grandeur, its scope was vast. The awesome beauty was astounding, overwhelming . . . a sublime spectacle. The landscape sculptured by some monumental event had been hammered into a mosaic of intertwined radiant colors, its buttes and mesas shaped in geometric terraces of turrets, spires and cupolas as far as the eye could see. Shaped by the elements, there was spread before her a world of savage but ethereal beauty. On the distant rim she could see piñon and juniper forests, and down below, at a dizzying distance, was the Colorado River wending its way between vertical red cliffs. Each subtle movement of the sun's light emphasized the brilliant golds, crimsons and purples and magically altered the shapes and forms before her. Standing apart, lost in contemplation, she failed to hear Horace calling her. She tensed as his voice finally penetrated, but as he approached he seemed subdued. "Come along, gel. We wouldn't wanta lose you. Sorry we gotta leave this God-given place, but we gotta get a campsite for the night. We sure wanta see this when the dawn comes up tomorrow."

She walked shyly by his side. "Yes, Poppa. Thank you for stopping here."

She was startled when he smiled down at her.

That night Amy dreamed she was telling Aunt Tina and Emmy about the Grand Canyon. It made her feel so good when Emmy leaned over and kissed her cheek. The kiss was so real she was astounded when she awoke to the muted sounds of the night and the starlit sky above her.

As they neared the California border, Horace grew irritable. From her place in the back Amy heard him grouching, "I wisht someone aside o myself had an idea in their head. Ted, ain't you studied nothin bout this area in your school? We got to decide on a place fur us to settle."

Amy was surprised to hear Deborah offer a suggestion. "Horace, you remember Cal Forbes? He even sent you a postal with that pitchur of where they settled. You gave him all those provisions on credit. He be bliged to you, and I recollect on the card he said so. Why don't we head there? His missus was a good churchgoing woman; I knowed her from the Ladies' Aid. I spect they'd be helpful."

Peering through the boards, Amy was happy to see a look of approval on Horace's face as he said, "You be right, woman! Dang it . . . what was the name o that place, you remember?"

Deborah was stymied. "I think it was Whit or Whitman . . . somethin like that."

"Jumpin Jehovah! You got it . . . leastways you made me remember it. Whittier . . . that's it! That's where we be headed—for Whittier, California."

They drove into the sleepy little town early in the morning. The scent of citrus blossoms permeated the air and Amy inhaled deeply. Horace pulled the truck to a stop in front of a diner. She waited impatiently for Ted to come to the back. As he helped her down, he grinned at her. "Come on, Amy . . . we're gonna have us a treat. Poppa says we can eat here whilst he looks for his friend."

Maxim's in Paris couldn't have impressed Amy more. For the first time in her life she was going to eat in a restaurant. Self-consciously the three of them filed into the little diner as Horace strode down the street toward a clump of stores in the distance.

By the time they had finished, they saw Horace returning, in animated conversation with a man. Carefully counting out the change, Deborah paid for their meal and they went out to wait for him. They sensed his excitement as he introduced them to Mr. Forbes.

Cal Forbes was a short, stocky man. He was friendly and his laugh was hearty. He was more than pleased to be able to direct them in their pursuit of a home.

There was a house available on a pretty residential street lined with small bungalows fronted by trees and flowers. Amy was secretly delighted and she could see that Deborah was pleased. She and Ted waited outside while Horace and Deborah inspected the inside. They came back shortly and Deborah announced: "Seems right fitten. Thar be two bedrooms—one for us, one for Ted—and thar be a sleepin porch to the back, Amy, right off the kitchen—do nicely for you. You kin go in carefullike and look about."

Amy saw with pleasure that the little porch, enclosed by glass and screens, was, to her way of thinking, the best room in the house. It looked out on a grassy yard that had orange trees and hedges of rosebushes.

They waited with eager anticipation as Horace went off in search of the landlord. He returned with a smile. "All righty, the place be ourn. . . . Git yourselves settled in. C'mon, Ted, give me a hand with this stuff."

Deborah and Amy set to work at once unpacking and cleaning. They had barely finished when Horace returned, triumphant with news: "You ain't gonna believe this! I got me a business awready. Hear, Deborah—a right good store, stocked and ready to open in a few days. Man what owned it took sick sudden and he made me a fine deal. I tole you, Deborah . . . this be the land o milk and money."

Deborah beamed at him with undisguised pride and admiration. "There you go, Horace! I tole you childrun . . . your poppa be a man in a million. Praise the Lord, Horace—and thanks to you for your good head."

For many the back-breaking work of taking over a neglected grocery store would have been a dreary prospect, but Horace found it a heaven-sent gift. In no time at all, with Ted's help, he had everything in shape ready to start business. The morning he opened, customers filed through the door.

Deborah and Amy worked harmoniously to set the little house to rights. They scrubbed every wall, and anything that wasn't nailed down was aired. The place soon had a lived-in feeling, and for the first time since she'd come to the Wilkersons Amy felt at home.

She'd been allowed to fix the porch the way she liked and Deborah even promised to make a pretty coverlet for her bed once they had more time. She looked round with satisfaction at the little table and lamp and the old ladder-back rocker. She hugged herself with delight. Impetuously she ran outside and cut some roses. She put a few in a milk bottle on her table and set some in a vase for the middle of the supper table.

It seemed as if the sun smiled down upon them. Deborah seemed easier and less tense; for the first time she had neighbor ladies who dropped in and urged her to do the same. Mrs. Forbes had taken her in hand, introducing her to the pastor of the church and the womenfolk of the Ladies' Aid. Neither Horace nor Deborah found it necessary to use Amy as their whipping block—and as long as she did what was expected, life was easier for her than it had ever been.

Ted attended the high school and Amy had been placed in the top grade of the nearby elementary school. She was thrilled when she realized high school was just a year away. She had not forgotten Aunt Tina and wrote little notes every few days, but she had no money for stamps. Every penny that came into her hands had to be carefully accounted for. She racked her brains trying to figure out a way to earn a few pennies.

This time her guardian angel took the form of a neighbor a few houses away. Mrs. Jung, a pleasant, talkative young woman with a flat midwestern twang, needed someone to watch her children on Saturdays when she cashiered in her husband's store. Deborah, hearing of this, volunteered Amy's services, and for this simple work Amy was able to earn fifteen cents. The jingle of coins in her pocket made her feel rich. She purchased stamps and mailed the first of what was to be many letters to Aunt Tina. She wished she could write her sister Emmy a note telling her where they had moved, but there was nothing she could do about getting her address, and resolutely she tried to put it out of her mind. It made life more bearable, for too many times Deborah still referred to "them trash that brung you into the world."

The Wilkersons would have been pleased had they known that Amy agreed with them. She only dimly remembered her real parents; they seemed like figments of her imagination. She knew now they couldn't have been good people to have done what they did. The thought gave her impetus to try in every way she could to be different from anything they had been.

Amy was a superior student and did well in the new school, and for the first time she began to make friends. Although she was painfully shy, she made timid overtures and tried to be more outgoing. Here no one seemed to care that she was adopted. She discovered there were others who were timid too and she bolstered herself with the knowledge that she was using her "guts." She was delighted when she found it brought results.

Her relationship with Horace was easier, although still guarded. He seemed less picky and argumentative, but Amy took no chances. There came an evening when Ted, who was his father's assistant with clerical matters, was out, and Horace was obliged to ask Amy to write a letter for him. Eager at the chance to prove she could be helpful, she wrote the letter just as he had scrawled it, changing a word which he had misspelled. He noticed the correction at once and took her to task. "Look here, gal, don they learn you nothin at school? I spelled the word s-e-p-e-r-a-t-e and yo spelt it wrong."

She wished she hadn't made the alteration, but it was too late. She froze with fear; the recollection of the spelling incident so long ago flashed across her mind. Suddenly she heard Aunt Tina's voice: "Use your guts." For the first time she determined to stand her ground.

"I know how you spelled the word, Poppa . . . but that spelling is incorrect."

Instantly she saw the old fury on his face. "Don give me any o yo lip, miss." He reverted to strong dialect when angry. "Fix it!"

"All right, Poppa . . . if that's what you want."

He smacked her across the face, sending her spinning. "Don yo ever use that tone o voice with me, gel! Yo askin for a beatin and yo gonna git it!"

Drawing herself up, she looked right at him and said quietly, "Poppa, it's not good for you to get so upset. I said I'd fix it the way you want even though it's wrong. And, Poppa, don't hit me again. Please don't raise your hand to me when I don't deserve it."

He moved toward her menacingly, picking up a chair which, to all intents and purposes, he was going to lower murderously on her head. Purple with rage, spluttering, he kept repeating, "Open that kind o mouth to me, will yo? Yo'll ne'er do it agin!"

Amy was terrified but steadfast. "Poppa, don't! I'm askin you not to do it. If you hit me with that I'm going to the police."

Momentarily transfixed by her outburst, he glared, outraged. Slowly he lowered the chair and glowered. "Yo agoin where? Yo be a dastardly ingrate, that's what yo be! Yo be a brazen hussy, that's what yo be! Git out o my house . . . out o my sight. I don want no tattletalers in my house. . . . Git! Go on! Git!"

Trembling, her cheek red with the imprint of the slap, Amy drew herself up with an attitude of self-righteous bravado, turned and walked out of the room, meeting Deborah on the way. "Git in your room, Amy, and don come out! Don you know you could be the death o him, talkin back to him that way? You be an ingrate . . . a no-good ingrate!"

Cold and shaken, Amy sat on her bed. The moment had been too incredible to take in all at once. Freedom . . . release . . . she had used her guts just as Aunt Tina had advised and come off the victor. She savored every second of it as she thought it over; it had been a victory, pure and simple.

For almost a week she endured silent treatment. Deborah and Horace pointedly ignored her, while Ted, ill at ease under their watchful eyes, took pains to avoid her. But she endured it stoically and went about her chores as usual, having the satisfaction of knowing there was a limit to how far she could be bullied if she stood her ground. She would never forget the wounded look on Horace's face when she had touched his raw spot; he was vulnerable too. She was willing to pay the price for this bit of power. She gloated inwardly when Horace broke the ice by asking her to pass something at table, and soon life resumed its normal course.

Some days later she was amazed when Horace again requested she write a letter for him. As before, she had reason to correct his spelling. Hesitating only a second, she did it, but this time he remained silent. Her triumph was complete; it was as though she had cauterized an old wound.

Outwardly Amy observed the civilities, remained obedient to their wishes, showed no open rebellion, but it was apparent she no longer wore her old yoke of submission. She knew for a certainty now that she was biding her time, and the day would come when all this would be behind her.

Even though Deborah and Horace were less harsh, she remained convinced they had no place for her in their affections. She had an obligation to them and gave them their due. Since leaving Aunt Tina, there had been no one with whom she could share the secrets of her heart, but she was hopeful that in time she would find someone else.

Without being aware of when it started, Amy and Ted had

developed a new and closer relationship. A keenly observant boy whose reticence prevented him from openly showing emotion, Ted for a long time had felt a mounting respect and affection for the young girl who shared so much of his life. Frequently, they would walk home from school together, talking over the day's events, and with subtle understanding laugh or commiserate about some of the episodes that occurred within their home. Always sensitive to the meaning of the word *family*, with Ted's open avowal of being her brother Amy felt a keen sense of pride. She had always admired him greatly, and now suddenly he offered her a recognizable familial link. Her spirits soared.

With the advent of high school, major changes became apparent. Amy's body had taken on a young woman's shape, and she had begun to flower. Tall and slim, she had prevailed upon Deborah for permission to bob her pale gold hair, and she wore it snug and close to her delicately featured and full-lipped face. Her huge blue eyes looked out at the world hungrily. Boys were beginning to notice her. She considered them strange creatures, pimply-faced, hairy and clumsy, and for the moment she had no interest in them. They were always making silly jokes, laughing and pounding one another on the back as if they alone knew a hugely funny secret. She thought their antics foolish, and it made her uncomfortable to see how contemptuously they treated some of the girls and practically stood on their heads for others to show how manly they were. She was grateful that she was not in either category. One or two would sidle up to her quietly as she was leaving a class and ask if she could help with a problem. With them she was relaxed; they were like her brother, Ted.

The first invitation she received for a date astonished her. It came about during a school lunchtime when Larry Newton, with whom she was working on a math problem, asked if she would like to go to a movie the next Saturday night. Awkward and tongue-tied, she stared at him perplexed, wondering how to explain she wasn't allowed to see movies. Taking her silence as rejection, he shrugged his shoulders and walked away.

She was better prepared the next time. As she walked alongside Phil Hagel after leaving a class, he asked her to go to an afternoon football game, and she was pleased to hear herself reply, "When and what time?" Arriving home, she asked, "Momma, will it be all right if I go to the football game next Saturday with Phil Hagel?"

Deborah considered and said reluctantly, "If you got nothin better to do, it'll be all right. Mind you, though, straight home afterwards. You remember you're not allowed dancin or movies . . . none o that stuff."

"Yes, ma'am, I know. I'll come straight home."

She had her first date. Phil was a gangly, lighthearted boy who had not yet begun to shave, and it was obvious he had a crush on Amy. Though they both were stiff and self-conscious when they started out, as the afternoon moved along they began to have fun. They laughed a lot at her ignorance of the game, and he patiently explained each play to her. Courteous and pleasant, he bought her a Coke and a hot dog. By the time he walked her home they were chatting like old friends. He thanked her profusely. "It was fun, Amy. I don't get to go out much because I work evenings at the service station, but maybe sometime soon we can do it again."

She smiled warmly. "Thank you, Philip. I really had a good time."

From then on, Phil sought her out and several times a week they ate lunch together.

She had her first setback when Phil asked her to attend a class dance with him. She'd had no reason to mention it before and, trying to find the right words to explain, she stammered, "It isn't that I wouldn't like to go with you, Phil . . . but . . . well, I can't. My family don't approve of movies and dancing." He looked at her in disbelief. "Okay, Amy, if that's how it is . . ." She suffered all sorts of pangs when she learned he had invited someone else, but there was nothing she could do about it.

She watched avidly as the others went to dances in the gym, and she wished she could participate. "I can see it'd be harder on you, Amy, than on me," Ted had said. "I don't date any of the girls. It isn't that I wouldn't like to, but I can't afford it. Look, kid, you've got to do the best you can. One day, when you're grown, you can make your own decisions as to what you think best. You'll be free to decide for yourself."

She looked at him seriously. "You mean when I'm older they'll let me dance and go to the movies?"

He laughed. "No, Amy, I don't mean that at all. I mean when you're old enough to live your own life, you can decide how you want to do it. You won't always have the folks tellin you what to do . . . you'll be on your own."

Of course, that had been what she'd been promising herself. It was out there, she was sure: that different world. She turned to Ted. "I never really thought about it that way. I'll be able to make my own judgments about right and wrong."

"Sure you will, Amy—and, honest to goodness, I can't see why there'd be anything wrong in dancing and going to the movies. I think it'd be a lot of fun. Don't worry your cute head about it, Amy . . . you've got a long life ahead of you."

He put an arm around her shoulder, a most unusual gesture, and smiled at her. "You deserve some pleasure. I've got to hand it to you for the way you've handled things." He left her dreamy-eyed.

Ted secretly admired his adopted sister for the way she had persevered and succeeded. He loved his parents, but there were many things he did not like, particularly their treatment of Amy. He had never been able to express how much he esteemed her pluck and courage. Recently in school he had found himself reflected in the light of her popularity. A serious, tall, clean-cut boy who had heretofore quietly plodded along unnoticed, he was amused when fellows asked him to act as intermediary for introductions to his cute sister.

Amy decided there had to be another way of handling her limited social life, and so she tried to compensate. She would join her friends for a Coke at the neighborhood drugstore and submit lightheartedly to their teasing when her feet would tap in rhythm to the music emanating from the jukebox.

A singularly pleasant event occurred toward the end of her sophomore year. When Mrs. Jung required some minor surgery necessitating a few days in the hospital, the Jungs asked the Wilkersons if Amy might stay over at their home during the time. Impressed with Amy's competence, Mr. Jung rewarded her with five dollars, an undreamed-of fortune. Sincerely fond of Amy, he consulted with his wife. "Florence, would it be out of place if we give the girl a gift of those new stockings just came into the store?"

Florence agreed. "It's a wonderful idea, Hal. Bring them home and let me give them to her. Imagine what the Wilkersons'd say if you gave them to her."

The magnificence of the gift overcame Amy. Her face lit up as she tried to express her gratitude. "Thank you so much . . . really, it's more than I deserve.

When she displayed the silk hosiery for her mother's benefit, Deborah sniffed. "That's a mighty handsome present, girl. Them Jungs is mighty nice people to treat you so good, although I can't say I admire their choice o what's suitable. I ain't never had a pair o them hose in me entire life."

Instantly Amy was moved to offer Deborah her choice of any one of the three pairs, praying silently that Deborah would refuse.

"No, girl, no need for 'em. You hold on to 'em for the proper time. Since I ain't never worn 'em, no need to start now. But see you don't start gettin any fancy notions in your head. Whatchu gonna do with your money?"

Amy had already decided. "If it's all right with you and Poppa, I'd like to open a savings account." When the Wilkersons agreed and she had her bankbook, she felt rich and secure. She was coming into her own, happy about her capabilities. The stockings were carefully rinsed, in accordance with Mr. Jung's instructions, and wrapped in tissue, to be saved for use on special occasions. Gleefully she wrote Aunt Tina about the change in her fortune.

It had become commonplace for Ted and Amy to solicit advice from each other, and now that he was nearing the end of high school he had begun to confide his future hopes to her. She felt very important when he told her of his plans to enter the ministry and asked if she would help in filling out the application for theological schools.

Although no mention was made in their presence, the older Wilkersons were aware of their children's closer relationship. Amy Beth had gained new respect in their estimation.

Serving supper one evening, Amy was startled to hear Horace ask Ted, "What's your rush to enlist?"

This was news—Ted hadn't mentioned it to her. It seemed inconceivable to Amy that Ted was old enough to take on military duty, but she listened attentively as he explained, "It'd be better for my chances; if I get in now before it starts, I get to choose my branch of service. I'd like the Navy."

She saw with what mingled pride and respect Horace regarded his son when he said, "You mean you think war's really goin to break out?"

Shaking his head affirmatively, Ted seemed positive. "I'm afraid so, Poppa. President Roosevelt is doing all he can, but I don't see how we can stay out of it. That crazy Hitler is dragging the whole world to the brink of it."

Horace looked grave. "Why don't you find out what the

reserves'll do for you? That way you could start your new schoolin and the whole thing might blow over."

Amy was shocked. She'd been so wrapped up in her own life she'd barely given much heed to what was happening in the outside world. She didn't want to lose Ted; he was important to her, a prop in her life. She could gauge from Horace's reaction just how serious a matter it would be for Ted to be in service.

As things evolved, Ted was accepted at a nearby theological college the same week he enlisted in the Naval Reserve. He told Amy, "Well, if war comes, I'll be in like Flynn."

The Germans were on the march. As country after country fell to them, the imminence of war was the all-consuming topic on everyone's mind. The boys in school talked of nothing else, and many planned to enlist before being called up. Amy wondered why going off to war seemed such a great adventure to them. Despite all the drumbeating, her mind was on other things. She had decided to become a teacher and pinned her hopes on winning a scholarship.

Since Sunday was the traditional day for sitting down to dinner together, the table was always specially set with a snowy white linen cloth and napkins, Deborah's best flower-patterned china dishes and their new silver-plated cutlery. Amy thought it looked festive and she enjoyed doing the tasks such a presentation entailed. Had everyone been less preoccupied, they would have noticed Horace's impatience for them to be seated. They had no sooner finished saying grace than he announced, "Got a bit o news for you. One o them newfangled food chains wants to buy the store 'n' made me a good offer too."

Gratified at the surprise he had caused, he continued, "Seems like it's gonna be hard to compete with 'em, so I'm thinkin o sellin."

At the dismay he saw written on his wife's face, he quickly added, "I been thinkin, now you children are grown 'n' bout ready to stand on your own feet, it's time for Deborah 'n' me to take us a rest. Might just look round a bit 'n' find us a spot in the desert to homestead. It'd be mighty pleasant to sun off our days."

Dumbfounded at this sudden turn of events, Deborah beat a nervous tattoo with her fingers on the table. "It's a smart idea, Poppa." Ted spoke first. "Soon as war breaks out you're going to have a rough time getting stock. Rumors are that the services are stockpiling food supplies. If the offer's a good one, it might be wise to grab it. You and Momma could do with a rest."

Amy's eyes were riveted on Deborah, whose face was running the gamut of emotions. Although she was as vigorous as ever, her face showed lines of age and her hair was streaked with gray. The hands drumming the table were knotted and gnarled, reddened with their constant toil. The vision of those hands kneading endless amounts of dough, paring and cooking, picking cotton, seemed to tell the story of her life. Studying her, Amy realized Deborah was a simple woman, whose sole pride was in her home. She wondered what Horace meant about Deborah resting.

Turning to her father, Amy realized with shock how he had aged. His hair was gray and thin, and he no longer seemed so tall; in fact he looked stooped, and his face had a gray pallor. Amy bent her head, ashamed of an impulse to cry.

In recent months there had been a radical change in their relationships. It had been due, Amy was sure, to the radio that Horace had presented to the family as his Christmas gift.

It had caused a hullabaloo, but Horace had been prepared with an explanation for this radical departure from the stricture of their normal life. He had told Deborah, in front of Ted and herself, "The minister said there be no harm in our havin one. Fact is, he thought it'd be good for the younguns. Surprised we ain't had one afore."

Aghast, Deborah had sputtered and scolded, and he'd jeered, "There you go, Deborah, thinkin the devil's agoin to take over. Minister said we had no cause to worry seein as how the children been raised so strictly in the good and righteous path."

The magical little brown box reminded Horace of a miniature castle with its squared bottom that rose to a rounded top. In the middle there was a glittery mesh inset covered by a thin wooden scroll through which a soft yellow light glowed when the set was on. Horace would stare at it in awe, unable to comprehend the miracle of radio waves that could not be seen or touched and yet were all around. He would examine the back of the box, packed with wires and little glass tubes, in hopes he could unravel the mystery of it. He was glad he had withstood Deborah's objections of heresy; he believed the invention of radio was a gift from God.

With a simple turn of the switch the little brown box

innocuously lured them into the twentieth century, opening
the door to the outside world, educating, enlightening and
entertaining them in a fashion they had never imagined. For
Amy and Ted it was an instantaneous boon, enabling them at
last to share something in common with their peers. But most
astounding was the transformation it produced in Horace and
Deborah . . . to hear their spontaneous laughter as they
became addicted to the comedy shows: Amos and Andy,
Fibber McGee and Molly. The dishes were washed hurriedly
so as not to miss the Eddie Cantor and Jack Benny shows. It
became routine for Horace to arrive home in time for the
Lone Ranger. For the first time, music became a part of their
lives—and if Deborah worried about its corrupting effect, she
couldn't bring herself to mention it.

It became a source of amusement to Amy and Ted as their
parents wrangled over program preferences; but, more
important, it began to loosen long-calcified emotions. Horace
had become fanatic about the news, spicing his speech with
Gabriel Heater's "Good news tonight" and taking as fact all
that H. V. Kaltenborn said. It was when he began to listen to
Father Coughlin that real dissension began—Deborah disliked the man and would go into high dudgeon at the things
he said.

Amy couldn't believe her ears when Deborah dissented,
saying the man was a troublemaker. She had never heard
Deborah take such serious issue with Horace before. Up till
now, she and Ted had stayed in the background, not wanting
to become part of their differences; but, with Horace
embroiling a reluctant Ted, and Deborah intent on standing
her ground, before long the entire family would be involved.
Basically Amy was in agreement with Deborah's views but
refrained from saying anything. It became a hotly contended
argument when, a few nights later, they had a set-to again
over one of the priest's arbitrary statements. Deborah
became riled, and after scoring what she felt were several
telling points, she looked to Amy for confirmation. Without
realizing that she was being drawn in, Amy impulsively
exclaimed, "Bravo! You're right!" and patted Deborah's
shoulder. To her amazement, Deborah reached for her hand
and squeezed it in thanks.

Seeing this, Horace shrugged and with a wry laugh said,
"Oho, so that's how it is. The women in my family against the
men! See that, Ted . . . see how them women stick together.

Well, I see, my girl, what I have to do to get in your good graces."

Everyone laughed, but for Amy it was a momentous occasion, and a warm feeling coursed through her. Horace had included her, had turned a key and made her part of the family. Impetuously, in the spirit of the moment, Amy leaned over his chair and gave him a hug. "That's for you, Poppa . . . for losing the battle so pleasantly."

There was a moment of awkwardness at the first show of emotion anyone had manifested in their family. Quickly covering, Deborah asked, "Ain't it time for milk and cake?"

Undressing for bed later that evening, it occurred to Amy that she hadn't written to Aunt Tina for a long while. She'd have to do so the next day. She felt a twinge of shame at having been so neglectful. She was too stimulated by the events of the evening to sleep. For the first time in her life she was experiencing contentment, and, as her thoughts rambled, she recalled Emmy and Polly Sue. It had been so long since she'd even remembered them. It struck her as odd that they no longer entered her mind. She'd never heard a word about them, but she hoped they were happy. It was just as well; life was full enough without them, and the Wilkersons had probably been wiser than she'd understood in cutting them out of her life the way they had. She drifted into pleasant dreams, forgetting the problems of the past.

Chapter XIII

><

EMMY ENJOYS THE REWARDS
OF THE RICH

AMY BETH'S UNDERSTANDING of why Emmy had never been in touch with her was partially true. The Wilkersons had not bothered to notify anyone in Brightwater where they had relocated, and Elizabeth was forced to tell her the truth. Emmy's angry reaction startled her. "It's not fair, Mommy. No one can stop us from being sisters. Isn't there something else you can do?"

Surprised at the adamant tone of her voice, Elizabeth said, "There may be, Emmy, but I think we should wait a bit and see if, in time, Reverend Jenson and Dr. Quenton get a lead on them. They promised they'd let me know if they heard." But this hardly stilled Emmy's fervor.

Elizabeth and Emmy had undergone radical changes. Following Max's advice, Elizabeth's entrée into a new social order had been accomplished smoothly and easily by serving as a patron of the arts. As word had gotten around that Elizabeth Fields could be counted on for substantial donations, she found herself inundated with invitations and requests to serve on various boards. The grand salon that had so discomforted her was now the scene of frequent evening affairs and Sunday teas. Beautifully gowned and bejeweled, she enjoyed the attention she received. The new symphony and art museum were special recipients of her largesse. She discovered a young and struggling artist and, with Max's concurrence, became his patron, having the pleasure of seeing him come to recognition. Free to indulge herself, she began to acquire sculptures and paintings, and, despite Max's handsome gifts of beautiful jewels, she added to them as whimsy dictated. It was as if Brightwater had never existed. Flattered by being the center of so much adulation, she confessed to Max, "I love it. I'm so sought after and catered to—I know it's because I can afford to do what I want, but it's fun. My only concern is how Emmy views this. I don't want her to lose her sense of values."

He smiled at her indulgently. "With you at the helm, there's small chance of that. Besides, what you do with your money should be of no concern to her."

Immediately defensive, she said, "The girl has no idea of what we've got—"

He cut in. "At her age, I don't think she gives it any thought—she probably just takes everything for granted."

Emmy grew and flourished, and it seemed to Elizabeth that almost overnight the girl had reached her teens. That spring Max suggested Elizabeth give thought to traveling. With his help, they decided on a tour of the eastern seaboard, to begin as soon as school closed.

"Behave yourselves—you're acting like giddy kids!" Max scolded as he helped them settle into the lush red velour train compartment. "You're two overly excited females. Take care of each other, have fun and don't forget to keep in touch!"

Their first stop was Washington, D.C. Oklahoma's senior senator had been told of their coming by his close friend Judge Esquith and had arranged for their stay in the capital. The itinerary he had planned excited and exhausted them. Despite the intense heat they maintained a rigorous schedule so they would not miss anything. They were awestruck at the size of the government buildings, imposing in their Roman and Grecian architecture, and they were amazed by the wide circular avenues and the impressively beautiful monuments. They visited the Smithsonian and spent a morning at Mount Vernon, after which they enjoyed a special tour of the White House, with Emmy craning hopefully for a sight of one of the Roosevelts. Finally, after a week of relentless sightseeing, they were relieved to be resting aboard a train again, en route to New York City.

From the moment they stepped into the cavernous Pennsylvania Station, the noise and the scurrying people overwhelmed them. Then, seated in a taxi, their eyes opened wide as their loquacious cab driver made his way through the jammed streets and rolling clothes racks of the garment center. They were incredulous as they passed the Empire State Building, its top looming into infinity. Bustling, theatrical Broadway, famous Forty-second Street, the Times Building, the Astor Hotel and the movie houses were mind-boggling. As they crossed town, the narrow streets seemed like cement canyons, the tall, tapering buildings shouldering one another, vying to reach the sky. They sat in trepidation at the traffic snarls and impatient pedestrians who dashed from one side of a street to another between moving cars. The cacophony of the busy city and the incessant din of horns rang in their ears. Elegant Fifth Avenue with its beautiful stores, majestic St. Patrick's Cathedral and Rockefeller Center came as a welcome surprise. The variety of New York City promised to be a unique experience, beyond anything they had ever imagined.

It was a relief to enter the shaded and quiet beauty of the Hotel Plaza's lobby. Installed in their luxurious suite, Elizabeth confided to Emmy her impatience to meet with her old friends, the Levinsons.

The next evening, immediately upon being introduced, Mrs. Levinson hugged and kissed Emmy, instantly making her feel she was part of them, and bridging the gap of years with Elizabeth in a matter of moments. Sitting quietly and observing as the three reminisced, Emmy thought it odd that they found her mother so unchanged. Mrs. Levinson kept repeating, "Liz, you're just the same; you're the same unaffected person you've always been." Emmy felt she was gushy and foolish; it was obvious Elizabeth had changed a lot. She wished they'd talk about other things. The conversation was making her uncomfortable. It was bringing back a lot of things she didn't want to be reminded of—her sisters, for one thing. A pang went through her as she realized she might not recognize them if they passed on the street. They'd be strangers! The tender spot of pain on her psyche opened anew and she was filled with confusion. She felt like an outsider—displaced and unwanted, set apart, not like other people. There was always something missing. Lost in a morass of self-pity, she didn't see her mother looking at her worriedly. Much later that night, as they were getting ready for bed, Elizabeth said, "Hon, when you're writing your postcards, include one to Amy Beth."

Startled and instantly irritated, Emmy asked, "How can I? I don't have her address."

Elizabeth nodded understandingly. "I know, but maybe by now the post office in Brightwater will have a forwarding address. You've nothing to lose except a stamp. Try it!"

Shrugging, Emmy agreed. "All right . . . I'll do it."

On her departure Max had asked that Elizabeth call old friends of his. When she had demurred, he'd insisted. "You'll enjoy meeting them. They're an old and prestigious New York Family. Bill Griffon's a diamond in the rough, a real chip off his father's block. The old man founded the fortune, made it in coal and oil. A word of caution, though: Eleanor—Mrs. Griffon—is the one apt to surprise you, but don't let her la-di-da fool you. She puts on airs, but underneath she's a good old gal. If she takes to you, and I'm sure she will, she'll show you the time of your lives."

Dutifully, the next morning Elizabeth called Eleanor Griffon, who responded by immediately inviting them to tea and sending her limousine for them.

As the car drew up before an imposing old house on Fifth Avenue, Elizabeth whispered to Emmy, "It's a good thing Max prepared me. I hope it won't be too rich for our blood."

Eleanor Griffon was a regal woman and she greeted them warmly, instantly proffering apologies. "Please forgive the confusion. Everything's in a dither here. Each year it's the same—we go to Newport for the season, and we're getting ready to close the house. You're dears to come and not mind the disorder."

Emmy wondered what she meant; she couldn't see a thing out of place and dared not look at Elizabeth for fear they'd break into giggles. The room they'd been ushered into was resplendent with Impressionist paintings and Aubrey Beardsley sketches on the walls. There were striking pieces of sculpture set around at vantage points, and Emmy wished she could see them at closer range. The silk striped couch on which they were seated was fronted by an intricately inlaid ivory and multicolored wood table on which there were crystal and silver dishes with a variety of delectable bonbons as well as a cloisonné bowl of fresh flowers. It became apparent that something was going on in the house as several uniformed maids passed back and forth before the door, intent on their duties. Emmy was fascinated by Mrs. Griffon's manner of speaking and the ramrod posture she maintained. A striking woman in a long print at-home gown, with her blond hair rolled in a chignon, she made every attempt to put them at ease and proved to be a charming hostess.

Before they realized what was happening, she was making arrangements to oversee their stay in the city. Discovering that they had not yet arranged to go to the theater, she had her butler call for matinee tickets and, smilingly, told Emmy, "Something suitable for you, young lady. You cannot be in the heart of great theater without boasting of one good play." She did not explain that the musical she had selected was currently playing to full houses and impossible to obtain tickets for unless you happened to be one of the Griffons' ilk.

There was no doubt she was a lady accustomed to having her way. To Elizabeth's astonishment, she added, "Mr. Griffon suggested that we put a chauffeured car at your disposal. It will be available to you at all times. As a matter of fact, our chauffeur is an excellent guide and you can leave sightseeing up to him. I promise you won't miss a thing."

Elizabeth tried to protest, but she quickly saw it was useless. Mrs. Griffon cut her off. "Nonsense; say no more about it. Since I can't be with you, I'm simply doing the next best thing. Not another word to the contrary."

After a few more minutes of chatter, Elizabeth said, "We mustn't keep you longer. You must be very busy."

As she rose, Mrs. Griffon added, "Before you go, there is one more thing, and you must promise you will do it. You must arrange to visit us in Newport . . . at least for a weekend. Max would approve of that. He loved the old place, and you'll be able to tell him about it."

At this Elizabeth's face reddened and she became obstinate. "Thank you for the invitation, but I really don't think we can do it. Our schedule is made up and it will not allow us to deviate. Every moment of our time is already accounted for, but thank you so much."

But she was no match for the indomitable Mrs. Griffon. There was no way to disentangle themselves from the woman's well-meaning clutches, and reluctantly Elizabeth was forced to give in with as much grace as she could muster.

Once out of the house and en route to their hotel, they each heaved a sign of relief. Back in the privacy of their suite, Elizabeth almost raged. "The very idea of her taking us over the way she did! It's one thing to be generous, but to smother us—it's awful. Wait until I get my hands on Max! He must have known she was like this!"

Emmy seemed to be considering as she said, "Maybe it's just her way, Mommy. After all, she's doing it for us, and it does sound very nice."

Surprised, Elizabeth asked, "You mean, child, she doesn't make you feel uncomfortable?"

Emmy laughed. "Yes . . . but Uncle Max did tell you she was affected. Mommy, did you get a chance to see the things in that house?"

Frowning, Elizabeth said, "She's too rich for my blood. I don't like being told what to do."

"She means well, Mommy, and I think she liked us."

"I'm sure she could get along quite well without us. You heard she was doing all this for Max."

"In that case," Emmy said, "I think we'll have to oblige. You wouldn't want to upset Uncle Max, would you, Mommy?"

For a moment Elizabeth considered and then, with a shrug, announced, "Oh, well, it won't kill us, I suppose. The chauffeur seemed very nice. It might be fun."

Despite the economic upheaval the country was enduring, those who came to New York City for pleasure found themselves with a veritable grab bag of delights. It offered something for every taste and inclination. Emmy delightedly told her mother it was indeed a Baghdad on the Hudson as she had heard it described. As the days passed, Elizabeth had good cause to be grateful for Mrs. Griffon's generosity.

Early each morning before being picked up, they would walk in the lovely green, tree-filled oasis of Central Park that bordered their hotel, constantly bemused by the diversity of architecture that framed its outskirts, trying to guess the age and period of the buildings by their outlines. Besides going to the theater, they rode the ferry to the Statue of Liberty and marveled at the New York skyline, enjoyed the precision of the Rockettes at the lushly ornate Radio City Music Hall and, clinging to each other fearfully, rode the rocking, speeding subway.

The days passed in a kaleidoscope of events and they were beginning to tire. Small irritations produced friction. Elizabeth missed Max, Emmy longed for her friends and they were both homesick. They began to fray at the edges, and the day the chauffeur pointed out the old Woolworth building, now a landmark, there flashed through Emmy's mind her association with the name. It was indelibly interwoven with the events that had occurred the day of her adoption. Wearily she leaned back, reflecting how naïve she had been at the time, believing it would be only a delaying action until she would be reunited with her family. She looked across at Elizabeth, wondering if she had any idea her adopted daughter had been masquerading . . . waiting . . . marking time until the day she would rejoin her parents, the people who perpetually haunted her dreams.

During the last week of their stay they attended an open-air concert at Lewisohn Stadium to hear a piano concert given by Artur Rubinstein. Swept up by the great pianist's emotional bravura and phrasing, Emmy sat enthralled. She was captivated by the little man whose short stubby fingers transported her into a world of melodic beauty and gave impetus to her dream of mastering the instrument.

Their remaining time was given to a shopping spree. A gift had to be sent to the Griffons, and at Tiffany's, after much debate, they chose an exquisitely chased silver bowl. At DePina's they selected a handsome shirt and tie for Max. They needed a few gifts for friends, and at Altman's they found silk scarves and embroidered Swiss handkerchiefs, and at Lord and Taylor's they found a pretty blue quilted robe they knew would delight Pearlie Mae.

At the last moment Elizabeth decided they had better look for a party dress for Emmy should the stay at Newport require it. They found a lovely violet chiffon which pleased them both. Finished with their errands, they strolled leisurely toward the hotel. Looking at the people coming opposite, Elizabeth noticed a woman and child and was struck by the little girl's resemblance to Amy Beth. She glanced at Emmy to see if she'd had the same reaction, but Emmy made no comment. A twinge of sadness ran through her—it would be possible for Emmy to pass her own sister and not know.

The lush green beauty of the Hudson River valley through which they rode delighted them. It was in marked contrast to their home country with prairie lands that seemed to stretch forever. Emmy enthused, "It's so beautiful, Mommy! How could you have left it? When I marry, I'm going to live here!"

Elizabeth agreed. "I'd forgotten how beautiful it is. When you live in a place you just take it for granted. That's how life is—everyone always seeks greener pastures somewhere else."

Traveling through the wooded and verdant Berkshire Mountains, fascinated by the areas that marked America's struggle for independence and the lore of the Mohawk Trail, they were spurred on to explore as much of the region as they could. Emmy found the speech pattern of the people they met engaging; they spoke with a nasal twang and sounded their As in the English fashion. One morning Elizabeth surprised Emmy with the announcement that they were going to visit her birthplace. As they drove through the rolling hills dotted with small villages and stony meadows brimming with buttercups and black-eyed Susans, Elizabeth sat quietly, lost in reverie. Suddenly she spoke. "Some of this looks the way I remember it, but most of the places are so changed I'd hardly know them."

As they wound their way through another small town, the driver slowed on the outskirts. "That was Massequa, ma'am. Where did you want to go?"

Amazed that she had not recognized the main street of her old hometown, Elizabeth requested that the driver let them off and wait for them at a small inn they had passed. She led Emmy to a turnoff, and arm in arm they walked along a country road shaded by huge elm trees. Emmy sniffed appreciatively. The air was redolent with summer scents emanating from heavy blackberry thickets, daisies and Queen Anne's lace bordering both sides; fluttering birds rose at their approach, quickly resettling as they moved along.

They had already gone past a few widely spaced houses, all the same saltbox shape, differing only in their settings—a broken go-cart with children's toys scattered on a lawn and the sound of their voices somewhere in the background at one; at another a sleeping dog that roused to bark at them—and Emmy wondered if Elizabeth would really recognize her old home. She was about to ask when Elizabeth stopped and pointed. The little white house, freshly painted, sparkled in the sun. It was surrounded by maple trees, bordered by peony bushes in full bloom, their tangy fragrance enveloping them. Looking around, Emmy tried to visualize Elizabeth as a child, doing all the things with her brothers she had described, when Elizabeth, her voice choked with emotion, said, "I wouldn't be surprised if my brother John's initials are still on the porch rail. That old elm . . . the one over there with the swing . . . is where Tom proposed."

Gently Emmy asked, "Don't you want to go closer, Mommy? We could ask the people if they'd let you see it."

Her eyes welling with tears, Elizabeth shook her head no and walked a few paces to look at it from another angle. There were white sheets flapping on a clothesline in the back. No one seemed to be about and the house sat quietly, drowsing in the noonday heat. Turning, Elizabeth reached for Emmy's hand and slowly began the walk back, saying sadly, "It's harder than I thought it would be . . . it brings back a flood of memories. Remember I told you I never saw any of my family after we left." She sighed. "When you're young, you don't realize what's in store for you. When Tom and I left for Oklahoma, we weren't so different from the people who came to America from the old country. In those years it was a common occurrence to have to leave one's family behind . . . but it's awfully painful. It's a wrench you never forget." She looked at Emmy sympathetically. "You can see, darling, your situation isn't as unique as you imagine. Many of us have had to deal with lost families."

Emmy stared at her without replying.

Reaching the main street Elizabeth said, "If you don't mind, I'll stop by the old cemetery for a moment, and that will be that!"

It had been an emotionally grueling day for Elizabeth. Worried by her drawn appearance, Emmy urged that she take a nap when they returned to their quarters.

Supper in the old-fashioned dining room of the inn was pleasant, and while they were eating, Emmy felt no restraint about touching on the events of the day. "You know, Mommy, I've been thinking a lot about what you said today and I'm not sure I agree with you."

The fork midway to her mouth, Elizabeth looked puzzled. "What are you referring to?"

Trying to keep an even tone, she continued. "It's true you were separated from your family, but it was your choice. When you left them you were old enough to know who they were and that they loved you." Her voice rose a bit to make her point. "You kept in touch with them and knew what was happening. You've told me about your grandparents and your uncles and aunts—you even receive letters from cousins." She paused and, looking straight at Elizabeth, said with emphasis, "I don't think it's the same at all . . . *I never even had that chance*. Every single member of my family has disappeared. I probably wouldn't know them if they sat next to me . . . I don't even know if they're living or dead. You *knew* you were loved and cared about—all I've got are feelings I wasn't wanted . . ."

Seeing Elizabeth's face pale, she hastily said, "Don't get yourself in a stew, please, Mommy." Feeling herself a culprit didn't help as she implored, "I thought I could discuss this with you honestly . . . after all, you told me I should feel free to come to you. There's something else I'd like to say, but maybe I had better not."

"What's that?" Upset at what she was hearing, Elizabeth had stopped eating and was staring at Emmy. "As long as we're on the subject you might as well tell me. . . . I'm waiting."

Faltering for a moment, Emmy blurted, "I've never understood it. . . . Why didn't you keep all of us . . . wanting children as much as you did?"

Elizabeth blanched in astonishment as she gasped, "Emmy, what are you getting at? I never dreamt . . ."

The die was cast and Emmy, intense with conviction, interjected. "Please don't get the idea I'm ungrateful . . . I've just never been able to figure it out. It would have made such a difference if you had kept my sisters and we hadn't been scattered to the four winds—always having to wonder."

There was such condemnation in her voice that Elizabeth's head reeled in turmoil. It took a moment to regain her wits and she countered curtly, "It's hard to believe you've been harboring such thoughts all these years without saying anything. I thought you understood that I wouldn't have been allowed custody of the three of you." There was a tinge of irony in her voice as she added, "I wasn't sure they'd let me keep even you because I was a widow."

Her mother's agitation plainly evident, Emmy attempted to answer, but Elizabeth brushed her off indignantly. "What else have I done that's bothered you, Emmalina? Do you blame me for the Corrigans' disappearance and the Wilkersons' refusal to let you see Amy?"

This was the first time Emmy learned about the Corrigans and she stiffened. Her eyes brimmed and, head bowed, she sat in woeful silence. Elizabeth's heart overflowed. "Oh, Emmy, my dear child . . . I had no idea . . . I thought my love would in some way compensate."

Raising her head, Emmy beseeched, "If you'll let me explain . . . I'm old enough to understand what having you has meant. I guess it's stupid of me not to realize you really couldn't have kept the three of us. It's bothered me, and seeing how you felt today just brought it all up."

Elizabeth sat mute, lips pursed, and Emmy, in an injured voice, went on. "You ought to know how much I love you, Mommy. Believe me, it has nothing to do with these other feelings. Sometimes it just comes over me and I can't help myself." She almost cried as she said, "It's as if I were missing a part of myself . . . as if I were different from other people. Can't you understand?"

Seeing the anxiety and pain on the girl's face, Elizabeth tried to sound convincing. "Of course I can . . . I do understand. In the main you've been good about it. On the other hand, I've tried to do everything in my power to make you happy. I thought we had a wonderful relationship. I had no idea you were missing something. What is it you would like me to do?"

Constrainted by what she felt was a rebuke, Emmy didn't speak for a moment, and irritatedly Elizabeth repeated, "What is it you'd like me to do?" Elizabeth couldn't believe it—the girl actually looked sullen. "I'm waiting for an answer, Em. At least give me the courtesy of a reply."

Keeping her head down, refusing to look at her, Emmy mumbled, "Nothing . . . there's nothing you can do. You really don't understand."

Astounded at the turn of events and her inability to fathom the mind of her adopted daughter, Elizabeth's voice quavered. "Well, where do we go from here? Am I to understand that your lost family takes precedence over me?"

Emmy burst into tears. "Oh, Mommy, you're talking foolishly. I can't talk to you. You made me believe I could. Let's just stop—that's not what I meant, and you know it. I don't want to talk about it anymore." Frustrated and pouting, she mopped her eyes and, looking at Elizabeth, said with great deliberation, "If I haven't made it plain, then let me repeat I love you and I know I'm the luckiest person in the world to have you to love."

They had traveled far enough; it was now time to make their promised visit to Newport. "It'll be unlike anything you've ever experienced, Liz," Max had said when she called him long distance. "Go and see for yourself what it's like. The entire place defies description. You won't regret it."

Once there, guests of the Griffons in Newport, Elizabeth was positive it would be the cause of a heated argument with Max. The entire locale was pointedly the privileged enclave of the very, very rich. The Victorian villas, the rococo mansions, the scope of planned and harmonious elegance made everything she had seen before appear bland. Her sensitivities were ruffled by the extravagance on display; she felt it artificial and unnatural.

But Emmy was enthusiastic. "It's truly beautiful. The

houses are museums . . . such taste and imagination. Have
you ever seen such magnificent grounds and flowers? This
house has so many servants I wonder how the Griffons keep
track. I keep thinking of Pearlie Mae and want to laugh. Can
you imagine her in all of this?"

Elizabeth said wryly, "She'd tell 'em off good and proper.
The way I see it, these lawns wouldn't dare have a blade of
grass blow the wrong way. They're so manicured they don't
look real." It was apparent, Elizabeth decided, that she and
her daughter did not think alike on more than one matter.

Understandably Elizabeth preferred the more casual way
people lived at home, but as for herself, Emmy found the
surroundings and style of life pleasing and was not at all
intimidated. Her years of finishing school enabled her to see
how this sort of insularity preserved its inhabitants from the
harshness of the outside world. It seemed to her evidence of
subtle refinement by those who could afford the best.
However, she had to admit that Mrs. Griffon jarred. The
woman's sense of social prominence gave her effortless
supremacy and caused Elizabeth's hackles to rise.

The Newport they saw was redolent with wealth. Shortly
after their arrival, Mrs. Griffon informed them they were to
lunch at the yacht club. As they entered the richly polished
wood-paneled quarters of the nautically decorated club-
house, the boats rocking at anchor were on full display:
yawls, yachts, sailboats, rich men's toys of every size and
description. Standing at the entry to the outdoor dining
terrace, screened by glass, they had a clear view of the gulls
wheeling against the cloudless blue sky and the sun brilliant
and glistening on the aquamarine water lapping at the rocks
alongside them.

Once they were ensconced, Emmy looked about at the
lovely scene, enjoying the soft laughter and conversation.
The women were simply but smartly dressed, and she was
pleased at their own appearance: Elizabeth in a pretty pink
lightweight suit and her own white and blue silk pleated skirt
and matching middy top. She thought, however, the ladies
paled in comparison to the men, suntanned and strikingly
handsome in their crisp white brass-buttoned, gold braided
nautical attire.

Their luncheon was interrupted from time to time by
people who stopped to converse with Eleanor Griffon who
reveled in the attention. As she listened, Emmy realized what
an incestuous relationship these people had . . . they be-

longed to the same clubs, indulged in the same sports and had gatherings to which only those who enjoyed their clearly defined social order were invited. Apparently it was a world unto itself.

During the cocktail hour, the evening before their departure, Bill Griffon Senior, a hearty, down-to-earth man, and the two Griffon sons—Bill Junior and Jonathan—joined them. The atmosphere lightened at once. Mr. Griffon and Elizabeth delightedly shared news about Max, and the boys, both affable, charming young men, put themselves out to entertain Emmy. It's not more than they should, Elizabeth thought; the girl's a breath of fresh air in this hothouse. Her heart swelled with pride as she looked at Emmy, who was growing lovelier by the day. Her large, expressive eyes were framed by shining black hair and her heart-shaped face with its petal-soft skin seemed almost breakable with its vulnerable, radiant beauty. Outwardly reserved, she was responsive and quick to show a sense of humor. Elizabeth was tremendously impressed by the way Emmy handled the situation; the girl was as poised and relaxed as if it were a daily occurrence.

In the course of conversation Elizabeth had disclosed that Emmy was an excellent pianist, and the Griffons insisted she play for them. She handled the impromptu recital with grace, and the Griffons plied her with compliments.

It was obvious that Bill Junior couldn't take his eyes off Emmy, and as the evening was drawing to a close he made his way to Elizabeth's side. "I hope you'll forgive me, Mrs. Fields. I must seem rude, but I've the feeling I've met your daughter somewhere before."

Smiling dubiously, Elizabeth asked, "How could that be? Where could you have possibly met?"

Honestly baffled, he admitted, "I don't know. I've never been to Oklahoma, but I'm certain I've seen her before this."

Eleanor Griffon joined their tête-à-tête and, overhearing her son, said, "I'm sure, Bill, you have Emmy confused with someone else." She smiled significantly at Elizabeth as she added, "But there would be a possibility of your seeing her again if I could convince Mrs. Fields to send her daughter to the Juilliard School of Music. She's so gifted that it would be a shame not to further her talent."

On this note, Elizabeth took the opportunity of expressing her appreciation for their hospitality, and she and Emmy bid their good-byes to the family; they were to leave very early the following morning.

It was the following day, long after the Fields had left, that Bill Junior remembered who it was that Emmalina had reminded him of—Polly Sue Corrigan, the strange girl at the ranch in Montana. They certainly bore each other a strong resemblance, but, he concluded, Emmy was a young woman of intrinsic refinement and much more beautiful. Satisfied that he had been able to recall this bothersome detail, he put the matter out of his mind.

Once they were resettled at home Elizabeth related to Max the incident of Emmy's outbreak . . . the anger so long fostered and the distress she had exhibited over her lost family.

He made little of it and reprimanded her. "It's only natural in such an instance—you so upset about your family—that the girl give thought to hers. She's not harboring any grudges against you. Land o goshen, woman, you're all she's got. Who else can she discuss it with? Better that it came out; this way it's over and done with."

But Max was wrong. It was far from forgotten. If Emmy made no further mention of her natural family, it was because she had vowed never to discuss them with Elizabeth again. Elizabeth had let her down, not understanding where a line had to be drawn. It was plainly evident that Elizabeth had put her own feelings first, believing Emmy's undivided loyalties belonged to her. Emmy could see no conflict. Her love and gratitude for Elizabeth were beyond question, but that had nothing to do with her concern about her real family. All Emmy wanted was to feel whole, to find surcease from the questions that plagued her. Somewhere off in the nebulous clouds of the future were the answers; she was sure of it, buoyed by it.

On the surface everything seemed normal and the pretense went on. The reality of the situation was too painful for the both of them.

Part III
YOUNG WOMEN
IN TRANSITION

Chapter XIV

〰〰

POLLY SUE

THE FRAGRANCE OF orange blossoms slowly diluted the stuffiness of the Pullman car corridors. Several hours before, the porter had informed Polly that they had crossed into southern California. As the novelty of the citrus groves and dun-colored hills they were passing wore off, she became restless, complaining that the plush of the seat irritated her skin. Her impatience mounted, knowing they were nearing their destination.

As the train jerked to a stop, she tried to figure out where they were. Through the dusty window of their compartment she saw an old freight building and made out the word Pasadena. She jumped up, wanting another view from the other side. Passengers were lined up in the aisle waiting to get off.

She squeezed through and pressed her face against the window. A crowd of people standing on the platform below caught her eye. As the passengers began to leave, she tailed along to the open train door, but the porter cautioned, "Don get off, miss. We pulls out in a few minutes. You can see good from here soon's I get de bottom half o the door locked. Look over dere. Some movie star gettin off fum de car back o us. All dem people waitin fo her."

Fascinated, Polly watched as the crowd surged forward to envelop a small figure, bedecked in a broad-brimmed flowered hat. A medley of sounds reached her ears, and the porter, who stood alongside her, grunted. "My, dey sho makes a fuss over dem."

Aquiver with excitement Polly asked, "Who is it? Do you know?"

"No, miss, but I kin find out once we pulls out. Dey stays locked in dere room most o de time."

The group broke apart and surged toward the lovely replica of an early California mission that was the station, the palm trees surrounding it waving and bowing in the brisk wind.

It was a made-to-order scene for the star-struck girl. People had gathered to watch as the lady luminary, shielded by a phalanx of men, made her way toward an elegant black limousine parked nearby.

Polly watched avidly until the train gathered speed and the porter said, "I'se got to close de door."

Eagerly Polly went back to report to Deirdre. "We're almost there, Mother—just another half hour. I can hardly wait. You should have come with me. There was a famous movie star on the train with us. She just got off. It must really be something special to be a star. You should have seen the flowers and the crowd. She was beautiful! I wonder who she was."

Deirdre wasn't impressed. "You left the door open—I caught a glimpse of the goins-on. I'm sure 'tis grand for her, but, after all, Polly, she be no more than any ordinary person, hardly deservin of such a fuss. Now, if you was tellin me o someone did somethin grand for her fellow man, I'd be excited too."

Polly glared in annoyance. "Oh, Mother, you just don't understand."

"Why not, me darlin? Actin like she's so important cause she's pretty and in pitchur shows is no cause, in my book, to be treatin her like she's special. 'Tis a lot of nonsense! I hope when you're a star you'll be behavin better, rememberin the people you come from and who put you there."

"You don't have to worry; I'll know how to behave!" Disappointed at her mother's response, Polly kept her head averted and her nose glued to the window. Sometimes her mother was a pain—always lecturing and robbing her of fun. But once Deirdre was gone, life would be a different story. Polly was like a thoroughbred prancing at the gate.

As the train began its final run into Union Station, they gathered their things. Polly could barely restrain herself as they walked down the long corridor into the impressive edifice. The Spanish-style terminal was bedecked in shining marble, tiles and massive wood beams that reached to the towering ceilings. Flowering patios were everywhere. It was more magnificence than either of them had ever seen, and Deirdre stared unashamedly. "Sure and it looks like a cathedral. 'Tis a marvel, Polly. I wish Sean could see it too." Embarrassed by her mother's behavior, Polly pulled her along to the baggage section. Waiting to claim their luggage, Deirdre asked, "Will they be lookin for you?"

"Who?" Polly snapped.

Looking at her daughter in surprise, Deirdre said, "Did the letter not say someone would be here to pick us up?"

Unable to disguise her impatience, Polly whispered vehemently, "No, Mother! I've already told you a thousand times the letter said we were to take a cab to the hotel. I don't have to let them know I've arrived!"

Deirdre was stung by Polly's arrogance, treating her as if she was a stupid nuisance. Her temper flared. "You're actin high and mighty, miss. I'm sorry me presence irks you. You'll jist have to be puttin up with it. I promised your father. 'Tis a shame the way you're carryin on. I don't like it a bit."

Realizing she'd snapped at her mother, Polly apologized, "I'm sorry, Mother. It's just my excitement at being in Hollywood!"

A short time later the cabdriver explained they were in Los Angeles and the Hollywood area was a distance from the train station. Leaving the downtown area, he rode along Wilshire Boulevard, slowing as they passed the famous Ambassador Hotel. Polly screeched, "Look, Mother, look! That's the place the screen magazines say is the favorite night spot of the movie people. All the big bands play in the Cocoanut Grove nightclub there."

The cabdriver grinned. Typical tourists, he thought. Several blocks farther he turned north, telling them, "Look up ahead. Those are the Hollywood Hills."

Polly's heart pounded with anticipation. He slowed again and pointed. "This here's Hollywood and Vine."

He had anticipated their disappointment. Perturbed, Polly asked, "Where are the studios?"

The man laughed. "Everyone feels the same way, miss. They're all around you . . . scattered everywhere. Whatchu do is take a sightseein bus. They show you the big ones. If you know someone, they might getchu a pass to go inside one. Gotta admit, they're mighty interestin to see."

Disappointed, Polly sat back glumly. They rode along Hollywood Boulevard until the cab turned down a street lined with palm trees and small stucco bungalows, at the end of which stood a large Moorish-style building. Turning into the driveway, the cabbie stopped before the entrance and announced, "This is the Hollywood Hotel for Women." Looking at Deirdre, he asked, "Are you gettin out here, ma'am?"

Puzzled, she said to Polly, "Why would he be askin that?"

He clicked off the meter and turned to speak to her. "No offense, ma'am, it's just that their guests are usually younger. It'll be four ninety-five for the fare."

Deirdre flushed with annoyance as she rummaged through her pocketbook looking for her purse, and he shrugged his shoulders by way of indicating to Polly her mother was a little foolish. She smiled at him, acknowledging agreement. Encouraged by this, he said to Deirdre, "Look ma'am, if you want me to wait while your daughter checks in, I will."

Deirdre handed him the money. "Thank you, 'twill not be necessary, mister." She added in a huff, "Ifn I be too old for these quarters, at least you'll be admittin I be female. Seein as how it's for women, I'll not be worryin bout their keepin me a night or two."

At that he jumped out in search of a bellhop to assist with their luggage. Following after him, they entered what appeared to be a huge, gloomy lobby with a glowing fireplace at one end. Momentarily blinded by the change of light, Polly finally made out a long, ornately carved wooden counter at one side.

After a long and elaborate discussion with Mrs. Clark, the manager, about the availability of a room for her mother, Polly was relieved when adequate arrangements were made. She was anxious to see her accommodations and Deirdre decided to freshen up in her room on the main floor, planning to go up afterward to inspect her daughter's quarters.

Pedro, a swarthy young man, was already moving Polly's bags into the elevator. Once he had them piled in, he signaled her to follow. Slowly, creakingly, the old wooden, black-grilled lift rose as she stood apprehensively squeezed into a corner. The young man smiled, allaying her fears. Since men were strictly excluded from the upper floors, it was obvious he was the exception, being all in one the porter, bellboy and elevator operator.

The dim hallway into which Polly stepped exuded the collective smells of age and dust, and when the door to her room swung open she was met by a narrow, uninviting cell. It contained the barest requirements—bed, dresser, lamp and straight back chair. Its only adornments were a once flowered, badly faded bedspread and a cheap print hanging on the wall. The washed-out sky-blue walls and worn braided throw rug made the room seem very uninviting.

The closeness of the space heightened the dank, musty odor and made her sneeze repeatedly. Her sneezing continued as a cloud of dust rose from Pedro's vigorous banging at the window as he struggled to open it.

When the last of her bags were in and a tip given, Pedro left, promising to return with towels. She walked to the window to get a breath of air and, looking below, saw a patio furnished with lounge chairs in which a few people were seated. It won't be too bad, she consoled herself; I won't be spending much time in the room anyhow. She frowned, knowing what her mother's reaction to the dismal room would be.

She opened the door to the adjoining bathroom and saw the toothbrush and soap of its other occupant. She hoped they belonged to someone friendly.

She was eager to get out and look around, but she knew her mother would scold if she didn't make some effort toward unpacking. Quickly she opened one of her bags and hung some dresses on the few wire hangers in the closet. The room was giving her a headache.

Her mother's expression of distaste at the sight of the room made Polly say quickly, "Let's go find a coffeeshop; you must be famished. I could do with something to eat myself. I've got a headache."

"Come along, then. I'm not too eager to set around here. 'Tis a terrible place. Not too clean from what I can see."

"Well, Mother, it is a hotel. I guess they do the best they can. I'll brighten the room up and clean it myself if it's necessary."

Deirdre grumbled; she understood Polly didn't want her interfering. This was confirmed later that evening when they entered the dining room and Polly stood apart from her mother.

The room was filled with large round tables at which chattering young women were eating. No one approached to direct them to a table and they stood uneasily, wondering what to do. Just as Polly had decided to seek out Mrs. Clark, a young woman who had come in behind them said, "Hey, you're new. Didn't Mrs. Clark tell you you're free to sit anywhere there's a place? Don't feel shy—everyone's friendly. Come on, there's an empty table over there."

Smiling pleasantly, she made Deirdre feel easier. Deirdre introduced herself. "I be Mrs. Corrigan, here for a day or two, to see the sights o this place."

Quickly Polly hastened to correct her oversight and make the proper introductions. Deirdre was fascinated by the striking young woman, who was so tall and thin and spoke in such a deep voice. The girl was beautiful in a way that Deirdre had never seen before, and as a light laugh escaped her full lips, her large, dark brown eyes flashed in amusement, setting off the angular planes of her face . . . the high cheekbones, the long, straight nose and generous mouth with dimpled chin. Her faintly olive skin was flawless, and the sleek pageboy style of her dark brown hair, burnished with copper, shone in the light. Extending her hand, she said huskily, "My name is Lillian Fazon and I'm one of the hopefuls who inhabit this ancient dungeon. I presume you've met the dragon keeper . . . isn't she something? Don't let her fool you, though, Polly; she can be very nice in a pinch."

Deirdre was relieved to hear this. "Well, she do have her hands full watchin over all o you."

"Say, Mrs. Corrigan"—Lilly smiled—"I think it's peachy you came along with your daughter. This is a great place for a visit. Take one of those sightseeing buses; they tour the city and you cover a whole lot of the place. Have you ever seen the ocean?"

"I crossed a mighty big one, me girl." Deirdre grinned. "Although standin and lookin at it on a piece o land should be a better experience. I do remember thinkin I never wanted to see that sort o water ever agin."

Lilly chuckled. "Ask Mrs. Clark. She'll be able to help you make the arrangements."

At the conclusion of what Deirdre thought was a miserable "mess o porridge," she excused herself. "If you young ladies will be pardonin me, 'tis my bed I'm needin. Goodnight, daughter. Don be stayin up too late—you be needin a good night's rest. 'Tis a pleasure to have met you—Miss Fazon, is it?"

Polly cringed at the familiarity of her mother's conversation, but Lilly seemed understanding. As a matter of fact, they became friends right away, and Polly confided her plans for acting school. Lilly told her she was lucky to have the chance, since most of the girls she knew could not afford the luxury.

As they sat, several girls came by and Lilly introduced them to Polly. Lilly took out a package of cigarettes and offered her one. "No, thanks. I don't smoke."

Smiling, Lilly lit a cigarette. "You'll start soon. It's good for the image . . . especially if you're trying for a sophisticated part."

"What work do you do?" Polly asked.

Sighing, Lilly said, "I'm a file clerk for an insurance company—but every spare moment I can wangle I'm at the casting agencies trying to get work as an extra. It's rough, let me tell you. I have an agent of sorts who keeps promising me something, but the something never seems to turn up. If things don't change, I may just have to give up."

Polly exclaimed, "Oh, you can't! You're so pretty . . . I'll bet you're talented."

"Thanks for your kind words, hon. . . . Talented? I haven't had the chance to find out. It takes so long to get a foot in the door. As for being pretty . . . look around, we're a dime a dozen. Did you ever see so many pretty girls in one place? Each one has the same idea. I've seen a slew of them pack up and leave this place, their dreams in shreds. Each of us goes to bed at night dreaming that tomorrow we'll be discovered."

Dismayed by what she was hearing, Polly insisted, "You can't give up. If you have a dream and stick to it, it has to come true."

"Sure, sure . . . but that won't buy you a roof and food, Polly. Everyone's password here is 'tomorrow.'"

Shaking her head in disbelief, Polly said determinedly, "I'm sure if you've got what it takes, you'll make it. Hang on, Lilly—you'll get a break. There's got to be a place for you."

Lilly chuckled skeptically. "Tell me that after you've been here awhile and learned the ropes. Of course, there's another way. Sometimes you get a big part in exchange. Two of those girls I introduced you to were being picked up tonight . . . heading for a party on the *Sirocco*."

At Polly's blank expression, Lilly explained, "Errol Flynn's yacht."

Polly gasped. "Errol Flynn? Gosh . . . does he help them?"

Lilly exploded in her husky laugh. "Oh, sure! The fee for

going is sleeping with him and his cronies. This place is lousy with those bums and their promises. I'd rather pluck chickens."

The shock on Polly's face amused Lilly. "Hey, Miss Innocence, you'd better wise up, and fast! That's one of the ways a good many of these girls try to get a break, but it rarely pays off!"

Exhausted, Polly tried to stifle a yawn, but her eyes were beginning to close. Lilly accompanied her to the elevator and to their amazement proved to be the other occupant of the bathroom. "That's great, Polly," Lilly said. "I'm up early so I won't be in your way when you get ready for school."

Undressing, Polly thought about what Lilly had told her. She wasn't worried. All this talk of failure was bound to be depressing; Lilly needed encouragement. As for herself, her future lay golden and rosy, and she was going to be ready to meet it.

Two days later Deirdre left for home. She'd taken a tour, had lunch with Polly at Musso Frank's and invited Lilly to join them at the Brown Derby for dinner. In each instance Polly was convinced they were surrounded by movie stars, and Deirdre's annoyance was plain. "I can't say I'm sorry t'be leavin other than t'be leavin you, Polly. If you were t'ask me, 'tis no place for livin, filled with all o this nonsense . . . everyone pretendin to be somethin they ain't."

Surprisingly Lilly concurred. "You're right, Mrs. Corrigan. It's hard to keep your feet on the ground here."

Deirdre was pleased that Lilly and Polly had become friends; at least her daughter would have someone to turn to in a strange city. The time for her departure came and she told Polly, "I'm lookin forward t'gettin back to the ranch and the outdoors. Another day and the smell o this hotel would drive me daft. I think I'd wither and die if I had to be stayin here. You take care o yourself. Be a good girl . . . and be bearin in mind you've a good home to come back to. Write! Your old father and I will be awaitin on your letters."

Polly smiled tolerantly, exchanging long-suffering glances with Lilly as Deirdre ran on full of last-minute admonitions until she stepped into the cab taking her to the train station.

Polly watched the cab drive out of sight around the corner, feeling a tremendous elation. She was free.

Adjusting to the school had kept Polly busy during the week, but she awoke to a Saturday that loomed bleak and empty. Lilly was off visiting someone, and she had her first pangs of homesickness as she ambled around the lobby in hopes of finding someone with whom she could talk, but no one acknowledged her presence. Remembrance pressed in; at home she'd have been astride her horse riding across the range. Suddenly an idea occurred to her and she went in search of Mrs. Clark. "Is there anyplace nearby where I could go horseback riding?"

The dour woman actually smiled. "That's the first time anyone's asked me for such a thing. Yes, there is . . . in Griffith Park. But you don't have a car, do you?"

Determined to go, Polly got directions for the trolley and bus. Mrs. Clark urged, "You'd better leave if you intend on getting there today."

Changing into her riding clothes lifted Polly's spirits. The ride was long, but eventually the bus driver indicated that they were almost there. She located the stables without difficulty, happily inhaling the familiar smells. This was more like it. Filled with nostalgia she looked around at the spacious grounds. There were several horse barns, and she was delighted to see a large corral.

It didn't take long before she was mounted and ready to go. The stableboy was solicitous. "Thees horse ees freesky . . . be careful. You sure you ride well, *señorita?*"

Waving at him and laughing merrily, she cantered off. The boy watched worriedly until her grace and skill became obvious to him.

The day was pleasantly cool and Polly was delighted with the wooded areas that crosscrossed the bridle paths. It was hard to believe the beautiful hills and great stretches of open meadows were actually in the city. Enjoying the exercise, the horse responded to her handling and she gave him his head.

All too soon the sun began to sink. Reluctantly Polly headed back, to be greeted by Mr. Havershaw, the owner of the stables. The huge, potbellied man dressed in cowboy clothes chawing on a hunk of tobacco seemed out of place in glamorous Hollywood. "It sure shook me up when I found out you were on Feisty. That horse can be trouble for someone who don't know how to ride. You ride real well, girly." He beamed at her.

Her pretty face quite serious, she boastfully told him of her prowess with horse and rope.

"You gotta show me next time . . . I'd like to see all that."

The day that had started so dismally wound up perfectly. Polly had found an outlet for her stored-up energy.

As the weeks slipped by, Polly found it fun living in a world of women. She was responsible only to herself, saying anything she wished without fear of contradiction. She and Lilly continued to get along well. Lilly was wiser in the ways of the world, and Polly was shrewd enough to depend on her counsel. In turn, Polly found it easy to be generous and was a welcome boon to Lilly who was struggling to make ends meet. It wasn't long before Polly was making small loans to several of the other girls. She could always be counted upon to lend a pair of stockings and other oddments, and the girls paid her court for favors given. On occasion she would be invited to attend a party some of the girls were going to, but at a sign from Lilly she would decline since it was likely to be a drinking and sex orgy.

School was her main challenge, and Polly was determined to absorb as much information as she could. The staff was composed of former movie actors who each taught a specialty. She was dubiously flattered by the lecherous attentions of aging Mr. Rawls, who put his hands all over her under the guise of instructing her in the art of walking, standing, sitting and turning. "The dirty old man's still handsome," she told Lilly. "He could have been a double for Robert Taylor in his heyday."

But it was Elaine Monte, a famous silent-screen star put out to pasture because of crippling arthritis, who impressed her the most. Seeing the girl's avid desire to learn, the woman worked diligently to correct her speech with its bits of brogue and western drawl, and Polly received superb coaching while picking up invaluable tricks of the trade. There was general consensus at the school that Miss Corrigan showed a real aptitude for acting.

It was the evenings after seeing a movie that she enjoyed the most. The girls would congregate in her room, sharing Deirdre's packages of home-baked goodies and gossip about the movie people involved in the production they had just watched. Invariably they would lapse into complaints about the difficulties they encountered finding film work. Without exception they all held down other jobs in order to keep going. A few talked of giving up. After a while she became annoyed as they repeatedly warned her, "You're just starting. Wait till your folks get tired of supporting you; you'll be in the same boat."

She saw their envy, and their assumption of what lay ahead began to rile her. It crystallized one day as, seated deep in a lounge chair while waiting for Lilly in the lobby, she overheard herself being discussed by two of the girls who frequented their sessions. They were ridiculing her studies to be an actress: they knew it was a waste of time; besides, professional schools never kept their promises, and she was sure to be fleeced. Barely able to control her fury, she confronted them. "It's obvious why you've never made it—you're losers! You're right about one thing—I'm not like you; I'm different, and one day you'll be laughing out of the other side of your faces!" She strode away, and from then on they avoided her. The experience strengthened her resolve. Anger steeled her; no matter what the price, she would succeed. The day would come when she would show them all.

Late one evening Lilly came bursting into the lounge with news. Triumphantly she told them her agent had gotten her a bit part in a film. He'd even hinted that if she proved satisfactory she might have the opportunity of speaking a few lines.

Everyone had to rehear each detail. When the chatter subsided, Lilly singled out Polly. "I owe it to you, kid. If you hadn't pestered me to keep on, I'd have given up." Lilly was rendering unto Caesar. It didn't hurt to give Polly credit; one never knew when her generosity might come in handy.

Tall, with the well-knit physique of an athlete, Jan Borge brushed aside the shock of blond hair that fell across his forehead, his hazel eyes admiringly intent on the slip of a girl riding around the corral, heedlessly swinging herself across the horse's back to hang from its side. He didn't hear Mr. Havershaw's approach. "Didchu ever see anything like it?"

"Who iz zhe?" Jan Borge's excitement heightened his accent. "Zhe's going to kill herzelf!"

Havershaw laughed. "You ain't seen anything yet—wait'll she works with the rope. The kid's a wonder . . . got her training at a ranch somewhere in Montana."

Mystified, Jan said, "All zat and heaven too . . . zhe's a beauty."

"Can't argue that. She's also a nice kid, been comin around two, three times a week for a month or more . . . wants to keep up with it. Want t'meet her?" He looked at the young man shrewdly. It never hurt to please these fellows, and he'd heard the stories circulating about Borge—a playboy who liked the ladies. He'd met him shortly after he'd come to the States, a refugee from Czechoslovakia, a protégé of John Madrix, the head of Major Studios. The young man had an important position as production assistant to Madrix.

Jan Borge grinned. "Yez . . . but don't interrupt her. I want to zee her go zrough her pacez."

From the corner of her eye Polly saw the two men watching; she'd become accustomed to people stopping to see her work out. When she finished working with the lariat, she dismounted and turned the horse loose. Sweaty and hot, she mopped her face as Havershaw opened the gate for her. "Hi, Miss Corrigan. Through for the day?"

She grinned up at him. "Not yet . . . still going to have my ride." She couldn't help but notice the fixed stare of the handsome young man next to him.

"This here's Mr. Borge, Miss Corrigan. He's been admirin your stunts."

Jan Borge's heart skipped a beat as the girl raised the biggest violet eye he'd ever seen to look at him. She was gorgeous. The wheels in his head began to click. "Voud you mind if I rode viz you, Miz Corrigan?"

By the time they concluded their ride, they had made a dinner date for the following night.

Telling Lilly about it later, she could see her friend's excitement growing. "My God, Polly! This could be the break of a lifetime. The guy's a big shot at Major Studios and *he* really can do something for you. Don't let this fish out of the net, kid—let your head be your guide with this one."

Their first two dinner dates were no more than that, but the third time he drove to the top of Mulholland Drive and made love to her. She was so simple and wholesome he hadn't wanted to frighten her off. Holding her in his arms, he thought: She's like a trembling moth, innocent and repressed. As his hands moved across her body, she pushed him away. Despite her desire to have him go on, she heeded Lilly's advice: "Don't be an easy mark. Make him feel he's the first; you've got to make him promise something in return."

Polly knew he was avid to have her and gave him just enough leeway to ensure his pursuit.

On their next date he told her, "Little vun, ve hafe dinner at my houze. I vant to talk privately."

This was it, she knew, and her mind reverted to the problem of how she could get him to offer something tangible in exchange. There was no doubt Jan Borge could be enormously helpful to her career. She had no expectations beyond that, since Lilly had already warned her not to look for any real commitment . . . Jan had a reputation for loving and leaving.

Her mind raced as she sat quietly in the luxurious black Cadillac convertible, her hand feeling its soft red leather seat. Tonight would test her ability to make something of herself; she mustn't fail. Her resolve heightened as she saw the envy on the faces of the other girls as they drove off.

Drawing up before his house, he drew her to him, nuzzling her ears, her neck and bosom. His kiss was long and lingering and as his tongue probed, her body arched toward his, anticipating what was to come. Her own desires were making it difficult to think.

Walking down the steps from his foyer, she was in awe. The room before her was unique. A large open space painted chalk white and huge linear paintings in golds, blacks and browns which coordinated with the angular modern furniture covered in beiges and browns. It was different from anything she had ever imagined. Seeing her reaction, Jan said, "Vhy you are zurprized? Iz home for a bachelor!" He escorted her to an outside patio where a candlelit table was set for two. Soft rhapsodic music drifted from a speaker above. After his manservant had poured the wine, Jan raised his glass to her. "To the joyz ahead!" The lemony veal was tart to her taste, but she forced herself to eat it, not wanting to offend him. As they ate, he pointed out the highlights of the view. From the cliff on which the house was situated high in the Sunset Hills, the entire city lay beneath them with lights twinkling like fireflies. A short distance from the patio she saw the blue of the lighted pool surrounded by a moonlit garden, and a sigh escaped her. It was a perfect setting for romance. He looked at her quizzically. "Vy do you zigh?"

She smiled coyly. "It's so beautiful here. I've never seen anything like this."

"Ah." He nodded knowingly, and she thought: No matter what he demands, I'll give it as long as he makes it possible for me to have a part of this world.

She was heady with the two glasses of wine she had drunk, and now the afterdinner liqueur was heightening her emotions.

The darkened bedroom was lit only by the moonlight pouring through the picture window, and as he slowly undressed her, caressing each newly disclosed part of her, she could barely restrain her ardor. He was delighted; she seemed to him the perfect incarnation of a wood nymph. She shivered in his arms as he took her, but to her astonishment he was a disappointing lover, not the least concerned with her needs. She was forced to pretend he had satisfied her. Fondling her, he said, "I haf a zurprize for you. Already I make ze arrangementz . . . you are going to be a ztunt rider in ze picture ve are making." He smiled down at her. "Unlezz maybe you prefer a zilver fox zcarf?"

Relieved that he had broached the subject but dismayed at what he was offering, she said sweetly, "Jan, darling, that's lovely of you, but I want to be an actress."

He stroked her face. "Vait, little vun . . . ztart zlow. I do vat I can for you . . . but zere muzt be a beginning."

It was exciting to arrive in front of the massive white gate that was the entry to the magical world of Major Studios. As they sat in Lilly's battered old car waiting for permission to enter, Polly worried lest Lilly be turned away. She wanted to keep her friend by her side this first day . . . it bolstered her morale, and besides, Lilly knew the ropes. They were directed to the lot where Polly was expected. Jan Borge was nowhere in evidence, but everyone treated her courteously. The picture being made was a feature film, titled *Western Saga*, starring Robert Morris and Illona Lassen. Polly was thrilled: it was a good omen that Illona Lassen, the sole person to have answered her query about a movie career, was to be present at her acting debut.

Lilly sat discreetly on the sidelines as Polly was taken to wardrobe and makeup, returning to join a group of extras standing alongside their horses. An assistant director came over to ask Polly if she would like to try the horse they had provided before performing her stunts. She thought it advisable, and a space was cleared for the purpose. Tremulously she began to put the animal through his paces. When she had concluded, she was astounded to hear applause led by Miss Lassen. Polly smiled shyly, delighted that she had impressed everyone. The day was spent rehearsing; because the actual filming was scheduled for the next day.

That night she had difficulty falling asleep, reliving the day's events and planning how, when the cameras went into action, she would surprise everyone with some trick riding that would surely amaze them and win their praise.

The scene she was in showed her fleeing from a band of robbers as she raced across a plain to escape their hail of bullets. At a signal Polly mounted and the action began. She rode like the wind, at one with the horse, doing hair-raising tricks that had everyone gasping. When it was over, the crew gathered around to compliment her and, looking up, she saw Jan standing quietly in the background. He motioned to her to join him. Putting a proprietary arm around her, he led her off to one side. "You vere vunderful, darling. For zat, you get to zay a few linez. Doez zat make you happy?"

Her eyes danced as she thanked him and standing on tiptoe gave him a little kiss, assuring him he would be proud of her.

Back at the hotel she waited for Lilly impatiently; thus far Lilly's advice had been excellent, and she wanted her opinion on how to proceed. At once Lilly urged, "Try to get him to make the part bigger. I'm sure he'll do it, particularly since he was so pleased with you today. Don't let down . . . keep after him, kid."

It was bad counsel as, visibly displeased, Jan's annoyance at Polly's nagging turned to anger. He refused to talk to her and after dinner took her directly home. At the door of the hotel he dismissed her with a brusque goodnight. Despite his rebuff, she threw her arms around him and kissed him ardently, apologetically trying to placate him, but he drove off without a backward glance.

The next few days passed in a blur as Polly prepared for the part, which was to be a confrontation with Illona Lassen. She arranged to spend an evening being coached by Elaine Monte, her speech teacher, so that she would be letter perfect. When the old woman was finally satisfied with Polly's delivery, she gave her some tips about camera angles but cautioned Polly to be careful about competing for the scene, warning that it wouldn't do to anger the star.

At the completion of the scene, with the director's words, "Good, cut!" Polly was bubbling with pleasure. She expressed her gratitude to Miss Lassen, who glared at her icily and walked away in a huff.

The picture of innocence, Polly stood in embarrassed bewilderment until the script girl said quietly, "Be careful . . . let it go. She thinks you stole the scene."

The projection room was filling as John Madrix joined his assistant, Jan Borge, to view the rushes of the past few days' shooting of *Western Saga.* "What's all the scuttlebutt I've been hearing about your new prodigy, Jan? Who's this fresh kid that's got Lassen in a tizzy?"

Jan said irritatedly, "Ze girl iz goot . . . very goot. Vait, you zee for yourzelf. You know I don't fool around vit ze work. Illona'z crazy . . . alvays vorried, but"—he grinned—"maybe in ziz caze she'z got reazon."

At the end of Polly's riding scene, John Madrix leaned over and whispered to Jan, "The girl can ride . . . pretty little thing."

"Vait!" Jan said. "She can act too. I tink ve got zometing zpecial . . ."

Madrix couldn't repress a chuckle at the scene between Illona Lassen and Polly. "By God, Jan, she sure stole that one from Illona—the girl *can* act. Tell me about her."

Had Polly used her head she might have been more careful about her relationship with Jan Borge. But as it was, assuming he was still angry, she accepted a double date for herself and Lilly when asked by one of the cameramen. Nothing was sacred on the studio lot, and Jan heard about it right away. He called Polly and arranged to take her out to dinner. His purpose was plain the moment they were alone in the car. He let her know what he thought of her behavior: not only could his affections not be trifled with, but he wanted nothing further to do with her cheap, conniving use of him. Aghast, Polly tried to explain that she had gone on a harmless dinner date with Lilly along and added, unwisely, that she hadn't been led to think there was anything serious between them.

He looked at her mockingly. "You are right, little vun. But now you got vat you vanted. Ve be frenz. I zink you go far, but I gif you zome advize . . . be careful who you zleep vit. Not everyone iz Jan Borge."

Her velvety eyes filled with tears. "Oh, Jan, I didn't mean to hurt you. Really, I didn't do anything but go out to dinner. You're the first and only man I ever cared anything about . . . you know that! I'm not the kind of girl goes to bed with any man . . ."

At the injured, wounded look on her face, he was almost tempted to believe her, but he knew better, recalling his surprise when he'd discovered she wasn't a virgin. "Iz all right, Polly . . . now iz ofer between uz. I juz don't like my vomen playing ze field. Mr. Madrix iz going to gif you a contract. But vun vord . . . vun vord only: the chief iz ztraight . . . no fooling around. He don't like it if hiz vomen starz got a bad reputation."

Her heart jumped; women stars was what he had said. Her face was a vision of loveliness as she smiled at him, reflecting the joy of her feelings. "Oh, Jan, how can I ever thank you?"

His heart almost melted but he said curtly, "Ve be frenz . . . from now on, juz frenz."

So it was. Jan never called or helped her again, although he always greeted her pleasantly when they met. She had no regrets, no remorse; he had served her well.

A few days after their showdown, she received word she was to report to the business office. Her heart pounded as she faced Mr. Lockhard, the stern-faced elderly gentleman who explained the terms of her contract. She would be considered a starlet and no longer have to attend her school since the studio would undertake her drama coaching. It was to be strictly understood that she was to abide by all the rules governing new actresses. The first hint of scandal or misbehavior and the contract would be automatically terminated.

Polly smiled demurely as she assured Mr. Lockhard there would be no cause for concern; she intended to dedicate herself to her work.

Satisfied, Mr. Lockhard handed her the contract for signing and wished her well. Watching as she left the office, he concluded this type of sweet and wholesome young woman was hardly in need of the prohibitions he had been required to lay down.

There was pandemonium at dinner that evening as the news of Polly's contract spread throughout the room. She felt a glow of satisfaction as she saw the dismay on the faces of the two girls who'd predicted she'd fail.

Later that night it occurred to her she had not written her family in a long while. But she knew that when they learned of her good fortune, that would be excuse enough. Her parents would be delighted at how much she had accomplished in so short a time. She felt a surge of affection for her father, who was always supportive and open in his love for her. Unlike her mother, who felt it wrong, her father never refrained from telling her she was beautiful. Looking at herself in the mirror after her bath, she posed and preened. Studying her reflection, she decided she really was someone special. She could not have wished for more than her slim and lovely proportions, violet eyes, thick lashes and provocative mouth. The only flaw she could detect was the faint splatter of freckles across her cheeks—but, considering her outdoor life, that was little enough. The image that looked back at her was nothing short of perfection, and she took herself off to bed completely satisfied.

There was no doubt Polly Sue was a beauty, but in addition she exuded a frailty, an ethereal quality, that completely belied her character. She was not at all frightened about her life undergoing a drastic change. Not a dreamer by nature, and limited in her horizons, she had latched on to an idea that appealed to her and decided it was what she wanted. Fate seemed to be a willing accomplice, bringing her to the fruition of what, for most, would have been an impossible dream. She felt no humility about what had happened; she had expected it, paid Jan Borge for it in coin of the realm, and it had come to pass. Basically a manipulator and pragmatist, she hadn't the least doubt in her mind that she would succeed as an actress. She knew that once she was launched, there would be instant recognition and acclamation. Her life would simply be an enlargement of what it had always been . . . she would continue to be the center of indulgent attention.

It never crossed her mind that this might not be the case. She would not be denied. Heedless of others unless they served her purpose, void of deep emotion or feeling, roused to anger when thwarted, she was prepared to stamp on anyone who impeded her path. There would be little joy in her success for the people with whom her life was intertwined. Dangerously deceptive, she was remarkably endowed for the glittering and glamorous world she was about to enter.

Chapter XV

❦⟨❈⟩❦

AMY BETH SEES
NEW HORIZONS

It SEEMED SHEER absurdity to believe that the bloody tentacles of a power-mad Hitler and his farcical partner, the braggart Mussolini, were reaching out to engulf the world. But as Europe heaved and pitched in its death throes, its once-great cities in charred ruins, depression-weary Americans rationalized, willing to be assured that the great sea between would keep them safe.

Refugees were pouring in and stories of horror and heroism filled the news. Once proud lands fell and the world's greatest holocaust was taking its toll. England fought to survive as the German Luftwaffe rained death and destruction on it from the skies while a handful of courageous RAF men miraculously held them at bay. Despite the painful reality of what was happening, the American people, presumably safe in their isolation, went about their normal routines, doing what they could to assist the war victims.

Deborah and Amy spent every free moment knitting socks and scarves to be given to Bundles for Britain. Horace had decided to sell his business while he still had the chance and then rest for a while, secure in the knowledge of having money in the bank. It wasn't easy having him around the house all the time, but at least he kept himself glued to the radio. Deborah wouldn't admit it, but she was relieved that he wasn't pressing her to look for "that place in the desert." She was happy just where she was.

Busy with their usual chores, their continual knitting, they were getting ready for Christmas when, on December 7, 1941, the world they knew went up in smoke. The Japanese bombed Pearl Harbor, and suddenly, America too was at war. Ted was called up and commissioned immediately.

The Wilkerson son was the first in their town to leave, and the family had the honor of placing a blue service star in their front window. Horace tried to hide his worry and concern for the boy's welfare. Deborah prayed constantly. They tried to maintain a brave front, and it pleased them when the minister made mention of Ted in his Sunday sermon: "He could have stayed and completed his studies for the ministry, but this brave boy chose instead to fight for his country." Their hearts swelled when, after services, people sought them out.

There came the day Ted returned home for a short furlough—his last before being shipped out. He looked so manly, so stalwart and handsome in uniform. Each in their way clung to him, fearing the moment of separation. The time was all too brief, and before they knew it they were at Union Station. Drawn and haggard, Deborah and Horace fought to keep their feelings hidden, but Deborah's tears slipped from her eyes. Choked up, Amy let her feelings well to the surface as she hugged and kissed Ted. She would miss him acutely; he had become her rock in an uncertain world. A little strained chatter, a wave, and then he was gone. They stood in quiet desolation, watching the departing train, bracing themselves against his absence.

It was a blessing that they could not see the years ahead. Ted would be gone for longer than they dreamed. Horace would never see him again. During his sleep one night, Horace experienced a quick stab in his chest, which was the last sensation he knew before death. Ted was away aboard ship and would not learn of his father's passing for a long time.

With Horace gone, there was a great gaping hole in the lives of the Wilkerson women. He had so dominated them that now they found themselves adrift in a sea of uncertainty, rudderless, without direction or purpose. Amy, whose great dream it had been to escape him, couldn't understand the extent to which she missed his presence. Deborah had disintegrated totally, becoming disoriented and incapable of performing the simplest task. He'd been her pillar, the mainstay of her life, and she was unable to make the smallest decision. Suddenly their lives rested upon Amy's shoulders. She had no choice but to regain her footing; someone had to care for Deborah, who overnight had become an old woman. Deborah had lost her will to live; nothing interested her.

Amy thought about it a great deal. Horace and Deborah had known each other their entire lives, and he had ruled her from the start. The realization that they had loved and cared about each other, really needed each other, was a revelation to the girl.

Without having anyone close to turn to for advice, Amy sought out their minister. "Be patient, child," he told her. "You'll see that time heals, and your mother, painful though it will be, will come around."

Weeks passed without any change in Deborah. Forced to take the initiative, Amy assumed a maturity beyond her years, and their roles reversed. Even though the tragic necessity of their relationship had never drawn on Amy's font of love, the moment she was needed she felt compelled to offer loyalty and compassion. Despite the cruel and cold emotional climate of their early years, the wear and tear of daily existence had forged a bond between them. Amy set up the appointments and drove Deborah to the lawyer's office; she contacted the Red Cross so that Ted could be notified. She took care of the shopping and finances. Deborah was totally dependent on her. Of necessity, Amy absented herself from school, jeopardizing the scholarship for which she had been working so hard and hopefully. She talked to her teachers about it, but they could offer small solace. She was desperate, but she had no choice.

One evening while they were doing the supper dishes, Deborah broke into tears. It had become so commonplace for her to do this that Amy was finding it hard to remain patient, but she took the weeping woman into her arms and let Deborah cling to her. This time, however, Deborah was trying to tell her something through her sobs. "I want to tell you, girl, I appreciate how good you been to me. What would've become o me if I didn't have you to lean on? God blessed us with your comin. Ifn I sinned gainst you I'm sorry."

Discomforted by this outspilling of guilt, Amy tried to quiet her, but Deborah continued. "These many nights I been on my knees pleadin for forgiveness. I been a sinner questionin the ways of the Lord." Then she straightened, trying to quell her sobs. For an instant revulsion rose in Amy and she wanted to brush off the hand Deborah put on her shoulder. "You oughta know, Amy, that Horace came to feel better bout you. He was glad you turned out so good. He weren't a man to show his feelings, but he came to care bout you. It weren't easy for him, but in his way he wanted to do what was right for you. Surely as he's in God's heaven now, I know he blesses you for how good you been to me and how you been tryin to comfort my sore heart. You and Ted is all I got, and with my boy gone Lord knows I consider you like family, even though you're dopted. I want you to stay with me. I need you." She broke into sobs again.

"Don't take on so, Momma . . . I'm here, I'm not leaving," Amy pleaded. "I'll just be a minute while I get a cold rag for your eyes and make some tea. Please, Momma, try to control yourself. I have to talk to you about some things."

Slowly Deborah began to regain her composure, and the two women sat quietly sipping their tea in the lamplit room. Resting her cup, Amy spoke hesitantly. "Momma, now that I've graduated high school, there are things we should consider. . . ."

Deborah looked at her in shock. "Graduated high school? When did you do that?"

Amy smiled sadly. "Two weeks ago, Momma. It was graduation then. Remember the day you were in bed feeling so poorly? Mrs. Cook, the girls' counselor, came to see me and brought my diploma. She told me I won a partial scholarship for the Teachers College if I wanted to go. . . ."

Instantly alarmed, Deborah implored, "Oh, Lord, you said you'd stay with me. You're not plannin to go, are you? Please—you promised."

It was all too much. Weary and drained, Amy slid down to defeat; she was trapped. Her voice was flat. "Don't get yourself all worked up—I know what I said." Grudgingly she forced the words, "I'll stay."

Deborah smiled wanly, and Amy despised herself for being a spineless coward. Everything had conspired against her. She fumed with hatred for Deborah, for Horace dying when he had and for the world that had wreaked havoc with her life. She stifled a sob as she thought of what she'd been made to sacrifice; she'd been asked to be valedictorian of her class, and she'd missed the accolades of her school faculty and classmates. She'd foregone all of this for a woman who hadn't even remembered the momentous event and wouldn't have cared if she had. She winced as she saw Deborah bow her head as if in prayer. Amy was certain she was giving thanks for her victory.

In turmoil over what she'd conceded, Amy made a quick decision. There was a way to retaliate. This time there'd be no giving in. Her voice was icily determined as she said, "Momma, I'm going to work. As long as I'm not going ahead with my schooling I'm going to look for a job. The aircraft factories are begging for help, and I'm going to do my bit for the war."

Roused again, Deborah opposed this idea as well. "There's no need for you to be workin, Amy—we can manage. You don need a job. With careful handlin we can do right well, and when my time comes, there'll be somethin for you and o course Ted."

Amy was resolute. She was not going to fall prey to any more of Deborah's wiles. "There's no need for that sort of talk, Momma. You might as well make up your mind to it—I'm going to work! I'm not going to sit around the house. Besides, you're perfectly capable of keeping it up. It's time I earned my own keep—and, what's more, it's my patriotic duty. I think Poppa would've approved what I'm planning to do. Everyone ought to pitch in and help our boys."

Deborah had no answer, and Amy quickly filled the breach. "I think it's time you stopped carrying on. It's not helping either of us." Deborah was about to retort, but Amy said, "Poppa would've been the first one to tell you to put your time to better use. You ought to be going to the Red Cross a few afternoons a week giving them a hand; they could use your help. Besides, it would do you a world of good."

Amazingly, the idea appealed to Deborah, and Amy's plan worked. Fearful of being left alone, Deborah was glad for someplace to go and something to do.

Losing no time, the next day Amy drove Deborah to the local Red Cross office, where she was welcomed and put to work. In a short while Deborah had made a niche for herself, and a new atmosphere permeated the house. The telephone rang frequently, and Deborah found herself in the midst of new friends and activities.

Having relieved herself of the problem of Deborah, Amy applied for work at the nearest aircraft plant, girding herself against the apprehension she felt on stepping into a strange world. She was hired, put through a training course and assigned a job in the assembly division.

Stimulated by the challenge of a new life, Amy was surprised how much she enjoyed working and how little she missed school. Her shyness waned as she met and talked with co-workers, people from every walk of life and faraway places, all wanting to aid in the war effort. What excited her most was the acquisition of a friend, Barbara Hopkins, a girl of her own age. They had been trained together and placed in the same division.

The block-long building in which the girls worked was given to tail-plane assembly. Huge patriotic posters covered every opening on the walls. The vast space, with everyone dressed in brown coveralls, resembled a beehive. The girls were positioned near one end, their job being to rivet together two small pieces of stamped-out steel. They managed to talk despite the clatter of machines and clanging metal. The work was simple, but it required stamina, since the parts were carried along continuously on a conveyor timed at regulated intervals. As each piece was finished it was placed back on the line to be taken along to the next section; and by the time the moving belt reached the end of the room, a plane tail had been assembled.

Barbara and Amy Beth took their breaks and lunchtime together, and their relationship cemented when they discovered they both enjoyed reading and listening to classical music. Amy felt great respect for her new friend when she found that she had put off going to college because she wanted to aid in the war effort. A vivacious, outgoing girl, Barbara was a marked contrast to Amy, who Barbara soon discovered had warmth and humor under her reticence. There was an innocence about Amy that Barbara couldn't resist teasing, particularly since Amy accepted it good-naturedly, finding her new friend a source of worldliness and fascinating information. Amy found Barbara a revelation, a key to a new door that she was anxious to go through.

Amy reveled in the knowledge that for the first time she was free to make her own decisions and pursue her own interests, and life at home assumed a comfortable pattern. The only concern that marred it was the continued absence of mail from Ted. He'd last been heard from when a batch of letters arrived shortly before his father's passing. Though she matter-of-factly assured Deborah they would hear from him soon, Amy was filled with foreboding: something was wrong with Ted. She was amazed at Deborah's willingness to accept her reasons for his silence and deemed it wiser not to press the matter. Debating what course of action to take, Amy discussed the problem with Barbara.

"One thing's sure," Barbara had advised, "if anything were seriously wrong, you'd have been notified. Stop horsing around and find out what's happened. Put your mother on the job. She works at the Red Cross, doesn't she? They'll help."

Relieved at what Barbara had to say, Amy promised she'd follow her advice. Barbara grinned. "Amy, you worry about everyone. But it's marvelous how close you are to your family. I'm the same way. My mom's like yours, a real pal. I can hardly wait till you meet my family."

Amy concealed a twinge of fear, wondering what Barbara's reaction would be if she really knew the facts of her relationship with her mother.

When Amy broached her plan, Deborah did not waver a moment in rising to the challenge, and Amy realized her fears of how she would react had been groundless.

The news all came at once: a short note from Ted, and communications from the Red Cross and the Navy. Ted had been wounded. He was recovering and awaiting transfer to a naval hospital—the one nearest to their home. They knew only that he was someplace in the Pacific and that his mail had been delayed or lost.

All Deborah's fears for her son were overridden by the news of his return. Ted now colored everything she said and did. Amy's spirits soared; a huge burden had been lifted from her shoulders. Ted's eventual homecoming would mean sharing the responsibility for their mother with someone else. Life held renewed promise and she even contemplated going to night school.

As she discussed her ideas with Barbara at lunch one day, Barbara interrupted her. "Gee, kid, I've been meaning to ask you if you'd be interested in going out on a double date."

Surprised, Amy asked, "Who with?"

Smiling knowingly, Barbara whispered, "Don't look now; he's sitting over there. Tom Worden, the new supervisor of our section, asked if we'd like to take in a movie. His friend works in another department."

Nonplussed, Amy blurted, "I don't know, Barb. I'll have to let you know." Seeing her friend's disappointment, she decided it might be better to explain. "There's something I ought to tell you. I hope it isn't going to affect our friendship, but you have to know."

Barbara looked at her expectantly as, shamefaced and reluctant, Amy admitted, "I've never been to a movie in my entire life other than the ones I saw at school."

For a fleeting second Amy was frightened by the expression on Barbara's face. In shocked disbelief, Barbara said, "Did you say you've never seen a real movie? You mean you don't know about Joan Crawford, Bette Davis, Tyrone Power, Errol Flynn . . . any of the movie stars?"

Her face red with embarrassment, Amy mumbled, "I've heard about some of them, but I've never seen them. You might as well know the rest. My family brought me up to believe that dancing, drinking and movies are sinful."

Barbara gasped as she asked derisively, "And you think that? Are you one of those religious fanatics?

Beside herself with fear at losing her friend, Amy entreated, "Oh, Barbara, I'm not like that . . . really I'm not. Barbara, you don't know what it means to me to have a friend like you. You're the first real friend my age I've ever had. Please don't be angry at me."

Barbara was embarrassed at the pain she saw on Amy's face, and her voice choked with emotion as she said, "I'm not angry at you. I'm sorry I got so carried away. I feel the same way; I've never had a friend like you, and it's wonderful to have someone all to myself that I can count on. We're friends, and that's all that matters."

They sat grinning at each other until Barbara said, "How about getting together Saturday? We could take in a movie and, if it's all right with your mom, you could come back to my house for dinner and sleep over."

Glowing, Amy said, "I'd love to spend Saturday afternoon with you. I'm not sure about staying over, but the afternoon's fine."

Grinning, Barbara teased, "I can hardly wait. You're about to see your first movie."

"I hope I don't embarrass you." Amy smiled ruefully. "There are a lot more things I have to tell you. Would you believe it was only a few years ago we got our first radio? It changed our lives."

"I'll bet it did." Barbara was fascinated. "You must have an interesting family. When did you decide to break away from the family tradition—you know, going to the movies and such? Won't it bother your mother?"

Amy sat quietly for a moment, considering, and then she said, "Barbs, there's something else you ought to know. When you come to my house, it'll be the first thing my mother'll tell you. I was adopted; the Wilkersons are not my real family."

Amy could hear Barbara's intake of breath at this information, and she watched with relief as Barbara nonchalantly tossed it off. "So what? Millions of kids are adopted. What's such a big deal about that? How come you didn't pick better?" Hearing what she'd said, she quickly added, "Oops, there I go again . . . my mouth ten steps ahead of my brain!"

"It's all right, Barb. I wish I'd had a choice, but that's a long story. I'll tell you about it some other time. I was lucky in some respects. I just didn't want you to be surprised when you met my mother. She uses my name in one breath—with 'dopted daughter.' For a long time I really thought that was my name."

Her eyes wide with compassion, Barbara asked, "Are you sure it will be all right for you to go to the movies? We can do something else, you know."

For a moment Amy considered the option, and then her eyes danced. "Nope . . . I'm dying to go. I feel like an idiot when I think about all the things I've missed. I've got a lot of catching up to do. Will you help me, Barb?"

"You bet I will, Amy. Oh, we're going to have so much fun."

Deborah was preoccupied and almost missed hearing Amy tell her, "I'm meeting a friend of mine downtown Saturday afternoon, Momma. I'll be back in time for supper."

Catching the word supper, Deborah reminded herself. "Amy, Mrs. Watkins is having some of us to her home for a little get-together. It's not really a party, else I wouldn't go. She told me it's just a quiet supper for some of the ladies she feels have worked specially hard."

Amy smiled at her mother's expediency. "In that case, Momma, you won't have to worry about me. I can have supper with my girlfriend. I'll be home later in the evening."

Amy couldn't wait to tell Barbara and telephoned her as soon as Deborah had gone to her room.

Whispering, Barbara said, "You won't be a virgin after tomorrow!"

Aghast, Amy asked, "What's that supposed to mean?"

Barbara giggled. "It means we're going to see Fred Astaire and Ginger Rogers, and I can't wait to see your reaction. Say, how about meeting me earlier and we'll have lunch together?"

There was no way Barbara could comprehend the import of

the day she had planned for her friend. It was to be a major milestone in Amy's life.

Cold and shaking at the adventure about to befall her, Amy let Barbara lead her into the darkened movie house. She had not imagined it would be like this. She bumped into someone as Barbara suddenly stopped in the aisle, having located suitable seats. Amy couldn't have spoken had she wanted to. She sat enthralled, entranced by the colorful images and sounds that filled her eyes and ears. She was breathless at the vision of the beautiful woman in the feathery gown and the man in his tophat and tails who moved so effortlessly, whirling about as if they floated on air. Once she managed to whisper, "It must be like this when a blind man regains his sight." Barbara squeezed her arm delightedly, moved by Amy's innocent exultation and joy. They sat through the movie twice and were almost to the end again when Barbara said, "Come on, hon, we've got to go."

Back in the light, dazed, Amy kept repeating, "I can't believe it. Why do you suppose people are told to live without such beauty in their lives? Why should it be a sin when it's nicer than real life?"

Pleased with what she had accomplished, Barbara consoled, "I agree. For the life of me I can't imagine why anyone would want to deny someone else such pleasure."

Amy said, "Let's do it again next week. Can we, Barb?"

Shaking her head in disbelief, Barbara agreed. "Of course. It's incredible in this day and age there's someone like you. You're special, Amy, and I'm proud we're best friends."

After boarding the trolley car that would take them to Barbara's house, Amy sat in a trance. It seemed impossible to believe all these wonderful things were happening to her.

"There it is!" Barbara pointed. The two-story Spanish-style house seemed palatial. It was surrounded by an emerald-green lawn and the path to its doorway was hemmed by bushes. Overpowered by its beauty, Amy slowed her steps and Barbara looked at her. "Come on—what's the matter?"

Smiling timidly, Amy confessed, "What if they don't like me?"

"Are you crazy or something?" Barbara snapped. "My family? They'll love you—come on! Mom's a nut about gardening. You'll have to see our Victory Garden in the back. My dad thinks it's silly when you can buy a bunch of carrots for a few cents."

"I wish we had one—it makes you feel better doing everything you can to support the cause."

Amy's encounter with the Hopkins family dissipated every preconception she'd had about families. They accepted her as if she were an old friend. Barbara's mother opened the door and, greeting both girls, took Amy into her arms. Kissing her, Carol Hopkins said, "It's about time! You're even prettier than Barbs said you were. You mean a lot to our daughter."

Looking at her, Amy tried to respond in kind. "Thank you, Mrs. Hopkins. You look young enough to be Barb's sister."

"Thank you. Barbs, hang Amy's things up. Did you enjoy the movie?"

The question disturbed Amy as she wondered if Barbara had revealed her confidences to her mother. She didn't have time to harbor the feeling as Barbara tugged at her arm. "Come on, Amy . . . you've got to meet the rest of the gang. See . . . through the door . . . that lazy lout on the couch. He's got his ear glued to the radio—that's my kid brother, Mike." As they walked into the room, Mike grinned. "Hi. You gotta be Amy. Scuse me, I'm listening to 'The Shadow.' It's my favorite program."

"Jeannie," Barbara called, "come out from back of the chair and say hello to Amy." A small girl popped out and plopped herself into a chair as Barbara grinned, explaining to her friend, "That's the baby of the family. She's almost as shy as you. Pesky as all get-out when she knows you. You're lucky you don't have any sisters. Makes a mess out of my drawers and clothes."

Suddenly, without realizing it, Amy found herself at ease.

There was no doubt, Amy thought, a house reflected the people who lived in it. This one was large and rambling, old Spanish with its wooden beamed ceilings and arched doorways. Its comfortable, nondescript furnishings, a large green cushiony couch and big easy chairs, were slightly worn at the edges, possessing a wonderful lived-in quality. She was delighted at the sight of a kitten curled up in a chair. The fireplace brass was darkened with soot and a fire burned cheerily amid the ashes. It was inexplicable, but she felt as if she belonged, as if, in this house, she was welcome. And it was an unfamiliar sensation to her.

Supper was a blur of fun which had Amy collapsing in giggles. Mr. Hopkins, a huge bear of a man, maintained a sober, serious face while teasing them all ceaselessly. It took

Amy a while to understand that he wasn't threatening or serious, but loved them all and communicated it this way.

Mrs. Hopkins refused to allow Barbara or Amy to help with the dishes and commandeered the two youngest children, who growled and groaned their dismay. Barbara whisked Amy away to her room to show her treasures. It seemed just a moment before Mr. Hopkins knocked at the door to remind Amy it was time to leave for home.

Hugging her father, Barbara plastered his cheek with kisses, while Amy watched enviously. Walking Amy to the living room to say her goodnights, Barbara hugged her. "Amy, I'll bet you're leaving here promising yourself you'll never come again. My awful family—imagine, this is their best behavior."

Mrs. Hopkins studied the girl, astonished at seeing tears well up in Amy's eyes. She hugged her. "Come soon again. You're welcome anytime."

Shyly Amy said, "Thank you all so much for having me." Turning to Barbara, she almost whispered, "You'll never know how much this day meant to me. I've loved every minute."

Mr. Hopkins tugged at her sleeve. "Come on, kiddo, we've got to get some speed on!"

He was a kindly man and he put Amy at ease, chatting as he drove. He pulled up to the stop and waited with her until the trolley came along.

Amy had never known such courteous treatment. She felt a pang of envy for her friend, who took such concern for granted.

Boarding the car, she settled into a seat in the back. She was very tired. The day had been a revelation. Her mind was a kaleidoscope, but she was sure of one thing: her life until now had been steeped in ignorance and misconceptions. She had lived in a world of fantasy predicated on wishful thinking. The Hopkinses had shown her reality could actually be a whole lot better than anything she had made up in her head.

She reached home a few moments before an abashed Deborah hastened up the front steps, her cheeks and eyes aglow with the evening she'd had. She was hardly through the door when she began to talk. "Amy, you'd never believe the lovely spread Mrs. Watkins laid. It was a sight, sure enough. She used sugar that must've taken all her ration stamps. Them ladies are all so nice. I sure enjoyed myself. I don spose it's right bein in mournin, but Mrs. Watkins said I got to look at it sensible. 'Life belongs to the livin,' she says, 'and you're not doin a thing wrong by socializin a bit.' What do you think, Amy?"

"I think she's right, Momma. After all, you only had a bite to eat and a chat with your friends. How could there be anything wrong with that? The Lord didn't intend for you to sit in sackcloth and ashes. How would that help anyone?"

Eagerly Deborah agreed. "I'm sure glad you think that way too, Amy. That Mrs. Watkins sure is a fine lady."

Amy smiled to herself. God bless Mrs. Watkins; she'd become the new arbiter of Deborah's life.

Excitement was burgeoning inside Amy. Life was opening up. No longer would she allow herself to be bound by the old rules. She'd been living in a cocoon, an anachronism far away from the present time. It was time to shed the past and shape her own destiny. She was no longer dependent on the Wilkersons for support. Since starting work she had accrued war bonds and her savings account had swelled. Aside from the ten dollars paid to Deborah weekly for her room and board, the balance of Amy's money could be used as she saw fit.

The knowledge that she could be independent gave her courage. She would buy new clothes, she would go to as many movies as she liked—she would never have enough of them. Spurred by her plans, she called to Deborah, who was readying herself for bed, "Momma, would you mind if next Saturday I invited my friend to supper?"

Deborah walked out of the room in her wrapper. "That'd be nice, Amy. I wouldn't mind atall. Do you spose it would be all right if I asked Mrs. Watkins and one or two o the others to join us? We could fix a real tasty meal." She waited hesitantly for Amy's approval.

Keeping a straight face, Amy pretended to consider the matter. "Why, Momma, I think it'd be only no more than right, seeing as how Mrs. Watkins had you over. We can plan the menu tomorrow. By the way, Momma, since Barbara lives a far piece from here, I might just ask her if she could stay the night. You wouldn't mind that, would you?"

Now the shoe was on the other foot. Amy was learning how to get her way.

"I spose not, Amy. Where would she sleep?"

Amy feigned consideration. "Well, Momma, there is Ted's

room, and for one night I don't suppose it would matter. Barbara's a lovely person and I'm sure you'll approve of her. In any case, you wouldn't want to be less kind to her than her family is to me."

It was an irrefutable argument. Deborah not only agreed, she also decided she would do all the shopping herself.

Stretched out in bed, Amy tossed and turned, overstimulated by the day's events. Suddenly the impulse to laugh overcame her and she was forced to bury her head in the pillow lest Deborah hear. The irony of their situation had struck her. It seemed absurd that she and Deborah should have been accomplices in their desire for a different life. There was no doubt Deborah was enjoying newfound freedom despite the pretext of mourning. Of course she missed Horace, but, without his domination, she had found other compensations. She was enjoying a social life that, with him, she'd never have known.

Stifling her laughter, Amy gave Deborah a mental pat on the back, thinking, Good for you, old Deborah, better late than never. She fell asleep dreaming she was twirling in the arms of Fred Astaire while her sister, Emmy, hazy and beautiful stood on the sidelines happily smiling approval. She often dreamed of Emmy, even now.

The huge cafeteria was jammed with people as Amy made her way into it. Usually she and Barbara ate in the lounge where it was easier to talk, but today Barbara had forgotten to bring her lunch. Looking around, Amy saw her off in a corner.

Their eyes met and Barbara motioned that she had picked up Amy's milk. As Amy approached the table, a strange woman seated alongside Barbara looked up and smiled. Barbara called, "What happened? I thought you'd never get here."

Smiling, Amy squeezed into the waiting seat and opened her sandwich bag as Barbara said, "Meet Mrs. Forbes; she's a newcomer to our division. Guess what, Amy—Mrs. Forbes comes from your neck of the woods; she has the same drawl."

Glancing disinterestedly at the slight, middle-aged person dressed in the same drab coveralls they all wore, Amy asked politely, "Where are you from?"

Her origins were apparent as she drawled, "Texas, Oklahoma, hon. Where you from?"

Taking a sip of milk, Amy nodded. "Oklahoma . . . a small town you probably never heard of—Brightwater." At that moment Barbara said something, and as Amy turned to respond she failed to see a look of surprise cross the woman's face. Not wanting to appear rude, Amy resumed her chat with Mrs. Forbes, who smiled, saying, "Would you believe I once went through there . . . kind of a cowtown, wouldn't you say?" She had put on a pair of thick-lensed glasses through which she peered intently at Amy. Unaccountably annoyed, Amy retorted, "I don't know that I'd call it that. It's more a farming community center."

Mrs. Forbes hastily explained, "Oh, I didn't mean to put it down . . . just what we call them towns. Well, if you'll excuse me, I've got to powder my nose."

Amy looked curiously after her retreating back and, noticing this, Barbara said, "She was telling me how glad she was to get work here. She's widowed and been having a rough time getting work. I think she's older than she looks, but these days I guess they're glad to take anyone."

Chewing reflectively, Amy said, "I don't know why, but she gave me the creeps. It's crazy, but for some reason she reminds me of someone. Did you see the way she looked at me? I got the impression she felt the same way."

"Oh, I think you're imagining it," Barbara said. "It's probably because you're both from the same area."

Despite Barbara's cheery patter, Amy remained pensive. Her thoughts had reverted to Brightwater and her sisters. She wondered what had happened to Emmy and Polly Sue and if they ever remembered her. Meeting that woman had brought back all those memories. It gave her an awful feeling to think that one day she might meet them and find them vaguely familiar. Figments of the past flicked through her mind, and vividly she recalled when Emmy had been so sick—how frightened she'd been, desperate for her parents to come and get them . . . that nice Mrs. Fields comforting her. Achingly, she felt again the fear, the slowly dying hope, the terrifying realization that her mother and father weren't coming back. Lost in the flood of her recollections of past miseries, she felt tears well up. She'd forgotten where she was until Barbara's voice penetrated. "Amy . . . hey, what's the matter? You haven't heard a word I've said."

Brushing the moisture from her eyes, she forced a smile. "I'm sorry . . . I've been thinking . . ."

Barbara looked at her sympathetically. "Well, it's certainly made you miserable. Come on, forget it!"

It was a few days later as Amy waited for Barbara in the lounge that she saw her friend come in, excitedly holding out an envelope.

"What's that, Barb?" Amy asked.

"I haven't the slightest idea. Just as I was leaving to come up here that Mrs. Forbes came by and asked me to give you this."

Gingerly holding the envelope, Amy had the strangest sensation; for a second a sense of premonition assailed her, as if trouble impended.

Impatient, Barbara scolded, "Aren't you going to open it? I'm curious—what's it about?"

Reluctantly tearing the envelope open, Amy unfolded the neatly written enclosure. As she read the contents she gasped, the color drained from her face, her hands shook and she had difficulty breathing. Alarmed, Barbara exclaimed, "What is it? What's the matter?"

Trembling, Amy extended the letter. She was unable to talk, floundering for words. Quickly Barbara scanned the sheet.

I hope this won't cause you any upset, but I just have to find out, because, your friend said your name was Amy Beth. If you're not the same one I knew, then this won't interest you none. I lied when I said I just passed through Brightwater. I was there awhile and know about three Beauford sisters left with a Mrs. Fields. They was Emmalina, Amy Beth and Polly Sue, the baby. I loved them girls very much and am sorry about what happened. If you is that same Amy Beth I have some things to tell. I do not want to make any trouble but if you are interested you can call me Pacific 2143. Please call daytime because I am transferred to the night shift.

Sincerely,
Mary Ann Forbes

P.S. You're a real pretty girl and remind me a lot of your daddy, my husband Dan Beauford.

Stunned at the disclosure, Barbara paled too as she realized the import of what she had conveyed to Amy. "My God, Amy, I had no idea. Oh, you poor darling, what a shock.

Amy, can I get you some water? You look like you're going to faint."

Amy felt sick. Her mouth filled with bile, she couldn't breathe. She winced as the pain became more acute. She wanted to run, to hide from this hideous revelation. It had been better not to know. Any illusions and fantasies she had harbored disintegrated at the vision of Mrs. Forbes' lens-distorted eyes boring through her. Her body contorted with bitterness. *Oh, God, to be back in the limbo of ignorance, wondering who I am. . . .* Her hands clenched into fists.

Frightened, Barbara said, "Let me take you to the nurse's office. You can't go back to work."

It was as if she'd been kicked in the stomach. Her head reeled, she was dizzy and now her body began to shake uncontrollably. She felt faint. Through a haze she saw Barbara, holding a glass of water. She tried to take a few sips; she had to regain her senses. Cold and hot all at once, she leaned back. Anxiously Barbara fanned her. Slowly the piercing pain receded and she finally managed to say weakly, "Just a minute, Barb, I'll be all right."

It took a few moments before Amy could get her mind to focus. She made herself start at the beginning. It was too incredible. That nondescript woman seated at the table . . . that Mary Ann Forbes . . . that woman actually her long-lost mother! Try as she would, Amy couldn't make herself recall what she had looked like—she'd been so commonplace, so colorless. Again her head reeled with a million conflicting thoughts and indignation began to rise in her. The gall of the woman, to strike at her like a lightning bolt and hope she wouldn't be upset. As if deserting your children, leaving them to face unspeakable agonies, was an everyday occurrence! Amy was overcome by the need to wreak violence, to smash at the deceitful, lying face, as if by doing so she could in some small measure revenge herself for the abandonment and the hideous suffering she had endured.

She felt Barbara's arm pulling and she snapped, "Leave me alone! I don't want anything to do with her." She saw Barbara's consternation and heard her pleading, "Please, Amy, come on. Let me take you to the nurse's office. All I want is to get you some help. Please, Amy, come with me."

Trying to rise, Amy felt as though her legs were rubber. Barbara instantly put a protective arm around her as Amy half sobbed, "This is a nightmare. Can you believe that woman—that Mary Ann Forbes—is my real mother?" Pulling herself upright, she snapped, "She loved us all, did she? She must have hated us! She's worse than a snake—striking the way she did!"

"Can you walk, Amy?" Barbara jumped as Amy let out a wail and broke into sobs. "I despise that woman! I loathe her!" Clinging to Barbara she gulped for air. "I never understood what family life was like . . . it's a miracle I am who I am. I'll always feel I'm not like other people . . . there'll always be a gap." Tears had begun to course down Barbara's cheeks as Amy shuddered. "I feel dirty, ashamed—when I think what kind of person she is . . . the things she did!"

They were drawing attention from other people and Barbara pleaded, "Amy dear, this is no place to talk. Let's get out of here. We'll go someplace where we can be alone. Okay? Come with me to the nurse's office."

Giving in, Amy let Barbara lead her to the nurse's office, where she waited while Barbara went for their things.

"The air feels good, Barb. I'll be okay, please don't worry," Amy said as they left the plant. They reached the coffeeshop where they usually stopped after work. Barbara watched as Amy drank the coffee. It was a relief to see her normal color returning. Amy felt better and reached across the table to pat her friend's hand. In response, Barbara said, "In a way I feel responsible for what's happened. It's weird when you think I introduced you."

An ironic laugh escaped Amy. "How could you know, Barbs? Don't feel that way. It's fate or one of those crazy things. Do you remember I said she looked familiar? Do you realize what that means? My own mother looked familiar!"

Cringing at the thought, Barbara sat silently, letting Amy talk. "It's coming back to me now. In my mind I always thought she was pretty. She had black hair and rosy cheeks. Isn't it crazy, the things you remember? I was so little. I'm not sure what I really remember or what I made up. She used to laugh a lot . . ."

Amy sat morosely, and Barbara cautiously ventured an opinion. "Give yourself a chance to think this over. You can't tell; maybe there's lots of reasons for what she did. Maybe you'd feel better if you hear what she has to say."

The pain in Amy's stomach was returning. Her voice was vehement. "After I'm through telling you a few things, then tell me what you'd do."

Barbara sat in horrified silence as the stricken girl poured out an account of her early life with the Wilkersons.

Eventually drained, she asked, "Well, now that you know, what do you think I should do?" Without waiting for an answer she said sorrowfully, "That woman frightens me. Can you think of anything she'd have to say that wouldn't bring more grief into my life? I thought I was free of the past, especially now when I'm finally able to do what I want."

Distressed, Barbara said, "I can understand, Amy—really I can. The only advice I can give you is to be sure; don't do anything you'd regret. Maybe she could answer some questions. The way I feel is that she shouldn't get off scot-free. She should be made to suffer too."

Amy looked at Barbara dubiously. "If she didn't feel guilt over what she did to her children, how do you imagine I could accomplish it?"

Barbara shook her head, commiserating. "I realize, but I'm thinking of you. Just be sure there's nothing you want to find out from her."

Amy conceded, "All right, Barbs. I won't make a snap decision. I'll think it over."

Worried about her friend, Barbara pleaded that she go home with her, but Amy resisted. She felt a desperate need for time alone to sort out her thoughts.

The house was empty when Amy reached it. Deborah wouldn't be home for several hours. It would give her time to think. Bathing her eyes, she stretched out on the bed, but rest eluded her. Her anger began to surface again as she read and reread the note. She seethed at the recollection of the woman's soft voice, repelled at the thought of how devious she'd been denying any knowledge of Brightwater, and of her callousness in assuming Amy might be one of her children—one, in fact, that resembled her father. Another wave of hatred for that woman—her mother—ran through her.

Mixed in the welter of emotion was the sound of the Wilkersons telling her over and over again about "the trash that borned you, them kind of critters who'd abandoned their own flesh and blood."

Today she'd suffered the pain she'd always had at those words . . . the guilt of having been so bad she'd driven her parents away. It had come back to overwhelm her . . . the hurt and punishment she'd endured in retribution for being the evil fruit of their loins. She recalled Aunt Tina's words as she'd offered consolation: "Don yo worry, chile. Cose o what's happen, yo gonna be a diffrun person, a betta one cose o it." She wondered if that was really possible . . . she had tried so hard to be good.

The shrilling of the telephone startled her. Barbara's voice, asking if she was all right, was a welcome relief.

As Amy spoke with her, the cumbersome weight of the past began to slide from her back, and the chaos of her mind began to quiet. She knew what she was going to do; her mind was made up. There were no questions she wanted answered; she had no curiosity, no need to know what had motivated anyone to such a miserable act. Better to leave it dead and buried. Mrs. Forbes could rot in hell for all she cared. That chapter was closed. It was too late for anyone to erase the anguish of a shrieking, beaten little body. Those memories had to stay buried, best forgotten forever, except for their scars.

A weight had lifted; she felt better for having made her decision. Locked in her thoughts, Amy had not heard Deborah's key turning in the door. She started when she heard her voice calling, "Amy? You home already?"

Quickly Amy ran to the mirror to run a comb through her hair. She was amazed to see how normal she looked. Her face was flushed, but otherwise she gave no sign of what she'd undergone.

For the rest of the evening Amy was proud of how artfully she concealed her feelings. Then, as Deborah busied herself turning out the lights in the living room, Amy suddenly asked, "Momma, did you ever see my real mother? Did you meet her when she was in Brightwater?"

Amy's heart leaped at the way Deborah recoiled. "Lan sakes, of all things, Amy, what in the world's gotten into you askin such crazy questions?" Suspicion immediately surfaced as Deborah said, "Why? What makes you want to know now?"

Amy retorted, "Why can't you answer without making such a fuss?"

Deborah drew herself up, her feelings hurt. "No call to be sassin me, girl. Yes! I saw that woman, if that's what you be wantin to know. No. I never met her . . . thank the good Lord. It was that Fields woman knew her. I believe I saw her onct or twice, that's all. Now, if you don't mind, would you be kind enough to tell me why suddenly you have such a need to know?"

Amy grinned mischievously, making a pretense of hunting for a book, relishing the tormenting, delaying action. Deborah was about to receive a small token repayment for the cruelties inflicted on a helpless child so long ago.

Amy savored the moment. She knew her adopted mother well, and what she was about to reveal to her would create havoc. Deborah Wilkerson would fight to the last to keep Amy away from Mary Ann Forbes.

There was another reason behind Amy's plan. Deborah's resistance would be Amy's support in her plan not to see the Forbes woman.

She felt justified in her actions, and the sensation of sweet revenge was satisfying. It felt good to have the power to hurt and hit back. Long ago she had forfeited any innocence of heart and had harbored the dream of just such a thing. Now she had the instrument, the capability to execute it. As far back as she could remember she had been forced to give way to the pressure of others, supposedly good people who, under the guise of sacrifice and charity, had wreaked their will upon her. She had been taught at the feet of masters.

Confused by Amy's behavior, Deborah had gone into the kitchen to get her nightly glass of water. Amy followed. As Deborah rinsed the glass, she said, "What's got into you tonight? You look kinda like the cat that swallowed the canary."

Pulling out a chair, Amy smiled at her. "Maybe you're right, Momma. A funny thing happened today."

Alert at once, Deborah waited.

Calmly and with deliberate slowness, Amy related how she had met the woman who might be her natural mother. "I'm almost sure of it, Momma. She knows where we were left. You wouldn't have any way of knowing, of course, Momma, but she says I look like my father. You wouldn't believe, Momma, what a sweet, attractive person she is . . . real soft-spoken."

Deborah stared at Amy, mesmerized. The color drained from her face and her eyes grew large with apprehension. Her fingers intertwined as she struggled to regain some composure. Her voice was hoarse when she asked, "What you gonna do about it, Amy Beth?"

"I don't know, Momma. Not yet, at any rate. It's been a long day, Momma; let's go to bed. If you want, we can talk some more about it in the morning."

"You gonna call her?"

Amy turned at the door. "Maybe. Maybe tomorrow, Momma. I'll sleep on it. Are you coming? It's late."

Deborah rose. "Amy . . ."

"Yes, Momma?"

"You ain't gonna . . ."

"Not now, Momma . . . it's been a difficult day. Sleep well . . . pleasant dreams!"

She had no idea when Deborah went to bed.

By morning, as Amy had anticipated, the situation had altered. Deborah was geared for battle.

She saw when she walked into the kitchen that Deborah had spent a sleepless night. Helping herself to coffee from the pot on the stove, Amy drew out a chair and sat down opposite her.

"You got to give up that job, gal. You'll find somethin elst."

Sipping her coffee, Amy didn't answer. Instead she reached for the telephone.

Deborah screamed, "Not in my house, you don't!"

Ignoring her, Amy placed the call and, when the connection was made, asked to speak to her supervisor. She explained she wouldn't report for work that day. Putting the telephone away, she smiled teasingly at Deborah. "Who'd you think I was calling, Momma?"

At that moment the phone rang, and as Amy picked it up she saw the beads of perspiration on Deborah's upper lip. The call was from Barbara. Intimating that she couldn't talk, Amy told her, "I'll call you this evening. Everything's under control . . . don't worry, hon. I'll tell you all about it later."

She looked up to see Deborah white-faced and shaken as if she were on the verge of hysteria. "What is it, Momma? You look ill. Can I do something for you?"

"Amy Beth, we got to talk . . . you and I got to have a talk. I got to know."

"Know what, Momma? You can't be this upset because you think I might call my real mother. It's flattering; I never knew you cared this much. If I'd known you were going to be this upset I'd never have told you."

Deborah exploded, and Amy sat quietly while she raged. Finally she shoved her chair back. "Momma, it's exasperating to hear all those old horror stories again. I'm too old for that, I know better now. Let's wait until we can talk reasonably. I assure you I have no plans to call her now. I'd like to go to my room, close the door and think this over. When you're calmed down, we'll discuss it."

Frustrated at Amy's stance, Deborah could do nothing about it. Amy held firm.

Barricading her door, Amy placed a chair under the doorknob. She dozed off, only to be awakened by knocking and Deborah's voice. "Amy . . . are you up? I been thinkin and wanta talk to you."

"Just a minute, Momma." Amy gathered her wits, removed the chair and invited Deborah in. "Come in, Momma. Did you rest?"

"Looka here, Amy, we got to get this settled. I'm agoin to have my say. Maybe you don like the way I talk bout that woman—the one that birthed you." She stopped as if expecting Amy to interrupt. Instead Amy sat looking up at her from her bed where she'd perched, knees drawn under her chin.

Plaintively Deborah continued, "You got to think, gal . . . where she been all these years? We stayed in Brightwater long enough for her to seek you out. We got you dopted fair and square. You remember, legal and right. She been needin to see you or her other childrun, why she wait so long? 'Tain't fair to you or the others! Plain ain't fair for her to come bustin in on other folks' lives."

Amy nodded at her as if encouraging her to go on.

"What she got to tell you now after leavin you those many years ago? You can't blame Horace or me for thinkin poorly o such folks. From your count she been doin fairly well. Gal, I don care what you gonna say for her . . . a woman who birthed three childrun and thrown 'em to the winds ain't got any cause to come awhinin after them now. You got to see what I'm talkin about . . . her leavin t'others the dirty work o raisin and rearin her younguns."

She glared at Amy, shaking her forefinger at her. "Like it or not, you is my daughter more than you is hers. All I got to say is, if you be a fair-minded gal, such as I think you is, you'll say I'm right."

For answer, Amy smiled.

Incensed by Amy's noncommittal attitude, Deborah's voice took on an angry edge. "What she agoin to tell you, Amy—sad stories bout where she's been at? Why? 'Twere up to me the likes o her'd be horsewhipped, that's what! The more so what she done to us these past hours. I'm bound to say this to you, Amy . . . ifn you see or talk with that woman, I'm through. I won't never want to see or talk to you again." Here Deborah paused. Turning her head so Amy couldn't see her face, she said almost ashamedly, "You oughta know you mean a heap to me. I just couldn't stand it, thinkin bout it. . . . I ask the Lord's forgiveness but that's how I'm made."

For a second, Amy felt remorse, and then the absurdity of it struck her. All this fuss over a woman who had deserted her and another who had brutalized her within an inch of her life. She put down any guilt she felt about Deborah's admission of feeling for her. Neither of them were worth the agonizing she'd been putting herself through. She had her own life to live—the future, hope and a new world.

Her face wore a grin as she said, "Momma, there you go, getting yourself all worked up again. If it'll make you easier, Momma, you can go get your Bible and I'll put my hand on it . . . that way you'll be sure I won't call that woman. What more do you want?"

"For you to burn that paper up. Do it here and now in front of me. That way I'll be able to sleep. Are you willin, gal?"

Amy rose from the bed, got her purse and extracted the note from it. She extended it to Deborah, who cringed, refusing to accept it. Sadness suffused Amy as she turned the note around in her hand. She said in a whisper, "Good-bye again, Mother . . . you who birthed me . . . you gave up your rights, you missed your chance." It was more grimace than smile as she looked at Deborah and said out loud, "Reason's on Deborah's side . . . she worked hard to make me good . . . you owe this to her!"

She walked out to the kitchen and struck a match, holding the note over the sink, watching as the link to her unknown past curled and writhed into ash. She hated herself because her heart sobbed.

As if in compensation, in some unspoken knowledge, Deborah was kinder and gentler to Amy than she'd ever been before. It was, Amy thought, as if she were trying to make up for all the miserable, wasted years.

For a while, Amy felt as if she were frozen in time, as if she walked on another planet. Nothing Deborah could do or say about Amy leaving her job altered her intention to stay on. She returned to work and to Barbara's loving warmth. The only thing she could bring herself to tell her friend was, "I made my decision, right or wrong; that's how it stands. The best thing you can do for me is not to talk about it, Barbs. It's too painful."

Deborah decided to postpone the impending dinner party to the following week. She'd been too upset by Amy's news.

The letter from Mary Ann Forbes was not the only unusual event of the week. As if to counterbalance what had happened, Amy was notified she'd been promoted to supervisor of her department. Barbara took it good-naturedly. "You're really much more competent than I am. I'm glad."

"What would I do without you, Barbs?" Amy asked. It had been Barbara who had soothed and reassured her when she had returned to work, worried about Mary Ann Forbes suddenly confronting her. Barbara had insisted, "She won't, Amy. There's one good thing you can say on her behalf—she knows where she isn't wanted."

As the days passed Amy's fears began to recede. The best thing in her life was having Barbara as her friend. Their co-workers, laughing, referred to the inseparable girls as "The Bobbsey Twins."

Thus it was surprising that the Saturday-night dinner party produced their first major altercation. Amy had grown slightly edgy at Barbara's reaction to Deborah and her lady friends.

They'd no sooner gotten into Amy's room and closed the door than Barbara had commenced to laugh, remarking at the way Deborah had put on airs. She was startled as she realized Amy was not in sympathy with her viewpoint. She tried to cover, but Amy wouldn't let it pass. "I can appreciate how well mannered and considerate you are, Barbara, but I think you've forgotten something. You're a city girl and we're hicks. Okies, isn't that what most of you folks term us? For sure you already know, I'm one."

Concerned at her own insensitivity, Barbara tried to apologize, but Amy refused to listen. Heatedly she went on to explain, "I'm not angry—I'm surprised. After all, Barbara, I never pretended we were any different than you're finding us. What did you expect? This is the first house we've lived in that has inside plumbing."

Embarrassed and hurt, Barbara retorted, "What's that supposed to mean to me?"

Having worked herself up at the imagined slight, Amy snapped, "It means that, in spite of the hardships, we still went to the toilet and kept ourselves clean. Not everyone lives in fancy houses and has fancy manners!"

The entire scene was uncalled for, and Barbara felt betrayed. She sat in silence, staring sullenly at this new and touchy Amy.

As if impelled, Amy rattled on, "We had an outhouse, or a privy if you prefer. We used a big metal tub and pumped the water for it from over our sink. It had to be heated on our old iron stove. We bathed at least once a week and always on special occasions. I find it hard to laugh at people who have to go to a bathroom in rain and freezing cold. While I'm at it, I suppose you ought to know I wore my first silk stockings only a couple of years ago. Deborah's never worn them."

What stunned Barbara was Amy's sudden defense of her mother. She studied her in surprise, confused at what was going on in her friend's mind. She'd never dreamed Amy would assume she'd been insulting Deborah when all along it was she herself who had criticized her mother.

Opening a closet door, Amy pointed. "See those middy blouses and skirts? I wore them all through high school. Deborah sat up nights making them. Don't for a moment think I don't realize how we appear to you, but you ought to know that what you've been seeing at dinner is a giant step for my mother." Suddenly wrung out, she looked at Barbara in contrition.

Barbara walked to the door. "Will it be all right if I make a call, Amy? I want to find out if my father can pick me up."

Startled at what she had done, Amy entreated, "Don't go, Barbs, please. I know I sounded horrid. I never meant to hurt your feelings. I don't know why I'm carrying on like this. I guess I'm just self-conscious about everything. These past weeks have unnerved me completely. You must think I'm crazy defending Deborah—it surprises me too."

Hesitantly Barbara said, "Are you sure you want me to stay?"

"Of course I'm sure. You're my best and dearest friend. I could kill myself when I think how I'm behaving."

"Forget it, Amy. I don't bear grudges. You're right about something, though. I take a lot for granted and I shouldn't."

Smiling, Amy confided, "You've no idea how great it is that Momma has friends. They're the key to my freedom. They're the first ones she's ever had, and they keep her off my back."

Considering what Amy had said, Barbara rejoined, "Please don't think I'm prying but I have to ask. Why do you stay with her? You're independent now, you could find a little flat and live your own life."

Hesitating for a moment, Amy answered, "It's really strange, but I can't walk out on her—she needs me. Despite everything you know about my life, I feel I owe her something. She's the only family I have. Once my brother Ted comes home I'll be off the hook."

Barbara found Amy a constant source of surprise. Hearing her refer to Deborah as her only family, she wondered why Amy made no effort to locate her real sisters. Curious, she blurted out, "Have you ever thought of trying to find your sisters?"

Amy looked at her in surprise. "At one time my older sister Emmy tried to keep in contact, but we both moved and lost track of each other." Instantly her mind conjured up the picture of Emmy the last time she'd seen her in the schoolyard, and then her mind went blank as she tried to imagine Polly Sue. "I wouldn't know my baby sister; I don't even know her adopted name. Maybe one of these days Emmy'll find me."

Barbara opened her mouth to ask why Amy didn't make the attempt, but the conversation ended abruptly as Amy said, "Want to give me a hand with the dishes? It'll give you a chance to hear more of their silly chitchat."

"Lead the way," Barbara said.

Chapter XVI

✦✦✦✦✦

EMMALINA HAS TO COPE

A FREQUENT EXCHANGE of correspondence had developed between Eleanor Griffon and Elizabeth Fields upon their return to Oklahoma. Of late, Eleanor Griffon's letters had been pointed in their reference as to how Elizabeth planned on "bringing Emmalina out." It was only right, she insisted, that the girl make her official debut into society.

Troubled by the fact that she had not given any serious consideration to such a matter, and not wanting to omit anything that would properly launch the girl into the proper circles, Elizabeth took the matter up with Emmy and Max.

It was true that several of the girl's classmates were going to have debutante balls and a special cotillion was being planned for those who preferred to do it en masse, but Emmy was adamant. She would not be a party to any such nonsense. Max refused to venture an opinion, secretly relieved at Emmy's stance. After considerable wrangling, as a concession to Elizabeth, it was decided Emmy would hostess a luncheon for her friends at the club. "Only," the girl insisted, "if you let it be known as a farewell party."

Emmy had been accepted at the Juilliard School of Music and would reside in New York. Her impending departure was causing major changes in their lives. They had been so secure and content that it was hard to contemplate the upheaval that was to affect them all. There were distant rumblings in the world: a strange little man in Germany was making warlike noises, and trains were running on time in Italy. The shock waves of impending events were beginning to be felt everywhere.

Elizabeth was uneasy about allowing Emmy to live such distance away, on her own in a strange city. She refused to admit she could not stand the wrench of having Emmy so far from her side.

For once Elizabeth consulted no one and made up her mind that for a year at least she would also take up residence in New York. Max was appalled but Elizabeth was ready with an answer. "It's time you gave some thought to retiring. If you don't want to stay in New York the whole time, then plan to remain with us for a few months."

No argument budged her; she was determined to make the move. Emmy kept her own counsel, knowing that any word to the contrary might launch a chain reaction. If a disconsolate Max couldn't change her mother's mind, she knew, it was a lost cause. Elizabeth had already written to Eleanor Griffon soliciting advice about locations and apartments. Pearlie Mae would close the house and join them in the East.

Grumbling, Max had no choice but to capitulate, promising he would join them as soon as he could get away.

Once again Eleanor Griffon had worked her magic and procured an apartment in what she deemed a sufficiently fashionable area facing Central Park and accessible to Emmy's school.

Arriving in New York City in early fall, they settled in quickly. Elizabeth seemed to be invigorated by all the wonderful activities the city afforded and by the resumption of her friendship with the Levinsons. To her amazement Eleanor Griffon seemed intent on maintaining a relationship with her. Emmy was enthusiastic about the school, and their happiness knew no bounds when Max arrived. He seemed to be ailing, and Elizabeth was concerned; but, between the ministrations of herself and Pearlie Mae, he began to regain his vigor and their lives seemed complete.

They were being exposed to alarms that had not touched them at home in Oklahoma. Max was gloomily certain war was going to come. The headlines and the radio were filled with the brutal invasions taking place in Europe. But everyone determinedly pursued their normal routines, not wanting to envision what might happen.

The Griffons were intending to leave for Palm Beach in late January and invited Max and Elizabeth to visit them. They declined, preferring to stay in New York with Emmy, and invited the Griffons for Christmas day.

The big city seemed infused with the holiday spirit as Elizabeth and Max scurried about on daily shopping expeditions, joining the happy throngs in the festively decorated stores. Hugging their packages, they were swept along in the crowds to the accompaniment of jingling bells as Salvation Army Santa Clauses on corners reminded everyone of the less fortunate. The sounds of Yuletide carolers and melodious carillons hung on the air. Rockefeller Center with its towering spruce tree ingeniously hung with glittering balls, baubles and twinkling lights was breathtakingly beautiful and Elizabeth was thrilled at the scene, complemented by the ice rink below filled with colorfully dressed skaters gliding to and fro.

Max was surprised at how exhilarated Elizabeth seemed by the faster pace and he wondered if she was laying the groundwork for a permanent move.

Her expression altered when he confronted her with the question and she looked at him forlornly. "No, Max. For one thing, Emmy's old enough to stand on her own feet. I know that and I have to accustom myself to the thought." She grinned at him. "You old darling, don't you know how grateful I am to have you? I'm coming home for the summer, Max. This is sort of a last fling."

He heaved a sigh of relief, but he longed for the more leisurely tempo of his home.

They were like two children as they carefully selected gifts for each other; for Emmy, for Pearlie Mae and for all of the Griffons. They chose a huge pine tree and had a marvelous time decorating it with the help of Emmy and some of her school friends. Good cheer was in the air. Pearlie Mae, in her element, reigned over the kitchen, deep in preparations for Christmas dinner.

Snow fell Christmas morning, covering the park in a mantle of white. It was an exuberantly happy day filled with high spirits. The Griffon boys, home from their respective colleges, couldn't repress their glee at being released from their studies. Emmy had left an indelible impression on them after her Newport weekend, and it quickly became apparent that Jonathan was smitten with her. Bill Junior didn't miss an opportunity to tease him about it. "Come on, Jon, what's your excuse? At least I had a valid reason for staring at her. Or do you think she reminds you of someone?"

Blushing, Emmy asked, "Do you still insist we'd met before?"

Laughing, Bill said, "No, you reminded me of someone. She's in movie pictures."

"Really?" Emmy looked at him coyly. "Are you sure I look like her?"

Joshing, he said, "I never forget a pretty face, and if you'll forgive my being brash, I think you're prettier."

Laughing, Emmy asked, "What's the girl's name?"

Thinking for a moment, Bill shook his head. "I'm terrible at remembering movie stars' names. She was good in the part, though."

Emmy persisted. "Do you remember the movie?"

He shook his head. "Sorry . . . it was some western, I think. I'll tell you if I remember. I saw it several months ago."

They were caught up in the conversations around them and the matter was dropped.

The holidays were a whirl of activity, and to her surpirse Emmy found herself spending most of her free time with Jonathan. Their families seemed to approve, and the situation gave rise to amusing speculation when the adults were alone together.

Jonathan was the proud owner of a vintage red and black Auburn Cord convertible with a stunningly vented hood and spare-tire case which he kept in shining condition. Emmy instantly fell in love with it, adding to Jonathan's already high estimation of her. Weather permitting, they drove everywhere, and Jonathan planned trips to every out-of-the-way place he could think of, including a thorough tour of Staten Island.

One morning, when he picked her up, he asked, "Em, have you been to the Fulton Fish Market? If not, I thought we'd combine that with a stop in Chinatown for lunch and see the lower East Side."

"You're the tour guide, Jon. Whatever you decide is fine with me."

Opening the door for her, he said, "In that case, hold your hat. I'll lower the top. I have a hunch you'll get a kick out of these areas; they're very different and colorful. Personally I think they're what make New York so special."

He drove through sections where different nationalities lived and congregated, each with neighborhood stores that stocked goods from their country of origin. They passed famous ocean liners in dock, and she marveled at the giant

French liners *Île de France* and *Normandie,* which he told her were like floating cities. Cutting through Greenwich Village, Jonathan pointed to a raggedly dressed man holding court on a streetcorner, telling her he recognized him as a well-known poet and writer.

Looking at the disheveled group standing around him, she asked, "Are they bohemians, Jon?"

Exaggeratedly nonchalant, he said offhandedly, "I guess so. A lot of them are very talented. I've been to some of their studios . . . they're really very interesting people."

As far as Emmy was concerned, Jonathan Griffon was the most sophisticated, worldly man she'd ever met.

Approaching the lower East Side, Emmy couldn't believe her eyes. Crowds of people in a steady stream were pushing and shoving along a street straddled by pushcarts. She couldn't help but exclaim, "Jon, it's like another world! I had no idea such a place existed."

Pleased with her reaction, he located a parking space. Instantly the car was surrounded by screaming children, all trying to get ahead of one another. "Watch your car, mister . . . a nickel to watch your car!"

Locking the car, he selected two boys, promising each a dime for their care of it.

Taking Emmy by the arm, Jonathan steered her toward a street packed with people, gesturing toward the old brick tenement buildings that lined it. "Can you imagine having to live in one of those? People jammed together like sardines. Maybe one bathroom for thirty people. I've heard those places are firetraps. It must be hell."

Her eyes danced with excitement and he could feel her tense as they moved in the midst of the hubbub. Tightening his grip on her arm lest they be separated, he raised his voice to make himself heard over the din. "After they got off the boats, this is where most of the Eastern European immigrants settled. Here's where they got their start."

Emmy looked at him in open admiration; he was so young to be so knowledgeable. In the short time they had spent together she'd come to respect his judgment, feeling totally safe with him. He was always willing to put himself out for her, and she appreciated his desire to expose her to such a novel experience. She pressed closer and Jonathan felt the pressure of her arm as she clung to him. Looking down at her, he thought she was the most beautiful girl he had ever seen. Her face was filled with wonder at what she was seeing. His chest swelled with pride as he protectively pushed people out of their path and shouted to make himself heard. "Em, hold your purse close."

They slowed as a gathering group made the street impassable, watching a woman argue vehemently over the price of a pot which she was waving wildly. He managed to make a path through the crowd as Emmy looked back to see the outcome. Laughing, he said, "Don't worry, they're not going to kill each other. It's just the way they do things here."

She shook her head in amazement. "It's a real, live show, Jon."

"I suppose it is, Em, but for these people it's a way of life."

They had turned the corner where they could talk normally and she asked, "What language are they talking?"

He grinned. "I think it's called Yiddish. They're mostly Jewish."

Instantly she was interested. "Do you know there are still places in Oklahoma where after six at night Jews, Negroes and Catholics are not allowed? Doesn't that seem absurd?"

He smiled at her, thinking how adorable she was in her innocence. "Well, each to their own! I hear the Jews are very clannish people. I really don't know too much about them; supposedly they're very industrious and ambitious."

Pointing to a building they were passing he said, "Look!" Women were hanging out over the windowsills. Some were shouting at children running about in the street. "It must be rough trying to play in these conditions."

The pungent smell of fish and aromatic foods mixed with sweat assailed her nostrils, and she stopped for a moment to get a handkerchief from her purse. A little boy sidled up to her, talking, his hand outstretched.

Motioning to him to get out of their way, Jon urged her along, but the youngster, his large olive-black eyes imploring, tagged alongside. "He probably wants money. If we give him any, we'll be mobbed by others. I know—I did it once."

Emmy let herself be led as she asked, "Was he Jewish, Jon?"

Amused, he replied, "I think so, although he spoke a different language."

She seemed to be considering what he'd said as she asked, "If you saw him in a different place, differently dressed, and he spoke English, would you know he was Jewish?"

He smiled at her in tolerant superiority. "Of course. It's common knowledge."

For some reason his answer annoyed her and, piqued, she persisted. "That's what I mean. How do they give themselves away? I understand how you can recognize them here, but in other places it puzzles me. Why do people oppose them so?"

Sensing her irritation, he tried to placate her. "I think it's all tied up with the idea that they killed Christ."

She looked at him curiously. "Do you mean after all these thousands of years they still have to bear the mark? We're supposed to be intelligent, civilized people, and as Christians we're supposed to turn the other cheek." She shook her head dubiously. "It's very depressing."

They walked along in silence, each locked in thought. Reaching the car, he paid the waiting youngsters who helped him lower the top. "Hop in, Em." He could see she had become serious, and some of the edge went out of the afternoon. Putting the car in gear, he pulled away from the curb. "Hey, Em, did what I say bother you? I don't disagree with what you say, but it is a fact that, even when those people leave all this behind them, they're still considered undesirable. It's just one of the facts of life. My mother hasn't a Jewish friend amongst her acquaintances." At this Emmy's eyebrows raised, and he didn't miss the implication.

Her face was expressionless as she said, "I guess that makes us unacceptable, since a lot of my mother's closest friends are Jewish. Of course, Jon, where we come from we're considered hicks . . . not in the know, so to speak. Do you suppose we're contaminated because of that?"

He was upset at the turn the conversation had taken. "I didn't mean to sound like a bigot, Em—I hope you understand that. I was just trying to tell you that's how things are."

"I see." She smiled but she did not see. "I can't tell you how much fun I'm having." She wanted to make amends for the tension she'd caused.

For answer he picked up her hand and held it.

At the end of the day, as he drew up in front of Em's apartment building, she asked, "Would you like to come up, Jon?"

He suddenly leaned over and kissed her on the cheek. "I don't think I'd better, I promised Mother I'd be home for dinner tonight. Em, I might as well tell you, if you haven't guessed . . . I've got a crush on you."

Her face suffused with red as she looked up at him.

"Want to go to the movies tomorrow night? I only have a

few more days left, so let's make the most of it. Would you come up for the prom?"

She was blushing when she reached the apartment. She enthused about the day's events and, hardly pausing for breath, she asked Elizabeth, "Did you know that when they first arrive here most of the Jewish people settle in the lower East Side of the city? It's indescribable—teeming with people. Jonathan and I had a disagreement; he insists no matter where they go they're recognizable. According to him they're considered undesirables."

First amused at the gush of words and then surprised at their implication, Elizabeth rebuked her. "Aren't you able to think for yourself? Since when has Jonathan become your judge and jury? You know very well how I feel about attitudes like that. I'm shocked at Jonathan; I thought he was more intelligent than that."

Emmy instantly rose to his defense. "I don't think he meant any harm—he was just explaining how things are. Really, I don't think he'd given it any thought until I brought up the subject."

Exchanging a look with Max, Elizabeth grumbled, "You're smart enough to know where he gets that nonsense from, Em. I'd have hoped that by now you'd realize you make judgments about people based on their character."

Laughing, Max cut in. "Hey, you two, you're just like pecking hens. Be fair, Liz. Jon can't help it if some of that sort of thing has rubbed off on him. You know how full of nonsense our friend Eleanor is. Say, Em, did Jon take you to the Bowery? Did you see the breadlines?"

"We just passed by," Emmy told them, glad of the chance to change the subject. "Some of the lines are blocks long. It's terrible to see people suffering that way."

Later, soaking in the tub, Emmy reflected on the day and her mind reverted to the little boy with the olive eyes and outstretched palm . . . a beautiful little boy. She shuddered as an odd thought flitted through her mind. What if my family was Jewish? How do I know they didn't come from a place like that? Disturbed by the track her mind was taking, she tried to dismiss it and stepped from the tub. "Emmalina," she said out loud, "you're crazy on that subject, you know—quite crazy."

Emmy's first year at Juilliard was coming to its conclusion, and Elizabeth decided it was time to return to Oklahoma. She told the girl, "I owe Max some allegiance and he needs me. Having been with you all these months, I won't be half so worried about how you take care of yourself."

Studying her mother, Emmy couldn't resist the impulse to ask, "Why haven't you and Uncle Max married, Mommy? I don't mean to pry, but it does seem odd."

Startled by the question after all this time, Elizabeth tried to be matter-of-fact. "You've a right to know, child. It's not because Max hasn't asked me. Next to my Thomas he's the dearest, best man in the world. I'm lucky to have had two such men in my life. At the start of our relationship I just didn't think it was fair to him to have me for a wife. We had lived so differently up to that point. Truthfully, when we made the move to the city, I was frightened to death. Afraid of the life he lived, sure that I wouldn't fit in, that I'd be an embarrassment."

Astonished at this disclosure, Emy scolded, "Mommy, I can't imagine how you of all people could have felt that way."

Wondering what had prompted Emmy's question, Elizabeth said, "Thank you, dear. I appreciate your high opinion of me, but my reasons weren't so illogical. Maybe it seems foolish now, but at the time I considered those things obstacles. Happily, they had no effect on our lives. Since marriage would complicate our business affairs and nothing can alter what we mean to each other, we're content this way. Please tell me truthfully, does it bother you?"

Hurt at the question, Emmy implored, "How can you say that, Mommy? I adore you both, you know that!"

Troubled, Elizabeth persisted. "I know you love us, but that's aside of the point. Does our status present problems for you?"

As she tried to determine what Elizabeth meant, it dawned on Emmy that she had opened a can of worms. "Mommy, please, don't ever say things like that. It never presented problems before and it certainly won't now."

Elizabeth was unable to let the matter rest. "Emmy, let's talk this out. You know, darling, you have such a sharply defined idea of right and wrong it's possible you're not even aware you feel we're doing something dishonorable. You do realize that at this time of our lives Max and I are just close companions."

Discomforted by her mother's revelations, Emmy tried to end the conversation. "Mommy, believe me, you misunderstood. I don't know why I started this. I was just suddenly curious. Nothing you or Uncle Max could do would ever embarrass or hurt me. I mean that with all my heart. I'm not as narrow-minded as you think. I understand a lot more than you give me credit for."

Laughing with relief, Elizabeth said, "It's good to be able to talk to you this way, Em. It's hard for me to believe we're two adults. I've often wondered and worried what you thought about us. You and Max are my world, and I wouldn't want to do anything to harm either one of you. Max has made me a very happy woman and I'm deeply grateful to him; he's a wonderful man. I hope one day you'll find such a person."

Emmy smiled shyly. "I hope so too." She paused. "What do you think of Jonathan?"

"Aha! So that's the lay of the land. Well, do you think you're in love with him?"

"I don't know, Mommy. I like him a great deal. We have a lot of fun together, but I'm not sure."

Immediately protective, Elizabeth advised, "If you're not sure, Em, don't let yourself be rushed into anything. Take your time; you're still very young."

During the year that followed, Emmy returned home to spend the long holidays with Elizabeth. Over the Easter vacation plans were set up for Emmy to join a group of classmates for the summer touring Canada. She had been gone about five weeks when a telegram reached her. Elizabeth had suffered a fatal heart attack. As quickly as possible, arrangements were made for Emmy's transportation to Oklahoma, but Elizabeth had been laid to rest long before she reached there.

Far away from familiar surroundings, Emmy found that the words telling her of Elizabeth's passing had no reality. She could not grasp their finality, so, despite her shock, she managed to hold on to herself while en route, staying the torrent of emotions inside her.

The terrible brunt of what had befallen her struck when she reached home. There, the realization came—Elizabeth was gone . . . never to be told how much she was loved by her or to be confided in, laughed or quarreled with again. Stunned, numb with anguish, Emmy seemed frozen; the loss was too great. She had never envisioned life without Elizabeth and she could not accept it. She began to disintegrate.

Max, grief-stricken, tried to do what he could for the bewildered girl. But, inconsolable, Emmy clung to Pearlie

Mae, refusing to venture from her side. Haunted and bereft, she cut herself off from everyone, refusing to see callers or leave the house. Rebuffed, her friends gave up. Their hearts were heavy enough anyhow; the world was about to explode. The fires of imminent war colored everything.

Slowly, inexorably, the absence of Elizabeth's presence bore in on Emmy and took its toll. She had no one. Desolated, she verged on total breakdown, raging at a fate that had done this to her. The cruelty of her first abandonment would have destroyed her had it not been for Elizabeth, always at hand when needed, loving and compassionate, unyielding in her support. Now, without her, the very pillars of Emmy's life were gone. Closeted in her room, Emmy sank deeper and deeper into depression.

Pearlie Mae grew increasingly alarmed and called Max. "Judge, you gotta do sometin. She don even dress no mo. Won eat, won even talk wif me. I think dat precious lamb gonna follow Miz Lizbet. Yo gotta do sometin fast or she gonna go too."

Max rushed over and was appalled at what he saw. Pearlie Mae was right: Emmy was seriously sick. Entering her room, he found her sitting in a chair, gazing vacantly into space. She gave no indication that she knew he was there. Pulling up a chair, he sat down in front of her, imploring urgently, "Emmy, can you hear me? Get a grip on yourself, girl. For God's sake, think what Elizabeth would say about the way you're carrying on!"

The shell of Emmy stared back at him with blank eyes.

"Emmy, stop this, answer me," he entreated.

She gave no sign that she heard him and he said, as much to himself as to her, "A doctor . . . we've got to call the doctor!"

At that her eyes closed, and Max, who had never raised a hand to anyone or used a strong word to a woman, lost control and slapped her face. "You're a selfish inconsiderate girl!"

Remorseful at once, he was relieved to see she reacted. Opening her eyes she questioned, "Uncle Max?"

Harshly he began to berate her. "You're a weak-kneed ninny. I'm glad Elizabeth never knew. Selfish! You don't give a damn about anyone but yourself. Have you given a thought to me or Pearlie Mae? Elizabeth didn't belong to you alone!"

She mumbled, "Leave me alone. I have no one. It doesn't

matter if I die . . . there's no one to care. I don't want to live."

Roused, Max shouted, "Okay! Go to hell if you want! I'm through! I want no part of you. I counted on you; you were all I had left. I needed you, Pearlie Mae needed you, but you're too damn involved with yourself to know anyone else exists!"

The impact of his words broke her down; suddenly she was crying hysterically and talking at the same time. Max had difficulty understanding what she was trying to say. "No . . . I love you, Uncle Max. Pearlie Mae too! I need a little more time . . . give me a little time."

Remorseful but firm, Max said, "You need a doctor, probably a hospital."

She sat sobbing as he left the room to telephone their family doctor. Shaken, Max called Pearlie Mae. "Go to her, Pearlie Mae. Freshen her up and put her to bed."

The doctor arrived within the hour. Emmy lay passively as he examined her. When he had finished, he spoke to Max. "Grief and shock, Max. Dehydrated, skin and bones. Nothing that can't be helped with care and determination. If she continues to resist, I told her, she would need hospitalization. I think she heard me. See what you can do. If she's no better in a few days, we'll hospitalize her."

Emmy's reaction had been long overdue. Elizabeth's sudden passing unleashed deeply buried years of anger and resentment. In her irrational grief, time kaleidoscoped and she saw her life with Elizabeth as a tantalizing interlude—a postponement of the inevitable. She was doomed to be alone—an exile, an outsider.

In the aftermath she gave way to an orgy of self-pity. Wallowing in misery, thrown back to the trauma of her childhood, she became that same little girl without the resources to fight back.

Standing over the sleeping girl, Max ruminated. What had Elizabeth wrought? She had come into the child's life to become her rock and her strength. She had made the decisions, run interference, guided and instilled values, channeled her thinking, shielded her from emotional hardship, smothered her with love and attention—and unwittingly crippled her.

Looking down, Max was startled to see Emmy's eyes open, looking at him, no longer vacant. She gave him a small smile.

He leaned over and kissed her cheek. Her hand reached

from under the blanket to lightly hold his. A tear coursed down his cheek. Then he moved toward the door, saying, "I want to call Pearlie Mae. She has some broth for you."

Propping her up, Pearlie Mae spooned the soup into her mouth. "In anuder hour, chile, yo gonna have mo."

Sitting down on the bed beside her, Max began to talk quietly. "You've got to get it through your head, Emmy, that there are people who need you, who depend on you. You have a place in the scheme of things."

Tearfully she said, "But, Uncle Max, I'm alone in the world."

He exploded. "Rot! There you go again. I had no idea I counted for so little. I lost as much as you, but I know Elizabeth would have gone on without me just as she would have expected both of us to do. What you're doing is selfish and self-centered. You're thinking only of yourself. All Elizabeth did for you amounts to nothing if you can't carry on for her now. The way you live your life is the only way you can show she mattered."

She stirred. "I have no family, no one who cares about me."

Angrily he snarled, "I care, damn you! Okay, so I'm old and now you figure my days are numbered, but can't you see that you're young and your life stretches ahead of you? Marry and make a family of your own!"

Surprisingly, she grinned at him as she asked, "Do you think I can manage for myself, Uncle Max? Mommy always took care of everything."

Grumpily he said, "Yes, don't you think I know that? However, as long as I'm around, you can count on me. Aside of that, let me tell you, you have a helluva lot of strength. Use that strength to live instead of die. Don't be such a darn coward!"

She studied him, thinking, and he said softly, "Get yourself back together, and then we'll make plans."

Raising herself, she kissed him on the cheek. "Thank you, dear Uncle Max," she whispered as he left her.

It was a flabbergasted Pearlie Mae who watched as a wasted and frail Emmy sat herself down at the kitchen table the next morning and asked for breakfast. She hugged and kissed her as Emmy grinned. "I love you too, Pearlie Mae. You can stop worrying, I'll try to do what I'm supposed to."

Slowly Emmy fought to regain a grip on life. She avoided the piano—music in general produced tumultuous pain—but at least she had begun to talk with Pearlie Mae about Elizabeth. The poor woman was so relieved with the change that she praised the judge as if he were a miracle worker.

Several weeks later Max called and told Emmy he was bringing someone over with him. She protested but he insisted. "I know how you feel about company at this time, but this is someone you have to see, someone special. I suggest you pretty yourself up."

Piqued, Emmy couldn't imagine why, under the circumstances, Max gave anyone such importance. The answer was obvious when Jonathan Griffon walked through the door. Max's formula worked; as if by magic, Emmy's desolation began to dissolve.

It had long been planned that Jonathan would serve his law internship in Judge Esquith's office. He would begin learning how to handle the family's interest. "This is promising country for a young attorney," he told Emmy. "I'd like to settle here, so my next project is to find a girl who'd consider being my wife."

She smiled shyly. "I'm happy you're here, Jon. I had no idea how much I missed you until I saw you."

On the side, Max confided to Pearlie Mae, "Elizabeth knew about Jonathan's plans for coming here. She'd have been happy about the way things seem to be working. She liked the boy and, if it comes to what I think it will, our problems'll be solved."

Her wrinkled face showed concern. "Judge, dat's fine. I's glad for our chile . . . he seems a good boy. What'll become o me? I hopes dey keeps me wit dem."

He smiled and patted her shoulder. "Pearlie Mae, I'm surprised at you. You should know better than that. Emmy wouldn't want to be parted from you for any reason . . . you're family!"

Her face broke into a big grin, and he continued. "That's a big thing to Emmy. Family matters to her; besides, she truly loves you. There is something else about which I'd like your opinion. Don't you think this house is getting too big for you to take care of? I don't imagine if the kids marry that they'll want the upkeep of such a place at the start."

"Dat's foolishness, Judge. Dis place is no bigger now den when I first came, and Miss Emmy can afford it."

"She can afford it, Pearlie Mae, that's true—but it might be a deal healthier for her to have a fresh new place to fuss about." Cleverly he proceeded to swing her to his side. It was important that she help to persuade the girl in his plans.

Emmy was surprisingly receptive, feeling, as Max did, that a new start deserved a new place. She had begun to regain vitality and take an interest in things, and the judge felt it was time to resolve the affairs of Elizabeth's estate. Briefly he explained that the matter could no longer be deferred and arranged a time for her to come to the office. Seeing her apprehension, he assured her it would take only a little time, explaining how important it was that she sign papers and begin to acquaint herself with some of the business. He added, "Being an heiress is one thing, but handling the matter such status involves demands some understanding."

"But, Uncle Max, you always took care of these things for Mommy. Aren't you going to continue for me?"

"I will, as long as I can. But if you marry, your husband may have other ideas. Aside from that, the estate is vast and complicated and it behooves you to understand its intricacies. One day you may have to handle it yourself, so let's start now."

Astonished, Emmy couldn't begin to comprehend the extent of what she had inherited. "You're a very wealthy young woman, Emmalina," Max admonished. "You've got to make some sense out of this so you can use your money wisely. Your dear mother was wise about money and she wouldn't want you to squander it foolishly."

"Uncle Max, knowing me, do you think I would do that? I have no intention of being foolish, so you needn't worry on that score. Besides, I've got you and Jonathan to keep me on the track. There is something else, though, that I want to talk over with you. It may call for an expenditure, but I feel it's important. I hope you won't be upset about what I'm going to say."

He looked at her in surprise as she struggled to say what was on her mind, finally blurting out, "I think this is important for my future life, Uncle Max. I want to look for my real family. I want to find out what became of my parents and sisters."

Only the sound of their breathing could be heard in the quiet room. He could see the effort such a confession involved and he responded gently. "We had no idea, Emmy, you were so troubled about this. You've certainly kept it well concealed."

Tears sprang to her eyes as she prepared to explain. "You have to know, Uncle Max, Elizabeth Fields was the most wonderful thing that ever happened to me. She was the most dear and precious person in my life—in my world! I don't think I could have loved my own mother more. I never wanted to hurt her. It isn't out of love I seek these people . . . it's out of need. If I marry, if I have children, it will be important for me to know about my real background. I want to learn as much as I can about who my people were. Do you see what I mean?"

He smiled as he searched her earnest young face. "Tell me, Emmy, are you planning to marry Jonathan?"

She laughed coyly. "Isn't it proper to wait until you're asked?"

"You mean he hasn't asked you yet? I'll have to light a fire under him!"

"Oh, you mustn't, Uncle Max! Please don't say anything. I'm certain it's coming to that, but—" She blushed fiercely and hesitated before going on, not certain how he would accept an implied criticism of the Griffons. "You know Jonathan's mother. She's such a stickler for 'proper background,' she may be very disturbed to discover I'm not really a Fields."

He bristled. "Indeed you are, all signed and sealed; you're a Fields, young woman. However, Em, I see what you're driving at, and there can't be any harm in finding out whatever we can. This is as good a time as any—and, child, I do understand how you felt about Liz . . . don't worry on that score. While we're on the subject, I hope I've made it plain that you're as dear to me as you were to Elizabeth, and since I was in at the beginning, I hope it entitles me to feel you see me in the light of a father."

"Darling Uncle Max, I've always thought of you that way—I've been doubly blessed."

"Em . . . I'll get the wheels in motion for a search, but I want to caution you—don't get your hopes up. Years ago when the trail was still fresh we couldn't uncover anything. There's another point I want you to consider carefully. Sometimes it's better to let sleeping dogs lie. There's no guarantee you'll uncover good things."

Emmy shook her head resolutely. "I don't care, Uncle

Max. It's probably hard for you to understand that, loving Mommy as I did, my desire to find them still persists. I'll never get over missing her . . . she'll always be a part of me—probably the best part—and nothing can touch the love and regard in which I hold her. That side of my life has nothing to do with this. I'm willing to take the risk of searching out my real family because there's a big hole . . . a big question inside me. It never goes away; it's there night and day, all the time. I need to have some answers, even if they are bad."

"In that case, Emmalina, we'll get on it. What are you going to do about Jonathan? Are you going to tell him or shall I? He should be told, you know. I wouldn't want him to discover it through the office action."

Pondering for a moment, she made up her mind. "I don't feel it's necessary to tell him anything unless we have an understanding—you know, an engagement. However, I wouldn't want him to stumble across it, so I guess I'll have to tell him."

Clucking like an old hen during their move to smaller quarters, Pearlie Mae fussed and fumed until they were properly installed in the new apartment. She didn't like it. "I's cooped up in dis heah box—it ain't fit foh proper-bred folks to live dis way. I hates dat service elevator man—he tinks he be sumpin."

Sympathizing, Emmy agreed. "I miss the house too, honey. But honestly, Pearlie Mae, this place is easier on you, and safer for both of us. We just need some time to get accustomed to it."

"Sho chile, sho. I's a old fool complainin about dis. I sho misses Miz Lizbet . . . I know you does too. She was da bes fren I ever had—magine her leavin me all 'dat dere money." Pearlie Mae had been shocked at the size of the bequest Elizabeth had left for her, and worried too. "Ah hopes she didn inten foh me to leaves you, cause I sho gonna stick close to yo like glue, money or no money. Yo knows dat, don yo?"

Chuckling, Emmy assured her, "I knows it, honey lamb . . . I knows it! Now help me decide where to put this lamp."

Emmy had given up any thought of returning to Juilliard. Music would always be an integral part of her life, and once the piano had been installed in the new apartment she resumed playing, enjoying the comfort and solace it gave her. Her life was now bound by the prospect of marriage and children—and that seemed fulfillment enough.

Jonathan was in constant attendance, and although they were restricted by her period of mourning, they occasionally dined out. Jonathan had not yet proposed, and while she knew it was only a matter of the right moment, she felt reluctant to tell him what she and the judge had discussed.

One day when it had rained heavily, they dined cozily at home. Pearlie Mae had decided to visit a sick friend and they were alone with little likelihood of interruption. As she flicked on the lamps in the living room and drew the drapes, she heard the rain pelting down and shivered as if she were cold. Jonathan, standing nearby, drew her to him. "What's the matter, hon?"

Impulsively she decided to tell him. "Jonathan, there's something I have to say. Let me give you a brandy to sip while I talk."

She looked up at him towering above her. Smiling teasingly, he said, "I have something to tell you too. Do you know your eyes are like pansies? Have I ever told you that I'd like to bite your nose? And—I don't recall—did I remember to tell you I love you?" He pulled her close to him, cutting off any reply she might have made. He tilted her face upward and kissed her long and lingeringly. Locked in his embrace, her body responded as he pressed her to him. She throbbed at his touch. Her senses wavered and the world was blocked out. Nothing but this moment mattered. She wanted him to go on forever. He murmured against her lips, "I want to marry you."

He released her but held her by the arms. Suddenly concerned, seeing the strained look on her face, he said hastily, "Hey, I'm serious, Em. I'm not in the habit of rushing around proposing to strange girls. You haven't said a word, and I know why. Well, hear this: I want you to know I do things properly. I got hold of Uncle Max at his club today—he was enjoying a snooze. I explained that, since he was your legal guardian, it was necessary that I obtain his permission to marry you. Would you believe the old coot put me over the coals? Really, I'm not joking . . . he's known my family since—oh, you know when—but he played it for real."

Smiling up at him, Emmy thought she understood why Uncle Max had done that. Jonathan couldn't get over it. "He wanted to know if I would stick by you through thick and thin and a whole bunch of other silly things. He's hardly the romantic type, don't you agree?"

"Well . . . what did he finally say?" Emmy asked.

Jon shook her playfully. "He said yes, and now I'm waiting for your answer. Come on, Em . . . what's this mystery all about?"

"Well, if you'll just sit down as I asked—here, take your brandy—and be patient . . ." She sat down across from him, and when she saw he was ready she began.

She could see the astonishment spread across his features as she related her story. He sat motionless, as if he were stunned. It was difficult for her to gauge his reception of her tale. He didn't open his mouth and the silence became oppressive. She became angry and rose from her seat. "I won't hold you to your proposal, Jonathan. I can see you're disturbed by what I've had to say."

He reached out and pulled her to him. "Emmy, Emmy, how could you think that of me? By God, I'll admit it was a shock—you knocked the breath out of me. I just can't get over what you endured. Thank goodness Elizabeth was the one who adopted you."

The look of irony that crossed her face was lost on him as he repeated over and over, "You're my girl . . . my one and only girl." Finally he said the words she'd been waiting to hear: "I love you, and no matter what, I pledge my troth to thee . . ."

She wondered—was he being facetious? His fingers pressed into her arms. "I'm not joking, dearest. I wouldn't joke about such a thing. Please tell me you'll be my wife." She pulled away from him. "Yes, Jonathan, I want that more than anything in the world. You know that . . . but there will have to be an 'if.'"

"A what? What in the world are you talking about?"

"Your family, Jon . . . your mother in particular. Do you really believe she'll welcome me into your family under these circumstances?"

He seemed to consider what she'd said and then brushed it aside. "They're not marrying you—I am! I don't care what they think!"

"That's well and good, Jonathan, but you will have to tell them about me, and if I'm still acceptable we'll announce our engagement."

Alone in the warmth of the softly lit room with the sound of

blowing wind and rain as accompaniment, the couple in love
presented a very sober image. His long legs stretched out
before him, Jonathan lazily wrangled, attempting to convince
Emmy she was unreasonable. Watching her face, the set of
her little chin and the spark in her eyes, he reached over and
pulled her to the couch beside him, smothering her protesting
mouth with kisses. Roused, he held her in his arms, exploring
the lovely contours of her body while the touches of his hand
and mouth blotted out everything but the sound of their
breathing until she suddenly pulled away, fending him off.
"No, Jonathan . . . you can't convince me this way. I meant
what I said—there'll be no public announcement until we
have your family's blessing."

He could not change her mind and finally he consented to
do as she requested.

The following day Max made him privy to the search he
had already caused to be instituted for Emmy's family. He
further recommended that Emmy and he, together, make a
trip to Brightwater to speak with some of the people there.

Emmy was ashamed to admit how much she looked
forward to making the trip to Brightwater; between nostalgia
and hopeful anticipation she had difficulty keeping her
feelings hidden. The morning they left was overcast, and as
they reached open country the plains stretching away on both
sides of the road were overhung by a grayish mist, the
branches of the great old oak and ash trees hanging limply in
the moist air. Herds of grazing cows were silhouetted in the
distance. Jonathan extended the chocolate bar he was munching on. "Want a piece?"

Emmy grinned; he was like a little boy. "Thanks!" She
broke off a square, and as the sweetness flooded her mouth a
quiver of desire ran through her. He was so handsome, so
masculine—she loved the feeling of security he gave her.
Studying the set of his face, she wondered why he asked so
few questions. She wished he'd open the subject of her lost
family; there were so many things she wanted to confide . . .
things that lay close to her heart that she felt he ought to
know. It was as if he deliberately avoided bringing it up.
Pondering as he chattered, she reasoned he was probably
trying to keep her from being sad.

Her heart skipped a beat as they approached Brightwater's
main street. Excitedly she pointed out familiar landmarks—
the little white frame building that housed the library, the
weathered wooden front of the Wilkerson general store, the

rickety slat-boarded old stable that was now a feed and grain warehouse, its walls covered by tattered old posters. She caught his expression of disdain as he glanced at the Brightwater Hotel with its porch chairs occupied by men in galluses and straw hats, the spittoon in evidence. Quickly, as if to make amends, she showed him the tall-spired white church they had attended. "It's set on the highest spot around, and the rectory where Reverend Jenson lives is alongside it. We'll stop there later."

Jonathan was stupefied with amazement. Nothing in his background had prepared him for what he was encountering. He could not reconcile the woman he had first met in Newport with such an environment and the people he saw on the street of this dowdy small town. At least it was impressive that the main street bore the name of Fields, and he listened intently as Emmy related some of their history to him. Looking at Emmy, he tried to imagine what it must have been like for her growing up in such surroundings, but he found it impossible. She was talking and he realized she was asking him to make a turn. He could see how tense she had become. Maneuvering the car along the narrow country road lined with stately elm trees, he braked as she exclaimed, "Stop! I'll open the gate."

Barring the road up an incline was a wide wooden gate with a large wrought-iron nameplate that spelled out *Fields* in curlicued letters. Emmy's eyes blurred, and her heart spilled over with memories. There it was, the sturdy old graystone house, its creaky rooster weathervane moving in the wind and the pecan trees standing guard, shining in the sun that had finally broken through. Welcomed by the Hovaks, Jonathan chattered congenially as Emmy tried to suppress her tears.

The day passed rapidly with Emmy renewing old acquaintanceships and becoming teary-eyed with condolences on Elizabeth's passing. But their main objective, the mission they had come on, was fruitless. Their meeting with Reverend Jenson resulted in no new information. The Corrigans had never been heard from, and old Father McGurdy had retired to a monastery in Colorado. As for the Wilkersons, it was believed they had headed for California, but there had been no word or forwarding address.

As they settled themselves in the car for their return trip, Emmy's disappointment was obvious and Jonathan attempted to bolster her spirits. "Look, Em . . . Max has hired a man who's an expert in these matters. Be patient . . . give him time; he'll leave no stone unturned. Believe me, if anyone can find your family, this man will. Besides, you've managed without them this long—a little more time won't matter."

She looked at him in mute appeal and for the first time wondered about his sensitivity.

Shortly after their trip to Brightwater Jonathan surprised her by requesting that they make a joint trip to New York to meet the lion in his den. He had to report to his draft board and felt it would be better all around if she accompanied him. Despite her reluctance, he convinced her by insisting she could see for herself how happy his family would be to welcome her. It would put her mind at ease.

Jonathan had wondered how his mother would receive the news of Emmy's adoption, but as the days passed he'd convinced himself he was being foolish. She was too good a mother, she cared for him too much, to jeopardize his happiness by putting any obstacles in his path over such a silly thing. He had resolved to prove to Emmy how pointless her fears had been.

It was a most loving and warm Eleanor Griffon who awaited their arrival at the station. She couldn't have been kinder and more sympathetic. Shortly after dinner, Emmy asked to be excused so that she could retire—she was worn out from the trip. Besides, her absence would allow Jonathan freedom to talk with his parents.

Upon coming into the breakfast room the following morning, she found Mr. and Mrs. Griffon in heated discussion, which ceased the moment of her appearance. Bill Griffon was the soul of affability as he welcomed her. "Good morning, Emmalina. I hope you rested well. Have a good day, you two. I'll see you early this evening." With that he rushed off.

There was tension in the air. Something in Eleanor Griffon's voice told her a crisis was brewing. "Help yourself, dear. There are scrambled eggs in the covered dish . . . bacon too. If there's anything special you wish, Rose will be glad to make it for you."

"No, this will do nicely, thank you. Did you sleep well? There was a lump in Emmy's throat. She tried to drink her juice but found it impossible. Suddenly she wanted to run. Coming on top of everything she had endured, a confrontation with this woman seemed more than she could stand. She looked up as Eleanor spoke. "It's cozy like this, just the two of us. Jonathan's told you, of course, he's gone off to see his pesky draft board. I hope you won't mind if we have a girl-to-girl talk. . . ." She stopped and waited.

Emmy hastily said, "Of course not."

Eleanor Griffon refused to meet Emmy's eyes as she began. "Jonathan told us the wonderful news last night, about the two of you wanting to marry. We were delighted; naturally, we'd seen it coming a long time. Of course, Emmalina, we never suspected—we never had an inkling you were not Elizabeth's legitimate daughter."

Emmy carefully set her coffee cup down. Keeping her voice on an even keel, she said slowly and deliberately, "Your use of the word 'legitimate' is incorrect, Mrs. Griffon. Of course, you mean 'natural.' If I was anything, I was Elizabeth Field's legitimate daughter . . . legally."

There was a curl of contempt on Eleanor Griffon's mouth as she said, "Under the circumstances, how would you really know about legitimacy? I'd certainly be interested in hearing further about that."

A cold shiver ran down Emmy's spine as she fought to keep her anger under control. "I was not an illegitimate child. I had parents—a mother and father whom I remember well."

Eleanor Griffon gave a derisive laugh. Blind with inchoate rage, Emmy managed to spit out, "Under the circumstances I think we have no reason for further conversation."

The look of scorn on the woman's face made her add, "You are the most hateful woman I have ever met . . . the last thing I'd ever want is for you to know any more about me than is necessary!"

Rising, shoving her chair back, Emmy glared at the woman who sat in sardonic composure. "Will you be good enough to have a cab called for me? I'll be leaving in a few minutes. I'm sure you'll be able to explain to Jonathan the reason for my sudden departure."

She was gratified to hear the woman's gasp as she strode out of the room. Hurriedly she packed her bag and, without a word to anyone, left through the front door. She hailed a passing cab and, within a few minutes, the life she had planned for herself lay in shreds. She knew with certainty Jonathan would hear and see only what his mother intended. Her mind was in turmoil; how right she'd been about not wanting to announce their engagement. With Eleanor Griffon in the picture she should never have allowed her relationship with Jonathan to have reached this point. Under the circumstances it had been foolish and hopeless from the start. Memories of their stay in Newport came back in full force. How right Elizabeth had been in her estimation of Eleanor Griffon. The woman had a cruel lack of heart under an artful genius for appearances.

Reaching the station, she remembered that Jonathan had retained their return tickets. Fortunately she had sufficient cash to buy her passage, and she retired to the waiting room for the three-hour wait that lay before her.

Once in her drawing room Emmy collapsed in tears of frustration and anger. Her pride had been hurt and insulted. Her rage festered; the entire episode had been a nightmare. She arranged with the porter to send a telegram to Max informing him of the time of her return.

Max was hardly sympathetic when he greeted her. He seemed phlegmatic, almost as if this was what he had expected of her. "It's not that I agree with the woman, Em. Believe me I know how wicked she can be. But you went knowing full well inside yourself that this was a possibility. You let me down . . . I daresay old Bill Griffon too. Turning tail and running . . . that was childish. You should have stood up to her and let her have it—that is, if you really loved Jonathan. He counted on you. What do you think Liz would have done under similar circumstances? You let Eleanor get away with her form of madness. Well, it's done now. . . . Come along, Pearlie Mae's waiting for you."

Expecting sympathy, she was crushed at the words with which he had greeted her. Was Max right? Had she behaved spinelessly? Maybe she really didn't love Jonathan. In the car she turned to Max. "Uncle Max, I see your point. I told her a few things, but I should have forced a showdown. Forgive me, but she's a horrible person, intimating the things she did. Honestly, darling, as things are now, I really think I'm better off this way. It would be awful having to deal with her as a mother-in-law."

He mumbled, "All right, if that's how you see it. I have one other word of advice for you. If—if, you hear?—you really intend to marry Jonathan someday, wait until you've had it out with Eleanor!"

Late that night Jonathan reached her by telephone. His

voice was tight. "I'll be back in a few days. I've gotten a deferment—something to do with oil for the government. Please, Em, nothing's changed between us. Keep your chin up. I feel just as I did before. No one can come between us. Remember, I love you."

She moped around the apartment until Jonathan telephoned he was back, and they arranged a meeting. He was unsmiling as he opened the car door for her.

"How are you, Jon?"

"Disgusted and tired, if you must know, Em. I thought you had more spunk than you showed."

Wailing, her voice rose. "Jonathan, if you'd heard the things she said to me—"

"I don't care what she said, Emmy. You owed it to me, if you loved me a little, to stand up to her and make her understand."

It was so confusing. Everyone was angry at her—the blame was being put on her shoulders. Dismayed and upset by his reaction, Emmy showed her anger in her voice. "What do you mean, it was up to me? What a terrible thing to say! Jonathan, as far as I'm concerned, it's over between us. Get someone with a suitable background for your mother. Do be sure there are no bastards in the bloodline!"

He paled at her words; his face was grim and his jaw was set. He turned to look at her. "Do me a favor, Em—shut up!"

She slapped his face. "Take me home! This instant! Turn this car around and take me home! I never, ever, want to see you again. I've had all of the Griffons I care to take!"

He drove steadily, not speaking, until he reached a roadside inn and restaurant. He pulled the car in and, taking the keys, got out. "Stay here! I'll be right back!"

She sat stiffly, her face averted. She heard his footsteps on the gravel but didn't turn around. He started the car, turned it around, drove a short distance and stopped. He put the car keys in his pocket as he said, "Get out!"

She didn't understand what he meant. His voice was hard and menacing. "I said get out. We're going to settle this here and now!" He came around to her side of the car and unceremoniously pulled her out. He yanked her along to the door of a small cabin, inserted a key and pulled her in, flicking on the light. It was a small, shabby room and she looked at him in amazement. "Just what is this all about? I don't want to stay here." She turned to leave, but he pulled her back. She fought him with all her anger, but he held her fiercely.

The touch of his lips sent voluptuous shudders through her, and as his hands savagely caressed her she had no will. He was rough with her as he tore her dress off and pushed her onto the bed. She struggled . . . to be pure and inviolate had been absorbed by osmosis . . . she mustn't let him. His teeth bit her mouth as she screamed, and as his body met hers she clung to him, dissolved in the fire that consumed them. . . .

It was much later that she heard him say, "This is a helluva place for a honeymoon—but face it, Em, you gave me no choice."

She murmured, "What would your mother say? She'd be right—I'm cheap, no good . . . no doubt a bastard does this sort of thing."

He turned over, raised himself and slapped her so hard on the rump that her buttocks hurt. When she tried to pull away, he pinned her down. His voice was hard and flat. "Listen, Emmalina, I never want to hear that word from you again. Get it through your head: I don't give a damn about anyone or anything but you! You! My mother will come around—if she doesn't, that's her loss. You and I are not going to be her sacrificial lambs. If you'd had half a brain in your head, you'd have understood it from the start. I'm sorry if I hurt you, but you deserved it. We're even now."

Much later Emmy remembered that Pearlie Mae was probably frantic with worry about her. She telephoned and explained they'd had car trouble.

Jonathan loved her; he'd overridden his mother's objections. She should have been happy but she wasn't. She had misgivings. She had difficulty looking Max in the eye when she told him that she and Jonathan had straightened things out and wanted to be married at the end of the month. She refused to allow Jonathan any more intimacy; she told him, with embarrassment, they didn't have long to wait. He had been masterful, taking the matter out of her hands, settling their relationship, but she didn't want him to assume she was that kind of girl. There was a great deal to be done for the wedding. A week before their marriage he told her he had spoken with his parents, and while they wanted to attend their nuptials, his father was tied up with some high-priority matters in Washington. In a way she was relieved; she wasn't ready to face his mother yet. Happily he told her his brother,

Bill, would probably meet them in Los Angeles if their arrivals coincided.

Everything was in readiness. Emmy had gone over the list of things to be done innumerable times, but she was still beset by doubts. She found it hard to believe it was actually the night before her wedding. Memories of the past kept intruding on the present, and anxiously she tried to convince herself that once she was Jonathan's wife the slate would be wiped clean. She would be beginning anew, magically sinking roots in the start of her own family. Seeing how nervous she was, Pearlie Mae consoled her. "All brides be dis way. I'm goin t'getchu some hot milk to hep yo sleep. Yo wants t'look yo bes . . . yo gonna be de mos beautiful bride ever was . . ."

Tossing and turning in her bed, she tried to concentrate on Jonathan. He loved and understood her . . . gave her confidence. From here on, he would be by her side when she faltered. For so long she had yearned for her father, and at last she could put him behind her. Musing in this vein, she fell asleep, dreaming she was back in the midst of her family and was filled with joy when her father smilingly told her what a good girl she was.

Judge Esquith's secretary had seen to it that Emmalina Field's wedding portrait and pertinent data about the impending nuptials had been sent to Oklahoma's leading newspapers. It made news when one of the state's most beautiful young oil heiresses wed the scion of an old-established Eastern mining and oil family, and the wire services picked it up. Eleanor Griffon was delighted to see how patrician and lovely her daughter-in-law appeared in print. No matter what she secretly thought, the outward appearances of the Griffon-Fields merger were good and she regretted not being able to attend the event.

The simple and intimate wedding ceremony, held at high noon in the country club, was marked by quiet elegance. The exotic and fragrant flowers, brought all the way from Hawaii, made a perfect backdrop for the bride, who wafted down the white-carpeted aisle on the arm of her beaming uncle, the famous Judge Esquith of Oklahoma City. The strikingly handsome groom, Jonathan Thomas Griffon, thought he had never seen anyone as breathtakingly beautiful as his bride. Looking at her as she approached, he was reminded of an angelic madonna as she returned his gaze with a small smile on her lips and luminous eyes filled with trust.

Emmy's chiseled beauty and well-proportioned figure were set off by a long-sleeved, high-necked ivory alençon lace sheath underlaid by a figure-contouring satin slipdress. Her softly curling dark hair was capped by the lace that half veiled her face and draped about her, falling gracefully into a train. Her only adornment was a single strand of shimmering pearls left to her by her mother for the occasion.

Looking up at Jonathan, Emmy's heart beat tumultuously. Never had he seemed more manly, more handsome. Here at last was safe haven—this man would care for her forever.

As Max left Emmy at Jonathan's side, a load slipped from his shoulders. His charge was over, and Elizabeth's sadly troubled girl was in capable hands.

The vows were recited, and a happily crying Pearlie Mae had the honor of holding the bridal spray as Emmy and Jonathan exchanged rings.

When the receiving line was ended, the party adjourned to the reception area where champagne, a sumptuous luncheon and music awaited them. After the three-tiered wedding cake had been cut, the newlyweds gaily made their adieus.

Jonathan was beaming as they came down the staircase. Emmy threw her bridal bouquet and, running through a hail of rice, she and Jonathan left on their trip to California.

Snuggling contentedly in the car seat alongside her husband, Emmy looked at her shining new wedding band and marquis diamond engagement ring, Jonathan's surprise gift to her. A tingle ran through her. She was married . . . Mrs. Jonathan T. Griffon . . . it would take time to absorb. Jonathan was smiling as he maneuvered the car through traffic and at a light he turned to give her an ardent glance and squeezed her hand. "Happy, angel?"

"Very, darling!" Suddenly she was shy. They were committed to each other forever, but despite their long courtship they really knew little about each other's innermost thoughts and needs.

"You and Uncle Max did a marvelous job. Everything went smoothly . . ."

She laughed. "Even Pearlie Mae—although at one point I thought she'd flood us out." She sighed with satisfaction, thinking that even his mother would have approved. Aside from Uncle Max there had been no immediate family present. It was sad that it should have been that way. She was about to mention it but stopped herself. Uncle Max had been right . . . he'd said this was not the time to dwell on that. But the feeling was too deeply entrenched; weddings—at least those she had attended—had joyous families in attendance, and she couldn't help but reflect how much more meaningful it would have been had her sisters, Amy Beth and Polly Sue, been present.

Chapter XVII

◖◦◦◦◦◖

POLLY SUE'S
METAMORPHOSIS

FOR THE FIRST time in her life Polly Sue was acquiring self-discipline and learning how to get along with people. The classes provided by the studio covered a broad spectrum of the dramatic arts, and she was being taught singing and dancing as well. Preoccupied by her work, she gave little thought to anything else. She was cognizant of the golden opportunity she'd been given and was determined to forge ahead. She applied herself zealously, and as her skills improved she was rewarded by small acting parts in B pictures. It became commonplace for her to work late, and when she returned to the hotel in the evening she looked forward to being with Lilly, who would be eagerly waiting to hear her account of the day's events.

Despite her persistence, poor Lilly Fazon's hopes for a movie career were dimming. Clawing and scratching for any sort of break, she seemed to meet with failure no matter what she tried. In desperation she'd even resorted to an affair with a man who held out rosy promises of work. An assistant director at a small studio, he kept stringing her along, but nothing of substance ever materialized and, disillusioned, she refused to see him any longer. As Polly seemed more and more indifferent to her plight, Lilly's envy over her friend's good fortune began to increase. She was sure that Polly could help if she wanted to, but Polly never volunteered and, in angry frustration, Lilly was driven to ask, "In your position you're like one of those Wampus babies. I'm sure you could get me something. There must be someone you know who could pull strings . . . get me work, even as an extra."

Polly protested, "You of all people ought to know how powerless I am. I haven't any influence; I'm just a small cog in a wheel."

Lilly didn't attempt to disguise her derision, and, seeing this, Polly vowed contritely, "I'll do what I can . . . you just don't understand, but if anything comes up, anything at all, I swear I'll try for you."

Lilly knew it was a lost cause and, too proud to insist, she dropped the subject. From past experience she knew Polly didn't credit any of the good fortune that had befallen her to luck, believing totally that she'd earned it because of merit. It followed that, since she'd made it on her own, Lilly ought to be able to do the same thing. In small ways Lilly made it a point to retaliate, but a bond remained between them, because each in her own way was dependent on the other.

Polly Sue refused to believe it the night Lilly announced she was leaving—giving up and going home to Arkansas. She sat in stunned silence as Lilly explained that she was tired of struggling, that girls like her were a glut on the market and her dreams of a movie career were at an end. As Polly opened her mouth to say something, Lilly cut her off. "It's no use, Polly. I'm going home. My sister's sick and needs to go to the hospital. My mom's been bedridden for years and I'll have to take over." As Polly stared at her openmouthed, she added, "I have a job waiting. I'm going to substitute for my sister . . . she's a secretary for the sales manager at the mill."

Unable to restrain herself, Polly exploded, "Are you crazy? Giving up now after all the effort you've put in—you're stupid! It's plain selfishness for your family to expect you to sacrifice your life. They have no right! You'd be a fool to give up everything for them!"

They fought bitterly, but no amount of persuasion changed Lilly's mind. Polly became sullen, and Lilly, reduced to tears, was humiliatingly forced to ask Polly for a loan. Tempted to refuse, but knowing it would be to no avail, Polly offered Lilly more than she needed, and they were glad of the chance to make up. Lilly planned to leave the following afternoon and this was their last evening together. It was a forlorn farewell; they parted sadly, promising to keep in touch.

Much to her dismay, Polly quickly discovered what a boon Lilly had been to her morale. Once she had gone, Polly hated returning to her barren room. She had depended on Lilly for more than she was willing to admit, and losing her left a large hole in her life. Forced to look elsewhere for companionship and having fallen heir to Lilly's old car, she invited some of her classmates to join her on excursions to the beach or the park. The fledgling acting group occasionally went out to dinner together, and in time Polly made a friend of Ron Douglas, a young man with whom she shared kindred aspirations. They were keenly competitive and ambitious and, having worked together in several films, had high regard for each other's abilities. From the onset Polly made it plain that their friendship was purely platonic. She hadn't forgotten how her innocent dinner date with Lilly and the cameramen had gotten back to Jan Borge, and she took every precaution to show propriety. She had no intention of jeopardizing her career for anyone or anything.

Polly had been away from classes working in a picture, and when she returned rumors were rife that casting was under way for a big production, with the strong possibility that a few of them were under consideration. During the lunch break, Ron Douglas confided to Polly he had already been tested and given the secondary lead. It was to be an epic film similar to *Gone with the Wind*. The more he talked the more depressed Polly became, afraid she'd been overlooked.

Reporting to work the next morning, her spirits at low ebb, Polly was called aside and given the ingenue script for *Southern War*. Her drama coach told her, "Frankly, your chances are slim. someone else is already under consideration, but give it the best you've got. You'll have to be ready for the screen test later today."

Quivering with excitement, she tried to pull her wits together. It was crucial that she succeed. One of the attributes Polly had developed was the ability to memorize lines while focusing in on the underlying character the part called for. Oblivious to everything else, she set to work. All too soon, it seemed, she was notified it was time to report to the costume department.

Dressed and made up, she studied herself in the mirror. Bewigged with long black curls, in crinolines and bonnet, she had been transformed into the girl she was about to portray— outwardly prim, with a promise of fire.

Polly Sue was as yet unaware that she possessed an incomparable mixture of innocence and sensuality—qualities that she projected with startling clarity on film. As she readied herself, her only qualms were whether she'd remember the lines. Flushed and lovely, she appeared the epitome of the part.

Determined to triumph, not wanting to leave a stone unturned to ensure her chances, she began at once to charm the cameramen on the set—they could be very instrumental in showing her to advantage. To Hal Cranston, the veteran character actor who was to share the scene, she girlishly confessed her fears. Beguiled by the frightened, forthright young woman, he promised to do everything he could to assist her.

Action was called. Her nerves under steel control, immersed in the part, Polly flowed through the scene as she and Cranston performed together like violin and bow.

There was silence as the scene concluded, broken only when a voice from the darkness in front of the stage called out, "Thank you. You'll be notified in a few days."

Smiling sweetly, Polly responded with a sweeping curtsy as Hal Cranston offered her his arm to escort her out. It was a deft touch.

Time hung suspended and Polly found it difficult to keep her mind on anything but the impending news. When the announcement came that she had won the part she was elated, certain this would be her breakthrough to stardom.

The next few days passed in a blur as she went from fittings to makeup evaluation and at last to the film set, a replica of a small Southern levee town on the banks of the Mississippi. Upon being introduced to the cast, she was startled to find herself confronting the hostile eyes of Illona Lassen. She was horrified to learn that the star had been cast as her mother, and a tremor ran through Polly as she realized how many intense scenes they would share, including one in which the mother angrily slapped the daughter's face. Managing to maintain her composure, Polly moved along to greet the others, making a silent resolve to let nothing interfere with her goal of stardom.

Rehearsals had been under way several days when the director singled Polly out for a compliment. This served to stimulate Illona Lassen into a campaign of overt harassment, and she devised all sorts of malicious mischief to throw Polly off stride. It brought the desired results when the director openly reprimanded the girl several times. Sensing she would be considered troublesome if she complained, Polly suffered in silence, and the situation worsened. In the scene calling for the mother to slap the daughter's face Miss Lassen unaccountably fumbled her lines, and it had to be repeated again and again with Polly enduring the blows. By now, however, several people on the set had become aware of what was going on and word got back to the director. He immediately had a talk with Polly, who admitted things had been difficult. Angrily he asked why she hadn't reported this before. Teary-eyed and contrite she explained she had not wanted to cause difficulties on the set. The only thing she worried about was her ability to turn in a creditable performance. An ultimatum was issued to Miss Lassen, who knew, finally, that it was time to desist. Polly emerged from the fray with kudos for good sportsmanship and cooperation.

Polly happily resumed work. If anyone noticed that she failed to express her thanks to those who had intervened on her behalf, they made no mention of it. It didn't occur to her to express gratitude or appreciation; she had long ago become accustomed to accepting good fortune as her due. But in thinking about what had taken place, it struck her that by feigning forbearance and childlike simplicity she had won her victory over Miss Lassen, and she decided to maintain the demeanor. It might eventually bring her even greater advantages.

Gene Madrix, president of Major Pictures, received daily reports of the progress and events on the set of *Southern War*. The name of Polly Sue Corrigan appeared with increasing frequency, and he heard the stories circulating about the unusual young woman who had won the ingenue role. He decided the time had come to check out this "incredible find" for himself. For one thing, she had taken the role away from someone highly competent, and if she had a promising future, he wanted to meet and evaluate her on his own. If this budding actress was as good as everyone said, it might be worthwhile to offer her a better contract.

The glowing reports of the girl's character left him dubious. It seemed unlikely she could have reached this point and remained as innocent and naïve as she had been described.

He recalled when Jan Borge had first brought her to his attention and he'd assumed she'd been one of Jan's ladies of the night. His assistant's proclivities for attractive young women sometimes got in the way of his judgment, but after seeing the girl's rushes and expert horsemanship, he'd understood Borge's enthusiasm. Priding himself on being a reasonable man, he'd given the girl the benefit of the doubt.

Madrix was a burly man in his mid-fifties, with a firm
mouth and crisp black hair graying at the temples. Awaiting
Polly Sue's arrival at his office, he signed some papers and
leaned back in his chair to reflect. He considered himself a
good judge of character; experience had taught him well. In
this business there were few angels, and he'd done and seen a
lot of unsavory things. These last years he'd removed himself
from the run-of-the-mill movie world and it had made him
prey to gossip. There were those who considered him a
hypocrite, and he'd grant, in a way, they were right—he'd
done his share of womanizing and now seemed to have
become a self-righteous prude. They didn't understand he'd
called quits when he'd had his fill. The truth was he didn't
give a damn what anyone did as long as it didn't conflict with
business. His moralizing was an industry necessity—Hays'
code and the Board of Film Censors were on everyone's back.
He'd fought hard to get where he was; to be at the helm of
Major Pictures was a great achievement. He had taken a
second-rate company and made it into one of the top five. He
grinned with satisfaction as he thought of the substantial
quarterly profits the company now paid its stockholders. As
long as he was in control, he kept a sharp eye on everyone.
There'd be no scandal attached to Major Pictures. He knew
the sycophants around him secretly conniving and baying at
his heels, always ready to grab what they could to achieve
fame and fortune. They were on a par with suppliant women
eager to give themselves in exchange for a break. At this
point in his life, he was relieved to be free of entanglements.
He had made an excellent marriage and was proud of his wife
and family. Madrix looked at his watch. The Corrigan girl
should be along any moment. He grinned; it was a far cry
from the old days. If the girl was as unworldly as she was
reputed to be, she'd be as safe with him as a newborn babe.
His sole interest in her would be as a potentially marketable
commodity.

It had been a late night. Since their call sheets did not
require them to be on the set until early afternoon, Polly and
Ron sat discussing the Tyrone Power movie they had just
seen. When Polly found a message ordering her to report to
Mr. Madrix's office she became alarmed, fearful that the
after-midnight session might signify dismissal for breach of
contract. She was miserable at the thought of all her hard

work having been in vain; her mind churned with plans for her defense.

Flushed with trepidation as she was shown into Mr. Madrix's office, she was breathless as she acknowledged his greeting. Wary and on guard, she seated herself where he indicated, facing the long, highly polished desk behind which he sat as if enthroned in an imposing high-backed chair. It seemed an interminable time before he stopped taking her in, and she could feel her color rising with resentment. He was about to say something when the telephone buzzed. Swiveling his back to her, he became involved in conversation.

Polly took advantage of the momentary interruption to look around. It was a novel experience to be in the office of the studio chief. Although the brown and beige decor was too subdued for her taste, she was impressed with the deep plush pile of the carpeting and the oil paintings of Major Pictures' leading stars hung on the dark walnut paneling. It was a huge suite complete with dining table and chairs and an amply stocked bar in a far corner. At the opposite end there were beige leather couches, a coffee table and an intriguing bookshelf hanging from the ceiling holding movie scripts in custom leather bindings. Turning back to the desk, her eye was drawn to a silver tray holding a gracefully shaped silver carafe with gold monogram and matching silver goblets. It seemed too elegant for mere water. Her eyes kept exploring and she caught a glimpse of gold-framed pictures showing a beautiful woman and several children. At that moment, Gene Madrix replaced the telephone and smiled. "These are pictures of my family, and, if you wouldn't mind, I'd be interested in having you tell me about yours."

This was not at all what she had expected, and tremulously she tried to gather her wits. Her timidity lessened as she began to talk about her parents and the ranch in Montana. She was visibly moved by nostalgia and he said kindly, "It's not easy to be far away from one's family. I can understand—you must be homesick."

At his sympathy, she nodded in agreement, as if too choked to speak, but regaining her voice said softly, "I miss them all the time."

Changing the subject, he asked when her interest in acting had begun. As she talked he observed her intently. Her beauty was like a breath of spring; her almond-shaped eyes were remarkable, deep wells of violet with changing hues reflecting the depths of her feeling. He was captivated by her ineffable quality of innocence; she seemed so artless and honest that his skepticism began to dissolve. Without doubt, the girl had a combination of assets which, if handled right, were star material. If her acting ability lived up to its claims, and her unspoiled sweetness and simplicity could be retained, she had great potential. He decided to take the gamble and offer her a feature-player contract. It would be laced with the proper clauses for the studio's protection; the risks would be minimal.

He allowed her to finish what she was saying and then, without more ado, told her of his intentions. He had seen people surprised before, but never the equal of this—the look of shock on her face followed by bewilderment, as if she wasn't sure what he had said. He smiled and said, "You heard correctly, Miss Corrigan. We're intending to make you a feature player—and one day, if you're good enough, probably a star." He pointed to the paintings on the wall. "It would be nice to have you grace a space there."

Her eyes welled with tears. Her relief was intense. She'd come with fear and anger, hopeful she'd escape with a reprimand; instead she was being offered a chance to become a star. She sat shaken and speechless, and Mr. Madrix became concerned. "Are you all right? Would you like some water?"

As she sipped from the goblet she realized the silver carafe actually held ice water, and she grinned. Seeing this, he smiled back at her and said, "Why are you so surprised? All reports indicate that you're very hardworking and ambitious. Isn't this what you've been working toward?"

Shyly, her face beaming, she replied, "Yes, of course, Mr. Madrix . . . but when it actually happens it seems unbelievable."

"Of course, I can appreciate that, but, my dear"—and his voice turned serious—"you have to understand this is another beginning. You have a long, hard road ahead of you . . . harder than you can imagine. It isn't easy to reach the top, and even more difficult to stay there. Your real efforts are just beginning. Now tell me who your agent is."

At this she became flustered, and he had to lean forward to hear her. "I don't have one. Will that change things?"

He couldn't repress a laugh at her naïveté as he assured her it wouldn't alter matters. "We prefer to deal with an agent. If you like, I'll be glad to recommend someone."

Her face alight with happiness, she burbled, "Oh, thank you. Anyone you suggest will be fine."

It had been a long time since he'd met anyone so unworldly and trusting—the girl amused him. Checking his watch, Mr. Madrix rose. "We'll find out if Mr. Michalson will take you on. He's the best man in the business. An appointment will be made for ten o'clock Saturday . . . my secretary will give you the details. Before you go, there's one other thing: you're not to mention this to anyone until we say so. Do you understand?"

She readily agreed but was disappointed that she couldn't share it with Ron Douglas and see Illona Lassen's face when she heard. As Polly left the telephone buzzed and he was pleased to hear the familiar male voice at the other end. When he'd relayed the information about the Corrigan girl and the conversation terminated, he thought about the man with whom he had just spoken. He'd been lucky to have found a counterpart in Ralph Michalson. A man of discernment and taste, Ralph had risen to become Hollywood's top agent. They'd been through a lot of adventures together, but now he too was happily settled and content. They were close friends.

Polly felt as if she were floating on air. She'd heard about the agent she was to meet when she'd first come to Hollywood. He handled only top stars, and if he took her on it would be a feather in her cap. His outer office was empty when she arrived and as she waited, hesitant, a tall, distinguished man came through a door and graciously introduced himself as Ralph Michalson. He was extremely dignified and she knew it would be important to impress him properly.

Ushering her into his private office, he took stock of the diminutive girl, wondering what there was to her, aside from her beauty, that had so intrigued his friend Gene Madrix. As they made introductory talk she seemed ingenuous, but he felt there was more behind her lovely face than was apparent.

Ralph Michalson knew his business—he'd learned it from the ground up—and his clients fared well in his hands. He hadn't been interested in acquiring another female client, but his friend Madrix had asked him, as a favor, to represent the girl. Nevertheless, before he committed himself he wanted to be sure she was someone with whom he could deal. Adroitly, he manipulated the conversation in order to draw her out. In response to his questions, Polly related the story of Jan Borge's assistance and instantly saw his flicker of skepticism. Relieved to have gotten that hurdle out of the way, Polly felt she could convince him she was really an unsophisticated little farmgirl.

He couldn't pin her down; despite her openness, he felt there was something that didn't ring true. She appeared unaffected and wholesome, and in comparison with most of the women with whom he dealt she was like a babe in the woods; but it didn't add up. She had to be smarter than she seemed; she'd been in Hollywood too long to have maintained the aura of innocence she projected. It occurred to him that if she was pulling the wool over their eyes, she had one thing to her credit—she was an exceedingly good actress. There was no use trying to break through her facade; he'd have to accept her at face value until she proved otherwise. He got down to business, explaining the agreement she would sign with him, and then began a discussion of the part she was playing in *Southern War*. At his mention of what he thought her salary should be her mouth flew open in astonishment, and she was instantly concerned that it might be too much. He assured her it was commensurate, saying, "Leave the business end to me. Your job is to prove to Major Pictures you're worth every penny."

There was something in his attitude that warned her she hadn't convinced him of her simplicity, and the smile on his face mocked her as he added, "Above all, Miss Corrigan, don't change. Don't let this go to your head!"

Slightly intimidated, with utmost seriousness she promised, "I'll work hard . . . believe me I will. It won't go to my head. There's nothing that can change me."

Clearing his throat, he said gruffly, "Madrix's epic pictures are usually big successes, and there's a good chance this one will make a star out of you overnight. A word of caution: don't promise him anything you can't do. Be honest with him and he'll treat you accordingly. If you do exactly as you're told, your future is assured."

With all the fervor she could muster she said, "I'll follow your advice to the best of my ability. I won't give you any trouble, Mr. Michalson."

Showing her out, he thought: At the start they're all eager

and willing. . . . He was almost certain this one wouldn't be an exception.

Each day Polly went to the studio dressed in her best clothes, expecting to be summoned for the signing of the new contract. She was delighted that the call came when she was wearing a new lilac jumper and frilly blouse, handmade gifts from her mother; the outfit heightened her girlishness.

Mr. Madrix and Mr. Michalson greeted her cordially, and she was no sooner seated than Mr. Madrix said, "Well, young lady, this is a special day. To start with, we hope you're going to like your new name. From now on you're going to be known as Tana Corgan."

Startled, she repeated, "Tana Corgan?"

"It's perfect . . . suits you to a T." He smiled. "Clever isn't it? It's a contraction of your home state and your last name."

She felt a twinge that she hadn't been consulted, but the name did please her—it sounded special and would be easy to fit on a movie marquee. She murmured sweetly, "I like it . . . it sounds very nice."

"Well, my dear, that's just the beginning. We have several surprises for you. Along with your new name, you will begin a new life. Right here, let me say that if you have any objections we will expect you to say so at once." He paused, and she turned to Mr. Michalson for clarification. Reassuringly he said, "Gene, how can she express an opinion before she knows? Spell it out and then ask."

Polly settled back, looking at them expectantly. She had already made up her mind that no matter what they asked, she'd agree. To get where she wanted was her sole purpose.

Pondering a moment, Mr. Madrix began, "We want you to understand that a great deal of study and effort has gone into what we want to achieve for you, and I hope you will appreciate this. First on the agenda: Tana Corgan must live in suitable style, so, as of today, you will be moved into a home that is being readied for you right now. As part of that change, you will break all your past ties—which means you are not to see or maintain contact with anyone you are involved with at the present time."

The wind went out of her. Perplexed, she blurted out, "What about my folks . . . my clothes? Can't I have time to get myself ready?"

Instantly disappointed, Mr. Madrix showed his annoyance,

and Mr. Michalson intervened. "That doesn't include your family, Tana; of course you'll be free to maintain those contacts. Your personal things will be brought to your new home."

"Oh, I see . . ." she said, but she didn't. She was totally confounded.

Impatient, his fingers drumming the desk, Mr. Madrix resumed. "I guess an explanation is necessary. I hope you recall that at our last meeting I talked about your embarking on a totally new career. We've decided since you're young and impressionable—too inexperienced to handle yourself in this type of situation—the studio will take upon itself the responsibility of acting as your surrogate parent."

She looked blank. "What does that word mean?"

Both men laughed and Madrix said kindly, "It means that in the absence of your real parents we're prepared to take over their role. That's one of the reasons we want you to break your past ties—it will be easier for you to assume your new identity and responsibilities."

She seemed hesitant and protested feebly, "I'm not sure my folks will like the idea."

"Nonsense." Gene Madrix overrode her objections. "They will be pleased knowing we have your best interests at heart. You're still a minor, and our legal department has already forwarded papers to them for their consent. Be sure you mention that when you speak with them." He paused, considering an idea. "Would your mother be willing to come here and live with you?"

She shifted uneasily. "I don't think she could leave my dad."

"Exactly what we thought," he said dryly, "and for that reason we have engaged a woman to act as your companion and chaperone." He smiled at Michalson as he said, "We've also hired a housekeeper and will underwrite the salary for a while. Any objections so far, Tana?"

Her face crinkled as if she were about to cry but she smiled wanly. "No, Mr. Madrix."

"Good! There is another important thing to get out of the way." Pointing his index finger at her, he became stern and admonishing. "I want to make this very clear so there is no misunderstanding . . . there are to be no exceptions to this rule! So that you realize how seriously we view this, it's been made part of your contract." He paused and she looked terrified as he boomed, "You are not to have any male relationships without express studio permission. There are to be no men in your life—none . . . other than your father and business associates! If and when you require male escorts, the studio will supply them."

Involuntarily her hackles rose. She couldn't believe her ears—it was ridiculous. What did they mean by such a thing? She was suffused with anger at the way her life was being ordered out of her control, and her face flushed red.

Seeing her color change and assuming he had offended her modesty, Mr. Madrix softened his tone. "This sort of talk is probably unnecessary, but it had to be said because of the image you will be creating." He smiled and, leaning back in his chair, said dreamily, "Our plan is to have you become every man's ideal girl . . . the sweetheart he dreams of . . . to be worshiped from afar. That's a big responsibility, and we cannot allow anything to blemish that illusion. Not one word, not one action, must tarnish your name!"

Fortunately he couldn't read her mind and she sat expressionless and stiff, fighting to keep a grip on herself, her mind racing. She might as well have entered a convent . . . she was being made into a nun anyway. Through a fog she heard the insistence in Mr. Madrix's voice. "Tana, do you understand what we want to accomplish? Is it clear to you? Do you agree?"

Raising her head, she looked at Ralph Michalson, but he remained dour and silent. Almost stammering, she forced herself to say, "I understand . . . I agree." She was angry at herself; she had overplayed the little-girl role. A sigh escaped her. She had almost botched it . . . it had been a close call.

Gene Madrix's face was wreathed in smiles and as she looked at him she knew she'd have to be careful and that for now at least she'd have to go along with this nonsense. There was no doubt she'd gotten herself into something she hadn't bargained for.

He felt sorry for her. Watching the play of emotions cross her face, Madrix had a hunch she wasn't liking this much; kids didn't like to be told what to do, to be ordered around, particularly at her age. He had a daughter just a few years younger and he very much doubted if his child had the stuff to accomplish her aims the way this little girl had pursued hers. He had to hand it to her—all alone, working, ducking pitfalls, she was plucky . . . no doubt about it.

Michalson placed the contract in front of her. "It's all in order, Miss Corgan, but take your time and look it over and sign it when you're ready."

Tana fingered the pages of the contract. It was long, and despite her attempts to understand the legal jargon, the wherefores, therefores and legalese, it was completely indecipherable. She was relieved to see the salary was exactly as Mr. Michalson had said, so, after making a pretense of scrutinizing the material, she looked up at him and said firmly, "I guess it's all right—I trust you." Nervously she bit her upper lip, hesitated a moment and, taking a deep breath, signed.

Polly Sue Corrigan officially became Tana Corgan. Fact had been replaced by fantasy . . . she had crossed into a strange new world, and it was too late for regrets.

Genially, Mr. Madrix extended his hand. "Good luck, Tana Corgan. When you are finished on the set today your car and chauffeur will drive you to your new home, where Grace Burke will be waiting. Sign the release my secretary has prepared so that Mrs. Burke can get your possessions from the hotel. Your old car will be stored on the lot; give the keys to the chauffeur. Don't forget to contact your family and inform them of your new address."

Her teeth clenched as loathing for this overbearing, paternalistic man consumed her; he acted as if he owned her. . . . Her spine bristled; she felt as if she were a puppet being manipulated at whim and by his will.

Ralph Michalson walked out of Mr. Madrix's office with her and, sensing her unhappiness, said consolingly, "You'll get used to it. Look at it this way: it's a small price to pay for something you want so much. There are a lot of compensations. Major Pictures is making a big investment in you—" He was startled by the mercurial change in her, the expression of bitter anger that flicked across her face, and he warned, "You'd better be certain you're willing to make the sacrifice."

Instantly she resumed the guise he'd become accustomed to and unflinchingly replied, "Of course I'm willing, Mr. Michalson!"

She was excited by the prospect of her new home and she realized the flower-lined streets they rode along denoted Beverly Hills. She had not expected this . . . it was beyond her wildest dreams.

As they drove along a broad avenue bordered by huge palm trees with mansions set back on lush green lawns, her heart beat with anticipation. The car slowed and turned into a curving driveway, stopping in front of an imposing house that appeared to be a fantasized version of French Normandy design, with high pitched shingled roof, gables and stained-glass leaded windows. It was built of white brick partially covered by thick yellow-flowered vines that extended over a high wall surrounding the property. She sat staring at it until the chauffeur said, "You're home, Miss Corgan."

Hesitantly she stepped out. The front door opened, disclosing a dark-hued woman in maid's uniform who smiled and said, "My name is Maria, ma'am. Miss Burke's waiting for you."

Suddenly she was terrified, overwhelmed by the impulse to run—to be free of all the restraints about to descend on her. There was nothing in her life that had prepared her for such an experience, for this sort of living. She found herself standing awkwardly in a dim foyer lit by a soft light from a brass lamp on a wall table holding a bowl of richly scented roses. Her feet seemed to be stuck to the gray slate floor and she was about to flee when a voice stopped her. "Hello and welcome, Tana. I'm Grace Burke. Do come in."

A tall, matronly woman extended a hand. "You must be tired. Let me show you to the den. I've looked forward to meeting you—I'm sure we're going to be great friends."

Docilely Tana followed Mrs. Burke into a cozy room that looked like a picture from a magazine with its elegant, countrified decor. A down-pillowed couch and wing chairs covered in floral-worked crewel made her want to sink down and rest. Potted fluffy green ferns were placed about on stands and a large over-leaf–patterned hook rug set off by glowing lamps and a small fire in the grate added to its inviting appeal. A smiling Mrs. Burke said, "Make yourself comfortable, dear. While you relax, we can have a little chat. Would you like something before dinner?"

Tana's eyes blurred with weariness; the entire day had been too much to absorb. Tiredly she sank into a soft-pillowed chair, slipped off her pumps and, with a start, realized she had not as yet said one word to Mrs. Burke. "Oh, I'm sorry . . . excuse me. Everything's so strange, and I'm exhausted. Nothing for me, thank you."

Tana thought the woman's blue eyes twinkled as she

laughingly replied, "Of course, dear . . . I understand. In a few days you'll feel at home. You're going to love it here, and you can count on me to do all I can to help."

At this point Tana was not surprised to learn that her belongings had been picked up, unpacked and put away in her bedroom. Through half-opened eyes she watched curiously as Mrs. Burke tugged at a long woven piece on the wall, which proved to be a bell that quickly brought the maid. Solicitously Mrs. Burke insisted, "A tiny bit of wine would do you a world of good. Let Maria bring you a glass." Tana shrugged resignedly—another parent taking over. She had a pang of longing for home where no one pressed her to do what she didn't want to do.

Sipping the nut-flavored sherry, Tana studied her chaperone, who was arranging a log on the fire. The statuesque woman, past middle age, was still trim and pretty despite the old-fashioned way in which she wore her blond hair—puffy and piled high on her head. Tana had reservations about sharing her life with a stranger, but so far the woman had been comforting and seemed anxious to please.

Reseating herself, Grace Burke began to talk, catching Tana's interest when she revealed she had been a silent-film star whose career had ended with the advent of talkies. The reason was obvious: her voice was nasal and high-pitched. But despite her efforts to stay awake, Tana's eyes were closing. Since dinner was almost ready, Mrs. Burke suggested it would dispel her sleepiness if they made a tour of the grounds before night fell. The sight of the blue-tiled swimming pool and tennis court roused Tana from her fatigue. As she looked around at the well-tended grounds bordered by stately cypress trees, flowering azaleas and hibiscus with smart lawn furniture, she knew she'd made the right decision—here were some of the visible compensations.

Standing at the doorway to the formal dining room, Tana was even more amazed by the richness of the life offered with her new status. A long, highly polished grayed oak table surrounded by wine velvet chairs was set for two, with intricately hand-embroidered rose linen runners and mats on which delicate china and crystal glistened in the reflection of twinkling pink candles in a porcelain centerpiece. The array of silverware next to her plate was confusing, and she watched to see which fork Mrs. Burke selected for the salad. Despite Maria's and Mrs. Burke's concern, Tana barely touched her food. She was secretly amused when they urged her to tell them her food preferences. She wondered what they'd think of Irish stew, and at that remembered she had to telephone her parents.

The Corrigans registered mixed emotions at the news of their daughter's changed role and surroundings. It was difficult reassuring them at such a distance, and she was forced to ask Mrs. Burke to come to the telephone and confirm she was to be her live-in chaperone. More than anything else they were disturbed by Polly Sue's changed name, and their repetitious questions brought her to tears. "I can't help it . . . it's what the studio wanted. Please don't nag me—I'm terribly tired. I have to hang up now, but I'll call you again in a day or so. Believe me, everything's fine—and, Daddy, I won't be needing your check. I almost forgot—please sign the studio's papers when they come."

Too tired to protest, Tana allowed Mrs. Burke to help ready her for bed. Worn out, she slid between the pink satin sheets and sank into sleep. It would be morning before she could admire the attractive Provincial bedroom done in soft greens and rose with a dressing room lined with mirrored closets bigger than her former hotel room.

The sudden change proved too dramatic, and the next few weeks worked a hardship on Tana. She cried easily without reason and would have floundered had it not been for Mrs. Burke's steadfast assistance. Grace Burke was subtle and tactful, quietly pointing out how things should be done, so that the girl could fit into her new background. Although she was humiliated at having to be so dependent, Tana accepted her aid, suddenly aware of how much she had been lacking and yearning for attention.

Grace Burke was a patient woman who, to her credit, tried to make the girl comfortable and happy. But, removed from everything and everyone personally familiar to her, Tana seemed quiet and withdrawn, growing animated only when Mrs. Burke regaled her with stories of the old days in films, confiding her adoration of Valentino and an affair with Francis X. Bushman. She was given to embellishing her tales with romantic interludes, whether true or not. She had endless anecdotes about famous screen personalities; she had worked with Theda Bara and Mary Pickford and been friends with Clara Bow, the *It* girl. A storehouse of fascinating lore about old films, she inadvertently taught Tana much about the origins of making movies. She'd worked in *The Covered Wagon, Ruggles of Red Gap, The Vanishing American* and many more.

It was in her limited spare time that Tana's loneliness became acute. It was then she missed people of her own age most keenly. Grace Burke tried to fill the gap as best she could, but they were generations apart and it wasn't easy for either one of them.

Listed on the call sheet every day, Tana was occupied from dawn to dusk. Accompanied by Grace Burke, she would arrive at the studio in the early morning and go directly to makeup or the set. Her life was now completely enveloped by the studio. She worked intensely, calling on her drama coach for special assistance, driven by her compulsion to have *Southern War* make her a star.

In time she grew accustomed to being addressed as Tana Corgan, and Grace Burke, always close at hand, reprimanded anyone who failed to remember. As she regained her footing Tana chafed at having her every move shadowed and being watched over as if she were a helpless infant. She grew increasingly surly at Grace's intrusion, particularly when the woman well-meaningly prompted her answers to questions. They had their first blowup when she saw Grace's disapproving eyes glued on her as she conversed with Ron Douglas before a scene.

Tana began to suspect that Grace Burke was not only her chaperone but a watchdog for the studio as well. Her suspicions were confirmed when one afternoon Grace, bursting with impatience, gave her news that could only have derived from someone on high. As soon as they were alone she excitedly told Tana, "You're about to be launched!"

Irate at how puffed with importance Grace seemed, Tana snapped, "What does that mean?"

"Oh, Tana, you should be thrilled." And as if she'd had a hand in it, Grace declared, "Your progress has been so excellent, the publicity department's been given the go-ahead. News of your discovery is going to be released—pictures and stories telling all about you will be everywhere. Isn't it exciting?"

Tana's pleasure was tarnished by the fact that she had not been told about it directly. She was being handled as if she were a workhorse—and despite her youth and stamina she was always exhausted by the daily routine that was totally devoid of fun.

The story of Tana Corgan broke and made front-page news: "Rags-to-riches girl soars cometlike through the Hollywood skies in her first feature role." It made excellent copy, and the newspapers and magazines were full of stories about her. Radio newscasters and columnists discussed her meteoric rise, and she became a symbol of hope for hundreds of other young aspirants. Since she was kept under wraps, away from everyone, and no one was allowed to interview her directly, speculation about her ran high. The Cinderella girl's tale had human appeal for everyone, and mail began to pour into the studio.

Tana had little time to revel. The lengthy rehearsal period for *Southern War* had honed cast and crew to a fine edge, and the actual filming of the picture had begun. It was as though Tana walked a high wire, pushed to the limits of her ability.

Renowned for his past successes, Norman Shaw, the director of the film, was a tyrannical perfectionist who demanded the utmost from everyone.

The fledgling actress found it nerve-racking and she would finish the day's work worn out and anxious, too tired to do anything but have a hot bath and tumble into bed.

Her emotions worn thin, Tana was often too weary to eat, and Grace would plead with her, "You must try, dear. It won't do to lose weight . . . it will show, and they want you just the way you are." But no one really gave a darn about her; even Grace's solicitude was for the sake of the almighty studio.

As the pressures increased, Grace's proximity grew more intolerable and Tana's thoughts often reverted to her mother. She wished that she'd asked her to come when Mr. Madrix had suggested it. The more she thought about it, the more it seemed Deirdre might be her key to freedom.

The idea took root and she wrote a calculated letter to her parents, trusting that their reaction would bring about the desired result. Just as she hoped, Deirdre replied at once: preparations were already under way for her to visit and find out firsthand what was going on with her daughter. It would take a little time to get things in order so that she could leave Sean, but she would try to stay at least a month.

The moment she learned of her mother's coming, Tana arranged an appointment with Mr. Madrix; she had to manage things so that he would see the wisdom of releasing her from Grace Burke's guardianship.

As the secretary ushered her into the office, Mr. Madrix

rose to greet her. "Sit down, Tana. I continue to receive excellent reports about your progress."

Smiling modestly, she said, "Oh, I'm so glad. Thank you. I know how busy you are, but I just had to tell you my wonderful news. Remember when you asked if one of my family could come to keep me company? Well, my mother is due to arrive any day, and dear Grace will no longer have to stay."

He studied her for a moment and then looked out a window as he dashed her hopes. "That's good news, Tana; I'm happy for you. About Grace Burke leaving, well, I don't think so, not just yet. I don't think you're ready to stand on your own two feet. As you know by now, Grace is very knowledgeable about what we want for you. She's doing an excellent job. Your progress is due in part to her supervision. Without her help and guidance over the next few months you'll have a difficult time getting over the rough spots. She has an instinct for this sort of work; that's why we trust her judgment." He paused and looked straight at Tana. "You should be very grateful to her; you owe her a lot."

Trapped, Tana tried to hide her disappointment. "Yes, of course. She's a darling and I am grateful to her . . . to you too for having her assist me. We've become good friends."

Smiling in a fatherly fashion, he said, "By this time I should think so. She really is very fond of you and has your best interests at heart. Now, little girl, I appreciate your telling me the good news. You must set up another appointment when your mother gets here; I want to meet her. As long as you're here, I guess it won't hurt if I let you in on a secret. We've found another excellent part for you and the script is in preparation. That should make you happy! Now, dear, I have a conference waiting. Take care . . . keep up the good work!"

Tana could barely resist saying, "Thank you, Poppa Madrix." Instead she smirked, murmured something unintelligible and walked out, restraining an impulse to hold her skirt and skip. The situation was becoming untenable; her frustrations were at boiling point. Desperately she cast about in her mind for a solution and decided that if the situation didn't alter soon, she would speak with Mr. Michalson and ask him to be her intermediary with Mr. Madrix.

On the studio lot the following day, Gene Madrix encountered Grace Burke. "Well Grace, your girl seems to be coming along, although I get the impression she's not happy."

Instantly alert, Grace protested, "Oh, no, Mr. Madrix,

she's fine. She's a darling, very cooperative and hardworking. But she could do with a little relaxation. Would you consider permitting her to ride? I think she misses it."

"Of course she does! That's an oversight. Call my office this afternoon and we'll see to the arrangements. The child should have her riding—by all means! Too bad we can't arrange for it right here, but maybe the change of scene'll do her good."

Tana had garnered a small victory. When not on call, which was infrequent, she would be at liberty to ride. Arrangements were for Mr. Havershaw and a studio guard to accompany her on the bridle paths; and even though neither man presented temptation, their company was preferable to the steady diet of Grace Burke and the studio.

Mr. Madrix was unrelenting. He took no chances and Tana was wrapped in cotton wadding, manipulated, seen but not heard, continually treated as if she were an empty-headed doll, unable to make decisions on her own behalf. The gall of it was corroding and revolt began to brew.

There had to be a way out and she scoured every possibility. An avenue opened up when, one cold and chilly dawn, half asleep in a makeup chair, Tana opened her eyes to find herself the center of concerned attention. The people around behaved as if the roof had fallen in—she had an erruption on her chin. The studio doctor would have to be consulted, and Grace, all atwitter, was being blamed for having been lax with Tana's diet. Seeing the seriousness with which a few pimples were being regarded, Tana broke into a fit of irrepressible giggles and immediately began to plot mischief. What would they do if she complained of pains in her side? They were in the middle of the picture and she could hold up production . . . she didn't want to do anything so radical, but if things continued this way, she'd resort to it. However, the idea gave her incentive, and as a first step toward breaking loose she spoke to Grace about her cousin Lilly Fazon whom she planned to invite for a visit. She wrote Lilly a long letter and took the precaution of omitting a return address and mailing the letter herself.

Tana's skin cleared up. Life was unremittingly boring and she had just about decided to risk open rebellion when, by chance, she overheard Grace on the telephone setting up an appointment with Dane Haddra, one of the film colony's foremost couturiers. Seeking her out when she had finished, Grace informed Tana, "Plans are afoot to bring you out socially, and we're at liberty to order an entire wardrobe for you. You're a lucky girl—it isn't just anyone who gets Dane Haddra to design her clothes."

Tana was in high spirits as she and Grace walked along the quiet Beverly Hills street lined with exclusive shops. She was like a child gazing at enchantments as she peered into the windows of the fashionable shops.

Inside the Haddra establishment, the elegant atmosphere and haughty sales staff made her feel out of place, and for the first time in a long while she was happy to have Grace by her side. The tall, suave man who awaited them as they stepped out of the elevator took Tana's breath away as he kissed her hand. "Welcome, mademoiselle . . . you are even more beautiful than I have been told."

Ill at ease, she blushed, reminded of the stories she had read about the famous designer. Handsome, blond Dane Haddra with the physique of an athlete was also known as an international playboy. Women vied for his attentions and he was considered a ladies' man, always in demand at fashionable parties and soirees. He'd been married to a rich, much-publicized society debutante from whom he was presently being divorced. Constantly mentioned in gossip columns, he enjoyed being in the limelight, singling out daring and well-known beauties to escort. Tana had never dreamed of meeting anyone like him and she found his charm and attention exciting.

As soon as the amenities were over, he got to the business at hand, explaining, "Your studio has laid down guidelines for the way they think you should be dressed. However, now that I see you, I'm not in accord. I will probably do your clothes differently, but possibly we can compromise and please everyone."

Tana nodded, hanging on his every word. Picking up her hand, he asked, "Are there any ideas in your lovely head that you would like to suggest?"

As he talked he removed his jacket and tie, and his monogrammed silk shirt, open at the neck, clung to his chest, making it difficult for Tana to concentrate on what he was saying. Taking a champagne bottle from an ice bucket, he filled three glasses, handing each of them a goblet. Smiling, he ordered, "While you sip, Miss Corgan, remove your dress . . . we are ready to work."

Flustered, Tana hesitated, looking around. The private salon they were in was hung from floor to ceiling in soft-hued silk draperies, but there was no fitting room to be seen. He was waiting. She handed Grace the glass and slipped out of her dress. Embarrassed, she felt nude, although she was wearing her prettiest silk slip.

He stood to one side appraising her and then motioned for her to step on a raised dais that stood in the middle of the room. Her heart was beating like a trip-hammer . . . the nearness of this man and champagne at eleven in the morning made it difficult to maintain her poise. He moved toward her, holding a measuring tape, and said, "Now, turn slowly until I tell you to stop . . . here!" He took her glass from Grace and returned it to her. "A small figure but excellent proportions. All right, we begin."

Without more ado he proceeded to take her measurements. Handling her as if she were an inanimate statue, he turned and twisted her, measuring bosom, waist and crotch to legs, making notes as he went along. Disconcerted by the liberties he was taking, she blushed, and he chuckled. "You ladies are all the same. For the moment it's your dimensions I'm interested in . . . and I must compliment you—for such a small figure they are excellent."

Wanting desperately to impress him, and humiliated by the studio again interceding with orders for how they wanted her dressed, she suddenly blurted, "Who is to pay for this wardrobe, Mr. Haddra?"

He looked at her curiously. "Such a strange question, Miss Corgan. I assumed the studio was planning to pick up the cost. They've given me carte blanche . . . what did you think?"

Laughing sheepishly, she tossed her head as Grace intervened. "Of course, Tana. Where did you get the notion you might be responsible?"

"Of course . . . the studio. Wherever did I get the idea I might be responsible?"

Catching the implication, Haddra winked at her as she added, "Knowing your reputation, Mr. Haddra, I was worried that, with all you are going to design for me, I might not be able to afford your prices." Her laugh tinkled through the room. "Since the studio is picking up the bill, the sky's the limit, and I leave myself in your hands."

He handed her more champagne. "You are even lovelier when you worry . . . but you mustn't crease your forehead. Now I'm going to have one of my assistants show you some of the fabrics we will work from . . . and, if you don't mind, we will throw that out . . ." He pointed to the dress she had been wearing . . . "I have a little frock that will look divine on you—a nip and a tuck and it will fit you perfectly. What do you say to that?"

Not in the least offended at his reference to her taste, she beamed at him delightedly. "I'd love it."

"Splendid! From now on, little one, you will be a stunning example of Haddra design."

Turning her back to Grace, she said softly, "It will be my pleasure, but please, Mr. Haddra, please . . . no matter what the studio says, don't dress me like Shirley Temple."

He doubled over with laughter. "No fear of that, my adorable one."

When the fittings were concluded, Grace, giddy from the amount of champagne she had imbibed, surprised Tana. "What do you say, dear, to our celebrating? As long as we have this free day, let's have luncheon out."

Tana was thrilled and Grace asked, "Would you like to try Chasens? I could call for a reservation. Do you like chili?"

The idea of going to an elegant restaurant for chili astounded Tana—it was a common staple back home in Montana. It made no difference; the important thing was that she would be lunching in a restaurant frequented by Hollywood's famous.

She felt transformed. Dressed in the simple but modish mauve silk dress that clung to her figure like a glove and heightened the color of her eyes, she had a new cloche hat, bag, shoes and gloves, topped off by a long strand of pearls that Dane Haddra had clasped for her along with a quick kiss on the back of her neck. Grace's admiration bubbled over. "I've never seen you look this beautiful! The man's a genius . . . isn't he a darling?"

Tana grinned, feeling happier than she'd been in a long while.

As their car stopped in front of the restaurant, a tour bus pulled up behind them, rapidly disgorging its passengers. They and a group of passersby lined up to gawk as the chauffeur helped the two women alight. A buzz of excitement ran through the crowd, and as Tana followed Grace through the entrance she looked back in amazement and asked, "Grace, who are they waiting for?"

Grace tittered and whispered, "You precious silly, they were watching you. Everyone wants to see film stars."

Tana looked at her in disbelief. "Come on, Grace—the picture isn't even completed yet."

"My dear, with the exposure and publicity you've had people are bound to recognize Tana Corgan. It won't matter if you do nothing for a while; you're a celebrity!"

Grace Burke had no way of knowing she'd set a buzzer off in Tana's head. Up to this point the embryonic actress had felt compelled to acquiesce and comply, but with this sort of recognition things were certainly going to change. She wasn't going to have to play games, pretend to be sick—no more of that! She felt a surge of power course through her. What sort of idiot did those studio people take her for? What right did they have to control her every move, deprive her of the right to choose her own clothes or see her friends and keep her locked up as if she were a prisoner? Her brain began to click as she realized the weapon she now had over them.

Back at home later that afternoon while Grace was otherwise occupied, Tana made a call to her agent. It took a few moments for him to realize the angry voice he was hearing emanated from young Tana Corgan. He was shocked when he realized the import of what she was saying, and when she'd finished he tried to make her see reason. "It's too soon, Tana. Don't make them angry. Remember when we discussed all this and you agreed not to let this go to your head?"

"Yes, but they're not being fair."

He said quietly, "I really think it's in your best interest to go along as you've been doing. Don't rock the boat. Take my word, you might regret it."

Badly disappointed, she ended the conversation. She had banked on Mr. Michalson's being her ally, but there was going to be little help from that quarter. Her only hope now was her mother. If she could get Deirdre's dander up, they'd be forced to listen. There was no doubt in Tana's mind about the feasibility of this plan. Her mother wouldn't pussyfoot around; if anyone could straighten matters out, she'd be the one to do it. Much to Tana's disappointment her mother had had to postpone her departure date, but she'd be on her way soon. Until then Tana had no recourse but to put up with things as they were.

One evening, bored and looking for something to do, she wrote to Lilly Fazon again, hinting that she would soon be in a position to do something for her if she was still interested.

This time Tana was no longer afraid to enclose her return address. Lilly answered quickly, saying she wasn't certain she cared to pursue a movie career any longer but was giving thought to returning to California where work opportunities were better. She was thrilled at her friend's success; she'd always known that if anyone could make it she'd be the one. Tana had put the letter in a dresser drawer and subsequently saw it had been taken out of the envelope. She was furious at the thought that Grace had gone through her personal things and for days after was hardly civil to her.

There was no break in the monotony of her life. Even though she enjoyed her work, she needed company of her own age and the chance to enjoy the good things that had happened to her. She couldn't understand why living a normal life would destroy the image the studio wanted to create. It was small satisfaction knowing the charade she'd played had fooled everyone.

One evening when they arrived home earlier than usual, Tana suggested to Grace, "Why don't we go to a movie? I'm dying to see that new Joan Crawford picture."

Instantly Grace was all aflutter. "I'd love it, dear, but I don't know if we dare. The studio might not like it. I have to ask and I'm afraid it's too late to catch anyone. I'll send Maria out for some ice cream and we can have it while we listen to the Jack Benny program. How about that?"

Disgustedly Tana snapped, "Forget it—don't bother! How long is this going to go on? You'd think I was a prisoner. Aren't we supposed to have any fun at all?"

Surprisingly Grace was sympathetic. "You're right, honey. It's not fair to keep you cooped up this way. But, if you promise to keep it a secret, I'll tell you something I heard. Just today I got wind the studio is planning to have us attend a major opening next week. That's when your new gowns are going to be ready."

Distracted, Tana forgot her irritation. "Tell me about it. Do you know where we're going? Who do you think they'll get to escort us?"

Grace promised to get as many details as she could. The anticipation of finally being free to see and be seen was foremost on Tana's mind. At last she would have a chance to savor her newly acquired status. Movie openings were gala events, with crowds of fans, newspeople and cameras; she visualized herself making a grand entrance and pictured how she would look with her hair swept up, a gardenia nestling in it . . . silk slippers peeking out beneath her gown of violet chiffon encrusted with shimmering crystal beads and ostrich plumes on the flowing cape sleeves and hem. Her smile would be warm and embracing as she walked up the red carpet on the arm of the man escorting her through the cheering crowd. The man, of course, closely resembled Dane Haddra.

Maybe some of her former friends would be there watching. She often wondered what they thought when they read stories about her. She was sure they assumed she was snubbing them. She wished she'd been honest with Lilly when she'd first written and asked her advice. Even though Lilly couldn't help herself, she'd been smart when it came to helping her. Tana was often tempted to telephone her friend, but with Grace always close by, eavesdropping on her conversation, it would be wiser not to attempt it. Grace would surely report it to Mr. Madrix.

The thought of her mother sustained her. Her face was the bright light at the end of the tunnel, and Tana's joy knew no bounds when the letter came with the date and time of Deirdre's arrival. Her mother would join her the following Sunday. The girl could barely control her impatience.

Grace Burke planned to accompany Tana when she picked up her mother. It was late Saturday evening when she discovered the girl had no intention of letting her come along. Tana had deliberately waited until it was too late for Grace to notify anyone about her decision. It precipitated a fierce argument when Grace cheerily said, "We'll have to be up bright and early to meet the train, won't we, dear?"

"Not 'we,' Grace. You can sleep late—you deserve it. You're not coming with me when I pick up my mother. I plan to do that all by myself. I haven't seen my mother in a long time, and our reunion is going to be private. Nowhere in my contract is there anything that says the studio has the right to know what mother and daughter say to each other. Come on—be fair! Admit that I'm entitled to some personal life—to be with my own mother without someone snooping around. I'm fed up with it, Grace, and by now you should be too!"

Embarrassed by the girl's directness, Grace spluttered, "But, Tana, you know how the studio feels about your going anywhere alone. I simply must—"

Tana snapped, "To hell with the studio! I'm sick and tired of hearing 'the studio says, the studio wants.' I don't give a darn! Nothing is going to happen to me. The chauffeur is capable of keeping the wild hordes off my back. He can take care of anything that needs to be done. No more discussion: I've made up my mind—this is it!"

Tearfully, Grace wailed, "Oh, Tana, honey, what will the studio say? They'll have my job if I don't go with you."

"Don't make me sick. Do you think I'm a fool? I know better than that—you're a very good jailer. Tell 'em the truth. Tell 'em I'm tired of seeing your face, of having you hang over me, spying on everything I do and say, reading my mail. It's nauseating. My goodness, Grace, tell the truth, doesn't it make you crazy too?"

Flustered, the woman sniffled and dried her tears. "You're right, hon . . . absolutely right! It's awful for both of us. If you weren't such an angel I'd have lost my mind a long time ago. Go ahead. There's no need for them to know, but for God's sake stay out of trouble."

"Trouble? What kind of trouble? I'm being driven to the station to pick up my mother and bring her here. I haven't any plans to elope."

"Heaven forbid!" Grace tittered. "You go along by yourself; I'll see that your mother's room is prettied up, fresh flowers and sachets. What sort of candies does she like, Tana?"

Tana chuckled devilishly. "You know, Grace, you're going to have your work cut out for you with my mother here. Be warned, she's not going to like your breathing down my back. Remember, she's my mother and she's got her own ways. Take my advice and stay out of her hair."

Aghast at what she was hearing, Grace sensed something was afoot—rebellion in the making. She'd have to tell Mr. Madrix Tana was getting out of hand. As matters evolved, poor Grace got more than she bargained for, and it happened fast and furiously.

Alone in the quiet comfort of the car the next morning, Tana leaned back luxuriating in her privacy. Her excitement was mounting; she was at fever pitch to see Deirdre, to tell her all she had kept stored up. In spite of everything, she'd been homesick, she'd missed her family. It had been so long since she'd heard her dad's teasing, been free to roam and see the wide expanse of sky and ride the beautiful open spaces.

Mother and daughter flew into each other's arms. There was no memory of the unpleasantness that had spoiled their last days together as Tana cried, "Mother, Mother, you're a sight for sore eyes! I've missed you so much—been so lonesome for you and Dad!"

Deirdre held her daughter at arm's length, studying her. " 'Tis a sight for me old eyes you are, me gorgous darlin. My, my, don you look a pitchur. If 'tis possible, you be even prettier than you were. Who's that man hoverin round us—that one all gussied up?"

Laughing gaily, Tana explained, "Mother o mine, 'tis me chauffeur. Wait till you see me car." She motioned to the man to come nearer. "Ray, I'd like you to meet my mother, Mrs. Corrigan. Here are her baggage tickets. We'll wait for you in the car."

Smiling in response, the chauffeur said, "Pleased to make your acquaintance, ma'am. Miss Corgan, if you don't mind, I think we'd best be getting out of here. There's a crowd gathering. I'll see you to the car and we'll drive over to the baggage area. There's apt to be less disturbance doing that."

Tana gave him an impish grin. "Ray, don't fool me. I know Mrs. Burke put you up to this."

He grinned back at her. "Not at all, miss. See for yourself."

Tana and Deirdre turned to see a group of people standing nearby watching them. Tana conceded, "Right you are, Ray. Shall I wave as we go?"

"It's not necessary, miss. Just follow me, please."

He made a path through the growing crowd as the two women followed him. Deirdre gasped as she saw the limousine. "Saints alive, Tana . . . don't tell me!"

Ray opened the car door, and after they got in he ran around the other side to drive off.

Pointing to the curious faces staring through the car windows, Tana said, "Look, Mother, they're not even sure who I am, but like sheep they follow."

Deirdre's eyebrow raised. "Tana, m'darlin, 'tis no so long ago you'd've done the same. 'Tis the look o the car draws 'em."

They laughed heartily and Tana took her mother's hand to hold it in her own. As the car moved off, Tana turned to her mother. "You're in for a batch of surprises, Mother, but I've got to tell you about the biggest one before we get home. We can speak freely in here; Ray can't hear with the window up between us."

Deirdre squeezed her daughter's hand and said with amazement, "Daughter, 'tis a rich new life you be leadin. 'Tis a far cry from the way 'twas when I left you last. My, my, your dad and I often be wonderin if you be happy now you have what you been dreamin of. Can you tell me here what 'tis so urgent you have on your mind?"

"The reason I've got to tell you this before we get home is because I've a beastie hanging over me every minute of the day and night, guarding me."

Incredulously Deirdre asked, "This chauffeur man?"

"No, Mother darling, he's a good fellow, just the chauffeur doing his job. It's a dragon lady breathing fire and waiting for us to get home. You remember when I had her speak to you?"

Deirdre studied her daughter carefully; something was very wrong. "Start from the beginnin, me heart, and don be leavin the tiniest bit out. I be wantin to hear everythin. . . ."

The familiar face, creased with sympathy and concern, eased Tana's mind. She had only one fear: her mother might be swayed by the comfort and luxury she saw surrounding her daughter and the good intent of those supervising her career. Somehow Tana had to convince her that no matter what the studio said, she didn't need her to be a replacement for Grace Burke. It would be intolerable if her mother assumed the role of another watchdog . . . she had to see her child was capable of taking care of herself. But foremost she had to be persuaded that some aspects of her daughter's new life were a nightmare . . . that from the moment it had begun, she'd been made a prisoner—strangers had taken over, issuing orders, commands and ultimatums. She'd been pummeled, pounded and molded into something they insisted was for her own good. Her mother had to understand that even though it had been a difficult pill to swallow, Tana had been wise enough to cooperate, to submit and go along with it, and in doing so had suffered as she never had before, and now this programming of her life had to cease.

Thinking about it and overflowing with misery, Tana spewed out the story. The more her daughter's tale unfolded, the more upset Deirdre became. Finished, the girl crumpled in a heap on her mother's shoulder, crying. "Mother, darling, I've been needing you so badly."

"Deed you have, lass . . . that's plain to be seen. Sich nonsense—'tis hard to believe grown people carryin on so peculiar. Well, don be frettin longer, baby. Sure an we'll be gettin it all fixed up."

A smiling Grace Burke awaited them at the door, but, despite her cordial greeting, Mrs. Corrigan's response was cold and distant. Instantly Grace knew trouble was brewing. Tana's mother was already up in arms, and it was not Grace's job to tangle with her. Her charge had obviously been laying the groundwork. Mr. Madrix would have to be informed as soon as possible. Grace tactfully avoided the two until lunch was announced.

At the table Grace made several attempts at being friendly, but, although polite, Mrs. Corrigan resisted her overtures. Grace was startled when, after a while, Deirdre suddenly addressed her. "Mrs. Burke, I think you should be knowin I'll be seein your Mr. Madrix tomorrow."

Grace's face froze in a half smile as she said, "I'm sure he'll be delighted to meet you, Mrs. Corrigan, but Tana had better set up an appointment. He's a terribly busy man."

Buttering a roll, Deirdre took her time before answering. "I take your good advice kindly and me daughter can do that if she think it be necessary, but I'll be seein him one way or t'other tomorrow. There's lots o busy folk about, good lady. I take no offense your tellin me that . . . 'tis just that the makin o pitchurs be not the most importan thin in the world, leastwise to me."

Grace flushed with the rebuke. She was annoyed; instead of showing gratitude for what she had done on behalf of her daughter, the woman was intensely angry. Grace wondered what Tana had said to cause her mother to behave in this fashion. It was apparent Mrs. Corrigan could be pleasant if she chose. She seemed to have taken a fancy to Maria, who was serving them. Keeping her composure, Grace issued orders to Maria about the menu for dinner and caught a sympathetic exchange of glances between the maid and Deirdre. Discomforted, Grace rose and was about to excuse herself from the table when Deirdre spoke. "I'd like a word with you, Mrs. Burke."

Reseating herself, Grace said icily, "Of course, I'm at your service." She averted her head, not wanting to look at Tana, who sat watching as if she were an innocent bystander.

Deirdre said, with a touch of irony, "First, it'll be thanks I'll be sayin for takin sich good care o my girl here, and next I'll be tellin you we'll no longer be requirin your services."

Grace gasped audibly and retorted angrily, "I don't think you understand, Mrs. Corrigan—that's not up to you! You can't be dismissing me like some rude country girl."

Deirdre stared at her scathingly. " 'Tis my notion that Polly here, or Tana as she be called, be free, white and female and, if she be needin care, thank the good Lord, she's got a mother willin and able to do jist that!"

Resentfully Grace argued, "Good and all, but that's not what I'm supposed to be doing for her. It's the movie end of things I'm here to oversee."

Deirdre had her. "If that be the case, me good woman, how come you've been keepin her tied to your apron strings? 'Tis a lot o foolishness been goin on from what I can see. Where's the sense keepin a young colt like this locked up, with no fun, no laughter? She be but a broth of a girl. 'Tis inhuman you all are. We'll be puttin an end to that sort o thing!"

Deirdre seemed ten feet tall as she shook her finger at Grace Burke. Her voice was coldly furious as she scolded, "You be no friend for a young lass. 'Tis one thin to be carin for her interests, but tis another to be considered the only one fit for her company. My Polly may be suitable for a movie star, but she be human, not a thing."

Exceedingly upset, Grace pushed her chair back, hastily excused herself and tearfully left the table.

Gene Madrix had agreed to meet with Mrs. Corrigan after being alerted to the urgency of the matter by a distraught Grace Burke. Not a man who easily changed his mind once he had it set, he found this firebrand of a woman sitting across from him amazingly persuasive, with a tongue that went like a trip-hammer.

Captivated by her brogue, he chuckled inwardly at the quaint earthy way she put the problem and he decided a concession or two wouldn't hurt. The fact was that the studio was getting ready to show Tana in public, and although he remained implacable about her being seen in the company of young men, women friends wouldn't hurt. In fact it would probably enhance her press image; Tana could be presented as a loyal, unaffected girl who didn't forget family and old friends when success came along. Mother and daughter in tandem would provide a stimulant for a jaded publicity department.

Smiling broadly, he smacked the desktop with the flat of his hand. "Mother Corrigan, you've got a point. I'm willing to give a little if you will too. Be fair . . . despite your complaints, it's been a great responsibility to care for Tana. She is still a minor and she is young and inexperienced. How would you have felt if we had left her exposed to all the things that could have happened? You have no idea of the hazards surrounding her and what unscrupulous people will do to attach themselves to someone on the rise in this business. You're a practical woman, and even if you're unfamiliar with our procedures, you're sharp enough to understand we're not only protecting our interests but Tana's as well. Frankly, you should be grateful to us, and particularly to Mrs. Burke, who was only following orders. She will be leaving the house today."

Deirdre's face broke into a winning smile. "There you go. 'Tis a most kindhearted, reasonable man you are, Mr. Madrix. I won't be takin any more o your valuable time, now we've settled things."

She rose to go and Gene Madrix escorted her to the door, stopping her as a thought occurred to him. "Pardon my asking, but does your wardrobe include formal clothes?"

Her face crinkled in a wry smile. "Now what would I be doin with the like o sich on a ranch?"

"Of course, I understand. I hope you won't take this amiss but, since you will be chaperoning Tana to the opening of a new film next week, and there will also be a round of parties coming up, you will need a suitable wardrobe. I'll have my secretary arrange matters with Tana's designer so that you'll have the appropriate gowns. Will you like that?"

" 'Tis a windfall, Mr. Madrix. I'll look forward to it." She looked at him coyly. "I can't say me Sean will like anither man outfittin me, but I guess under the circumstances 'twill be all right." On this pleasant note, they parted.

Later that same afternoon, repentant and friendly, Deirdre made a point of expressing her gratitude to Grace Burke. " 'Tis me sincere hope you'll be forgivin me if I sounded harsh. 'Tis the truth I didna fully understand and I'm hopin we can be friends."

The moment was warm and Tana impulsively threw her arms around the woman. "Gracie, it will seem strange without you."

In the instant all the unpleasantness was forgotten and they parted friends, with Grace promising to do whatever she could to assist the two women thread their way into the new and glamorous world awaiting them. With a twinkle in her eyes she assured them, "You won't have to worry . . . I won't be stepping on anyone's toes."

In the days that followed, Deirdre Corrigan found herself enormously involved in caring for Tana's affairs. A meeting with Ralph Michalson left Deirdre in shock. She'd had no idea about the money Tana was amassing. He, for his part, was delighted to have someone personally involved with whom he could share the responsibility for its investment. At his suggestion, it was decided that if the studio was willing, Tana should buy the house in which she was living. Mr. Michalson also advised that Tana purchase a ranch in the San Fernando Valley, which he considered a good investment for the future.

The two got along amicably and Deirdre wrote Sean, " 'Tis the Lord's hand watches over our child. Good people have been interested in carin for her and furtherin her career. The agent man thinks 'twould be a good idea for yourself to come here and check out some thins such as the ranch and land he thinks to buy for our girl. Polly knows naught of business matters and just signs papers as ordered. 'Tis not much more I know meself, me darlin. 'Tis my opinion, Sean, 'twould be wise to be closer at hand for all these matters. Polly wonders if you might not like to move here to the new ranch. We can discuss all this, Lord willin, when you come for holiday."

Tana was occupied at the studio and Deirdre had her hands full with household and business affairs; matters were piling up. Ralph Michalson advised them, "Hire a secretary. From here on it will be necessary to have someone taking care of appointments and the hundreds of other things that will crop up. The studio will help where it can, but it's necessary you have someone close at hand to relieve you."

As Tana and Deirdre were debating the best way to go about acquiring someone, a letter arrived from Lilly Fazon announcing she would be in Los Angeles the following week. She planned to stay at the old hotel and start her search for work as soon as she was settled.

After Tana had read the letter aloud to her mother, they both reached the same conclusion. "Poor lamb," Deirdre commiserated. "All she be goin through . . . her mither and sister so sick 'n' all . . . 'twill be a blessin for you t'be takin her on . . . her bein your friend so faithful 'n' proud o you too."

It would be an excellent solution and, at Deirdre's urging, Tana happily raced to the telephone to ask her friend if she'd be interested. Lilly was ecstatic at the offer and couldn't believe her good fortune. Her own voice jubilant, Tana told her, "I'll be working but Mother will pick you up at the station . . . you'll be living with us. Oh, Lilly, I can't wait to see you!"

The night of Lilly's arrival Deirdre tactfully withdrew, leaving the two happy girls alone to catch up on each other's news. She was a contented mother as she saw the lighthearted change in her daughter. A load had been lifted from her back; with Lilly on hand, Tana would have competent assistance and a friend on whose allegiance she could rely.

Adapting easily, in a short while Lilly became a part of their lives, fitting into the household as if she'd always been there, ministering to Tana's burgeoning affairs quietly and capably. Mr. Michalson approved the decision and arranged a good monthly salary for the secretarial work.

Lilly seemed so grateful for the opportunity and happy with the position it never occurred to Deirdre that, as her dedication to Tana grew, so did an obsession. Lilly took a vicarious pride in Tana's success; she understood the pitfalls and problems attendant upon her friend's career. It was only natural that this bound them closer, gave them one more thing to share in common. As her possessiveness of Tana increased, she took over completely—whatever mattered to Tana was paramount to anything in Lilly Fazon's life. The more entrenched she became, the more her annoyance showed over what she considered incursions on her rights.

It became blatantly noticeable whenever Deirdre and Tana had occasion to exclude her. In time Lilly's attitude began to manifest itself toward Deirdre, who was at a loss to understand why suddenly it was so difficult to get along with Lilly. One day she overstepped herself when Deirdre forgot to give her a telephone message received when she was out. Lilly reprimanded her harshly. "You're very careless about your daughter's affairs, Mrs. Corrigan. It seems you can't be trusted with any responsibility. You were lucky this time. Don't let it happen again or I'll have to take it up with Tana."

Shocked at the manner in which the young woman took her to task, Deirdre walked off in a huff. She was becoming uneasy about Lilly's attitude. It seemed to Deirdre she manifested more than devotion—it was as if she wanted to draw every breath for her daughter. She circled around Tana like the moon around the earth and padded after her in worshipful obeisance. Lilly's behavior was certainly curious. Then Deirdre remembered Mr. Madrix's words about the peculiar behavior of people who latched on to celebrities.

A pragmatic woman, Deirdre was not one to put up with nonsense or nurse a grudge if it could be avoided, so when she calmed down she sought Lilly out and told her, "'Tis not that I don appreciate how good a job you be doin and how you care for me girl, Lilly, but 'tis another thin when you go too far and bite the hand that feeds you. There be no need to be threatenin me. I be Tana's mother and be expectin you to show respect. So, please, watch how you speak to me in future." She smiled. "We both be lovin the same girl, so let's make our peace and be friends." Deirdre was unaware Lilly would neither forgive nor forget.

Despite her desire to be free of restraints and do as she wished, Tana didn't have time. She was completely tied down by work, involved to the hilt of her capabilities.

It was mandatory for her to appear at film social events, and Deirdre was relieved that she was no longer obliged to act as chaperone. Escorts were provided by the studio, and bland young men, impeccably attired, would arrive at the door, proffering the proper corsage, to escort Tana Corgan, all expenses paid.

Expertly made up, exquisitely gowned, Tana was breathtakingly beautiful, causing a stir wherever she appeared. Everyone in the know predicted big things for her. The only remaining hurdle as far as she was concerned was the ban on dating men of her choice. The studio remained adamant, but fortunately, except for Dane Haddra, she had not met anyone who aroused her interest.

Southern War was in the final stages of production when the Japanese bombed Pearl Harbor and war was declared. Consternation reigned everywhere. Work on the film was halted temporarily and several young men in the cast were called up for immediate service. At the studio's request, Ron Douglas was granted a deferment so that the picture might be completed.

Wartime restrictions and blackouts were put into immediate effect and incursions on everyone's life became daily occurrences. Commonplace things normally taken for granted, such as food and gasoline, took on new importance. Tana's beautifully tended grounds showed neglect as her gardener and the other Japanese Americans were rounded up for shipment to Manzanar Internment Camp to be incarcerated in tar-paper barracks behind barbed wire and armed guards. War hysteria was at its height; inflammatory rumors circulated everywhere. People were beset by fear, and the blackness of the nights heightened the darkness pressing on everyone's soul.

In the midst of all this, Tana and Ron were enacting their final love scenes. Kindled by the knowledge of Ron's impending departure, both young people were moved by such genuine affection and tenderness that there wasn't a dry eye on the set.

Southern War was finished and those who previewed it predicted it would be a blockbuster. Instantly word got out that the love scenes between Tana Corgan and Ron Douglas were the most poignant ever filmed. Due to the precarious war situation, the studio made preparations for an immediate release. The trumpets blew, publicity heralded the event and, despite the horrifying battle headlines shadowing everyone's life, the film opened to rave reviews. It was what the public needed—good escape fare.

Tana Corgan had more than fulfilled Gene Madrix's hopes. The consensus was that a new star lit up the Hollywood firmanment—one with acting ability as well as beauty and style. The reviews without exception were laudatory. The critics lavished praise on the young woman who, in her first feature film, enraptured them all with her youthful beauty and convincing performance. Once again the name of Tana Corgan made headlines and she became the instant darling of the columnists and film magazines and was courted and fawned over by everyone.

Sean Corrigan, who had come on a visit, was amazed to find his family the center of such attention. He and Deirdre were no longer simply the mother and father of Polly Sue Corrigan, but had been promoted to the role of parenting Tana Corgan, movie star.

Despite the war and its intrusions, they were swept into a glittering tinsel world of glamor. Tana and Ron Douglas had become celebrities, and attendant upon this were demands for their time. Invitations poured in, the press pleaded for interviews and there were rounds of parties and events attended by the notables of the film world rounded up to pay tribute to the young people's newly achieved triumph.

Feted and lionized, Tana and Ron became for a while Hollywood's favorite breakfast topic as speculation about a romance between them ran high. Hedda and Louella vied with each other for scoops and inside information about the twosome. They made a stunning young couple, and the studio approved of their being seen together. It was disappointing to Tana that in their secluded moments, aside from a quick goodnight kiss, Ron made no other gestures toward romance. She gave him every opportunity, flirting outrageously, but he seemed content to leave matters as they had been before.

Ron left for service, and as the furor died down Tana was granted a few weeks of respite from work and she and her parents were free to do and go wherever they desired. For Tana the ultimate joy was being allowed to live her own life—of course within the bounds of discretion. It was assumed she had been properly inculcated in the things expected of her.

At the end of her vacation period she was called into conference with Mr. Madrix and introduced to the director of her upcoming picture. This time it was a poised and confident young woman who greeted him, and Gene Madrix was taken back by her new presence. It struck him Tana had a strangely contrasted nature: while she appeared innocent, she was not a guileless girl, but an avid, sensual woman with a sumptuous body. He felt better about the wisdom of his decision as he explained that henceforth she would be given a wider range of roles, more worldly and sophisticated. Her original image would be scrapped. She would no longer be limited by wholesomeness and innocence. At this her face broke into smiles, and once again he saw traces of a childlike girl. Her next picture would be a contemporary love story—she would be the star and a script was ready for her to study. Rehearsals would begin within two weeks.

Back on a set again, for a while Tana seemed the same sweet and willing person she had been, but occasional flashes of temperament began to appear. It was a though she would suddenly realize she was a star and certain things were due her. It would have taken a stronger nature than hers to have withstood the attention lavished on her. She made a fuss over her dressing room, demanding a larger one, but it was when the name of Illona Lassen was mentioned as a replacement for an ailing actress that she threw her weight around. She asked for an immediate appointment with the director and, trying cajolery at the start, asked him not to put Illona Lassen in the picture, describing their prior difficulties. When he seemed to dismiss this, assuring Tana he could handle the matter, she became autocratic and angry. "In view of what I've done for them, it's the least the studio can do for me. If that woman works in this picture, I won't!"

With a rueful smile the director conceded and agreed to

find someone else. Instantly she became pliable and cooperative again.

Overnight Tana had become the studio's darling. She was a
valuable property; her parents were accustomed to humoring
her, and Lilly was a constant source of fuel for her ego. She
was being spoiled to the point of corruption. At the moment
there was no one who wished to lower the boom, and with no
one to deny it Tana began to believe her own publicity. A
mother who doted on her, fulfilling every wish; a studio that
gave in to every request . . . she lived a capricious, problem-
free life and assumed she was God's gift to the world.

Breakfast in the studio commisary was eye-boggling for
the two Griffon men. Bill kept hounding his brother. "Jonathan you're not supposed to be looking—you're on your
honeymoon. Better not let Em catch you."

The young Griffons had all managed to reach Los Angeles
at the same time and the reunion the night before had been a
happy one.

Attired in a well-tailored, dashing brown captain's uniform, Bill was in the Special Services branch of the Army.
Surveying the room around them, he remarked, "I can see
I'm not going to suffer. Commuting from East to West won't
be hard to take."

Joshing, his brother remarked, "Well, apart from doing
your patriotic duty, it can't have hurt to come from a family
that owns a chunk of Major Pictures' stock."

"Darn tootin'. Don't think the army's dumb," Bill said. "It
gives me an inside track producing documentaries. Heck,
I'm sorry Em couldn't make it this morning. I think she'd
have gotten a kick out of seeing all this."

His mouth full, Jonathan nodded and swallowed. "We went
to bed so late I didn't have the heart to wake her. She'll see it
another time. Bill—look! Over there! That girl!"

Turning quickly to see where his brother was pointing, Bill
saw only the backs of a crowd of people leaving. "Which
girl?"

"That one, going through the door. She's out now. For a
moment I could have sworn it was Em."

Bill laughed. "You got it bad, brother. Everywhere you
look you see that wife of yours."

Jonathan shook his head, puzzled. "It was just a fleeting
impression . . ."

"I'm glad you two are married . . . Em's a special person," Bill said soberly. "I'm glad you stood up to Mother."

"Did she tell you the whole gory story?"

Chuckling, Bill said, "You know Mom. It sounded interesting."

Jon smiled. "Well, evidently Em has two sisters . . . they've been separated since they were children. She won't rest until she's located them. There's an investigator on the case now."

Nodding as he drank his coffee, Bill asked, "What's on the schedule for this afternoon? I've got a tank of gas and we can tour around a bit . . . want to do that?"

"Sure . . . we'll pick up Em and go. Don't forget we have a dinner reservation at Romanoff's tonight." And the beautiful young woman he had just noticed fleetingly disappeared from his mind.

Chapter XVIII

◅─◈─▻

AMY BETH:
THE RITE OF PASSAGE

THEY WERE DISAPPOINTED with her, Amy Beth could see clearly. Emmy frowned disapprovingly and Amy's heart sank as she reached down to touch the baby. Polly Sue let out a yowl, her little hands shoving her away. All that time, that woman, her mother—Mary Ann Forbes—sat there leering, watching as Emmalina scolded, wanting Amy to apologize. The woman, her face contorted in an ugly grimace, grabbed at Amy to embrace her. Screaming, struggling to push her away, Amy Beth woke with a start to find Deborah holding her, trying to calm her. Her nightmares were becoming recurrent, each one more horrible than the last. Deborah spoke soothingly, the concern visible on her face. "It's all right, Amy Beth—nothin here to fright you so. I gotchu some milk warmin on the stove. Sit up and clear your head."

Amy Beth leaned back on the pillow, exhausted. She was beginning to show the wear of sleepless nights. Barbara had suggested she see the plant doctor and get some pills to help her sleep, but Amy Beth was afraid they'd make her worse, she'd have trouble rousing from the horror of her dreams.

Deborah came in with the cup of milk in her hand. "Feelin better? Mebbe you oughta see a doctor. Whatever it is botherin you ain't gettin better, gal."

Wearily Amy Beth accepted the glass. "I'm sorry I woke you again, Momma. Was I screaming loud?"

"Betchu the neighbors at the end of the block heard you. What's gotchu afrightened so?"

There was no point in telling her. Amy Beth didn't want to reopen that hornets' nest again. It would only add to her difficulties. She made up her mind to see the doctor the next day.

Fortunately he was an older, well-seasoned physician, aware of what trauma could do to the mind and body. Gently he led Amy along and kept her talking until he had the substance of her story. "Nothing to worry about, my dear. You are not losing your mind. You've had a bad shock, and along with what you've already suffered, all those collective miseries, it's no wonder you're undergoing this ordeal. Believe me, just airing it will bring you relief. I'm going to prescribe something that will help you sleep. A few undisturbed nights and the episode will begin to recede."

Relieved, Amy's spirits lifted and, true to the doctor's word, she began to sleep through the nights. Deborah's clumsy efforts at consideration touched her and gave them a commonality of affection. Slowly the episode of Mary Ann Forbes began to fade. It had drifted into the limbo of all the wrenching experiences of her early life when early one morning she picked up the telephone and heard Ted's voice at the other end. She yelled for Deborah. "Mama, Mama, come quick—it's Ted!"

The news was wonderful. Ted was in San Francisco awaiting transfer to the nearby Long Beach Veterans Hospital, probably within the next few weeks. Charged with excitement, Deborah became a dervish working her Red Cross schedule and tearing the house apart. She refused to accept Amy's explanation about Ted's not being able to come home right away. "It makes no matter; mebbe he can and the house'll be ready for him."

Evenings were spent in an orgy of baking; months of sugar rations disappeared into batters of Ted's favorite cookies and cakes. Amy gave up wrangling, sampling and enjoying the fragrant aroma of good things to eat. Observing Deborah happily involved in her chores, Amy thought how changed she was—openly showing her emotions and exposing a caring person hidden beneath the barnacles.

The house shone and the supply of baked goods continued to grow. Looking around, Amy commented wryly, "If Ted doesn't get here soon the furniture will be worn out and we'll be buried under cookies."

Deborah took Amy's jibes good-naturedly, and the evenings in the kitchen were companionable and warm. Recounting the goings-on to Barbara, she said, "There's such a transformation in her I can't believe it—she's actually likable."

The girls continued to spend their Saturdays together, and in the process Amy acquired a new wardrobe. A little self-consciously she began to buy Deborah small gifts. Through the auspices of a co-worker, she was able to latch on to some nylon hosiery, an item in real scarcity, and presented them to Deborah. She was embarrassed by Deborah's delight and gratitude. "Thank you, gal." Reaching over she pecked Amy on the cheek. "I do preciate you, Amy . . . more than you know."

Amy developed her first crush when they saw the movie *Casablanca*. She fell in love with Humphrey Bogart. Up to then she'd idolized Nelson Eddy. Movies had a strong influence on her thinking. She became fashion-conscious and, along with her new clothes and high-heeled shoes, she wore her thick ash-blond hair in a sleek pageboy and touched her lips with pink. She had a winsome beauty; though she smiled often, her large blue eyes were shadowed by a touch of sadness when her face was in repose. Tall and slim, she was delicately boned with a fair and flawless complexion. There was a shy gentleness and grace about her that combined to give her an ethereal loveliness that set her apart. Having watched the caterpillar-to-butterfly changes in her friend, Barbara was impressed. "You've become a stunner, kid. Have you noticed that the guys in the plant whistle when you go by?"

Pleased at the compliment, Amy pretended indifference. "It's flattering, I guess, but I'm waiting for Mr. Right."

It had become customary for the girls to alternate weekends at each other's homes. One weekend, when Barbara came home with Amy, Deborah declared, "You two gals'll have to share your room, Amy. Ted's room took all my strength cleanin and puttin to rights."

Laughing, Amy protested, "But, Momma, it'll be a long time after he gets down here before he'll be able to use it."

"Never you mind, gal . . . that room's not to be touched. I set it up and that's how we'll leave it."

Teasingly Amy retorted, "There you go, Momma! I know I'm hundred percent again . . . you're feisty as ever."

"Now what's that sposed to mean, Amy Beth?"

Looking at her from behind lowered lids, Amy smirked. "Exactly what I said, Momma. You're fighting again! For a while you were so kind and gentle you had me worried, but now you're back to normal. I guess I should thank the Lord for that!"

Almost three weeks later, Ted called from the Long Beach hospital and informed them he could have visitors the next day. They were beside themselves with excitement, and Amy telephoned the plant to say she would not be in to work. Driving toward the hospital, Amy stole a glance at Deborah, who fidgeted and twisted like a two-year-old. "We'll soon be there, Momma. Just hang on and don't go to pieces before we arrive."

At first glimpse they weren't sure it was Ted. He was so wasted and wan the two women had difficulty hiding their shock. As they walked along the portico where Ted's wheel-chair had been placed, Amy cautioned Deborah, "Momma, try not to let him see how upset you are. Keep remembering how he'll fatten up with all those goodies you made for him."

It was hard to remember the boy who had left in the face of the haggard man looking at them from black-rimmed, sunken eyes. He waved his arms as they came nearer. "Mother! Sis!" Deborah broke down, kissing his face, his hands, again and again. Amy stood quietly. Finally Deborah, emotionally overcome, allowed Amy to come to him.

Kissing him gently, she said, "How we've missed you! You'll never know how wonderful it is to see you."

A flash of the old Ted was evident in his grin. "Missed me, have you? You'll never know the endless nights and days I've dreamt of this moment. God, how I've longed for a sight of you. My two best girls . . . you've no idea what it means to me! You're a sight for sore eyes. I can't believe Poppa isn't here. What a shock it was to hear about him . . . but I was grateful he didn't suffer."

Deborah's eyes overflowed again. "Oh, Ted, how he longed for this day. He was so proud of you."

Ted held her hand. "I know, Momma. Now, come on, you two . . . we've got a lot of catching up to do. How are you managing?"

They talked and talked until a nurse came along. "Now, Captain, you've had your visit allotment for the day. Your strength isn't up to much more."

The women saw that Ted was exhausted and assured him they'd return on Saturday, Amy's next free day.

As they were taking their leave, the nurse suggested they stop at the office where a doctor would explain Ted's case to them. Their apprehensions were put to rest when the doctor assured them Ted's prognosis was good. He would probably regain partial use of his right leg. It would, however, be some time before he would be able to return home, but, with his family in attendance and good care, his chances for a speedier recovery were enhanced.

Deborah was busier than she'd ever been before. If Amy wasn't available as chauffeur, Deborah would take the trolleys necessary to reach the hospital. She would go laden down with her cookies and cakes that were distributed to everyone: patients, doctors, nurses—anyone in sight. She had become familiar with the long, sterile corridors, the omnipresent smell of antiseptics and medicines and the wards lined with beds. At first she suffered acutely, horrified by the wounds of the war-torn young men; but, encouraged by their welcoming response, she would be brusquely cheerful as she greeted them all. The boys began to look forward to her coming, and, to Ted's never-ending amusement, she enjoyed their "sassin and teasin." She was more than capable of giving it back to them.

"I hardly get to spend any time with you, Amy, since your brother arrived," Barbara said one day. "Aren't you planning to introduce me to him?"

"Of course I am. It's just that there's been so much excitement, and truthfully Ted really wasn't up to it. He's improving every day. How would you like to go to the hospital with us this Saturday?"

Deborah wasn't pleased at the idea of Barbara's accompanying them but grudgingly agreed when Amy pointed out, "Ted might enjoy another face, Momma."

"I don't see where she should come in on our private family affairs . . . but sinct you already said she could, I don't spose you can back out."

When Deborah saw that Barbara carried a little gift package for Ted, her resentment dissipated. Arriving at their usual meeting place, they found Ted sitting beside his buddy, Peter Cooper. The young men had become fast friends and were almost inseparable. Amy had begun to wonder if she'd ever have a chance to speak with Ted alone.

Peter let out a whoop as they approached. "Hey, Ted, one for each of us."

When Deborah had concluded her greeting and gone off to tend her "boys in the wards," Peter urged, "Come on, girls . . . take us for a walk. Get us out of here. Barbara, you push Ted's wheelchair. Amy, you're in charge of mine. You can push Ted around as much as you want when you get him home. Come on, girl . . . get going. I need some of the spoiling you dish out to Ted."

Amy had decided Peter was good-looking, in a Van Johnson way. Of course, it was hard to gauge how he was built since she had never seen him standing; he was either stretched out in a hospital bed or seated in a wheelchair. Deborah called his close-cropped blond hair a bristle since it was cut in Marine style. He had been injured at Guadalcanal and gone through several operations. It surprised Amy that Deborah had become so fond of him, become, in fact, one of his most ardent fans, although his boisterous humor and incessant teasing seemed overbearing. She was a little frightened of him, never quite knowing how to talk with him.

At Ted's insistence, Barbara was already wheeling him down the ramp from the portico along the path toward the lovely green tree-shaded park on the grounds. It was a welcome respite from the hospital atmosphere—grass lawns with bushes, flowers and the chirping of birds. There were benches spaced around, and squirrels could be seen scampering about. Amy had no choice but to follow. As she pushed Peter's wheelchair, he seemed more subdued. Under the spell of his easy charm and glib chatter, she began to feel more relaxed.

By the time Deborah located them it was almost time to leave. Ted whispered to Amy, "Sis, see if you can persuade Barbara to come back. She's a knockout!"

Deborah's objections were overruled and Barbara began to join them in the regular routine of hospital visits. Amy was delighted to have her friend along; besides, it gave her a chance to be alone with Peter. They had developed an easy comradery, and he had told her a great deal about himself. "My mother's been widowed the last ten years; she's had a rough time supporting three of us boys. My older brothers are fighting overseas, Army and Air Force. She's had more than her share of difficulties."

It dawned on Amy that, beneath the bravado and gay banter, Peter was lonely. "Doesn't your mother get here to visit you, Pete?"

"Sure, but she comes during the week on her only day off. It's a distance from Santa Barbara and getting enough gas is a hassle. One of these times maybe she'll make it on a weekend; then you'll get to meet her. She's a great lady."

"I'd like to meet her."

"Good, because I've told her a lot about you."

Amy blushed, grateful she was behind Pete's wheelchair at the moment. She had begun to lose her timidity; in truth she found herself strongly attracted to him. It was a new feeling, one she was not quite sure how to handle.

"Pete, have you thought about what you're going to do when you're discharged from the service?"

"Nope . . . haven't made up my mind yet. I was called up at the end of my first year of law school. Boy, was that rough, working and going to school at the same time. I doubt whether I want to go through that again."

Amy placed the chair under the shade of their favorite tree and checked to see if Pete's blanket was secure. As she bent toward him his cheek brushed hers, and, blushing, she asked, "Warm enough? That breeze is a mite cool."

He grinned at her as she tucked the blanket around him and traced her cheek with a finger. As she straightened up, he reached for her hand and held it. Startled, she drew back. "That's foolish."

He held on to her hand. "What's foolish?"

She slid onto a seat bench alongside him. "Not wanting to go back to law school. You're going to have the GI Bill to put you through . . . you can go full time and get your law degree faster. Besides, I've heard you fellows are going to get disability pay. You'd be stupid not to take advantage of the opportunity. I wish I had it."

"The GI Bill or the disability pay?"

"Oh, Pete, can't you ever be serious?"

Fondling her hand, playing with her fingers, he said, "Yes, m'darling, very often. For instance, I think you're a very sensible cookie, aside from being a beautiful young woman. What are your plans . . . marriage, kids, all that womanly stuff?"

She sighed. "It's too late for me. I lost my scholarship. I wanted to be a teacher, but just at that time my father died and Momma wouldn't hear of me leaving her. Of course, now with Ted home, there might be a chance. But I think he'll go back to studying for the ministry."

"Do you still have to stay with your mother?"

There was a moment's hesitation before Amy replied: "A

lot will depend on Ted's plans. If he remains at home for a while, she might be willing to let me go. Actually I think it's that she doesn't want to be alone, even though she's busy enough. I'd sure like to get my teaching credentials."

"Well, why don't you?"

"I just told you—I have to wait until Ted's settled."

"Now you're being foolish. He's got his life to live; why should what he does affect you?"

"I just explained about Momma. She made me promise, and you don't know Momma when she makes up her mind to something. In any case, I'm working—it's a real good job, interesting too."

He looked at her with a quirky smile on his face. "You know what I think, Miss Amy? I have a hunch you're waiting for Mr. Right to come along."

Flustered, she turned crimson. "I am not! That's the furthest thing from my mind."

"Aw, come on . . . what's wrong with that?"

"Nothing! I wouldn't say never, ever, but for the moment that's not what I'm thinking about."

"You mean to tell me a gorgeous creature like you isn't swamped with eligible young men? I'll bet you could have a date every night of the week."

She looked up at him, disconcerted. "No, that's not the case. It isn't that I couldn't, I guess, but it's been difficult for me. It's hard to explain to most people; it has to do with the way we've been reared. Hasn't Ted told you anything about our background?"

"We haven't gotten to that yet, sweetie, but believe me, after today I'll make a point of finding out."

As the weeks passed, Barbara began to tease Amy about Peter. "Can't you see the guy is crazy about you?"

"Oh, Barbs, he is not! We're just good friends."

"Oh sure, friends . . . wait till you're lovers no more. You must be blind not to see the way his face lights up when he sees you."

"You're nuts, Barbs. It's nothing like that at all. If anyone's got a crush on someone, it's Ted for you!"

The truth was Peter had become a constant refrain in Amy's mind. She saw him everywhere, dreamed about him, yearned for the touch of his hand on hers. She adored everything about him . . . his gentle mirth, his good humor,

YOUNG WOMEN IN TRANSITION 271

his salient quips. As far as she was concerned he was
perfection. She couldn't wait to reach the hospital to be with
him. Evenings were spent mooning around the house. If she
tried to read, his face appeared on the page. Soft music set
her pulses hammering. She fell asleep dreaming of romantic
interludes with him. When she and Barbara were together
they talked of nothing but Ted and Peter. There was no doubt
that Barbara was smitten too, doing her share of daydreaming
as well. At lunch one day as they were talking they broke into
giggles, wondering if the boys spoke about them as much, and
Barbara said, "I'll bet they do . . . they've got more time. I'd
give a nickel to be able to listen in."

One week Deborah had a cold and slight fever and for once
the two girls were on their own. They went off, packaged and
bundled with Deborah's baked goods. It was a damp, misty
day and there'd be no walking in the park.

The jukebox was blaring in the recreation room as the girls
entered. The moment Peter saw them, Amy was amazed to
see he was attempting to stand up, struggling to show her he
was on crutches. To emphasize the fact, he was trying to do a
little jig. Amy rushed over. "Are you mad, Pete? It would be
just like you to fall and have to go back to bed because of
your craziness. Stop it, please!"

He grinned impishly at her. "So you care, huh? Think I'm
crazy, do you? It all adds up . . . I'm getting the feeling you
care."

"Oh, Peter . . . you are mad, you know." She found
herself looking up at him. "Peter, you're so tall. My
goodness, I had no idea."

"Well, all that bed rest stretched me out. If you had ever
asked, I could have told you I measured six foot three. Is that
too tall for you? You're a tiny thing, you know."

"You shouldn't take such chances, Pete—really. Sit down,
please."

He had an impish grin on his face. "I'll sit if you promise to
sit on my lap."

She laughed as he maneuvered himself down on a couch.

"Well, I'm sitting." He stretched his arms out.

"Oh, Pete, you're impossible."

She sat down next to him and he reached over and pulled
her close to him, putting his arm around her shoulder. Her
heart pounded; his nearness sent the blood tingling through
her Her unspoken desire for him had her quivering, and her

face was a dead giveaway. He put his face close to hers and grinned. Embarrassed, she asked, "What's so funny, you crazy man?"

He reached his hand around and tilted her face up toward his. "The only thing that keeps me from taking you into my arms and hugging and kissing you are these." He indicated the crutches. "But, come to think of it, this isn't too bad. I think I can manage."

She began to squirm, trying to pull away but not really wanting to.

He tightened his grip. "Stop it, Amy—it's hard enough to manage this. Why are you fighting me? Don't you understand? Oh, God . . . what a helluva place to tell a girl you're in love with her. Amy, if I'm crazy, it's you who's making me this way."

"Peter, stop talking nonsense." His face was so close to hers that everything was blurred.

He crooned in her ear. "I think of you every minute. Each time you leave I go through hell. I can't wait to see you . . . it's an eternity until you return. Tell me you feel the same way."

Tremulous, she leaned against him. "Oh, Peter . . . it's just because you're here . . . alone . . . sick."

"I mean what I'm saying. I'm in love with you. I dream of you awake and sleeping. I can't bear it when you're not near me. When I get out of here I'm going to devour you, crush the breath out of you. Now tell me . . . tell me you feel the same way."

She began to giggle and his fingers began cut into her arm. "Are you laughing at me?"

"Peter, you are crazy! How can you love someone you're planning to squeeze the breath out of?"

Then she raised her head, her lips parted slightly waiting to be kissed. When their lips met, he had his answer. Their ardor was unquenchable.

When momentarily he let her catch her breath, she murmured, "Peter . . . it's the same with me."

The whoop he let out turned every head in the rec room in their direction. Blushing Amy scolded, "Shush, Pete! Do you want everyone to know?"

"Yes! I want the world to know!"

He kissed her again. The sensation spiraled into her soul. Her hunger for love was suddenly insatiable and in this moment of commitment to him she became joined to him with all her heart. Joy transcending anything she had ever known coursed through her body, dazzling her mind with an intensity so great she felt faint.

He held her close to him, sharing an emotion neither could put into words. He was consumed by the need to show her tenderness, to express somehow to this gentle, delicate woman whose heart he could feel beating so wildly his desire to protect her, care for her and love her. She was like some frightened and beautiful bird.

"Amy, darling, you'll never have to worry again. I'll take care of you forever and ever. Just you wait—this is only the beginning."

He smothered her mouth with kisses. She didn't know or care where she was or who saw them. His lips made her want for nothing else. They would have remained in their embrace indefinitely but suddenly he winced. "Darling, I'm sorry. I have to straighten up . . . this darn hip and leg can still take only so much twisting."

Instantly she was all concern. "Oh, Peter, darling, you shouldn't have. I'm so sorry . . ."

He struggled to straighten himself. "Sorry for what? Sorry for letting me love you? Put your head here. Since I can't come to you, it'll be more comfortable if you lean across me. It's easier to kiss you in this position."

He pulled her across him. "Let's test it." He kissed her again. Lost to the world, she was startled when he suddenly laughed. She sat up in surprise. "What is it?"

"Look—over there—in that corner. It's in the air today."

Turning as he directed, she began to laugh too. Barbara was cuddled up next to Ted in his wheelchair.

"See, Amy, love finds its ways. I knew that was coming."

She snuggled closer to him. "I can't believe this is really happening." Her fingers caressed his face.

"For starters, supposing you tell me you love me. You haven't, you know."

Her eyes were wide, and he could see how bottomlessly blue they were—flecked with gold, the reflection of the lamp behind them. "Peter, I'll try . . . it's new to me. But I don't think I love you." She could feel him start with surprise as she went on softly, teasingly. "You see, Pete, I think it's more than that. I adore you . . . I worship you. You're my whole life. If that's love, Pete, then I love you."

He kissed the tip of her nose. "Aha, so you're a schemer too. You felt this way all along and planned to trap me."

She smiled contentedly up at him. "I have so much to tell you, Pete."

Caressing her, he drew her closer. "I know you do, Amy. I know . . . we'll have forever for the telling and forgetting. No one will ever hurt a hair of your precious head again, darling."

She put her head against his chest and let the tears flow. Wiping them away gently, he mocked, "They'd better be tears of joy, my girl. Not to change the subject, but do you think we should break the news to your brother and Barbara?"

Reluctantly she pulled away and handed him his crutches. "Whatever you say."

"That's a good start, sweetheart." He grinned down at her as he hoisted himself up on his crutches. "The honest truth is, Amy, this is about as much sitting as I can bear." He saw the look of concern on her face. "Don't worry, darling, it won't be long before you'll be pleading with me to let you go. By the way, in case you have any regrets about worshiping me, let me put your doubts to rest. I worship you too."

Amy wanted this feeling to go on forever. It was indescribable that Amy Beth and Peter were in love with each other, that both had survived to reach this pinnacle.

As Amy stood by, Peter made certain his footing was secure, and then he pulled off the insignia ring he was wearing. "Let me have your left hand, woman. I want to mark you as my own."

Shyly she extended her hand. As he prepared to put the ring on her finger, he said loudly, "Now hear this . . . hey, everyone—look! This woman belongs to me. You're all invited to witness the pledging of our troth."

There was a moment of silence and then a loud cheer greeted the announcement. Everyone hollered and applauded as he slipped the too large ring on Amy's finger. Blushing, embarrassed, Amy hung her head. "Lift your head up, darling. Look the world in the face . . . tell it, 'World, I'm pledged to Captain Peter Sidney Cooper—he's mad but I'm glad.'"

In a moment they were surrounded by a crowd—wheelchairs, crutches, walkers—they were hemmed in by happy congratulations. The room, whose walls had encased so much heartbreak and sorrow, was filled with joy. Then Barbara and Ted managed to push through to them. Pete squeezed Ted's shoulder. "Well, old scout, you thought you'd be getting rid of me, but see what I've gone and done. Wait till that termagant mother hears the news. Ted, you don't think I have to ask her for Amy's hand, do you?"

They broke into gales of laughter, followed by kisses and hugs.

When the crowd of well-wishers had finally dispersed, Ted looked at them sheepishly. "Well, kids, we didn't want to steal your thunder, but we think you should be the first to know, seeing as how everyone's doing it. You want to tell 'em, Barbs, or should I?"

Blushing prettily, Barbara said, "You tell them, darling."

Pulling himself up as far as he could, he asked, "Do I look manly enough? Oh, heck, I don't think we could stand that crowd again, so I'll keep it among ourselves. We're engaged too—show them, Barbs."

Barbara extended her hand, on which Ted's naval ring spun around. The hugging and kissing commenced all over again. As Amy hugged him, he said, "I'm grateful to you, sis . . . if it hadn't been for you I'd never have met her. If I haven't told you before, then I will now—you're the best sister a guy could have! Pete's a lucky man." It was a wild and glorious day.

Deborah appeared at the kitchen door when Amy arrived home, startled by her daughter's excitement. "What is it, gal? Everything all right?"

Amy laughed and spun around. "Look, Momma! Everything's super-duper—look!" She held out her hand so that Deborah could see the ring.

"What's that mean, Amy?"

Amy put an arm around Deborah. "It means, Momma, I'm engaged to Captain Peter Cooper, the handsomest, most wonderful man in the world . . . and, Momma, I'm so happy I think my heart's going to burst."

"Well, I shouldn't wonder, Amy. That's a mighty piece o news. Well, I never! And to think it happened when I wasn't there. Can't say I weren't expectin it, the way he's been amoonin over you. I'm real glad for you, girl. I magine Ted was pleased as punch. That Peter seems a right good young man."

It was on the tip of Amy's tongue to tell about Ted and Barbara, but she decided it would be better for them to break their own news. Besides, she didn't want to face Deborah's disappointment; she knew her mother envisioned keeping house for Ted when he returned to school. Amy resolved not to do anything that would mar her happiness.

Sleepless with excitement, she spent half the night writing the wonderful news to Aunt Tina, who had already been regaled with the minutest details about Peter in Amy's twice-monthly letters. Brimming with happiness, she promised that at the first opportunity she and Peter would visit her.

At work the next day Amy was moody and overtired. She wished the day was over. She was premenstrual and the noise of the plant and the huge overpowering posters pounded at her relentlessly. THE ENEMY IS LISTENING . . . SOMEONE TALKED TOO MUCH. She scoffed to herself. Who had time for talking in this place? There seemed to be no respite from the war. There was no avoiding it; it was a daily fact of life.

Lost in her thoughts, she barely heard the loudspeaker booming above the racket. She looked up in surprise, certain she'd heard her name. The announcement was repeated, and it was her name. Astonished she heard, "Incentive Award for the Month to Amy Wilkerson."

She looked around and saw the grinning faces. The next announcement floored her. "Congratulations to Amy on her engagement."

She wished she could disappear behind her desk. It had to be Barbara who had leaked the news; she'd get her for it. A group of people were moving toward her with Barbara in the lead. "Hey, you lucky nut . . . that's worth a two-hundred-fifty-dollar bond. Money goes to money. What'd you do to cop it?"

How could she be peeved with this friend? Everyone bunched around, extending congratulations. Mr. Bernadi, their supervisor, was coming toward them. Amy grinned at Barbara. "You can hear for yourself, you snitcher; the boss is about to tell me."

He extended his hand as Amy rose to greet him. "Congratulations, Miss Wilkerson. We're proud of you on both counts."

He eyed the group standing around with disapproval, but no one moved, eager to hear what the award had been given for, so he said, "The big brass approved your new form for expediting the inventory parts system. The changeover is being readied now. Good work!"

Thrilled but embarrassed at being singled out, she stammered, "Thank you, Mr. Bernadi. I never thought they'd really consider it."

He smiled. "Miss Wilkerson, the department is proud of you. Have you set the date?"

Confused, she asked, "Date? For what?"

"For your wedding. I hope this doesn't mean we're going to lose you."

"Oh, no, Mr. Bernadi. It'll be some time yet. My fiancé is recovering from his injuries at the naval hospital."

"Well, be sure and extend our best wishes to him." He turned and looked at the listening group. "Are you all through for the day?"

Amy had difficulty keeping her mind on her tasks as more and more people stopped by to offer congratulations. She was distracted by the novelty of so much attention. She wished there was a way she could share the news of her award with Peter before the weekend. It was getting harder and harder to be apart. The realization that she was engaged to be married was something she was not yet able to take for granted. While it filled her with pride, it gave rise to new torments. She told no one, not even Barbara, about her concern that Peter might suddenly realize how inadequate and unworthy she really was.

Alone at night, she would sit in front of the mirror and study herself, hoping that in her reflection she would discover the reason such an incredible man had chosen her. It was frustrating to be faced by plain old simple Amy Beth. The mystery remained—she was still the same nonentity she had always been. Often in these moments Aunt Tina would cross her mind and she would recall the old woman's words of support and encouragement, clinging to them in an attempt to bolster her self-esteem, which had never quite recovered from the disasters of her youth. She would look at her ring; it would confirm anew the reality of her status, and she would murmur a prayer of gratitude. Resolutely she would set her mind on what she could do to prove to Peter she was deserving of his love. She would fall asleep enumerating his attributes: he was intelligent, kind, understanding, gentle, handsome and humorous . . . a man beyond her wildest dreams. Eventually her apprehensions lessened as her visits with him brought more affirmation and slowly her confidence began to build.

There was no doubt Deborah had been rocked by Ted's announcement of his engagement to Barbara. On several occasions, she had made caustic comments to Amy, holding her responsible since she had been instrumental in introducing them. Amy tried to be patient, feeling Deborah would come around in time, but occasionally old resentments would flare.

Once, after an especially happy visit with Peter, Amy returned home eager to talk about him. Seeing that Deborah was in a mellow mood, she enthused, "Oh, Momma, he's so wonderful. I can't believe he's really going to be my husband. Did you feel this way about Poppa?"

Put off by the intimacy of the question, Deborah asked, "What way?"

Blushing, Amy answered, "When you and Poppa were courting, did you ever wonder what he saw in you?"

"Don't talk nonsense, girl. Don't look a gift horse in the mouth. It's said love is blind, and ifn he likes you, count your blessins. There's no accountin for tastes."

By contrast Amy had been envious when she'd heard how Barbara's family had reacted to the news of her engagement to Ted. Barbara had been indignant when she'd told Amy about it. "You'd think I had agreed to sell myself into white slavery the way they carried on. They were almost angry I'd consented to marry Ted before they'd checked him out."

Amy had listened in shocked disbelief. Although she didn't say so, she thought it incredible the Hopkinses hadn't considered Barbara lucky to have a fine young man fall in love with her. Barbara had confided, "My folks won't admit it, but they don't think anyone's good enough for me. It's a blessing they're so fond of you; knowing Ted's your brother made it easier. They're apt to be softer on him when they meet."

Something she couldn't put her finger on triggered Amy's response. "You know very well, Barbs, Ted's not really my brother."

Barbara's temper flared. "Holy mackerel! What's that supposed to mean? Are you telling me that after all these years and the way you were brought up together, you don't consider Ted your brother?" Eyes glinting icily, her voice sharp, Barbara went on. "The way Ted feels about you, I'm absolutely amazed you'd say such a thing. You've got some crazy notions, always complaining about the Wilkerson family."

"Please, Barbara, you know I adore Ted. He's very dear to me; I just meant we weren't blood-related."

In no mood to be mollified, Barbara grumbled, "Big deal! You're more related to him than anyone else. You're as silly as Mrs. Wilkerson with her 'dopted daughter' business. Do you realize you pull the same stuff?"

Barbara was unrelenting and for days after there was a strain between them. Amy suffered; Barbara was her dearest friend, her only one. She tried everything she could to bring her around, to no avail. Finally an opportunity presented itself when they discussed visiting the hospital on the weekend.

"I'll pick you up, Barbs," Amy volunteered.

"I don't think so this weekend. My folks are planning to go out to the hospital with me. Do you know, Amy, if Deborah is planning to go both days?"

Amy understood at once. "Would you prefer she not be there with your folks?"

Grinning sheepishly, Barbara nodded and Amy hastily said, "I'm not sure what her plans are but, if it will make things easier, I can at least arrange to delay our arrival."

Barbara smiled gratefully and they were back on their old footing. "That'd be great! We can be there by one so, if you could give us an hour, it'll give Mom and Dad a chance to meet Ted alone."

"Barbara, will you promise not to get upset if I ask you a question?" Amy went on. Barbara stiffened; her loyalties were all with Ted and she hoped it wasn't about him.

Not quite sure of where she stood with her friend, Amy hesitated but finally asked, "Have you prepared your folks for Deborah?"

Relieved, Barbara admitted, "I sure have tried. Have you any suggestions?"

"You could tell them her bark is worse than her bite. She's been fairly good considering her shock at Ted's decision to get married."

Barbara looked at her dubiously. "Well, at least having you as a sister-in-law will be a help."

It was a few weeks later that Amy met her intended mother-in-law. Dorothy Cooper was a petite, pretty, soft-spoken lady, and although her face showed lines of worry and struggle, she was much younger than Amy had imagined. Peter had her twinkling blue eyes. Mrs. Cooper hugged and kissed her, saying, "I'm sure we're going to be great friends. If my boy loves you that's enough for me. I can't tell you how thrilled I am to finally be acquiring a daughter."

Knowing Deborah would soon be joining them, Amy anxiously made an attempt to prepare Mrs. Cooper. She stopped short, seeing the quizzical expression on the woman's face. Peter jumped to the rescue. "Don't worry, darling. I've already prepared Mother for Old Ironsides."

"Peter," Mrs. Cooper chided, "that's not nice. Listen, you two, I appreciate what you're trying to tell me, but I can take care of myself. As long as Amy and I get along, we won't worry. All right?"

Amy smiled with relief and Mrs. Cooper said, "I don't want you to be concerned, child. You've no need to be ashamed if your mother's brusque and forthright. I understand that's her manner. Let's give credit where it's due. It seems to me she's raised some excellent children. You and Ted seem to have weathered her quite well."

Peter chuckled. "Mom, don't let on. I think it's in spite of her, not because of her."

Mrs. Cooper frowned and he quickly added, "Come on, I'm kidding. She's a good old admiral, a bit crusty, but you should see how she stands up to the razzing the guys in the wards give her."

As if to prove how perverse she could be, Deborah was as congenial and pleasant as it was possible for her to be. She had a mischievous twinkle in her eye as she seated herself in the car. She waited until Amy started the motor and declared, "You be lucky, gal! You gotchu a nice family there. I do believe I could take up with that mother o Pete's."

Amy drove, pleasantly dumbstruck.

A stark, white-tiled hospital, permeated by stringent antiseptics, peopled by doctors and nurses serving the sick, seemed an unlikely setting for romance. Yet despite all the odds, it proved an expedient backdrop for Amy and Peter's burgeoning love. Within its walls they fervently whispered their vows and made plans for the future. It provided an easy means of release for the inhibited girl.

Peter, invalided, acted as a catalyst drawing on Amy's long-suppressed need to express tenderness and care. In return for his love, Amy was prepared to lay her life at his feet. Peter loved her vulnerability, her gentle ways. It touched him when he looked into her eyes and saw the vestiges of hurt and pain that had been her lot.

Alone on the park grounds he would kiss her and feel the tremor of her lips giving promise of smoldering fires within. He hungered for her visits; each time he would catch anew the first glimpse of her sweetly smiling face, he was struck by her loveliness. As she would walk to him, he would be stirred by the grace of her movements. Amy's voice, soft and diluted by its Oklahoma drawl, made him ache with desire. Watching her face as she hung on his every word swelled his heart with pride. He thought her adorable, his to be cherished and protected. Teasing her with outrageous nonsense, he was tickled to see the flush color her cheeks. She would quiver when he put his arms around her, and he was desperate for the moment when he could embrace her totally.

Peter had come to know a great deal about Amy when, through the long and sleepless nights, he and Ted had talked, exchanging confidences. He had fumed as Ted unsparingly recounted much of what Amy had endured. Coming from a close and loving family, he found it incredible that the Wilkersons had behaved so cruelly to the helpless child entrusted to their care.

Although angered by the stories, Peter grudgingly came to respect Ted for his candor. It was obvious Ted had deep affection and admiration for his adopted sister. What puzzled him most as their talks continued was the loyalty Ted manifested for his parents. Provoked, he asked, "In view of the things you've told me, how can you come to their defense?"

It was Ted's turn to show surprise. "They're our folks, Peter; they raised us. There's another side to the coin. Not everything's just black and white. I didn't spare them when I told you how tough and cruel our childhood was; but, on the other hand, we were taught good values and respect for the right things. Sure, you're upset about Amy . . . all sympathy and pity—but don't underestimate her. Remember, we were molded in an iron forge. She may lack confidence, but that's because she's been kept close to home. You're getting quite a girl, and I want you to know she's A-number-one in my book!"

The announcement had been made at the start of the morning shift and anticipation filled the air. They waited expectantly until someone shouted, "There she comes!" Then bedlam broke loose as the workers left their stations, rushing to get a glimpse of Tana Corgan. The security guards were lined up to hold the crowd back as she and her entourage walked through the entrance gate of the aircraft plant.

Special clearance had been granted Major Pictures for the filming of their new picture, *Katy the Riveter*, in which Tana Corgan was starring.

Exclamations indicated the star was near and everyone shoved for a vantage point. The section manager climbed to the top of a ladder and, with bullhorn in hand, ordered: "Back to work, please. This means all of you. If you maintain quotas, Miss Corgan has agreed to speak to you when the filming is finished. Remember, this picture will show how the home front works. Let's cooperate. Don't let our boys down. If you are asked to work in the film, you will be paid in exchange for your signed releases. Please get moving. Thank you."

Stimulated by the unusual break in the workday, they dispersed slowly, reluctant to resume their routines. Walking back to their area, Barbara was excited. "She's oodles more beautiful in person than on the screen. Did you see what she was wearing?"

Amy was disappointed. "Yeah, one of our uniforms."

"Sure, she's in costume! But she looked terrific. Golly, if she really worked here the men would never get anything done."

"She'd be a distraction all right. She seems to be very sweet, though."

Barbara, who scoured every screen magazine, puffed with her knowledge. "Hah, who wouldn't be with all that attention—she's a very important star."

It became increasingly hard for them to keep their minds on work. Amy found it impossible to do anything, since a movie crew had moved her desk, setting up their cameras and equipment practically on top of her. She watched as a makeup woman stood over Tana Corgan, applying pastes and powders. Amy could overhear the conversation as a man lounging nearby talked to the star. "What do you think, hon? What say, shall we walk around, doll?"

Amy surmised it was the director talking, and she was amazed at the deference with which he addressed the actress. "If you're ready, sweetheart, let's survey the scene." He tucked Tana Corgan's arm under his and headed for the aisle, suggesting, "You pick out two or three you think suitable."

As they left, Amy decided not to take her break; the area was too exciting to leave. She tried to attract Barbara's attention in order to tell her, but her friend's eyes were riveted on the movie procession heading her way. Amy called, "Barb! Hey, Barb!"

Hearing her, Barbara signaled back that the group was approaching. As they neared, they stopped abruptly and Tana Corgan whispered something to the director. Scrutinizing Barbara, he asked, "Would you like to work in a scene with Miss Corgan?"

"Me?" she squealed. "I'd love it."

Amy had walked over and stood silently observing when, to her amazement, the director asked, "What about you, miss?"

Caught by surprise, she hastily said, "Oh, no, thank you, I don't think so."

Amy saw the instant scorn on Tana Corgan's face as she turned to her escort and announced to all within hearing, "She wouldn't do anyhow, too blah and Milquetoasty. Take this girl and the other one back there."

Banished and humiliated, Amy crept back to her desk. Barbara was unavailable for the balance of the day as the troupe moved off to a selected area to do their filming. Amy wished she'd been able to do it, but if Deborah found out, all hell would have broken loose. It would have been marvelous to tell Pete she'd been in a movie. She'd been stupid; she'd have made money and had fun! She could have risked Deborah's wrath. Well, it was too late for regrets now. At the end of the shift, Amy went in search of the film group. When she arrived at the site, there was such a crowd milling about she couldn't get near, so she gave up and went home.

Barbara was not at her accustomed place the next morning and it wasn't until the day was over that she reappeared, breathless and bubbling with her experience. "You're a goose, Amy! It was fabulous. Can you believe I'm going to appear in a movie and I'm being paid two hundred dollars for doing it? It was fun!"

With envy oozing from every pore, Amy entreated, "Tell me about it. I'm dying to hear."

Barbara needed little invitation and babbled on about what had occurred. As they walked to the bus stop, Barbara said, "I can hardly wait to tell Ted. You floored me when you refused the chance to do it. You're still afraid of what your mother will say. I'll bet for the two hundred dollars she wouldn't have made half the fuss you think. You were chicken."

Unhappily Amy commented, "I thought Tana Corgan was sweet when I first saw her, but she made me feel like two cents."

Barbara sympathized. "Well, I can tell you, she's not your friendly good-neighbor type. She makes everyone feel lower than a worm. I have to admit I didn't like her . . . the way she plays big cheese all the time, telling everyone what to do and ordering them around. You should have seen the leading man—whew, was he ever gorgeous!"

"Would you do it again if you had the chance?" Amy asked.

"Maybe. It's boring, though. They do the same thing over so many times and you have to stand for hours in the same place."

Amy laughed. "It must be something to be a movie star, to be waited on hand and foot as if you were something special. Well, Barbara Hopkins, don't get any notions. One movie does not a star make, right?"

They laughed as Amy's bus drew in and they parted.

Bursting with the news of the movie incident, the girls could hardly wait to reach the hospital. But their news paled in comparison to the excitement of what the fellows had to tell them. They were to be released in time for the Christmas holidays. As soon as Deborah heard, she took charge. "Ted, you tell your friend Peter he's to come home with you. He's apt to be thickheaded cause he's not too fond o me. He can't be going back to Santa Barbara till his therapy be through." She smiled, knowing she'd surprised them.

Impetuously Amy smothered her in a hug. "Oh, Momma, that's wonderful. We'll all pitch in and give you a hand."

"Deed you will! A parcel o limpin men about. Mind you now, Amy, you too Barbara, there'll be no hanky-panky in my house."

At this they all cracked up with laughter. Ignoring them, she said to Pete, "Your mother workin all day and bein such a fur piece from the hospital, it'll be better this way."

Pete took her work-worn hand in his. "Thank you, Mrs. Wilkerson. I really appreciate it."

With a mischievous grin on his face, Ted asked, "Now, Momma, explain what you meant about hanky-panky. I'm glad you didn't say that in front of the Hopkinses. Imagine what they'd think of us."

Deborah could never resist her son. "Ifn they stood me up

to now I imagine they'll let you marry their movie-actin girl. You just let them know you been brought up right and proper, you fixin to be a minister and all."

They knew it was implied criticism of what Barbara had done, but they let it pass.

Arrangements had been made for Mr. Hopkins to pick up and deliver the two invalids to Deborah Wilkerson's house and care. It was Ted who hobbled to the front door when the girls ran up the walk. Amy brushed past him in search of Peter, only to stop short, rooted to the spot at the sight of the handsome young man in Marine uniform, smiling with arms outstretched, awaiting her.

She stood for a second and then flew into his arms. Dimly she heard Deborah's voice calling, but it didn't matter, she was safe in Peter's arms. No harm would ever befall her again; the long arid years were gone. She belonged to Peter and in turn he belonged to her.

It was the most wonderful Christmas Amy had ever known. The old house was alight with laughter and love. A gentle Deborah, up to her elbows in flour, baked and cooked to her heart's content. She ordered everyone about but they accepted it good-naturedly. She was preoccupied with the menu for Christmas dinner. Peter's mother had been invited to spend Christmas weekend with them and the Hopkins family would join them Christmas day. The unfamiliar hilarity in the house made the walls ring.

The tree trimming seemed so much fun Deborah was reluctant to leave for church services, but her departure was facilitated by Mrs. Cooper's request to accompany her. The girls busily strung cranberries and popcorn, slapping their fiancés hands as they grabbed fistfuls of the corn. Barbara had found a little neighborhood shop that had a supply of old-fashioned Christmas bulbs and decorations, and with these, the garlands and candy canes, the tree had become a thing of beauty by the time the two women returned. The packages were piled high and wide, filling every nook and cranny.

The table had been set, the gifts opened, the food was ready and the dining room table stretched out to encompass all.

After dinner, amid the groans of guests who had eaten too much, Peter rapped on the table for attention. He rose and handed Amy a large box. She was surprised and he urged, "Open it, hon."

"But, Peter, we've already exchanged gifts."

"Sure . . . but what's wrong with another one?"

Everyone started to holler. "Come on, Amy . . . open it! Hurry up, open it!"

Carefully she began to untie the ribbon and everyone moaned. Mrs. Hopkins handed her a scissor. "Cut it, Amy. We can't wait forever to see what it is."

Amy went through five ribboned boxes until she reached the small velvet jewelry case. Opening it with trembling fingers, she gasped, "Oh, Peter . . . it's so beautiful!"

There were tears in her eyes but her face was radiant as she looked at the tiny diamond ring nestling in the box. It was her first piece of jewelry and its significance surpassed anything she had ever been given. Everyone admired it; even Deborah was overwhelmed. "Well, my gal, we've come a fur piece— you engaged with a diamond and all." She handed the box back to Peter, who took the ring out and, taking Amy's hand, slipped it on her finger. Everyone cheered.

He looked over to Ted. "You ready to tell them, pal?"

Beaming at Barbara, Ted said, "Well, old Pete and I figured long as we had you all together, we'd tell you our plans and hear what you think." He paused and then said dramatically, "Folks, it seems the service has some plans for us."

Instant protest interrupted him. Smiling, he held up his hand for quiet and went on. "No cause for alarm—there's no more active duty. Pete and I are going to be landlubbers for the duration. We just got the news a few days ago. We're being ordered to the same base up north when we finish our therapy treatments. Since this is the case, we've decided to make application for married quarters, and there's a good chance we'll get them. We thought—and we hope you agree—this would be as good a time as any to set the date."

The ensuing noise drowned out anything else he might have intended to say. Suddenly Pete's voice boomed out. "Hey, everyone! Now hear this! Our assignment starts in March and, if you like the idea, what do you say to our having a double wedding in June?"

Deborah and Amy invited Dorothy Cooper down for another weekend a few months later so that she could accompany them when Amy made her selection of a wedding gown. To Amy's utter astonishment, a surprise shower had been arranged for her; when they returned home later that day, Barbara was there to receive the guests.

Amy found herself caught up in an intensely emotional

period. It was difficult for her to handle Deborah's highs and lows—sadness or happiness suddenly altering her mood. She had dropped her guard and, for the first time, permitted Amy to see how deeply she cared for her.

With the arrival of March, both men departed to resume their service and the house seemed empty. Amy wrote Peter every day; without him life was hollow. His letters were loving and reassuring, bolstering her spirits. Their living quarters on the base had been secured and preparations were under way for the wedding.

As the date for their marriage drew nearer, Amy's nerves grew raw. She was certain something would occur to prevent the ceremony from taking place. Remarkably, it was Deborah who, in her no-nonsense way, proved supportive and comforting.

Time triumphed, the weeks passed. The eventful day arrived with the sun shining on all the participants. The brides were radiant and the grooms stalwart and handsome. It had been arranged for Amy to proceed first so that Ted might lead her through the arch of swords to the altar and Peter. Ted then waited as Mr. Hopkins brought Barbara to him. The mothers cried and Mrs. Wilkerson confided, "Losin both my children the same day, it won't be easy pickin up the pieces."

At the minister's words "I now pronounce you man and wife," the blur that had covered Amy's eyes lifted and her heart sang. As she put her face up to receive Peter's kiss, she trembled with the realization that she was married—the dream had become reality. The ceremony over, the wedding group lined up to receive congratulations in the officers' club where the reception was held. Pictures were taken, the cake cut and amid much gaiety Ted and Barbara left in a shower of rice for San Francisco. Peter whispered, "It's time for us to leave too, sweetheart."

With the assistance of Deborah and Mrs. Cooper, Amy changed from her wedding gown to a traveling suit. Seeing how carefully Deborah wrapped the wedding gown, Amy's heart went out to her. She looked at Amy and smiled, almost tentatively. "Where do you want it kept, Amy?"

"At home, Momma, if it's all right."

"Of course, child. I just thought . . ." She sounded so sad.

Amy went to her and held her for a moment. "Thank you, Momma. Thank you for all you've done these months. Take care of yourself. Try to keep yourself busy. I'll be in touch."

Deborah held her close for a moment and wiped away a

tear. Then there were last-minute hugs and kisses, and after their share of rice she and Peter were off.

She sighed with contentment as he smiled at her. Finally, at long last, they were alone. She suddenly felt bashful. Peter drove slowly. They held hands and quietly absorbed the magnificence of the rugged coastline and Big Sur country they were passing.

Within a few hours they reached the Highlands Inn. The hotel was set high on a bluff overlooking the ocean. A few people were scattered about, but it was as if they had the place to themselves. Peter had chosen well.

As they sat in the dining room over the excellent dinner, wine was brought to their table. "Compliments of the management," the waiter said with a grin.

Amy looked at Peter questioningly and he asked, "What is it, hon?"

"Should I, Pete? I've never been allowed to drink wine just for pleasure."

He grinned at her teasingly. "Say, Mrs. Cooper, have you forgotten so quickly you are now a married lady? You're free to do anything you wish. Within reason, of course. Test number one: We've been married six hours and thirty-seven minutes. Let's see if marriage has changed you. Do you recall what you said?"

"What did I say?"

He held her hand across the table. "You've a weak memory. You said you worshiped me."

She was so without artifice, so defenseless, he wanted to hug her then and there. "Oh, Peter, I do!"

"Honey, I'm teasing, but I want you to understand from now on you're to be yourself, do what you think best. Stop worrying about the past or what anyone else thinks is right or wrong. Rely on your own judgment."

She felt daring as she sipped the wine; it made her talkative and gay. They strolled around the grounds for a while and then Peter asked, "Tired?"

She could barely suppress a yawn. Hesitantly she admitted, "It's been a big day."

"Okay, my girl, let's go up to the room."

Shy and nervous at the thought of their impending intimacy Amy decided she would simply have to give herself up to Peter's understanding.

Her hair shimmered in the lamplight, her peignoir opened and her gown clung, revealing the contours of her body. As she walked toward him, Peter thought she was an illusion. He pressed her to him as she leaned against him, shaken and frightened. He kissed the top of her head. "Amy, darling, there's nothing to be feared."

She almost seemed resigned as she looked up at him, trusting and waiting. "I don't know what I'm supposed to do. Peter, will you show me?"

He held her tightly. "Sweetheart, we'll do what we feel. It's as natural as breathing when two people love each other. Remember, there's nothing to be ashamed of. Once the first part is over, I'm sure you'll want me as much as I want you. I promise."

As they stood silhouetted in their embrace by the moon's silver glow, the velvet darkness wrapped around them, Amy's senses merged with the roaring surge of the waves as they dashed and receded on the rocks below. Lifting her in his arms, Peter carried her to the waiting bed. Gently and tenderly he began to caress her. Tumultuous with sensations she had not known before, Amy responded, roused by feelings that drew her higher and higher in quest of rapture. They were so much in love, so suffused with desire, that when the pain came—unexpected, piercing and sharp—she fought him. A scream rose to her lips, and then it was over as her body, needing and warm with a will of its own, rose to meet and move with his.

Worried that she had displeased him, she snuggled up to him. Holding her close, he whispered, "It was wonderful, darling . . . honestly it was. The bad part is over. You'll never have that pain again."

Dawn was breaking when he made love to her again. This time she clung to him with joy, responding without restraint. When it was over they lay next to each other, talking softly. "I never knew there were such feelings, Peter. There must be lots of things I have no idea about."

He was amazed at the unrestrained way in which she responded to his fondling and pleaded, "Hey, give me a chance to recuperate."

She was like a smoldering fire that he had fanned into flame. Amy's sexual fusion with Peter had been cataclysmic; it had put the stamp of authenticity on their union and swept her to ecstatic heights. The questions and doubts had been swept away and she felt whole, complete. In their fire she had cauterized the pains of the past, melting the chains that had bound her to their miseries. Her body throbbed with the knowledge that she was a woman in harmony with her man. She was fulfilled and content.

Later that day, walking on a bluff overlooking the water, Amy exulted, "Peter, how can I tell you what having you as my husband has done for me? Suddenly I'm no longer afraid to care, to feel—it's so wonderful!" He smiled and kissed her. Carefree and happy, they held each other close, and nothing else mattered, because they were together.

The war in the Pacific ended. It was a triumphantly riotous day, and within hours the base grapevine was rife with rumors that service discharges would begin. Both Peter and Ted had sufficient points for early releases, and Peter soon learned he would be discharged at the end of the month. Ted was to follow two weeks later.

There was fresh hope in the air. President Truman had taken firm hold of the country and unconditional surrender terms were being offered to the Japanese. Everyone was filled with optimism and a sense of new beginnings; now their war-thwarted lives could assume shape and direction.

For the four whose lives had become so inextricably woven, it was a time of gladness tinged by poignancy. Their paths would separate; never again would they share this same sense of closeness.

Peter would receive disability pay and free college tuition. Amy had persuaded him to return to law school for his degree. Barbara and Ted would be leaving for the theology school in Kansas. Emotions ran high, and the parting was difficult for all of them.

Mrs. Cooper had asked Amy and Peter to visit with her a while before they settled down. It was interesting for Amy to see Peter in his home surroundings and to listen to his mother tell stories about him and his brothers when they were growing up. It had been a happy home. She pleased her mother-in-law by insisting that Peter looked just like the pictures of his father. Over dinner one evening Mrs. Cooper said, "Kids, I've been thinking. Why don't the two of you take a real vacation before you settle down and get caught up in school and work? You have a month. It'll probably be a long time before you'll be so carefree again."

There were endless discussions about where they could go until Peter exclaimed, "I've got it! We'll go to Oklahoma and see Amy's Aunt Tina."

"Peter, what a marvelous idea! But I hope she's still alive. She can't write, you know, I told you."

"Well, we'll find out. You write and tell her we're coming. We'll sightsee along the way. Mom, you can help. I don't want to borrow your car again—we're going to need our own anyhow. Your good buddy, Mr. Simpson, mentioned he might sell his son's car. Can you put in a good word for me?"

Cars were hard to come by, but Mr. Simpson had lost his son in the Normandy invasion and, with Dorothy Cooper's intervention, he agreed to sell the car to Peter at a price he could afford. Although gas rationing was still in effect, between all of them they were able to gather sufficient tickets. Amy worried. "Supposing we haven't enough and get stuck?"

Peter scolded, "You're supposed to leave the worrying to me. We'll manage."

It was the best time of year and the weather was magnificent. They were like children let out of school, exploring wherever they could. They reached Oklahoma and late one afternoon, sauntering along a side road, Amy shrieked, "Peter, look! There!" A small signpost indicated BRIGHTWATER—10 MILES.

Amy sat tense with anticipation, awash with memories. It was so much smaller and dustier than she remembered it. Peter drove along the main street. "Jeepers, Amy, it looks sorta sad and seedy."

"It wasn't much when we lived here, but I guess time has eroded it even more."

At the end of the street, Peter stopped in front of an old and shabby building marked *Hotel*. He grimaced. "Hon, do you want to spend the night here?"

"Darling, I'm afraid it'll have to be this or the car. But let's find Aunt Tina before we decide on anything."

He drove as she indicated until she spotted the break in the thicket of bushes for the backwoods path. "Here, Peter—stop!"

Her heart thumping wildly, she was transported back in time. Here nothing seemed to have changed; the same acrid bush-laden smells mingled with sun-drenched wild flowers. She pressed along the overgrown winding path and then she saw the roses, the same old roses. "Peter, if she's alive, she's got to be very old. I think my heart's going to burst."

He squeezed her hand. "Try to take it easy, puss; hold on to yourself."

Amy let out a screech. "There she is! Aunt Tina, Aunt Tina—it's me, Amy!"

Peter stood by as the two women flew into each other's arms. The old woman hardly matched Amy's description. Far from fat, she was old and bent, wrinkled and gnarled like a weathered tree. She held on to Amy as she turned a grimy, tear-streaked face in his direction. "Now I kin die happy. My little gel's come back to me."

She peered at him. "Yo mek my gel happy, yo be good man. Yo loves my gel, Aunt Tina loves yo."

It was difficult for Peter to understand why it didn't matter to him that the tiny room in which they sat was a mélange of untidy beds, old clothes and a stove covered with battered pots and pans. The heady scent of roses permeated everything.

After the kerosene lamp had been lit later that evening, the old woman rummaged through a heaped corner and drew out a dented tin box. From it she removed tied packets of Amy's letters, treasured and carefully preserved. Then her old arthritic fingers singled out a sealed envelope, which she handed to Amy. "Here, chile. I fin dis in de ol house mailbox—come for yo a long time ago, and jus recen a man come to ask about yo. The ole teachur, she be retired now, sen him here. She allays reads me yo letters. We tink it betta not to sen de letter counta mebbe it be trouble for yo. One o yo sisters lookin for yo. Mebbe dat's in de letter. Read it fo yoself. Now I members . . . believe it was Emmy. Yo knows bout dese chillun?" she asked Peter.

Sprawled lazily in the old rawhide chair, his long legs stretched out, filled with the supper of corncakes, squash and beefsteak Aunt Tina had provided, Peter felt far removed from the world he knew. Surrounded by relics and symbols of another time, the opiate perfume of the flowers and the motes of dust dancing above the lamp hypnotized and dulled his senses. Dimly hearing Aunt Tina, he nodded, but her piercing black beadlike eyes caught his, demanding a better response. Straightening up, he said, "Yes, I do, Aunt Tina. I know the whole story, and I'm grateful to you for what you did for Amy. Do you want to read us your letter, Amy?"

Amy's face was sober as she scanned it rapidly. "You're right, Aunt Tina. Em's been looking for me and Polly Sue. She's married too and lives in Oklahoma City. But this letter is over two years old. What did you tell the man, Aunt Tina?"

"I tol him yo livin in Californy—but I don tell him where, don wanna bring trouble on yo, chile."

For a few moments Amy sat lost in thought, and then she looked at the two of them. "All this brings back something I think you both should know." Rapidly she told them of the encounter that had taken place with Mary Ann Forbes.

Peter looked at her, perplexed. Aunt Tina moaned, "Chile, I unnerstans, but mebbe yo feel bettah ifn yo spoke wit her."

Amy kept her head bowed as she said, "I know that now, Aunt Tina, but at the time I was upset and angry . . . real mad. Besides, Deborah wouldn't let me. Honestly, I can't say I regret what I did, but in another way I was foolish."

She picked her head up and saw Peter's expression. Her eyes flashed defiantly as she said, "Peter, don't judge me. Aunt Tina can tell you what Deborah's like when she throws a fit."

He shook his head in bewilderment. "Amy, darling, it's just that I don't understand how you could have done that to yourself, punished yourself that way."

For a moment she stared into space and then turned to him, her expression both bitter and sad. "Being here, Peter, tells me more clearly than you can ever understand what would have made me do such a thing." Her voice rose in intensity. "In a million years you could never realize what hell and torture my real mother left me to suffer. It would be impossible for you to know what desolation and misery it was to live on sufferance . . . on someone else's charity. To be unloved, unwanted . . . to be a child surrounded by cruel monstrous giants who denied me the ties of a loving, caring family." Breaking into tears, she sobbed, "God bless Aunt Tina . . . she gave me the first real love I ever knew."

Peter went to her and tried to take her in his arms. Gently she pushed him away. "Let me say it, Peter . . . let me tell you. I think without Aunt Tina I would have been left an emotional cripple. I can remember losing all hope the day I was adopted by the Wilkersons. Lord, how it emphasized my rejection . . . marked my difference." She paused. "It's amazing I am who I am. I'm afraid down deep I'll always feel I'm not like other people. As a little girl there was always so much confusion and uncertainty in me—such bitterness and anger. I've always had a fear of anything that was different. I tried all my life to be good . . . to be accepted." She turned to Peter and clung to him. "Until you fell in love with me, I was not a whole person. Can you understand why I hate that woman? Talking about it makes me shudder. It's a miracle I survived."

Peter held her tightly until her sobs quieted.

The old woman sat rocking, watching them. Suddenly she turned on Peter angrily. "Now yo knows—but only de words. Dem Wilkersons shoulda been hanged, beatin dat lil one de way dey did. Never woulda treated dere animals dat way, I tell you. Folks woulda stopped dat! Amy be right not wantin t'see a mudder done sich a ting, but mebbe if she'd a heard de reason 'twoulda helped. Dat's what I means."

They remained with Aunt Tina for a day, and Amy took Peter to see her old haunts. She refused to give more than a passing glance at the old Wilkerson house. They stopped for a brief visit with her old schoolteacher, who told Peter, "You got yourself a bright girl, Mr. Cooper. Pretty too! She was the smartest of the lot, although Emmy wasn't any dummy."

As they were leaving, Aunt Tina tried her best to smile. "Write, chile. I looks forward to yo letters. Tank yo, Peter—yo made dis ol Indian lady very happy. Blessins on you bot. I be happy now I see my Amy and her Peter."

In the car, Amy cried. Her heart spilling over, she poured out her recollections of the times spent with Aunt Tina.

The miles sped by and the great plains stretched before them, marked by trees in riotous fall color; the wind brought their woody fragrance mingled with sage and the earth's growing things, and it was like balm. Drawing solace from Peter's presence, Amy sat quietly, her eyes upon the wide blue sky, seeing the wheeling hawks and plummets of smoke drifting lazily up from a far-off train. Her misery subsided. She seemed so intent that Peter sensed something else was on her mind. "What's buzzing around in your pretty head now, sweetie?"

Her brow furrowed. For a moment she seemed hesitant and then she asked, "What do you think I should do about my sister, Peter?"

Almost as if in disbelief of what he had heard, his lips formed a wry smile. "What do you want to do? Do you want to ask Deborah what she thinks you should do?"

Abashed, she said, "Why in the world would I want to do that?"

"Who knows, Amy? You might still want to be her good little adopted daughter. I'm trying to understand, Amy, but

I'm wondering what's happened to your spunk. If it were me, I'd be bustin to find out what happened to my family."

She smiled sheepishly. "Of course, Peter. I understand what you mean, but don't say you weren't warned. Supposing they turn out to be a bunch of jailbirds, really no-good people?"

"I'll take my chances. If any of them are like you, I'm on safe ground. Don't be so hard on yourself or your family, Amy; you might be surprised to find out they weren't totally bad." He pulled her close to him and they drove along in contented silence.

Reaching the outskirts of Los Angeles, they decided to visit Deborah. Peter asked, "Are you going to mention visiting Aunt Tina?"

"No. The only one who knew about her was Ted. It would only be raking over old coals and what would be the point? She was a pariah in their eyes."

Deborah was surprised to see them and amazed to hear they'd gone back to Brightwater. "Why'd you want to see that old hole? Ain't nothin thar but dust and musty memories. You take the cake, Amy Beth."

The discussion of their old home went no further. Amy and Peter remained with her overnight, and Amy was relieved to see that Deborah kept herself occupied and seemed content.

The newlyweds were happy to settle down. Amy found their apartment easy to take care of. Small but comfortable, it was furnished throughout in maple and had a young and cheerful feeling. With the addition of some of their wedding presents—pewter candlesticks, a small brass vase and some colorful, inexpensive prints that Peter favored—the compact space took on a warm and homey look. Most important, it was theirs; they were on their own. When the little teakettle whistled on the stove, Amy felt snug and secure; the world was locked out and she was safe in her own home. Peter had started school, and now she felt it was time for her to seek work.

Amy's qualifications for office work were limited but she could type and file and so, with a list of employment agencies in hand, she began her search. With manpower still in short supply, she had to go no farther than the first agency, where she was handed a list of openings and told to make a choice of those she felt best suited her abilities. Scanning the list, she became excited by the prospect of acquiring the job of

receptionist at Major Pictures studio. She was infatuated with
movies, so the work seemed tailor-made for her. She was
interviewed and hired the same day. Her supervisor, a
pleasant woman, explained her duties, emphasizing the
importance of screening the people coming into the executive
building against the daily appointment list she would have.

Elatedly Amy told Peter, "The salary's good, I've got
weekends off and it only takes me half an hour to get there.
Just think, Pete, I'll be rubbing shoulders with movie stars.
Boy, can you imagine how envious Barbara will be when she
hears about it!"

It took a lot of discipline for Peter to reaccustom himself to
school. He and Amy had set up a schedule so that after
dinner he could retire to the privacy of the tiny bedroom
where they had moved the desk and do his studying. With
Peter out of the way, Amy busied herself with household
tasks, and when they were done she would wait for him. A
book in her hand, her sewing box and radio on the little
maple side table next to her chair, she rested contentedly,
queen of her own domain.

One evening when Amy had finished earlier than usual she
decided to come to grips with the overdue letter to Emmalina. Just making the decision filled her with apprehension.
Having suffered so deeply after her reunion with Aunt Tina,
she knew that if Peter hadn't expressed such strong convictions about the matter she would have ignored it. She wanted
only to obliterate the past. Why couldn't Peter understand
she didn't want any intrusions on her present life? What could
she possibly have in common with this woman who had
obviously led a vastly different life from hers? Establishing
contact would only reopen wounds that were better left
untouched. Thinking about it, her lips became dry and her
hands began to sweat. It had taken her so long to develop her
own identity that it wasn't fair to expect her to open the door
to someone strange and remote from the past who might
diminish her, make her less secure again. Oh, how she wished
she could be left in peace! She had finally become a person
with a place in the world; she belonged, she and Peter were a
family. She was appeased in loving and being loved.

A sound from the outside snapped her back to the present.
She'd better think about what she wanted to say in the letter.

Her pen poised above the sheet of paper, she saw the sun
beating down on two little girls, heard the sounds of children
playing and saw the earnestness on Emmy's face as her lips

formed the words, "We're sisters forever and ever; no one can change that!" Amy sat back, strangely wistful, wondering if being sisters really meant anything special. Could it be better than having a friend such as Barbara? What could be so remarkable about having a sister or sisters? It was just linkage in the chain of a family, and, without the whole, how could the parts matter? She was letting herself do too much mooning. She shrugged and began to write.

Hopefully she speculated. Maybe Emmy had moved on, or, like all the times before, there'd be a void . . . no answer, nothing more, just the abyss that had always separated them. The note was short and omitted mention of any immediate desire to renew their relationship. Looking at the envelope, she noticed that her sister's married name was Griffon. It seemed familiar, but she had no idea why. Sealing the envelope, she failed to put a return address on the outside. She felt no qualms; she intended to preserve the tranquility of her life.

She sat quietly satisfied. She looked around at her little home, taking pride in the way she managed it. Peter was always glad to lend a hand and did the shopping before she arrived home. She couldn't get over his willingness to be involved in daily chores. She sighed with contentment. She was so lucky. At work she'd met other young women who were working to assist their husbands through school, and she felt it was a badge of honor to be a member of the clique. Life was perfect just as it was. Her cup was full.

Chapter XIX

❁

FROM WHAT ROOTS AM I GROWN?

DESPITE THE OVERHEAD fans, Jonathan found the heat oppressive in the darkened office. The work he had planned to get finished this quiet Saturday morning when most of the staff were off enjoying the beautiful summer day was going badly.

He had promised Emmy he'd be home by one, but he couldn't concentrate, his mind was distracted. Restless, he got up and walked out to the water cooler. As he did so, he heard a key turn in the outer office door. Wondering who had come in, he took a few steps down the hall and saw it was Judge Esquith. Surprised, he called out a greeting. "Hi, Max, what brings you in here today?"

The old judge peered through the gloom. "Jon? Well, I might ask you the same thing. I wanted to look through an old file for some papers and didn't want to bother any of the girls with it. It's a time-waster for them."

Smiling at the judge, Jonathan said, "Come on in and sit a spell. I'm not making any headway—guess it's the heat in here."

The judge followed him into his office. "What are you working on, Jon? Anything I can give you a hand with?"

"Wish you could, Max. I'm framing the brief on the Keeny case. Normally I enjoy doing it, but this case has so many loopholes I need to be more alert than I am."

The old man laughed. "I've been there, son, know what you mean. Put it away for today. Take a breather and go home to your beautiful wife. How's my Emmy?"

298

Jonathan's mind had been wandering and he brought his attention back. "What? Oh—Emmy. She's fine, Max."

Surprised by Jonathan's dispirited reply, the judge sensed something was not right. "Had a fight, have you? Don't worry, son, it'll blow over."

Jonathan smiled. "We seldom quarrel, Max. But to tell the truth, there is something bothering me. You know, you're about the only person I can talk this over with; the fates must have brought you in here today. Max, I'm worried about Em."

Leaning forward, Max asked edgily, "Well, boy, what's this about? Don't keep hedging."

Max studied the young man as he saw him attempting to put his thoughts in order. Jonathan's boyishness had been replaced by a pronounced Lincolnesque appearance. Tall and lanky, filling out with Pearlie Mae's cooking, in build and feature he was reminiscent of the famous man. Jonathan's aquiline nose fit well beneath his deep-set brown eyes, and his long narrow lips showed the shadow of the mustache he was growing. His chestnut hair, with a lock that always fell forward on his forehead, was beginning to gray at the sides. Max thought, He's young for gray, just about twenty-nine. He cared deeply for the young man; the more he learned about him, the more pleased he was with his character and the fact that he was Emmy's husband. In his opinion, they were a perfect match, made for each other.

Jonathan sipped his water. "Want some, Judge? I'll get you a glass."

"Dang it, boy, if I want some I'll get it. Now get on with what you're going to tell me." He saw the young man's reluctance.

"Well, Max, it's difficult. It's something I really can't put my finger on. You know I adore Emmy . . . I'm as much in love with her as ever; but, frankly, there are some things I can't understand."

Relieved, Max chuckled. "Women, my boy, the eternal mystery. What precisely is it that has you so concerned?"

"I want a family."

"Thank God! I thought I'd be dead and gone before you got to it."

Jonathan seemed upset. "That's just it! I can't convince Emmy. It's that darn missing family of hers. She's afraid."

At this the judge showed shock as he sputtered, "What in tarnation are you talking about?"

Jonathan rose from the chair. His shirt was wet and clung to his back. He walked around to sit on the rim of the desk near the judge. "She's convinced if we had a child it would bear the mark of Cain or some weird thing."

Stunned, the judge looked at him in bewilderment. "Emmy? Are you telling me that Emmy actually thinks that way?"

Jon nodded. The judge mumbled something and then said, "What kind of lawyer are you that you can't convince her how wrong she is? And forgive an old man taking liberties—what the hell kind of man? There's more than one way to catch a rat. Do you want me to spell it out for you?"

Jonathan stood up. "Now, look, Max, I'm not an idiot, but there's more to this than simply fooling Em or forcing a child on her. Of all the people who know my wife, you're the one who knows her best. Don't you know that Emmy is the most insecure, frightened girl in the world? Do you know how many times I have to assure her I love her and that she means everything to me? Max, it's clear she's still tormented by her past—and she gets worse each day, ever since we started the search for those damn people."

The older man looked at him askance. "Jon, you've sure knocked the wind out of me. I can't get over what you're saying. My God, with all that Elizabeth did to implant solid values and a sense of security and belonging, it's hard for me to believe the girl's slipped this way."

"Max, to my way of thinking, while Elizabeth was alive Emmy never gave way to this. For one thing, she knew it would upset Elizabeth; and for another, Elizabeth alive represented family to her. Now that she's newly married to me, in a new situation, with a new future, it's my opinion that all the old, hidden fears have surfaced and she can't fight back. It's like an unending nightmare."

The judge sat quietly for a moment. "Jon, would it help, do you think, if I spoke to her?"

The judge saw the concern deepen on the young man's face as he answered, "It might, Max, but it could be more serious than we think. I'm worried about her having a breakdown. Having a baby she isn't ready for might frighten the life out of her."

Shifting in his chair, the judge's voice was firm, belying his worry. "Look here, Jonathan, Emmy's a healthy girl—there's got to be a simple solution. You know as well as I, she's basically a down-to-earth person, takes after Liz in that respect. That talk about breakdown is nonsense—she's mentally sound. Something's got her going . . . just what I'm not sure."

Max Esquith saw Jonathan's relief at what he'd said. "You know, I was thinking of trying to convince Em to go to that clinic in Kansas. You know—the one those Menninger doctors have?"

"Bosh, Jon! Before you resort to that, there are a few other things we can try. Just how bad is this?"

"How bad is wanting to divorce me? How bad is her crying because she's depriving me of a child and worrying herself sick over my mother and what she thinks?"

Max Esquith stood up and faced him. "It's all clobberdash . . . it's her fears coming out. Eleanor, of course, is a real bogeyman . . . don't wash that away. Has Emmy seen a doctor here?"

"Yes, she has. Your old family doctor—but you know she's not going to discuss this with Dr. Cranson."

"Well, she's got to be made to see how she's blowing this out of all proportion. She needs to feel confident that it makes no difference to you what her real family was like. It would help, without a doubt, if we could unearth that gang, but in the meantime she should be able to live her life as she always has."

"I agree . . . but just tell me how."

Max put a hand on the young man's shoulder. "Let me think about this a day or two. Hang on, be patient; we'll find an answer to this. Have you heard from the investigator?"

"Not since the last report. I think he's onto something about the middle sister. He's pinned them down in California."

Max started to leave the room but stopped and turned. "Jon, I meant what I said about Em. Don't lose patience. She's going to be fine; this is just a temporary thing."

"Sure, Max. You don't have to worry. I love the girl; why else would I want her to have my baby?"

They both laughed and Max left.

"It's mental telepathy," Max said, when he heard Emmy's voice on the telephone. "I had been planning to call you today." Following his conversation with Jonathan, he had intended to invite Emmy to have lunch with him in order to gauge how things actually were with her. He loved the sound of her voice, mellifluous and musical. "How are you, darling?" she asked.

"I'm fine, honey. I was just thinking about our getting together and having some talk. We haven't had a good old confab in a long time. How about it?"

"I'd love it, Uncle Max, but the Griffons just got in. They're staying with us."

Astounded, Max asked, "What Griffons? I know Bill Senior's been planning to come in on business, but who else is here?" He heard the drop in her voice.

"Eleanor is here. She wanted to see us."

Max was keenly aware of the meaning of such a visit to Emmy. She hadn't been face to face with Eleanor Griffon since their encounter prior to her marriage.

"Well, now, isn't that an interesting surprise? How's the old witch behaving?"

He was relieved to hear Emmy laugh. "So far, so good. You'd be proud of me!"

He chuckled. Jonathan was crazy—this young wife of his was sound and sensible. She invited him to dinner and he readily accepted, feeling quite confident about Emmy's state of mind.

They'd been amazed when they'd gone to the station to pick up Jonathan's father and Eleanor had stepped onto the platform with him. Instantly Jonathan worried about how Emmy would react, and he'd been pleased at her poise and competence in handling the meeting. As they'd gone forward to greet his parents, Jonathan said, "Remember, hon, I'm on your side!" He could tell she was tense. Knowing how much this would matter to Jonathan, Emmy made every attempt to be as normal as possible. They heard Eleanor before they reached her. Loving and effusive, she swept Emmy into an embrace. "Dear child, you're more beautiful than ever! Marriage agrees with you." She hugged and kissed the unresisting girl until Bill Griffon interceded. "Let 'er go, El, I want to see my beautiful daughter." Bill Griffon was a gruff, goodhearted man and Emmy had a special place in her heart for him. Seeing the pleasure the Griffons were experiencing and Jon's joy at the reunion, she determined to let bygones be bygones.

It was a gay group that drove home together, talking and exchanging news. Eleanor was at her most charming, admiring and exclaiming over everything in their apartment. "Em, it's just beautiful. You have exquisite taste."

She laughed as if at a joke when Bill Griffon said, "Son, we'll have to go back to the baggage department. I forgot all about the crate your mother insisted we bring with us."

Jon groaned. "Dad, it'll be safe there for tonight. Can't it wait? We'll get it first thing in the morning."

Jon and his father were gone early the next morning when Emmy entered the kitchen to see what Pearlie Mae had concocted for breakfast. She stopped to survey the breakfast area, inhaling the spicy fragrance of the white and yellow peonies set in a deep crystal bowl on the buffet. The flowers were a reminder of Elizabeth, and she had a standing order for them when they were in season. She had worked hard to create a happy atmosphere to start the day. The sunny yellow wallpaper striped in silver and white and the long sheer curtains on the window were a perfect backdrop for the round white table and chairs covered in complementary fabric. She was pleased with the way Pearlie Mae had set things up. "It looks lovely, Pearlie Mae. Thank you."

Her sweet black face broke into a grin. "We'se got us special company, chile. We'se gotta put our best foots forward." They both turned as they heard Eleanor sing out, "Good morning, dear people. What a way to start a day. It's a bower of springtime. Those flowers are spectacular, Em. Such peonies! Where do you get them?"

The compliment pleased Emmy. "I thought you'd sleep late this morning, Eleanor. Pearlie Mae was all set to serve you breakfast in bed."

"And miss this? I should say not. I want to spend every minute possible with you. You've no idea how I've been looking forward to this visit. I've missed you children so much, and your letters are just teasers."

Emmy pulled out a chair. "Sit down, Eleanor; have your juice and coffee. I've no idea when the men will be back, so we might as well start."

As she seated herself, the fragrance Eleanor always wore wafted toward Emmy. It brought back in a rush the years past when she and Elizabeth had first met Eleanor. Studying her overtly, she saw that even without her window-dressing makeup her mother-in-law was still a stunning woman. The constant ritual of expert masseuses and beauty-salon ministrations kept age at bay. Her elegant morning gown blended with the decor.

As Eleanor sipped her juice, she reached over and patted

Emmy's hand. The affectionate gesture was not lost on Emmy. Obviously she wanted to make amends. Emmy smiled at her.

Eleanor was curious about Pearlie Mae, and when she left the room, she commented, "My land, she's been with you such a long time. She must be on in years. Aren't you going to retire her?"

"Eleanor, if I so much as suggested it, she'd die. We're her family, her life."

"You're lucky. Good help is impossible to get back home. Has she adopted Jon too?"

For a second Emmy was jolted at the choice of word, but she realized there was no malice behind it. "Why, she caters to him outrageously. I think he's getting a potbelly."

Chatting easily, they heard the men at the back door. Jon appeared. "Good morning, my two favorite girls."

He pointed an accusing finger at his mother as he laughed. "Mother, you're amazing. What in the world have you got in that box? Em, you can't believe what that woman has lugged halfway across the country."

Bill Griffon walked in, feigning exhaustion. "It's got to contain half the contents of our house. She wouldn't let me ship it; we had to bring it."

"Sit down, Bill," Emmy said. "You've earned your breakfast. Pearlie Mae's pancakes are the perfect reward for all your hard work."

Bill pretended to collapse into his chair, groaning as he said, "Tell 'em what's in that monster crate, you crazy woman."

Eleanor leaned over and kissed her husband's cheek. "You're a darling, Bill. Just stop it; you know you loved the idea as much as I did. Children, we've brought you some of the family heirlooms. We're dividing them between Jon and Bill Junior—his share when he gets married. We want you to enjoy them now. I didn't know how much silver you had, Em, but now you'll have more. As for getting you something else, I had to see firsthand what you might need."

Emmy understood her mother-in-law meant well, and she accepted the handsome gesture, trying to be gracious in return.

Jon's face showed his delight at the way his wife and mother were getting along. "Well, girls, we've got to get going. Ready, Dad?"

Emmy walked them to the door and Jon bent down and kissed her, whispering in her ear, "I'm so proud of you. You're my best girl. Thanks for everything."

She whispered back, "Don't be silly. How else can I show you how much I appreciate you?"

Bill Griffon laughed and opened the door. "Come on, son. We'll never get downtown if you two keep that up."

It was a convivial group that gathered for cocktails late in the day and Eleanor and Bill found themselves the center of happy attention.

Seated at the dinner table, Max Esquith quietly observed Emmy, taking pleasure in her loveliness. Emmy was a beauty. The soft glow of the candles heightened her alabaster skin and her almond-shaped eyes reflected the soft lights. He admired the way she wore her shining black hair. It was cropped short and the natural ringlets framed her delicately chiseled features. It set off her face even though it was not in the prevailing style. He thought how admirable it was that she had the independence to do what she considered right for herself. He knew Elizabeth would have taken pride in her girl tonight. He could hear her telling Emmy, "Be yourself! Don't follow along like a lamb just because the others do." He mused, My young friend Jonathan hasn't really fathomed his wife's depths yet. She may appear delicate and overly emotional, but she's made of stronger stuff than he imagines. It's only natural she's tormented at times by what's happened to her, but she'll come out of it. His reverie was broken as Jon rose to pull out Emmy's chair.

Later as the guests were departing, Emmy whispered to him, "Don't go yet. We've barely had time to exchange a word. Are you tired?"

"No, child, I'm not. I'll stick around for a while and have a catch-up session with you and Eleanor."

He turned and hailed Eleanor. "Come on over here. I'm waiting to hear what you think of our fair city; it's been a long time since you've threatened to visit."

She seated herself alongside him. "Right, Max, I've finally made it to Oklahoma."

"And? What do you think of what you've seen? Did Em have a chance to show you her old homestead?"

"Yes, and it's a beautiful place. I'm really impressed, Max. I had no idea you all lived in such civilized fashion."

Those listening laughed as the two jibed with each other.

Max said, "Oh, we've got some cowboys and Indians around, if that's what you were expecting. I'll drum some up for you before you leave."

Eleanor was happy and flushed from all the wine. "Emmy didn't have the time to show me the interior of the house, but I understand it's really beautiful. She will though, won't you, Emmy darling?"

Emmy was busily stacking the coffee cups and plates. "Of course, if you'd like. I thought we'd go to the club for luncheon tomorrow—the house is nearby."

Max interjected, "You know, Em, I'm glad we didn't sell the house. The neighborhood is excellent and the land appreciates every day. I wouldn't be surprised if one day you and Jon decide to move back into it. It'd be a wonderful house in which to raise a family. Wouldn't the thought of that have tickled Liz?"

Before Emmy could answer, Eleanor huffed, "Max, I'm surprised at you."

He huffed right back playfully, "At what are you surprised, old friend? What did I say that roused your dander?"

She hesitated for a moment, collecting her wine-befogged thoughts, and said, "About the children having a family. Aren't you butting in? I love and adore Emmy, you all know that, but I'm sure she's too sensible under the circumstances. We'd all do well not to encourage them in that direction."

It was as if a thunderbolt hit the room. Emmy reeled as if she'd been struck; for a split second blackness descended and the sound of roaring winds filled her ears. There was stunned silence until Bill Griffon, who had been sitting quietly, snapped, "You've had too much to drink, El. What business is it of yours to suggest to the kids what they should do? You just got through reprimanding Max for the same thing."

She looked at her husband, her eyes full of reproach. "Oh, Bill, how could you? I love Emmy, and I wouldn't be the mother I am if I stayed quiet about the risk they'd be taking."

Jonathan, who had been at the door seeing the last of their guests depart, walked back in time to see Emmy, rooted to the spot, holding a full tray on which the glasses were shaking. His father, brick red, was hollering in anger at his mother, "What in hell are you talking about? What risk?"

Eleanor, thoroughly besotted, sniffled, "You know very well, Bill. Do I have to spell it out for you?"

He rose and stood over her, a strong, stockily built man,

with a pugnacious jaw that jutted out. He seemed almost menacing as rage overtook him and he roared, "Dammit, yes! Stop talking in your crazy riddles!"

Red with embarrassment at what she sensed was going on, Eleanor was too far gone to contain herself. She blurted out, "It's because of Emmy, poor child. She doesn't have the slightest idea what sort of family she's out of . . . what her background was. It could have been awful."

Bill Griffon exploded so loudly Pearlie Mae almost dropped the dish she was holding way back in the kitchen. "Listen here, Eleanor, you cut this stuff out. I never heard anything so asinine in my life. You apologize to Emmy this instant."

At this, Emmy put the tray down and tore out of the room, with Jon in close pursuit. Bill Griffon lit into his wife. "Of all the cruel and callous things you've ever done, this is the worst. It's a miracle those children suffer having us around. What's gotten into you, woman?"

Reduced to tears, Eleanor was sobbing, "Oh, Bill . . . I didn't mean to be cruel, really I didn't. I meant it for their good."

Bill Griffon could never withstand his wife's tears, but he was really angry at what she had done. He lowered his voice as he said coldly, "Well, if anyone had better mind their own business, it's you! If you ever hope to remain on halfway decent terms with Em, you'd better apologize and mean it!"

Max had sat quietly throughout the episode, realizing he had been the innocent instigator of what had occurred. In a way he was glad it had happened, that they had all been witness to what went on in Eleanor's mind. He could understand Emmy's reluctance to have a child. Now this would give him an opportunity to get a few things straightened out, to clear the air.

He poured himself another drink from the Scotch decanter and said, "I have a few things to say and I'd appreciate your attention. First, let me tell you, Eleanor, I'm astounded at the things you've said, but I believe you're sincere. Apparently you've been harboring these feelings for a long time. Isn't this what you told Emmy in New York when you knew she and Jon were going to be married? You gave her a bad time then too. It's a pity you feel that way."

Bill Griffon looked at Max with interest; obviously he had not known the full story. He was about to interrupt, but Max signaled him to wait. Eleanor had something to say. "Max, I can't deny it, you're right. It worried me then, and now that the children are married, it worries me more."

A derisive smile crossed Max's lips as he said scornfully, "My dear Eleanor, you and your daughter-in-law have more in common than you apparently realize."

She looked at him, puzzled. "I don't know what you're talking about. I just have to admit the truth. I know what a marvelous person Emmalina is, and I know how wonderfully Elizabeth raised her—it's none of those things—I don't know why it worries me the way it does."

"Why don't you try to tell us, Eleanor . . . please."

"It's the story. It's the way those people, Em's natural parents, went off and left them. You have to admit those people might have had insanity or some other inherited disease in their family. People who would do such a thing can't be of a very high moral level. Maybe they did something evil they didn't want anyone to know about. Have you ever thought they might even have been robbers, murderers—or, at the very least, Jews, who knows? I can't imagine what could make people do a thing like that."

Max had frozen at her words, and he stared at her in cold contempt. He gave a small ironic laugh as he said, through clenched lips, "You're right, Eleanor, *you can't imagine!* You've lived too sheltered a life. How could you possibly know what would make people do a thing like that? They probably suffered from a disease you know little about—they were poor, maybe starving to death. Dammit, why don't you every try to put your foot in the other man's shoe? Did it ever occur to you they might have been good people? People without prospects or hope of any assistance, with three little tykes needing food and shelter. What would you know? Those were harsh and horrible times. My God, didn't you see enough of people standing on streetcorners trying to sell a lousy apple? Are you completely blind and bigoted?" His voice rose. "Where have you been? Locked away in your castles of comfort, have you ever concerned yourself with others, with decent people who might have wanted to give their children a chance at a better life? Have you any idea of the guts and bravery that would take?" His anger seemed to shake the room. "Think of the courage it would take to give up your children for such a reason. Why haven't you ever come to me before and asked what I knew? I've been mistaken about you; I always thought under all that silliness there was a more generous, humane person than you've shown here tonight."

Bill Griffon cut in. "Max, you've got to believe me. The things Eleanor's said never even occurred to me. If I'd known this was going on in her head, I'd have knocked some sense into it long before this."

The men exchanged smiles as Eleanor hid her face behind her handkerchief.

Max assumed his most judicial manner as he resumed his lecture. "Listen carefully, Eleanor, and see if the facts I put before you don't bear out what I've been saying. Elizabeth knew Em's parents."

Eleanor looked at him in surprise as he explained, "The family sought shelter in her home fighting their way to it through one of the worst dust storms ever to hit the area. She told me they were well-spoken, literate people. They were penniless; the father had lost his job and they were migrating in search of a place where they could resettle. Elizabeth's impression of them was that they had an overburdened sense of pride. They were caught in a terrible dilemma. Many times she told me how well cared for the children were." He paused and said sternly, "You're making mountains out of molehills with all that gibberish about inherited disease. How sure are you of your genetic background? I have a hunch there might have been a few washer women. Have you any idea what this calamitous war we're fighting is all about? There's something you should know. I regret you've already been contaminated by our long friendship. I never thought to tell you one of my grandparents was of the Jewish faith. I gather you assume that's a disease too. Would you mind telling me, since you're so concerned with bloodlines, what's so special about yours? Just how do you account for this blind and bigoted nature of yours?"

Bill Griffon rose and extended his hand to Max. "Put it there, old friend. I'm one hundred percent with you. Em's what this family needs. I'm ashamed of you, El."

Max added to his depleted Scotch glass. "There's a little more I have to say; we're all family here, and I think it's important you know what's going on. Em and Jon are having problems—and, El, I believe you're mainly responsible for them. Jon wants a family and Em's refused. Someone's put a bee in her bonnet about her murky background and the risks involved. After what you've said here tonight, I understand why she feels that way."

Both men saw shock on Eleanor's face but not contrition. Max's face grew grim. "You know, Eleanor, if Liz had been here tonight, you'd really have gotten it. She worked for years to build up Emmy's confidence and faith in herself, and along you come and blow the whole house down. Emmy trusted you—that child has an openness of spirit. She's a beautiful innocent who wants to embrace the whole world."

Eleanor squirmed in her chair as Max said, "I'm afraid you could seriously undermine their marriage. Before you ever entered the picture Emmy had started the search for her family. Now I must tell you Jonathan has been most supportive of Emmy . . . but, Eleanor, you are his mother, and some of his influence has to be felt. It gives me great cause for concern about their future."

Jonathan walked into the room, his face showing worry and strain. "Thanks, Uncle Max. I couldn't help but overhear a lot of what you've said. Emmy won't let me near her; she's locked herself in the bedroom. Mother, what you did to Em tonight was inexcusable. If you were so really worried, couldn't you have come to me or Uncle Max before this?"

Eleanor sat awash in her tears as the father went to his son. "Jon, I think your mother's just beginning to understand how badly she's behaved. Let her make amends the best way she can. All right?"

"Dad, I wish with all my heart this had never happened. I just don't know how Em's going to handle this."

Standing up abruptly, Eleanor almost fell over as she pleaded, "Let me go to her. Let me talk to her."

Everyone was startled as Emmy said, "That won't be necessary, Eleanor." She had walked in unobserved. "Whatever you have to say can be said here and now."

Suddenly haggard and drawn as the realization dawned on her that what she had perpetrated had ruined the happiness of their visit, undone their reconciliation, a wilted and beaten Eleanor implored, "Emmy, I didn't mean to be cruel. I hope you can find it in your good heart to forgive me. I had too much to drink. I'm so sorry."

Emmy couldn't disguise her scorn as she said, "In a way I respect your honesty. That's how you really feel. You love your son, and it was your concern for him—"

"No, not for Jon alone . . . for you too."

"I would like to believe that, but I can't. You've harbored these feelings for too long. But, in any case, put your mind at ease. I have no intention of putting any blot on the Griffon escutcheon. I have offered Jon his freedom, but that is a matter we must settle privately."

She walked over to Max, who looked up at her sadly as she sat down on the floor next to him. "Thank you, darling. What would I do, dearest Uncle Max, if I didn't have you? Without Mommy there'd be no one."

He tilted her head up so she had to look at him. "That's nonsense. You have a wonderful husband. What went on here tonight is not of Jonathan's making. You're one of the bravest, finest young women I know, and any child you'd have would do you credit. There's been enough talk for one evening. I'm tired . . . you all get yourselves to bed. I've got to amble along home."

Max's hopes for a peaceful resolution of the family situation were dashed when Emmy telephoned him early the next morning. "Uncle Max, I have to speak to you. Where can I meet you?"

"Come to the office whenever you're ready, Em. I'll wait for you."

In all the years he had known Emmy he had never seen her so cold and deliberate. She was filled with an anger that would brook no rebuttal. As she began to talk, he realized Jonathan had done the unpardonable: he had apparently risen to his mother's defense.

"I need to put some distance between myself and Jonathan, Uncle Max. I have to get this thing in perspective, think it over coolly. I think a divorce will be the only cure, but I won't do anything until I've had time to consider everything. Let's be fair, Uncle Max; even though I despise Eleanor for thinking the way she does, we can't deny she has a point. More so when you consider in what esteem she holds bloodlines . . . she'd have made a perfect Nazi. But think what she's going through over me . . . and it is entirely possible, you know, that there is something tragically bad in my background. Could be my baby would have black blood, Jewish blood, congenital heart disease or a horrible deformity."

Max stared in stony silence; he was having difficulty controlling his anger. "I'd be the last to refute what you're saying . . . George Washington Carver, Albert Einstein, oh, I could give you a list miles long—but why bother when any child of yours is already foredoomed? You, my dear Emmalina, are more like Eleanor Griffon than you can imagine. That's a cumbersome load you're carrying. Have you any plans for lightening it?"

Emmy was not impervious to his sarcasm; she knew he considered her behavior cowardly and far from anything Elizabeth would have approved. But Eleanor Griffon had eroded her strengths, hit her Achilles' heel; she made too much sense to be brushed aside, no matter how logically Max argued to the contrary. Jonathan was tainted by his mother's brush, a product of his upbringing, more so than he knew. If a child of theirs carried a defect it would never be attributable to anyone but Emmy. She studied Max for a moment and then spoke.

"I am no gambler, no matter what you think. I feel I'd be better off out of this marriage. I never should have married Jonathan Griffon in the first place. I want to live in an atmosphere where I can be free to struggle with the gifts and burdens of my own inheritance without bias or prejudice. If I remain in this situation, Jonathan is right, I will go crazy. I have to have the freedom to broaden my goals, to see my qualities and capacity for widening and opening up . . . aspects of myself that up till now have been hidden. I have more strength of character than you're giving me credit for right now, but I have to find breathing room . . . these people have the faculty for smothering any spark that ignites in me. I am going to leave Jonathan, Uncle Max, and the sooner the better."

Listening, Max decided perhaps it might be the wisest course, at least for the time being, to put some distance between the two. It would give them a chance to come to their senses.

Emmy related what had gone on after his departure the evening before. "I wish Jonathan were half the man his father is. Bill told me he didn't believe in meddling in his children's affairs and he would have given everything he had to have erased what Eleanor did. He insists they're clearing out tomorrow. I guess he's afraid she'll put her foot in it again." She paused and her face took on an indignant expression. "Uncle Max, I can no longer tolerate Jonathan's excuses for his mother. I realize he's in an awkward position, but you might as well know, any love and respect I felt for him are gone. In spite of his protestations that my family situation doesn't matter, I'm convinced that it does matter to him. Uncle Max, you did a wonderful thing; I heard you, but it's wasted. Nothing will ever change Eleanor Griffon's mind or heart. You don't have to answer, but think about it . . . if you were me, would you really want to have a child who would have her as its grandmother? She'd always be hunting for something. Any child I'd carry would have the mark of Cain. Can you imagine if the baby had something as common as crossed eyes? Heaven forbid, but if it were so, it would be due to my heinous background."

"That's ridiculous and you know it." But Max was no longer so sure he was right.

"You know better, Uncle Max. Don't think it hasn't rubbed off on Jonathan."

"My God, Em, come on—he's his own man. He married you in spite of his mother's nonsense."

"That was a mistake. I knew it then and now I'm certain. He left me no choice."

"Whatever that means, Em, I'll take your word for it."

"You know what he told me last night? Despite his seeming to agree with what I said, it wound up with his insisting I go to his mother, make peace and ask them to stay." She stopped as she fought to control her feelings. "When I said I'd only ask them to stay if he forced me to—and if they did, I'd go—he got very angry and said, 'Go ahead, leave—that's what you've been threatening to do anyhow. Running out on your responsibilities comes naturally . . .'" She broke down.

Shocked, Max tried to think of a plausible answer. "Em, under the circumstances you both said a lot of things you didn't mean; you were badly upset. I know what his saying that did to you, believe me I do . . . but remember one thing, he loves you."

Emmy laughed sharply. "Sooner or later it was bound to happen, Uncle Max. He's his mother's son; she reached him. Did you know, Uncle Max, Jonathan thinks I'm crazy? He's been urging me to go to the Menningers."

"Yes, I know, Em. He told me how concerned he was about you and felt they might reassure you about having a family."

Emmy dried her eyes. "I wish I could believe that was the only reason. I don't! I think he wanted to know if there wasn't a streak of lunacy in my background."

Max laughed heartily. "Em, that's bosh. You know better than that!"

"No, I don't, Uncle Max. Consider for a minute. Do you want me to live the rest of my life with a sword hanging over my head? Do you understand that anything I do, say or think that isn't in accord with the holy Griffons will be attributed to my tainted bloodline? I don't see much hope for us. I have to get away! I've made up my mind."

Max sat quietly, thinking. "You know, Em, I was wondering how Liz would have handled this, what she would have advised. She was not one to run away from a problem—but in this case, I'd say it's not running away, it's taking a gamble. It might be a good idea to let your husband come to his senses. Yes, I think so. Take a vacation. Where would you like to go?"

She crumpled in a heap in the chair. He rose and stood over her. "Child, you're all I have in this world, and I can't stand it when I see you like this."

Emmy murmured through her tears. "Uncle Max, it hurts, it really does."

He patted her head. "I know, child, I know. But one thing I want you to promise me. I never again want to hear you talk about your 'tainted blood.' You're as sane and as fine as any human being it's been my privilege to know, other than your sainted mother, Elizabeth. Your life is in the future, child. You've a whole lifetime to live without adding to your old ghosts. Find your family, that'll help—get it out of your system. What's gone and done is over with! Now, I have an idea. I have a marvelous old friend in California. He and his wife are just the folks to help you over this hurdle. He's a well-known movie agent, and she's really a doll—you'll love her. They'll show you a high old time."

Drying her eyes, Emmy asked, "Uncle Max, do you think he could help me find work?"

"Work? How long are you planning to stay? Do you mean in the movies?"

"There you go, being funny. No, not in the movies. Maybe something in the music line. I'd like to get busy and do something different for a while. If I could, I'd bring Pearlie Mae out there and stay for a time."

"You mean you don't mind leaving me?" He was joking but he realized she had no intentions of resuming her marriage; her mind was already made up. Well, it was too soon to be sure about anything. It was best to play along with her. He reached for the telephone. "I'll place the call now. When do you want to leave?"

"How about the start of next week? I want a change as quickly as possible. Do you think you could come and visit me while I'm there, Uncle Max?"

"You know, Em, there's a mighty big war going on. If you're so anxious to do something to keep your mind occupied, why don't you volunteer your services in some useful way? You certainly don't need any remuneration."

"Why didn't I think of that? Am I that selfish?"

"No, no, child, but you seem to be planning a long stay. I thought originally you meant about a month."

"Well . . ."

"Em, you're jumping the gun. In a way you're not being fair to Jonathan. You're not a faucet that runs hot and cold. If you cared for Jonathan when you married him, your feelings can't have altered so appreciably that you're ready to throw it all to the winds."

She wailed softly, "I thought you understood why we have no future together. I'm not walking out; I'm giving Jonathan his freedom to find someone more suitable for his needs and station in life."

"Em, you have to think this through very carefully." He tilted his chair back and studied her. She was being stubborn and childish. "Look, Em, I'm on your side. I understand what you're up against, but I still don't think it's without hope. I'm certain Jonathan already regrets what he's said, and I'm agreed a cooling-off period will be good for the two of you. All I'm suggesting is a vacation, not a permanent separation. Will you try it this way?"

Silently she nodded her head in acquiescence.

The call to California had gone through and Max picked up the telephone. Max Esquith and Ralph Michalson went back a long way. Their friendship had begun when they had been neighbors in Philadelphia. Max has been in his early teens when his family had taken the youngster in; Ralph's father had been killed in a tragic accident and his mother, hospitalized with tuberculosis, had been unable to care for him. It was to Max that Ralph came for help when the bigger boys bloodied his nose and bullied him. Max was the friend in whom the lad confided and whose advice he sought. It had been a painful time when Max had left to set up practice in Oklahoma, and over the years and across the miles they had remained in close touch. Ralph had unashamedly come to

Max for a stake when he had first gone West to make his way, and Max had been the one he had asked to be best man at his wedding. As far as Ralph Michalson was concerned, Max Esquith was father, brother and friend all rolled into one, and he was always mindful of the bond.

Ralph's voice pealed across the lines. "Hey, old buddy, if I lived ten lifetimes I could never do you enough favors. Tell that girl of yours she'll be as welcome as the sunshine. You know how delighted Betty'll be."

"That's wonderful, Ralph. Hey, I might even make it out there as long as Em's going to be staying awhile."

"Now you're talking—you've been promising for years. It's time! Takes a pretty young thing to make you do it, eh? Can't do it for the sake of auld lang syne, hah?"

"You know better, Ralph . . . you know what you and Betty mean to me."

Max, one thing: make sure your niece knows she won't be staying at a hotel. It's impossible to find crawl space—everything's booked for months. The war's filled the hotels to the gills. She'll have her own room with us. You've never seen it, but we have a huge, rambling old shack of a place. Give me her arrival date and time. We'll be there with bells on to pick her up."

It was almost an hour after Emmy had left that a knock on his door roused Max from his thoughts. He was more upset than he had let on to Emmy about what she had told him. At his "come in," he'd been surprised to see Jonathan. The woebegone face in front of him told Max he was in for another family counseling session.

"Well, I'll get right to the point," Jonathan said. "You remember the things I told you the other day—you know, about wanting a child. Well, it seems to me there are a whole lot of other things that are wrong. I've convinced there's something really wrong with Emmy . . . she's sick."

Max felt a shudder run through him. "What exactly do you mean by that? On what are you basing your medical diagnosis?"

"It's not easy to illustrate, but I'll give you examples. You know how involved Em's been with the Junior League, the Assistance League, all that sort of thing. Well, she seems to be well thought of and the other women appear to like her. She's been offered all sorts of jobs to do, but she flits from one to another. She's told me she thinks the work is silly or that she's not adequate. Then she carps if the women criticize her for this . . . says they're empty-headed and silly. She's so unsure of herself. She's fine when it comes to giving and you know how much she donates."

He paused and Max interjected, "Maybe she doesn't feel comfortable frittering her time away." Max was becoming wary; it was as though Jonathan were obsessed with the subject of Emmy's instability.

Jon looked at him in surprise. "Maybe, but in a way she does the same sort of thing with me."

"With you? How?"

"She's never sure with me. No matter how many times I tell her I love her, she doesn't believe me. I try everything, flowers, gifts—and the answer is always the same: 'Tell me you love me, Jonathan, make me believe you.' How the hell can I keep it up?"

Max sat quietly, twirling a pencil in his fingers, and then he looked across at the troubled face. "That cuts right to the heart of it, Jon. Isn't it possible Em intuitively senses something you're not aware of? Could it be that she feels you're making the best of a bad bargain, that she sees you're disillusioned with her? Be honest with yourself: how did you handle the situation with your mother? Did you really convince Em you were on her side?"

Jon shook his head impatiently. "That old saw again. Would I want a child if I agreed with my mother?"

"I'm not siding with Emmy, Jon, and I respect what you've told me; but somehow I get the feeling your wanting a child might be a cover-up . . . a sort of panacea to get Em off your neck. I'm inclined to agree with her: it might be better if you put it off for a while. There seems to be a big area of troubled communication between you. I get the feeling Em's insecurity is heightened not by what you do, but what you don't do. How honest are you with yourself?"

"For Pete's sake, Max! What the hell am I supposed to do? So my mother said she was disturbed by Em's background. My God, if she really knew what was going on there'd be hell to pay. I never thought twice about it until Em made it loom so large; and now, to tell the truth, I am wondering about it. After all, she's got everything a woman could ask for—and still she has trouble keeping friends, she's always worried about how she looks, what she's wearing, what I think about this one or the other. I think she's sick and—"

His irritation growing, Max cut in. "Hold it, son . . . stop using that blanket term for your rationale. On the assumption that you might be wrong, let me ask, have you ever encouraged her in other pursuits?"

"Why should I? I'm busy. She's got all the time in the world at her disposal. She knows I wouldn't stand in her way."

"Do you encourage her?"

"Now, forgive me, I don't mean to be rude, what's that supposed to mean? I don't recall my father ever having to suggest how my mother occupy her time. After all, Em is a grown woman; by now she ought to know the world is round."

"You are really angry at her, aren't you, Jon?"

"I don't know if it's anger, as much as I'm fed up."

At this Max leaned back in his chair and said quietly, "Well, Jon, it seems your crazy wife has a point. She was in here not so long ago telling me she thinks a separation is in order. I gather from what you're saying that it would be the best solution, unless you have any other ideas."

Max was sure he saw a surge of relief go through Jonathan as he responded, "It isn't that I've stopped caring about her, Max . . . I do . . ."

"Sure you do, Jon, but she's disappointed you. She's not living up to what you expected. I think the feeling is mutual on both your parts, so why don't you talk it over with Em and arrive at some sane conclusions?"

Jonathan looked at the judge, struggling to express something he couldn't quite articulate. "Max, I hope you won't think I'm a bastard, but I'm really finding it hard to cope with. Honestly, I think Em should have some professional help."

"You may be right, Jon, but she's an adult and she'll have to make her own decisions. Did you want me to recommend it to her?"

"It sure would be a help if you could."

Max leaned forward, a stern expression on his face. "Jonathan, you've undermined her enough without my adding to it. I appreciate how well intentioned you are, but I have a hunch a separation may do more for her than a doctor. You know, Jonathan, I was a judge almost more years than you were a boy, and I've listened to both sides of this case. There's much to be said for both of you; you're two fine young people, but—it's sad to think about it—you may not be good for one another. Try a separation; possibly it may work the cure. Now, young man, if you don't mind, I've got to get to work."

Miffed at the judge's attitude and the way he was being dismissed, Jonathan rose hastily, thanked Max and left.

After the door closed, Max sat exhausted. He was certain of one thing. Emmy was not mentally ill; insecure and unsure, yes, but not ill. He'd been certain Jonathan had not been influenced by his mother's attitudes, but now he was no longer so sure. He was angered by what Jonathan had said and muttered, "Young smartass." He put his desk in order, turned out lights and made his way out. Suddenly he felt old and disappointed; he had expected so much from the union of Emmy and Jonathan. With the way the situation was shaping up, it might be wiser for Emmy to extricate herself now, rather than later.

Immediately after his parents left, Jonathan moved to the club. Max spoke with Emmy and she told him, "Uncle Max, we're too sore and hurt with each other to be able to talk this thing out sensibly."

Max made a point of asking Jonathan to come to his office. "I hear you've moved out, boy. Things certainly seem to be in a mess. It seems a shame that because of a lot of nonsensical jibber-jabber you're both prepared to throw the whole thing over. You've each got an overburdened sense of pride."

Jonathan was gentle with him. "You may be absolutely right, Max, but for the time being this seems to be the best solution. We couldn't make any headway talking to each other. We just don't see things the same way."

"Well, what more can I say, boy? What are your plans? Are you going to stay at the club after Em leaves?"

"As a matter of fact, no, Max. I was planning to tell you. I'm going to join the Ambulance Corps. I have no business sitting the war out despite my deferment. I've given it a lot of thought, and this is what I want to do."

"Well, my boy, I can't dissuade you from that either. You have to do what you think is right."

Alone Max mused. In his generation young people had taken responsibility and commitment more seriously. The way Emmy and Jonathan were handling their difficulties—it didn't bode well.

The young Griffons maintained a politely frigid front with each other. On the day of Em's departure for California, Max accompanied Jonathan as they drove her to the train station. It was painful to watch as they bid each other good-bye.

They exchanged pecks on the cheek. Max couldn't bear what he was watching and scolded Emmy: "You're behaving like a child. Stop it! Don't you realize that this crazy loon of a husband of yours is about to go off to war? He may be killed—you may never see each other again. Do you want to part this way, knowing that?"

She flushed and put her hand on Jonathan's arm. He looked at Max compassionately. "You're being overly dramatic, Uncle Max. One chance in a million . . . don't make me out a hero."

"Fool!" Max muttered.

Suddenly Jonathan took Em in his arms. He held her closely without speaking and she said, "Take care of yourself, Jon. Keep in touch."

"You too, Em . . . take care. You're a wonderful, marvelous girl—and no matter what, I love you." He kissed her long and lingeringly.

She drew back and asked, "How will I know where to contact you?"

"Uncle Max will have my address. You be sure to write! Hey, don't you fall for any of those handsome Hollywood guys."

She almost faltered. Max had the feeling it was a crucial moment; if Jonathan had pressed the point, the matter might have straightened itself out right there.

The conductor was impatiently signaling for her to mount the steps. She didn't look back and in a moment the train began to move. Both men slowly walked away. It hurt Jonathan to see how old and bent the judge seemed. It wasn't until they were back in the car that the judge spoke. "Why didn't you just drag her off and put all this foolishness behind you? Seems to me she'd have been willing."

Jonathan didn't answer at once; he sat thinking and finally said, "You might be right, but I tried that once before. That's how I got Emmy to marry me. You can see where it's got us. Look, I shouldn't have said what I did about her always wanting to run. I'm sorry about that."

Max was moved by the entire experience, watching the two part, hearing this from Jonathan, and he sat quietly considering it. Jonathan broke the silence. "Remember when I first spoke to you about Em? At that time she wouldn't let me touch her and I practically raped her twice." Jon could see the shock on the older man's face and he added, "It'll probably surprise you even more to know she liked it. Once in a while it may be stimulating, but who the hell wants to live that way?"

Embarrassed by the disclosure, Max asked brusquely, "What do you really think the future holds for the both of you, Jon?"

"At the moment, I wouldn't venture a guess."

Max felt a wrenching sense of loss as Jonathan put the car into gear and began to drive. The world, as he knew it, was being blown to bits, falling apart.

Matters had moved with such headlong speed in the time before she'd left that Emmy had not really given herself a chance to make an evaluation of the steps she was taking. When she was alone in her train compartment, the impact of what she was doing hit; she saw herself forsaken and bereft and gave way to waves of self-pity. She pitched from one emotion to another: anger and resentment at Jon and his mother, at Max's audacity in telling her how to behave saying good-bye to Jonathan. When she had run the gamut, she quieted down and tried to put her thoughts into some semblance of order. She knew that when Jonathan had taken her into his arms that last minute, she'd weakened, almost changed her mind about going. In a way she had hoped he would overpower her, forcibly make her remain. Was this a sign she loved him? She couldn't answer herself. She wondered what kind of game she was playing. Maybe she was unable to recognize love, didn't know what it was all about. Jonathan had been the first and only man in her life. Her conscience plagued her; how awful to have parted from him the way she did, knowing he was going to face heaven only knew what sort of peril. Suddenly she missed him, the sight and sound of him; she wanted him desperately. She had brought this entire thing on her own head. Damn Jonathan, he'd been right—in a way she was crazy. Well, it was too late for regrets; it was time to calm down and face facts. She picked up a magazine and flipped through the pages. Suddenly an advertisement gave her an idea: she'd put a call through to Jonathan as soon as the train had a long enough stop. She buzzed for the porter, who gave her the information about the station stops. She felt better; given a chance, she'd get herself straightened out. In trusting her instincts, she's regain her balance.

She heard the call for dinner and realized she was ravenously hungry. Walking through the rocking corridors, she was impressed with the well-appointed train. Passing through the attractive club car, she saw it was occupied by a convivial group. Stars glittered on its ceiling and the subdued lighting gave it a nightclub atmosphere. She'd stop later and have an afterdinner drink from the bar. It would be more interesting to pass time here than alone in her compartment.

The maître d' welcomed her to the dining car. She felt better, ready to enjoy a leisurely dinner. The table was set, covered in white linen, and there were fresh carnations in a slim vase. The waiter hovered at her elbow making suggestions. After she had written her order she relaxed, enjoying the company of the two naval officers who had been seated at her table. As she chatted with them, her self-esteem rose as she saw how eager they were to make an impression. They invited her to join them for a drink in the club car and remained by her side until the train made its long stop.

She raced for the telephone, heedless of the time. She tried not to cry when she heard Jonathan's sleepy voice. She could hear his surprise when she poured out her apologies and protestations of love. Roused from sleep, he did his best to assure her. "It'll be all right, Em. I'm sure we'll work it out. Just remember I love you."

"I will darling . . . please write."

"I will, Em, as often as I can. Just hang in there and try to get yourself straightened out."

She heard the conductor's call; the train was huffing, ready to pull out. She had to go. "Good-bye, darling. I love you very much. Come back to me."

"I will. Good-bye, Em."

Back in her compartment she watched the empty faces sliding by as the train gathered speed. She was suddenly consumed with regret at what she had done. She had foolishly given way to an impulse, reassured Jonathan she loved him when down deep something told her it wasn't true. An inner voice nagged at her, and it hit; she saw with clarity what she had allowed to happen. She had given way to her insecurities, and Jonathan had been her anchor. She had married him because she had needed to make herself part of something— to belong, to be part of a family. She had not been fair to him; they each saw things from different viewpoints, came from such different places. She was filled with self-contempt; she had used Jonathan, and while he had tried to love her, she was probably incapable of accepting love. As she settled herself in bed, the doleful whistle of the train sobbed as it made its way through the night.

Ralph Michalson's attention would have been drawn to the attractive young woman in any case, despite Max's accurate description of Emmalina. Observing her as the passengers moved along the corridor, he felt certain they'd met before. He tried to remember where as she stopped nearby, looking around. He approached. "Hello. You must be Mrs. Griffon."

Her face broke into a warm smile as she said, "How nice that Uncle Max described me so well. You are Mr. Michalson?"

Escorting her by the arm, Ralph Michalson couldn't rid himself of the insistent impression of familiarity. He knew her, he'd met her before—her voice, her manner, all convinced him. "We'd better move along, Mrs. Griffon. It looks as though we're holding up the war effort. All the trains are loaded with service people."

The two naval officers came along at that moment and hailed Emmy. She waved in response and said, "Wonderful men—it breaks your heart to know what they're facing."

He nodded. "We do our best here to send them off happily. Do you have baggage checks? Would you like a cup of coffee while my chauffeur waits for your luggage?"

She felt at ease with this warm and friendly man, and within minutes they were chatting like old friends. As they stood in line waiting to be assigned a table, he took the opportunity of telling her what plans had been made in her behalf. "We want you to feel completely comfortable and at home with us. It's impossible to get a hotel room for more than two nights. Betty, my wife, is looking forward to having you stay with us. It'll be a joy for us to have a beautiful young lady like yourself around."

Emmy protested prettily, "I hope I won't be in your way. I really hate to impose."

He assured her that her visit would be a breath of fresh air in their lives as the hostess motioned them to a table. "Tell me about that old weasel, that wonderful friend of mine—how is Max?"

"You're right, he is wonderful . . . and, thank goodness, he is fine."

Once seated with the order placed, Ralph asked, "Are you related to the Esquith family, Mrs. Griffon? I don't recall Max ever mentioning nieces or nephews."

"My name is Emmalina—Emmy for short—Mr. Michalson. It would please me very much if you'd call me by my first name. Uncle Max is my uncle by love. He was the dearest friend of my mother and probably the nearest person in my life to a father. He's grown even more precious to me since the passing of my mother. He's all the family I have."

"Mrs. Griffon—rather, Emmy—it mystifies me . . . I can't rid myself of the feeling we've met before. Am I being foolish? Do I look familiar to you?"

She looked at him dubiously. "I don't think so, Mr. Michalson." She smiled at him archly. "You're so distinguished I'm sure I'd recall if we had met."

He shook his head in wonderment. "It's the strangest thing—you must remind me of someone." As the words left his mouth he knew immediately. "Of course! Tana Corgan! You resemble each other enough to be sisters."

She chuckled. "I have heard that from time to time."

He thought, It's going to be interesting seeing what impression others get when they meet Emmalina Griffon.

As the car drove up the driveway, Emmy couldn't help being impressed by the beautiful landscaping and interesting architecture of the stately old house.

"You see, young woman, you have but to look at this humble abode to know we have more than ample room for a mite like yourself. Despite its outer grandeur, don't be misled. We live unpretentiously and have just a couple to help us out. The chauffeur and his wife take care of everything. Ah, there's Betty now."

Standing in the doorway was a smiling woman who called out a greeting. "Hurry, you two! I'm dying with impatience to meet Max's niece."

As she moved forward to welcome Emmy, it was apparent she was lame; one of her legs was shorter than the other. The two women took to each other instantly. Almost at once Emmy felt herself completely at ease, at home.

Betty Michalson was not a beauty. She had been a dancer in her youth, cute and pert, and then polio had struck. Notwithstanding that she was lame, Ralph Michalson had fallen madly in love with the charming girl, and their marriage had been a huge success, the talk of Hollywood. Everyone knew they adored each other, and Ralph had eyes for no one else—Betty made his world complete.

Despite the numerous demands on his time, Betty lived a fairly secluded life; her interests were different from most of those around. Childless, she had filled her days with quiet philanthropic work and painting. She was a recognized artist whose work hung in museums throughout the world. A woman of warm and vibrant personality, those who knew her loved her.

Emmy exclaimed with delight as Betty showed her to the quarters that were to be hers. "How beautiful! Mrs. Michalson, I feel guilty putting you to all this trouble on my behalf."

"Please"—she laughed—"don't feel that way. Believe me, you're just what Ralph and I need. We're such recluses, it's a joy for us to have you with us. Not for one minute are you to feel you're imposing. You see for yourself we're like two beans rattling around in this cavern of a house. If that old bear of a Max ever decides to visit us, we've plenty of room for him as well. I implore you, relax, feel at home and call me Betty. I'll let you unpack and then we'll give you the grand tour. Ralph has such plans for you, and if what I do interests you, you'll be more than welcome to spend time with me. If you don't mind, one day I'd like to sketch you."

"Watch out, Emmy." Ralph Michalson stood at the open door, grinning. "Once she nabs you, you'll be stuck. Don't let that sketch talk fool you; it'll be an oil painting and you'll be hanging in galleries everywhere."

Relaxed and happy, Emmy felt totally comfortable with her new friends. They reminded her of Elizabeth and Max.

Later as they showed her about their spacious grounds they were struck by her lack of affectation and honest admiration for the beauty that surrounded them. Emmy reacted with childlike delight to the vine-covered gazebo and the tinkling fountain in which two whimsical cherubs perpetually splashed one another, and then surprised them by her sophisticated discernment of the paintings in Betty's studio. Oohing and aahing at the sight of the huge swimming pool which Betty used daily as therapy, she said disappointedly, "I never thought to bring my bathing suit."

"Fear not," Betty quipped, "there's no shortage of them in our fancy Beverly Hills stores. It's amazing how well stocked they remain through all these shortages."

Emmy looked around in wonderment. "It's a little bit of

Paradise . . . one could almost forget there's a war going on."

Betty, who had been studying Emmy's facial structure, suddenly exclaimed, "My God, Ralph, look! Emmy, did anyone ever tell you that you're a double for Tana Corgan?"

"What took you so long, Betty? You surprised me. I saw it at once. Did you ever see such a resemblance?"

Shaking her head vehemently, Betty said, "It's uncanny. I had the feeling we'd met before, but I knew we couldn't have—and then it's such a cliché to say that, I just let it go. But studying you, it struck me. Do you know, you could be twins?"

Emmy looked at her curiously as Betty said, "You certainly have to have heard this before . . . particularly since Tana's become such a hit."

"Not as often as you assume. However, there have been instances. My brother-in-law had the same impression."

Emmy looked at them, pondering; she seemed far away and Ralph asked, "Is something bothering you, Emmy?"

She hesitated for a moment. "I know this has to seem out of place on such short acquaintance, but I'd like to ask a favor. Is there someplace we can sit down and talk for a moment?"

"Of course, dear. Come along," Betty said, leading the way. "Let's sit in the den and have a cool drink or some wine. What's on your mind?"

As she entered the room behind Betty, Emmy exclaimed in delight. It looked like a page out of an English novel. It was a replica of an English clubroom to the last detail. The dark inlaid floors were covered by wine-colored Persian throw rugs; upholstered red velvet couches and chairs framed in mahogany were juxtaposed in front of an antique, intricately carved wood fireplace on whose mantel there was an array of charming Toby mugs. Interesting groupings of drypoint prints and etchings covered the walls, and there was lots of fine china and unusual pieces of brass from India. Emmy was captivated by a life-sized china Pug dog used as a doorstop. Completing the impression was a small but authentic bar, straight out of an English pub with a dart board alongside it. Emmy was filled with admiration as she realized it was a perfect background for Ralph. The room exuded dignified masculinity from the red velvet portieres to the aromatic scent that emanated from the inlaid humidor that flanked the chair he had seated himself in. Just as Emmy moved to sit down, she was waylaid by the sudden appearance of a gentle, inquiring, shaggy old sable collie. Dropping to her knees she cooed and petted him, looking at Betty questioningly; his large soulful brown eyes were almost sightless. Betty smiled at her. "You've acquired another friend. Robin's been with us since he was three months old, and that yelping you hear from the outside is his progeny. He's the only one we permit in the house—his arthritis is bad. I hope you're a dog enthusiast . . . we have three of them."

Emmy hugged the animal. "I adore them."

"Good. Come, sit down."

Ralph whistled softly and the collie moved slowly to lie at his feet.

They were waiting for her to tell them what was so urgently on her mind, and as she seated herself she could see Ralph was concerned. Almost beseechingly she said, "I've no right to burden you with my problems, but, under the circumstances, I feel you ought to know why this close resemblance to Tana Corgan disturbs me."

Their curiosity roused, Emmy told them the circumstances of her childhood. "So, you see, after my adopted mother's death, at my request Uncle Max and Jonathan, my husband, agreed to institute a search for my missing family. We've not had too much luck so far, although there's a possibility they're onto the trail of my middle sister who's somewhere here in California. Our baby sister, however, disappeared without a trace. This resemblance you talk about to Tana Corgan could have more significance than I ever realized. I remember now how struck Bill was by it. Just the same as the two of you."

Ralph moved to refill the women's wineglasses. He looked at Emmy compassionately. "Emmy, it's a possibility, of course. Just don't get your hopes too high. It's a shame she's not in town; she's gone home for a while. It's interesting how the similarity stops at the physical. Tana Corgan doesn't seem like you in any other respect."

At that moment Emmy jumped as she reminded herself, "Oh, my goodness, I forgot that I promised to call Uncle Max." They directed her to the phone, and after she had talked with him, Ralph Michalson took over. When he had concluded he returned to the den. "Young lady, you've worked the magic. Max is coming. I can hardly believe it. He told me to reassure you that he would have a Mr. Saperson get on the Tana Corgan angle as soon as he can contact him."

Emmy smiled. "Uncle Max wouldn't have any problems if it weren't for me. Mr. Saperson is the man in charge of searching for my family."

She looked at them appealingly. "Would you mind telling me a little more about her, what you know of Tana Corgan?"

The Michalsons seemed discomforted by the request. Betty said, "Emmy, you've been so open and candid with us, I'm going to take the liberty of giving you some advice. Don't solicit other people's opinions of Tana Corgan. You'll be better off forming your own judgments. Ralph has known her a long time . . . since she started here. But I can say truthfully, we only know her superficially—and to be quite honest that's enough. She's an exceedingly self-indulgent young woman whose opinion of herself is way out of proportion to her merit. Apparently she's surrounded by people whose sole purpose is to wait on her hand and foot and keep her thinking she's perfection."

Emmy smiled wanly. "I gather she's not your most favorite person."

Ralph considered for a moment and said, "It's not fair for us to prejudice anyone in regard to her. In all honesty, I have to admit I think Tana conforms to what she feels movie stars are supposed to be. Although we see her from time to time, it's purely a matter of business. There's a great deal of that in this town."

Betty agreed. "Ralph's right, Emmy. If you meet her, you may find her very different from our estimation. I can tell you she's not my cup of tea."

Ralph added, "She's changed a lot from the timid slip of a girl she was when I first met her. I had the pleasure of meeting her parents, and it was hard to believe she belonged to them." He looked at Emmy, startled by what he had said. "It's true, though; the Corrigans were the simplest, most charming little Irish couple."

Emmy paled and swayed and both Michalsons made a move to go to her. She smiled. "I'm all right, really. It's just that it's got to be Polly Sue."

"Who? What name did you say?"

White, shaken, Emmy said slowly, "Polly Sue . . . Corrigan became her adopted name."

Betty stood up and moved to the couch alongside Emmy. She put an arm around her and, trembling with her own excitement, said, *"She is your sister!* It's too wild . . . I can't believe this story is true! You come here, after all the time you've been searching for her, and in a few hours, we find her. It's too incredible!"

Emmy sat speechless, stunned. Finally, when she could manage, she said, "Mr. Michalson, would you be good enough to call Uncle Max again and tell him what's happened?"

"I will. Of course. What an exciting piece of news this is going to be!"

Turning to Betty, Emmy entreated, "Are you certain she isn't here?"

"I'm positive. Ralph told me when she left. You know, she recently lost her husband. They'd been married such a short time and it was supposed to have been such a love match. He was a handsome, talented young man . . . such a waste. She went home to spend some time with her family. However, from what Ralph's told me, I think she's in for a rough time. It's a strange story . . . we inadvertently heard that her mother had passed away and we've gathered that, for some reason that we do not know, Tana was not informed."

Emmy's eyes grew dark with pain. "My goodness, how could that be? Poor girl, that's awful."

"That's partly what we meant when we talked of her before, Emmy. The plain truth is, Tana Corgan's a hard nut to crack. It seems there was a little incident when her mother visited some time back; they apparently parted angrily, and from that time on Mrs. Corrigan never returned. As far as I know, Tana's never gone back to her home before this."

The Michalsons' adverse description of Tana hadn't really registered. Emmy was too overcome with the knowledge of her disclosure. The realization that Polly Sue was close at hand, alive and well, was all she could absorb at the moment.

The two women sat in reflective silence until Ralph walked back into the room and began to switch on the lamps. He reported quietly, "Max finds it astonishing. He wants you to keep him posted on developments. Would you girls like a fire?"

He saw that Emmy looked at him without hearing and added, "This is the desert—it gets cool at night, did you know, Emmy?"

Betty caught his attention and nodded without speaking. He put a match to the kindling laid out in the fireplace. As it caught and flared they could see that Emmy's thoughts were a million miles away. The flames and the setting rays of the sun played on the walls and draperies of the room, illuminating them in flashes. It seemed a fitting accompaniment to the revelations of the day. As the firelight glinted and played across Emmy's face, each piercing light brought another image to her mind: her father's laughter, her mother's chatter and the baby crying . . . mixed in with images of Elizabeth and Jonathan. Her mind was a well of memories bubbling over from the recesses of her heart. She didn't know tears were coursing down her cheeks. Dimly, as if from a great distance, she heard Ralph Michalson's voice. "Do you think Tana knows she was adopted, Emmy?"

Emmy was bemused by the question, and an odd little smile crossed her face. "I'd have no way of knowing; she was just a baby. Unless the Corrigans told her, she'd have had no way of finding out."

The kindness of these people touched Emmy. They had been strangers a few hours ago, and now an intimacy had developed that made them feel like close friends. Later that evening, as they prepared to part for their respective rooms, Emmy impetuously embraced them both. "Thank you for everything. I feel as though I've known you all my life. I don't know how I can ever express my gratitude—but believe me, I'll try."

Ralph was embarrassed at the girl's effusiveness. "We've done very little, but the feeling is mutual. Now try to get a good night's sleep. I'm taking you off to Major Pictures tomorrow, and you'd better look your best. You're apt to get an offer to be Tana Corgan's stand-in."

The idea amused them all and they parted laughing.

At breakfast the next morning, high with excitement, Emmy chattered like a magpie, particularly thrilled at the prospect of Max's visit. The Michalsons were equally pleased that he would be joining them, but Betty joshingly scolded the girl as she continued to talk about it. "It's simply marvelous, but time you stop flying and eat some breakfast. You're in for a long day and I don't want Max to think we're not feeding you. Have a slice of toast and jam with your coffee."

Emmy grinned. "I do get carried away—I'm sorry. It's hard to settle down."

Passing the jam to her, Ralph said, "Emmy, we've been discussing the events of yesterday. Betty and I don't want to put a damper on your feelings, but we think it would be wiser if, for the time being, you kept the knowledge of your relationship to Tana Corgan under wraps. In this place, if the newspeople even got an inkling, all hell would break loose. They'd drive you crazy."

Puzzled, she looked at him in surprise. "Really? Why? I don't understand. Of course, I'll do what you say, but why would they be interested in my personal affairs?"

Astounded at Emmy's naïveté, Betty said, "A star like Corgan has little privacy. She lives in a fishbowl . . . everything about her makes news. Obviously it hasn't occurred to you that you also bear a well-known name. The Griffons don't make the sort of flamboyant headlines that screen people do, but nonetheless their activities seem to be newsworthy."

This seemed odd to Emmy; where she came from they'd just been everyday people. "I really had no idea, but of course I'll do whatever you think best."

She's really a simple girl, Ralph decided; it'll be interesting to see what Hollywood does to her. He watched her for a moment and then said, "You know, Emmy, if this is disclosed to Tana she may not want it made public."

"What?" Betty interrupted. "The way she courts publicity, I can hardly believe that."

Lowering his voice, he put his coffee cup down and looked at Betty significantly. "You of all people, knowing what you do, shouldn't take anything for granted. There's always the possibility that, whatever her reason, Tana Corgan may reject this relationship. But"—and he turned to include Emmy—"in the event she should accept it, you'd better be prepared. With the Griffon name, its prominence, and her film fame, you'll be besieged."

Aghast at this new twist in her affairs, Emmy blurted, "Oh, my God, my mother-in-law would have a fit. I'm sure Uncle Max has already told Jonathan, but I hope he doesn't tell anyone else."

"Max?" Ralph scoffed. "Don't worry about that old fox; he's too sharp to be loose-tongued. My dear, why do you suppose he's arriving here in such a short time? He knows how complicated this situation can be."

Embarrassed at her lack of understanding about how involved a matter this could be, Emmy said sheepishly, "I had no idea about all the trouble I'd be putting you people to . . . I'm dreadfully sorry."

"Nonsense, young lady," Betty said. "We love it. It's the most interesting thing that's happened to us in a long while."

"Do you know the Griffons?" Emmy asked.

Ralph nodded.

For a moment Emmy sat quietly thinking and then made the decision. It wouldn't be fair to keep these kind people in the dark. In the brief time she'd known them they'd inspired her trust and confidence, and under the circumstances maybe they wouldn't think too harshly of her. "I'm married to Jonathan; he's the youngest." She sighed, and they looked at her curiously. "You're going to hate me . . . I seem to do nothing but impose on you but . . . since I know you're apt to hear about it from Uncle Max, I'd rather not deceive you. My reason for coming to California is that Jonathan Griffon and I have decided to separate." She paused and looked at them imploringly. "Please believe that I had no intention of weighing so heavily on your generosity. I really didn't intend to make you party to all my troubles. I've behaved inexcusably."

Mortified, she sat with her head bowed, missing the commiserating glances the Michalsons exchanged at this new revelation.

The tour of the studio was an eye-opener for Emmy. As Ralph has predicted, almost everyone, upon being introduced to Emmy, commented on her resemblance to Tana Corgan. By the time they had finished their tour, it was the lunch hour and Ralph took her to the executive dining room to meet Gene Madrix. After the preliminary pleasantries had been gotten out of the way, he could no longer restrain himself. As Ralph smirked, Gene said, "Mrs. Griffon, has anyone told you of your resemblance to our star, Tana Corgan?"

Ralph and Emmy broke into laughter. "No offense, Gene," Ralph managed to sputter, "it's just that it took you a little longer than the others. Everyone on the set and off has talked about it. Isn't it amazing?"

Gene Madrix seemed a little touchy at their response, but he smiled balefully and said, "Mrs. Griffon, if your illustrious in-laws were not put off by it, I'd offer you a contract."

This brought on more laughter as Ralph said, "Gene, you're doing exactly what I predicted. The Griffons are big stockholders, but what would that have to do with keeping Emmy from signing a contract with you if she was so disposed?"

Gene looked knowingly at Emmy. "I don't think it would be in line with their family standards."

"You're probably right, Mr. Madrix," Emmy said, "but in any case, it would be the farthest thing from my mind. I have no movie aspirations."

"I imagine you'd test well. You know, even though the two of you bear a remarkable resemblance, you're very different in type. You're more of a lady . . . you know, the Irene Dunne type. If you ever change your mind, say the word."

"That's a lovely compliment, Mr. Madrix. I appreciate it. Coming to California has been very good for my self-esteem. You're all so kind to me." She laughed girlishly. "I can imagine what my husband would think, to say nothing of Uncle Max. He'd absolutely do a flip-flop if I ever entertained such an idea."

"By the way, Gene," Ralph interjected, "I almost forgot to mention, Max Esquith is finally coming here next week and Betty's probably going to cook up some mass entertainment . . . a cocktail party or something so we can all get together."

Gene nodded as he continued to observe Emmy. "You know, I'd love to do a screen test with you. It would certainly shake Tana up."

"Give up, Gene; don't you know when you're beaten?" Ralph cut in. "Besides, Emmy's not sure how long she's going to remain here."

At this Emmy surprised them both. "You know, I've been wondering, do you suppose it's possible to find a small house for rent here? It would be fun to settle in Hollywood for a spell. I'd like to bring my housekeeper and find something to occupy my time. Since my husband's joined the Ambulance Corps, I wouldn't mind remaining for a while.

Smiling broadly, Gene Madrix said, "I've already told you we have a way for you to utilize your time. Do you realize how many girls would die for the opportunity I'm offering you?"

Puzzled at his persistence, she said earnestly, "But, Mr. Madrix, really, I don't want to be an actress; it doesn't interest me at all. I appreciate your offer very much, but that's not what I meant about doing something. I'd prefer to do something to aid the war effort."

Ralph was about to say something, but Gene waved him quiet. "I may have a solution for you."

"No more of that Tana stuff, Gene," Ralph cautioned.

"All right, old buddy, I know when I'm licked . . . that's not what I have in mind. See what you think of this: Joan called from the Hollywood Canteen office yesterday and asked if I knew of anyone who could give them a hand managing the Canteen. It might just be what our little friend here needs."

Emmy's eyes opened wide and her face flushed. "Are you talking about the famous Hollywood Canteen? My goodness, do you think I could fill such a position?"

"Why not? It's really not difficult; it just takes some charm and common sense if you have the time to give it. How does that appeal to you?"

"Hold your horses, Emmy," Ralph cautioned. "Don't let my rascally friend here fool you. It means a lot of work, and, with gas rationing and finding a house, don't say yes so quickly."

Waving his hand pontifically, Madrix grinned. "Use your head, Ralph. The house problem is licked."

They looked at him in astonishment as he continued. "No one's living in the Tana Corgan house, and it would be perfect for Mrs. Griffon—of course, if she'd like it."

Chuckling, Ralph could see Emmy's delight, and he thought, Gene'll get her to take that screen test one way or the other. "Gene, are you forgetting Tana owns the house? Wouldn't we need her consent?"

"I surmised you'd use that as an obstacle. Let me remind you, good agent that you are, she doesn't own it yet. The studio holds the mortgage. In any case, I'm sure she'd prefer to have it occupied and taken care of rather than standing empty. You can determine a proper rental fee, and as a moving-in gift we'll have the paint shop freshen it up."

Stupefied at the turn of events, Emmy sat openmouthed as Gene Madrix said, "You see, I'm like a genie; you have but to ask. Already you have a house and something interesting to fill your days. It's the least we can do for Bill Griffon's daughter-in-law."

Ralph sighed in resignation. Gene Madrix was phenomenal. Despite the thousands of complicated matters he dealt with on a daily basis, he had an encyclopedic mind that could come up with data and solutions at a moment's notice. For sure Emmy wouldn't refuse such a magnanimous offer. He assumed correctly as he heard her say, "Mr. Madrix, it's all too wonderful. You're so kind. I certainly can't turn this offer down."

Gene smiled paternally. "Delighted to be of service. Our good agent here can take care of all the details."

"On one condition, boss man . . . Emmy's to understand she's to remain as our houseguest for a few more weeks. She can check out the Canteen deal, but she can't start until the beginning of next month. Do you think they'll be happy with that arrangement?"

"I don't see why not, Ralph. I'll just pass the word along. Then everything's settled?"

"Oh, yes, Mr. Madrix. I can't wait to tell Jonathan all about it. I'm sure Uncle Max will approve. It sounds so exciting."

As they were leaving, Ralph reminded Madrix, "Make a note, kiddo . . . pass it on at home, although Betty'll be in touch there. Two weeks from Sunday—a big shindig at the Michalson's for the guests of honor."

Ralph ordered the chauffeur to drive by the Corgan house so Emmy could see it. "It's beautiful, Mr. Michalson. I just don't know how to thank all you wonderful people. Do you realize what's happend to me since I arrived? I can't get over it! My head is whirling with everything that's taken place."

"We're the magicians of the world out here, Emmy. We bottle and package everyone's dreams. Of course, since you're so special, yours have come about more quickly than most. I'm delighted to have a part in all of this, and I know Betty is too; you've already acquired a good friend in her."

"Mr. Michalson, that really means more to me than anything else. I honestly feel the same way about her. You're both wonderful people, and I'm indebted to you already for changing my life."

He changed the subject suddenly. "Look! Over there! See all those towers? They're air-raid sirens. We had a bad scare a few months ago; it was rumored a Japanese sub was off the coast. The war's got us all at fever pitch. I'm an air-raid warden—do I look the part?"

"How's an air-raid warden supposed to look? Whatever you do, I imagine you do well, and we're in safe hands."

From the time of her arrival in southern California she had been too absorbed and excited over what had been taking place to give much thought to the war. In truth, she'd given it meager attention from the time of its inception, but other things had been paramount on her mind. She'd been so insulated in her own problems that the cataclysmic events of the war had not made real inroads on her consciousness. It had been a huge black cloud floating off somewhere on a distant horizon . . . a muffled sound of drums urging the purchase of bonds and the use of ration books. Even that had not been an imposition; the merchants of the stores where she usually shopped were always ready to make concessions. Suddenly the significance of what was happening on a global scale began to penetrate, but it had taken Jonathan's enlistment to awaken her. A veil had lifted from her eyes, and now newspaper headlines and mounting casualty figures had meaning in personal terms. She was filled with shame at her indifference and recalled how envious her friends had been at Jonathan's deferment due to his involvement with strategic materials. As the car proceeded and Ralph pointed out some of the obvious war measures such as camouflage over important buildings and signs for defense shelters, it dawned on her how self-involved she'd been. She promised herself to rectify that and make every effort to do what she could for the war effort and her job at the Canteen.

In the short time she'd been on the West Coast, she'd learned the war was of top priority to everyone. It dominated conversations; people seemed to take pride in abiding by the restrictions and the use of their ration books. It made no difference what position the person held, each one seemed to be intensely involved in doing his bit. Blackouts were rigorously maintained; posters cautioned about loose talk, and detailed directions were posted everywhere about where to go and what to do in the event of an air attack.

During dinner the night before, Betty had discussed the internment of the Japanese people in California, and Emmy'd been embarrassed when Betty asked, "Do you have any internment camps in Oklahoma?"

Emmy had been ashamed to admit she didn't know and Betty had added dolefully, "Most of the Japanese are loyal Americans. It's really awful they've had to give up their homes and businesses, but opinion is running dangerously high against them. Our gardener and his family were taken."

Emmy decided then and there she'd learn more of what was going on around her as well as in the world at large.

Her insulation had not been lost on Gene Madrix, who, in a conversation with Ralph Michalson later that night, asked, "Where'd you acquire your distinguished houseguest?"

Replying, Ralph said, "I thought I had mentioned it to you: she's Max Esquith's niece. She's a sweet person; we're happy to have her."

"The girl doesn't know the world's round; she vacuous."

"Come off it, Gene—just because she's not interested in movies? She's a fine young woman."

"Okay, okay . . . maybe I'm being too quick to judge. I don't mean to get your dander up. She struck me as being a cold cookie. She's got more style than Tana, but Corgan's got a helluva lot more fire and intensity. This one reminds me of the "Sleeping Beauty—you know, never been kissed."

"She's not too worldly, but I imagine she's led a very sheltered life. There's a lot more to her than appears on the surface. It hasn't all been a bed of roses."

"You'd never think so, listening to her. You know, Ralph, it's really peculiar how much those two resemble each other. They could be sisters."

"I'll go along with that—it is strange."

"Are you going to set up the Corgan house for her?"

"You sure put me on the spot, Gene. How am I supposed to get in touch with Corgan?"

"Don't worry about that. Was she serious about working at the Canteen?"

"Absolutely—she's thrilled to pieces at the idea. She'll probably do a good job too. Did you call Joan?"

"I will, got a note on my desk—tomorrow morning."

It was shortly after Ralph's conversation with Gene Madrix that a call came through for Emmy from Jonathan. Immediately he informed her that the call was limited, but she tried to tell him about all that happened. He told her, "Honey, I'm happy for you, but we don't have the time for all this discussion. Max has my APO address. Write me everything."

She tried to keep from crying. "Jon, take care of yourself."

"I will, Em. Glad you're getting yourself together. Sorry, but I have to hang up now."

It was the only damper of the day. His call had left her aggravated and frustrated. He was always admonishing her.

She explained to the Michalsons, "Jonathan couldn't talk any longer."

Consolingly, Betty said, "You'll see him sooner than you think, Emmy. This darn war won't go on forever. Will he be calling again?"

Emmy choked up. "He didn't say. He's in training now and think he'll be shipped off soon."

IRalph looked sad. "All our wonderful young men what a waste."

Betty tried to change the line he was taking. "He'll be fine. Emmy's got to think that way."

"Oh, sure he will . . . I don't mean that. I meant the whole damn war—that lousy Hitler and Hirohito!"

Betty changed the subject. "You haven't told me, Emmy: what did you think of the movie factory?"

The Michalsons took Emmy everywhere they could in an attempt to familiarize her with Los Angeles and Hollywood. Ralph, at her request, had already put out feelers for a car for her. He had held off doing anything about the Corgan house until Max Esquith's arrival, feeling he should put the stamp of approval on their plans.

The following week was taken up with preparations for the party to be given on Sunday and Max's arrival. Max was immediately given all the details on Tana Corgan's background and agreed there was little doubt that she was the missing baby sister. "Saperson is checking it out, Em. We should be hearing from him shortly."

He was surprised at how quickly she had made up her mind to remain in California, and they had a long discussion. She explained how much the change had already benefited her—how it had given her a new perspective. She confessed to him that the work she had done at home had seemed meaningless and a waste of time. Here it seemed that willing hands were needed everywhere, and she would feel useful, able to make a contribution to the war effort, even if it was a small one.

Max couldn't argue with her, since this had been her aim from the start. He found her enthusiasm infectious. It was the first time in years he'd seen her excited about doing something. He asked, "Won't you miss your friends?"

She looked at him quizzically. "Friends? With the exception of you, there'll really be no one I'll seriously miss. The best thing that could have happened is my coming here. I feel a thousand times better already."

"Em, I've a serious question to put to you. If by some strange freak of fate Tana Corgan doesn't turn out to be your sister, will you be able to handle your disappointment?"

Without a minute's hesitation she said, "Impossible, Uncle Max. It's her without a doubt . . . the resemblance, the name, the circumstances . . . it's her, all right."

"Assuming you're right, what if she's never known she'd been adopted?"

This possibility stumped Emmy. "You think her family might never have told her?"

"I do.. Remember, they never picked up the adoption papers, and the story is they stole away in the middle of the night. It is something you have to consider very carefully. Tana Corgan could be very upset at such a revelation at this time in her life."

He could see Emmy's spirits deflate. "But, Uncle Max, do you mean I shouldn't tell her?"

"Emmy, Emmy, you can't color her with your dreams. You have some idea she's just waiting to hear such news and that you'll put your arms around each other and be sisters living happily ever after. If she has no idea she'd been adopted, the repercussions could be awful. This could prove a very distressing position."

"You're right, of course, Uncle Max." The dismay on Emmy's face told him what he had said had registered. "As usual I'm painting things the way I want them to be. What do I do in such a situation?"

"Well, for one thing, you move very slowly. You have to ascertain if she knows; if not, don't spring it on her. A lot will depend on the kind of person she is, and then . . ."

"And then what?"

He sat considering. "Honestly, I don't know, Em. You'll just have to wait and see. You'll have to exercise caution until you have the situation sized up."

"As usual you're right. I promise I won't behave like an impetuous child. It was plain stupid of me not to realize what a terrible shock this could be. I'll try to use my head."

Thankful that she was showing judgment, he brought up another matter. "Em, I think you ought to drop the Griffons a note and let them know where you are."

Instantly she stiffened. "Really, Uncle Max, for what reason?"

"Em, you don't have to be Eleanor's friend, but she's still Jonathan's mother, and if something happens to him, they have to know where to reach you."

Jolted, she looked at him in silence. "What are you talking about?"

"The war, Emmalina, remember? Jonathan's work is very precarious; he's going to be in the thick of it. Just because everything's coming up rosy for you doesn't mean the world's your apple. People are suffering and dying everywhere, and you live in a bubble. I hate to be the one to do this to you, but it's time you woke up."

She sat silently, like a chastened child.

Betty remarked to Max a few days later, "You know, Max, I find Emmy changed since your arrival."

"How do you mean?"

"It's almost as though she grew up overnight."

He grunted, "I hope so. It's about time."

Chapter XX

◦◦◦◦◦◦◦

TANA'S COMET

TANA'S MUCH-VAUNTED SUCCESS began to make an impact. She had become good box office and fan clubs were springing up throughout the country. No longer worried about the course of her career, she shed the role of amenable innocent she'd feigned at the beginning. The first manifestations of the change were felt by those in more lowly positions such as wardrobe and makeup; but it wasn't long before she began to wield the influence of her new status with her directors and co-workers.

The older, more experienced people surrounding her were patient at first, attributing the personality alteration to her meteoric rise and the stresses of her work. In short order, unfettered by any restrictions, she became a temperamental, imperious, self-willed young woman who expected instant gratification of her every wish.

As Tana Corgan saw it, she was riding the crest of a wave. She had been acknowledged a star and saw nothing wrong in being herself. With the accolades for *Southern War* continuing to pour in, she assumed the world was hers for the taking. Willful and vain, day by day she became more difficult to work with, and word went out that she had to be handled with kid gloves. The least rebuke or reprimand would bring about a temper tantrum: her beautiful face would turn red, she would stamp her foot, toss her head, her eyes would flash fire and if there was no conciliatory offering she would lapse into sullen, moody silence until it was forthcoming.

341

Totally wrapped up in herself, she was indulged for expediency's sake, since denial by anyone roused immediate anger. Even had she wanted to, there was no way Tana could have perceived what she had become. Her entire life up to this point had been precedence for this behavior. Love and attention had been poured upon her abundantly; she had never known their lack, but neither had she been led to feel that anything was expected in return. On rare occasions she would be prone to displays of sentiment that were often construed as evidence of deeper feeling.

She continued to be the pivot of her mother's life, the precious darling of her father and adoringly admired by Lilly Fazon. After the first flush of pleasure at having her parents close at hand had worn off, she took them for granted. Now they were less troublesome than they had been before, more eager and willing to do her bidding. There were times when her mother thought her behavior ugly, but she was hesitant about speaking out, fearful of Lilly's reprisals. Deirdre didn't want to risk alienating her daughter and consoled herself in the belief this was a temporary situation.

People in daily contact with Tana suspected that any charm and amenability she displayed were usually for her own self-serving design. It reached a point where the only pretty thing about her was her face. She had become a bully, without conscience; remorseless, she stored up grudges for future retaliation against anyone who dared to oppose her. It mattered not one whit that colleagues and acquaintances looked at her askance; she ascribed it to envy, totally convinced of her own invincibility.

The holidays long over, Sean had extended his stay, hoping that Deirdre would return to Montana with him, but Tana was not yet willing for her mother to go. Sadly, Sean left without his wife, but it was agreed she would return by spring.

A new film was being readied, and Tana was to star in it along with a famous leading man, old enough to be excluded from military service. Tana was now weighted down by her preparatory work for the new movie, heavy social obligations and bond-selling appearances. It all began to make inroads on her stamina. The slightest thing would set her temper off, and she began to engage in fierce quarrels with her mother. Deirdre, sincerely concerned about her daughter's health, felt that the girl was being forced to function in a state of exhaustion, and excused the abuses in the belief that her daughter could not help herself. Her child might be Tana

Corgan to the outside world, but it didn't alter the fact that, as her mother, it was Deirdre's obligation to understand and care for her.

Conditions worsened, and Deirdre found herself living in a hostile atmosphere. Lilly Fazon, in her role as Tana's secretary, assumed more and more of the responsibilities and used every means at her disposal to make Deirdre feel unnecessary. It was becoming apparent that Deirdre's primary function was to serve as a whipping post. The poor woman never knew what she would say or do that would cause either of the young women to fly off the handle. Deirdre yearned for her husband and the quiet homespun quality of life on the ranch. She was fed up with this artificial life, the foolishness of the glitter and pomp that surrounded them.

Deirdre was seriously considering leaving for home when she unwittingly precipitated a crisis.

One afternoon, doing an errand for Tana, she was selecting some merchandise at the counter of a fashionable store when she was suddenly confronted by a well-known lady columnist. Deirdre was on guard at once, for the lady was known to be formidable and more than once had demonstrated her power to make or break movie careers.

They had been introduced at some function, but a renewal of their acquaintanceship didn't improve her in Deirdre's opinion. For her part, the newswoman found this an opportunity too good to miss and plied Deirdre with questions which the good woman found offensive.

The newslady wasn't about to let her escape. Finishing her transaction, she attempted to leave, but the woman blocked her way. It was an awkward situation; people were watching, and Deirdre's ire was growing. The woman persisted in a question that Deirdre considered impertinent and exasperated, finally lost her temper. "Look, miss, 'tis not me can answer your questions. 'Tis not seemly nor polite o you to insist when I be in a hurry. If you don mind, I'll be about my business—and good riddance to you." She brushed the mighty lady aside and left, not staying long enough to recognize the offense she had caused.

It was commonly assumed by those in the know that no one in their right mind would offend such a prestigious and powerful person. For being so importunate, Deirdre would be taught a lesson, one she would never forget.

The woman's vengeance followed quickly on the heels of

her encounter with Tana Corgan's mother. Her column was carried in the leading newspapers throughout the country, and two days later it appeared bearing the headline POOR TANA CORGAN. It was a mischievously cruel and vitriolic piece expressing sarcastic sympathy for the talented girl who so successfully belied her shanty Irish background. It commiserated with Tana's difficulty in hiding her mother's fishwife behavior and concluded by recommending that Deirdre Corrigan leave town before she ruined her daughter's career.

It caused an explosion that sent out shock waves.

Deirdre had thought nothing more about the woman after leaving the store. It had seemed of no consequence and she had not felt it necessary to report the incident to either her daughter or Lilly. In truth, these days she avoided bringing up anything that might produce controversy.

Those people who had met Deirdre Corrigan held her in high esteem. An unassuming, friendly person, she was well regarded by everyone with whom she had come in contact. The people at the studio considered her reasonable and considerate; in every way she'd been cooperative with all they'd requested.

When the story of the column was relayed to Gene Madrix, he was baffled. He immediately put a call through to Deirdre, who tearfully told him what had occurred. She was distraught, wanting to know what, if anything, she could do to make amends. He consoled her and advised, "Mrs. Corrigan, don't take on so. We have situations like this every day. It won't hurt Tana—it's another means of keeping her name in the limelight. Do me a personal favor: just forget it. Keep your head up and pretend it never happened. I'll tell you a secret . . . it's my hunch that everyone in this community is siding with you right this minute. Go about your normal business; in a few days it will die down and things will be as if it never happened."

After Madrix had put the phone down, he thought the matter over. He put a call out for Tana Corgan to come to his office. As it happened, she was unreachable at the moment. She never got the message, and he failed to see her that day.

When Tana reached home later that evening, having been on a locked set all day, she found Lilly awaiting her in tears. "It's outrageous, Tana, simply awful. It can ruin your career . . . all your work down the drain."

Deirdre was in her bedroom unprepared for the storm about to be unleashed on her head. The confrontation, when it came, was horrible. The air around them exploded, fragmented. Tana's venom and accusations filled the room. Deirdre couldn't believe her ears; she was being torn to shreds by her beloved child, whose beautiful face was ravaged by fury and hate.

Weary and disgusted with it all, Deirdre said sadly, "Tana Corgan, whoever you are, 'tis for sure one thin you are not, and that is my darlin daughter Polly Sue Corrigan. My true daughter would ne'er have disrespected so those who raised her. 'Tis God's truth, me heart is broken. I'll have no more of this and 'tis good-bye I'll be sayin."

Weeping quietly, Deirdre closed the door as Tana stormed out. She quickly packed her bags and telephoned the train station for a reservation. She obtained a space for later that night and then arranged for a cab to pick her up. Distracted by worry and grief, she waited in her room, hoping that Tana would relent and come to her. Instead a knock on the door showed Lilly Fazon. "Did you call for a cab, Mrs. Corrigan? It's here."

Gathering her things together, Deirdre said, "I'd appreciate it if you'd ask Maria to come here. 'Tis good-bye I'd like to be sayin to her."

Lilly went to do as she had asked, and when the maid came she wept with Deirdre. Deirdre pressed cash into her hand and told her, " 'Tis the God's truth, Maria, you be the most carin person in this house. There be some things on the bed for you. Take care o that Tana Corgan, leastwise as much care as she'll be lettin you. If ever you want, you can write me to this address. Now, if you'll be a good lass and help me with the bags . . ."

Lilly Fazon stood stone-faced at the door as Deirdre went through. "Good-bye, Mrs. Corrigan."

Angrily Deirdre turned and faced her. " 'Tis sure I am o one thin, Lilly Fazon: you want to be ownin Tana Corgan. You need not have worried so about her love of me, cause she be not the same as me daughter—sweet lass by the name o Polly Sue Corrigan. She be gone from here a long while. Yes, 'tis good-bye and good riddance!"

There was no turning back, no making up this time. Deirdre wept without restraint in the darkness of the cab; her heart was broken.

When she reached the station, red-eyed and shaky, she had her baggage checked through and went in search of a telephone. She could not resist calling Tana. She was older and wiser; this was no way to part, and she would be conciliatory. Hearing her daughter's voice at the other end, she summoned all her self-control to speak. "'Tis a decent good-bye I'm callin to say, daughter. Take care o yourself . . . and for your own sake, be mindin what you say. You've the great fire o the Irish in you, my girl. Be careful lest it turn on you one o these days. Polly Corrigan, cause that be your true name, you be overtired and overworked . . . but 'tis no excuse for you being too big for your britches. Be careful you don get your comeuppance."

Deirdre waited to hear a reply, but there was silence. She asked, "Be you there, Polly?"

The voice was cold with indignation. "No, it's not Polly Corrigan. This is Tana Corgan. Since you're so free with your advice, ask yourself if what that column said about you isn't true. Isn't that why you ran? I'll thank you to let me be!"

Filled with sorrow, Deirdre said, "Please try to remember how you was reared, child . . . not rude and bad mannered as you are now. If what you be sayin you truly mean, then 'tis the saddest good-bye o me life I'll be sayin."

With a heavy heart, Deirdre hung up the telephone. She boarded the train in a daze. The events of the day unreeled before her like a nightmare until exhaustion overtook her and she fell into an uneasy sleep. Stiff and rumpled, she was awakened by dawn breaking across the rolling horizon. After freshening herself and ordering coffee, she tried to sort things out. It was imperative she put matters into perspective for Sean.

The more she agonized about her daughter, the more she felt the girl had been absorbed by the creation of Tana Corgan. True, she was still young and impressionable; but it appeared that, without the few restraints of her upbringing, she had shed the veneer her parents had imposed upon her. The thought tormented Deirdre; had she and Sean been so blind to Polly Sue's true nature? Was it possible that, in assuming the role of Tana Corgan, she had felt free to reveal who she really was, a self-centered, selfish creature, uncaring about anyone else unless they served her purposes? Deirdre forced herself to face what for so long she had refused to see. She and Sean had deceived themselves. Their beloved child, the center of their universe and light of their lives, had the potential to destroy them.

Her disillusionment would not have been mitigated had she been present to see what took place after her departure.

Tana had known nothing about the column until Lilly had broken the news to her. Upon reading it, she had lost all control; she saw her future going up in smoke, all her work gone for naught. No one had reached her in time to tell her matters were not as bad as she believed, and Lilly certainly was not going to play down anything Mrs. Corrigan might have brought upon her daughter's head. Since it was her mother who bore sole responsibility for the awful event, it was upon her Tana vented her fury and frustration.

Originally Tana's sole purpose in having her mother come to California had been to have her act as intermediary on her behalf. When Deirdre had successfully accomplished the personal and necessary business tasks, Tana had felt it advantageous for her to stay on longer. On a personal level, Tana would sooner have died than admit it was comforting to have her mother close at hand. She refused to acknowledge how necessary it was to have someone to depend upon, who remained patient and supportive, defending and excusing her no matter how badly she behaved.

At the realization that her mother had actually left, Tana exploded again, raving and ranting as if she'd lost her mind. Lilly and Maria stood by helplessly. Finally, when she had spent herself and calmed down a little, Lilly tried to console her.

"It's outrageous, her running off like this. But, Tana, darling, in a way it's the best thing she could have done for you."

At this, Tana picked up an ashtray and hurled it across the room, shouting, "Outrageous! . . . Outrageous! . . . Don't you know another word? Are you so dumb you can't see she'll make that bitch of a columnist look right? What the hell did my mother do to her anyway? Does anyone know? Do you know? What do I do now, can you tell me?"

Maria spoke up. "Miss Tana, it's not so bad as you think. Mr. Madrix spoke with your mother today. She told me she feel much better after. He say is silliness . . . is nothing."

Tana stopped her pacing and looked at Lilly in disgust. "Did you know about that? Why didn't you tell me that before? You bitch! You really hate my mother, don't you?"

Lilly turned white as she backed off. "How can you say that, Tana? You know it's not true."

"Liar!" Tana sneered. "I've caught you doing a lot of mean things. Well, now she's gone and you've got your wish!"

For a moment Lilly was frightened. "Tana, please don't

worry. You can depend on me. I'd lay down my life for you. I'll do everything I can to help you."

They were interrupted by the sound of the doorbell ringing. Maria hurried to see what it was and returned at once carrying a huge bouquet of flowers and a handful of telegrams. "Look, Miss Tana . . . all are for Mrs. Corrigan. What shall I do with them?"

Tana looked at her in surprise. "For my mother . . . from who? What's this all about?"

For the balance of the evening and several days after there was a flood of messages, telegrams and floral tributes for Deirdre Corrigan. Everyone wanted to congratulate her for apparently having told the infamous newswoman off. The columnist had as many enemies as she had readers, and the vitriol she had spewed spurred some of them into letting Deirdre know of their support. There was a wire from the Irish Society saying they were instituting suit and boycotting the newspapers that carried the column. Unwittingly Deirdre had produced a flurry of publicity for her daughter that a million dollars could not have purchased.

In the furor that ensued, Tana conveniently failed to remember the way she had sent her mother off. Her anger had subsided. It pleased her that Deirdre was the heroine of the moment and had inadvertently made the Corgan star more conspicuous.

The morning after Deirdre's abrupt departure, Gene Madrix called and spoke with Tana. "Tell your mother we don't have to do a thing about the column . . . just as I predicted. The Irish of the country are in an uproar and one ugly newslady is on the hot spot. All you have to do, Tana, is remain quiet. Give no interviews . . . we're handling everything from this end. We'll want some pictures of you and your mother together for press releases. This matter's going to come out smelling like roses."

Tana didn't dare tell him her mother had left. She'd have to think of something—and fast. After much frenzied conjecture, Lilly concocted a plan. "We won't tell anyone that Deirdre's already gone. Later this afternoon you call Mr. Madrix and say your mother received an urgent telegram from your dad. He's taken sick and needs her at home."

It seemed weak and transparent, but Tana agreed it was the only solution. They'd have to take their chances. Then she remembered. "What about Maria?"

"You'd better handle her, Tana. She's not too crazy about me."

Tana went in search of the housekeeper. Maria knew what was going on and wasn't fooled by Tana's performance. She knew, however, that if she reported the truth to Mr. Madrix, it would only make matters worse for Mrs. Corrigan with her daughter. One day she'd have the chance to tell him the truth. She wondered just how much Mr. Madrix knew about his precious movie star. Maria had good cause to dislike Tana, but the position paid well and she was there primarily on Mr. Madrix's behalf. She stared noncommittally at the pretty face appealing to her so sweetly. "I know how fond you are of my mother, Maria, and I hope I can count on you not to say anything. It would make Mother look foolish if people knew she'd run away. Please promise you won't tell anyone."

Maria's face didn't change expression as she said, "I promise. There *is* one condition, Miss Tana . . . write your mother a letter and tell her what's been happening."

"Oh, I will, Maria. I will! I'll tell Lilly to do it at once."

Maria looked at her disgustedly and, turning her back, walked away.

Seething, Tana called out, "Maria . . . you knew Mother was planning to leave in a month, didn't you?"

The woman stopped and looked at her. "Yes, I knew. Your mother is a wonderful lady, and I'm glad to see so many people think so too. Those letters and flowers are for her . . . did you forget that?"

"Of course not. You don't have to tell me my mother is a wonderful lady."

Shaking her head at this, Maria made her exit but not before she heard, "Insolent bitch!"

Lilly had been listening, enjoying the manipulative way Tana handled the maid. She couldn't have done it better herself.

Fighting to control her fury, Tana went back to find Lilly. "I hate that woman . . . I'm sure she's a sneak and a spy. Did you hear her?"

"I certainly did . . . but I have to hand it to you, you handled it magnificently. One day, when you think it's time, you can give her notice. You can always get someone else."

"Yes, but not now . . . it won't help if we get her dander up. For the moment it's better to humor her. Listen, Lil, it might be a good idea if you wrote Mother a note for me. Tell her what's going on. If she knows, I'll have less trouble from that end. Maybe you ought to enclose a few of the notes and telegrams so she can see for herself what's actually happened."

"Okay. I'll get right to it." Lilly Fazon was happier than she'd ever been.

What had started out as certain disaster resolved itself, and within a few weeks the excitement subsided and the story was forgotten.

Tana and Lilly worked harmoniously as a team, glad to be left to their own resources. Deirdre's presence began to recede as Lilly made every effort to substitute for her. It came as a surprise when one morning Tana requested that she write weekly letters on her behalf to her parents.

Still indignant at her mother for having humiliated her by leaving, Tana felt this would be a means of punishing her . . . it would let her know she had not yet forgiven her. As the days had passed without word from her parents, she felt a qualm, but she was convinced they'd come around. She was certain Deirdre had prejudiced her father against her. Mulling it over, she decided it was time they showed some respect for what she had accomplished; any conciliatory gestures would have to come from them.

Outwardly she seemed unperturbed, but as the weeks wore on and there was no acknowledgment of the letters being sent to her parents, her anger intensified. In the past they'd always been proud of her, taken pleasure in her achievements; she couldn't understand the stubborn silence. She resolved that if they could bear it, she would too. But lurking in the back of her mind was the feeling that this time she might not come off the victor. They had never done this to her before. She might have to resort to a ruse to bring them around.

Her mother's parting words had rung a warning bell, and for a while she adopted a new demeanor at the studio. She made attempts at being friendly and cooperative and took pains to explain her mother's sudden absence. But with her parents' continuing silence she began to lose her temper over trivial matters and lash out at the very people whom, days before, she had tried to befriend. She became so insufferable on the set that word reached Mr. Madrix. She was notified he wished her to come to his office.

The moment the message reached her, she knew she had the means of breaking her parents down. Mr. Madrix would be the instrument for bringing them around.

"What's this I hear about you, Tana?" he began. "Fighting with your director, your co-workers, with everyone. We can't have this! It's bad for morale. Any more of this and we'll have to discipline you."

Instantly Tana was the picture of contrition; her eyes brimmed tearfully. "Oh, Mr. Madrix, I wish I could tell you what's at the bottom of this, but it wouldn't be fair."

Concerned about the temperamental girl, he insisted she reveal what was upsetting her, playing right into her hands. She looked at him woefully. "You're so wonderful to me, Mr. Madrix, but I don't think it's fair to involve you in family matters."

Persisting, he finally managed to extract Tana's version of what had happened. "It started with that awful column. Truthfully, I lost my head with mother. It was unkind of me, since she was also terribly worried about Dad, and we had some cross words. She's not the kind to forgive or forget, and I guess she influenced my father to think the same way. I just can't bear it. Even though I write frequently, I haven't heard from either of them since Mother left." She broke into sobs, crying as if her heart would break.

The upshot of the meeting was that Gene Madrix took it upon himself to write a personal letter to the Corrigans. He implored them not to treat their daughter so harshly, especially since she regretted what had taken place and longed for their forgiveness and understanding.

Sean Corrigan, already unhappy at what was going on, was further upset when Deirdre laughed mockingly at Mr. Madrix's letter. "The girl's worked her tricks again, Sean."

Sean looked at his wife wonderingly; he had never known her to be so adamant and upset with their daughter. "If you say so, Deirdre, then 'tis the way it is, I'm sure . . . but 'tis a hard thing to be doin. However, since 'tis not our intent to die this way, I'd say 'tis time we drop her a note."

"A note and that be all, Sean, since it be your wish," Deirdre said curtly.

Sean had never seen Deirdre as distraught as when she'd returned home. Astonished, he'd listened to the story; and, although he believed her, he assumed his wife was exaggerating things out of proportion. As time went on, however, and there was no direct word from Polly Sue, Sean began to have an inkling that his precious child was not all he had assumed her to be. But, he reasoned, she belonged to them nonetheless, and having made their bargain long ago, they'd suffer her, one way or the other.

The day he decided it was their responsibility to write, he put his arm around Deirdre, saying, "Darlin, I'm only beginnin to understand what you been tellin me, but there'll be no turnin our backs on her. She's ours even though the pain is hurtful. To be sure, she's got no cause to be treatin us this way, but we've got to count our blessins. . . . Thank the Lord we've each other and no need o her. It can't be hurtin us to drop her a line an a bit o chat. We'll see what comes o that. All right, me darlin?"

Deirdre gave him a pat on the cheek. The piercing hurt inside her never went away; it was something awful. She was careful to keep it hidden from Sean, but her heart was broken. It leaked tears at night when he was asleep. It was bad enough Polly had treated her as she had, but how could she do this to her darling dad? No matter how she faced what her daughter had become, it was beyond comprehension that their little girl, their beloved angel of a child, had been transformed into such a cold, unfeeling creature.

Deirdre had aged rapidly after her homecoming. Sean was aware of it despite all of Deirdre's efforts to prove otherwise, and he worried greatly about her. They were helpless, caught in the web of love for their child.

Matters eased somewhat when, in response to Deirdre's note, they received a short scrawl from Tana. It was totally about herself, containing press clippings and reviews. She did close by saying how often she longed for them and to be back at the ranch living the good, simple life. Deirdre yearned to believe it, but warning bells made her suspect it was another of Tana's shams.

The war was making great inroads on their lives, and fortunately they were kept busier than they had ever been before. It kept them from brooding and Deirdre was grateful for that. It was futile to continue beating at themselves; they'd had their gratifications. Each had been party to their own form of selfishness, given way to indulgence with their child, and now, if the girl was void of compassion, it would be senseless to play the game of retaliation.

Deirdre knew it was important to preserve whatever emotional resources she and Sean had left. She resolved they would not crawl, they would not beg at their daughter's shrine for crumbs of affection; that would leave them wrung-out relics, entirely at her mercy.

Ceaseless in her quest to understand, Deirdre finally concluded there was no deliberate motivation in Tana's behavior. It was clear the girl did not understand the responsibilities and obligations, emotional or otherwise, that a parent-child relationship entailed. It was ironic that, despite their efforts and sacrifices to be good parents, they had gambled and lost. Their so desired and beloved foundling had already given all she had; for them her well had run dry.

Sean too waged his secret battles. With the arrival of each infrequent note from Tana, he grew more disturbed. The girl seldom questioned or remarked about anything concerning their lives. She took no notice when they informed her of old Pete's passing and never again mentioned missing them or the good, simple life. Standing at the corral in the clear morning air, Sean would rummage through his mind back to the old days when his "darlin" would be at his side eagerly asking questions of him and Pete. It hurt to think she had ignored the old man's going; he had adored her.

Unlike his wife, he was not beset by guilt about his daughter. He ached in the thought that in all probability she was a throwback to her origins and nothing they could do would change this fact. But deeply secreted in his mind was the belief that God was punishing him for what he had perpetrated so many years before when he had stolen the baby away from Brightwater.

One day, when he had completed some errands in town, Sean stopped in to pass the time of day with his cousin, Mike O'Rourke. His cousin was as close to him as any man he knew, and Mike sensed that all was not right with the Corrigans. A hearty, jovial man, he hailed Sean as he entered the empty barroom. "Jist the man I'm lookin to see! 'Tis Providence sent you today, m'boy. I was wondering how to get a message to you. 'Tis no more than an hour ago her ladyship, the movie star, telephoned."

He saw the shocked surprise on Sean's face. "Are you sayin Polly called? How come not the house? Is she all right?"

"Seemed so, Sean. 'Tis them dang party lines always hung up with them chatterin females . . . she couldno get through. She was a bit o sweetness with me, jist asking how everything was and if you be awright. Took the breath outa me, I'll admit. Can't blame her callin here anyhow, Sean. That biddy o ourn Miss Jenny'd notify the county, what with the lass being so famous and all, if she'd made the connection to you."

Forcing a smile, Sean said, "You sure everythin was all right. You know how Deirdre worries."

The big man's face turned serious. "Sean, on my honor 'tis how it seemed to me—jist as if the lass was wantin to pass the time o day."

Sean was pensive. "Did she want me to call her back?"

Mike shook his head dubiously as he refilled Sean's glass. "She did no say . . . but 'tis nothin wrong with you afindin out. Put a call through to her now."

Rummaging through his wallet, Sean looked for the paper that carried his daughter's unlisted telephone number. Then he asked Jenny for the long-distance operator and was relieved to hear her ring for the connection and cut off; she was a notorious eavesdropper. His heart was palpitating— Polly had never done this before. He heard the line ringing and then an unfamiliar voice answered. "Miss Fazon speaking."

"Hello, 'tis Sean Corrigan here. 'Tis my daughter I'd like to be speakin with."

"Hold the line, Mr. Corrigan. She's just leaving—I'll catch her."

He heard voices and then the voice that tickled his heart. "Daddy, dear old Dad . . . are you there?"

" 'Tis me, darlin. Here at Mike's. Is everythin all right?"

"Everything's fine, Daddy. I just had a hankering to speak with you, and you know I can't call direct . . . that Jenny tells everyone everything. How are you and Mother?"

"We be all right, lass. We miss you."

"I miss you too, Daddy. Why don't you write more often?"

Sean sighed. "Darlin, we don hear from you often as we'd like, and 'tis not good for your mother. 'Twould be a blessin if you'd find a mite more time to keep in touch."

"Oh, Daddy, it isn't that I wouldn't like to, but you have to understand I'm just so busy. I'm hoping to find time to get home one of these days. I'd sure love that."

Sean smiled. " 'Tis good to hear that, darlin."

"Daddy, why don't you just call me collect when you feel like it?"

Sean laughed. " 'Tis no need for you to be payin for our call. I may just get your mother to do that come one o these Sundays."

"That'd be great. For the next few weeks I'll be on a bond-selling tour, so wait a bit."

"All right, darlin. Any special message for your mother?"

"Just tell her I miss her and give her my love. Here's a kiss, old Daddy darling."

Sean heard the sound. "Good-bye, Daddy dear; I've got to run, I'm late. Oh, I almost forgot . . . check and find out if the picture is going to play in Butte. I think I wrote you about *Katy the Riveter*. It's a new kind of role for me . . . doing my war bit. I think you and Mother would enjoy it."

"I'll find out, me darlin, and if it's playin we'll be sure to see it . . . mebbe even take old cousin Mike along."

"That'd be great, Dad. Let me know what you think when you see it. I really must run. Good-bye, darling."

Sean hung up the receiver. His hand was wet with perspiration and he took out his handkerchief to dry it and blow his nose. His eyes were suspiciously moist, and Mike averted his head.

Lilly watched as Tana checked her makeup in the mirror nearby. She saw Lilly's reflection and turned, grinning at her. Lilly handed her a letter to sign. "Feeling good, Tana?"

"Like a million! I ought to call home more often. You wouldn't believe how my old dad loved it. You know, I don't believe I've ever heard him say a cross word to me or my mother. Sometimes I get real homesick for them; I wish they lived closer. You'd love the ranch, Lilly. Maybe this summer we can get some time off and get back home. How about it?"

"I'd adore it, Tana. It must be beautiful out there. Why don't you try to work something out with the studio?"

Tana was pleased with herself, pleased with the affirmation she was still her parents' adored little girl. Everything was great!

She arrived at her dressing room late and the reporter who was to interview her was already waiting. She was charm personified as she apologized for her tardiness. He had not met her before and was captivated by her sweetness. The publicity department no longer worried about Tana's ability to handle newspeople.

There was no doubt the war had expedited Tana Corgan's climb to the top. Her films were in great demand, and pinup pictures of her hung from sea to shining sea. Only the month before she had been voted the girl most GIs wanted to come home to. The studio treated her accordingly, and she lived the life of a princess, receiving the homage of her courtiers. Her continuing success was something she was keenly aware of, and she frequently confronted Ralph Michalson with demands for new contract negotiations involving substantial monetary increases. The agent had been surprised at Tana's shrewdness, but he knew better than to dispute what she said: "I'm worth every penny I ask for. After all, who knows how long I'll be able to command this money? Getting here hasn't been easy."

Michalson smothered a grin. "It was often difficult to hide his reaction when Tana quoted the glowing lines picked from the articles written about her. He had followed her development closely, and he knew she was doing her job; but he could not say he had grown fond of her. He felt an allegiance to all the people he represented, but something about her alienated him and he would not have cared if she opted for another agent.

Looking at her, he marveled at the change in her appearance. From a pretty, wholesome little girl, she had blossomed into a ravishingly seductive young woman. Nature had splurged on Tana. Her facial contours, enhanced by perfectly chiseled features, were set off by wide, almond-shaped eyes, a velvety mixture of blue and violet, thickly fringed by black lashes. Her luscious mouth, shaped like a rosebud, seemed designed to be kissed. She had a luminescent beauty magnified tenfold on the screen. She projected a softness and vulnerability that tugged at the heartstrings. She seemed the essence of fragile femininity, making one want to protect and shelter her from the hazards of the world. In effect, she was designed for happy endings. It made no difference that she was not an actress of great depth. She applied the techniques taught to her and, with an excellent sense of mimicry, proved versatile enough to convey whatever the director asked of her. She's been blessed with the proper components, Ralph Michalson thought; she's lucky. In beauty and ability she's the epitome of a movie star. He couldn't deny she was riding high and he knew for the moment the world was hers for the asking.

Mike notified the Corrigans that Tana's film *Katy the Riveter* was to be shown at the movie house in Butte the next week. They arranged to attend the Saturday matinee.

Sean self-consciously acknowledged the greetings of some of their neighbors as he stood in line waiting to buy their tickets. Shortly after they settled in their seats, the lights went out. They sat through two cartoons at which Mike and Sean laughed riotously. The Pathé News which followed was grim with pictures of the war, sobering even the youngsters.

At last the preliminaries of the feature film flashed on and there, printed for all to see, was Tana Corgan's name, larger than any of the others—she was the star of the film. Sean reached over, groping for Deirdre's hand, as much to reassure himself as to warm hers, which was cold and clammy. She had never seen her daughter on the screen despite the time spent in Hollywood. She let out a gasp as Polly looked out at them. Sean muttered, "I wouldna believe it . . . look there!"

Mike whispered, "'Tis Polly . . . real and true . . . 'tis hard to believe."

They were rooted to their seats as the simple little story of a young girl's efforts to aid in the war unfolded. They were gripped by the love story of the young soldier shipped overseas and the villainous executive who attempted to win the affections of the girl by fair means or foul, and the way in which she spurned him and remained true. There were snatches that showed Tana at home with a make-believe family and mischievous younger brothers. Comedy and drama in equal parts held the audience spell-bound, grief-stricken with her when she was mistakenly told her lover was lost, elated when finally they were reunited.

Sean had long since released Deirdre's hand in order to surreptitiously mop his eyes and nose. Deirdre was totally absorbed watching her daughter move across the screen.

They blinked as they came out into the sunlight. Deirdre was quiet and subdued, listening as Sean and Mike chattered. A neighbor woman approached smiling and said, "Your daughter is a good actress, Mrs. Corrigan. You must be very proud."

"Oh, yes, indeed we be . . . 'tis proud we are."

Some of the children standing about overheard the conversation and one more bold than the other approached. "Mrs. Corrigan, could we get her autograph?"

She smiled. "I don't see why not. 'Tis not me that has it, though. You'd best be writin to the studio for it."

They walked to the restaurant a few blocks away. Mike was filled with wonder at the movie. "'Tis a miracle to see the lass that way. 'Tis a beauty she is for sure . . . a love of a girl. Be that her betrothed? The one with her?"

Deirdre laughed. "Oh, Mike, me boy, 'tis just make-believe. 'Tis a story sure and fine . . . but 'tis all it is."

Sean shook his head in bewilderment. "But, wife, that kissin and all . . ."

Now Deirdre was the authority. " 'Tis part o all them movies . . . like stories . . . they just be playin them out. That's what movie-pitchur makin be about. You act out them stories so all seems real as life. 'Tis like a package o dreams. Polly be very good and convincin. It's me feelin she be good at this work." The men bowed before her superior knowledge.

"Seems to me it'd be right embarrassin to be kissin and huggin a stranger like that," Sean persisted.

"Seems so to me too, but from what I seen o Polly, it don't bother her a bit," Deirdre replied. "I heard her say onct 'twas all in a day's work. Matter o fact, I onct heard her complainin her leadin man et garlic afore one o them scenes and it bothered her plenty."

At that the men broke into gales of laughter and the matter was dropped.

That was not the case with Deirdre. This was the day she finally realized the things she had suspected about her daughter were true. Polly was shallow. She could handle love with dispatch if necessary; she could put it on and take it off as easily as she did her clothes. Her daughter was either incapable of real love or had not been touched by it yet.

The studio complied with most of Tana Corgan's demands, since it was in their best interests to keep her happy and satisfied. In return she did try to be cooperative with most things they asked of her. Her bond sales were huge, and she never refused a request to make an appearance for the servicemen. The White House had recently sent a letter to the studio commending Tana. Grateful, they coddled and catered to her.

Tremendously excited, Tana had finally been rewarded with a film considered a choice plum by everyone in the business. Overnight she was the envy of every actress in town. She had been found to have a small sweet voice, and the movie was to be a musical war story in which she could make her singing debut. To top it off, she finally had a leading man she thought worthy as a counterpart.

Tony Vacchio had become an overnight sensation on the New York stage and had been signed to make his film debut with Tana Corgan. There had been apprehension when his agent insisted he have top billing. Mr. Madrix had called Tana to his office for a conference, and Ralph Michalson was present when she arrived.

Expecting a temperamental outburst at this injustice, they

were surprised when she proved totally understanding and cooperative. She listened intently as Mr. Madrix explained the problem, and when he finished she shrugged her shoulders. "Heavens, let him have it. As long as I rate tops with you, what difference can it make? My name will appear anyhow, so if it's not on top, it will be next."

She tilted her head in what was now fast becoming a Corgan trademark and laughed in her little-girl way. "You're all so wonderful to me and this is such a little thing. I can't understand the fuss you're making. You're my family, my own dear family."

Michalson, observing the scene, thought it was one of Tana's better acting jobs. He filed it away for future reference. Her generosity augured something, of that he was sure; of what, he had no idea at the moment. He'd begun to suspect the girl, particularly when she was all sweetness and light in respect to a business matter. He'd come to have a different measure of Tana Corgan through their business encounters. He was not as enthralled with her good qualities as others seemed to be, and there were other qualities . . . she was devious and intractable.

He knew Gene Madrix was shortly going to be called upon for repayment of Tana's generosity in regard to Tony Vacchio. She had too much of an unerring sense of self-preservation, and the act of sweet cooperation was a connivance toward those ends.

Before the meeting broke up Gene Madrix decided to tell them something else. "Tana, there's one more thing I think you should know. It's strictly confidential; may I have your word you will tell no one?"

She nodded her head to signify agreement and waited as he went on. "We're in a bind on this film because Tony has only a limited deferment. We're going to have to get it out right on schedule."

She looked at him, waiting to hear the secret, and he grinned at her. "Tana, darling, not even Tony knows how short a time he has. We are going to be even more in your debt because we want you to keep everyone on their toes, lines letter-perfect, cut-downs on rehearsal time, that sort of thing. If you set an example, they'll follow suit. Tony will need all the help you can give him. This is his first picture, and you're the pro. I have no doubt he'll be grateful for all the assistance and tips you can give him. Poor kid, he won't have much time to enjoy his career."

Tana sighed sympathetically. "Of course, Mr. Madrix. You can count on me. How much time do we have?"

"I'm not even sure yet. We're waiting word from Washington."

Tana was happy as she and Ralph Michalson left the big man's office. Slipping her hand through his arm, she asked, "Ralph, have you met this wonder boy yet?"

"Not yet, Tana. You have a tall order there, though. If you can pull it off you'll have all the big brass eating out of your hand. Do you think you can do it?"

"I hope so, Ralph. It's going to be a challenge, but I'm going to try." She laughed merrily. "I'm off! Got to get the wheels moving. I'm late for my voice coach. Be seeing you, Ralph."

He remained standing, considering her as she ran down the path. In many ways he had to hand it to her. She had come a long way from the timid little bird she'd been the first day he'd met her.

Tana finished her voice lesson and called Lilly Fazon to say she would have dinner at the studio. Although she was tired, she was too stimulated to go home, and tonight she was expected at the Hollywood Canteen.

Tana Corgan's appearances at the Hollywood Canteen came to be known as stampede night. The boys adored her and she danced with them until her feet were numb. She played no favorites and her affection for all of them was plainly apparent.

There was a huge crush as she, Lilly and her makeup girl made their way through the crowd. The place was jammed, and as she looked around she thought, It's a dream. Scattered throughout the room were the greats of Hollywood: Betty Grable, Bette Davis, Joan Crawford. So many of their male counterparts were already serving overseas. She saw Jack Benny talking to Gene Kelly. She looked up as Carole Lombard called out a hello as she whisked by in the arms of a sailor boy. Walking to the sidelines she was suddenly pulled to a stop and whisked into a bear hug. She looked up as the man in uniform pulled her closer, starting to move in time to the music as it resumed. She loved the song, "For All We Know," and melted into the rhythm of it. One serviceman was the same as the other and she was amazed when she heard the tall stranger say, "How are you, Polly Sue?"

She leaned back, trying to get a better look at the man in

the Special Services uniform. He looked vaguely familiar but she couldn't place him. He wore large horn-rimmed glasses and was good-looking in a rugged way. He laughed down at her. "The last time you saw me, you were very, very angry at me. I hope you've forgiven and forgotten by this time."

Her feet dragged and she misstepped as she looked up at him quizzically. "You look familiar, but I can't place you. Forgive me, but how do we know each other?"

He looked at her skeptically. She smiled. "Will you excuse me? There's a long line waiting for their turn. Maybe we can dance again later."

He didn't release her, moving her along slowly as the others made a path for them. "Come on, Polly. You can't still be carrying a grudge. Don't you remember your old friend Bill, of the range? How are your folks?" He didn't wait for an answer but pulled her closer to him. "You're gorgeous, more beautiful in the flesh than on the screen. I've seen you a few times—you're really talented."

She moved a few steps with him and then stopped dead. She looked up at him blankly. She now knew very well who he was. Who did he think he was, dragging her around like this? She was annoyed at his assumption she'd be glad to see him. She'd teach him—and fast. "Thank you for all those lovely compliments, but, really, you mustn't monopolize my time. I'm sorry I didn't recall who you were, but then I meet so many people it's hard to recall them all."

She moved back and gave him a frigid smile. "Thank you. Take care of yourself and come back to us." This was her standard parting speech at the end of each dance. She turned and left him standing in the middle of the floor. She was immediately swept away again, and as he made his way through the crowd, he heard her peals of laughter. For some unknown reason he'd swear she was laughing at what she'd done to him. What a witch she is, he thought, as he watched her dance away into the crowd. Well, it didn't matter; it had just been awkward for the moment.

The film was finished on schedule with two days to spare. It was released quickly and earned rave reviews: *Forever and Ever* was a runaway hit, the love scenes intense and convincing. Already Tony Vacchio was being called "the torrid lover." He was setting female hearts aflutter with his lyrical voice, dark mobile face, brooding eyes, and clear-cut features. Tana Corgan and Tony Vacchio were Hollywood's newest romantic pair. It was a war story so romantic and touching that people lined up for blocks waiting to see it. The film was a stupendous money-maker, and the studio projected long-range plans for co-starring the two again. They were trying to get Tony Vacchio an indefinite deferment. The love song he and Tana had sung in the picture was sweeping the country. Tana was more radiantly beautiful than she'd ever been before. She and Tony were an item, and Walter Winchell was predicting they'd be wed. Louella and Hedda had pieces about them frequently. They were photographed together everywhere; coming out of Ciro's one night, they caused a traffic jam on Sunset Boulevard.

Outstanding on the agenda for the board meeting at Major Pictures one morning was the subject of the romance between Tana Corgan and Tony Vacchio. On Gene Madrix's pad the notation was underlined: *How serious is it? Should we permit it to go on?* He never got to discuss the matter due to the lobster he'd eaten the night before; he developed an acute case of ptomaine poisoning and had to be rushed to the hospital.

The parties under consideration had no idea they were of such concern to the studio. They were taking care of their personal concerns themselves. Maria was standing guard as Tony Vacchio peeked out. It was five thirty in the morning and it wouldn't do for anyone to catch him leaving the Corgan home at such an hour. Rumors were rife as it was. He turned as Tana nuzzled his back. He kissed the top of her head. "Be ready, sweets. We can make Tijuana and back just as I planned if we do everything as arranged."

She stood on tiptoe and kissed him. "I'll be ready. Don't you worry."

As far as she was concerned Tony Vacchio was the handsomest man she'd ever seen: tall, virile, with a cleft in his chin. She thought he looked like a taller version of Tyrone Power, and he was all she had ever dreamed of having as a lover. Girls swooned and screamed wherever he appeared. He had a fine baritone voice, which imparted itself to his speaking tones and sent shivers up Tana's spine. She had made up her mind after the second day on the set that she was going to marry him.

They reached Tijuana on schedule and were married at four that same afternoon by a Mexican justice of the peace.

Maria and Tony's valet were their witnesses. Lilly had consented to stand guard as a cover-up at the house. On their return trip they stopped for dinner at Victor Hugo's in Laguna Beach. It was not crowded and they were seated in a dark corner at a table overlooking the ocean, but it wasn't long before they were recognized. People began to bother them with requests for autographs. It was common consensus in the room that they were a stunning, storybook couple.

Tony Vacchio had been a refugee from Italy. He'd escaped the Fascists by crossing the border into Switzerland, where an American producer had made arrangements for him to come to the United States. He'd been coached arduously in English and in two short years had been brought to Hollywood where a great future awaited him. Falling in love with Tana had not been in his plans but it didn't seem a detriment. On her part, obsessed by him, she had no hesitancy about using any means to entrap him . . . getting him into bed with her was her main objective.

Their first time together was a passionate, erotic orgy. She was a clawing and sensual tigress who drove him wild. Madly intoxicated with each other, they were unquenchable in their fierce, driving need. Never sated they explored thirstily, savagely seeking any way to reach higher peaks of sensation. Consumed by her desires, Tana gave vent to her most honest emotions. She was a taunting, provocative temptress with an innocent lewdness about her that totally enthralled Tony . . . he had never imagined such a woman existed. More than anything else he wanted to possess her, but to do so marriage was mandatory; neither one could jeopardize their careers by scandal. He knew the studio would not sanction their union, but in the long run it would prove an advantageous match, serving a twofold purpose. Tana would belong to him, and, since he was going into the Army, her fame would keep his name in the public eye, thus ensuring his future.

At the start, they hoped to keep their marriage secret and had pledged the Mexican justice of the peace to secrecy, binding it with a handsome cash gift. Unfortunately the man knew where he could get even more for revealing the secret. He'd recognized the couple the moment they'd walked through his door, and as soon as they left he placed a call. The announcement of the marriage would knock the war head-lines off the front page the following morning.

The newlyweds knew immediately something had happened when they reached the corner of the street on which Tana lived and saw the crowd of press people and cameramen on the front lawn.

"Slide down, honey," Tony ordered. "If they haven't seen us, we'll be able to get away." They had already dropped Maria at her aunt's house and the valet at Tony's apartment. A distraction at the other end of the street enabled Tony to swing the car around at the corner and they were safely away, at least for the moment. He urged Tana, "Stay down until we get further out on Sunset. You never know who might be driving by."

Tana didn't mind. She was having fun seated on the floor, stroking and rousing him so that he could barely keep his mind on the driving. The newsmen would have had the story of their lives that night if they had been able to follow them, although it wouldn't have been publishable.

Tony pulled the car up on a vacant lot as soon as he spotted one. He turned the car lights out and drew Tana to him. "Don't let's go, Tony," she murmured into his ear. "One more time here—it's fun." He obliged her and the motorcycle policeman who thought he saw the outline of a car on the lot decided he was foolish to chase some kids when there were so many speeders on the highway to go after.

They were tired afterward but they had to get out of town. They drove as far as the palatial Biltmore Hotel that overlooked the Pacific Ocean in Santa Barbara. The night clerk, drowsy with sleep, did not recognize the good-looking man who registered himself and wife as Mr. and Mrs. Maxwell. He gave them a secluded private cottage.

He was off for two days and it wasn't until he returned that he realized who his early-morning check-in had been. At his first opportunity he knocked on their door. After a few minutes' conversation, Mr. Maxwell gave him a hundred-dollar bill. It was a windfall for which he'd sooner have had his throat cut than talk. The promise of two hundred more earned his undying gratitude. He knew it would make great story anytime. He'd had a peek and seen how beautiful she was curled up on the couch in front of the fire. He was a romantic and he gave them his silence as a wedding gift.

He was not there the morning they departed, but Tony left a sealed envelope and a thank-you note, with an invitation to visit the studio anytime he came to Hollywood. Tony paid the bill. The cashier recognized him, and the moment he left the desk the woman called the newspaper.

This time when they pulled into Tana's driveway there were only two newsmen on hand to notify the others. They were able to get inside the house and freshen up before presenting themselves for the barrage of questions.

Michalson found the perfect house for them in the Bel Air hills and hired a decorator to put it in shape. They hid in the luxuriant, rolling green hills, but still they made news copy for weeks. People ate up stories of romance and love in contrast to the daily diet of the cataclysmic war.

For over two months the newlyweds lived in a dream world, wined, dined, adored and envied—and then their world crashed. Tony was served with a presidential greeting for military service. In response to Tana's tears he had one answer. "I must be an example to others. I have a debt to repay this marvelous country." The studio tried every ploy to delay his going, but it was to no avail.

For once Tana was stymied; there were no wiles she could use to prevail. Despite their brief time together she had to face his leaving, and the thought of parting with him drove her wild. Even Lilly was forced to admit Tana was mad about her husband, head over heels in love with him. There was some small consolation for Tana that Tony would not be in the fighting lines but would serve in a Special Services entertainment group. She clung to him in desperation until he left for training and then threw herself into anything that kept her busy, outdoing herself in personal appearances for bond sales.

The period of her elopement had been so hectic that she had overlooked asking Lilly to notify her parents of her marriage. It was almost five weeks later before she found the moment to send them a letter explaining how deliriously happy she and Tony were and telling them at the first opportunity she would bring him home for them to meet. With everything that had gone on it never occurred to her that there had been no word from them; time had slipped by and over two months had passed without a letter. Preoccupied with Tony's departure, she never noticed their silence. Her mind now was on one thing: the news that Tony had completed his basic training and that she would soon be able to join him. At last it came; he had a two-week furlough before being shipped out. Immediately Tana flew out to be with him, forgetting, again, about her family.

Tony had reserved a suite in a hotel in a nearby city and for two weeks they were lost to the world. When his time was up they returned to the small town that bordered the Army camp and were swamped by crowds and the press. They could not make a move without photographers dogging their heels. The major newspapers carried the picture of their good-bye kiss on the front pages. Everyone could see how Mrs. Tony Vacchio courageously bid her brave young husband of such short duration farewell. Tana carried the picture with her as if in some way it could bring Tony closer to her.

Two months later Tony Vacchio was killed when a Japanese enemy barrage hit the small island on which he was stationed, destroying the canteen in which he was having a beer.

Tana's world crashed into smithereens around her. When the notification reached her, she broke into screaming hysterics. Grief-stricken, in despair, she collapsed. The doctor did what he could for her, but for a long time she lay like a rag doll, wasting away. Everyone rallied around to do what they could, but she was inconsolable. Eventually her bitterness at a fate that had deprived her of the one person she wanted more than anyone in the world ignited a spark of anger, and with that anger as a stimulant, she slowly began to recover.

Gene Madrix had been puzzled by the absence of Tana's parents at such a time. In a discussion with Lilly about this, he was amazed to learn there had been no word from the Corrigans from the onset of Tana's nuptials. He was peeved at how unfeeling they seemed to be and secured a telephone number from Lilly; he would ascertain why they were ignoring their daughter's plight.

A telephone call was put through to Mike O'Rourke's bar. It was a poor connection, and the thick Irish brogue of the man at the other end made conversation difficult. When Madrix realized he was not talking to Tana's father, he requested that the man deliver a message: "Please ask them to return my call. It is urgent that Mrs. Corrigan contact me. Her daughter is ill—her husband has been killed in the war. I'm sure you've seen it in the newspapers."

There was a pause at the other end of the line and then Mike O'Rourke said, "Polly's mother canno call. She died two months ago."

Madrix was dumbstruck, but he realized the man was about to end the conversation. He pleaded, "Don't hang up, sir . . . just a moment. Who am I speaking with?"

"You be talkin to Sean's cousin, Mike O'Rourke. Poor Sean ain't fit fur anythin, bereft o the best wife God iver give to a man. That gel you be tellin about stuck the knife in her sure as God made the world . . . niver lettin them know she be married, forgittin all about them."

"That can't be true, sir—there must be some explanation. I'm upset at hearing about Mrs. Corrigan; please convey my sympathies to Mr. Corrigan. Believe me, we had no idea such a thing happened."

"That'll be all I'll be sayin to you. Good-bye, mister."

Stunned, Madrix was unable to believe what he had heard. He tried to put the bits and pieces of the last months into sequence. He remembered how the feisty little Irish woman had come to him standing her ground so valiantly on behalf of her daughter. He'd had no idea Tana had severed relations with her parents. Dismayed and unhappy, he tried to understand, from the little he knew, how such a deplorable situation could have come about. In retrospect he felt ashamed of the letter he had written to them on Tana's behalf.

He telephoned Ralph Michalson, and at the club later, having a drink with him, he related the story.

"She's surely pulled the wool over your eyes," Michalson said. "Haven't you any idea what Tana's really like, Gene? That girl is so wrapped up in herself she rationalizes everything she does. At first I felt her parents were important to her, but I've come to realize she has other priorities, and out of sight, out of mind."

Madrix looked at him in astonishment. "But, Ralph, she led me to believe she adored her mother, and with good reason. I can't get over it."

"That beautiful face covers a selfish, spoiled, self-centered child—she's an inconsiderate, mean little soul. Frankly, if it weren't for you I'd have dropped her long ago."

Amazement was written all over Madrix's face. "I can't understand that you never intimated these things to me before."

"Why? She's doing a good job for you. Her personal life is not our concern. I wonder what happened to her mother; she didn't seem ill when she was here. I liked her—she was quite a lady."

Madrix nodded. "That's what I thought too. I assumed the apple didn't roll far from the tree."

There was silence between them for a few moments and

then Ralph Michalson asked, "How are you going to handle this? I gather from what you've said she probably hasn't heard about her mother. With Tony gone and now this news, you're going to have your hands full."

Madrix seemed to be deliberating. "I got the impression she was crazy about her parents. I can't believe this is a case of deliberate neglect. There must be some explanation."

Ralph thought, The bigger they are, the easier to fool. "Did I ever tell you what went on after that infamous episode with Mrs. Corrigan and the columnist? Tana literally threw her mother out of the house."

"That can't be the case," Gene Madrix said defensively. "She left because Mr. Corrigan was ill."

"That's what she wanted you and everyone else to think. If it hadn't been for Maria I'd never have known differently."

"You're being very hard on her, Ralph. She's young. Be fair: too much too soon. I believe she loved her family."

Ralph didn't reply and the two men sat reflecting until Madrix said, "I'm positive she has no idea what's happened to her mother. What do you think we ought to do?"

Putting down his drink, Michalson said, "I think maybe you should do as her father wishes . . . nothing. As sad and messed up as this whole thing is, you'd better not get involved. It's a family matter and they'll have to handle it their own way. I agree with you, Tana's young—in my opinion, infantile. It's time Tana began to learn a few facts of life. Do you know a better way than having your nose rubbed in a mess? It's not your job or mine to always run interference for her."

A week later Mr. Madrix received a call from Lilly Fazon. "Mr. Madrix, Mrs. Vacchio asked me to call. She would very much appreciate it if the studio could give her a few weeks off. She's planning to visit her family."

Gene Madrix wondered if they knew. "Why, Miss Fazon? Is there any special reason?"

"Tana hasn't been home in some time, and with all that's happened to her she feels it might do her some good to visit with them for a while."

"All right, tell her she's free for two months. Will that be sufficient time? I expect you'll keep in touch with me. Are you accompanying her?"

"Yes, she's asked me to go along. We'll keep in touch. And thank you."

"Let me know when you're leaving and advise me when you expect to return. All right?"

"Yes, sir. Thank you."

There was no doubt Gene Madrix was unhappy about the way he had been compelled to handle the matter. He felt guilty and called Ralph Michalson. "Ralph, she's going to be a sick girl when the news hits her."

"Possibly, but my hunch is that Tana Corgan has a buoyancy that's going to surprise you. I don't doubt she's going to be very upset . . . after all, this is her mother we're talking about—but mark my words, Gene, Tana'll give you a Joan of Arc performance that will outdo any ever done. She'll hurdle the loss of her mother and her husband. She's a converter."

"What's that supposed to mean?"

"She turns debits into credits. In some form or fashion, this period of grief will be turned to her advantage. I sound awful, I know, but that girl's incapable of real love or gratitude."

Gene Madrix was miserable with the entire situation; he had a sick feeling in the pit of his stomach. When he saw the newspaper pictures of the recently bereaved war widow as she boarded the train for home, he was in a way glad that Tana Corgan was out of town.

Sean was unable to accept Deirdre's passing. Without his cousin, Mike, he might never have survived. He'd known Deirdre hadn't been herself for a long while; he knew she'd been eating her heart out over Polly. When the girl had married without notifying them and the whole world knew about it, she'd been completely overcome.

Sean had tried everything to brighten her up, but nothing roused her from the listless stupor. One morning she'd had a stroke, and she'd been rushed to the hospital in Butte, where she lingered for several weeks. He had not left her bedside, but nothing he could do seemed to prevail. She had just faded out like a flickering candle.

Sean was a madman for weeks, and it took all of Mike's care and attention to keep him from doing something to himself in order to follow Deirdre. In the end it was his fury at his "darlin Polly" that kept him going. Stubbornly he refused to permit Mike to notify their daughter of Deirdre's illness and her ultimate passing. He'd told Mike, "She didno care enough to let us share her joy; she surely wouldno want to know her blessed mother's gone to her reward. 'Tis the Lord's truth, Mike, I could tear the lass limb from limb. 'Tis sure certain, she be the instrument took my Deirdre from me."

An unkind fate had stepped in and worsened an already bad situation. Tana's letter informing her parents of her marriage, late as she had written, at least would have alleviated some of their unhappiness; but the letter had dropped behind Lilly Fazon's built-in desk and no one ever knew of its existence.

It was almost two months after Deirdre's death that Sean sat down one evening and tried to compose himself for the ordeal at hand. It was an obligation long overdue. He had no idea whether Father McGurdy was alive and still in Brightwater, but the compulsion to write him was overwhelming. It was a hard task he had set himself. Opening wounds that had long been covered, he wept as he wrote:

Dear Father,

Tis no doubt you will be surprised to learn who tis is finally writin to you as promised so long ago. I hope this finds you well and enjoyin the fruit o your good life. Tis much I have to tell you.

I'm no too clear in me mind. My darlin Deirdre, me blessed wife these many years, has gone to her rest just these weeks past. Tis inconsolable I am alone without her by me side.

In the years past the good Lord blessed us and the child grew beautiful. She was the light o our lives as you well knew and for a long time gave us much happiness. She studied actin and got to be Tana Corgan, now a famous movie star. In the doin seems like she forgot her poor mither and dad. It broke me Deirdre's heart. Like so many years ago when I tol you takin the child from her would kill her, so it came to pass. Deirdre couldno live without her Polly, and Polly did no have time for us. She got married and niver let us know. Tis that I think took me Deirdre. Tis clear, Father, our sins catch up with us. So tis this way I be confessin to you whats been so long overdue. Tis plain what I did those many years ago stealin away with the child caused all this painful grief. Tis your pardon I'm askin and the good Lord's too. I hope he

forgives Deirdre and lets her into heaven, twas all my fault. She were no to blame for anythin at all, bein the bist wife and mither God himself made. Tis me fault entirely.
   I hope this letter finds you in the best o health.

                              Your old friend,
                              Sean Corrigan

Chapter XXI

◅─◈─▻

THE SEARCH

MANY MILES AWAY, high in the Colorado Rockies, Mr. Saperson, a private investigator for Emmalina Griffon, had been waiting impatiently for permission to see Father McGurdy, who was in residence at a monastery. When finally he received word, he rushed to the office and was greeted by the abbot who told him, "Remember, please, he is very weak and frail. He may not even recall the information you are seeking, so please do not persist."

Mr. Saperson was shown to a small, walled terrace to await Father McGurdy. It was a beautiful summer day; high in the mountain air the birds wheeled and sang as they soared over and around the mountain peaks. Masses of flowers bordered the walls, and he sniffed appreciatively at their perfumed fragrance. He turned as he heard the creak of a wheelchair on the stone floor. An old man whose skin was like parchment grinned from what had once been a cherubic face.

The young monk who had wheeled Father McGurdy out placed and braked the chair and then turned and left. Saperson was lucky: the priest was alert and curious today. His quavery voice reached across the short distance. "How do you do, young man. I see you appreciate the majesty of our countryside. Father tells me you are seeking information." The voice wavered and stopped. It had been a long speech for him.

Saperson could see he would have to move quickly and

carefully lest he wear the old man out too soon. He began, "Father McGurdy, I do not want to impose on your rest, but the information I seek is vital. My client, Emmalina Fields Griffon, is desperately seeking information that might lead to the whereabouts of a lost sister, Polly Sue Corrigan. A Dr. Quenton, formerly of Brightwater also, told me you might have some knowledge about the family."

The old man sat with his eyes closed; he seemed to be asleep. Mr. Saperson was worried. The minutes were flying and their time together was almost up. He saw the shadow of the young monk waiting behind the window.

Slowly and wearily Father McGurdy raised his head. "My son, I wish I could be of help, but I know not where they disappeared. Many years ago I had one letter from some small out-of-the-way place en route to heaven only knows where. I recall some of my parishoners thought they might even have come here, Colorado, but who knows? 'Tis sure, though, it would have been someplace with land. Sean, dear fellow that he was, would have wanted land. How is little Emmy? She was a dear child." His head bobbed and it was apparent he had fallen asleep.

The interview was over and the young monk approached. As he released the brake, the priest roused and said, "You didna tell me."

"Emmy is fine, Father. She sends you her greetings."

The old man smiled gently as the monk moved the chair and he feebly waved his hand as if in benediction as he said softly, "God be with you in your mission. Please leave Emmy's address in the office. 'Tis unlikely we'll ever hear, but if we should . . ." The monk had wheeled him through the door.

Saperson had come with high hopes; he had expected some more precise information. He was a determined man: he'd find that Corrigan family, they couldn't have disappeared off the face of the earth without some trace. At least he had a good lead on the Wilkerson girl. This was proving a tough case, but he'd crack it yet. Judge Esquith and the Griffons were good clients, and he knew it would rank him high if he could please them. The young man, Jonathan Griffon, had implied his wife's health was blighted by her inability to locate the missing members of her family. He sighed; sometimes this was heartbreaking work, and one came up with strange endings. He headed for the office of the monastery. While he figured it unlikely that anyone would contact Father McGurdy at this late date, he would take no chances. He left his address.

It was some weeks later when Sean Corrigan's letter to Father McGurdy reached the monastery. It had traveled a roundabout way, having had to be forwarded to the main diocese and then readdressed and sent out to him.

Now almost blind and failing rapidly, the old man was amazed when the letter was handed to him. Events of the past were much sharper and more present in the ruminations of his mind these days. He was grieved at what had happened with the Corrigans, but he was weary, and it was all so very long ago. He would try to remember to offer a special prayer on their behalf. He remembered the young, sweet wife. He must make an effort to have a mass for her. There was something else in connection with these people, he tried to recall—oh, yes, he would ask the young monk in attendance on him to forward the letter to the man who had visited him.

Exhausted by the exertion of his thinking, he dozed off, and the letter slipped from his frail fingers, to be picked up by a gust of wind and borne off, high and far.

As his head bobbed he awakened and it occurred to him that the Lord worked his wonders in mysterious ways. He felt a wave of pity for poor Sean—so much trouble and his guilt weighing so heavily all these years, catching up to impale him now. He must see to it that someone dropped Sean Corrigan a note.

He died in his sleep before the opportunity presented itself. Weeks later, Sean's letter, still in readable state, was found and returned to the monastery office.

Chapter XXII

❧❦❧

EMMY FINDS HER NICHE

EMMALINA GRIFFON FELT the need to pinch herself to be sure this was happening to her. Laughter was coming more easily and she was filled with a new sense of anticipation. Life with Ralph and Betty Michalson had given her the feeling she'd been transported to another world; and with the arrival of her Uncle Max, she experienced a contentment unimaginable to her before.

She looked around the elegant room now filling with handsomely dressed people. The Michalsons did not entertain often, but when they did, the elite of Hollywood turned up in splendor. The day of the party had dawned clear and brilliant. The caterers had arrived early and Emmy had watched in amazement as bars and tables were set up so that by noon everything was in readiness.

As Emmy prepared to join Uncle Max, who was in his element with old friends, Betty Michalson intercepted and took her in tow. After introductions had been made, she stood chatting with some people, while Betty excused herself to greet newcomers. As Emmy's eyes followed her, she saw her hostess embracing a strikingly handsome man in uniform. Their eyes met across the distance. She had difficulty averting her glance; there was something so compellingly attractive about him. Excusing herself, she moved toward Gene Madrix and his wife standing in a corner. She was curious to know who the man was. He had a raffish sort of swagger, a devilish nonchalance. Apparently he was well known and people seemed delighted at seeing him. He was stunningly attractive. She saw the man looking at her and became self-conscious at her unusual forwardness. She felt foolish at her reaction; she hadn't even met him. But she wasn't alone in her feeling, she saw, as women began to surround him. Obviously others felt the same way, and he became the target of their flirting and teasing. His presence was distracting, and she found it difficult to keep her mind on the people around her. His voice, deep and authoritative, could be heard from where she stood.

Chatting with Mr. and Mrs. Madrix, she was unaware that Betty was bringing the man toward them. His voice close behind startled her. She fought to make herself appear calm, certain that just by looking at her he would know the effect he had upon her.

Betty was introducing them and his eyes seemed to pierce through her. She hadn't caught his name but he smiled impishly at her as he said, "I know, of course, you're not Tana Corgan, but everyone's talking about your resemblance. You're beautiful in a different way." She blushed to her roots as he said, "Is Bill Griffon your husband?"

She looked up, only to be locked into his eyes, and she stammered, "N-no, Bill is my brother-in-law. My husband is serving in the Ambulance Corps."

His smile was shattering; no one had ever had such a sensual affect on her. "In that case, Mrs. Griffon, you must allow me to be of service. I'm fortunate enough to be stationed around here for a while, and since these are my stamping grounds, I'd be happy to show you around."

She murmured some unintelligible reply and he continued. "Betty's told me you're an accomplished pianist and that you studied at Juilliard. I had a year there a long time ago."

Her voice quavered as she replied, "Betty's too kind. I don't think I'm that expert, but I love the instrument, Major—I'm sorry, I didn't get your name."

She noticed they were standing alone, Betty and the Madrixes having moved off. He stood scrutinizing her. "I'm Larry Bayless; please call me Larry. I'm hoping to hear you play. Betty's asked me to dinner Tuesday evening. She tells me you're their houseguest."

She couldn't avoid looking up at him . . . into a pair of knowing, derisively amused eyes that saw through her pretenses.

Larry Bayless was accustomed to being fawned over by

women. He was a sophisticated man-about-town, and women were openly aggressive in their pursuit of him. A ruggedly handsome man, his superb physique was set off by excellently cut clothes. His tanned skin and back hair shot with silver accentuated the piercing blue eyes that seemed to Emmy to be devouring her.

"Is it true you're planning to settle here?"

She hadn't been listening and was disconcerted. "I'm not certain, but there is a possibility I may remain awhile."

"Betty tells me there's talk of your working at the Canteen."

Obviously Mrs. Michalson had been doing her press-agentry. Emmy wished she were not behaving like a moon-struck girl. She desperately wanted to appear nonchalant and indifferent. She made an attempt at changing the subject, asking him about his background in music. He was widely conversant with musical personalities, some of whom they discovered they knew in common.

The flow of people around them was a constant interruption as they maintained the amenities and he suggested, "Let's move . . . it's less crowded in the garden."

Taking her by the arm, he steered her through the French doors. A tremor ran through her at his touch. She asked, "Are you in the movie business, Major Bayless?"

He smiled at the question. "Yes. Very much so. I was a producer before the war."

In a flash it came to her. She had heard about him. He was considered the youthful creative genius of the film world. Everyone talked about him with awe and admiration. She was bowled over with embarrassment. "Of course! You must think I'm an utter idiot, Major, not to have recognized your name at once."

Laughing heartily, he assured her, "Movies are not the world, Mrs. Griffon. You've no idea what a pleasure it is to be able to impress you without my titles and pedigree. I hope I've won your esteem without them."

Smiling gratefully, she said, "Indeed you have, Major. You're a most knowledgeable man."

For a fleeting instant they stared at each other. Then he said, "Would you take it amiss if we left quietly and went somewhere for a drink? The party is almost over and they'll never miss us."

"That would be very nice, but I'm afraid I'll have to take a rain check. After all, I am one of the guests of honor."

"Stay right there . . . don't move . . . just practice the name Larry. I'll get the Michalsons' permission and off we'll go."

She was astounded at herself, at how shameless she was; she was as smitten as a teenager with a crush. Watching as he walked back to her, she knew she wanted him to touch her, hold her, kiss her. For a fleeting second she felt a pang of conscience—she was being immoral, she was a married woman, what had come over her? But she didn't care; the moment—now—was all that mattered. She had found a catalyst to enchant her most exotic fantasies; her mind was swept clean of anything else.

Seated in the car with him, chatting easily, she relaxed enjoying the breathtaking vista of the ocean as the winding road cut through the foothills of the verdant Santa Monica Mountains en route to a little beach restaurant he frequented. She could feel his eyes on her, and it was as though he was blatantly undressing her. A tingle ran up her spine; he made her feel so feminine, so daring. She'd never been the recipient of lascivious attention from a man, and she was curious, filled with a strange, heart-quickening anticipation.

Over a light supper and wine they talked of many things. He told her about his home, which was just a short distance away. "Would you like to see it? I have a marvelous piano. Regrettably, I must admit, it's German, but I bought it long before the war—a Bechstein, the pride of my life." She could not force herself to say no.

The house was on the beach facing the ocean, and as they climbed the steps to the deck she stopped to take in the view. It was pitch black everywhere, the only light emanating from the distant shimmering silver stars and bright moonlight reflected on the churning waters. The brooding velvet darkness held them in its grip, and they stood in silence until he said softly, "It's as if we were in another world . . . as if we were standing on the edge of the unknown."

He saw that she trembled. "Cold? Come here!" He put an arm around her, and she felt faint. He held her by the shoulders and then turned her to him, holding her face in his hand, her head tilted back. The kiss, when it came, drained her. Her veneer cracked—her infatuation was complete. She could feel the swell of his thighs, and she had no control of her body as she responded to him. She lost all sense of time and place as he made love to her. She wanted him to go on forever. Her feelings had never been invoked with such physical passion. She had abandoned the world and everyone in it. He kissed her eyes, her neck, her breasts . . . she throbbed with desire.

When he drew her toward the house she demurred. "I can't—I mustn't. Larry, please . . ."

She was locked into intense blue eyes filled with eager expectation, at once mocking and laughing. He held her to him as if she were a baby. She wanted to resist, to fight him off, but she was aching for him too. He undressed her slowly and she tried to rise from the bed, but she was powerless as he fell on top of her and pressed his lips on hers. Feverishly, greedily her body moved in rhythm with his. Her senses sang . . . the world exploded. As he thrust himself into her for the last time she dissolved in ecstasy. She had never known, no one had ever told her, such feelings were to be had—it was the most unimaginable pleasure. This man had conjured a sweet and magical distillation that had cleft the very earth she had stood upon. Love or lust, she abandoned herself to it. Every inch of her body pulsated in this stirring crescendo of joy. She wanted more . . . to know it again; she was insatiable, and it was only when she kissed her hard and brutally that she regained her senses. He was sitting up and stroking her. "What a woman you are, Emmalina."

He brushed a hair from her eyes and she looked at him, saying so softly he had to bend near to hear, "I never knew, Larry."

He stretched out next to her, moving his hand across the sheen of her skin. "What a waste if that is true, my darling. It's the secret of life."

She turned her head. "I never knew love was like this."

Fortunately she missed the cryptic look that crossed his face. "How do you know it's love, Emmy?"

She turned back to look at him and her eyes opened wide in surprise at his question. "I fell in love with you the moment I saw you, Larry. I'd never have been able to do this if I hadn't been in love with you."

He lay back without answering. She rose on an elbow to look into his face. "Did I say something to upset you, Larry?"

"No. Of course not. It's been an unusual experience for me too."

How could he tell her that sleeping with adoring women was a commonplace experience for him? This woman stirred and disturbed him. Long ago, he'd promised himself he'd make no lasting commitments; he wanted no involvements or protracted entanglements. She put her hand on his body and he drew her to him again.

Theirs was a fantastic coupling. She could make him do things he'd never believed possible. As they sank back in repletion, she heard him say, "By God, I think I've met my match."

She laughed breathlessly and curled up next to him. They slept for a while. She awoke to see him dressed and staring down at her. Suddenly she was overcome by shyness and pulled the sheet around her. He said quietly, "We'd better get ready if I'm to get you back before dawn. The dressing room is over there. I hope we're not stopped because of the curfew."

Hastily she scrambled up, draping the sheet around her. He watched with amusement and reached for his robe, handing it to her. "What's to hide? I know every part of you."

She giggled. "I know; it's silly, of course."

Surprisingly, she felt no remorse. Showered and dressed, she walked back into the room toweling her wet hair. He was stretched out in a chair, smoking a cigarette. The sight of him recharged her again. He sensed it as he watched her through lowered lids. "You know, my dear Em, you are a voluptuary. If you keep this up we may never get you home."

She said softly, "I don't care."

He was rough as he pulled her down to him. "You'd better stop this, or there'll be nothing left of me. Beats all how you can do this to me."

Holding her face tightly, his fingers cut her skin. He kissed her so hard the breath left her. She was about to suffocate when he released her. "You're a wench, Emmalina—a wench! By God, who'd ever have thought it? A prim and proper lady on the outside, but in bed . . ." They both laughed.

"Come on, woman. I promised the Michalsons I'd get you home early, but I'm sure they never bargained for this early. I have a key, though. Betty thought to give it to me."

She smiled coyly. "They know I'm reliable, Larry. They won't worry about me."

He looked at her archly. "That's just it, Em, just it! They know me and they'll worry."

She stood her ground. She was about to answer him, but he pulled her to him again and she murmured in his ear, "I'm over twenty-one and you're not responsible."

"Em . . . I have a reputation for being a playboy, and everyone in town knows it."

She pulled back, but this time she didn't look at him as she spoke. "I'm not asking you for anything, Larry. Please don't worry."

As they were leaving, she ran her hands over the keys of the piano and he said, "Next time, Em."

They drove homeward in silence. As he escorted her to the door, he said in a whisper, "I'll be back for you this evening. I don't think I can stay away from you. But one thing you'd better get straight: if I fall in love with you, I'm an all-or-nothing guy. Please, Em . . . don't let's get into something we'll both be sorry for. Do you understand?"

She reached up and kissed him lightly on the lips. He put the key in the door for her and ran swiftly down the walk.

She slept late the next morning, to be awakened by Betty's knock on her bedroom door. She sprang up. "Oh, Betty, I'm sorry. What time is it?"

"Don't be foolish, darling. I'd have let you sleep longer, but I absolutely couldn't wait another minute for you to see the hothouse of flowers that's come. Such an embarrassment of flowers has to prove only one thing—you've made a conquest."

Blushing fiercely, Emmy wished she could disappear. She was a dead giveaway. "Oh, Betty, I don't know what hole to hide myself in. What must you think of me?"

Betty stood leaning against the doorjamb as she smiled innocently. "Think of you? What are you talking about?"

"Betty, I'm about to confess something to you. I guess the way I'm feeling would be apparent to a mole. Please, don't tell Ralph. For the first time in my life, I'm helplessly, hopelessly in love."

Closing the door behind her, Betty moved into the room and sat down. It was like being sunstruck looking at the girl's incandescent face. She said easily, "Look, hon, get showered and dressed. Ralph has taken Max off to the studio. We'll talk over coffee. There is something you should know, right from scratch: Larry Bayless is a wonderful, marvelous, talented man, and we all adore him, but he has a reputation when it comes to women."

She was amazed at Emmy's response. Laughingly she called out as she went into the bathroom, "I know; he told me. Betty, he's in love with me."

Betty got up. "All right, Emmy . . . get dressed. We'd better talk."

Showering, Emmy looked at her body, examining it as if seeing it for the first time. She had not one regret. She had never been in love with Jonathan, never! Her feelings for him had been totally different from those she had for Larry Bayless. She knew there was a word for her, for what she had done; she was an adulteress. Well, so be it, she didn't care. She had never felt so complete, so whole, in her entire life.

For the entire afternoon Emmy and Betty talked. The whole sad tale of her marriage from its beginning to its end was related. Betty was both sympathetic and understanding. She tried to reason with Emmy but made no headway. "Emmy, you have to give yourself more time. Goodness, you and Larry have only just met. Be certain you're not confusing passion with love. What you have now the world doesn't have to know about." She paused and looked at Emmy. "Normally what's happened to you wouldn't show, but I'll be darned if it's not written all over your face—you are in love. If you don't want Ralph and Max to know what's going on, you'd better change that expression on your face."

The men were arriving as Larry drove up to call for Emmy. He joined them in the den for a drink while Emmy dressed. When she walked into the room, the conversation ceased. Inwardly on fire, she was beauty incarnate. Greeting them, she walked over to kiss Max, who stared up at her. "I must say, Emmy, there's something about this California air agrees with you. I've never seen you look so well. Don't get in late tonight, hear?"

She patted his cheek. "There you go, Uncle Max. You complain about my being childish and you treat me as if I were twelve." Everyone laughed and she and Larry made their departure.

Max was no fool; he had seen and felt the current between the two.

In the days that followed, Emmy tried desperately to hide her feelings, but she couldn't suppress them. She talked about Larry at every opportunity. They saw each other every day. Finally Max could stand it no longer, and he took Betty aside. "I'd appreciate it, Betty, if you'd talk to Emmy. It's unbecoming for her to be behaving in this fashion."

Betty tried to ease his apprehension. "Max, she's just a young woman having a harmless fling. The gossipmongers are always with us. Larry Bayless is a fine young man, and they're young people in the midst of a terrible war. It will all work out. Please don't worry."

They were fervent lovers. Emmy thrived and blossomed. She had never dreamed a man could be so gentle and compelling; his every touch made her tingle. She was filled with an ardor and intensity that were new to her. They were heedless now, they no longer cared to keep up appearances; it was as if they challenged the world to know they were madly, passionately in love. For Emmy it was as if Jonathan had never existed. Every song they heard was their song, every place they went was their place.

Three weeks had gone by. One morning, at breakfast, Emmy and Max found themselves alone. He looked at her in dismay as he said, "Emmy, are you preparing to divorce Jonathan?" His face was set and stern. "I'm not sitting in judgment, but you seem to have forgotten you are a married woman. I'm delighted with your new sense of self-worth, but let's put things in their proper perspective. You seem to have forgotten also that you are the Michalsons' houseguest and what you are doing may be an embarrassment to them. Until you are under your own roof, I would suggest you conduct yourself with more propriety."

Humiliated, she didn't respond. When he saw that she intended no reply, he said, "If you can bring yourself back to reality, I have some other news for you. Mr. Saperson says that Tana Corgan is probably your sister Polly Sue. His letter intimates she has some problems too."

Emmy was startled at his use of the word *too*.

"From what he writes, it may be some time before she returns. I think, therefore, that if you want to resolve the matter of your relationship with her, it might be advisable that you get yourself properly settled here. You can notify Pearlie Mae to come. And you should at least keep up some pretenses of respectability."

"Uncle Max, please." Emmy winced. "I had no idea."

"That's the first sensible thing you've said in a long while. Of course you had no idea."

The old man reached into his jacket pocket and slapped down a thin packet of APO letters from Jonathan. He shoved them at her and angrily stomped from the table. He took great pains to avoid her in the days that followed.

Reading Jonathan's letters in the privacy of her room, she

felt she'd had a narrow escape. They were not the outpourings of someone who loved her; it was instead as if they were from an old and good friend, a devoted brother. He had erected barriers of reserve between them. She might have been willing to make adjustments, find a way to keep the peace, but she had met Larry Bayless. Thinking about what had happened, she felt no guilt, no shame, no sense of deception.

Emmy felt as if she had been reborn, a woman roused from a somnolent state, awakened to see herself and the world around her with eyes that suddenly perceived. In giving herself to this man it was as if she had been stripped to the bone, and there was no artifice left. There was at once pain and bliss and, most amazingly, freedom from the shackles that had held her tied to the past. The chrysalis in which she had been bound had fallen from her, to reveal a woman in full possession of her faculties. Her resolution had not faltered, it had strengthened. She would find her family, she would resolve the mystery; but in doing so there would no longer be the same panic . . . she had retrieved her balance. Those muted ghosts of the past floated freely in the reservoir of her memory, but, while baffling and besetting, the unanswered questions were now illumined by hope. With Larry by her side, there was no need to dredge them from the recesses of her mind. He understood and accepted her as she was; she could be her own person.

Larry Bayless had been the wizard who had freed her from bondage by his love. Released from the pressures of standards alien to her, the need to conform, to fit in, she was finally and truly free to be who and what she was.

Larry colored her days and nights. Poor, perplexed Uncle Max was right; she had been heedless and inconsiderate in allowing Larry to obliterate everything else. She would have to talk matters over with him so that they could arrange things differently.

At the first opportunity she talked to Ralph Michalson about arrangements for the rental of the Corgan house and then telegraphed Pearlie Mae with instructions for packing and a date for departure to come to California.

Larry had been called back to his base where he would remain for a month, so she was able to concentrate on matters at hand. Betty told her Uncle Max was making preparations to return to Oklahoma. He continued to glower at her, and one day, with a lowering expression he told her, "If you ever really need me, Emmalina, of course I'll make myself available. Please remember I'm not as young as you imagine and not as inclined to think for you as I once was. I speak honestly when I say you've been a big disappointment to me."

"Uncle Max, I insist you give me a chance to say something. You're not being fair to yourself or me. In your heart you know very well I'm not a loose woman, a fly-by-night. I'd like very much to tell you what's happened if you'll just listen."

Coldly implacable, he refused to listen. "No, Emmy. Maybe there'll be a time, but for the moment I prefer not to hear it. After all, who knows, you might have a change of heart again, and then how would you explain that?"

"Uncle Max, you've made up your mind about me without giving me a hearing."

"Maybe . . . maybe you're right, but that's how I feel. I would like to suggest to you, if you have any heart left, that you do not send Jonathan one of those 'Dear John' letters."

She gasped. "Uncle Max . . . no matter what you say, I'm not the heartless woman you make me out. I've fallen in love with Larry Bayless. I didn't intend to—it just happened. It's done more for me than anything in my life, other than you and Elizabeth. Please listen . . . Larry's freed me from the past. I'm happy, at peace with myself. I feel whole, healed. I don't know what the future holds, but at this moment I must trust my instincts. If I have any remorse, it's in the thought I might be hurting Jonathan; but, in a way, I have a feeling he'll be glad to be free of me."

He looked at her and sat quietly. He was too old and weary for the passionate complexities of the young. As he sat thinking, habit and affection rose in him. He knew Emmy still needed an anchor; the future wasn't one where love conquered all. As yet he knew too little about this man who had become her savior.

He held her close to him the morning of his departure. "Take care of yourself, Emmy. Try not to do anything too foolish and brash."

She clung to him, crying. "I'm sorry, Uncle Max, sorry that I caused you grief. I realize I've been inconsiderate. I'll speak with you every Sunday. Please, try to take care of yourself."

Max had taken for granted he knew every facet of her nature, her empathy and compassion, and been astounded by the startlingly independent and enigmatic woman she had become. He said ruefully, "Emmalina, get yourself in hand. Don't let Elizabeth down."

Without Larry and Uncle Max, life took on a different aspect. The Corgan house was hers, and within a few days she was able to move into it. Betty Michalson, who had not been swerved one iota in her affection for Emmy despite all that had gone on, gave her as much assistance as she could, and Emmy found herself comfortably installed. With Pearlie Mae's arrival, the house began to feel like home. Before he'd left, Larry had managed to secure a car for her and she was ready to go to work.

Her co-workers at the Canteen welcomed her warmly and she quickly made a niche for herself, learning easily what was required of her. She proved equal to the new responsibilities of her life and found pleasure in the daily order of things. She awoke each day to the joy of purpose and direction. Larry telephoned whenever he was able and wrote short notes assuring her how much he missed her.

No one was more surprised than Larry Bayless at this alteration to his life. Footloose and carefree until his involvement with Emmy, he found himself adrift in a sea of emotion, baffled by the hold this childlike woman had on him. She was beautiful, but for a man of his intellect that would not have been sufficient. She had a good mind too, but it was her innocence that touched his heart. She needed him but she didn't clutch and tear, and as their relationship had deepened he had discovered his dependency on her. She had untapped strengths. He admired her style and grace and her enthusiasm for life. He associated her with music he loved, the strains of which were wild and melodic. Away from her now for the first time, he could not forget her.

There had been one brilliantly flawless afternoon when they walked hand in hand along the ocean shore. The breeze had stirred the sand, although the water stretched like glass to the horizon. The air was thick with salt spume and the gentle swells had unfurled frothy edges that splashed their feet. Emmy had matched his stride.

Hurrying clouds scudded across the horizon and a stiff gust

whirled the sand around them. She had told him about her life and some of the episodes of her marriage.

He throbbed as he thought about her: her legs, long, slim and strong; her thighs, slender, sensuous in their set from her tightly molded hips. He remembered when he had flopped down in the sand beside her. "Emmy, I get the feeling you were really not in love with Jonathan. If you were, none of this would have mattered; you'd have made it your business to fight back, overcome it. You're a lady of integrity, and I believe you when you say you love me. It's different between us. And I don't give a damn about your family—although I have to confess I'm not too crazy about the idea of Tana Corgan being related to you."

He could see her mischievous, laughing eyes and he ached at the remembrance of her body as she snuggled closer to him and said, "Darling, I want to have your children. I want to bear your name."

He'd smiled and squeezed her. "How can I refuse such an offer? Now, about bearing my name"—his eyes were slits from the sun—"how does Emmalina Balishefsky appeal to you? Isn't it musical?"

Surprised, she giggled. "You're not getting rid of me! A rose by any other name smells just as sweet."

They'd laughed together; laughter came easily to them. "I can see it's not going to be easy shaking you. I'll have to find a better reason. My father's a retired dress cutter . . . my folks were poor but honorable and education for their children was the light at the end of the tunnel. I went to CCNY and they dreamed I'd become a lawyer. I had other ideas, which fortunately worked out well. Now, my sweet, if we marry you may have in-law problems of a different kind."

Instant concern showed on her sweet face. "Larry, won't they approve of me?"

He'd kissed her nose and told her, "Silly girl, they'll be thrilled to know I'm going to be married—they've almost given up on me. They'll treat you very formally until they really feel comfortable with you. After all, we're of different faiths . . . they'll be concerned about how we intend to raise our children. Em, I'm telling you all of this in the event you have any reservations about marrying a Jew . . ."

She'd reached up and kissed him, murmuring against his lips, "Nothing matters as long as we can spend the rest of our lives together. Now I've some questions for you. How will

your family feel about your marrying a divorced woman?
That might automatically mark me as a 'bad woman.'"

He'd held her by the shoulders, looking down at her,
searching her face. "Someone once said love is just a poetic
word, but for me it sums you up. You've hypnotized me. I'm
mad about you and, yes, you're captivatingly bad. My family
won't tell me if they're disturbed about your being divorced.
Besides, they won't care when they realize how I feel, so
forget about that. There's no doubt we're meant for each
other . . . we have no choice!" The sun had gone down when
they'd finished making love.

He had consoled Emmy. He'd been luckier than most to
have been stationed so near, but now his time at the
California base had come to an end and he had been notified
he would be shipping overseas in ten days.

Emmy had arranged to take time off from the Canteen, and
they drove to a lodge high in the pine-forested mountains.
Everything merged in that one week before he left. They
moved together in a trance. Nothing would be remembered
as commonplace: the sparkling clarity of the air, the fragrance
of the rain-washed forest, the symphony of birdcalls, the
heartening chill at night, the crackling of wood . . . the
brilliance of sunlight filtering through the trees . . . a plaiting
of sight and sound that had spread a magic mantle over them.
When they returned to the world there'd be peaceful resignation in their good-bye. He could see her face as he'd held
it . . . a last kiss.

These nights, thousands of miles from home, exhausted
after the missions he'd been on, in a strange, harsh environment made ever present by the sound of planes taking off and
returning, hearing the muted voices of the men around him,
he would draw the memory of her to him, remembering how
brave she had been. He would hold close to him the image of
her face as she'd said, "You will come back to me, my dearest
friend, my tender and gentle lover."

He was grateful for her to the innermost depths of his
being . . . the more so since he was compelled to face the
hazards of this cruel and hideous war: His one thought
was that he had her to go home to and, God willing, he
would.

As for Emmy, there was no other recourse but to wait. It
was as if time hung in abeyance. She spoke with Max, who
remained unsympathetic and sent her Jonathan's sparse little

notes, which she answered in kind. Mr. Saperson wrote he hoped to have news of Amy Beth shortly. As for Polly Sue, that would have to await Tana Corgan's return.

There was no way for her to know that just a few short miles away her sister Amy Beth lived happily with her husband, Peter Cooper.

Amy and Peter were...

Chapter XXIII

◦⟨═⟨◦⟩═⟩◦

AT HOME
WITH THE COOPERS

THE COOPERS' APARTMENT was easy to care for, and Amy took pleasure in keeping it spotless and shining. Both she and Peter were occupied during the day, and weekends were given to whatever relaxation they had time for. On occasion Deborah would come for a Sunday visit, more rarely Dorothy Cooper when she could manage the time. Amy Beth and Peter were content.

Peter had found a buddy in a young man, also a veteran, who attended classes with him. Jules was also newly married, and it was not long before Peter suggested Amy call and invite Jules and Sally Leven over for a Saturday evening. The young wives liked each other, and the couples became a foursome, interchanging visits frequently.

It was on one of their weekend evenings together, as Sally and Amy were in the kitchen preparing coffee and dessert, that the men overheard them discussing the Hollywood Canteen. The girls were comparing notes and discovered that neither had been there. When they returned to the living room, Peter surprised them. "Okay, you lucky girls. Jules and I have decided to don our detestable uniforms and next Saturday evening we'll take you to the Canteen. However, there's one condition: I'm absolutely not saluting Jules. Can you believe, Amy, this jerk made Lt. Colonel in the Army?"

Saturday night came, and dressed in their finery for a gala night out, they arrived to find the Canteen jammed. After the entertainment, Peter maneuvered a space for them on the dance floor. Despite his limp he enjoyed dancing, and Amy, to her joy, had proved an apt pupil. As they moved onto the dance floor, she bumped into a couple and turned her head to apologize. Amy felt certain the woman was well known, perhaps famous; she looked familiar. She nudged Peter, whispering, "Who is she?"

"I don't know. Could she be Tana Corgan?"

Amy was dubious. "I saw her once—remember when Barbara made that movie? Although maybe . . . she looks a lot like her."

Later, when they rejoined the Levens, she asked Sally, pointing out the woman standing in a group not too far away. Sally wasn't sure. "It could be her. They say they look different off the screen."

"Come on, you two stargazers," Jules said. "You've had enough thrills for one night. I wanta get out of my uniform—it's gotten tight."

Peter agreed. "I'm with you, Jules, my boy. I'd hate to tell you where mine is grabbing me."

They began to shepherd their wives through the crowd toward the door, unaware that the woman under discussion had began to move hesitantly toward them. Before she was able to reach them, they were swallowed up by the crowd.

Emmy Griffon was certain she knew the pretty girl from somewhere. The feeling of familiarity was so strong it was as though it reached out and touched her, yet she couldn't place her. Why was it so significant . . . why did it bother her so? She tried to dismiss it, but that night, as she readied herself for bed, a scene from the past floated into her mind. Oh, God! Of course! A shiver ran through her—it had been Amy Beth! The little girl in the schoolyard . . . the bow in back of her hair like the flower she'd worn there tonight . . . the face that looked out of the woman was the grown version of that child . . . those same sensitive, questing eyes. It had to be! She was sure—it was her sister, Amy Beth!

She'd have to contact Mr. Saperson. Talk about coincidence! Her sisters were apparently close by, based somewhere in Los Angeles. Her heart thumped at the prospect of what must soon be a reunion.

Chapter XXIV

TANA'S TROUBLES

THE TRACK WAS rough and the train, moving at high speed, swerved and jerked.

"This damn train is driving me crazy, Lilly. When do we get off?"

Lilly had just begun to doze off when she heard Tana's whine. The lights were dim in the compartment. Again Tana expected her to climb down out of bed and find the timetable. "Tana, dear, the porter promised to wake us an hour before we get to Butte. Try to get some rest, even if you can't sleep."

It was no use. She heard Tana scrabbling about and complaining in the berth below. "Hold still, Tana! I'm coming down. Would you like to play some cards?"

She was amused at the expletive as Tana bumped her head. "Oh, shit, Lilly. Stop humoring me like I'm an idiot."

Lilly lay back, wishing, for other reasons, that they were out of this confinement. Again as she dozed off she was roused. "Are you coming down?"

Wearily Lilly pulled herself together and, hanging on for dear life, struggled down the ladder. "Whew, that was a close one."

The grousing stopped. "Okay, now that you're down, let's have a dinky-winky and play some cards."

Lilly groped for the main light; she could just discern Tana's face. As the light came on she saw how frowsy and bloated Tana looked, her features distorted and swollen. Was it from tears or from drinking? Lilly wondered. Lilly was becoming increasingly concerned. Tana had discovered that gin eradicated memories, and she had wholeheartedly resorted to it to ease her unhappiness.

"What're you so slow about? Get the bottle. I know you put it in the night case."

There was no use arguing. The entire train would hear Tana if she got upset.

"Okay, honey, give me a minute. It's hard to reach anything in this cramped space."

She was being rocketed about as the train sped around curves. Gratefully she located the bag and the bottle, which she handed to the now whimpering woman. Tana no longer used a glass in private. The bottle was more direct. Lilly remained crouched in the corner of Tana's bunk, where she quickly fell asleep. It seemed a short time when the buzzer sounded at their door along with a hard rapping. "Train's due in Butte in forty-five minutes."

Lilly cracked her head sharply as she hastily arose. "Thank you," she called to the porter. She put all the lights on, hoping to awaken the completely collapsed woman who was snoring sonorously, with the empty bottle tucked in her arm. Lilly got a wet cloth and began to apply it to Tana's face. She couldn't help muttering, "My God, if anyone sees you in this condition! You're a mess."

She raised her voice and tugged at Tana's arm. "Come on, Tana. Get up! We're getting off!"

There was no response. Lilly finally resorted to slapping her face. "Get up, Tana! Wake up! For God's sake, get up!"

Frantically she pulled the supine form up and, grabbing her blouse, struggled to get her arm into it. Fortunately they had not undressed entirely. Lilly managed to get Tana's blouse buttoned and her shoes on. Finally Tana opened one bleary eye.

Desperate now, Lilly pleaded, "Help me get your coat on, Tana. The porter's waiting to take our luggage."

It was useless. She pulled the woman upright and got her into the coat. Propping her up, she scrambled into her own clothes. Just before opening the door for the porter, she remembered the bottle and tucked it back into the case. It wouldn't do to leave any telltale evidence. Under the circumstances anyone spotting Tana Corgan could ascribe her condition to extreme grief. She held on to Tana's arm tightly, saying to the porter, "It's hard to stand with the way this train rocks."

The porter helped them down to the platform, where the cold night air began to revive the drunken woman. "We here, Lilly? Where's the car?"

The train moved away. Lilly looked about. The station was desolate, empty. There was a small light in a shack a few yards down the platform. She saw that their luggage had been deposited there. "Come on, Tana. We can't stand here."

Tana looked down the now vacant track and called as she staggered, "'Bye, 'bye, train."

The porter's grinning face had told Lilly he knew what was going on. How could he not, with the reek of gin all over the compartment and them? She hoped he'd be charitable. Impatiently she propelled Tana toward the light. Fortunately the telegrapher opened his office door and allowed them inside. "Blowin a bit, ain't it?"

Lilly saw the clock above the desk. It was four thirty in the morning. Thank goodness for that. Outside of this man, there'd probably be no one else to witness Tana Corgan in this condition. She steered Tana to a bench on the side wall, where she promptly sprawled out and went to sleep. Lilly removed her coat and tossed it over Tana's shoulders.

She turned to the man, who stood staring at them, trying to make out what was happening. Lilly said sadly, "She's been awfully sick. . . .We were expecting to be picked up."

The man looked at her dubiously. "I ain't heard naught o that. Who you expectin this hour?"

Smiling engagingly, Lilly said, "My friend's family was to be here. They live a distance away, I've heard."

He looked at her with disbelief. "Wal, make yourself comfortable. 'Tain't much but better'n standin outside. Help yourself to coffee. Pot's over there."

Lilly was grateful. "Thank you very much, sir. I could do with a pickup; it's been a bad trip."

He snickered. "Seems to me your friend's had one too many pickups."

Lilly ignored the remark as she walked to the coffeepot and poured the bitter brew into the cracked mug that sat alongside it. The man settled himself at his machine, which was beginning to rattle, and Lilly tiredly sank down on the floor, her back against the bench on which Tana slept. She must have fallen asleep, because suddenly she heard voices.

"Says they be expectin somun to pick 'em up."

She opened her eyes to broad daylight, sun streaming and another strange man looking down at them. She roused herself and stood up. "I'm so sorry. I guess I was just exhausted."

The men stood silently. Embarrassed, she looked at them. "I can't imagine what's happened to my friend's family. I'll wake her now."

She bent over Tana and shook her gently. "Wake up, dear. We're here, and no one's come to call for us."

Grudgingly Tana opened her eyes. Thankfully Lilly saw that she had slept off the worst of the drunkenness. "Where are we, Lilly?"

"In Butte, honey. Don't you remember?"

Lilly made a point of addressing Tana as honey in public, particularly since her drunken bouts. It helped to keep her anonymity.

"Let's see if we can't find a place to freshen up and contact your family. All right?"

The station was now open and Lilly made arrangements for their baggage to be kept there until they called for it. She and Tana walked through the awakening town until they found a café. Lilly helped Tana to the rest room to freshen up, and then she ordered bacon and eggs, toast and coffee. Tana turned green at the sight of the food when it was brought to the table. Lilly hissed, "You'd better eat. You were quite a case last night, and if you don't pretend to be normal, that telegrapher will broadcast your condition all over the country. Don't give me any back talk—just sit up and eat!"

She managed to peck at the food and drank two cups of coffee. She'd been angry at Lilly but on reflection thought better of it. The waitress noticed Tana's half-eaten food and asked, "Anything wrong, miss?"

Lilly interposed. "Oh, no, it was real good. My friend's been awfully sick. Thanks."

As she walked away, Tana muttered, "Pig! What business is it of hers?"

"Look here"—Lilly spoke through clenched teeth—"until we get where we're going, we'd better have no more of this and no scenes—that is, if you know what's good for you. This isn't Hollywood; no one here gives a damn about you except a great big newspaper headline. Get yourself under control!"

Tana spat like a cat. "How dare you?"

Lilly spat back just as quickly. "Would you like me to leave? It would suit me fine the way you're carrying on!"

At the threat the wind went out of Tana, and she sat deflated and sullen. Finally she looked at her friend and said,

"I'm sorry, Lil. I can't imagine what's happened to Daddy. You did send the wire, didn't you?"

"Of course I did. I didn't dare ask that man in the office. He probably handled it. I surely didn't want him to know who you are. Is there anywhere in this godforsaken place we can rent a car or a taxi to take us to your house?"

It cost Lilly a hefty sum, but she arranged with the mechanic at the gas station to get them a car and a driver. It turned out to be an old truck driven by a retired miner who was unfamiliar with the countryside. Tana had to direct him most of the way. At the sight of the now familiar terrain—the lofting hills and haze-covered mountains against the limitless sky—her spirits lifted. Approaching the outskirts of her hometown, she tensed. "Lilly, do you suppose they didn't get the telegram? Won't they be surprised?"

Tana had the truck stop in front of the old café where Mike O'Rourke was just putting his key into the door lock.

"Lan sakes, who have we here? Saints alive, 'tis you, Polly Sue! Whatchu be doin here like this?"

She ran to him. "Cousin Mike, what a joy to see you! Where are the folks? I sent a telegram—didn't they get it? This darn war and all, it must have gotten lost."

Mike stared dumbly at the young woman. He was non-plussed about what to do and say. "C'mon in, Polly—you too, miss." He indicated Lilly. "I'll git me boy to bring in them bags. Hey, Tom, grab them bags and stick 'em in the back."

The two women followed him into the dim interior, empty except for them. Polly sniffed appreciatively at the alcoholic fragrance. She could do with a pickup, but she caught Lilly's look. She turned coy. "Cousin Mike, you're a sight for sore eyes. You haven't changed at all. Tell me about the folks. How are they?"

He stared at her. "Sit down, Polly." He pulled a chair. "Who you be, miss?" he asked Lilly.

"Oh, Cousin Mike, this is my friend and secretary, Miss Lilly Fazon. I'm sorry. I should have introduced you."

He stood there looking at them indecisively and then said, "'Tis plain you really don't know. You're in for a wee shock, missy."

Lilly grew apprehensive as he went on. "'Tis a shame you ne'er wrote. Your poor dear mither sick and ailin and nary a word from you."

Tana paled and grew frightened. "What are you saying,

Cousin Mike? Of course I wrote. When I was too busy this
lady here took care of it for me."

He glanced at Lilly and then back at Tana. "You got real
fancy, Polly Sue, with your writin lady and all that! 'Tain't
right you being too busy for us poor folks back here. Seems to
me you went to school and had your larnin. A word in your
own hand woulda done the poor bairn a world o good afore
she left this earthly place."

Polly's head reeled; he was being cruel to her. "What are
you talking about, Cousin Mike? Where are my mother and
daddy?"

He grimaced at her with distaste. "Your daddy's as all right
as he's ever agoin to be agin, but your mither, like I told you,
is havin her well-earned rest. She be dead and gone these
many months past."

He didn't make a move to catch her as she fell to the floor.
Lilly jumped up. "My God! Oh, my God, what a terrible
thing to do! Get some water—get something! Is there a
doctor in this godforsaken place?"

Mike walked behind the bar and filled a glass with tap
water. "Here you be, miss. She'll come to; she's a hardy one,
that one is. I'll be callin her father. 'Tis only right he know she
be here. For sure, miss, though, he may not come. He be cold
angry at this daughter o his."

Lilly was exhausted and overwrought—it was too much.
Tears welled into her eyes. "Oh, please, Mike. Do something.
We can't just let her lie there like that. Shouldn't we get a
doctor?"

Mike shook his head. "Let her be. She'll come round. I'll
be callin Sean."

Lilly bathed Tana's head and neck in the cold water. She
had bruised her cheek where she had fallen and it was
discoloring. "Come on, Tana, let me help you up."

Ashen, numb with shock, limp as a rag, she could barely
whisper, "Lilly, is it true . . . did he say my mother is dead?"

"He did, Tana. I'm sorry. I wish there was something I
could do." Lilly couldn't speak; she was choked up. She
managed to raise the stricken girl, who put her head down on
the table.

Mike returned. "Hear now, Polly, carryin on won't do
Deirdre any good—beautiful lass that she was. She be at
peace in God's good heaven. Your dad be sendin his man fur
you."

Tana mumbled, "Old Pete's coming?"

"Saints alive, lass, git yourself togither. Ol Pete's been dead and gone these past two years. What's got into you? You jist writ us all off. You had a right good home here and a fine God-fearin upbringin. You be a disgrace to one and all!"

So saying, he turned and strode off, leaving them to look at his back. They sat in somber silence.

It took almost an hour before a strange man walked in and looked at them inquiringly. "Miss Corrigan?"

Polly nodded yes and he said, "I be Jim. Your father's sent me after you."

The two women squeezed into the front of the truck as Jim loaded their luggage in the back. They drove the entire distance without a word being spoken. As they drove down the rutted road with the cattle and corral in the distance and reached the great wooden gates, memories tugged at Tana's heart and her hands began to tremble. Lilly took a hand, trying to calm her. The truck stopped in front of the main house and a wizened little man came to the door. Lilly heard Tana's gasp as she said, "Dear God, what's happened to my daddy?"

He didn't smile or greet them as he helped Jim unload the baggage. "Take 'em into the house, Jim. I be not sure how long the ladies'll be stayin."

When Jim had deposited the bags and driven off, Tana threw herself at Sean. "Oh, Daddy, please don't. I can't bear it. I had no idea, I didn't know. Please, Daddy, please, speak to me. I came home grief-stricken and find this."

His face was distorted with hatred. "You come here lookin fur comfort? You be worse than I iver thought. We be not good enough to share your joys, but you come draggin your trouble fur us. You'd best be gone gal. I've naught to give ye!"

Lilly tried to intervene but he cut her off. "I don recollect who ye be, miss, and this moment I be sorry fur ye. We be a family unaccustomed to airin our troubles and grief in front o strangers. I appreciate you be discomforted, but there be naught can be done to ease that."

He turned to Tana. "What you be wantin to do, Polly? You kin stay the night and be gone tomorrow."

Tana raised her hands beseechingly. "Daddy, please don't. Let's talk it over. Give me a chance to explain."

This served to further enrage Sean. "Talkin? About what? How your mither died o mournin over you? Dyin for the lack o word from you . . . readin all them stinkin stories about how you got married to some fancy Eetalian who got hisself killed. Everyone cryin and carryin on fur poor Tana Corgan . . . and poor Tana Corgan niver givin a tinker's damn fur her poor, sick, ailin mither that woulda given her life for her. All you ever had fur us was use. You ain't got a givin, lovin bone in your body. You be like the people who borned you!"

Tana's grief was so intense the words didn't register, and he stopped short, as if puzzled at what he'd said. He looked at her coldly. "'Tis too late fur talkin, Polly Sue. Yer poor mither be done and gone."

She looked at him imploringly, the tears coursing down her face. "But you, Daddy . . . what's to become of you without Mother?"

His face was torn with pain and grief. "'Tis not fur the likes o you to be worryin what's to become o me. I'll make my way till I join my darlin Deirdre—and fur sure 'twill be without the likes o you at my side. 'Tis fur sure, Polly Sue, the pain o losin you come afore the pain o losin m' Deirdre. She and I suffered together, only she couldno bear it and so she went where she could have peace. 'Tis no wonder God tested us so. We did a bad thing and we paid the price. 'Tis all I have to say. You be my daughter no longer. Me daughter be gone a time ago."

Tana became hysterical. Lilly tried to take her into her arms, but she pushed her away. "Leave me be, please, leave me be. Oh, Lilly, to think this could have happened and I didn't know. Daddy, I beg you . . ."

She slid to the floor, her arms outstretched. "Daddy, please find it in your heart to forgive me a little."

Unmoved, he turned and left the room. "I've things need tendin. You kin help yourself to food and stay the night. Jim'll drive you to town tomorrow. There'll be the afternoon train leavin Butte at four. You remember that, Polly Sue, don you? 'Tis the same ol train goin west at the same ol time."

Lilly watched helplessly as Tana, still on the floor, continued to implore her father. Somehow the sight of Tana prostrate and begging seemed ludicrous, and she had to restrain herself from a mad impulse to laugh. She was unable to decide whether this was a genuine act of contrition or partly a performance, and she wondered if Tana really knew herself.

As far as Lilly was concerned, the matter was grossly exaggerated. It was sheer stupidity to blame Tana for neglect.

She sincerely felt they were in the clear, guiltless, absolved and exonerated. Having been witness to what had occurred here this day, Lilly felt there was justification for Tana's attitude toward them. Judging by Mr. Corrigan's display of outraged anger, it was no wonder Tana kept him at a distance. He was obviously an ill-tempered, inconsiderate man, totally without understanding and compassion for his daughter. They had to get away from this place as quickly as possible.

Tana was getting up. Lilly quickly went to assist her and received a stinging slap for her efforts. Rising to her feet, Tana hissed, "I hate you, Lilly. I despise everything about you." Gulping for breath, she went on. "If you ever breathe a word of this to anyone, I'll hound you to your grave. Remember what I'm saying."

The slap had brought tears to Lilly's eyes. She looked at Tana reproachfully. "How can you talk this way, Tana? I'm not just your employee, I'm your friend. From the looks of it, your only friend."

Lilly's voice became cold and insinuating. "Do you think I'd be foolish enough to hurt the goose that lays my golden eggs? Damn you! Why do you think I keep trying to stop you from becoming a lush? Now, if you can get a grip on yourself, let's decide how to get out of this hellhole."

At this, Tana shoved her and spat. "My father's right. I deserve you. Don't go getting any ideas—there'll be no blackmail. Don't try it. You're no match for me."

Lilly snickered. "We're two of a kind! Okay, we understand each other. Do you want to stay the night?"

Shuddering, Tana looked around the old familiar room and, sighing, asked, "What time is it?"

"It's almost one thirty."

"There'll be enough time to make the train if we leave immediately."

Tana walked outside and called to Jim in the corral. Sean was nowhere in sight. At their urging, Jim drove them hell-bent back to Butte, and they arrived with fifteen minutes to spare. Tana's only words to Lilly were: "Buy tickets with a connection to Denver."

Sober throughout the remainder of the trip, Tana talked to Lilly only when it was absolutely necessary. She maintained a steely exterior, and Lilly knew when not to push. Upon their arrival in Denver, Tana ordered Lilly to make reservations for an indefinite stay at the Colorado Springs Hotel.

As they checked in late that same night, the manager of the elegant hotel appraised his guests. He recognized that they were people of substance but, not being familiar with film personalities, he gave them their due without fuss. The Depression and the war years had changed the element that had formerly visited the hotel. The guest list had been famous for the patronage of the rich and important, some of whom preferred anonymity—and into this category he placed the two women. From their appearance and demeanor he assumed them to be nouveau riche. It was obvious that Mrs. Vacchio had been a beauty, but she showed the ravages of illness and drink. It was all to the good that she was accompanied by a paid companion.

In the days that followed, the hotel staff learned that Mrs. Vacchio was rarely sober. However, the matter was kept discreetly quiet, since the considerable bar bills were paid promptly. Fortunately the two chose to remain in seclusion, seldom venturing out.

It was about two weeks after they had settled in that Lilly found it necessary to confront Tana. "Please, let's not have a scene, but when do you think we should contact the studio? We promised to give them an address where you could be reached."

"The hell with them! The only reason they want it is so they can call me back to work. I'm tired, and they can wait till I'm good and ready."

"Okay, Tana. It's all right with me, but you're going to have to contact your bank or Ralph Michalson shortly. We're running out of funds, and you can't remain here without prompt payment."

Tana eyed her suspiciously. "Why'd it take you this long to tell me? Write a note to the bank and have them transfer five thousand to a bank in Denver. Ask Mr. Hoity-Toity, the manager here, for the name of their biggest bank. That'll impress him. Anything else?"

"Yes, there is one other thing." She turned her back and walked to stare out the window. "I don't know why you picked this spot, but if it was to hide out, you couldn't have done better. Not that it matters—no one would recognize you."

She took a deep breath and turned around to face Tana. "You look a mess. You've let yourself go completely. When was the last time you really took a look at yourself? You're bloated and flabby; your face and body show the drinking. If you care a hoot about your career, you'd better get yourself in hand."

She waited for the explosion, but it never came. Instead Tana moved to look at herself in the full-length mirror that hung on the bedroom door. "You're a mean bitch, Lilly, but you're right. Am I too far gone, or have you any suggestions as to how your golden egg can be put back together again?"

Lilly released a sigh of relief. "The first thing you have to do is lay off the bottle. You need air and exercise. Once you begin to get rid of the bloat you can begin massages. If you're willing we can start tomorrow. After I take care of ordering the money we can get out and walk."

Tana walked back into the room and looked out the window. "How about swimming? The pool looked great when we checked in."

Lilly laughed. "Take another look out the window. The weather's changed; its gotten cool. Look at the aspens— they're turning gold. It's too cold for swimming."

A quizzical smile played on Tana's face—the first in a long, long while. "Lil, old girl, I guess I've been a handful. I appreciate your hanging on, whatever your reasons. You know, I like this place. I wouldn't mind staying in these parts forever."

Lighting a cigarette, Lilly scoffed. "At these rates, sweetie, you wouldn't last long. Why don't you look around and find a little cabin? You could probably pick it up for a song. You'd be able to come back here whenever you wanted to take a break."

"That's a marvelous idea. Since I won't be going back to Montana"—she paused and Lilly saw the hurt—"this would serve instead. Who'll know the difference?"

Lilly was so grateful for the change in Tana's mood that she'd have agreed to anything. "Hey, how about dinner downstairs tonight?"

She saw Tana was hesitant and she urged, "Look, wash your face . . . put some lipstick on . . . and you'll pass. The place is almost empty anyhow. Besides, no one looks at anyone here . . . the air is too rarefied."

"Okay, Miss Fazon, you may take me to dinner downstairs."

It was some days later that Ralph Michalson telephoned Gene Madrix. "What do you make of this, Gene? The silence has been broken. I have a letter from Lilly Fazon telling me that Tana's decided to buy some property in the Colorado Rockies. An attorney in Denver will contact me with the closing papers; they're to be in the name of Polly Sue Corrigan. It seems Tana wants to remain incognito. Lilly was generous enough to say a few other things. Here, let me read it: 'Have had a terrible time with Tana. She's been ill and really in a bad way. She found out that her mother had passed away, and the shock of that on top of Tony's death did her in. It's been a rough job just keeping her alive. She's finally coming around, but it will take more time before she'll be in any condition to return to the studio. I promise to keep in touch. In the meantime, leave things to me and don't worry. Say hello or not as you think best to those we know.' It's signed Lilly Fazon."

Madrix let out a whistle. "We may have trouble, Ralph. Tana at best is not the most stable human being."

Michalson assured him, "I don't think you have to worry. Lilly's a very practical girl. The thing I'm surprised at is how they landed in Colorado. What do you suppose happened?"

"My hunch is the little Irishman pitched them out. I don't want a word of this to get around."

"What's gotten into you, Gene? Remember, it's me you're talking to. There's no need for any talk about this at all."

"Sorry, Ralph. I just can't believe this story. She's been scheduled for a remake of *Western Skies;* we may have to recast. What's your hunch as to when she'll be back?"

"Haven't any. We'll have to play it by ear. I'll try to speak to Fazon when the lawyer contacts me."

Tana was improving daily. She had stopped drinking and followed a rigorous health routine: riding, walking and resting. Her appetite returned, her color was better and she had almost regained her figure. As she stepped from her bath one night with the towel wrapped around her, she paraded in front of Lilly. "Well, what do you think?"

"I think you're getting there."

"Lil, if ever I go soft again—stop me cold!"

Struggling through her pajama top, Lilly popped her head out and asked, "Soft? What's that in reference to?"

"I don't want anyone to ever matter again. No relationships. I almost destroyed myself. I'm never going to give a damn about anyone again."

"Does that mean you're through with men?"

"I didn't say that. I meant no real involvement. From now on it's going to be head over heart."

"You've no control over that." Lilly laughed.

Tana stopped brushing her hair and looked at Lilly. Her eyes flashed. "Oh, don't I? You're wrong. You forget I'm a chip off the old block. Do you think I can ever forget what my old dad did to me?"

Lilly waited as Tana went on tremulously. "They were the rock of my life. I was a louse, I admit that . . . but I would never have turned away if they needed me."

She remained silent, as if needing affirmation from Lilly, who sat thinking and then offered her opinion. "Believe me, Tana, I know how you feel. You know, there are a lot of families that don't demand that sort of closeness. I have to tell you I don't really understand a lot of what happened. Why do you put yourself in the wrong? I seldom hear from my family and they don't carry on."

"Well, you have a sister. I was an only child and close to both my parents."

"What kind of closeness was it when your mother ran off?"

Tana's face flushed as she snapped back, "That's crud and you know it. You were partly responsible too. You were jealous of my mother. You knew that newspaper thing wasn't as bad as it seemed, and you let me carry on—you encouraged me. It was only natural for my mother to be terribly upset. I was really rotten to her."

Lilly remained silent and Tana went on. "I'll never get over my dad throwing me out—telling me I'm 'like the people who borned me.' If I'm so much like him, why wouldn't he give me a chance—hear my side?"

Hesitating, Lilly said, "Tana, that wasn't my impression . . . that's not what I thought he meant."

"Are you nuts? What in the world did you think he meant?"

"Really, Tana, I don't know. It was the way he said it that confused me. I guess I misunderstood."

"No matter how you interpret it, it adds up to the same thing. He doesn't like me. I killed my mother and he wants no part of me, his 'darlin daughter.'" Her face was dangerously puckered as if she wanted to cry, but instead, with an air of bravado, she said, "He's through with me—so from now on that's how it's going to be. I have no family—it's just me, myself alone!"

Reaching to turn off the bedside lamp, Lilly muttered, "So what's so different about that?"

Tana had found property she wanted to purchase, and the Denver attorney the bank had recommended agreed to meet them there with the final papers. The magnificent and rugged Colorado Rockies surrounding her were reminiscent of Montana and the awesome scenery acted as an opiate that calmed her nerves. It was an excellent buy: several acres with hunting lodge, sheds and barns. She was enthusiastically planning changes when Lilly called her attention to the car just appearing through a grove of shivering bright golden aspens. "There's the attorney, Mr. Hutchins."

He walked toward them. "How do, ladies. If I hadn't lived here half my life I'd think the altitude'd got me today."

He was huffing as he handed Lilly a folder. "If we can get these papers signed I'll be on my way. I've got another appointment."

Lilly rapidly checked through the forms. "It seems in order, Tana . . . Mr. Michalson has put his okay on them."

As Tana prepared to sign, Lilly whispered a reminder. "Don't forget . . . sign Polly Sue Corrigan."

Putting the papers back in his folder, Mr. Hutchins exclaimed, "Gee, I almost forgot! Your Mr. Michalson asked me to tell you to call him soon as you could. Something important."

"Something to do with this?" Lilly was alarmed.

"No, ma'am, absolutely not! You saw he marked the papers okay. He didn't tell me what, just asked me to deliver the message. Well, I'll be going. Good luck."

They explored the old house. Tana was delighted with it. "I just love it, Lilly. Look at that great fireplace. We can have some wonderful parties here."

Lilly was examining closets and cupboards. "When do you plan to start the renovations?"

"Not till late spring, Lilly. I'm an old country girl, and I know this place will be buried in snow soon—see that sky? I'm going to have the plans drawn up this winter, and by next summer the place will begin to look like new. You know, Lilly, I've been thinking. I'm going to name it after us: Tota, for Tony and Tana."

A hug told Lilly that Tana was in unusually good spirits.

Upon their return, the lobby of the hotel was filled with

officers from the nearby Army camps. As they walked through, all eyes turned their way. Tana was jubilant. "Let's celebrate . . . get dressed up tonight and give the boys a thrill. Want to?"

"Sure thing. It'll be a good chance to see if they recognize you."

Tana looked at her balefully. "What do you think, Lil? The truth, please—do I look like my old self?"

Lilly put both hands on Tana's shoulders, pretending to check her out. "Kid, I'd say you not only look like your old self but ten times better. Go on, get your shower. I'll call Ralph while you're at it."

As she listened to Michalson she winked at Tana. "She's fine. In fact, I just told her she's more beautiful than she's ever been. What? Hold the wire a minute, please." She cupped her hand over the speaker and asked, "He wants to know when we're coming back."

Tana did a little jig. "Tell him we'll be back in town by the end of next week."

The moment the two women entered the dining room a buzz ran through it. Tana and Lilly were pleased; there was no doubt the military men had recognized Tana Corgan. Shortly after they were seated, a bottle of wine was brought to their table. "Compliments of the officers sitting over there," the wine steward told them.

Tana raised her glass in the direction of the smiling men, feigned a sip and mouthed thank-you, to their delight. Dinner went well. Tana seemed full of her old spirit and enjoyed being the center of all eyes.

It had begun to snow during the night. Next morning a filigree of iced white branches showed ghostly through the veil of falling snow, and the air had turned bitingly cold. Tana announced, "It's time to pack up and leave."

It was during their homebound trip that Lilly brought Tana up to date on all the gossip she had missed during her period of grief. Tana was astonished to learn that Ron Douglas had lost a leg in his first war action and that his affluent homosexual mate had assured everyone he would oversee his recovery and help him regain his career. Although it wasn't openly acknowledged, most people knew about Ron's sexual proclivities. Tana was floored—it never occurred to her why it had been so easy to maintain a platonic relationship with him.

"How's this?" Tana smiled somewhat sadly. "Do I look grief-stricken but brave?"

They both laughed and Tana said seriously, "How long do you think I have to maintain the mourning-widow image?"

"That's up to you, hon. You can begin by intimating a change of attitude, saying it's your duty to be an example for everyone else who's lost a loved one in the war. You've decided to go on bravely and face life."

Grinning mischievously, Tana said, "Darling, you've just given me the material for my press interview. Thanks!"

"Don't mention it! And don't ask me how you look again!"

The crowd that surged toward them was large enough to tell Tana the publicity corps had done its job. She was relieved she hadn't been forgotten.

Ralph Michalson pushed his way through and took each of them by an arm. Once they were safely inside the press office he blocked the door for a moment and stood back to look at Tana. "You look sensational. Your vacation did you a world of good . . . I was sorry to hear about your mother, Tana."

Lilly replied instantly, "When did you hear about Mrs. Corrigan's passing, Mr. Michalson?"

"From your letter, Miss Fazon. Only Mr. Madrix knows besides myself. We didn't think it wise for Tana to endure the additional publicity such news would bring."

Tana looked at him soberly. "You're right; it belongs to my private life. It's time to face the future and put all this grief behind me. Life is for the living, right, Mr. M?"

He agreed with a nod of his head. "It won't help to carry it further. Now, are you ready to resume your public life? It sounds as though they're going to break the door down."

He stepped aside and the newspeople poured in to talk with Tana Corgan.

Later, driving toward Bel Air, Ralph took the opportunity to tell them about Tana's old house being rented. "So, you see, since we couldn't reach you, we took the liberty of supplementing your income. Your tenant, Mrs. Griffon, is paying you the hefty sum of three hundred and fifty dollars a month, plus caring for the house and grounds."

Tana hid her surprise at the name of the tenant and received the news with no further comment than "Thanks. I suppose it might as well be lived in as not."

Ralph Michalson was relieved to have that over and done with; he was never quite sure what tack Tana might go off on. In a jovial mood he continued, "You ladies are in for a bit of a surprise. When you meet Mrs. Griffon you won't believe your eyes. Everyone's talking about your resemblance to each other, Tana." He chuckled. "No cause for worry, though—she has no screen aspirations. But it's amazing how much you look alike."

Tana looked at him in amazement. She was annoyed by the conversation. "That's absurd! How can she look just like me?"

Ralph backed off. "Of course she's not your twin, Tana; I didn't mean to imply that. There are differences of course—she's a bit older, and your ways are different—but you bear each other a striking resemblance. You could be sisters. You'll be able to judge for yourself when you meet her."

Lilly interjected wryly, "I'm surprised Mr. Madrix didn't want to sign her to a contract."

Laughingly, Ralph said, "Even if she dreamed of it, she wouldn't dare. She's married to one of the Griffon boys. They're very high society—stockholders in Major Pictures too."

"La-di-da," Tana mimicked. "I'm sure, Ralph, when you see us together you'll find there's not as much likeness as you think."

Ralph turned to look at the disquieted girl. "I guess you're right, Tana. She takes it as a great compliment. You'll like her, I'm sure. We've all grown very fond of her. She's quite charming and accomplished. She's looking forward to meeting you."

With a derisive look Tana said curtly, "I couldn't care less! Thanks for the run-down."

Ralph saw how irked she was, but he had felt it important to prepare Tana for what had to be a shock. With what was at stake, it would be wiser to lay some groundwork.

As the car climbed the hill to Tana's Bel Air home, Ralph reconsidered the advisability of extending an invitation to the dinner party that Betty had deliberately planned. Then the car stopped and Maria appeared at the front door.

At the sight of her Lilly exclaimed, "Oh, thank you, Mr. Michalson. I was worried about notifying the help. I'm glad to be back! Gosh, Tana, isn't it wonderful to be home?"

Ralph winced, shocked at Lilly's insensitivity, but he quickly saw that the remark was not out of turn. Tana was all smiles as she replied, "It's great. You've no idea how I've looked forward to it."

Accompanying them to the door as the chauffeur carried their baggage into the house, Ralph said, "I hope you're going to be free this Sunday. Mrs. Michalson thought it would be pleasant to have a small welcome-home dinner for you, Tana. Of course you are included, Miss Fazon. Cocktails at five."

He saw Tana's hesitation and quickly added, "It's all very proper. Just a small dinner party that will help to break the ice. All right?"

Tana really didn't want to go, but an invitation from the Michalsons usually meant a command appearance. She accepted reluctantly. "If you're quite certain it's a small group, Ralph. I don't think anything too festive would be right just yet, do you?"

"No, of course not. We all understand. Come early so we can break at a decent time since it's a Sunday night. We'll look forward to seeing you."

The house seemed strange and unfamiliar, but Tana was relieved to be home; she'd had a long and strenuous journey. The impact of Tony's face staring at her from photographs was disturbing, but Lilly quickly gathered them together to be put away. As Lilly watched, Tana sifted through the mail stacked high on her desk. She opened a few envelopes and then stopped. Lilly said quietly, "Tana, we'll have to hire someone to help with these condolence notes."

"Sure, do what you think best. I don't want to see them." She walked over to the stack of photographs that Lilly had collected and picked up a large framed picture, studying it. "He was a handsome man, wasn't he?"

Lilly's voice rose in caution. "Tana . . ."

She smiled sadly. "Don't worry, Lil. I can handle it. Seeing all these pictures again reminded me. What a waste. You know something, Lil? We'd probably never have stayed together. We were both too egotistical and temperamental."

She put the picture down and said, "That's a closed chapter. Get rid of them . . . it's not healthy to have him staring at us wherever we go in the house. Lil, do you think I need a new gown for Sunday?"

Chapter XXV
TANA CORGAN VS.
EMMALINA GRIFFON

THE MINUTE BETTY Michalson heard that Tana Corgan was coming home she set the wheels in motion. She knew what this signified to Emmy—at long last she was going to come face to face with her baby sister.

The love and trust between Betty and Emmy had grown even deeper, and as soon as Betty told Emmy what she had in mind, great discussions ensued. Emmy was apprehensive. "Do you think we ought to meet like this, Betty?"

"What do you propose to do? Call her on the telephone and try to make an appointment? Take my word for it, she won't see you. Believe me, Em, your best chance of getting to her is by being introduced to her first. Pray hard she likes you. I'm not trying to dissuade you, but, believe me, she's very difficult to get close to—she's going to keep you at arm's length. More so if she suspects you might want something from her."

Betty saw the dismay on Emmy's face. "I never dreamt it would be anything like this. After all this time, I thought . . ."

"You imagined you'd fall into each other's arms with love and kisses. I hate to be the one to remind you, but I have to since Max isn't here . . . she probably has no idea she was adopted. Keep that in mind, for heaven's sake, and let that govern your actions."

So the dinner party was arranged. It was a well-known fact that everyone invited to the Michalsons' was expected to arrive punctually. They deplored the who-could-come-last game that was commonplace in Hollywood. Nonetheless, Tana and Lilly were the last to arrive.

The intake of breath was audible as Tana stood posed in the archway. Her entrance was stunning, and she knew she looked particularly beautiful in a simple clinging black dress accented only by pearls at her ears and neck. "Hello, everyone. I'm sorry we were detained."

Betty Michalson made an effort to greet them warmly. "Tana, dear, welcome under any circumstances. So delighted you could come, Miss Fazon. Come, let me introduce you."

Putting an arm around each of the women, she took them around. Ralph and Mr. Madrix were talking with someone seated in a chair. As they approached, Gene Madrix turned and put his hands out to greet Tana. "Well, well, our wanderer has returned. I must say even more breathtakingly beautiful, if that's possible. It's good to have you back, our little Tana."

"Thank you, Mr. Madrix." She smiled and tossed her head in her accustomed way. "It's really good to be back." Her smile froze as she looked past him into what seemed a mirror. The face looking up at hers was her twin. The two men watched, fascinated by the strange encounter. Emmalina rose. She was a fraction taller than Tana and wore her hair differently, but their similarity was striking. Lilly Fazon gasped.

Every eye in the room was on them. Emmy smiled and nervously extended her hand. "Since everyone seems so stunned at seeing us together, let me introduce myself. I'm Emmalina Griffon. I must say, my dear, no matter what anyone says, I don't do you justice. No one could . . . you are divinely beautiful. It's the rarest of compliments to have been compared to you."

The guests were all intimates of the Michalsons and had known of Tana's coming. They were naturally curious to see how Tana would react to meeting someone who looked so much like her. She didn't disappoint them.

Tana had turned to stone in what seemed indecipherable shock, staring at her counterpart, speechlessly. Emmy turned to Ralph. "Would a drink be in order?" She smiled at Tana, trying to break the silence, and said, "Now you can imagine how I've felt all the time you've been gone, with everyone telling me how much we resemble each other."

Ralph put an arm around Tana, breaking the spell. "Isn't this amazing, Tana? You two gorgeous creatures must get together and check your backgrounds. You must have some very beautiful relative in common."

Caught off guard, Tana visibly struggled to regain her poise, finally managing a smile. "You must excuse me, Mrs. Griffon. My life seems full of shocks these days. Seeing you made me think I'd looked into a mirror. It's an eerie feeling." She turned to face the others in the room. "Well, they say everyone has a twin, and here's mine. We *must* compare notes, Mrs. Griffon. Ralph may be right—possibly we have an ancestor in common."

"Yes, indeed we must," Emmy said sweetly. "I feel very fortunate. I repeat, if I look at all like you, I feel very blessed."

Tana was not immune to compliments and she appeared mollified. "Ralph, you're really naughty. You should have prepared me."

He protested. "My dear, I tried. But, you know, until I actually saw you both together I wasn't even certain you were such look-alikes."

Betty Michalson's voice cut in. "Come along, everyone. Dinner will be ruined if we put it off another moment."

Each woman was mesmerized by the other. Every time Tana looked up, Emmy's eyes were on her. Tana was uncomfortable. Thank goodness, she thought, we don't talk the same way and we carry ourselves differently.

At the conclusion of dinner, when they had retired to the terrace for coffee and afterdinner drinks, Emmy approached Tana. "Miss Corgan, I do want to thank you for permitting Mr. Michalson to rent me your former home. I don't know what I should have done; there was simply no other place to be found."

"It's all right, Mrs. Griffon. There was no way he could have reached me. Did he tell you I may be moving back? My present home is much too large for my needs."

Emmy was taken aback. "No, he didn't. Oh, I'll be sorry to have to give it up."

"Well, it won't be tomorrow. I've just gotten back and my plans aren't definite."

Nodding sympathetically, Emmy said, "Of course, I understand. Well, whenever . . . I'll have to make other plans. Wouldn't you like to see it? Would you come to tea?"

Tana's patience with the situation was frayed. "No! I'm quite familiar with the house. I'm going to be very busy for a while, but thanks just the same."

Emmy persisted. "There is something important I would like to discuss with you, Miss Corgan. Do you think you could spare me a moment in the next few weeks?"

Tana looked at her blankly. "You can check with Miss Fazon, my secretary. She keeps my schedule."

Emmy was distressed at the way things were going, and her mind was in ferment. For so long she had yearned and hoped for this wonderful moment of revelation. It had been so crucial to her—was it all to be for nothing? Her dreams lay in ruins. Her sister was rude and arrogant. She wanted to pursue her, shake her; she had no right to behave this way. The worst part of it all was that Tana wanted nothing to do with her. Torn between disappointment and humiliation, Emmy nursed her hurt. Her cheeks were flushed and she thought, How will I ever be able to tell her? What would this cutting, imperious creature do when she learned of their relationship? Confused and filled with misgivings, Emmy turned at a touch on her arm. Betty stood next to her. "We warned you the resemblance ended facially. Tana Corgan's a tough one. Got a change of heart about your newfound relative?"

Her dismay evident, Emmy said soberly, "Yes, I'm really concerned about her reaction when she finds out."

Piloting Emmy off to an inconspicuous corner, Betty advised, "Please don't be in such a rush. You have time; it might be wise to think it over. Maybe you'd be better off to forget the entire thing. You're so full of love and nostalgia, and she's like ice. Did Ralph tell you the story of her mother?"

"Yes, he did. It's very sad."

Betty whispered, "Ralph and Gene are convinced Mr. Corrigan threw her out."

They saw Gene Madrix walking toward them. "What are you two ladies doing huddled in a corner?"

Emmy was offhand. "Discussing how strange it is to find I have a counterpart. You know, it puzzles me that Larry made so little mention of it."

"Because it's easy to forget the resemblance when one gets to know you," Gene said, smiling.

She looked at him and asked, "Did Larry ever date her, do you know?"

He broke into laughter, and Betty said softly, "You'll have to ask him. However, I don't think your relationship with him has anything to do with Miss Corgan."

Gene said brusquely, "She's a spitfire. Difficult as all hell to handle. Sometimes I wonder if she's worth the effort."

"Oh, come on, Gene," Betty retorted. "She's proven her worth . . . a million dollars' worth."

Grinning, he said to Emmy, "As you can see by that marvelous new antique cabinet. Ralph's her agent."

"Touché, touché." Betty chuckled.

"What's the news from Larry, Em?" Gene asked. "By the way, Bill Griffon Junior is coming in. He's interested in getting into the producing line."

Emmy's face lit. "He's a fine man, Gene. I like Bill very much."

When he was out of hearing, Emmy whispered to Betty, "Do you know she wants the house back?"

"You're kidding!" Betty was appalled. "What for? She's got that magnificent new house in the hills."

"She said it's too big, but to be fair she said I didn't have to leave tomorrow."

"Isn't that generous? Wait till I tell Ralph about this turn of events. You can always stay with us, Em. You know I mean it."

Emmy reached over and kissed Betty's cheek. "Thank you, dear, but I've done my share of imposing. There has to be another solution. If only Larry's house wasn't so far out."

"We'll find you something nearby, Em. That Tana . . . the worst part of her is that she can't be persuaded to change her mind about anything."

"Who knows, Betty? It may all be for the good."

"Have you resolved anything with Jonathan since we last spoke?"

"No. His call was brief and he was going to be in New York for just a short time. Say, how about lunch with me tomorrow?"

"Good idea. I'll be over at oneish. You don't go in until late afternoon, do you?"

Later, as they were getting ready for bed, Ralph said, "Betty, Tana's trouble . . . there's no other way to describe her. Leave it to her to find it amusing to upset the apple cart . . . wanting the old house back is sheer spite. If I were Emmy I'd disavow her as my sister. It'll be an adversary relationship at best. Em will be opening a can of worms, and no good will come of it."

Betty seemed lost in thought. When she finally spoke she said dryly, "Dear, it's not our decision to make. We're going to have to watch from the sidelines and let the chips fall where they may. I don't think Emmy will be easily dissuaded."

The morning air still retained a nip from the overnight cool, and Ralph leaned back appreciatively studying the cloudless blue of the sky. He waited for Betty to pour his coffee. The serenity was broken by the jangle of the telephone, and shortly the maid appeared with the phone in hand. "It's for you, Mr. Michalson. Miss Fazon's on the line."

He grimaced. "Ah, it starts." He lifted the receiver and Betty heard the shrill tones emanating from it. "It's not Lilly, it's me—Tana. I hardly slept a wink last night. I'm very upset, Ralph. I want to see you right away."

Ralph's face turned grim; he hated her when she spoke in this peremptory fashion. "It will have to wait, Tana. I have a very busy day scheduled."

She shouted angrily, "It can't wait. What I've got to say won't hold. You make it up here as fast as you can."

"What sort of talk is this, Tana? If you have something to discuss with me you know where my office is. Call the office and set up an appointment."

"You've got to get over here." She spluttered. "Or—"

"Or what, Tana?"

"Or I see my attorney and charge you with misrepresentation!"

Ralph straightened in his chair, his face reflecting his anger. "Is that so? Well, young lady, if that's how you feel, you go right ahead. I suggest you do whatever you think is best! Good-bye, Tana."

Putting the phone back in its cradle, he said to Betty, "I won't have her ordering me around."

"I think it has to do with meeting Emmy here. Last night must have really thrown her. It's absurd, but it's obvious she took an instantaneous dislike to Emmy."

"Imagine the gall! Threatening to see her attorney, telling me I've misrepresented her."

Betty gasped. "Oh, she couldn't mean that."

"If you don't think so, then you don't know Tana Corgan. After all, I merely wet-nursed her from the beginning of her career—but what about the mother who adored and raised her?"

Betty looked stricken. "Oh, Ralph, why is she looking for trouble when she's already had so much?"

"I don't know, but she's surely ruined a beautiful morning. . . . What are your plans for the day?"

"I'm meeting Em for lunch. Do you think we'd better keep her posted?"

"Yes. It might be wise not to have her caught with her guard down."

Ralph could hear her voice through the door of his private office. When his secretary buzzed, he geared himself for what was to come.

His secretary had no sooner closed the door behind her than Tana exploded. "You've got a nerve treating me the way you do, Ralph Michalson. Don't think I'm going to let you get away with it."

Indignantly she swept into a chair. "I can't believe you'd do such a dishonorable thing. My attorney says I have grounds for suit."

He banged his hand on the desk. "Just hold it . . . now start from the beginning. You can't waltz in here and insult me without at least explaining what you're so upset about."

"You had no right to rent my house without my explicit permission. If that woman isn't out by the end of the week, I'll sue you and everyone in sight."

She saw the look of derision on his face, and it further infuriated her. But he interrupted her tirade. "Hold it, Tana." He picked up his phone and ordered that no calls be put through. He had made up his mind—he'd terminate their business relationship. "I've had it, young lady. There's not enough money in the world to induce me to put up with you one minute more. I think you *had* better take this up with your attorney. You might also tell him you are not the titled owner of the house which has you so up in arms. The mortgage is not fully paid, and under the terms of the sale the studio still retains options."

She glared at him. "That's not so, and you know it."

Ralph rose and walked toward the office door. "I will not put up with any more of your ugly inferences. I have never misrepresented you and I have no intention of doing so now. You and I are through! When you leave my office, see Mr. Edison, our office manager. Your audited statements and accounts are all in order in our files. Your contracts and other legal papers will be delivered to your attorney tomorrow, unless you wish them sent elsewhere. Let me say that, though this has been a long and interesting business relationship, it is one which I am not sorry to terminate. Good-bye, Tana, and good luck!"

She sat, momentarily stupefied by his dismissal. Ralph opened the office door and called his secretary. "Miss Mavis, we are terminating Miss Corgan's account. Will you notify Mr. Edison to get all her files in order. She is leaving now."

He held the door open. Tana was about to say something, but he turned his back on her. With as much dignity as she could muster, she left his office, whereupon he closed the door.

He picked up the telephone and immediately dialed Emmy's number. When she answered he wasted no time. "All hell's broken loose. She wants you out of the house and, since I've terminated my business with her, she's apt to really come down on you. Start getting your things together. You and Pearlie Mae prepare to stay with us until we find something else."

"Oh, Ralph, I'm so sorry to have caused you all this trouble. We'll get going right away."

"Listen, Emmy, she really can't put you out on the street, but she's such an ornery witch there's no telling what she's apt to pull. Tell Betty what I've told you; she knows how it all got started this morning. Another thing, Em: don't ever worry about my giving up Corgan's business; you gave me the excuse I've been wanting for a long time."

The next call Ralph made was to Gene Madrix, who was astonished at the story. "What the hell, Ralph, she can't throw Em out. You tell her to stay put."

"No, Gene, I won't do that. Em doesn't need anyone's charity. There's a lot more underlying this than I've been at liberty to tell you, but I think Em will agree to it now. We'll meet for lunch and I'll spill it."

"Wait'll I get my hands on that little snake!"

Ralph laughed. "Be my guest. It'll be a relief not to have to defend her."

"What? You mean to tell me you terminated her?"

"Yes, my friend. Candidly, it was one of the few pleasures I've had in my association with her."

There was no doubt that Madrix was upset. "Ralph, how could you have done that to us?"

"It won't be any problem at all. She'll have a new agent by tonight. Everyone in town will be fighting to grab her."

"Sure, but you're the only one can handle her. They'll fill that devil's head with dreams of millions, and I've no intention of going along with that."

Ralph said quietly, "Gene, you know I'm not a betting man, but I'll give you odds you've already had the best of Corgan. I have it on good authority the girl's a drunk."

"I've heard the stories. Do you think we've got two years left? That's the contract run."

"Look, Gene, you know how to deal with her. What happened here today may make her watch her step. She'll probably be businesslike for a while. I'll see you for lunch tomorrow; we'll discuss it then, all right?"

Aghast at what Emmy reported, Betty immediately began to caution her. "Emmy, you've waited this long; wait a little longer. This Tana thinks in a way you wouldn't comprehend. She can play underhanded and dirty. She doesn't understand what you're like as a person, and for some reason she took an instant dislike to you. It's emanating from her in waves of anger. She's awful! If she ever finds out about you and Larry she'll do everything to make your name mud. She's like that!"

"Betty, why? She doesn't even know me. Are you telling me that all this came about as a result of our meeting last night?"

"Do you have a better reason, Emmy? The fact that you look alike could be burning her up. Unfortunately no one can really figure out what makes her tick."

Emmy sat thinking over what Betty had said. "Then," disappointment edging her voice, she agreed. "I'll do what you say, Betty. Under the circumstances there's certainly no way I'm going to tell her she's my sister—not now."

"Right, let her feelings subside, Em. At the moment she's in a rocky emotional period. Give the devil her due, she's been through a bad time. I honestly don't thinks she's in any condition at present to handle what you'd have to tell her. Possibly later on. Given time, who knows? You may get a totally different reaction."

Once again Emmy and Pearlie Mae began to pack. Emmy called Betty Michalson. "Hon, we're leaving for Oklahoma on Monday. We're going back there for a while. Larry's not due back before the first of the year, and this will give me an opportunity to clear matters up with Jonathan. He's meeting me there. Also, I want to spend some time with Uncle Max. He's been ailing and I'm worried about him."

Emmy took a leave of absence from work at the Canteen and wound up her affairs. The last Sunday was spent with the Michalsons. Emmy confessed that she feared Jonathan's reaction to her request for a divorce and didn't expect help from Max.

Betty mistook what Emmy was saying. "If Jonathan won't agree to the divorce, are you saying you'll go on this way?"

"No, of course not. I'm concerned about Larry, however—about how he will feel if I give the grounds for the action. I may have to agree to being the adulteress."

Ralph, who had been listening quietly, interrupted. "That's not necessary at all. Six weeks' residence in Reno and you'll have it neatly wrapped and tied. You could get it in Mexico, but it won't have the same validity."

Vastly relieved by Ralph's advice, Emmy laughed. "I wouldn't dare get a Mexican divorce. Jon's mother would certainly spread the news that Larry and I are living in sin."

"She wouldn't at all," Betty disagreed. "She wouldn't want the Griffon name besmirched. I'm surprised at you for even thinking that. In fact, I'm sure his mother will have feelings of guilt about this entire thing."

Emmy smiled ruefully. "Maybe, but I doubt it. In any case, it no longer matters. But listen, you two darlings, it seems to me that since we've met I've done nothing but burden you with my problems. I want you both to know I have no words to express my love and appreciation for all you've done for me."

Betty sighed. "Emmy, in the short time we've known you, you've become very dear to us. I just hope this is the beginning of a long and lasting friendship."

"Well, then, I'll tell you one more thing, but this seems to be on the good side. I told you about the young woman I saw at the Hollywood Canteen and thinking she was my other sister." She paused and her face lit with happiness. "The note I received yesterday from Mr. Saperson says it's entirely possible. He's checking into it now."

Betty and Ralph were intrigued by Emmalina Griffon. Though possessing all the social graces, the soft-spoken young woman had seemed so helpless when they first met her. They had discovered she was completely honest and sincere and had come to admire her lack of artifice and her ability to stand by her convictions, but Betty felt she was apt to put her head in the lion's mouth a bit too often. She sighed and said, "I'm honestly curious, Em: what will finding another sister do for you? After all, with the complications you've run into with Tana, don't you feel the least bit hesitant?"

"No. If she turns out to be another Tana, I'll just have to suffer it. Let me explain it as best as I can. Imagine if that was really my sister at the Canteen. We saw each other and didn't even know we were sisters. I can't live this way—it plagues me. I've got to put all the pieces together, for better or worse. At least I'll have found out once and for all."

The Michalsons sat in silence until Ralph broke it. "Emmy, has it ever occurred to you that your sisters might not like your busting into their lives? You're opening a Pandora's box. Will life be easier for you if you persist in finding them knowing they may want no part of you."

Emmy didn't hesitate for a moment. "Absolutely! They can do whatever they please once I find them. You might as well know that Mr. Saperson thinks he has a lead on my parents too. As for them, I have every intention of digging them out and hearing from their mouths just what made them cast our three fates to the wind."

They looked at her in astonishment and she said, "I hope I don't cause anyone unnecessary hurt, but in either case it will be small recompense for all that I've been through on their account."

Betty chuckled. "Bravo! One would never suspect such strength just by looking at you, Emmalina."

Smiling, Emmy said softly, "I know I may be playing with fire and it may consume me, but having come this far, I'm not quitting. I want you both to know something . . . what I'm doing is in its way a tribute to my adopted mother. Elizabeth Fields was a marvelous woman, the most remarkable person in my life. She would have encouraged me; she never wanted me to quit on anything. I'm not afraid to tell the world she was responsible for my existence, she breathed life back into me. Anything that is good and decent about me she is responsible for. More than ever I know that now."

Chapter XXVI

❦❧

DECISIONS AND
DEPARTURES

TECHNOLOGICAL ADVANCES BEING what they were, Emmy arranged to fly back to Oklahoma with Pearlie Mae. For the old woman the magic of plane flight was incredible; and she sat in fearful silence, clenching Emmy's hand most of the way. Fortunately the apartment had been vacated by the time of their return, and Pearlie Mae beamed with pleasure at once again being happily installed in what to her was home. She took the news hard when she learned of Emmy's intention to dissolve her marriage. She adored Jonathan, and for the first time in their lives together, she offered Emmy no word of encouragement. "All these changes, chile, ain't no good fur you. 'Taint fair to dat boy." There was nothing Emmy could say to console her.

More difficulties ensued as soon as Emmy saw Max. He was delighted at the knowledge that she would now be close by, but Emmy was shaken at the change in him. It seemed that in the time she had been away, Max had become a very old man. He looked so wan and fragile. Pearlie Mae tried to take it in stride, scolding him. "Jedge, you jist wait and see. Now Pearlie Mae here to tend you, yo gonna be strong agin no time."

He tried to please them and for a while made efforts to eat what they brought to him, but Emmy could see he was failing. She was devastated at the thought that he would soon be gone. She couldn't imagine life without him; he had for so long been her rod and staff. She had no delusions about what he'd been to her. He'd been the only real father she'd ever known; he'd stood by her when she'd needed him; this stalwart, gallant old man had given her immeasurable love and understanding. . . . She couldn't have hoped for more if he'd truly been her own. He meant more to her than any words could impart. She spent part of each day with him and took the opportunity of telling him forthrightly about her feelings for Larry Bayless. One day, when she had once again discussed him, she looked up to see tears in Max's eyes. His voice was so faint when he spoke she had to lean close to hear him. "Emmy, darling, my Elizabeth's girl, if this young man is all you think, and means as much to you as you say he does, then what can an old man say? You have my blessings. Remember, Em, no matter how you love each other now, it won't stay that way. Life changes us. Be sure you have the strength to weather it. Remember, you thought you loved Jonathan."

Holding his frail, parchment hand in hers and stroking it, Emmy said softly, "No, Uncle Max. I know for a certainty I was never in love with Jonathan. I liked him very much; I still do. He's a fine and wonderful person, but my feelings were not love. Uncle Max, it was never right. I know that for sure. Jonathan deserves more than I can give him. Uncle Max, believe me, with Larry the world is another place. I will never know defeat with him because we give to each other, we need each other. We mesh like two gears. If I had never met Larry I might never have known the truth. I might have remained with Jonathan and cheated him."

He sighed, and seemed to be asleep. She was about to rise when he said, "I know what you're talking about. Liz and I had it together. Our time was short because she was so stubborn, but I'm happy for you, girl. If I'm not around to see the two of you together, give him my blessings. Tell him he's a helluva lucky guy."

When Jonathan arrived and had checked into the club, he telephoned Emmy. She asked him to come for dinner and he did. He looked well, and they greeted each other with pleasant restraint.

His demeanor toward her could best be described as formally friendly. She was inwardly grateful that he seemed so distant; it would be easier telling him of her decision. After their separation and her early hysterical protestations of love on the telephone and her first few letters, it must have become apparent to him she'd had a change of heart.

Pearlie Mae hovered over them during dinner, and the talk was light and inconsequential. When they finally settled by themselves in the living room, he seemed more relaxed. He appraised her and smiled. "You look wonderfully well, Em. In fact, I suspect you've grown more beautiful."

She poured his favorite liqueur, smiling archly. "Every woman enjoys hearing that; thank you, Jon. You also look very well. The touch of gray in your hair makes you so distinguished. It'll be eminently suitable for a judgeship."

"Well, that's a far piece. Speaking of that, I was shocked when I saw Uncle Max this afternoon."

She nodded soberly. "I'm afraid we have to face the fact he's failing rapidly. The doctor says there's nothing they can do. He seems to have lost the will to live."

He looked at her sympathetically, knowing what Max Esquith meant to her. "Em, Uncle Max is touching ninety."

"I know, Jon, but we're never willing to let go of those we love."

Silence hung, and then Jonathan leaned forward. "Em, this may be a bad time, but there's something I have to tell you."

She leaned back. She had a feeling of jubilation: he was going to ask for his freedom, she knew it.

He faltered only once at the start. "I don't know how to tell you this, but I honestly believe the sword is better than the kiss. I have the feeling, Em—I got it from your letters too—you've changed. I don't think our marriage can survive."

It was out in the open. She sighed with visible relief, and he grinned sheepishly before saying, "I gather you're of the same opinion."

She looked at him, smiling understandingly. "Jonathan, let's not be unhappy. The fine thing about this is that we're good friends. You're absolutely right about our marriage, but it makes me happy to know we can discuss it like two civilized beings."

He looked at her, obviously baffled by her reaction. She teased him. "Is it just that you don't want me, or have you found some other wonderful girl you're head over heels in love with?"

She was tickled to see the look of incredible wonder on his face. He couldn't figure out why she was taking it so well.

"Emmy, you're a brick. I'll take the responsibility. I'll settle half of everything I have on you so you won't have to worry."

"Thank you, Jonathan, that won't be necessary." She laughed merrily. "You know I could never use up what I have in ten lifetimes. You haven't answered my question. Who is the lucky young woman?"

This was such a different Emmy from the one he had known that he couldn't figure her out. It was an extraordinary situation. She was accepting the breakup of their life together as if she too wished it. She was so changed, so forward and aggressive. He squirmed under her barrage of questions, astonished at how unabashed she was about broaching what he considered intimate matters. She would not let him off the hook. Awkwardly he began to relate the story. "Believe me, I never intended—it happened by pure chance. It was when I first went back East. She was a nurse in the Ambulance Corps. I never suspected I would fall the way I did. Em, I respect what we had. In my heart I'll always love you for the beautiful things you are."

She looked at him fondly. "Jonathan, my dearest Jonathan, please don't apologize. We were two babes in the wood, and what we had for each other was good but not enough. I know that too. I'm happy, deeply happy, and touched that you have found someone to fulfill you and your life."

"Em . . . what about you? What will you do? What are your plans?"

She smiled enigmatically. "I've become a very capable lady, Jonathan. I really did a man-sized job at the Canteen. I've found that I can stand on my own two feet. . . . And there's something else. I think, if I play my cards right, I too may have found someone to fill my life."

As soon as it was feasibly possible for Emmy to leave Uncle Max, she would take up residence in Reno.

The barriers down, Jonathan told her that he planned to resume his law career and that as soon as the divorce was final he would remarry and bring his new wife to Oklahoma. Hesitantly he asked, "Are you planning to live here, Em?"

Once again she made him happy. "I doubt it, Jon, I think I'll resettle in southern California. I hope we'll get to see each other from time to time. I'd be interested in meeting your new wife."

Emmy made a point of telling Pearlie Mae the news after Jonathan had departed. It amused her that Jonathan had not wanted to know anything about the man in her life. She could hardly wait to tell Uncle Max the next day. She cabled Larry, "All's well, legally and lovewise. Come back, make it legitimate."

Early the following morning she telephoned Betty to tell her what had happened and to inform her and Ralph about Max. Ralph cut in, and in response to his questions she said, "If you want to see Uncle Max again, Ralph, you'd better come very soon."

She was surprised to hear him say he'd fly out the next morning. "Have you time to pick me up, Em?"

She was delighted to see both Ralph and Betty making their way from the plane. As they hugged and kissed, she held Betty's arm. "You must have read my mind. You'll never know what your coming means to me."

Emmy drove them directly to Max's house. "You're going to be shocked at the change in his appearance, but his mind is as sharp as a bell."

As they were ushered into the bedroom, Ralph thought, Max looks like an ancient Chinese seer—parchment skin, almost transparent. Max was delighted to see them, but they could see it was an effort for him to sustain any conversation. They left shortly, promising to return.

Max slipped away in his sleep that same night.

Emmy was fortified by having the Michalsons at her side. Jonathan took care of all the arrangements that Max had ordered, and he and Emmy represented the judge's family at the large funeral. It was as if all the city turned out to pay their last respects to a beloved citizen and friend.

Later that evening Jonathan presented himself at Emmy's apartment to be properly introduced to the Michalsons. After the first few amenities, they were surprised when he wasted no time in getting down to what he apparently felt was the business at hand. With no qualms about discussing Emmy's personal affairs in front of the Michalsons, he revealed that she was the judge's major heir.

Betty Michalson thought him crass when, as Emmy crumpled into tears, her feelings did not seem to deter him at all. He merely said, "I realize you're upset, Em, but you've known for a long time it was coming."

She looked at him reproachfully through tear-misted eyes. "Yes, of course, Jonathan, but nonetheless I'll miss him. He was the only father I've known."

"Then you shouldn't be surprised that you're his heir—you were also all he had. Would you believe that, with all he left to charity, you'll still come into millions?"

Ralph could sense that Betty was having difficulty restraining herself. He made a motion to rise so they could leave the room, but Emmy stopped them. "No. If you don't mind, please stay. There's nothing about this you can't hear, since you've already been made party to it."

Jonathan missed the innuendo; he seemed oblivious about talking out of turn. Emmy looked at him coldly. "Since you're in such a rush to get this taken care of, Jon, go on."

"The way I see it, Em, this will probably make you one of the wealthiest women in the world. I hope you realize this much money entails grave responsibilities."

She restrained an impulse to slap him. "I'm well aware of what you are trying to tell me, Jonathan." Ignoring him, she turned to the Michalsons. "Maybe you can suggest how I can use some of this money to mark Uncle Max's memory. You know—something that would carry on his wonderful spirit and fairness?"

There was silence and Emmy added, "It should be something that conveys the essence of the man . . . one who gave so much of himself to others."

Ralph perked up. "Isn't there a way a foundation could be set up for needy students who wish to study law? I have a hunch Max would have liked that idea. Do you know, Emmy, I can't count how many practicing lawyers there are today that Max financed through law school. There's a judge or two who would consider it an honor to administer such a foundation."

Emmy was enthusiastic. "That's perfect, Ralph. That's what I want! Jonathan, I'd like you and the others in the firm to draw up the plans so that I can make the endowment. It's an excellent idea. It must be called the Max Esquith Endowment Fund. If you'll put your heads together, you'll know best what qualifications and other things are necessary. Yes, that's what I want."

If Jonathan was surprised at Emmy's decisiveness, he gave no hint. She smiled at him icily. "Jon, I'm sure you won't be offended if I say we're all bone-weary."

He rose instantly. "Of course. I'm sorry. It's been a trying day." He left shortly.

As Emmy escorted him to the door, Betty said softly to

Ralph, "Can you see why a man like Larry swept Em off her feet?"

The Michalsons remained with Emmy for another day and then left for home. There was no reason for Emmy to delay any longer. But now she had another decision to face. Emmy knew that even though Pearlie Mae was in good health, it wouldn't be fair at her age to transplant her again. Oklahoma was home to her and it was where she belonged, to live her days out in care and comfort. Without a hint to the old woman, Emmy, assisted by a realtor, located a suitable house and arranged to have it furnished with everything she imagined Pearlie Mae could want or need. Once that had been accomplished, she sat her down for what proved to be a long and tearful discussion. Pearlie Mae was insistent that her place was at Emmy's side. When she finally realized that Emmy was not going to give in, she extracted a promise. Once Emmy was permanently located, she was to permit Pearlie Mae to rejoin her.

Emmy was consumed by guilt; the joy of her plans dissipated, she was miserable. She felt as if she were deserting her best and oldest friend, leaving her to a life of loneliness and desolation.

When the appointed day came for the move, Emmy was dismayed as she drove Pearlie Mae to what was to be her new home. She had been the culprit and she was besieged by worry. Pearlie Mae had no one, no immediate family at all. Oh, there had been distant cousins brought in to assist on special occasions, but Emmy knew that she was in effect Pearlie Mae's only next of kin. The poor darling had lived her life vicariously through her. The only time they'd been apart had been on Pearlie Mae's days off and when she'd gone to church. As far as Emmy knew, that had been the extent of her outside life.

It cheered Emmy to see that Pearlie Mae was pleased by the house. As the day wore on she became amazed at how filled the house was with people come to welcome Pearlie Mae.

She stood off in a corner observing as one after another they came, people drawn to the remarkable old woman by the magnetic quality of her love and caring. Emmy smiled to herself as she realized that some of the ladies present were still garbed in hand-me-downs given to Pearlie Mae by Elizabeth. Vaguely she recalled clothes in a giveaway box in a corner of her room. This woman whose well of giving was bottomless and in whose arms she had found sanctuary through so many crises had also been a relay in another world that Emmy had never suspected. A load was lifted: Pearlie Mae need not be worried about any longer, she had a whole and distinct life apart from anything Emmy had ever imagined.

Emmy knew she had been lucky to have been loved so selflessly. She knew Pearlie Mae would continue to love her so regardless of what life brought them. Impulsively she reached out to hug the old woman. The room was silent for a moment at the display of emotion, but the visitors smilingly turned away so as not to embarrass them.

Soon Emmy prepared to make her departure, and Pearlie Mae made one more attempt. "Chile, no matter what yo sees here, yo is my family."

The dam broke and tears poured down their cheeks. Pearlie Mae seemed inconsolable. "Chile, I won be a nuisance . . . yo is my baby."

Emmy was gently firm. "Darling, where I'm going now, there is no place for you. As soon as I'm settled, I promise I'll bring you if you still want to come. You know how much I always need you. The telephone will be installed tomorrow, and we'll speak often. You'll be so busy you won't miss me. Besides, you're entitled to some time all for yourself." Emmy finally broke away, sad and bereft.

The friends that she and Jonathan had no longer called. Busy in the routine of their lives, they had shut her out since she had informed them of her imminent departure and her separation from Jonathan.

One afternoon, arriving at the law offices for some signatory purposes, she bumped into the husband of a friend with whom she had formerly been close. At first the man seemed embarrassed and then overly cordial as he made a hasty retreat, but not before clumsily calling out, "Don't forget, Jon . . . dinner on Friday. Jan's expecting you."

As they walked into his office Jonathan asked, "Did you girls have a falling out, Em?"

She looked at him artlessly. "Not that I know of, Jonathan. Did she say that we did?"

Startled, he replied, "No, not a word, but I wondered. I never run into you with any of the old crowd."

She smiled. "These days, Jon, it seems I'm on the outside

looking in . . . but no matter. I guess they know I'm pulling up stakes, so they've cut the cords. Remember me to them."

When he didn't reply she said, "Eligible men are never a fifth wheel on the wagon, Jon. It's always easier to fit in a bachelor than an unattached woman."

He looked at her in surprise. "I'm sorry, Emmy, I had no idea they were cutting you."

She was annoyed at his passivity. "Believe me, Jon, I no longer care. Once they had the information they wanted from me, the curtain descended. You've always gotten along well with them, and besides, your future lies with them. Let's get to business."

The process of ripping up her roots and tying all the ends together wore sorely on her nerves. She wavered over each decision about what to take or leave. Her heart was heavy at leaving all that had once been near and dear to her. Finally, in lonely desperation, she telephoned Betty. "Am I losing my mind? My feelings are so ambivalent. How can I love Larry the way I do, and yet be so upset about cutting off my life here? I'm miserable. I had no idea this would be so painful."

"Stop tearing yourself to pieces. You're not losing your mind and you're not crazy," Betty said. "You're a sensitive, feeling person. It isn't easy to turn your back on everything that made up your life. It's a way of growing. Think of what you mean to Larry. Get through and out of there. You're having a healthy attack of emotional roughage, that's all."

At last everything was sorted and packed. Sleepless the night before her departure, she wrote Larry a long letter, relating her feelings about the move. She concluded by telling him, "I don't take to changes easily, so you'll know and be forewarned by what it means when I say . . . with my whole being, I love you!"

Jonathan drove her to the station, and she sensed his awkwardness. It was her strength that helped them over the last difficult moments. When the all-aboard call came, he held her close and quickly kissed her good-bye. "Thanks for everything, Emmy. I wish you love and joy. If you need me for anything, don't hesitate to call. Keep in touch."

"I will. . . . Keep an eye on Pearlie Mae. Be happy!" She watched him wave until he was out of sight. Her eyes misted, blurred . . . another portion of her life disappearing into a memory. She looked around and sank into her seat. She was free—unencumbered. Those who had truly loved her, aside from Pearlie Mae, were gone, but their wisdom and counsel would always be part of her. But the others . . . all of them were left behind: Jonathan—the things he'd expected of her, the blemishes he and his family saw in her that she could never have lived down—the meaningless friends . . . all were being swept away with each passing mile.

Suddenly she felt happy and carefree. She said aloud, "Here's to us, Larry." Her spirits soared with anticipation at the new life awaiting her.

She arrived in Reno and was driven to the guest ranch by the chauffeur awaiting her. The attorney representing her had chosen a comfortable dude ranch for the six-week stay. Little was required except her residence, and she filled her time by reading, writing to Larry and exploring the countryside. The nip in the air, the lofty snow-topped mountains rising in the background, the towering redwood trees witness to centuries of men's exploits, the turbulent streams that broke the wide fields still spotted with late wild flowers were all companion to her reveries.

Outside of a casual greeting, she kept to herself. As the days passed and guests came and went, she became impatient awaiting her own time for the hearing. It was hard to break the bonds of her recent past and its social strictures. The realization of her adulterous relationship with Larry had never assumed the proportions it did now, and she worried whether it had diminished her in his eyes. She was tormented by the knowledge that she had indeed been a loose woman. A divorce was synonymous with easy morals. She endured torturous hours mentally punishing herself. She couldn't bring herself to write Larry of her ordeal. He was too far away, too burdened with his own immediate problems, for her to add to them by what he might construe as a lessening of her strength and feeling for him.

Then she awoke one morning with the realization that she had only ten more days to wait. To add to her joy, a letter arrived from Mr. Saperson with extraordinary news. He had finally located the correct Wilkerson family and been able to ascertain Amy Beth's married name and address. Most astounding was that he thought he'd located her natural mother. It had been difficult, since she had been widowed and remarried several times. He'd written, "I believe it advisable to leave the final identification up to you. The woman's not too well and grows easily confused. You will be more apt to recognize the facts she can recall. I have little doubt, however, but that she is your Mary Ann Beauford."

He had enclosed their addresses and suggested she make immediate contact. Also, he asked her to inform him as soon as possible so that he would know if his work for her was at an end.

Overwhelmed, she sat lost in reverie. Dusk fell and she turned on the lamps. Looking out her window, she saw snowflakes gently drifting through the air. It was already November and Larry was due home at the start of the new year. She would have just enough time to establish contact with her family before his return. Her excitement mounted and she telephoned Betty, who agreed to come to Reno for a few days. The date and hour were arranged, and at the appointed time Emmy drove into the city to pick her up.

Betty listened as Emmy vented all the thoughts she'd stored up for so many weeks. When she had spent herself, both agreed enough time had passed for Tana's anger to have subsided. Emmy would invite her sisters to meet her at the St. Francis Hotel in San Francisco. The letter to Tana would say, "You come or face the chance of public exposure about a personal matter concerning the possibility of your having been adopted."

When they had composed the letter to their satisfaction and were relaxing, Betty remembered her own news. She had found out that a beautiful house on the same street they lived was going up for sale. In her opinion it was an excellent buy, and she felt it would be a home of which Larry would approve. Instantly excited, knowing what superlative taste Betty had, Emmy requested that Ralph act as her agent in the purchase, insistent that he take his agent's fee. Betty was sure Ralph wouldn't hear of it, but Emmy explained that she had intended asking him to act on her behalf in other matters as well, and that was the only way she would permit the matter to be handled. Reluctantly Betty agreed to convince Ralph.

Emmy sighed contentedly. "I don't think my heart can stand any more excitement. Finding my family and a house to boot—I can hardly wait to write Larry and tell him what's happening."

The day before the hearing Emmy received a note from Amy Beth. She ripped open the envelope to read, "I can't tell you how happy I am to know you're fine. My husband, Pete, thinks it is the most wonderful thing that's happened since our marriage. He's very excited at the thought of meeting you. You'll love him—everyone does. Did you ever receive the letter I sent to you in Oklahoma? About your thinking you have found our mother, I have to tell you honestly, she's of no concern to me. It's hard to believe that Tana Corgan is our baby sister, Polly Sue. Peter said I should call her, but I won't because you may not want me to do anything like that until we meet. Also, I don't think she would like it."

The following day a terse, badly scrawled reply came from Tana. It was angry and minced no words. "I will come to San Francisco because I think you would like to cause me trouble. I don't believe a word of what you say. I was not adopted and I am sure you have no proof, and I have already advised my lawyer about this crazy story. He says you better be able to back up your claim or you'll be in trouble. He thinks you have me mixed up with someone else. I will meet you at the hotel on the day you mention."

The divorce hearing went smoothly and the decree was granted. Emmy clutched the papers to her and rushed back to the ranch to pack and telephone Betty, saying she would call again from San Francisco after the reunion.

That done, she telephoned Jonathan to advise him he was a free man. He seemed startled at the glee in her voice but thanked her for letting him know. They talked about Pearlie Mae, their one common neutral ground, and Jonathan assured her the old woman was happily surrounded by assorted kinfolk. He implied it was probably due to her being a rich lady's ward and wondered if Emmy realized how many children she was planning to send to school. At this Emmy reiterated what she'd already told him about her willingness to do anything that made Pearlie Mae happy . . . all he had to do was send her an accounting. With that out of the way, he inquired where she was heading and Emmy decided she should tell him. He was genuinely surprised at her news and happy. She couldn't resist teasing him about what he thought his mother's reaction would be at hearing that Tana Corgan was her sister and, she added significantly, the possibility of having found her mother. He ignored her tone and asked her to let him know how it all turned out.

They said their good-byes, and that was that. Cheerfully she packed for her trip to San Francisco. She was glad to be leaving on a triumphant note. She had regained her freedom, and she was on the verge of a reunion with her family—all the loose ends were coming together. She was bursting with happiness and expectation.

Chapter XXVII

MYTH BECOMES REALITY FOR AMY BETH

THE MOMENT SHE saw the name on the envelope Amy became distracted . . . finally the mythical past was becoming a tactile present. Almost reluctantly she opened the letter to read Emmy's warm and loving sentences. She was neither elated nor surprised at its news. She'd felt their making contact was only a matter of time. In truth, she was ambivalent in her feeling about her lost family; they were vague and shadowy figments she hardly remembered. Although more secure now, she was still afraid of the complications that might ensue . . . apprehensive about what it might do to the peace and tranquility of her present life. She did not want or need any other ties than her husband. She was just coming into her own, acquiring the strength to think and act independently. These newly revealed relationships might require obligations and responsibilities for which she was not ready. In short, she wanted no intrusions on her recent wedded state and the joys which she and Peter shared in such wonderfully full measure.

It took her husband's interest and excitement to make her see that she was on the brink of a remarkable adventure that could add a whole new dimension to their lives. His support enabled her to shed her anxieties, and with that came a sense of anticipation and exhilaration about the meeting. As the reality bore in on her she was moved by long-buried feelings, kindled anew by curiosity about her real family.

Amy tried to describe to Peter how she felt. "Whenever I

think about it I have butterflies in my stomach. It's almost the way I felt before our wedding when I was afraid something would stop it."

He grinned. It had become a standing joke between them after she'd confessed her fears that he'd change his mind about marrying her. He'd joshed, "Of course, with all the girls after me, it was only natural you'd feel that way. You better watch out. I still might trade you in for a new Ford."

They were seated at the kitchen table finishing their supper and he saw she was fidgety. She said, "It's silly, I can't settle down. Today I had to retype a letter twice before I got it right. Miss Korel—she's Mr. Madrix's secretary—said I could have the time off. They're bringing someone in from the typing pool to cover for me."

Peter watched her. "Puss, it's going to be fine. You know what Emmy looks like—you saw her. I can't get over how the two of you looked at each other."

"It's scary, Pete, isn't it, to have a sister standing next to you and not know it's her?"

"It sure is, but I think the craziest thing about all of this is that Tana Corgan turns out to be your baby sister. It's incredible! Has she been in recently?"

"No, as a matter of fact she hasn't. I'm going to feel peculiar when she does come in. What should I do?"

"Just say, 'Hi, sis.'"

"Oh, I wouldn't dare. She barely looks at me when she walks through. She's really not very pleasant with the peasants, Pete. All the girls dislike her."

"Don't worry about it, Amy. It won't be long before you'll be meeting and straightening matters out. You know, darling, behaving a certain way only because it's always been done can be changed."

Amy rose to carry the dishes to the sink. Her face wore a soft glow; marriage had dissipated the furrowed brow, and her body had taken on softer curves. "Peter, I can't get over Mother. It's so amazing that she broke down and told that man where I could be reached. When I asked her about it she almost snapped my head off." She mimicked Deborah's voice: "'You be a married woman, Amy Beth, and if you want to go traffickin in that direction, 'tain't my business to stop you. If 'twere me, now, I'd say I want no part of it. No tellin what you'll be gettin into.'"

She paused and, shaking her head in wonderment, said, "I'm surprised she even spoke with him."

Peter looked up. "No doubt he was outstandingly hand-some and charming, like me. You know how Deborah falls for that type of man."

Amy couldn't resist him. She grinned and then turned sober. "Pete, I know she was upset. In her way she cares about me. It's got to be the first time in our lives that she'. allowed anything about my real family to come into the open. You can't imagine what they did to keep Emmy from having any contact with me."

Peter stopped chewing. "Look, puss, she's no fool. She probably figured the investigator would find you in any case, so she might as well get the credit."

Amy laughed. "Pete, we're awful about her."

"No, we're not. We're just calling it the way it is."

Suddenly she lowered her eyes, embarrassed, ashamed to meet his eyes. "I called her back today. It's been bothering me. I know somehow in her crazy way she's worried about my feelings for her. When I told her again how I appreciated her telling the man about me and said, 'It has nothing to do with the way I feel about you, Momma; it's just after all this time I'm curious about Emmalina and Polly Sue being Tana Corgan . . . '"

Peter choked. "My Gawd, I'll bet she had a fit."

Amy broke into giggles. "She about did, Pete. I told her I was going up to San Francisco. It beats all how she can't break down and say a nice word."

Peter smiled. "I'll bet she's dying of curiosity. Amy, if you want to get back at Deborah, just keep all that's going on a secret from her."

Amy tossed her napkin at him. "Peter, I'm not through. I asked Momma to come to dinner Sunday, and would you believe she started a new line: 'No, thanks, you're sure to be busy with your newfound family. Don worry bout me—now I done my share you can forget bout me.' I tried to tell her one thing had nothing to do with the other, but she wouldn't budge."

Peter scowled. "Amy, stop trying to reassure her. She probably had other plans for the day. Don't let her do this to you. Did she hear from Ted and Barbara?"

"Of course . . . she gets her letter faithfully every week. Thank God she's got one good child."

A rueful smile crossed Pete's face. "I told you she only has eyes for men. But about her feelings for you . . . she loves you in a strange way. She's going to be devilishly jealous.

She's too old to change, darling; she's a product of her upbringing and her life. Just be grateful it didn't rub off on you."

Amy drew back in surprise. "Rub off on me? Oh, Pete, maybe it has . . ."

"Well, if that's the case, there's nothing can be done about it, dear heart . . . we'll just have to suffer you. Where's that newspaper article about your rich sister you were going to show me?"

Amy went in search of it and gave the newspaper to Pete. "It's in the society section. The picture isn't too clear."

He scanned the article and looked up amazed. "Wow! How come you didn't tell me Emmalina Griffon's one of the richest women in the world?"

Primly Amy said, "It's interesting, but it doesn't alter the fact that she's my sister. I also happen to be one of the richest women in the world—I have you!"

He pulled her onto his lap and nuzzled her neck. Laughing, she picked up the paper. "Did you read this? She's started a foundation for needy law students. See here . . . read it."

He looked at her questioningly after he finished. "Did you have anything in mind about this?"

"No, not in our connection; we don't need it. But, Peter, what do you think her opinion of me will be? I'm happy, you know that, but compared to her, what'll I be?"

He turned her face toward his. "You'll be her long-lost sister whom she's finally found. Doesn't it occur to you that she needs you? All the money in the world can't make up to any of you for the separation you've suffered . . . what you went through . . . agonizing and wondering all these years where each of you were. I'm sure she's going to love and adore you—she'd be crazy not to. Don't give yourself any nonsensical ideas."

Shoving her off his lap, he rose and made a courtly bow. "To my wife, younger sister to one of the wealthiest ladies in the world, and older sister to a famous movie star. I had no idea when I latched on to you where I'd be heading."

She hugged him. "Oh, Pete, I love you!"

He held her close. "That's all that matters. However, I have a suggestion. Since you will be traveling in such fancy company, you'd better get yourself a few new things to wear."

"No, Pete!" Her face showed consternation. "I'll make do—we can't afford it."

"Yes, we can! You'll take money from the savings account. We can manage. This sort of thing doesn't happen every day, my pet. Mrs. Cooper, you are going to do your husband proud. You're to pay your own way. Mrs. Griffon may be able to buy and sell us, but we're able to stand on our own two feet, got it?"

Amy didn't argue. She knew that when Peter made up his mind the matter was settled. Instead she said, "Pete, I can't imagine what it will be like. I adored Emmalina when we were little."

For the first time, with almost startling clarity, she saw herself marching in back of Emmy through tall corn . . . she heard voices and, as if in a silent film, her father mouthing words to a song they were singing . . . she could feel his tug as he lifted her up on one hip, and she saw Emmy's laughing face confronting hers on his other . . . there was a roomful of laughing people and a baby crying . . . Emmy was helping to button her dress . . . she could recall having her hand pulled back from a lit candle . . . she heard Emmy scolding . . .

He saw she was way back in time, and as he watched he saw tears well up. She said haltingly, "Do you think I should tell them about the meeting and the letter from our mother?"

There was to be no retreat as he said firmly, "Of course you should!" In a lighter vein he added, "It's going to be something with three gabby women catching up on all the past years. Now, how about our clearing up this mess and letting your hardworking husband get to his studies?"

The following Saturday Amy arranged to go shopping with Sally Levin. Amy thought she had excellent taste and, since their budgets were on a par, she knew Sally would help her to make the right choices.

It was when they stopped for lunch that Sally could no longer curb her curiosity and asked Amy what had happened since she had learned Tana Corgan was her sister.

Amy was too filled with apprehension and nerves about the upcoming event to talk about it, but she did explain that she hadn't approached Tana Corgan since her older sister had said that she doubted she even knew she'd been adopted.

Sally was wide-eyed, and Amy took the opportunity to tell her that this wasn't the time and place to relate the story but she would one day. Disappointed, Sally said, "Gosh, Amy, one day you could write a book about all of this."

Her brow furrowed as Amy replied, "Oh, sure. It would be some book of horrors, with a lot of miserable bones rattling around in my closet. How about splurging? Let's have some dessert."

Chapter XXVIII

◗━∞◆∞━◗

GRIFFONS ARE ANATHEMA TO TANA

EXUBERANTLY HAPPY, FILLED with halcyon dreams about the coming reunion with her newly found sisters, Emmy hadn't a doubt in her mind that Tana's hostility could be turned around once she knew the truth. Even if she was upset at the indisputable revelation of her adoption, once the shock wore off there would eventually be acceptance. The wish was so strong, so much father to the thought, that Emmy refused to face the possibility that things might work out otherwise.

There was no way Emmy could have known that the confrontation at the Michalsons' dinner party had provided the goad that propelled Tana upon the worst behavior of her life. The young actress was more out of hand than she'd ever been. It was as if the meeting with Emmalina had ignited all the aggravations of the months before.

Lilly was at a loss to understand why, without provocation, Tana suddenly gave way to unwarranted paroxysms of rage. She only knew it had begun upon their departure from the Michalsons' when, in a cold fury, Tana had screamed, "I hate that Griffon woman. I never want to see her again! The airs she gives herself, acting as if the world belongs to her!"

Lilly'd had the sense not to pursue it further. The next day, when Tana continued to carp, she'd tried to put an end to it by remarking, "For heaven's sake, why are you making such a thing out of it? Frankly, she didn't strike me as much of anything. Why are you letting her get to you this way?"

This was the fuel Tana needed and she flared, "Just what

439

I'd expect of you! You never understand! The woman is an affected ass and, whether you like it or not, I'll say what I think. This is my home and I'll say whatever I darn please!"

Lilly tried to nip the matter. "Okay, okay—don't get yourself in an uproar. I didn't mean anything by what I said. You certainly don't have to see her anymore."

"I sure as hell don't—and won't! I want her out of my house. What a helluva nerve they had renting it to her behind my back!"

Upset by Tana's odd behavior and worried by what it might induce, Lilly tried to placate her. Lighting a cigarette and trying to appear sympathetic, she said, "Look, Tana, all I'm concerned about is you. It hurts me to see you getting upset over nonsense. I'm really worried at the way you're carrying on. Not just with me, but with Ralph Michalson this morning. I couldn't help hearing you give him hell on the telephone. Scream at me all you want, but not at him. Agents like Michalson are hard to come by. I'm sure he thought he was doing you a favor by renting the house—it was a good deal."

Her eyes glinting with fury, Tana snarled, "When I want your opinion I'll ask for it. I want that woman out of my house, and that's that! I'm about to take care of it, and him too for that matter."

It was futile trying to reason with her, so Lilly dropped the discussion. Shortly after, Tana stormed out of the house. When she returned she closeted herself in her room. Lilly got the message: Tana had taken to the bottle again. It was a big binge, and for the next few days Lilly had her hands full. Exhausted by her ministrations and disgusted with the slobbering woman, she finally got her sufficiently sobered up to issue an ultimatum. "I'm not your keeper. If you ever pull this again, I'll leave. You're ruining your career and your life. You'd better see a doctor. I don't know what's gotten into you, but I'm sure as hell not going to hang around to find out. The servants know, and heaven alone knows who else. Don't you understand, if the studio gets wind of this they'll put you on suspension? This is my last warning. Don't touch that damn bottle again!"

To her amazement, Tana was contrite, almost repentant. "I'm sorry, Lil . . . really I am. I don't know what's gotten into me. The craziest things bother me. I'll try, I promise."

Tana couldn't explain it to herself. For one thing, the Griffon name compounded itself in her mind; it brought back memories of things she was trying to forget. And for another, the piercing pain of what her father had done continued to plague her. The fight to get where she was had suddenly become a hollow victory. Who was there to honestly appreciate her, whose words could she believe? She had fought and clawed her way to the top. She was Tana Corgan, and no one seemed to understand that on her pinnacle she was continually menaced—it was as if dogs bayed at her heels, biting and scratching to get at her.

Lilly looked at her coldly. "Do you recall that Ralph Michalson is no longer your agent?"

She bristled. "Yes!"

"Well, who do you suggest we replace him with?"

"They're all the same. I don't care. Anyone you think is good, Lil, will be all right with me."

Lilly studied her; she couldn't make her out. "Are you sure you have no preference?"

Fumbling with her cigarette lighter, Tana wouldn't look at her as she replied, "What the heck, one is as good as another. How long does my contract have to go?"

Disgustedly, Lilly said, "It's got nothing to do with your contract. It's all the other things Ralph did for you. He's the top man in his field and he did a super job for you. There's not another Michalson around."

Irritated by what she already knew, Tana lost her temper. "What's that supposed to mean? Did you expect me to kiss his ass? He's another of those pompous prissies. I told you how I feel about those people. He had no right to do what he did."

Wearily Lilly leaned back and closed her eyes. "Okay, we'll pick someone else."

For a change Tana was as good as her word and tried to keep an even keel. She even professed an interest in what was going on around her.

Then, out of the blue one morning, a letter arrived bearing the return name of Emmalina Griffon. Instantly Lilly was on guard. Opening the letter and reading its contents, she sat in stunned silence. It seemed incredible, but it was unlikely Mrs. Griffon would have fabricated such a story. Pulling her wits together, Lilly racked her mind for the best way to handle the matter. The letter had to be given to Tana—there was no way of avoiding it. Maybe, if she took the line that the resulting publicity from a relationship with Mrs. Griffon would be beneficial to her career, Tana could be made amenable. The more she thought, the more she believed Mrs. Griffon's claims could have validity.

Girding herself for what she was sure was going to be a renewal of fireworks, Lilly buzzed for Tana on the intercom.

She seemed pleasant and relaxed as she walked through the door. When Lilly motioned to her to close it, Tana seemed surprised. "What's up, Lil? Why all the hush-hush?"

"Because what I am going to show you is something you'll probably want to keep confidential, at least for the moment. But first I want you to promise, and mean it, that you won't start a tantrum."

"Well, get to it! What are you talking about?"

"Do you promise?"

She grinned. "I'll try. Tell me what this is all about."

Lilly handed her the letter, but the moment she saw the signature she flung it back at her. "Are you crazy? Is this the reason for all your buttering-up?"

Her voice strident, Lilly ordered, "Read it!"

As if she were being contaminated by it, Tana held the letter in her fingertips. She read and reread it, and then, her face white, she asked, "What is this? I've never heard anything so absurd in all my life. I told you that dame was creepy. This is crazy!"

Lilly sat without expression and Tana looked at her appealingly. "My God, you don't think there's anything to this, do you?" Disdainfully she crumpled the letter and threw it on the desk.

Lilly snapped, "Stop it, Tana! Grow up, think! That woman doesn't want to be related to you any more than you want to be to her. Hell, she doesn't need you."

Tana looked at her incredulously. "That's so, I guess. But, Lil, how can this be true? You know who my parents are. In my entire life there's never been the slightest word about such a thing. Sean and Deirdre Corrigan are my parents!"

Suddenly Lilly realized Tana was frightened and she said softly, "Look, hon, stranger things than this have happened. When I first read it, I felt the same way, but then I recalled the remark your father made, about 'the people who borned you' . . . remember?"

Tana sank into a chair, her mind awhirl. In a barely audible voice she said, "Yes, I recall, but I didn't think he meant anything like this. What reason would I have to think such a thing?"

Carefully considering her words, Lilly said, "The way you reacted to meeting Mrs. Griffon, maybe it was an intuitive feeling you had about her. Maybe that's why you wanted no part of her."

Tana looked at Lilly, startled. "Who knows, Lil . . . maybe. What do you think I should do about this?"

"Go! Meet her, hear what she has to say. You've got nothing to lose."

At this Tana roused. "Nothing to lose—are you kidding? Can you see the headlines?"

The pressure was off. Grinning, Lilly said, "Yes, I can! Wow, kid, it's billions of dollars' worth of free publicity. You the sister of the wealthy, oil-rich society heiress Mrs. Griffon. Think about that!"

"Not now. . . . First I want you to write my father a letter—now, this minute! Send it special delivery. Tell him what's going on and ask him if he has a dot of mercy to let me know if there's any truth to it. Next, I've made up my mind. I will go to San Francisco—and I'll write that answer myself."

Lilly grinned appreciatively. "That's the spirit, Tana! Good for you! I'm proud of you."

"Lil, there's even another sister involved. Someone by the name of Amy Beth who lives here in Los Angeles. What a kettle of stew this is! If, for some crazy reason, this should be true, there'd be a whole new family and all their troubles. . . . Ye gods, who wants that?"

Lilly said blandly, "Maybe there'd be no troubles and they'd be nice people."

"Not for me, darling, not for me! Lil, it can't be—I don't believe it! I remember Mom telling me stories about the old country and my grandparents there. Everyone always said I looked just like my dad when I was growing up. He always teased me about how I was like his older sister back in Ireland. Even cousin Mike. Be reasonable, Lil . . . somehow, sometime, I'd have had an inkling of such a thing before this."

"I have to agree with that . . . unless they were very careful never to let on. How do you account for your resemblance to Emmalina Griffon."

Tana grinned ruefully. "My luck! Well, everyone has a twin somewhere." She looked at Lilly hopefully, and when no answer was forthcoming she said, "If you want my opinion, she's got a screw loose somewhere. But it'll be a lark listening to her explain how I'm her sister. Feature that! Lil, get that letter off to my father."

She walked to the door, stopped and turned around. She hesitated for a moment and then said, "Lil, he probably wishes I was adopted. It'd be easier for him to be quit of me."

Lilly watched Tana leave, thinking, She's fortunate in one respect: if the world doesn't suit her, she pummels it into the shape she wants or escapes by drinking. She's really an outrageous person. She slipped the letter paper into the typewriter and began the letter to Mr. Corrigan. At least she'd be around to see the outcome. Lilly was convinced the story of Tana's adoption was true. It would be small retribution watching her get her comeuppance.

Outwardly at least, in the days that followed, Tana gave no further sign of being disturbed by the import of the letter. In passing she commented briskly to Lilly, "There's no point giving it any thought until my father answers."

She was busy, occupied by the routine of her work. She was scheduled for a starring role in the remake of an old and famous picture, *Old-Fashioned Girl*. She was swept up in all it entailed: script, costume fittings and rehearsals. Tana was back in her element, and, to top it all, the Hollywood Canteen was having a special evening featuring her as the main attraction. At least that night she wouldn't be asked to help with the dishes, although it was usually in good company—Bette Davis, Joan Crawford . . . it could be any one of the great ones. Even Walter Pidgeon had helped to dry them one night.

The Canteen was thick with sweaty crowds of adoring men, and she enjoyed the excitement that her appearance on the platform caused. She was startled to see Bill Griffon standing close by grinning up at her. What was he doing here again? She bridled at the thought of how high-handedly the Griffons encroached on her life. They symbolized humiliation for her. She definitely wanted no part of them, but since they seemed intent upon intruding, it was time she showed them a thing or two. If Bill Griffon was Emmalina's brother-in-law, it would be amusing to teach him a lesson he'd never forget. For starters she had an idea that would prove to him it was not wise to trifle with her. When the dancing resumed, she extricated herself from her partner and went in search of him. Spotting him in a group, she walked over and with her most beguiling smile said gaily, "Bill, you old fool! Did you really think I didn't recognize you the last time you were here?"

He looked at her in amazement as she went on. "You look twice as handsome in your uniform. What brings you to Los Angeles again?"

Bewildered, he grinned at her. "I'm taking care of some matters for the military and, by good luck, got out here again. I'm stationed in Washington these days—got a good berth. But let's not talk about me, let's talk about you." They moved to the side where they could talk privately.

Smiling sadly, she said, "I guess you heard about my husband."

"Yes, it was in all the papers." He was grave, and she stood as if waiting and then smiled up at him. "You know, we have a lot of catching up to do."

He stared, not knowing what she meant until she said coyly, "Aren't you going to ask me out—a drink, dinner . . . something?" She pouted adorably and said softly, "Of course, on one condition—you have to call me Tana."

"Absolutely, Tana. It will be my pleasure. When?"

"What's wrong with this evening? I'll be through in half an hour."

Poor Bill Griffon—all he remembered was that Polly Sue Corrigan had been an adorable little girl, a breath of fresh air and innocence. As he escorted her through the door he was the envy of every man around.

At Tana's suggestion, they secured a quiet table at the Brown Derby. Its comfortable, soft leather banquettes, its walls adorned with autographed pictures of Hollywood's famous, its good food and service made it a favorite hangout for many of the stars, several of whom Tana greeted in passing. She was the soul of affability and charm as she led him on. He fell victim to every one of her wiles. When she asked him if he was related to Emmalina, he was delighted to tell her, "Luckily, yes. She's a wonderful person—married my kid brother. She looks a bit like you, although not half so beautiful." He stared at her and said, "I ask myself how I could have been such a fool. I could kick myself, I was such a dumb kid. Although I guess I'd do the same thing all over again. Recall what I'm talking about?"

She smiled at him in wide-eyed innocence. "No, I don't. What are you referring to?"

Reddening, he said, "Oh, I'm being foolish. Of course you

wouldn't remember. I was crazy about you, did you know that?"

"Oh, Bill, we were just children."

They talked about her family and the ranch, and then she said, "You haven't told me anything about yourself. Are you married?"

Grinning boyishly, he confessed, "I'm promised, but nothing's definite. Now that I'm with you, Tana, I'm glad. I'm not sure it'd be right."

She wanted to laugh in his face but instead smiled demurely. "Oh, Bill, don't tell me you're still carrying a torch for that wild Polly Sue?"

Completely captivated, he succumbed to her blandishments. When he returned her to her door she invited him in for a nightcap. She was languishing and seductive, returning his hesitant lovemaking with ardor. Roused until he was at fever pitch, he tried to push her down on the couch to consummate what she so obviously was inviting. She slid from his grasp. Laughing, she held him off. "Bill, stop. Just because I'm Tana Corgan now doesn't alter things. You'd better leave, you mustn't bring dishonor on the Corrigans . . . after all, I'm still their daughter."

Filled with desire for her, he persisted. She teased him, urging him on until he was blinded by his need. He grabbed her and pulled her down, and at that moment she kneed him viciously, slapped his face and raked his cheek with her fingernails. Her teeth were clenched with fury as she said, "Who the hell do you think you are? Did you think I'd been waiting around for you? You're a stuffed-shirt ass! I want nothing to do with the likes of you. Your being a Griffon doesn't give you the right to treat me like a whore. Get out!"

She thought she heard his agonized "Bitch!" as she left the room. She was delighted with her little plan of revenge.

As the waves of pain receded and he could once again stand upright, he looked around the darkened room and shivered. There wasn't a sound in the house. The heavily brocaded furniture gave no evidence of what had occurred other than the disordered cushions on the couch. The heavy scent of wilting roses from vases everywhere made his nausea increase. Taking a few tentative steps, he found he could walk. Locating the front door, he let himself out into the night.

Humiliated and in pain, he rested on the seat of his car, staring up at the dimly lit window he saw on the second floor. A figure was outlined on the shade, and he wondered if she were looking down and laughing. The only thing he could conclude was that Tana Corgan was a little bit crazy. If this had been retaliation for the incident so long ago, she must really have thought about him a lot to have borne such a long-seated grudge. Well, he was through with her. The sooner he could conclude his business and leave Hollywood, the better he would feel. He started the motor and drove off.

Bill Griffon's next appointment with Gene Madrix was two days later. As he was ushered into the luxurious anteroom he was told there would just be a few minutes' wait.

He heard voices and noticed that Madrix's office door was slightly ajar. To his astonishment he overheard his name being discussed, and in a moment he realized that the female voice belonged to Tana Corgan. Listening, he heard Madrix's voice rise in protest. "What's your objection to him? He's a decent enough young man. You're being unreasonably disagreeable."

She answered sharply, "I'm not being disagreeable. I merely said I'm not interested in putting myself out for him even if he is your big stockholder's number-one son. Besides, he's not really interested in women; he prefers the company of men." Chuckling nastily, she added, "He looks like an owl."

Bill's fists clenched. What was that she-devil up to? Torn with the urge to leave lest he be discovered eavesdropping, he couldn't tear himself away. Madrix's voice was annoyed. "I'm surprised at such talk from you. By God, Tana, you're making a case out of a simple request. It's important to us that he escort you to this shindig. He's a darn sight better escort than anyone from your stable of gigolos. It's just for an evening."

She laughed. "I see you're still trying to run my life. The man makes me sick; he's dull and an insufferable snob. I hate the type. How can it help my image when everyone knows he's not a man?"

Madrix's voice registered surprise. "I don't know where you get your information from, but if that's the case then you have nothing to be concerned about as far as your person is concerned. You will be doing your patriotic duty by appearing with a man in uniform. You'll be obliging us and making a small repayment for the many favors done for you. You'll cooperate, and that's that!"

Bill jumped to his feet as he heard her scream, "All right! I'll go with the fairy if you insist."

"Cut it out, Tana!" Madrix's voice was angry. "That's a contemptible thing for you to say."

All sincerity, she replied, "You'll just have to believe I have it on very good authority."

The silence was heavy, and Bill sensed she was beginning to convince Madrix. There was a conciliatory tone in his voice as he said, "Tana, all I'm asking you to do is to go to the awards ceremony with him, not to bed. I can't affirm or deny what you're saying, and I'm really not interested in his sexual preferences. You're listening to vicious rumors."

"You know I'd do anything in the world for you, Mr. Madrix, but I just can't help myself. Men like that make my flesh crawl." Her voice rose girlishly. "Take my word for it, it's no idle gossip."

"All right, Tana. I'm appreciative of your cooperation. We'll be in touch. Now, if you'll excuse me, I have another appointment. I'll have Bill Griffon telephone you."

Hastily Bill let himself out of the office and left the building. He had to regain his composure before he met with Madrix. He turned a corner and walked along the tree-lined path, seething. The woman's venom could have nasty repercussions. He had to get himself in hand; his disappearance from the office would have been noticed. He turned back in time to see Tana's car drive off, her omnipresent secretary at the wheel.

Reaching the outer office, he managed to smile at the pretty receptionist. "Is Mr. Madrix ready for me? By the way, wasn't that Tana Corgan getting into her car?"

"Yes, it was, Mr. Griffon. Isn't she something special? She's every inch the star, if you know what I mean. She's always on—the perfect movie queen. The studio likes it that way, I guess."

He pretended to enjoy the exchange. "Is she making a picture now?"

"Yes, she's been away."

"I guess it's time for my appointment. Will you check for me, please?"

Bill was certain that Madrix studied him on the sly, and he took pains to be as composed as he could. At the conclusion of their business, Madrix said, "I thought you'd enjoy attending the award ceremonies, so we've made arrangements."

Bill knew it would seem strange if he refused, so he

appeared enthusiastic. "Say, that would be something! My fiancée would never forgive me if I had the chance to go and didn't."

At the word *fiancée,* Madrix seemed to relax. He smiled. "I have another surprise. How would you like to escort Tana Corgan?"

"Who could turn such an offer down? How would I go about arranging that?"

"Leave it all to us. You just take care of the amenities. We'll even supply the limo."

"No, that won't be necessary. I'm driving a Caddy. If that'll do, you don't have to bother."

"Sure—however you like, Bill."

Normally a quiet, even-tempered man who rarely lost his temper, Bill Griffon was consumed by an implacable rage. He was determined to wreak revenge on the silly creature. Tana Corgan had acquired a formidable enemy. If she had been a man, he would have beaten her to a pulp; but something else occurred to him. Now it remained to see if it was workable. He set to work to iron out the details. He gloated; it would be the perfect way to give her a dose of her own medicine.

He made several telephone calls. When matters were arranged to his satisfaction, he shopped for an assortment of items. That done, he made the telephone call to Tana Corgan's secretary to confirm the appointment.

He could barely contain his impatience and forced himself to check and recheck his plan so that nothing would go awry. The evening of the affair he dressed carefully. He checked the valise to make sure it contained all his purchases and then stowed it in the trunk of his car.

He arrived at the Corgan home on schedule. He and Tana greeted each other with cold correctness and drove off in silence. During the ceremonies they exchanged only perfunctory and necessary words. At the conclusion, after the news pictures had been taken, he assisted her into the car. He drove with the traffic until it thinned out and then unobtrusively turned the car around and took another route, in the opposite direction. At first she didn't seem to notice. Then, aware that it was not a familiar road, she said, "This is not the direction we should be taking."

He turned and smiled at her. "I promise to get you home in good time. I want to show you something."

She remained unalarmed, pulling her wrap closer and

slouching down in the seat. He was gaining the outskirts of the city when she suddenly became annoyed. "Where the hell are you going this time of night?"

He gave her an odd smile. "I told you I wanted to show you something. It's a little way off; be patient."

She became nervous. "Take me right home! I'm not interested in anything you have to show me. Please turn the car around at once!"

It became necessary for him to manhandle her. He did it deftly and with pleasure, driving with one hand while he subdued her with the other. She was out, totally unconscious, by the time he reached the turnoff for the road up the mountain. Slowing, he covered her with a blanket so that she appeared to be sleeping comfortably. He pulled up at a small roadside stand and gas pump and had the attendant fill the car. He took the opportunity to make a telephone call. He assumed it was the maid who answered and was gay and charming as he entrusted her with a message: "We've been invited to a house party in honor of the winners. We'll return no later than Monday morning."

She promised she would deliver the message. He knew there would be no problems in that area; he had personally arranged Lilly Fazon's appointment for the evening and, if things went as he hoped, she'd be occupied for the night.

His pulses were pounding as he drove up the narrow mountain road searching for the dirt lane leading to the hunting lodge. It was a good thing he had reconnoitered during the day; it could so easily have been passed.

Cutting the motor, he turned to look at his passenger. Her breathing seemed normal and even. He grinned sardonically; even if she screamed her head off, there was no one within miles that would hear. There was no point in taking chances. He was looking forward to being as brutal and cruel as it was possible to be; he'd relish every moment of torment he would subject her to.

Once he'd heard himself described by his English nanny as a boy without a malicious bone in his body, and all his life he'd been proud of that characterization. It had never occurred to him that he could be otherwise. However, his encounter with Tana seemed to have unearthed passions he'd never considered in himself. He was pleased at the perverse pride he felt in being able to prove himself savage and ruthless. He was afire for the moment she would awake and understand he could vent his rage on her at will, on her much vaunted body. He'd spent hours imagining what it would be like, devising ideas of what he would do once he had her in his power. The time had come.

He left her in the car as he took out his bag and entered the lodge. He turned on the lights and saw the wood laid in the fireplace. He read the note his friend had left: everything was as he had requested. He returned to the car and saw that she was beginning to come around.

He carried her to the bedroom and quickly stripped her to the skin, enjoying every moment. He hoped he'd brought everything. He pulled his equipment from the bag. He placed long woolen mittens over each of her hands beyond her wrists, and then he wrapped them tightly with cord, tying them separately to each of the bedposts.

She was beginning to stir, so he squeezed her mouth open and inserted a gag, over which he placed tape. That done, he padded her ankles and spread-eagled her legs, roping each one to the bottom of the bed.

He surveyed his handiwork. Satisfied that she would be unable to do more than squirm, he threw a blanket over her and went about starting the fire, since there was a chill in the air.

He was exhilarated. This promised to be the experience of a lifetime. His adrenaline pumped with the anticipation of her reaction. As he fussed over the coffeepot, he heard her making sounds. Once he had set the pot on the stove, he walked to the bedroom door. He smiled as he saw her struggling helplessly against the restraints. Her face was red and perspiring. He spoke quietly as he ordered, "Lie still, Tana! You'll have to put up with it."

Her eyes bugged at his approach, and he saw her tense. "I'm not going to hurt you if you cooperate and behave yourself."

He looked down at her. He'd have to be careful—she was a tiny, fine-boned thing. He pulled the blanket off. It would have been hard for anyone to believe, seeing the delicacy of her body structure, that it encased such crudity and meanness.

Her face was streaming with perspiration from her efforts, and he mopped it with a handkerchief. He saw by her eyes that she was trying to tell him something. "It won't help to struggle, Tana. There's no one around to rescue you. At the moment, you're completely at my mercy. There's a lot we have to settle. Think about it while you're resting."

Seeing the fear register on her face, he had a fleeting moment of compassion, imagining what she must be going through. He was basically a gentle, good-hearted man, an ascetic given to intellectual pursuits, but his rage had transcended reason. His actions with this woman were foreign to anything he had ever done in his life. He knew he held the power of life and death over her—in his hands, at his will. That in itself worried him; he had committed himself to an act of violence on another human being. He had no intentions of harming her beyond using her and frightening her. He was surprised at the titillation of his senses. His need for revenge would not be slaked any other way.

He ran his hand over her body and watched coldly as she thrashed. The thought of how venomous she had been made him feel an aversion for her, an abhorrence that she could have driven him to this point. He thought of her blandishments the night she had sensually wooed him, and his voice, when he spoke, was harsh and cold. "I imagine you can figure out why I've done this. Even though it sounds melodramatic, you're mine to do with as I wish. For one thing, it will be necessary to prove my manhood. I'm sure, with your precious conceit, it never occurred to you that you could repel me, but I'm going to try to overcome that."

She writhed and pulled at her bonds, but they held firmly. She tried desperately to push the gag out of her mouth, grunting and groaning.

He laughed. "I wouldn't do that. I imagine it's hard enough for you to breathe as it is. Make up your mind there's no way you are going to escape what I have in store for you. We're going to make up for all the time we lost. I've a few things to say." He saw her expression change, her eyebrows rose in plea or disdain, he couldn't tell. "Tana, don't taunt me. Don't make me angrier than I already am. I really don't want to hurt you unnecessarily. If I take the gag out, will you promise not to scream?"

She bobbed her head. Well, it wouldn't alter anything. If she were reasonable maybe they could settle matters less brutally. He lifted her head and removed the tape, dislodging the gauze pad with a finger. She gagged for a moment, then took deep breaths of air. Her voice was shrill. "What about the rest of this? Get me out of these ropes!"

He looked at her in derision. She was doing the worst thing

she could, ordering him about. He said contemptuously, "God, you're stupid. I told you I wanted to talk."

She struggled. "Didn't you hear me? Loosen these ropes! Free me!"

He sat down at the foot of the bed smiling at her and she screamed, "Bill Griffon, are you crazy? Have you lost your mind? Do you know what you can get for doing this?"

Running his hand up her leg, it pleased him when she cringed. "Tana, I like you less than you like me. But you'll have to accept it. A few things are going to be settled before I release you."

She sneered. "The sight of you makes me sick. Your name's going to be mud." She ranted and raved using every vituperative word she could think of.

He heard the coffee boil over and strode out of the room. Her screams pierced the air. He knew no one was around, but, just in case, he rushed back and replaced the gag in her mouth. She bit his finger, and he slapped her face. She tossed and threw herself as far as the ropes permitted.

"Hang on there, my buckaroo. This is no game where you order me around. I am not going to let you go. I'm going to keep you quiet, because if I don't I might be tempted to kill you, and you're not worth it. You're cheap, vulgar, crude. You've got a pretty face with nothing behind it. We'll find out about the great body . . . that's about it. If you look at me like that I may just blindfold you . . . in fact, I will." He retaped her mouth and wound a scarf around her head.

Finishing his coffee, he stood against the doorjamb, looking at her. He put the cup away. She heard him coming. He could see her body go rigid. "I've got a fire going, Polly. Oh, forgive me—Tana." He began to remove his clothes as he talked. "You know, it's interesting to see what you've achieved with your notion of life. It's strange that a simple little country girl who loved horses and the wide-open spaces would wind up making movies."

He noticed that her struggles had brought the scarf over her nose and she was having difficulty breathing. He removed the scarf. "Now you're using your head. Just keep calm. If you do as I say, you may have a good time too. Nothing bad is going to happen. You see, what I have in mind for you is in the way of apology. This old bird—'owl' was it you called me?—is going to make up to you what he neglected so long ago. I'll bet you never knew that a man who respected you, even though he hungered after your body, didn't have to be a fag. I've stored up one big appetite, and we're going to make up for lost time."

He was naked, and she closed her eyes and tried to turn her head. He chuckled. "It would have been more pleasant if you'd been cooperative and let sweet nothings come out of your mouth, but as it is your vocabulary offends me. You're safer this way. Are the ropes too tight?"

She wagged her head and he smiled. "I think you're lying. You are a liar, you know. I'm a careful guy. Those mittens you're wearing keep the ropes from making any marks. That ought to tell you I'm planning to let you live—that is, if you don't anger me. Just stay quiet. I'll be back as soon as I get more wood for the fire."

He tucked the blanket around her, picked up a robe and left. She struggled for a moment, then gave up. Fear was beginning to erode her defiance. Her body began to shake uncontrollably, and tears coursed down her cheeks. She saw him return and closed her eyes. She could not keep from shaking. He poured some bourbon in a glass. He removed the tape and let the bourbon drip through the gauze into her mouth. She gurgled and gagged but he was unrelenting. Her eyes implored and he thought he heard the word *please*.

"No, honey, you had your chance. This is it for the duration. You're just not reliable, Tana. And it's a good idea to keep that mouth of yours shut, because you deserve a lot worse."

He began to examine her body, probing where he pleased. Her writhing whetted his appetite. "This is just the start. You must be ticklish. Get used to it, darling. I really don't want to bruise or disfigure you, but it'll depend entirely on you."

Her body shook violently. He stood considering for a moment and then said, "I know what'll relax you . . . an oil bath."

He picked up a bottle of baby oil and slowly began to oil her from head to toe. He took pleasure in her resistance, swabbing the oil over every part of her, penetrating every area he could reach. Finished, he stood back and surveyed his handiwork.

He stretched out beside her. She turned her head away. He pulled it back and held it. He taunted and teased her as he played with her body. When he saw the fury in her eyes change to fear, he forced her to look up at him. "Little Tana Corgan, you are never going to forget this . . . never in all your life. It'll end when I see you begging for mercy . . . when I see you groveling on the floor, humiliated, debased, like the foul creature you are. This old owl has a few treats in store for you."

When he climbed on top of her, she fought him in every way she could, her muffled screams and moans subsiding only when he had taken his pleasure. After he had rested he was delighted to find he could do it again immediately. He'd never felt this potent before. His adrenaline was really pumping; he'd never be satiated, he felt that strong. He rose from the bed and took a swig of bourbon. "Want some? No, it might make you sick. I wouldn't want you to get drunk and miss a moment of this."

He swathed her in more oil. "It helps, don't you think?"

He took pictures of her. Her eyes kept pleading, and he laughed.

Ruthlessly he used her again, this time forcing her to pleasure. Then he slept awhile. When he awoke some hours later, he saw that she had fallen asleep. He rose and went to the bathroom where he adjusted the shower water. Releasing her hands and legs from the bedposts, he tied them together. She still fought him, and he slapped her sharply on the rump. "Don't try anything you'll be sorry for."

He carried her to the bathroom, where he held her under the shower. He soaped her from head to toe. When he had rinsed her off and dried her, he laid her on a sheet, which he then proceeded to wind around her in mummy fashion. He laughed. "You've never been more appealing."

He picked her up like a sack of potatoes and dumped her in a chair near the fireplace. "Romantic, isn't it? I'm going to give you something to eat. If you scream or yell, I promise the gag will go in twice as far and tight."

The moment he released the gag she came down on his hand, biting with all her strength. She screamed.

He pushed her head back and pinched her nose. He was rough as he replaced the gag. "Bitch! I told you! No more chances! Starve, for all I care. You still have to learn I mean what I say."

He dumped her back on the bed, face down. He unwound the sheet and retied her to the bedposts. "You're a foolish woman. You think you can ride roughshod over everyone and get away with it. Well, this is one time you're learning a lesson. What the hell, this is more fun for me."

He tried every erotic thing he had ever imagined . . . every fantasy that he had read or dreamed about. There was nothing he left untried in the way of taking his pleasure from her. When he tired, he left her.

When he returned in the morning, he saw that she was still full of fight; she had amazing energy. "Good morning, wild Polly Sue. Would you like to play Beauty and the Beast? You could sit up and beg. Maybe we ought to try it in case you ever have a part that calls for it. There's no substitute for experience; you learn how creatures feel when you endure things yourself."

She was terrified when he wrapped a towel around her throat and put a rope leash around it. He tied her hands behind her back, making her crawl as he tugged at it. He smacked her when she resisted. When she was near collapse, he put her back on the bed. "You can rest now. I don't want to lose my playmate."

But he was getting tired of her; he was getting tired of the entire thing. He had wreaked his vengeance. He covered her and left her to her own thoughts. During the night he took her again but derived no pleasure.

Early in the morning he put her in a tub and scrubbed her. She tried to catch his eye, but he refused to look at her. When he had dried her, he dressed her. He slipped gloves over her hands and restrained her again. When she was ready, he covered her with the evening wrap she had worn. He carried her to the car. As he placed her in it he said, "I'd like to remove the gag, but you can't be trusted. I guess it'd be safer to knock you out again."

She shook her head vehemently, indicating she'd cooperate. He removed the tape from her mouth but left the gag in. It would take time for her to dislodge it. She was totally submissive, and the drive back was uneventful. She fell asleep. She had reason to be exhausted. At a red light near home, he spilled bourbon over her dress and cape. As he drove through the gates of Bel Air he saw she was waking.

"You're home, Tana. This is no idle threat. If you don't want a repeat performance, remember what I'm saying. If you ever say a word about this, or call me a fag again, the pictures will go out on the instant. The only person who'll know about this is a buddy of mine who's thoroughly reliable. If anything happens to me, he'll know what to do with the negatives."

He pulled up a short distance from the front of the house and removed the gag. She gulped for air. He untied her hands and ankles, removing the protective coverings. As the front door opened, he reached down and kissed her . . . long and hard so that anyone watching would see them.

Smiling, he jumped out of the car and opened her side. He pulled her out. She staggered for a moment. When he saw that she could stand, he called, "Good-bye, darling. Thanks for a wonderful time!"

Without a backward glance he jumped back into his seat and drove away.

Dizzy and weak, she staggered again as the car roared down the hill. Maria thought she'd been drinking and ran to her side. She hung on to the woman, who put a supporting arm around her. "I'm not drunk, Maria. I think I'm sick, coming down with something." Her voice was hoarse, her throat sore and dry. "I'm dizzy. I really don't feel well. Help me upstairs, please."

Concerned, Maria asked, "Shall I call the doctor?" Tana was surprised that Lilly was nowhere in sight. Maria said, "She had an early appointment. She'll be back this afternoon."

That was a relief. It would give her a chance to get her story straight and account for the weekend. Every muscle in her body ached.

Under Maria's solicitous care, it wasn't long before she was propped up in bed with a tray of soup, sandwiches and tea. She was famished; Maria was astonished to see how she wolfed the food down. When Maria had removed the tray, Tana stretched luxuriously. Just being free to move her arms and legs was a relief. She kept inhaling great gulps of air. Maria was certain she had a pulmonary ailment. She hoped Miss Fazon would return soon. Then Tana fell asleep.

She awoke to see Lilly's worried face looking down at her. "How do you feel, Tana? I've telephoned the doctor—he should be here shortly."

Smiling, Tana said, "I feel much better. I'm sure it's unnecessary for him to come. It's probably just a bug."

Adamantly Lilly said, "It's better to have him check you. You must have had quite a weekend. It was certainly a surprise, your going off with Bill Griffon. You must have had a sudden change of heart."

Tana looked up at her and said quietly, "It was a crazy

thing to do, but we were just in the mood. You know how those things come about with everyone urging. We went to this fabulous lodge in the mountains . . . really marvelous, a crazy assortment of people."

Lilly eyed her dubiously, not wholly convinced. "I hope you didn't make a fool of yourself. No wonder you're sick—you had nothing to wear. Maria says your dress reeks of whiskey."

"I didn't drink—someone spilled a drink all over me. You should have seen how funny we looked, everyone running around in borrowed snow clothes. It gets real cold in the mountains this time of year."

"It sounds crazy. Who was there?"

To Lilly's astonishment, Tana broke into tears, crying hysterically. Lilly said hastily, "I'll see if the doctor is on the way. Just try to rest."

She left the room and Tana's tears subsided, to be replaced by angry frustration. The pain and torture Bill had inflicted upon her, her inability to fight back, enraged her. Her mind raced. She would get him if it was the last thing she ever did. Her body was a mass of pain; she was seared with the memory of her indignity, her humiliation. She held up her wrists—that demon, there was not a mark. What if he had impregnated her? What would she do?

Lilly peeked in. "Dr. Jarson's here, Tana." He had taken care of her since she had started at the studio.

"Well, hello there, Miss Corgan. Hear you've come down with something. Can you sit up?"

He stuck a thermometer in her mouth and, after a routine check, he assured her, "You're fine, Miss Corgan. Your throat's a little red. You probably overdid things a bit and picked up a bug. A few aspirins and a day or so in bed should have you fine again."

She thought he was through, but he continued with his examination, lifting her gown and checking her body. It wasn't every day one saw the likes of Tana Corgan in the nude. What he saw didn't surprise him too much. These movie people were tramps.

Dr. Jarson was studio-connected, and the following day he and Gene Madrix were locked in private conference. "I tell you, Gene, there's more to it than drunkenness. You can't imagine the condition of her body. It looked to me like she had one helluvan orgy. There's no accounting for their strange sex habits. You'd never guess it from looking at her. Didn't she lose her husband some time ago?"

Madrix looked at him angrily. "Are you positive?"

"Her body is covered with bites and bruises. She apparently likes them rough. Somebody had a time! Let me put it to you straight, Gene, I didn't do a vaginal. I didn't have to, I've seen a few in my time. Whores don't show that much wear and tear."

"There's no limit lately to her nastiness. I'm in a quandary." He looked at the doctor thoughtfully. "She's signed to do a big part, and there's still a long way to go on her contract. We'd better not make waves right now. We'll take action at the proper time. Meanwhile, not a word of this to anyone."

"Strictly confidential, don't worry."

Tana's youth stood her in a good stead. It didn't take long before she improved. It was a day later that a huge bouquet of yellow roses was delivered to the house. She winced as she read the card: "Thanks for the time of our lives. Owl."

Bitterly she tore the note to shreds. What bothered her most was how Bill Griffon knew what she'd said to Gene Madrix. They had been alone, and she was positive he had not repeated the story. She tried to recall if there had been anyone else around at the time. The only one she could remember was the innocuous receptionist in the outer office. Mr. Madrix's secretary had been off on an errand for him. Woe to that receptionist if she somehow proved to be the one. Given the time, she'd find out.

As the days progressed, Tana's changed demeanor began to confound the people around her. Her behavior was in marked contrast to what it had been. Lilly quietly worried as she observed the subdued, withdrawn woman. She surmised it had something to do with the weekend Tana had been on, but subtle questioning bore no more results than a variation of the original story.

Deciding that a man must be at the core of it, Lilly figured that Tana had met with rejection by someone she might have fancied. Not one to give up without a fight, she began to offer the usual mundane consolations one offers a friend under such circumstances, until Tana grew vexed. "What in the world are you getting at? Why are you consoling me for something that has never happened? What drives you so crazy about that silly weekend? I wish you'd stop it—you're making me angry. Stop harping on that house party—it bores me."

In reality Tana thought about Bill Griffon all the time; the memories of what had gone on never lurked far beneath the surface. For no apparent reason her face would suddenly flush and beads of perspiration would appear on her forehead. Maria and Lilly thought it a result of her illness. Awake, Tana was angry, rankled by the humiliation of what had befallen her, yet at night she had erotic dreams. She wondered why she hadn't been more frightened; he might have killed her, yet something told her that despite his savagery and manhandling he would not have gone that far. This man had accomplished what no one else in her life had been able to do—he'd stood up to her and had the audacity to master her. She despised herself for feeling as she did, and she tried to convince herself she hated him; but in her heart she was moved by admiration. She was fearful lest she encounter him at the studio and was relieved when she heard he'd gone East. She was uneasy at the thought that he might have gone back to be married. Desperately she fought to put him out of her mind; yet, half ashamed, she would fall asleep at night awaiting dreams of him. It was with bittersweet sense that she acknowledged that Bill Griffon had won his revenge. She wondered that that didn't gall her more.

Lilly couldn't get over how untemperamental Tana seemed these days. If anything, she had gone into reverse, moping, daydreaming and conversing in limited fashion about her work. Lilly decided that Tana was more worried about the adoption story than she'd assumed. The visit to San Francisco was coming up.

Hesitantly Lilly asked, "Tana, are you all set for the weekend in San Francisco? You're still planning to go?"

"Yes, but I can't get over the fact that my father hasn't answered the letter. It's possible something may have happened to him and Mike wouldn't notify me since I'm no longer part of the family. But I have the feeling he's punishing me by not replying. You'd think he'd have the common decency to let me have the straight truth. I'll be honest—I am upset. I think his silence is a way of getting back at me, and maybe there's something to the adoption story."

Lilly considered what Tana had said. "Why don't you call Mike and ask him about your father? That way you'll know for sure there's nothing wrong with him."

Tana acted on the suggestion and Mike, while surly, at least confirmed there was nothing wrong with Sean. Tana tried repeatedly to get through to the ranch, but either Sean was not there or he was not answering the telephone.

Lilly drove Tana to the airport for her trip to San Francisco. Dressed simply, Tana made every attempt to be incognito; she was in no mood to please her public. Lilly could see how tense she had become. "Tana, for your own sake, try to stay calm, listen to what Mrs. Griffon has to say. I know that no one can fully appreciate what a shock this is to you, but who knows, it may be all for the good. Don't lose your temper so you'll have something to regret. Give the woman a chance. Another thing: I've been thinking—now please, don't get angry at what I'm about to say—you haven't lived at home in the bosom of your parents, for a long, long time . . . so what difference does it actually make if you were adopted? Know what I mean?"

"Thanks, Lil. I suppose that is one way of looking at it. I appreciate your kindness. I wish I could feel that way, but I can't. If by some miracle Sean Corrigan decides to write, you know where to reach me. I'll be back by Monday, if not before. I'll telephone. Are you seeing Herman Johnson again this weekend?"

Blushing fiercely, Lilly said, "We have a date."

Tana smiled. "I've never known you to go so steady before. Looks like this might be serious, eh?"

"I can't deny it, Tana, although he hasn't really said anything yet. I have a hunch he will. I have to admit I'm crazy about him."

Tana smiled wearily. Her world was slipping away. Now it seemed likely Lilly would be shutting her out, leaving to live her own life. She had better be prepared for that. One by one all her old standbys, safeguards and props were deserting her. She'd have to learn to stand on her own feet.

As she seated herself in the plane she prayed silently: "Lord, give me the ability to face Emmalina Griffon and accept whatever she has to tell me calmly. I don't want to have been adopted, Lord, please let Deirdre and Sean have been my parents."

Chapter XXIX

◇◆◇◇◇◆◇

PANDORA'S BOX

EMMY MANEUVERED THE curves carefully as she drove down the treacherous mountain road from Remo. She had little patience for the concentration it required, but it helped keep her mind off the impending meeting.

She breathed a little easier once she reached the flat land. It was a good omen; she had managed the dangerous roads without incident. As the days had passed and the time for the convening of her sisters had grown nearer, she had become convinced that something would occur to prevent it; after all this time she was haunted by the feeling that it was not meant to be. But now only a day separated them. If she could keep her wits about her, she'd arrive in one piece to have her dreams materialize.

Her mind ran like a reel conjuring up pictures of how they would greet each other, the way each would react to the other. Finally, annoyed with herself and her inability to think of anything else, she tried panaceas, stopping at historical roadsites, even dawdling for a torturous hour touring state buildings in Sacramento. Nothing worked and, exasperated, she gave up and drove determinedly through to San Francisco.

She checked in at the hotel and, since it was late afternoon, she assumed any messages of cancellation would be there. Her heart skipped a beat when the desk clerk informed her there was nothing.

After selecting a suite and unpacking, she ordered a light

dinner from room service and drew a hot bath. She was weary from the drive, and tonight would be a good time to get a letter off to Larry. It might be several days before she would have the opportunity to write him again. She wished there was someone to talk to, but Betty and Ralph had gone to Coronado, and she certainly didn't want Jonathan to suspect she couldn't handle the long-awaited event.

After forcing herself to write a few lines to Larry, she gave up and, taking a book, propped herself up in bed in hopes she'd fall asleep. She slept fitfully through the night and was delighted when she saw dawn creeping through the draperies. The day had arrived and now she had only to wait until late afternoon. Amy was arriving by train and Tana an hour later by plane. Emmy planned to fill the intervening hours by looking into where their mother, Mary Ann Beauford, lived.

The bell captain explained the route and her car was brought around. She found it more easily than she had anticipated. It proved to be a dingy area on the periphery of the city, an old and run-down formerly middle-class section. It was obvious their mother did not live in luxury. Most of the homes had gone to seed, with signs advertising rooms for rent. She cruised slowly when she reached the street, trying to make out the house numbers. When she reached the number on the address she was tempted to stop, but there was such a sad, forlorn look about the decaying building that she was dissuaded. Besides, she convinced herself, it wouldn't be fair to her sisters; from now on they would act together as a unit. The thought buoyed her. No one could ever stop them from being a family again. It was a wonderful feeling.

The afternoon was waning. For the hundredth time Emmy walked to the mirror to check her appearance. The heavy smell of furniture polish mixed with the effusion of flowers permeated the rooms, making her feel slightly ill. The portable bar and hors d'oeuvres had already been placed in the corner. She looked about, giving the elegant living room a last-minute check; everything was in order.

She moved to the window as lights began to flicker on and jewel the nearby buildings. She watched people below scurrying along like ants drawn to some mysterious destination. How she envied them. She yearned to find a niche in the life that pulsated around her. For a long time now she had been without ties, an outsider looking on from the fringe. She had Larry—he was the beacon light of her existence—but, as things were, he was like frosting on the cake. Their time together had been so brief, their experiences together so emotionally climactic, that they had not yet established a reservoir to draw on for mundane living.

It seemed to Emmy that if she could regain the ties that were her very own, familial, she would instantly have a place in the broader tapestry of people that would be marked as hers. She would be secure, entrenched behind the armor of family that in her mind was somehow synonymous with fortress. *Family.* The word seemed to reverberate in her mind: those who cared whether you lived or died, to whom it mattered when you were sad and who took joy when you were happy. Seeing the steady stream of people on the streets beneath, she thought, You don't know, you take your relationships for granted without understanding how meaningful they are. Her heart quickened as she said softly, "In an indifferent world it gives you place and status."

Somewhere in the inner recesses of Emmy's mind a warning bell sounded. She knew she was putting too much hope into this reunion with her sisters, placing too much emphasis on their being out of the same seed. What if they did not have the same need? She thought about Tana and wondered. Supposing none of them had anything in common . . . were too entrenched in their own lives to have room for each other?

Well, it was too late for these considerations now; what she had done was irrevocable. She thought about Elizabeth, and the note she had written when Emmy had left for Canada. It applied now: "God be between you and harm through all the many places you must go." The thought of Elizabeth warmed her; she realized her hands were cold with nerves. Sharply a sound penetrated her reverie—the phone was ringing. As she picked it up, she heard the soft rapping on the door and called out, "Just a second—coming." Holding the phone, she heard the operator announce, "Mrs. Cooper is on the way up."

Trembling, she opened the door to face Amy Beth. For a split second they looked at each other in silence, and then Amy flew into Emmy's arms. They stood in a shaken embrace for a long moment.

Emmy flicked on the main light switch. "Let me look at you. Can you believe we didn't recognize each other that night? You've grown into such a beautiful woman, Amy Beth."

Their eyes were filled, and Amy had difficulty talking.

"Emmy, after all these years we're actually together, free to be with each other. How did you ever find me?"

Emmy laughed exultantly. "It wasn't easy, Amy. I've been looking for a long time."

"I had no idea." Amy looked at her sister shyly. "I gave up hoping a long time ago."

"But I wrote," Emmy protested. "I tried to keep in touch. My mother did everything she could to convince your folks to let us see each other."

"They didn't want me to see you, to remember you. It's the most amazing thing to Peter and me that my mother broke down and told your man where to find me. It was the wonder of wonders. Their whole idea was for me not to remember the past or have any contact with anyone from it. Oh, Emmy, it was awful!"

"It's all over, darling, all over." Emmy's eyes glowed. "We've found each other. I never stopped thinking about you, wondering and hoping. It's my dream come true, at last."

Amy asked eagerly, "Is Tana Corgan really Polly Sue?"

"Isn't that incredible? Isn't this wonderful? I can't get over our sitting here and talking. But let me tell you what's happened with her."

Briefly Emmy told about the search for the family and her encounters with Tana Corgan. "At the start, of course, I had no idea who she was, but then it all come to light. It seems, from what we can make out, she was never told she was adopted. Even with the evidence, she may decide to reject us. One thing's sure, she disliked me on sight. She practically threw me out of the house I had rented, which by some strange streak of fate belonged to her. I must tell you honestly, up till now she's given me very little reason to like her . . . but I've made up my mind to give her a chance."

Amy's eyes bugged through the recital. "Hey, what a coincidence! I work at the same studio. I'm a receptionist and I get to see her from time to time, although I doubt if she even knows I exist."

Emmy grinned broadly. "Isn't life crazy! All three of us being so close and not knowing it. I'm so excited I'm forgetting my manners—are you hungry, would you like a drink?"

Hesitantly Amy said, "I don't drink too often . . . you know I was reared so strictly."

"Yes, I know. I heard about your upbringing. Oh, Amy, I was so fortunate. I wished so often you'd been lucky enough to have had Elizabeth for a mother. She regretted not taking you to her dying day."

Wistfully Amy said, "I didn't know she had died. She was a sweet lady."

"She was a marvelous person."

"You know," Amy said, "in honor of the occasion I'll take a glass of wine. Peter and I have wine when we celebrate special things. What could be more special than this?"

Emmy rose to serve the wine. "You're a sweetheart, Amy Beth. I can't tell you how good it feels to be sitting here with you. I have to pinch myself to be sure it's real." She struggled to open the bottle and then filled two glasses. "Help yourself to some of these." She indicated the platter and stood back to study her sister. "You're a lovely young woman! I can still see that skinny, bandy-legged little girl from the schoolyard so long ago."

Amy looked at her in surprise. "I'm far from beautiful, I know that!"

"Why do you refuse to believe you're beautiful? You're really a lovely woman. It's interesting, your coloring is different from ours. Do you know that everyone thinks Tana and I look a great deal alike? I'd been hearing it for years but never made the connection."

"You do look alike." Amy shook her head emphatically. "Yet there's a difference. It'll be interesting to see you together. Somehow, Em, I think you're softer looking. She's always so made up. I think she looks hard."

"Well, I look older in any case. It riled her no end that everyone thought we resembled each other. Tell me about your Peter—I'm dying to hear."

The two sat in cozy closeness talking until the telephone interrupted them.

As Emmy replaced the phone on the hook, she was amused as she told Amy, "Tana's traveling incognito; she's announced herself as Miss Corrigan. Get ready for the fireworks—our baby sister is en route."

Amy could barely repress a gasp as Emmy, responding to the knock at the door, revealed Tana Corgan posed in the doorframe peering at them through sunglasses. Amy was magnetized by the sight of the two women together. Both so strikingly attractive, she thought; it's true they look alike, but yet they're so different.

Any attempt Emmy made at cordiality was met with quiet rebuff as Tana reluctantly removed her coat. "Let me introduce you," Emmy offered, as Tana moved toward the couch. "This is Amy Beth Cooper." Before she had finished, a frown crossed Tana's face. Staring down at Amy's upturned face, she asked, "Haven't I seen you somewhere before?"

There was no doubt she intimidated Amy, who replied abjectly, "I'm the receptionist at the studio executive offices."

Tana drew back in obvious disdain as Emmy hastily interjected, "Will it be all right if I call you Tana? Please sit down. No matter how you feel about us, you will have to admit this is an odd series of coincidences. I had no idea you two had met. Tana, if we're right, Amy Beth would be your middle sister."

Tana Corgan looked at them in amused skepticism, and Amy seemed to shrink into the cushions. Emmy tried to alter the mood. "Please, make yourself comfortable. Can I get you something to drink?"

She was relieved to see she had hit the mark as Tana answered with a miserly smile, "Yes, please—a vodka martini would do nicely. It was a bumpy trip. I don't know why I fly, I hate it so."

Tana watched closely as Emmy, making attempts at small talk, put the ingredients together. "I'm not too good at this—coach me if you like."

"One more jigger of vodka, please. I like them strong."

Emmy complied and handed her the glass. "Help yourself." She indicated the tiny sandwiches.

Sitting as though she had been turned to stone, Amy felt her mind racing. Both her sisters behaved as if they were princesses; she felt as if she was Cinderella. Those two were bound to clash, and Emmy was going to have a difficult time handling the situation. Enthralled, Amy was like a moth drawn to a flame; she couldn't take her eyes from Tana's face.

Coldly scrutinizing Amy, Tana said meaningfully, "You sit in the outer office at the front desk, don't you? I'll bet you hear a lot of gossip. Tell me, didn't you recently meet another Griffon?"

Amy looked at her as if she were crazy. She had no idea what Tana Corgan was referring to. Catching Emmy's glance, she shrugged her shoulders to indicate this.

Scornfully Tana turned to Emmy. "I believe the gentleman in question is your brother-in-law, Mrs. Griffon."

Surprised, Emmy said, "If you're referring to Bill Griffon,

why, yes, he's my former brother-in-law. Pardon my asking, Tana, but neither Amy nor I understand what you're getting at. What has all of this to do with us?"

"Don't you know, Mrs. Cooper?" she asked pointedly as Amy regarded her in astonishment.

Finding her voice, Amy said, "I know the man you're talking about. He's come through a few times, but that's the extent of what I know about him. I didn't even know until just now he was Emmy's brother-in-law. . . . Emmy, did you say former?"

"Yes, I did, darling. Last week, with my divorce decree, Bill became former."

A round O formed on Amy's lips and Tana smiled derisively. "That's interesting. I had no idea." She sipped her drink and seemed to be thinking, and then she said loftily, "I'm not too fond of the Griffon men myself. How's that for a starter?"

Emmy was genuinely puzzled by Tana's strange conversation, but Amy, whose courage had been restored by the wine she was rapidly sipping, said, "Isn't it remarkable that we're all together again? I can't get over your turning out to be our baby sister, Polly Sue."

As if snapped back to the reality of the meeting, Tana said tartly, "That has yet to be proven. Quite frankly I think, in my case, you've made a mistake."

Musing out loud before Emmy could answer, Amy said, "I remember now . . . it was in the schoolyard you told me, Em, you'd been to see Polly Sue at the Corrigans'."

"Yes, you're right, Amy." Emmy caught the surprise on Tana's face at the mention of the Corrigan name. "It was after I recovered from diphtheria. My mother had promised to take me to visit you both. I remember we drove out to the Corrigan farm. I recall your mother, Polly Sue. She was a warm, sweet little Irish lady. I can still remember how intrigued I was by her Irish brogue. You were a darling, chubby little girl, and, young as I was, I could see how much she loved you."

Tana sat expressionless and Emmy continued. "I distinctly remember I didn't mind your being with her, even though I was upset at our being separated from each other."

Attentively studying the glass in her hand from which she had already drained the contents, Tana refused to look at either of them. She set the glass down and toyed with the olive. Finally she raised her head and her voice was edged as she spoke. "This is creepy. Look, you two, I came here more as a lark than anything. I believe you're sincere, but it has to be a case of mistaken identity. I don't deny my real name is Polly Sue Corrigan, and it's also obvious we look alike, Mrs. Griffon, but I'm certain I was not adopted."

Amy was jolted, but Emmy had been expecting this. She kept her voice gentle as she said, "Of course this has to be a tremendous shock, and you are free to think whatever you wish, but I believe it would be in your best interest to hear the full story. Before you slam the door, please be reasonable. You can't attribute all of this to coincidence—my knowing your family's name, remembering your mother, that we all lived in the same town. That is where we were abandoned."

At this Tana looked at her in amazement. "Abandoned?"

"Yes," Emmy said. "We were abandoned by our parents."

Tana's face flushed and she looked at her curiously as Emmy said, "You were just a baby. I think under the circumstances you wouldn't have known what was happening. Now, let me assure you, if after hearing the facts you decide you want nothing to do with us, we won't argue with you; you'll be free to do as you wish. No one is going to make a federal case out of this. I've been searching for my lost family too many years to be put off now."

Assuming an air of suffering patience, Tana extended her glass for a refill and leaned back, saying, "If it's a long story, please freshen this."

Amused, Emmy said, "Why don't you make yourself at home and help yourself? I'm not very good at mixing drinks."

Uncurling herself from the couch, Tana walked to the bar. Amy and Emmy exchanged sympathetic glances as they watched her pour almost a full glass of vodka, add a dash of vermouth and an ice cube. When she had reseated herself, Emmy commented, "It's interesting seeing us together. There's a strong familial resemblance."

With a contemptuous toss of her head, Tana said wryly, "Hey, you're not going to pull that. This woman here"—she pointed at Amy—"looks nothing like us."

Amy giggled. "That's true. You're both so dark and stunning. If I didn't know you were the baby, I'd take you and Em for twins."

Instantly roused, Tana glared. "Don't be stupid! We just have a superficial resemblance. As for you, you're completely different—blond and bland."

Amy wilted under the rebuke. The sting lashed and Emmy

retorted icily, "It's silly, Tana, that you're so bothered by our resemblance. We may look alike, but that's where it ends. Amy and I know we are sisters, and, although you're not giving us cause to be happy about it, we also know you are our baby sister."

Tana was not the least put off. "Fire away, Mrs. Griffon. As long as I'm here I might as well listen to your precious story."

Angered, Emmy snapped, "I'd appreciate it if you would try not to be snide about something so serious."

Step by step Emmy began to recount the story of what had befallen them: the terrible Oklahoma dust storm, the car breakdown, their struggle to shelter with Elizabeth Fields, the diphtheria epidemic, the separation—each to a different family—the town of Brightwater and the suffering and anguish at the realization that their parents were not returning. As she concluded, Emmy said, "If you still have any doubts about what I've told you, I brought along documented proof. Also, in the county building in Towana, Oklahoma, there are papers still waiting the Corrigan signature signifying your legal adoption."

Suddenly it seemed as though Tana's assurance had begun to dissolve. She looked at Emmy questioningly. "Tell me more of what you know about my family, please."

Spurred by her interest, Emmy said, "Father McGurdy, who was their priest, passed away before I could meet with him, but it seems the monk in charge at the monastery had it on good authority that your father had written to him. They found a letter from him confessing that you had never been told the circumstances of your background. It seems your father and mother were afraid you might be taken from them and ran away; they pulled up stakes and moved to Montana."

Emmy paused, moved for the first time by compassion for Tana. Despite the effects of too much alcohol she had paled, and it was obvious she was experiencing a painful bewilderment.

Amy's eyes were filled as she said softly, "The shock has to be awful, Tana, but it has to help to know how much they loved you."

They saw how her throat constricted. She sat shaking her head back and forth as if in denial. They couldn't know, as they sat quietly watching in sympathy, what a welter of pictures coursed through her mind: Deirdre tying her hairbows, Sean lifting her onto the back of a horse, the sound of their brogue, prayers at night, stories of Ireland, the horrible news of her mother's death, her father's fury. The pain was almost unendurable. She didn't want to give way to the hurt. . . . She felt ill. She struggled to push the feeling away. Suddenly her voice was strident in the quiet room. "It can't be true—it's all a lie! You've got your nerve trying to sell me that story. You can't expect me to swallow it."

She attempted to stand and staggered. Amy jumped to assist her. "Get your hands off me. I can take care of myself."

Emmy whispered, "Let her be, dear." Raising her voice, she spoke firmly. "I understand, Tana, what's happening here tonight won't cause you to like me any more than you do, although I don't really know why you dislike me. Maybe it will help to change your feelings if I tell you that all my life I've been looking for you, wanting to know you, to be your sister with whatever that word can mean. Today is sort of letting blood for each of us. We're uncovering heartaches and wounds that still bleed. At least that's the way it seems to me. It's like a knife in each of our hearts dredging up the past—but maybe, if we can share this with each other, we'll have something in common . . . something to tie us together."

Tana's jaw tightened in fear at the proof to come, to be revealed. Emmy saw it was time to let the matter rest awhile. Tana pushed her glass toward Emmy again and, seeing it, Emmy said, "Hon, I think you've had enough to drink for a while. Let's arrange for dinner."

Eager for a brawl, Tana scolded, "Donchu dare order me around! I've had as much of you as I can stand for one day. I don't like you—you make me sick!"

She rose but tumbled back into the seat as they watched in consternation.

Emmy walked to the telephone. "Amy, there's a menu on the table next to you; decide what you want. We'll have room service bring it up. Our sister is in no condition for a public appearance."

As if in reply, Tana kicked off her shoes and sprawled out on the couch.

Emmy asked, "Tana, is there anything special you'd like?"

She mumbled, "Order for me" and closed her eyes, seeming to fall asleep.

Picking up the vodka bottle, Emmy showed it to Amy. It was almost empty. She put it out of sight and then placed their dinner order.

Amy and Emmy sat talking quietly, exhausted from the ordeal they had been through with Polly Sue. Some time later, when the knock sounded on the door, Amy gently roused Tana. "Dinner's here. Wouldn't you care to freshen up?"

It was a relief to see she responded without a fight. When all was in readiness and the waiter had left, Emmy called, "If you're ready, Tana, dinner's waiting."

She looked better when she reentered the room, and Amy said, "Doesn't that dinner look sumptuous, Polly Sue?"

Instantly she rasped, "Don't call me Polly Sue!"

Seating herself, Emmy said, "Oh, come on. Whether you admit to being our sister or not is beside the point. Your real name is Polly Sue. What's the harm?"

It was apparent she was full of quick contradictions as she countered amiably, "True! It's just that no one calls me that anymore. I'm hungry."

As they ate, Amy and Emmy reminisced about old times in Brightwater, and Amy told how she and Peter had made the trip to visit Aunt Tina.

Emmy asked, "Didn't she know I was there? It was the last time Jonathan and I went back. Your old schoolteacher told us about Tina Ondinka and how she befriended you. She told us what a well-kept secret it was because of the brutal way the Wilkersons treated you and no one wanted you to get into trouble because of her. She never mentioned knowing where you were."

Amy winced and Tana, who had been eating steadily, looked at her with new interest. Swallowing what she had in her mouth, she said, "I've been told suffering's good for the soul. Experience is the best teacher . . . you should be very kind. Is it true?"

Impatiently Emmy snapped, "Don't you have any sensitivity for anyone but yourself?"

For answer she got a smirk. Ignoring Tana, Emmy said, "That old Indian lady must have been very special. The schoolteacher told us just a bit of what you endured. You must have lived through years of torture."

Tana was regarding Emmy with an indignant stare and she cut in. "Why don't you stop being so superior? You act as if you know everything. Would you mind telling me, were there three girls who each got placed in a different family? Amy, from the sound of it, you took the prize."

Amy nodded sadly and Tana said matter-of-factly, "That

accounts for your being so Milquetoasty. Each time I've seen you I thought you looked terrfied of your own shadow."

Emmy showed her irritation. "Now who's being superior, Miss Movie Star? I thought you heard the story. Our parents abandoned us, and each of us was given to a different family."

The conversation was heating up, and Amy's eyes glinted angrily. "I wasn't as fortunate as either of you, Polly Sue. I lived in constant fear, and for your information, I was a very little girl . . . not much older than you. I was beaten near to death . . . I lived in hell. From what I've seen of you I doubt whether you'd have had the *guts* to live through it."

Tana wasn't insulted; she seemed to take it equably, studying Amy, and then, satisfied, said, "Really, who would think it? You don't look capable of swatting a fly."

They broke into laughter, after which Emmy asked, "How much of what I told you registered, Tana?"

"I heard you, I didn't miss a thing. I still don't believe it has anything to do with me. I'm curious: why are you spending all this time and money looking for parents who pulled such a stinking thing? Who'd want to know them, let alone find them?"

Trying to frame an answer, Emmy was startled when Amy banged her fist on the table. "Geez, Tana, you're a case. Why don't you stop denying what you know is the truth? They were your lousy parents too! *You are our sister,* and I'm frank to tell you, the way you're behaving, I'm not too happy about it. You surely didn't learn any manners where you came from."

At this, Tana jumped up, upsetting her water glass. Her teeth clenched and she spat, "Don't you dare talk that way about my folks. They were wonderful and they brought me up good and proper. I don't give a damn if you don't like my manners. For my part, you can both go right to the devil."

"Sit down, Tana . . . stop squabbling," Emmy said. "Let's try to be kinder to each other."

When they had simmered down, Emmy resumed. "I've been told our real mother is alive and living here in San Francisco."

Tana snickered. "You must be kidding. Are you sure this isn't a movie script?"

At this, Amy flushed and said, "Em, there's something I have to tell you."

They listened quietly as she related the encounter with

their mother at the aircraft plant. When she finished, Tana exploded. "Are you saying this woman told you who she was and you weren't curious enough to find out what it was all about? God, you're a milksop!"

They were at it again. Tana poured it on. "You didn't have the backbone to face that woman and let her have it. What kind of person are you?"

Amy's eyes filled and Emmy interceded again. "It's easy for you to talk, Tana—don't be so quick to judge. You didn't have to live with Amy's family. Please, let's stop this bickering."

Suddenly Amy came to life. "I want to know, since you're sure this has nothing to do with you, why you're so upset."

Tana stared at her without answering. Then, in almost a whisper, she asked, "Could I see the papers you have? You said you had letters and things."

The first breakthrough. Emmy rose to get the folder. As she moved to leave the room, Tana grabbed her by the arm. "Do you know what you've done to me today? My father—at least the man I always thought was my real father—only told me recently I was 'like the people who borned me.' I didn't know what he meant." Her voice broke. "I thought he meant I was like him. I wasn't a very good daughter . . . I'd probably make an even lousier sister. You'll be sorry you found me. I adored my folks—they were the world to me. I knew I meant everything to them, but I took them for granted. I neglected them . . . I was too busy to think about them . . ." Tears were pouring down her cheeks. "I didn't have time but I thought they understood I loved them."

She looked at them, appealing for some sort of absolution, but no one said anything and she continued. "I was always a fresh kid. My mother did the best she could to make a lady out of me. They spoiled me rotten. It seems natural to be the way I am."

Emmy moved away and returned with a folder of papers. Tana immediately began to look through them, passing them on to Amy as she finished. Her face ran the gamut from shock to anguish as she bit her lip at the realization of the truth. Her eyes were filled with tears as she looked at Emmy and said softly, almost to herself, "It's hard to believe, but I can't deny the evidence. Why didn't they ever give me a hint? It's awful finding out this way."

A tear dropped, and she muffled her voice in her handkerchief. "They loved me a lot, I know that. It must have been terrible for them."

Emmy tried to console her. "Listen, they were your parents in every way they could be. I'm sure they knew you loved them."

Mercurially her manner altered and she blustered, "Don't be a fool! I told you how I treated them."

Emmy said, "We were lucky, you and I. At least we knew love. You know, even though I dislike the Wilkersons, seeing Amy Beth here and knowing she's a happily married woman, I have to admit we probably were all lucky."

Amy sighed. "What's the use of rehashing old miseries? We're all grown and free to do as we wish. I for one am thrilled to have found you, to be with you both."

At this Emmy looked up and said reluctantly, "There's one more thing to be settled . . . in any case, for me. Would either of you be interested in going with me to meet our mother?"

There was dead silence and Emmy said softly, "I'll understand if you don't. I want to hear the story directly from her lips. That's the least she owes us."

Amy didn't look up; her fingers drummed on the tabletop. "You remember our parents, Em? Do you recall anything about them?" She raised her head. "When I met that woman at the factory I would never have known she was our mother . . . of course, she was much older. Sometimes I think I remember our father. Did he have black curly hair?"

"Yes," Emmy said. "It was a long time ago and I was little also. But there are some things I remember. The clearest memory is a birthday party."

Amy's eyes glowed. "I think I remember that, Em. There was a cake and a candle . . . wasn't there another man?"

"You do remember," Emmy said excitedly.

"I don't remember a thing," Tana said.

They laughed. Amy said, "You were an infant," and Emmy added, "I remember you crying. Momma said you had the colic. She was pretty. Our daddy was strong and laughed a lot. I remember he used to throw us up in the air and catch us."

Amy's face was wreathed in smiles. "Em, it's such a relief to know I didn't dream that. For so long I was afraid to even think of them. I was told over and over again what terrible people they were."

Emmy's voice was resolute as she replied, "My adopted mother, Elizabeth, always told me our folks appeared to be decent people who got trapped in awful circumstances. I don't say they were right to leave us, but I don't think we ought to be ashamed. We don't know what really happened. Elizabeth drummed that into me. She never said one harsh or unkind word about them, Amy. She always tried to make me understand they probably couldn't help themselves."

Scornfully Amy said, "Try to tell that to Deborah Wilkerson."

Roused, Emmy snapped, "Well, don't you ever permit yourself to feel ashamed again, hear, Amy? No matter what, you're not responsible for what they did."

Following this, their mood became easier. While Emmy and Amy reminisced about what they recalled of their family, Tana sat brooding, drinking her coffee, seemingly listening. Suddenly, without warning, she cut in on what they were saying. "Ladies, I have something to say. It'll be better if I give it to you straight. I'm willing to admit that I'm probably your long-lost sister—but seeing as how you've lived without me a long time, why complicate your lives again? It's interesting and all that, but it isn't going to change or make the least difference in my life." She paused, looking at their shocked faces. "I'm Tana Corgan and that's all that matters to me. You might as well know I don't give a damn anymore about family. I've already spelled it out: I gave the two best people in the world a kick in the ass. If I were you, I'd say good riddance to bad rubbish."

She laughed ironically as they looked at her, dumbfounded. "You could say, if you're ever asked, I'm the black sheep of the family." She stood up. "It won't affect you one bit if I just go on my way."

Disbelievingly, Emmy and Amy stared at her until Amy said sharply, "How can you talk that way? Doesn't it mean anything to you that we've just found each other after all these years?"

Tossing her head, Tana shrugged. "See! That's just what I mean. You have to understand, I'm not the least bit moved by all this corny stuff. There's no room in my life for this kind of sentimental attachment. All right?" They couldn't realize her anger had demonic energy fed from despair. She swayed with it and her voice edged each word sharply to give meaning to her hatred—at the agonizing stripping away of her roots—at the horrible discovery they had forced upon her this day. "I don't want anyone hanging on Tana Corgan's coattails. I've got all I can do just pulling myself along. I'm dedicated to my career; that's my family. I don't want any entanglements or anything to interfere. Besides, face it, you don't like me, you said it before, and just because I turned out to be your sister doesn't change things. Why don't you both pretend you never found me?"

The callousness of Tana's rejection was too sharp a blow for Emmy. The frustration, disappointments and heartbreak of the past years welled up; she felt as though she were crumpling. It couldn't be; it was too bitter a pill to swallow. It was beyond her comprehension, she refused to accept it, to believe this jeering woman's unfeeling attitude. Blind fury took over at the realization that this woman who was their sister intended to turn her back on them and smash their newfound world to smithereens. Emmy screamed, "How dare you? Do you hear what you're saying? You treated the Corrigans the same way! You're a miserable ingrate! Do you really think your career can be a substitute for caring people? You're right. You're an inconsiderate, conceited, empty-headed ass! I'm sorry we ever bothered with you. Get out!"

There was silence. Then, with an air of insolent bravura, Tana moved to pick up her bag and coat. Turning to them with a contemptuous toss of her head, she said mockingly, "Thanks for your hospitality and the interesting stories. There's one other thing . . . if you see that woman you said was your mother, don't mention me. I don't want some old sop telling the world she's my neglected old mom."

Scorn flicked across her face as she lashed out at Emmy, her voice shrill. "All you Griffons are pompous fools—hypocrites! You can't face the truth. You think the world belongs to you. The thought of being related to you makes me sick. Ta-ta . . . see you around."

She left without a backward glance, and stunned silence filled the vacuum. The cyclone that was Tana Corgan had whirled in and whirled out of their lives.

Tears stung Emmy's eyes as desolation overcame her, and she murmured, "It's turned out so differently from what I dreamed. I'm great at self-delusion."

Amy looked so forlorn that Emmy immediately reproached herself. "Oh, Amy, I'm sorry. I wish it had been different. I just couldn't take any more. How could she sluff us off the way she did?"

Raising her head, Amy stared fixedly at Emmy. "Maybe

she's wiser than you think. She could be right about herself, you know. You have to understand, Emmy, we've all lived different lives, and you can't just wave a magic wand and make us automatically love and care about each other."

Fear filled Emmy. Was Amy right? Had she expected too much of them? "Amy, I was sure there were moments when she felt the way we did. Whatever her reasons, she didn't want to, I guess. . . . I was wrong to lose my temper."

Amy got up and walked around the room, studying the paintings on the wall. Suddenly she turned and said, "She's very unhappy. She's got more of a conscience than we give her credit for. She tried to keep it under wraps because she wants to appear hard. We were a little rough on her, considering it was only a short time since she learned she'd been adopted. Maybe I'm crazy, but I feel sorry for her."

Emmy was desolated at what she felt was Amy's reproach. "Maybe you're right, but I have to be honest—I don't like her, she's been awful to me from the first moment. . . . And this vendetta with the Griffons—I don't get it."

Amy smiled. "Don't blame yourself. She wasn't going to take us on any terms. You did exactly what she wanted; you played right into her hands by giving her an excuse. She's got to have some reasons; otherwise how could she live with herself? It must be awful for her finding out the Corrigans weren't really her parents."

"What difference would it have made if she'd known?"

Sighing, Amy said, "Obviously, she has a conscience, Em, and it kills her. I hear she drowns it in drink."

Emmy looked at Amy with new respect. "You've really got it figured out. I hate myself for losing my temper. Maybe if I'd handled it differently . . . given her a chance."

Shrugging, Amy said, "Try to forget it. She told us plainly she wanted out, no ties."

"True, but maybe she'd have reconsidered."

Amy was adamant. "I don't think so. Not at this time anyhow. I'm sure she felt if she acknowledged us in some way she'd be obligated."

Regretfully Emmy gave way. "I guess so. She probably feels she'd have to rearrange her life. Well, it's her loss—she won't get to spend time with us; share Christmases, our children and all those good things."

Amy laughed. "It's too bad. You know, it's going to be a ticklish situation when she comes into the office. I wonder how she's going to handle that."

Emmy snapped, "Just the way she always has."

Amy turned solemn. "In that case, I won't have to worry. She's not the most popular lady around with the commoners." She shook her head with dismay. "They make such a fuss over these people it's hard for them to keep their feet on the ground."

"Does she really have a drinking problem?"

Perplexed, Amy stared at her. "I don't know for sure. It's been rumored. The studio frowns on anything like that."

"Well, I think she does. Did you see the way her hands shake? She drank an awful lot in a short time."

Amy rose and stretched. "Well, it's not our responsibility. I say let's be grateful for what we have."

"Have you given any thought to what I asked you before, Amy, about visiting our mother?" Emmy waited hopefully.

Hesitating for a moment and grimacing with distaste, Amy said, "I guess so, Em. I couldn't face Pete if I didn't . . . which reminds me, I have to call him."

Emmy sighed with relief. At least Amy would accompany her to see their mother.

Chapter XXX

◦⟨⟩◦

MARY ANN BEAUFORD

EMMY STRETCHED AS the sun hit her eyes. She had slept so well. All the tensions and pressures of the day before were gone. She rolled over to see Amy's blond head pillowed on the other bed. She called out, "Sleepyhead, it must be late."

Amy rolled over. "I'm awake. I just didn't want to disturb you. It looks like a great day. You know, Em, I've never been to San Francisco before."

"In that case, let's shake a leg and we'll make a tour of the city. "

They both avoided mentioning the appointment they faced later that afternoon.

As they dressed, Amy asked, "Sis, shall I wear a dress or my suit?"

For that appellation, Emmy was prepared to give her the world. "Wear your suit. It may be chilly this time of the year. We'll go out for dinner and you can wear that pretty dress. I've got a coat you can wear over it. Okay?"

"Fine!" Amy was pulling her slip over her head as she asked, "Do you feel as happy and proud as I do that we're sisters?"

"I feel ten times that way, Puss," Emmy said.

Laughing, Amy said, "I must resemble a cat . . . Pete's favorite name for me is Puss."

"Is that so? I don't know why I called you that, somehow it just came out. I'm interested in hearing more about your Peter—how you met, everything about your life."

480

Amy poked her head out of the bathroom door . . . "We've got a lot of ground to cover. It isn't every day one finds a sister who's just been divorced and has a Larry. Do you know, I've never met a divorced person."

Busily applying her lipstick, Emmy watched Amy's face in the mirror. She stopped and asked, "Does it bother you? You know, with your background and all?"

Coming into the room, Amy said, "No. It's just new to me. I'm not prying . . . you don't have to tell me anything if you don't want to . . . "

"Why not? I'm not going to keep any secrets from you. It's a long story, but I'll tell it to you."

Amy smiled shyly. "Pete says I'm unworldly. Boy, won't he be surprised when he finds out I have a divorced sister."

"You're a card. I think your Pete's a lucky fellow to have you."

After a leisurely breakfast, Emmy ordered the car and told Amy, "We'll hit all the high spots, Amy. I want you to see as much as we have time for."

They traversed the streets of the city and to Amy's delight began the crossing of the Golden Gate Bridge. She exclaimed at the view: the beautiful blue circle of the bay beneath, its waters dotted with small craft moving briskly under wind-filled sails, ships and boats busily plying back and forth; grim and forbidding Alcatraz sitting squat and stolid, isolated on its rock; the picture-card outlines of Sausalito ahead; and in the background San Francisco's buildings framing it all. Amy felt relaxed and comfortable. It was easy to be with her sister. "You know, Em, we're turning out to be the kind of friends I always imagined sisters could be. I have to confess, after being apart so long, I was frightened about getting together . . . but it's been wonderful. I can talk to you so easily. I can tell you anything."

Deftly turning the wheel, Emmy rounded the corner. "It beats all, Amy. I have to pinch myself to believe we're really together, saying the same things. In a million years you'll never know how I've longed for this moment. My only regret is you never got to really know Elizabeth. You two would have loved each other." She paused and then grinned sheepishly. "I'm still ashamed of the way I acted with Polly Sue yesterday. I keep thinking if I hadn't lost my temper things might have turned out differently."

"Forget it, Em. She was determined to do exactly what she

did. Do you know when she made up her mind to cut out on us?"

"When?"

Amy smiled ruefully. "It was when you asked if we'd go with you to visit our mother. I honestly think it was more than she could bear. It was the straw that broke the camel's back. After all, she didn't do too well with the one she had, and you must have frightened her out of her wits without knowing it."

Openmouthed, Emmy looked at her sister in astonishment. "I can't get over how clever you are. I wasn't thinking. How could I have behaved so stupidly?"

Grinning, pleased at the compliment, Amy giggled. "Well, I think I have an answer for that too. It was only natural—you were so eager to gather us into your arms you just assumed we'd feel the same way." Seeing Emmy's expression alter, she hastily added, "Of course I felt the same way, but Polly Sue didn't even know she had sisters. Em, give it time . . . maybe she'll change her mind."

Shaking her head dubiously, Emmy said, "No chance. She already had a hate for me. Why should she ever reconsider?"

Thoughtfully Amy concurred. "I wouldn't bank on it, but who knows? Maybe she'll have a change of heart. We'll just have to wait and see."

Emmy had manipulated the car into a parking space and, opening the door, declared, "Okay, no more of that today. Come on—last stop. Fisherman's Wharf. After which we'll head for our mission."

Amy grimaced. "I get queasy when I think of it. It's like turning back the pages of a book."

"Listen, hon, maybe you shouldn't. I'll drop you back at the hotel and you can wait for me there."

"No, Emmy! If you can do it, so can I. I'm not running away this time. She belonged to me as much as to you. In the long run, I have to be the better for knowing the truth, don't you think?"

"I can't give you any guarantee, Amy, but I hope so."

The pungent aroma of seafood and shellfish displayed in the different stalls lining the wharf beckoned as they made their way down the street.

On the drive to the meeting with their mother, they sat in silence. The area they were entering was different from the bustling atmosphere they'd just left. Amy seemed withdrawn as she stared out the window. Emmy remarked, "We're almost there."

Amy turned to her. "It's an awful-looking area, Em."

"Yes, it's seen better days. It's a very old section, probably been here since the earthquake."

Her voice wistful, Amy commented, "It looks so sad. The houses seem ready to fall down."

"Everything's so neglected; rotting wood and peeling paint don't help. I'm surprised the houses aren't condemned—they must be firetraps."

Amy said reflectively, "Although she wore a uniform when I met her at the plant, she seemed well put together. Somehow I can't picture her living in such a poor and shabby neighborhood.

Just then Emmy said, "Hold on to your hat—we're here! This is the street."

She turned a corner and pulled up in front of a decrepit two-story house. They sat still for a moment and then Emmy said, "Ready? Come on!"

Reluctantly Amy opened the door as Emmy came around. She looked at her sister. "Emmy, I could cry. It's like the last stop for hopes and dreams."

Emmy didn't answer. They held each other's hands as they started up the rickety steps. When they reached the stoop, Emmy declared, "I'm frightened! What are we going to find?"

Her face showed how panic-stricken she was. Her heart pounded; her mind was in tumult. What had she expected; what was she really seeking? Her senses conveyed how foolishly she'd colored her dreams. She'd always envisioned a trim little white house surrounded by colorful flowers and a white picket fence. Inside, sitting in a chair, would be the figure of the mother she dimly remembered—a young and pretty woman, smiling with a warm, welcoming embrace. Shaking, she cautioned the trembling Amy, "Be prepared. None of this is going to match our dreams."

Desperately Emmy took a deep breath and, summoning her courage, turned the handle of the outside door. The mélange of odors that met their nostrils made them gag. Amy pulled back. Emmy also wanted to, but determinedly she grabbed Amy's arm. They could not come this far without accomplishing their purpose. No matter to what end, she had to see what all the years of search and hope had to disclose. They would see it through.

The hall was dark and unlit. Emmy peered at the nearest door and checked with the paper in her hand. She had memorized the address and apartment number, but she wanted to be sure. Holding Amy in an iron grip, she entreated, "Help me find it. It's Neely-Forbes, number 3." Fervently she hoped it wasn't on the upper floor.

Stumbling against each other, they moved down the gloomy hall, trying to decipher the numbers. At the very end they found it. Emmy was unable to control her shaking; she was overcome by fear of what awaited them. She was disgusted with herself. Why had she persisted; why was she allowing her dreams to disintegrate? Filled with regret, her mind was suddenly flooded with visions of Elizabeth. Why hadn't she listened to her? Why had she done this? Where had she gotten all those crazy ideas: charming interiors, Christmas trees, gaily wrapped packages saved through time, smiling faces—whose? She'd had to have been insane all these years. She stood, mesmerized by her thoughts. How could I have brought this upon myself and Amy? Why couldn't I have left it as it was? Dear God, Elizabeth, save me from what's coming! The premonition of disaster was so strong she could barely raise her hand to rap on the door. She broke into an icy sweat and her eyes blurred. Too late; her hand, seemingly with a will of its own, had knocked on the door. She could hear Amy's breathing over the hammering of her own heart. This torture was ridiculous. She turned to grab Amy's arm and run, but someone was fumbling with the knob.

Emmy stood paralyzed as the door cracked open. Through a haze she discerned a tiny figure, a skeletal apparition that seemed to waver as it stared out at them. She heard Amy's gasp and she reached back to pull her close. As the door swung wider, the face that looked at them wrinkled into a smile. Emmy's instant reaction was, My God, she looks like a little monkey. Amy's stomach heaved; it couldn't be the same woman, it's a joke, she's made up like a clown. The shrunken, wrinkled little face was thickly pasted with garish makeup in a pathetic attempt to cover the years, to hide the ravages of illness and time. Bright red streaks of lipstick had been applied over and below the lips. Eyes dim with age and wavering hands had not been able to ascertain their mark. The total effect was bizarre; the housedress and the old-fashioned spike-heeled shoes which caused her to totter were grotesque.

Emmy wasn't sure how many minutes elapsed before she realized the quivery sounds she heard were emanating from the weird little creature standing before them. The voice was thin and reedy. It kept repeating, "Come in, come in. I got your letter a few days ago."

Emmy turned wooden. If it hadn't been for Amy's shove, she'd have remained rooted to the spot. It was only with the greatest effort that she was able to put one foot after another to follow the tottering figure into the room. She drew strength from the knowledge that Amy was close behind her.

The room's interior was almost as dark as the hall; a dim, unshaded lamp bulb served as the sole light. She almost tripped over the woman, who stopped abruptly and gestured, "Sit down—sit there." She pointed to a small, broken-down couch.

Gingerly they sat down as directed. She perched herself on an old wooden rocker next to a cluttered table. They watched speechlessly as the woman reached for her glasses. Once they were in place, she leaned forward to study them. She shook her head as she murmured, "I can't believe it. After all these years. You must be Emmalina." She pointed a finger at her and then leaned toward Amy. "Who are you? Are you the one I met? Amy, Amy Beth, is that you?"

They were dumbstruck. Still scrutinizing them, she said, "It's a miracle. Who'd o thought it? Bend nearer—I want to get as good a look as I can."

She peered into each of their faces and, finally satisfied, sat back. "What good-lookin girls you are."

She turned to Emmy. "You were the oldest. I remember. You were the firstborn—Emmalina, aren't you?"

She pointed at Amy, who was almost rigid. "You be the second one. Danny was certain you'd be a boy. You sure was a disappointment when you came, but he said you was the spittin image of his mother and he loved you special for that."

The sight of tears rolling from the rheumy eyes shocked them back to reality. Emmy was startled to hear Amy say, "Yes, ma'am."

She saw Amy flinch as the woman's claw-like hand reached out to touch her. The woman drew it back and now sat quietly, tears coursing down her cheeks, distorting the makeup and her face even more. Emmy forced herself to think; I've got to get myself in hand. I came here looking for her, she didn't ask for this.

The mixture of odors in the room and the suffocating

closeness made Emmy dizzy. Her head reeled. Amy's face told her how concerned she was, but she was beyond control. The physical distress and the shock of the meeting overcame her. Emmy broke down. She cried piteously, for herself, for Amy, for the sad, wasted years of yearning and the disillusionment of their dreams embodied in this little woebegone creature, confused and helpless—their mother, who sat wringing her hands at Emmy's unhappiness.

Finally Emmy's tears were spent and she put a hand out toward the pathetic little woman huddled so sadly in the chair. She had to do it; she willed herself to smile and thankfully it worked the magic. The little lady perked up happily and smiled at both of them. "Don't cry, dearies. It'll be all right. It must be very hard on you. So many times I wondered what it would be like to have one of you girls near me, to talk to. It's hard for me to realize who you are."

She leaned toward them and confided, "You know, sometimes I think I'm a little disconnected, so if I don't sound reasonable you'll understand. But most times I can manage."

Emmy nodded as an involuntary shudder ran through her. At least, she thought, she talks sensibly. The woman piped up cheerily, "We can still have cozy talks together, can't we? First off, though, I want to be sure of something . . . there's another one, isn't there?"

She leaned back as if trying to remember. Emmy began to regain her composure, and the irony of the situation began to make its impact and steeled her resolve. The years of hope leading to this moment pierced her; she needed answers. "Ma'am!" She stifled the impulse to laugh at the way she addressed this woman, her mother.

The woman roused and looked at her with bird-bright eyes, expectant and waiting. "What you want to say, Emmalina? You are sure a good-lookin woman. I'd never knowed you—all grown up. You know, Emmalina, I remember once seeing one o your sisters. Now, I don't recall which one it was. She was a very pretty girl. It was a long time ago. Since I had the stroke, I sometimes don't remember . . . things get mixed up. I don't recall what happened when I saw her. I think she didn't want to see me. That's it! She never called . . . that's it!" Her voice trailed off, and her eyes closed.

Emmy looked at Amy in commiseration. A wave of compassion washed over her for all of them as she spoke.

"Yes, ma'am, you're right. I believe you did see Amy Beth. It isn't that she didn't want to see you, but her adopted mother wouldn't permit her to call you."

The eyes opened. Her face flushed and she became indignant. "Why did the girl have to tell her?"

Amy surprised Emmy as she spoke up. Her voice was hard. "You're probably right, ma'am, we all do things we have cause to regret. But now we're here, and there are many things we'd like to ask you."

The woman studied Amy with interest. "You got some spirit after all. What would you like to ask?"

For Emmy it was a relief to see the woman's show of interest. It was incongruous that this tiny creature had once been the sole focus of their world. This small spark of soul had fought and labored to give three of them life. Amy was about to speak when their mother leaned forward anxiously. "It's comin back to me. Polly Sue, darlin little Polly Sue." She almost crooned the words. "I remember now. Lord forgive me, how I missed you all. You were so precious to me. My darlin Emmalina . . . what a sweet, good little girl you were."

This time when she reached out for her hand Emmy let the parchmentlike fingers hold hers. "You were such a serious little girl. Mother's helper, that's what you were. Oh, my dear, sweet, gentle Emmalina. You were all so little, so frail and helpless. Such little mites . . . how could I take care of you? I couldn't take care of myself and he left us. He promised he would take care of us. He always told me you were the world to him. 'My girls,' he'd say. He'd find a castle for you to live in and he'd always watch out for us."

She broke into a maniacal laugh that changed to hysterical sobbing. Emmy and Amy tensed as they saw the rickety body shaking. Their presence had unleashed a flood of excruciating memories.

Emmy tried to calm her. "Please, ma'am, it was a long time ago. Please don't take on so." She extended her handkerchief, which caught the woman's interest. Still tearful, she took it, examining it eagerly before drying her eyes. "May I keep it?"

Smiling, Emmy replied, "Of course, please do."

Amy poked Emmy as she asked, "Ma'am, maybe this excitement is too much for you. Would you like us to return another day?"

Holding the handkerchief tightly, she cackled sardonically, "Oh, no, my dear. In my state, there's no knowing whether there'll be another day. Every minute counts. Let the chips fall now. Let's talk; I'm fine."

The sisters exchanged amazed glances. The woman veered from one mood to the other. She was obviously quite ill, and her mind had been affected by the stroke, but when she had lucidity, she kept on the track. "Tell me why you looked for me . . . tell me everything."

Emmy said softly, "We'll be glad to fill you in on everything, ma'am, but before that we'd appreciate it if you would tell us what happened way back there in Brightwater."

Amy showed her approval as Emmy went on to explain. "I've been looking for you for a long time. We'd like to know why you and our father left us, where you went. We'd like to know about your families. It's important to us. It would mean a great deal to hear the story from your lips. You would be doing us a great favor if you'd tell us."

She paused and saw the woman looking at her overtly, as if considering. Emmy would swear later that at that point Mary Ann had squared her frail shoulders, inhaled and taken the plunge. At first her voice was weak, but it grew stronger as she went along. "You've got a right to know. I'll tell you every blessed thing I can remember. If my memory lags and I fall asleep, you just wake me. For starts, pour a snip o that wine in this glass . . . that'll give me strength for this journey. Help yourselves girls, if you want some . . ."

Emmy poured the wine into the dirty, stained glass as the woman leaned back, closed her eyes and began her story.

"It was a long time ago . . . back in South Carolina . . . where it began. Your granddaddy was a prosperous merchant. Your grandmother and kinfolk all came from them parts." She sighed. "It was a good life. There were lots of kinfolk—aunts, uncles and cousins. It was a pretty time."

"Ma'am?" Emmy asked softly. "What were their names—your name then?"

The woman opened her eyes in surprise. "My name was Mary Ann, of course. Oh, you mean your granddaddy's name . . . it was Donald David Webster, and ifn I recall right, your grandmother's name was Pollyanna. Her kinfolk, the whole parcel o them, were Parkers and Rutlands. Out o Scotland and England, most of them—real uppity folks they were. The town we lived in was called Rutland after your grandmother's father. We had deep roots in that place. How many times I yearned to go back there—but you can see, I couldn't. I didn't dare. With everything that happened, I couldn't do that!" She paused, lost in reverie. Emmy leaned over to refill the wineglass. She had to be careful; too much wine might put her to sleep.

The woman sipped appreciatively and she seemed to ramble. "She was a right pert child, and accordin to most accounts very pretty. She didn't lack for beaux from early. She was her daddy's darlin."

She frowned as a thought occurred to her. "How many times later on I wisht I'd listened to my folks, but I didn't and I wound up with that scoundrel . . . that charming, rascally scoundrel, Daniel Defoe Beauford."

Her face was suffused with pleasure as she said, "Handsome! He was so handsome he turned every gal's head. But I'm gettin ahead o myself. One day this troupe of players came to town . . . they was actors doin plays and entertainments as they went from one town to another. Daniel, he was the star, the lead actor, and he could act so's you'd really believe he was who he was playin up there on that stage."

She opened her eyes and looked squarely at them. "That was it! From the moment I laid eyes on him, that was it! Strange enough, the marvel of it was that he felt exactly the same about her." They were disconcerted at the way she referred to herself, but they listened intently as she went on. "Even when they moved on to the next county, he'd come acourtin her. Her daddy didn't take to him, nor for that matter her mother, even though she agreed he was a good-lookin boy, nuff to turn any girl's head. It made no difference anyhow cause she loved him so. She couldn't hear, see or care what anyone said. When the time come for the troupe to be leavin the area, Danny came right and proper and asked her daddy for her hand. There was a row that day! Danny was ordered out o the house, and there she was all snivelin and cryin, weepin her heart out. She was sent to her room, and when she looked out the window, there was Danny standin under the tree. She opened the window and he threw up a note wrapped around a rock. It said he'd be back that night, to get ready. They'd elope and be married the next mornin."

It was confusing and difficult to follow her ramblings as she continued to refer to herself in the third person, but Emmy felt at least they were getting the story. It wouldn't be wise to distract her and set her off on another tangent. She poked Amy, wagging a finger indicating not to interrupt.

As they watched, the little face no longer seemed quite as grotesque, enraptured by the sweet memories of love experienced so long ago. It seemed to Emmy that the wrinkles vanished and she could once again see the vision of the curly-haired girl with rosy cheeks and laughing eyes. She must have been a beauty, Emmy thought.

The woman rocked contentedly, her mind back on some happy pathway. Amy stirred as if to rise, and she snapped, "Where you goin?"

Amy tittered nervously, "Nowhere, ma'am. Just changing position."

Mary Ann opened her eyes and looked angrily at Emmy. "I remember when you was born. You gave her a rough time of it . . . but that Danny, he never left her side other than to get the doctor. You was named after his grandmother. You know, he was real good to me, Danny was. My, how they loved each other. As much as she missed her folks, she never resented goin off with him. Did I tell you the mornin they was married, Danny took her back home so's they could tell her folks and get their forgiveness and blessins? That mean old daddy wouldn't let her mother come to the door. She never forgot how fearsome he looked, his face so red and ugly. Danny had to hold her up, she was so afeared. Her daddy just looked at them and said 'Go away. We never want to see or hear from you again. You died for us when you married that man.' The awful thing about it was that he meant it. Her daddy never went back on his word. You know, after you was borned, Emmalina, she wrote her mother to tell about you but she never got an answer.

"All them years and there was nary a word, not from any of them. I guess they wasn't the forgivin kind. We moved around a lot those days. Some places we'd do real well, and I learned to help with a lot of things. When you was a babe, I'd help out and keep your basket next to me while I'd collect tickets for the shows. We saw lots of places, and for a while things was agoin good. But times got bad, and it got so that folks would trade off eggs and vegetables to see the shows.

"You know, now that I think of it, all you girls was born in different states. I know you, Emmalina, was born in Georgia. Amy Beth, I do believe you came along in Kentucky; and then Polly Sue, that was in Texas. Poor little thing, that was when all the trouble started. She was real poorly from the moment she was borned . . . never had a good day after that. That was when Danny decided we'd give up troupin."

Emmy'd had no idea Polly Sue'd been such a sickly baby. And she learned something else: their having been born in such wide-apart places was the reason they'd never been able to find their birth certificates.

The woman's voice droned on. "The troupe was barely makin out long bout that time and everyone agreed we'd best split up. There was a real nice older couple, and Timothy, a young fellow—real good—could play any part. It was real sad partin from each other. We all cried, but Danny was a good fellow—he sold the horses and the wagons and whatever else folks would buy and divided everthin up even so we'd all have a bit to get along on. Danny was a real charmer and made friends with the rancher who bought most of our stuff, and he offered Dan a job.

"For a while life was heavenly. No more travelin from town to town. We had a little house where I could bed you down every night. It wasn't much but it didn't move, and each day we'd know where we were. Dan did right well for a spell and laid off the bottle too. Every man has his faults, and your daddy was a drinker. Understand, of course, only when he was upset or for sociability's sake. We even made friends roundabouts. Maybe you remember that a bit, Emmalina; seems to me you was old enough to recall some o that. How your daddy loved you girls! Every night afore you'd be put to bed, he'd throw you up in the air and catch you. I can see you alaughin now. Do you remember, Emmalina?"

"Yes, I remember, ma'am. That's one of the memories I've carried all my life." It washed over her, the way she had adored her father. The tall, dark, dashing man—she could see him vividly when her mother described him. She snapped back as the voice resumed.

"It's funny, Emmalina, but it seems to me, when I recall it, that was one time for sure when Danny was happy. He never showed he was restless. Sometimes we'd talk of the old tourin days and he'd say he was glad we was settled and were all together in one place. He was even puttin a little money aside. Mr. Collins, the boss, was a decent man and he was pleased with the way Danny caught on. Danny'd been a farmboy as a little one, so it wasn't new to him. But then it started . . . things got worse. There was lots o sickness and many passin . . . the drought . . . the winds, the hard times. Danny wasn't fit for anythin, him grievin the way he did. It was awful hard on me. Poor Mr. Collins, it was a short time after all that happened and he couldn't pay us. He was worried about foreclosure. Decent soul that he was, he gave Danny his car and agreed that we should go some other place to start over again where things wouldn't be so hard. We had a few dollars stashed away and one mornin we started off. Danny had an idea that the Oklahoma area might prove better and maybe we'd even find a spot of land for ourselves. . . ."

She stopped to ruminate, and the only sound in the room was the soft breathing of the sisters. Now the old woman looked at Emmy almost apologetically. "You oughta remember some o what happened to us there. You and Polly Sue was too little, Amy Beth. We feared for our lives when those winds came at us. We was lucky your daddy got us to shelter on her land when he did. What was that woman's name? Can't recall it now."

Emmy said softly, "Fields, ma'am . . . Elizabeth Fields."

Mary Ann nodded with satisfaction. "See there, girl, you have got a memory. Sure enough, that was the name. That's where your father disappeared, girls. That's where and when my Danny went . . . never to be seen or heard o again."

Her voice broke with the pain of that memory. "Oh, my heart was sore and broken. There I was waitin . . . just waitin in all that wind and dirt. Waitin for Danny to come back and get us . . . but he never did. After a while I just couldn't wait anymore. I had to do somethin. We had to eat and I had to look for Danny. I was sick with worry over what might have happened to him. That nice woman—Fields, was it?—she helped me get a job waitin on table and cleanin up at the hotel there in Brightwater. I remember givin her a dollar a week for the care o you girls. I had half a day off a week and then could barely make it back to see you between the windstorms and everythin else goin on. . . ."

She paused and looked intently at both of them. She took a deep breath and her voice quavered. "I know you're goin to find this hard to believe, but it's the truth, so help me God . . . up till that time, my Danny and you children were my life. I loved you all so much. In all the years since I never could understand what happened . . . what came over me . . . why I did what I did. The best I have been able to tell myself was I was scared—plumb scared out o my mind—and when that man came along and offered me a ride to look for my Danny I went, I didn't think for a second. I knew you was all being cared for, and I guess I thought I'd find your daddy and we'd come back and get you."

Her voice dwindled off, her eyes closed, and they sat, expectantly, hopefully. Emmy's hand groped in search of Amy's; they needed to hold on to each other. With her free hand, she leaned over and touched the woman's skirt, imploring, "Ma'am, please . . . go on."

They both heard her; she mumbled but they heard. "That's it. There's nothin more to tell." She smiled as her head bobbed and she dozed again.

A shudder of fear ran through Emmy as every fiber of her being protested. This couldn't be it . . . this rambling, crazy story, the whole of it! She wanted to scream, to pummel the limp body in front of her. No! It couldn't be—there had to be more. They waited, willing themselves to believe she would resume and tell them of some great climactic event to justify their lives of frustrated belief and hope. But it was not to be as the emotionally spent will-o'-the-wisp of romantic illusion, this derelict, their mother, slept, her mouth open as she snored.

Revulsion overcame Emmy. She felt as though she were standing on the brink of an abyss through which she was plummeting into darkness. For a moment she lost awareness, but the pressure of Amy's fingernails brought her back. Amy's face was twisted in fury as she hissed, "I told you! You deserve this! That's it! My God, that's all of it! I hate her!" Amy reminded Emmy of a crazed animal.

Grief and disappointment assailed Emmy. She felt as if her heart would burst with the pain of it. It was all a delusion. The gauzy retrospect of her memories was disintegrating. She was wrenched with distress and shame at the realization of what she had so willfully sought. She was filled with remorse at the thought of how Elizabeth and Max had fought to keep her from this knowledge. Well, now she knew; she had come to the end. She had no recourse but to face it. A cry of utter desolation from deep inside her rose to the surface and she fought to repress it, heaving silently, shaken with sorrow.

The musty old room was closing in on them. Their tensions mounted and it seemed they would explode with the intensity of their feelings. A sudden move would precipitate it. Emmy turned slowly to see Amy's face grim, her body rigid with passions dredged from a vortex so deep she couldn't give vent to them. Poor Amy—what had she done to her? Amy recoiled at Emmy's touch and snatched her hand away. Her teeth clenched, her voice was hoarse as she panted, "They were right! They were right all the time! You with your crazy ideas had to prove it . . . you couldn't leave it alone . . . you had to hear it from her lips . . . that ugly devil . . . I despise the sight of her!"

Emmy moved closer. "Don't, darling . . . please don't do this to yourself. I'm so sorry . . . please, it's over. Nothing we can say or do can erase those years."

Furiously Amy pulled away. "Sure! It's easy for you to talk, to forget—but not for me. I'll never forgive her!" She shook with scorn as she looked at the crumpled creature. "I loathe her with every part of me. It's sickening to think such an evil creature gave birth to us!"

Weighted by misery, Emmy rose. She stared down at her mother's face. What was wrong with her? Why, having heard this awful story, didn't she feel as Amy did? She felt torn as a wave of pity washed over her for all of them. This worn and withered creature, aged beyond her years, desperately ill, looked so crippled and defenseless. A feeling of terrible dejection ran through her as she searched the ravaged desert of her visage for some vestige of the pretty laughing face she had so dearly remembered and treasured through the years. It was gone forever. In its place there would be, for as long as memory held, the image of this lined and furrowed stranger.

Standing there, Emmy felt overcome by incredulity. Amy had said it and it was true . . . this woman had once been the repository of their seed . . . how absurd to think she'd had the audacity to say she'd loved them. A spark of jealousy flared in Emmy as she thought about Mary Ann Beauford's love for their father. That love had been a hideous deceiver, it had stripped her barren. Driven by its compulsion, she had sacrificed every bulwark that might have offered solace.

At this point, depleted and drained, Emmy couldn't even gird herself with anger. She felt empty, her senses dulled. This woman, the vessel into which she had poured such high hopes, had long ago fulfilled her destiny. Who could measure the pain she had endured and the price she had paid? She had been more servant than master.

Their mother had been a capricious, selfish creature; she had borne them and then heedlessly mangled their lives. Emmy recalled sorrowfully how, driven by her fantasies, her own compulsion, she had diminished Elizabeth Fields by whom she had been nurtured and blessed. She had not understood how sustained she had been by the quality of love she had been given. Her sights had been fixed on the gap . . . in the secret place inside herself she had single-mindedly focused on what she had been missing. Now the ties of memory and association had come full circle and been joined, and the realization of what she'd had washed over her.

The thought of Elizabeth gave rise to a surge of gratitude. It had been at her hands that she had learned civility of heart, at her knees that she had acquired the ability to distinguish right from wrong; had developed compassion and drawn strength from what might have been weakness. She had been reared to face commitment and responsibility and not shrink from them. Somehow, in thinking about this, her spirits lifted. But her sister . . . poor Amy, there had been nothing in this experience to vindicate what she had endured. But, Emmy realized, Amy had been better prepared to deal with this than she. Her hide was tougher, her sights more realistic.

Turning, she walked over to her and, putting an arm around her, said gratefully, "I'd never have made it without you. I thank you from the bottom of my heart for coming here with me."

Angrily Amy snarled, "What are you talking about? I was their child also . . . we're both cursed!"

"Don't say that, Amy! In some way, we're lucky. As awful as things were for you, at the base of it the Wilkersons were caring people; they thought they were doing the right thing. We were both cursed and blessed at the same time. Who knows how we might have turned out in the hands of this woman? You've been too furious at what's gone on here to realize our time hasn't been wasted. We've learned a lot. Even as disappointed as you are, you have to admit our people weren't all bad; they were weak and irresponsible, and we can profit from what we know. Please, darling, try to understand that for your own sake."

Amy looked at Emmy warily; she didn't want to be fooled again. Then, reluctantly, she managed a wan smile. "Okay, have it your way, Em. I'm sorry if I've been mean to you. It hasn't been a total waste—we've got each other."

Miraculously her mood altered. "Before we go, let's take a look around. Maybe we can find a picture of our father."

The dust-filled room was glutted with memorabilia; faded pictures, mementos of the past everywhere. Emmy felt a lump in her throat. The puzzle of what had happened to their father persisted. Damn that Daniel Defoe Beauford. Had he been blown away by the winds, dead under dirt and silt, or had he too escaped with never a backward glance? His story had reached a dead end; there was not a clue to what had become of him. Obviously Mary Ann's efforts to find him had been futile, and she had tried to make some sort of life for herself. She'd remarried twice. Emmy's eye was drawn to a picture in an old gilt frame. She picked it up and tried to discern the man's faded features. It reminded her of Polly Sue . . . was Polly Sue like their father? Her musings bore fruit as Amy, looking over her shoulder, said, "That's him!"

They studied the faded picture in silence, until Amy said, "It's hard to make him out, but I believe you and Polly favor him. He was handsome."

Emmy's eyes bored holes in the fragile yellowed picture as a tear coursed down her cheek. She quickly brushed it away. "I think he must have died."

She put the frame back in its place. Turning to Amy, she said resolutely, "If this has done anything, it's proven one thing: we're our own persons. By the accident of birth these people may have sired us, but we're the products of other people's ideas and values. I have to say we haven't turned out too badly." She poked Amy playfully. "Although you could do with a little more humor. . . . Come on, let's get out of here."

Emmy walked over and picked up her bag. Extracting a checkbook, she began to write a check.

Amazed, Amy snapped, "What in the world are you doing?"

Sheepishly Emmy said, "I'd do it for a stranger. I can spare it, and I'll feel better if I leave it. I have a hunch she can use a few dollars. What's the difference? One sec, while I scribble a note."

Emmy placed the check and note under the wine bottle. As she did so, Mary Ann stirred and opened her eyes. She stared up at Emmy intently as she asked, "Did I tell you he married me? He was a real good man, justice o the peace with Mr. Collins to witness. Pour soul, I don know what he'd a done without me all that time she was ailin. I sure was crazy bout him . . . runnin off . . . leavin my folks and home just so's I could be near him. But, as God is my witness, I never did a thing to harm your dear mother."

Astonished, shocked, both girls gaped until Emmy blurted, "Aren't you our mother?"

Indignantly nodding her head negatively, the old woman said querulously, "Ain't you been listenin?"

Amy returned to her sister's side and in a voice choked with emotion said, "We didn't understand. What happened to our mother?"

Emmy asked, "Where did you come from?"

Straightening up in her chair, the old woman glared at them. "Sit down, you two!" She glared at Amy Beth. "Why didn't you call me when I asked way back? You coulda learned all this then."

Emmy said consolingly, "Please, ma'am, we didn't understand. We thought you were our mother."

Apparently pleased at this, the old woman smiled. "I coulda been for the way I cared for you. Your little mother was a darlin, but she started sickly from the day she carried you, Emmalina. It was a good thing I ran away to join up with 'em. I took you little ones under my wing from the day you was all borned. I loved your daddy from the moment I first saw him, and I guess you could say I paid the price. After your poor mother passed, he married me, I guess out o gratitude. He never cared a whit bout me, but he sure was wild about her. I know he loved you girls. . . . The way I figured it, somethin must o happened to him to have kept him from comin back. He was a good father . . . Danny Beauford was a good man." She was about to drop off again but Emmy roused her.

"Please ma'am, what was our mother's name?"

She indicated to Emmy she wanted more wine. As she sipped at it she caught sight of the check. Picking it up, she squinted at it. "Well, that's right nice, girls. But no more'n what's due, you could say." Her face was wreathed with pleasure and Emmy entreated, "Ma'am, if it's not asking too much, could you tell us about our mother . . . what her name was, what she was like?"

"Well, her name was Sue Ellen . . . and she was a pretty slip of a thing. Blond and blue-eyed—sorta like you there, Amy Beth. Soft and gentle . . . helpless as a bird, you might say. Her folks was right fancy—rich too! Poor little thing, she died afore she growed, you'd have to agree. No more'n twenty or so. We lived on the other side o the tracks, but I used to see her when I'd pass. She never shoulda run off with Dan Beauford. That kind o life was too hard on her, and I do believe the poor lamb never really got over missin her family. We got to be real good friends and she used t'tell me stories about them all the time."

A tear trickled down her cheek as she said, "When she lay adyin she made me promise I'd look after you, and I did. I mean, I tried. It just weren't fair o Danny to leave me with the whole kit and kaboodle. You understand that, don't you, girls?"

Tears were coursing down Amy's face as Emmy asked, "Where is our mother buried?"

"She was laid to rest in that little town o Porto where we lived. Danny saw to it she had a decent burial. I told you he was a good man."

"Was her family name Webster?" Amy asked.

"Yes, I told you so. Don't go lookin for those folks. They was mean and ornery . . . I remember."

Emmy stood up. "Thank you, Mary Ann, thank you very much. You can expect a check each month. If you want to move from here, there'll be enough. There's one more thing . . . would you mind terribly giving us the picture of our father?"

There was a moment's hesitation, and then the old woman smiled. "Take it with my blessins. Won't be doin me no good anymore." She sighed as she looked at them. "I sure loved him a lot. You had real good folks, you girls . . . real good. You can rest easy on that score."

Her head nodded and she was sound asleep. Emmy walked back and picked up the picture, frame and all. "Are you ready, Amy?"

They walked through the door and Amy asked, "Are you planning to see her again, Emmy?"

"I'm not sure, Amy. One day, if I should be in this part of California again, I might . . . maybe, who knows?"

Vehemently Amy hissed, "I'd never come back! That woman makes my flesh crawl."

Emmy looked at her in surprise. When they reached the stoop, they stopped to breathe deeply. The day had changed and the sun was veiled by clouds; fog was beginning to drift in. As Emmy unlocked the car door, she said, "Amy . . . if I weren't ashamed I'd scream and shout. Isn't it marvelous?"

For answer Amy slid into the car seat, her face registering unmistakable disgust.

As she sat herself down behind the wheel, Emmy leaned her head back. Her mind was a melee of confusion; she needed to get her wits together. Turning to her sister, she was startled by Amy's gaze: it was blank, dull, unreadable.

Putting the car into gear, Emmy's movements were automatic. She was bursting with emotion—happiness, exultation and, overriding everything, relief—vast, colossal relief! She was suffused with joy at the knowledge that Mary Ann Beauford was not their mother. It colored her every feeling. As she moved the car out of the parking space she remembered with what trepidation she had come here seeking the confrontation with Mary Ann Beauford. The results had been more than she had hoped for. There was poignant irony in the happy knowledge that this woman did not belong to them. The albatross was gone from her neck. Her good dreams had been restored; she was free to imagine the mother they'd had. She knew she should have been saddened by what had happened to that young woman, so many years ago, but she was a symbol whose physical being she couldn't remember. Unlike Amy, she had no ax to grind with Mary Ann; in a way she'd been sorry for her. Instinctively she'd felt from the first moment there'd been nothing to bind them. Mary Ann had seemed so removed from what she'd felt that she'd sensed she and Amy were different deep inside themselves.

She felt a heartening sense of pride. There was no reason for shame in their origins; instead there was a sense of continuity. Her mind raced as she imagined those stern grandparents who had barred their only daughter from their door. They reminded her of the Wilkersons. Her mind ranged back and forth and she could no longer contain herself as the urge to talk about it with Amy overcame her. A spate of words flowed from her lips as she poured out what she was thinking.

Amy sat quietly, trying to grasp what her sister was saying. The experience had been an ordeal and she was exhausted, tired of it all. She was relieved it was over and she no longer wanted to think about it. She wished Emmy would get hold of herself. In her mind she gave it a name; Emmy's Crusade. For what—for whom? From her perspective the past was over and done with, and for that she was grateful. Emmy could be annoying; she was one of those idealists who predicated her feelings on some inner vision that Amy sensed hadn't touched her the same way. Anyhow, it wasn't really that important. She stirred. Probably Peter would have a better grasp of what Emmy was trying to convey; as for herself, she was content to let it ride until another day.

Emmy lowered her window. The bay air was salty and invigorating. The wind tousled their hair. She turned to look at her sister, who seemed so dismal, and she said cheerily, "Isn't it great to be free? You don't have to apologize to anyone for your background . . . for what our parents did. Doesn't that make you feel good?"

Amy gave her a rueful smile as she said quietly, "It's a little late for that—at least for me. No matter how poetically you put it, I had to suffer the consequences."

Put off by Amy's sullenness, Emmy tried to explain. "Oh, Amy, I'm not excusing Mary Ann or our father. She was unkind and selfish not to have told someone about this before, but it's not fair to place all of the blame on her. The reason I'm so out of my mind with happiness is that, thank God, she is not our mother. Whoever she is and whatever motivated her, we can only guess at . . . the shadows and shadings can't be filled in."

There was a glint of anger in Amy's eyes as she replied, "That's her—but what about him? I was taught that the sins of the father are visited on the children. I don't suppose you believe that, do you, Emmy?"

Emmy couldn't believe what she was hearing. After all they had been through and learned, this girl remained unhappy, unwilling to concede they were victims of circumstance. Her voice rose. "No, I don't! Emphatically not! I remember something Larry told me when we talked about my former mother-in-law: ''Tis of no consequence of what parents a man is born, so he be a man of merit.' When it's all said and done, Amy, can't you see it depends on what you make of yourself? The man who said that lived a long time ago. I'm sure you've heard of Horace."

Amy looked at her quizzically. "Are you trying to tell me such things have happened and we're not alone in our predicament?"

Amy was such a stickler for fact that it struck Emmy as funny and she began to giggle. Before long her laughter became contagious and, unable to resist, Amy joined her.

When they had quieted down and were nearing the hotel,

Emmy said, "Hey, I'm in the mood for some fun. How would you like to go to Chinatown for dinner? We have to celebrate! In a way, today's the first day of our lives . . . let's have a make-believe birthday dinner."

Resignedly Amy decided she couldn't refuse to be happy with her.

Chapter XXXI

GETTING TO KNOW YOU

Chapter XXXI

GETTING TO KNOW YOU

IT HAD GROWN dark by the time they reached the hotel. Emmy walked to the desk to check for messages and learned that she had just missed a telephone call from the Michalsons. As soon as they reached the suite, Emmy put a call through to them. It was good to hear Betty's cheery voice and, after assuring her that everything had gone well and that the news about Tana would have to wait until they were together, she let Betty take over. "I can't wait to tell you—that's why we called. The deal on the house is consummated. It's yours. When are you coming down here?"

Emmy said, "Hold it, hon . . . I want to check with my sister. How are you going home—by train?"

Amy nodded. "Yes. I have to leave tomorrow."

"I'm taking the train with Amy tomrrow, Betty, all right?"

Betty giggled. "Are you sitting down? The most important news is about to come. Larry telephoned. He'll be home in two weeks and he wants you to pick out your wedding dress!"

Emmy screamed. Amy ran to her side. "Is everything all right?"

Shaking her head yes, she said to Betty, "I don't know if I can stand all this wonderful stuff. I can't wait to see you and talk over everything."

Ralph cut in. "You're not alone, pet. Betty can't stand waiting another two minutes. Hurry up and get back. We'll be at the station to pick you up."

"Okay, darlings. See you tomorrow."

She hung up and grabbed Amy, dancing her around the room. "Larry will be home in two weeks! Oh, Amy, now I can't wait!"

Amy stopped and, catching her breath, asked, "Are those *the* Ralph Michalsons? Are they good friends of yours?"

"I thought I told you about them—they're wonderful friends. You're going to love them."

Amy didn't answer. As they were dressing for dinner, Emmy chatted on about the new house and her plans for the future. It took a while before she realized how unresponsive her sister was. "What's the matter, puss . . . something bothering you?"

"No, not really, Em. I'm happy for you. It's just that . . ." She stopped.

"What? Say it!"

Amy's reddened face gave her away; she was embarrassed. "Please don't think I'm not thrilled for you . . . it's just that we live in such different worlds. Pete and I, we're just getting started. We don't own a grand house or any of that kind of thing. We don't travel in your sort of circle. I was just wondering how we'll get along."

It hit Emmy like a lead weight. This could be a sensitive, touchy situation if it wasn't handled with care. She said soberly, "Okay, Mrs. Cooper, what suggestions do you have? Do you want me to call this 'family thing' off? Do you expect me to say that now that I've found you I have to give you up because you're not rich, don't have fancy friends and a big house?"

Amy looked at her dubiously. Fighting to think rationally, Emmy's emotions roiled over. "Don't you see what you're doing? Why must rejection be such a natural part of our lives? Isn't there another way . . . another solution?"

At this Amy started in surprise and Emmy exhorted, "Where is your generosity of spirit? Doesn't the tie that binds us have any meaning to you at all? Hasn't what happened to us made our need for each other override every other consideration?"

Her voice beseeched. "Can't you see me—the inside me? Nothing else ever mattered to me as much as finding you! Doesn't it matter we can have a relationship rich not in money but in love? Can you imagine anything more wonderful than being wanted? Is there anything equal to that? You found that in one way with Peter . . . but there's room for more."

Her eyes filled and Amy put out a placating hand as Emmy said resignedly, "Would you allow your pride to stand in the way of this? Isn't it possible for the four of us to have a relationship in spite of your living in a modest house on a budget?"

The dam broke as tears spilled from Amy's eyes and she managed to sputter, "Oh, cut it out! I wasn't thinking about any of that. You know very well what I meant."

"Does it bother you that Ralph will see you working at the studio? He's the last man in the world to judge anyone by such things. Come off it, Amy. My Larry's the most wonderful, easygoing man in the world. I'll bet you anything that he and Pete are going to be buddies. I can suggest this: if ever you feel uncomfortable with us, in our home or yours, with our friends or yours, speak up . . . that way we can take care of it."

Amy seemed relieved and happier.

It was drizzling the next morning and they had to rush. They took a cab to the station. After securing her ticket, Emmy asked, "Amy, want something to read? How about a candy bar? We'll lunch on the train. I love eating in the dining car."

Amy was agreeable to anything and they settled into their seats to enjoy the view of the ocean on one side and, as the skies cleared, the sun-dappled hills with their convoluted carving on the other. Swaying fields of green bespoke the fertility of the land they were passing through. After a while Emmy opened the newspaper she had bought, scanning the pages. Suddenly she exclaimed, "Amy, look!" She passed the paper, pointing to a headline that read, "Movie mogul Madrix reports Big Silver shooting delayed. What's wrong with Corgan?"

Amy considered. "Do you think it had something to do with our meeting?"

Emmy was dubious. "I don't think so. Maybe she's gone on a binge . . . although she'd be crazy to jeopardize her highly prized career. I hope it's not that. Who knows? Maybe she has a toothache. You know these crazy columnists. I'll ask Ralph when we get in; he usually has inside information."

Amy shrugged. "She's stupid. It may sound crazy, but I'm convinced our beloved sister is determined not to grow up."

Surprised, Emmy asked, "What do you mean?"

With a look of smug superiority Amy said assertively, "Just what I said. It's obvious she doesn't want to assume responsibilities she's not interested in . . . why should she? Think about it: all her life everything's been done for her. She never has to cope with problems. I see it at the studio—they do everything but go to the bathroom for her. I don't mean to be vulgar, but it's true. I have a hunch our meeting really threw her, so it was probably easier to forget with a drink. . . . Shades of our father!"

At this, Emmy stiffened. "I doubt that—she's not a complete fool. She does manage to take care of some things."

"Yes," Amy insisted, "but everyone makes allowances for her because she's so talented. I think she's heading for trouble unless someone does something."

Emmy sat thinking for a moment and then, studying Amy, said, "If you have any notion of volunteering our help, forget it. I'm sure the biggest favor we can do is to pretend we don't know her."

Amy shook her head emphatically in agreement and Emmy added, "Tana Corgan may be gifted, but whatever she's got doesn't come packaged and tied with a bow . . . she's got to keep herself in the running. I wouldn't worry about it. I think she can take care of herself. By the way, do you know she has a great love affair going?"

"She does?" Amy asked in surprise. "Who with?"

Emmy smiled. "With herself!" They both laughed. "Come on, let's forget about her and see if there's room in the diner."

The well-appointed dining car was crowded and the maître d' ushered them to a table where an attractive middle-aged man was finishing his meal. He smiled at them, and Amy was taken back by Emmy's geniality as she urged, "Please, don't rush on our account."

Charmed, the man beamed at them. "Thank you, I'm just about through. Pardon me, miss, but I must say you bear Tana Corgan a striking resemblance. You're not her, are you?"

Responding gaily, Emmy said, "No, of course not, although I'm accustomed to hearing it. Thank you for the compliment."

Enjoying the company, the man lingered a little longer than he might have and babbled on about inconsequential things. It took a few moments for Emmy to see how discomforted and prim Amy had become.

Glancing at the man briefly, she concentrated on Amy. "Have you decided what you'd like? I'll write it down."

The man excused himself, rose and left.

"Well, I never!" Amy exclaimed.

Emmy's eyebrows rose. Putting her menu down, she looked at her sister. "Are you serious, Amy? Do you think passing the time of day innocently has any meaning?"

"Well, you certainly were encouraging him. Talking about your personal appearance and all is rather out of line, don't you think?"

Emmy couldn't help smiling at her sister's unworldliness. "No, I don't attach any importance to it. I think you're blowing this out of all proportion. Just being civil doesn't mean an invitation to an affair."

Amy turned brick red.

Ignoring her reaction, Emmy asked, "What would you like, sis?"

After Amy had decided and the waiter had gone off with their order, Emmy saw her sister's continued uneasiness. With a look of amusement she asked bluntly, "Do you think I'm a loose woman, Amy?"

Amy's audible gasp told Emmy she'd guessed correctly about Amy's line of thinking. It riled Emmy, and she decided Amy Beth was really prudish. She was a Wilkerson! An imp of perversity egged Emmy on and she asked, half mockingly, "Are you really sure you want to hear what has happened to me in my life?"

She watched Amy's face as, in all innocence, the girl looked at her, saying, "Of course I do. I'm very interested."

Emmy had second thoughts; she'd have to be careful or their relationship might end right here at the table. It would be best to be tactful and not offend Amy's sense of morality. "Well, it's not too exciting, Amy. I'll tell you what brought about my divorce. There are many things I could reveal, but frankly I'm afraid it might shock you. You've been so cloistered and I'm afraid your good opinion of me might alter. I do feel there are some dreams worth keeping."

Amy flushed as she protested, "That's not fair, Emmy. After all, I've told you all about me. I don't understand what you're getting at. How can you assume what my reaction will be before I hear what you have to say."

Emmy smiled enigmatically; she was tempted but she knew better. "That's the hitch, Amy, darling. Your attitude indicates your inability to handle my convoluted drama."

Amy flared. "I don't understand what you're talking about and I resent your putting me down."

Hastily Emmy said, "Lord forbid, I'm not putting you down. It's just that we've lived such different lives I think you'd probably judge me harshly."

Amy's eyes opened in surprise. "I know we're different, Em, but you have to realize a lot of things are new to me."

"Right, darling, I understand." Emmy was grateful she hadn't opened up and confided everything. She'd been skating on thin ice.

Unaware of what was going on in Emmy's mind, Amy said, "You can understand, where I come from divorce is unheard of . . . it's considered scandalous. Not that I think you're a bad woman, Em—really I don't."

Amy missed her sister's intake of breath as Emmy laughed lightly and said, "I do understand, Amy." If she was going to build up their friendship it wouldn't do to bruise it right at the start; she'd have to exercise caution and patience. "I guess all the things you've been exposed to these past few days have turned your world upside down. But honestly there's nothing too shocking about my story. It's just that Jonathan and I agreed to part because our differences were too numerous and deep for us to mend."

Wanting to mollify her, Emmy began by filling her sister in on her early life and her interest in music. "I never would have been concert material, and it all came to an end when Elizabeth died."

She explained about her former mother-in-law and suppressed a grin as she saw that Amy sympathized with what had been her plight. She followed this by simply stating she had met Larry on the coast and they had fallen in love after she and Jonathan had separated. It would have been too much of a burden for Amy to know anything more.

As it was, Amy was exceedingly curious about how she had been able to fall in love with another man so soon after her parting from Jonathan. Emmy didn't belabor the point and concluded the matter by saying, "Larry Bayless is the love of my life, the man I'm going to marry and live happily ever after with."

Looking at her earnestly, Amy said, "I'm glad you've found the perfect man. Once you two are married, no one will remember your first marriage—it will be forgotten."

Emmy smiled, thinking, I want to like you, puss, but your pious pronouncements make me feel you're a prig.

When they finished their lunch, Amy reached for the checks. "Please, Emmy, don't fight. I'd like to take care of this." Emmy gave in; this was another area where she'd have to watch her step. "Thank you very much, Amy. Thank you for everything."

Seated back in their car, Emmy sat reflecting. She had opened a Pandora's box, all right. Her sisters were a far cry from what she had envisioned: Amy's piety and smugness, Tana's insults and rejection. She laughed at herself. My concern about them goes back a long way; even at a very young age I must have been their umbrella . . . as Mary Ann said, Mommy's little helper.

When they arrived in Los Angeles, Amy eagerly ran into Peter's arms. Happily she introduced her sister to the handsome young man. He reminded Emmy of a huge puppy, and instantly she was sure it would be easier to build a bond with him than with her sister. The Michalsons were nowhere in sight and, since Amy was eager to go, she urged them on their way with promises she would call them.

The moment the Coopers had departed the Michalsons appeared. Good people that they were, they had hung back, not wanting to complicate Emmy's introduction to her new brother-in-law. They took for granted that Emmy would be their houseguest until Larry's arrival and new plans were formulated.

Emmy was overflowing with things she had to tell them. It seemed to her the Michalsons were more her family than her sisters. She admitted to Betty, "I have to get it in perspective. It isn't going to be easy. I own up . . . it's not at all the way I imagined it would be. I wouldn't want Amy or Tana to be the arbiter of my taste or make my choices for me."

Betty patted her arm consolingly. "Could anyone have convinced you that having 'a family' is not all milk and honey, Em? Do you feel being natural sisters overrides the differences in your backgrounds?"

Emmy shook her head in perplexity. "That's where I made the first mistake, Betty. But it is strange, there are similarities in other ways . . . all three of us are very honest and straightforward. Obviously Tana and I share the creative side. But it's really not fair to evaluate us yet. Amy's moving out of the nineteenth century into ours. She's so indoctrinated by her Wilkerson upbringing you can feel it's in the marrow of her bones. Our sensitivities are so different. Peter must have his hands full. I get the feeling she's like the Sleeping Beauty whose prince came along, kissed her and woke her up."

"Are you able to find common ground?"

"Yes, surprisingly. Amy's bright and perceptive. She's a paradoxical mixture of prudishness and curiosity, but, given time, she'll learn. She's really intelligent. I like her and I think she likes me—so that's a good start, don't you think?"

Chapter XXXII

◦━◇━◦

PICKING UP THE PIECES

AT THE MOMENT, Tana's mind was precariously perched as she
wrestled with every ounce of her will to hold on to herself.
The events of the past months culminating in today's revelations had stripped her reserves. It was as though her soul had
been picked bare. She was emotionally exhausted; the din of
the assaults upon her had left her deafened and confused.
What did everyone want of her? What had they expected of
her? What should she have been? Her only memory of solace
in this maelstrom was Tony, and there too she suspected she
had failed: their only bond had been their lust for each other.

In the plane flying back to Los Angeles her mind ranged
back and forth. Her father and Bill Griffon had been
instruments that, against her will, had exorcised the past. In
cutting her they had forced her to see herself for what she
was. Whatever it was that had welded them together against
her—love or hate—they would forever be the Gorgons
standing guard on the sins of her past. Bill Griffon had called
a halt to her egocentricity, made her see for the first time she
was just a cog in a wheel, forced her to eat humble pie as
dessert for her wanton behavior. In a fearsome way he'd done
her a service. It was hard to admit she didn't hate him—that
would rob her of the last vestige of pride. In him she'd met a
master teacher who'd robbed her of her youth. Her father—
for that he would be till the day she died—had ripped her
painfully from her roots, shorn her of every vestige of
belonging. The anguish of this pierced her through and

through. She wanted to go home . . . to a place of peace where she would not have to hide, where she could be something of value to someone and have the luxury of knowing someone really cared. She desperately needed solace and a haven.

She was grateful for the familiarity of Lilly's affectionate embrace when she entered the airport building. Theirs too had been a stormy relationship, but she was the only safe port Tana had left. She sighed wearily. She had alienated everyone . . . Lilly was her last hope.

Curbing her impatience to hear what had gone on, Lilly saw that Tana was more than physically tired—she was drained.

Tana Gorgan had been through the mill, withstood more than most people could have. She was haunted by everything that had happened to her, but with a supreme effort she made up her mind she would not resort to drink. She knew it was time to face up to herself.

As her conversation with Lilly deepened and broadened, Lilly was amazed at the alteration in Tana. Over the weekend she had grown from child to woman. For the first time they were able to talk candidly without fear of Tana's temperamental outbursts. Lilly was able to say, "You've lived in a make-believe world so long you became emotionally retarded. You never put yourself in the next person's boots."

A chastened Tana sat quietly thinking and asked, "Have I been that mean and selfish?"

Hesitating only for a second, Lilly said, "You've ridden roughshod over everyone . . . you can't expect them to like you. You need people, Tana—not just for what they can do for you but for care and affection."

When Lilly told her she was going to be married Tana teetered on the brink of disaster. It was during the hours she contemplated suicide that she went through a scalding dissection of her soul. She had been debased and humiliated; she had received accolades and reached heights few people ever achieved, and yet she had made a mess of her life. She writhed at recognition of the truth. Could she pick up the pieces? More important, could she change? Could she humble herself and make a fresh start? She couldn't do it alone.

On the fringe of her consciousness was the knowledge that there was an alliance waiting for acquiescence. It was a ray of hope. It was difficult to think of those women as her sisters, but they were. She had to face it. It offered an alternative pathway, and maybe, if she trod lightly, she'd accomplish a twofold purpose. She'd acquire people who would care for her and be genuinely interested in her . . . in a strange new way, a family. Maybe with them she could learn to be open; maybe she would not have to hide her fears and aspirations, her worry about the people who snapped at her heels when she stumbled on her pinnacle. She had a resurgence of hope. For some reason she wasn't worried about her sisters' recriminations. They'd wanted to be kind; maybe they'd forgive and forget. With this as incentive, the thought began to supersede all else.

The first day of her return to the studio she walked into the executive building. She saw the surprise on Amy's face as she stopped before her desk. The girl flinched as if expecting she might be slapped. Obviously disturbed, Amy asked, "Can I help you, Miss Corgan?"

Tana smiled. "I hope so, sis. I don't have an appointment with anyone here. I just wanted to say hello and ask if you'd like to have lunch with me in the commissary."

Amy looked as though she might faint, but when she regained her voice, she said, "I'd love it."

Incredible! Unbelievable! The impossible had happened. Amy telephoned Emmy at the Michalson house, where preparations were under way for the wedding.

After she had finished telling Emmy about Tana, Amy sat stupefied, wondering if it had really happened. How amazing all of this was and—she had to admit—how gratifying. All her fears and apprehensions had been washed away in the renewal of her relationship with Emmalina. In a shorter time than she had imagined possible, they had built a bridge to each other . . . and now, if they would let her, Tana would join. . . . How astonishing that after so much devastation, there was illumination.

Chapter XXXIII

◇━◇

FULL CIRCLE

WAITING WITHIN THE visitors' confines for Larry to disembark, Emmy tried to distract herself by watching the others. A sudden babble of voices could be heard; then the gate swung out as an MP cautioned the surging crowd to stay back; and at last the men came through. Frantically Emmy sought for a glimpse of Larry. For so long now she had had no sharp picture of him, only collages of the way he had looked.

She couldn't mistake him; she saw the familiar outline—tall, dark-haired, breathtakingly handsome in officer's garb—moving down the line, his eyes searching.

"Larry, Larry, over here, dear . . . darling!" And then she was lifted off her feet in a bear hug and heard the wonderful timbre of his voice. "It's you! It isn't a dream. Darling, I don't want to ever let you go."

She wriggled. "If you don't loosen me, darling, this well may be the last of me."

Laughing, he put her down. "I'd forgotten how really tiny you are—and how beautiful!"

They went to the hotel in Santa Monica where Emmy had reserved a suite according to his instructions. There were to be no outsiders intruding on their first hours together. After the first edge of their passion had been satisfied, they spent hours talking, exploring, probing . . . making certain each was the one the other imagined. Then there came a quiet exhilaration knowing nothing had altered.

After listening to her account of her family, he gave her his

513

version of Amy. "There are different layers of love . . . affection . . . whatever you want to call it. Each of us is really like a mine with veins running through. You have to be patient with Amy. Give her the opportunity to stretch out. I have a hunch you'll win her allegiance. We'll all be friends; you'll see."

She snuggled up to him and he smiled. "You know, honey, the three of you remind me of a game I play—Anagrams. Everyone starts with the same letters, and you make as many words as possible out of them. It's interesting to see what happens. Now, take for instance the word *made* . . . right off I see *dame*. . . . Another word: *now*—reverse it, you have *won*. . . . Get what I mean? You sisters are made from the same letters, but there's no end to the number and combinations of words that can be derived from the three of you. . . .

"Maybe, with another rearrangement one of you will uncover the root you have in common, and with that, in time, you'll begin to trust and rely on one another." He held her in his arms, and she turned her face up to him to receive his kiss.

EPILOGUE

THE SOCIAL EVENT of the new year was the Bayless wedding. Most of Hollywood was amazed at the announcement of the marriage of Emmalina Griffon and Lawrence Bayless. Invitations were prized, and those that received them were the envy of all the others.

The ceremony and wedding reception were to be held at the Michalson home. It was a bower of flowers as the guests began to arrive. Both Larry and Emmy had insisted that Betty be the bride's sole attendant. Ralph would have the honor of giving Emmy away. The day was spectacular and the garden was jammed with all of Hollywoods' notables as well as other friends.

As the music began and the procession started, Emmy's eyes blurred. She saw Larry waiting, and her heart sang. She kissed Ralph as he gave her to Larry. She looked up to see the judge smiling at them. They were wed! As they walked back down the aisle, she saw Amy and Peter smiling at them.

The newlyweds stood happily in the reception line, receiving the good wishes of those who passed before them. It took Emmy a moment to realize it was Tana Corgan who had reached up and pecked her on the cheek. At Emmy's insistence an invitation had been sent, but no one had really expected her to put in an appearance.

Tana smiled at them. "Congratulations! I wish you both the best of everything."

Smiling back, Emmy said, "Thank you for coming."

Laughing shyly, Tana said softly, "This has special significance. I wouldn't have missed it for anything. Thank you for including me."

Larry laughed. "Tana, you'll find Amy and Peter somewhere up ahead in that crowd."

She grinned back at him. "I've already seen them. I sat next to them. . . . I mustn't hold up the line."

As she started to move away, Emmy pulled her back and kissed her cheek. "Thank you for this beautiful gift."

Larry saw Emmy's glistening eyes and whispered in her ear, "You're the most beautiful of the Beauford girls—and they're a very handsome family."

They were off on their honeymoon, headed for Washington, D.C., and New York City. It was as if the events of the day culminated in the powerful roar and surging thrust of the plane as, airborne, it nosed upward, reaching for the star-studded sky.

Sitting quietly, Emmy put her left hand out to see the diamond wedding band sparkling on her finger. Turning, she saw Larry grinning at her. "Happy, Mrs. Bayless?"

She reached over and kissed him tenderly. "My heart is overflowing—you'll never know what you mean to me."

He pressed her shoulder. "I feel the same, Funny Face." He leaned back. "Ralph and Betty have been marvelous; we're forever in their debt. Did you catch Tana talking to them?"

Emmy smiled reflectively. "I couldn't get over it. The fact that she came left me gasping—although Amy told me how warm and kind she's been to her. I wonder what happened, Larry. She's gone into total reverse."

Chuckling, he said, "Whatever brought her around, my sweet, dear heart, she won't be the loser for it. You and your stubborn dream came out the victor. The Beauford sisters are reunited."

A gossamer flicker of worry crossed Emmy's face. "You know, Larry, in a crazy way the idea weighs on me. For so long I lived with the idealization of what it would be like. It's been a mirage, always there, just out of reach; and now that it's happened, I feel responsible—as if there's something special I'm supposed to do."

Studying her for a moment, he picked up her hand and said, gently but firmly, "You turned a page in your life today, Em. Each of you has other priorities, and the responsibility has to be shared. You're all grown women . . . don't try to bite off more than you can handle. Be content! The way I see it, a family is a viable, growing expression of many things. If your love and respect for one another are valid, time will bring about change and a wonderful expansiveness of feeling for one another. . . . Give it time to grow."

She sat pondering what he had said. Looking into his piercing blue eyes, she could feel the force of his dreams, the restlessness of his ambitions. Being wife to this man would require her concentrated effort. He was right: she had done all she could single-handedly; now it would be up to each of them as sisters to make their contribution. A spark of recognition coursed through her. It was as though the bud had burst into flower . . . her seed had fulfilled its destiny. Almost as if it had been ordained, she had fulfilled what her mother before her had not been able to do: she had regained her family.

Emmy sighed with contentment. "You're right, darling." She snuggled up to him and he kissed the top of her head.

There was sudden turbulence, and the plane lurched. Instantly alarmed, Emmy clutched at Larry's arm, and he smiled at her in calm reassurance. She leaned back trying to relax, and the steady drone of the engines brought back to her the whining accompaniment of those wayward winds, whose inexorable passage so long ago had drastically altered her life. She knew there was no reason to worry, the Beauford girls, each in their own way, were lucky. A benificent fate had always gentled the tempests that had beset them. They were meant to be survivors.